Acclaim for Earl Thomps

# A Garden of San

"Brilliantly evokes the sad decade of the Depression and dramatizes the lives of some remarkably feisty and tenacious people. . . . Distinguished by a fluent, conversational style, powerful and accurate dialogue . . . *A Garden of Sand* is a raffish and exuberant book that movingly asserts the strength of a boy's will and spirit."
—*New York Times Book Review*

"Earl Thompson has you by the lapels and before long you're hooked by a story that has style, swagger, raw sexuality and a seduction straight out of Oedipus. . . . This is crisp, incisive writing with a sardonic overview and a sharp cutting edge that impresses itself on your memory. . . . His characters are intensely alive and his prose crackles. A genuinely powerful and impressive novel."
—*Saturday Review*

"The time-span is the Depression and first years of World War II, and Thompson has captured the raw gusto and grimy despair of those years."
—*Washington Post Book World*

"A big, blistering sexual odyssey in the down and out days of the thirties. . . . A realistic and captivating novel."
—*Chicago Sun-Times*

"A rare novel—tough, honest, uncompromising and yet heartening."
—*Newsday*

"A brilliant, brutal and enormously exciting novel."
—*Los Angeles Times*

"A raw shocker of a bestseller."
—*Cosmopolitan*

# A Garden of Sand

## Earl Thompson

CARROLL & GRAF PUBLISHERS
NEW YORK

First Carroll & Graf trade paperback edition 2001

Carroll & Graf Publishers
A Division of Avalon Publishing Group
161 William Street
New York, NY 10038

Library of Congress Cataloging-in-Publication Data is available.
ISBN: 0-7867-0946-4

Manufactured in the United States of America

*This book is dedicated to Nelson Algren,*
*who doesn't know me from Adam,*
*and so should not be held responsible*

# A Garden of Sand

*Every family has its problems.*
CANDY MOSSLER

L OVE a place like Kansas and you can be content in a garden of raked sand. For ground it is the flattest. Big sky, wheat sea, William Inge, bottle clubs, road houses—Falstaff and High Life, chili and big juke road houses—John Brown, Wild Bill Hickok, Carry A. Nation, cockeyed Wyatt Earp, Pretty Boy Floyd, and shades of all those unspoken Indians. Out there on the flat, in a wheat sea, on the spooky buffalo grasses where the ICBM's go down into the shale and salt of a prehistoric sea wherein the mighty mosasaurs once roamed and the skies were not cloudy all day.

Where John Brown and Pretty Boy Floyd could have run one-two in any election through 1937, there are still more members of the Townsend Clubs than anywhere else save Long Beach. And professional baseball can't make a dime, while semipro can draw 25,000 fans to a swing-shift game getting under way at 1 A.M. of a Tuesday between the Honolulu Hawaiians and the Boeing Bo-Jets. The state was strong for Bryan, and it *had* Alf Landon. It went for Nixon and dug Goldwater. It admired John L. Lewis for his stubbornness but never let labor unions get more than a toehold anywhere. It built one of the best educational systems in the land, then let the Boy Scouts set miniature Statues of Liberty on *all* the lawns.

Where traditionally, though as Republican in taste as Ike's sport jackets, a governor of the state rarely succeeds himself in office even if the electorate has to go for a Democrat. It is the same with all public office holders. And should the incumbent's opponent be of such a known unconscionable quantity that they trust the governor for a second term, he could pay his own carfare and postage and still not go for three. Which is why Willkie could have carried the state with a picture postcard.

9

Where ministers preach against "The Carnal Knowledge of Women" as if it were a Communist plot and seek legislation against smoking and obscene literature as if one were crypto-cover for the other; the girls are prettier than those across any of the bordering state lines and only slightly less willing than those up in the hills on the Missouri side, and virginity before marriage—or puberty, for that matter—means less than regular church attendance. Calvinism still runs deeper than the missile sites bore, and the Amish are ever more respected than Papists. Women who were taken in by Jackie Kennedy will never be fooled again by Jackie O.

Where the displaced progeny of rebels fleeing for their lives after the Battle of Culloden in 1746 came walking out of the American highlands after the Battle of Shiloh looking once more for a place where a man tired of war and rumors of war might live once and for all on his own terms. It is a place where carny hustlers and storefront gypsies can still work the shell game and the money switch every day of the week and Hadacol outsells Johnny Walker.

Calvinism gets its test every summer by any erstwhile Gantry who can rent a tent and con the local funeral parlors out of folding chairs and cardboard fans on a stick. Attendance at regular churches thins out appreciably as soon as the revivalist's sound truck has gone once around, and Christians, whether they sprinkle, pour, or half drown, are hard pressed to get up a quorum until the Bible-banger pulls the plug on the last electric Christian guitar and beats it out of town with the tent and awning company wanting to know who is going to pay the last week's rent on the tabernacle.

Then all those abandoned souls who had made passionate, spontaneous decisions for Christ down on their knees in the sawdust under canvas shake out their cuffs and come penitently back as from a week's vacation at the Sodom and Gomorrah Hilton, looking straight ahead, seeing in the eyes of their preacher above that superior, all-forgiving-smile their sin—*idolatry!* Confessed and forgiven, they are ready once again to bear the winter's long hymns while a high, bright, cold winter sun illuminates the stained glass. There is that dry prairie cold in which you can freeze to death feeling only a warm drowsiness.

So, though any Kansan knows in his heart that in the end *all* those dandy saviors go South, there is a kind of displaced black, Highland-Scandinavian hope into which any sort of witch doctor or witch hunter can worm. Sitting on enough nuclear explosive to blow his ass to atoms, the collective Kansan tunes in "Let Freedom Ring" and sincerely believes the only Christian thing to do is obliterate Peking. And many still want a shot at Rome, too. "Voice or no voice, the people can always be brought to do the bidding of the leaders. That is easy. All you have to do is tell them that they are being attacked, and denounce the pacifists for lack of patriotism and exposing the country to danger. It works the same in every country" is how Hermann Göring put it.

Which leaves Kansas just about the same as anyplace else that hasn't as yet had the benefit of the civilizing influence of the Mafia operating on the local level. Where ordinary man's sins, repentances, and hopes are of no more consequence than some long gone Indian vision quest. The record is yet more important than the private man.

This is a story of ordinary, hardworking, often out of work Christians who are Kansans until they die.

# 1

JOHN MACDERAMID was not important in any way. He was merely an honest man of whom the worst that could be said by those who pitied his wife was: "He's a fool." For he knew so much and his talents were so varied, yet his history was an unbroken string of failed investments, abandoned homesteads, broken schemes, and bankrupt hopes. His great folly—in spite of all accumulated evidence to the contrary—was an unshakable faith in the American dream that if a man is honest, law-abiding, and willing to sweat a dollar's worth for a dollar's pay, his success should be guaranteed.

He simply could not conceive of a world less logical. He was aware of the many imperfections in the one he lived in, but he was sure the Democrats would ultimately get it straightened out. It was with such faith he went to vote for Roosevelt in 1932. Of all his regrets, being on the side of the winner in that one was the most rancorous and abiding. Not that he later preferred Hoover. It was simply that he felt Roosevelt had connived to hoodwink him personally. Nor was there any forgiveness in Mac's heart. "A greater liar never had a gut!" was his unqualified indictment.

The year before Roosevelt was elected, MacDeramid's first grandson was born on the kitchen table into the hands of a Dr. Nodruff in the electrified prairie Gothic house that sat on a quarter of a section of land straddling Wichita's Ninth Street, between the canal and the interurban tracks. His daughter was there because the boy's father was in jail and his family would not have her. MacDeramid didn't know whom to blame for that one, Hoover or Roosevelt. He only knew that even at marrying off his daughter—and a damn pretty girl, too—he had somehow failed again.

He had never seen a woman as pregnant as his daughter had been. Wilma was a small-boned, gentle girl no taller than five feet three inches. That great long Swede, Odd Andersen, must have planted her with a calf. He was one foot one inch taller than MacDeramid's Wilma. When the girl let go the first blood-curdling scream behind the brown kitchen door, Mac fled the house and hid in the barn until he saw the doctor come out to get in his car. When he got to the house, he found the calf had been named John after himself and Odd after his father. By the next morning everyone except the boy's mother was calling him Jacky.

And it was Jacky that stuck while he toddled about discovering their big half-German-police-half-collie, Buck; Imo, the hired man; Nelly, their gentle secondhand race horse who could not outrun his Grandmother Mack; and all the other aunts, uncles, cousins, and friends. Rumors filtered down to him that somewhere he had a father. His mother told him, "Your daddy is away right now. Daddy's gone ahunting to get baby a bunting." He was doing a year for kypping $200 worth of postage stamps from Harwi Hardware Company, where he had been a clerk. He had never confessed why. But that was not the kind of news to tell a child, though his mom had no more notion what a "bunting" was than did baby.

Wilma liked to think Odd decided to lift the stamps so they could get married after she turned her pretty face up under a harvest moon and confided, "Iay hinktay eway areay inay hetay amilyfay ayaway, Odd honey"—Pig latin being the native language then. He could have stolen the stamps to buy an abortion. But if that was the case, *his* family was certain it had to have been the girl's idea. In any event, there hadn't been time to do either before he was salted away. But the girl made certain that by the blank for the father on the child's birth certificate the name Odd Ewal Andersen was dutifully recorded. It was this that the Andersens held against her the most. They just weren't that certain.

Odd had been a good boy. An assistant Scoutmaster in his step-father's troop at the First Lutheran Church, he had, until his mother re-married, handed over his pay envelope to her every week as cheerfully as if it were a bouquet. And even before Old Odd died, Young Odd was the binding force in a family of nine children whose father spent most days moodily closeted over some invention to change his own destiny, emerging only to plant another kid in Mother Andersen's elastic womb or kick hell out of those he had for making too much noise in the house. He had invented something that had to do with windmills. But that had been long ago, and his royalties did not leave his widow rich. It was always Young Odd who had the tenderness and patience to comfort the others while Old Odd was closeted with his turbulent thoughts and his mother gnashed her teeth in the face of a world which rewarded her Christian virtue and dedication to duty with ever yet another Viking in the womb until duty and a little pleasure became a weight that pulled her helplessly to her knees in utter, undignified despair. So her entire bearing was an upright, unbending challenge to the Christian proposition that there *is* life after death. In her heart that heavenly hope had turned into a due bill. Her eyes, always burning with the dry flame of a temperance activist, bore through every moment toward some mental wall on which she chalked again and again: *By God, There Had Better Be!* It was only Odd, an Eagle with a sash full of merit badges, who had time for the buttons and laces, the scrapes and tears of his brothers and sisters.

Then there was the theory held by Old Man MacDeramid and his son, Kenneth, that Odd did not lift the stamps for anything more honorable than the purchase of an old roadster he had his eye on. If anything, he was even keener for cars than he was for getting between Wilma's quick, slim legs. Or one thing was somehow all mixed up in his mind with the other.

When Odd got out of jail, he came to marry Wilma and stay with the MacDeramids until he had enough to get his little family a place of their own. Everyone kept telling him the baby looked just like him. And it truly did, to such a degree that the fact he personally knew two others who could have fathered the child raised a doubt in his mind only at odd moments. "Naw. That baby is mine," he concluded every time. After all, one of the other guys had bright red hair, the other black. The baby was so blond Wilma put olive oil on its eyebrows lest it be mistaken for a honeydew.

Odd had a tan roadster on which he had made a down payment parked in Mac's side yard. The fact that he had found reason to buy it before finding means to move galled Mac enough, but when, every time he wanted Odd for work, he had to pull him away from the car, Mac began to equate him in particular and Swedes in general to matter lower than whale shit, which if once surfaced and dried would have the consummate worth of a fart in a maelstrom.

"He's a romantic," Wilma claimed. "He's the most gentle man on earth."

"He's a dreamer," Mrs. Mac decided.

"Well, he sure as hell ain't no farmer!" Of that MacDeramid was certain.

Nor did Odd confess to harboring a vision of some perfect little place somewhere in the future when the independent farmer got his just due. He would like to have driven at Indianapolis in the 500, flown the Atlantic, written his name in the sky. And he was good with machinery.

One day the old man wanted Odd to go with Kenny to cut brush along the tracks, a contract the old man held with the railroad, and could not find him. He was under the car with the bell housing down and did not want to leave until he had it back up. So he lay still until the old man went away.

That night at supper Mac cursed the boy with a venom that could have stripped paint. Somewhere between the first "goddamn" and the last, the old man explained that he considered Odd's labor around there at that point of value which might be expected from someone several degrees lower than a thief, liar, and sonofabitch. When Odd allowed that perhaps the old man might have overstated the case, Mack told him to pack his fucking things and get out.

When Odd paled and wordlessly left the table, Mack really moved into high. There was no alternative. He actually did not want the boy to leave. He deeply regretted almost everything he had said. Yet his pride demanded he get some signal that he had not been totally wrong. He was ready to shake and call it square if Odd would say he was sorry. Mac's instinctive tactic ever being to force the ante against another man's pride beyond that which he was able to call, thereby saving his own.

"Well, you go on then, goddamn you! Good riddance, you goody-goody, Anabaptist, egg-sucking, useless layabout! You can just *go*, goddamn you! I won't stop you! But you ain't takin Wilma and that boy with you unless you can show you'll take care of them!" He hoped a pitch-player's hope he could play an off-jack like that for a trump.

While Odd took the stairs two at a time, Wilma tearfully flew at the old man to implore him to relent.

"I'll be damned if I do!"

She ran to bundle up the baby and gather a few things to go along, too.

"You aren't leavin this house. I raised you, bought your clothes and books and sent you to school, got the doctor for your baby, paid for the wet nurse when you went dry, dideed you both, and the only way you're goin out that door is stark naked and alone."

"You can't stop me!"

John MacDeramid had stopped a stampeding herd of two thousand longhorns once on the Chisholm Trail. He could stop anything but time and his own rage, which had to run their course.

Odd, curiously, felt for the first time since being apprised of his impending fatherhood like a man with full title to himself. Had he been less gallant, he might have whistled.

He had done his time for the stamps. Now he had done his time for the warm wonder which had held him so fast for too long when a cold car seat on the long prairie grasses was a couch for love beyond compare. For the thoughtless moment when his heart beat without care, free of all earthly need, for the length of one joyous, silver yawp that went out as far as it could go and then turned snakelike and slithered deliciously back upon itself.

Going up the stairs, he felt in his heart like calling it square. After all, he *hadn't* been the only one was a constant nagging point.

When Mrs. Mac slipped out to go talk to Odd, Mac warned, "Now you keep your nose out of this or I'll kick your ass out, too!"

But he let her go, secretly counting on her to smooth things over. He was left at the table with his namesake, who was busily puddling a plate of gruel, while Kenneth's wife, Elfie, who had presented him with his second grandson eleven months after his daughter produced his first, tried to curb the child and continue the dinner for the sake of her husband.

Mrs. Mack told Odd upstairs in the room he and Wilma shared, "Listen, he don't mean nothin by it. That's just his way. You know hardly a day goes by he don't blow up at somebody. It was just your turn. In fact, all told, you've been running a long streak of luck in that regard. Don't let the first time get you down."

"I don't want there to be a second time. No one ever talked to me like that. No one's ever called me names like that. No, Missus Mac, I can't stay." And tears were squeezed out of his anger, even as happy devils danced and clapped hands all around him in teasing inner-earshot.

"What about Wilma and the boy?" She had raised one family.

"Soon as I can, I'll get a place and they can come to me."

"But what are you going to do?"

"I don't know. There's a guy I know wants to go partners in a gas station. Maybe I can trade my car and go in with him. I was never cut out to be a farmer."

"Still, you know Wilma loves you. I would liked you two to have gotten started off on the right foot, everything nice and proper, but that don't mean you can't make a go of it."

"I sure want to."

"So does Wilma."

"Just as soon as I get set up. . . ." He was in a hurry then to go, in case the old man decided to apologize and so trap him forever.

Wilma clutched at his coat at the door and got a fleeting cold kiss and just as fleet a promise.

The tires of his roadster spun on the dirt drive when he let out the clutch and spun again when he had backed and filled and took off up Ninth.

"I think he thinks more of that damn car than he does of his wife and child" was the old man's judgment. "Gimme a piece of that pie, even if it is cold."

"Sometimes I *despise* him!" Wilma confided to her mother.

"He can't ever learn to control his temper. Now he'll sulk and grump around feeling sorry for himself until Odd comes back."

But Odd never returned. And though he did trade his equity in the tan roadster for a piece of a Skelly station on Thirteenth Street, he never got set up well enough to send for Wilma and the boy.

His sister Inga assured Wilma it was only a matter of time and acted as go-between, since he could not show his face at MacDeramid's and she could not get off the Andersen front porch. They dared not call one another directly for fear Mac or his mother would answer.

Yet, if he loved Wilma and the boy so much, everyone asked, what the hell was he doing the day he got killed trying to take the intersection at Emporia and Waterman on sheer good faith at 40 mph in a stripdown he and his partner had put together which had no brakes at all and with Miss Wichita of 1933 on the other end of the seat?

He was doing a favor for a friend, Inga was quick to maintain. Characteristically. He was running the fifteen-year-old darling to the Union Station to say good-bye to her boyfriend, who was off for one of Roosevelt's forestry camps. It was October 27, the sky was clear, the pavement dry when Odd creamed the unsuspecting citizen in a tight little sedan that had all of its original components and had until that instant run like a watch. The last thing the guy at the wheel would have suspected was that the apparition of no discernible breed flapping toward him had no way of stopping save low gear and wind pressure.

It was the accident of the year! The *Beacon* and *Eagle* both kept it on the front page from that afternoon's extra until Odd was planted. "Bathing Beauty & Young Scoutmaster." There was hue and cry for banning "collegiate cars," as the stripdowns being put together in gasoline alleys all over town were called, from the public roadways.

So there was Odd's heap plastered all over the pink front page with pictures of him and Miss Wichita inset. Hers had her sash cutting diagonally across her bathing suit the same way Odd's merit badges did across his. A picture of the wreck had a dotted line arcing from the driver's seat of the stripdown to a fat Maltese cross on the curbing where Odd came down splat—right on his head. Miss Wichita got out with a fractured collarbone, cuts, and abrasions that would keep her from ever running for a beauty prize again. Her boyfriend left for the woods feeling like the loneliest woodsman on earth. On the train he got drunk on a fellow recruit's home brew and made a vow to stay off women forever. She hadn't been any virgin, either.

There were close-ups of the wrecked car to show how it was covered with hep sayings like *Kiss Me Quick, I'm Hot & Steamy! Don't Laugh Lady, Your Daughter May Be Inside! Air Brakes!* And on the back the admonition: *Speed On Big Boy. Hell's Only Half Full.* Odd was twenty-two years old, which some felt was a little long to remain an Eagle Scout.

There was a grotesque row in the hospital with the Andersens on one side of the bed and the MacDeramids on the other, with Odd stretched out between, his head completely wrapped in bandages and no further known cares in this world.

The argument raged over whether or not the surgeons should go into his head in hope of keeping him alive, even though they assured them he would never be "right" again even if they were successful.

"He isn't in any pain now," they swore. He was in a coma. It wasn't even a 50-50 chance he would ever truly waken again even if he lived.

"He wouldn't know us?" his mother asked.

"Not likely. There has been a lot of brain damage."

"Please try!" Wilma begged.

"And who will pay for the specialist?" Mrs. Andersen was forced to ask. "Who?" No one volunteered. She had a little doughnut business she ran out of her kitchen. Her next to youngest, Bjorne, hustled the things door to door. Her second husband serviced Singer sewing machines and collected the seamstresses' quarters. All the kids had to work. There was no money for specialists. "Will you take care of him for the rest of his life? Him like a helpless baby?"

"Yes. Yes, I will!"

"No. You wouldn't. Someone has to face the truth. Maybe what you and Odd did when he came back is called a marriage, but in the eyes of God it is condoned fornication. A girl like you isn't going to sit home nights with a husband who is a vegetable." She began to weep, dabbing at her bright black eyes, a strangely dark Scandinavian woman whose roots reached back to some captive of Vikings, a woman with the dark corners of a hut in her eyes. "I *can't!* I just can't. I haven't the strength. I haven't the money. It's *silly* to talk. *Silly!*" Her tears were gall, and they fell mostly inside, where they burned without consuming.

What did that hot-assed little bitch know? Her decision to let her son die was like something ripping her very sex out of her. He lay there with life still in his lungs, and she had to be the one to say, "We can't afford no specialist." She had to be the one to commit her heart to his death. "Let him go. For God's sake! He has paid enough!"

It was all retribution. He had been a good boy. A clean boy. A Christian leader. An Eagle. And he had lain with that silly girl, got her with child. He had stolen for her and been put in jail. He had been scorned by her family. He had been killed. And in her heart she wondered, as did everyone else, what *had* been his plans for Miss Wichita?

Inga tried to bring peace between the families during the two-day vigil it took Odd to die and ended up going to sleep at the MacDeramids' until after the funeral.

Jacky got a new pair of patent-leather shoes from Robough-Buck's basement for the funeral. His uncle Hans came in from a forestry camp up in Minnesota. He was the brother closest to Odd. Wilma and the boy rode with him and Inga and Bjorne to the funeral in spite of Mrs. Andersen's objections. She was driven by her husband and escorted by her youngest son, Billy, who was the only child dark and myopic like herself. Mrs. MacDeramid thought the boy looked a lot like Mr. Allen, the woman's second husband, but she was quick to say it was probably only a coincidence.

The Boy Scouts and Odd's Young People's Sunday School class were there to bury him. Reporters from the papers were there. They got a picture of the pretty widow and the little towheaded boy in an itchy blue wool sailor suit. When it was time to go past the coffin, the boy's mother held him up for a last look. The boy wanted to kiss his dad and make him well. Wilma, ever an optimist, a reader of horoscopes, gave the boy a shot at it. Nothing happened. They put down the lid. Everyone began crying again. The music came up. The Sunday school bore him out between an honor guard of Scouts.

They ran a picture of the boy with a wrap-up on the story and an obit in that afternoon's *Beacon* under the headline: BABY'S KISS FAILS.

Little old ladies came around to tell Wilma and Mrs. Mac what a lovely funeral it had been, bringing covered dishes, looking to do the dishes, sweep up, help out.

"Why, he looked so natural," one whispered, "I expected him to sit right up and say, 'Hello there, Mrs. Stevens,' just like he always did. Just to give me a fright. He was always jokin. It's so sad. He was such a lovely person."

"And like all Swedes, one of world's worst drivers," the old man would mutter in the other room behind his newspaper.

"I guess little Jacky doesn't really miss him yet, does he?"

They stared at the boy playing with a spool-wheeled wagon on the floor.

"I don't know. I think he understands," the woman said.

"I tell him his daddy has gone to live with Jesus," Wilma said.

Longing to see his father became part of a general feeling of deprivation on the part of the boy rather than a remembrance of any specific good time together.

"I want him to know his father," Wilma said. She swept the boy up in her arms, kissing his cheeks.

Mrs. MacDeramid said, "Wilma, stop babying him. Now's the easiest time to spoil him of all."

"Oh, Mom, but he's all I have left now."

She didn't ask what it was she thought she had before. She said, "Well, you better watch it. I don't care how much you do for that boy, he's never satisfied."

# 2

THERE came a loud, thigh-slapping, black-haired woman from St. Louis in a '29 Ford, with a boy that should have been weaned long ago fastened to her big breast, a hole in the muffler, and a boot in every bald tire. No other woman in the world other than Stella Coker, Aunt Elfie's sister, could have made the trip. Left her worthless husband for good this time and come home to her mama. When her mama would not let her in the house, she came to stay at the MacDeramids'.

"Mom never did like Gus because he was a Catholic. Said she would as soon seen me married to Satan. After six years with that philanderin, drunken sonofabitch, so would I!" Stella explained.

The boy stared at her there at the kitchen table, her pig-faced brat,

Claude, sucking on the biggest, whitest tit he had ever seen. Claude was as big as himself. He was amazed.

There were strange sounds and inflections in the woman's voice that tickled and thrilled him through the awe that filled him. So when she interrupted his gaping reverie by slipping her nipple from her kid's lazy mouth and giving him a squirt warm and sweet, full in the face, across the length of a harvest table with both leaves in, the thin, blue-white trajectory became a mortal contrail across his mind, the big raspberry nipple a lasting standard. The boy thought he had been shot.

And then he heard that raw, wonderful, loose St. Looie laugh. Where else do women laugh just like that? It made St. Louis one of this nation's great cities for him, forever. A tough, white broad of a city with a big swart laugh that may have come upriver from New Orleans, but it was those St. Louis women, black and white, who honed it to a new edge. It was "Daddy now you're signifyin', let's see you do some qualifyin' " blues. "Power to you, Daddy!" Where women would drink from the bottle like men.

"What's the matter, honey? Cat got your tongue?" she hee-hawed like a jenny. The bray went clear through the child. He stood there looking as if he had to go to the bathroom, with her milk running down his face.

"Want some titty, too?" She waved her unoccupied breast at him. She gave Claude a jog. "Eat up, buster, or I'm going to give it away."

The kid woke up, growled, waved a threatening paw, and went back to his lunch with a vengeance.

Jacky's mother hadn't nursed him. She had tried, but her milk wasn't any good. Mrs. Mac claimed it was just she wanted to get back in circulation and not be tied to a schedule. So they put the kid on raw cow's milk until he nearly died. Then they hired a colored girl who came every morning and milked herself with a breast pump but had a transportation problem and was replaced by a couple of goats the old man rented from a neighbor, promising to trade work at hay time.

"There's sure as hell enough here for two," Stella said. "I'd of weaned him long ago, but times are so hard and I got so much. Never known no one to keep milk as long as me. Seems a shame to let it go to waste. OW! But I wish the bastard wouldn't bite! I think he does it just to be mean. I really do. Just like his goddamn father, may his tallywhacker rot off for all the dingy places it has been in instead of me. OW! Damn it! Cut it out." She gave the kid a little shot on the noggin to make him quit biting.

"They say," Elfie said, "if you keep nursing you'll continue to produce milk for years."

"Look, Elfie, he really does want some. Poor little mammaleft, papa-left fella. He is a beautiful boy, ain't he? Think I ought to give him a little? Bet he wouldn't bite. You wouldn't ever bite a girl's titty, would you?"

He solemnly shook his head that that was the farthest thing from his mind.

She whooped. "Comere." She drew the boy to her, just nuzzling the corner of his mouth with her nipple. "Ummm, good," she hummed in his ear. Claude stopped to watch what was going on. Stella giggled deep inside. Jacky took a tentative taste. The milk was warm, and sweeter than any milk he had tasted. He took a deep pull. It filled his mouth. He could feel her breast filling back of his lips, the juice sucked from her body. There was a warm mad moment of utter calm when he felt connected to the woman in some everlasting way. Then Claude let out a growl and kicked him right in the face. He instinctively gave the other kid a punch. Stella held him off.

"Here! Here! Boys!" Then she laughed. "Oh, you're a jealous little fart, aintcha!" She rocked the piggly-eyed kid against her huge, squashed breasts.

Elfie laughed, too. They did not notice or care that the tears in the boy's eyes had not been drawn by the kick. He hated the other kid, hugging up there to her front so satisfied, clutching the woman with arms outspread to hold her for his own.

When she lifted a pint of whiskey and took a big belt from the bottle, her face tilted up under the naked, mothblown bulb, her soft deep throat metering the flow, and both big breasts hanging out there, he shivered so one would wonder if he hadn't a touch of epilepsy. From then on, in waiting for a glimpse of Stella, time in all its agonizing spread and fearful brevity was born in the boy. She was too long coming, and too quickly gone away.

He hung around Stella until it became an embarrassment for everyone. She could not lift her arm to drink without giving him a shot in the eye with her elbow. His grandmother and aunt became so ashamed of him they took turns trying to interest him in something else, giving him empty spools and tins to play with until they saw he was luring little Claude over into a dim coal bucket's corner with the stuff so he could beat it back to Stella while the other kid was hung up on the Clabber Girl on a baking powder box.

"I simply don't know what's got into that child," Mrs. Mac said.

"I've never seen him act like this around anyone before," Elfie corroborated.

When Stella looked down and found him under the table on all fours gawking up between her carelessly crossed legs at her big black muff, there was no longer any doubt in her mind.

"He wants to see my pussy! And by God, he's doin it, too!"

She scooped the boy up and bent him backward over her knees and pinched his sunsuit where it wasn't even manly enough to have a pee hole yet and shrieked, "Elfie! Lookee! He's got a little-bitty old hard-on."

And dropped the kid as if he were on fire.

"You ought to see a doctor or something about that kid" was her advice.

"They're all like that," Mrs. Mac said, though not so sure Stella might not be right.

"Yeh. But I never seen one so cocksure where it's at! I always did say he had a kind of old look in his eye, even when he was just a baby."

"Stella, he's just a baby now."

"Listen, he was lookin where he was lookin, and whatever he was thinkin, it wasn't no goo-goo baby thoughts. Listen. Nothin surprises me. They have them mathematical genuises can do arithmetic in their heads, why not a sex genius?"

"Oh, Stella."

"Well, you never know."

The boy's grandmother and grandfather discussed it in bed that night. She wondered seriously if perhaps giving him that colored girl's milk could have done something to him. The old man thought if there was a problem, it could just as easily be traceable to the goats. He was much too tired to give a damn either way. The only thing the boy was likely to catch up to then was old Star the cat. And she had been laid by every race, creed, and color of tom from both sides of the tracks, as well as by a purely wild, full-blooded American Indian cat from the Reservation School way out on Twenty-first Street who had been too wild even to meow, making his intentions known by hisses, spits, and growls. Star could take care of herself.

With the boy, it was only Stella. He haunted her shadow right up to the minute she slid into her car with Claude rattling around the back seat like a pea in a colander, hiked her hem into her lap, advanced the spark, and headed back toward St. Louis with her knees spread wide to catch the breeze, leaving the boy with nothing but a nagging desire, some slobbered-over spools, and a baking-powder box that smelled of urine.

Her husband had sent her a letter with some money in it, asking her to come back. It was the letter that was the main thing.

"That sonofabitch never wrote nobody a letter in his life," she mused, studying the tortured hand on the child's tablet paper. He had signed it "Yrs truly, Augustus P. Coker."

The main thing was the letter. The boy hated that letter.

The morning after she had gone he was out early astraddle a hay hook with the point down, plowing rings around the front yard, with one eye out on the unlikely chance she would come back and the other searching ahead for those ball-breaking stones, clumps, and roots, which could just make him sick if he plowed into them full force.

The sun was straight up. His shadow had dwindled around his dusty bare feet. As he looked up, he felt as if he were toppling over backward. As if the house were falling on top of him. Beyond was a flat horizon broken only by roofs and an occasional tree. The blue sky was everywhere and teeming with invisible things. He thought he felt the earth turning.

He knew she was not coming back. She had been gone too long for the little hope he had harbored all morning to come true. She had been gone too long for any forgotten thing to draw her back.

He hated her then with the envy of an orphan. He would have been so much better for her than Claude. He dropped the hay hook and ran for the house and into the kitchen as if being chased.

"My land! What is it?" his grandmother wanted to know.

There were no words that he knew that would convey his ache.

He began to sob, "I want my mama!" It was a demand. He meant—now!

"Well, your mama ain't here now, and I don't know when she's coming back. She don't tell *me* no more."

"You mad, Grandma?"

"Not at you. You just hop up here and eat some of this good tater soup. Then you take a nice nap and you'll feel better."

All her life she said things like that without believing them herself. And still found strength to be demonstratively disappointed when her ministrations never made anyone feel any better.

The boy fell into fitful sleep with his chest full of tears and an undigested ache in his throat.

# 3

THE boy snuffled awake to a house still asleep in the afternoon. He peeped into rooms where his grandmother and aunt were down for naps. Elfie's new baby slept in his old baby bed in their room. The men were down in the fields. The house was silent, shade-drawn to save the morning cool. The boy went on tiptoe, for there was something secret and illicit in a house asleep in the afternoon.

He prowled softly about, poking into things. He opened the tobacco-smelling drawer in a rickety, copper-lined humidor beside his granddad's chair in which he found decks of playing cards, some pencils, and an old-fashioned, fat, broken, tortoise fountain pen that smelled acrid and made him wrinkle his nose. The pen had been Mrs. MacDeramid's father's. It had been made in France. Once part of a set in a velveteen-lined box, the clasp and the nib were 24-carat gold. It was the only personal possession of her father's she had left. Though MacDeramid could never get it to write, she kept it as a remembrance. Because she was a practical woman, she did not keep it in any secret place.

There was one deck of cards in a box better than the other two decks, which were held together by rubber bands, the bands brittle and granulated with age. The cards smelled of tobacco and face powder, with which MacDeramid dusted them to make them slip easily when he dealt. Pitch was his game. He played High, Low, Jick-Jack, Joker, and Game. It was an old cowboy game, a railroad game sometimes called Coon Can. On days when it rained too hard to work, he and Imo, the colored hired man, and a neighbor or two would set up a board out in the barn and play all day, keeping score on another board the old man had whittled clean for the purpose. The boy was always finding their scoreboards out in the barn. He saved them for the hieroglyphics.

The pencils in the drawer had all been carefully sharpened with the small blade of the old man's pocketknife. Just looking at the points, the boy could see in his shade-drawn mind the old man meticulously whittling a pencil to a perfect point as if the world were really in no hurry to see all the pictures a boy could draw.

The old man had been taught to write by the wife of a rancher down in Texas who took him in when he was twelve, after he had been a year alone on the trail. He took pride in his penmanship, often practicing it on the margins of newspapers after he had finished the news and sat mulling over its many implications. He would write the full names of the entire family in a beautifully pointed, flowing old script that went back to Lincoln's time.

He also saved small bags of the size one got penny candy in. He usually had a bag of horehound drops in his coat pocket, or lemon drops. He saved the bags. He saved twine, rolling it into a ball. He saved envelopes on which he had penciled some long forgotten reminder. It was all there in his humidor drawer. In the big bin below, there was a tin of twisted tobacco hanks he could chew or smoke. There was a box of King Edward cigars. And a few bags of Bull Durham smoking tobacco with yellow drawstrings. He used tobacco every possible way except as snuff. The boy got the empty Bull Durham bags for marbles and treasure.

He went to the Victrola and pulled out a lot of records and pushed them back in their flocked stanchions just to feel them slip. The records were a quarter of an inch thick.

On the shelf beneath the Victrola there were the family albums. Watery old brown pictures crumbling in the front, mostly of his grandmother's kin. There were only a few photos of his grandfather's relatives, all pretty new. The old man's folks all looked like Abraham Lincoln, even the women. He had run away from home in Tennessee when he was eleven, after the Civil War had left his family destitute and headless. It was only when he was a grown man, married and a father, that he made an effort to let his brothers and sisters know he had survived out West.

Mrs. Mac's parents, Jesse and Sarah Coxe, were in twin sepia ovals decorated around with a scrollwork of loving doves. The birds in juxtaposition to those faces were as incongruous as a cradle in a Shaker sitting room. He had a beard like a spade. She had a face like a clenched fist. They were Quakers. He was a baker who had gone West and opened a bakery and rooming house in Dodge City when it was a big cattle town and Katie Coxe, the boy's Grandmother Mac, was a little girl. There were four other daughters, Katie was next to oldest, and a younger brother, born during "the change," who was never quite right. "You know," women whispered behind their hands about Mervin.

And neither was his old man. They both ran off. Coxe heard voices. Moreover, he believed them. It was a gift, was his view. And they did get him out of the house more than he ordinarily might go. Though the voices always told him to take off, they had, until Mervin was born, also told him to wander back. After the boy was born, Coxe had to be fetched home.

When Mervin reached puberty, he started cutting out, too. For some reason, he and his old man never went in the same direction. Mervin got so bad they had to put him away in the state hospital, where he was employed molding plaster of Paris figurines which everyone in the family was expected to buy at Christmas and Easter.

Neither father nor son ever struggled to remain where they were found, each returning home or to the hospital as docilely and unashamedly as a straying cow.

The last time old man Coxe heard a voice, it sent him off headed East without a satchel, an overcoat, or a change of underwear, to be dug up a couple of months later in New York, where he had signed on as cook on a cattle boat bound for Liverpool. The boat was due to sail on the next tide when they found him. He raised some slight objection about missing his chance for an ocean voyage, but it was against his religion to fight. Liverpool was where the voice had told him to go. It had guided him to the very ship. He never revealed what, if anything, the voice had in mind for him to do there.

Probably the voice did not give him instructions of that nature. Probably the voice took one look at Great-grandmother Coxe's kisser and told him, "Man, cut out! Even if it's too late for you, you've got to try!" Not that she was ugly. Just bitter as scald. And where would a guy married to a woman like that for all those years run off to? Not Tahiti. Coxe could never make a jump like that. He would have to work up to it by stages or get the bends. That voice knew what it was doing—Liverpool. It was always that kind of family.

There was a wedding picture of John and Katie MacDeramid. They were better-looking people than any two people the boy had ever seen. She was beautiful. Truly! That was a tremendous shock. Those two great-looking people were actually his grandma and grandpa. She had lost the most since. Only in her eyes was there still a resemblance to the girl she had been, standing there behind his chair in a yard somewhere with a flowering trellis framing them. She had on a long white skirt and a white puff-sleeved shirtwaist with a dark band around her waist, her hair swept up in a gigantic Gibson Girl pompadour. She was twenty, her face radiant yet demure, her eyes alive and mischievous. Even the boy could see in the picture why they had married each other. Before reason became questions. Her breasts swelled the nipped-in shirtwaist to precisely the full-spinnaker running before the wind, flying pennants, that had been Gibson's obsession.

Mac was handsome, a foot taller than his wife at six feet two inches, with a ready smile of good teeth, dark wavy hair breaking over his ears, and shy, bright eyes even more mischievous than her own. He had thought at the time he was about thirty. At least, that is what he put on the license and saw inscribed in the family Bible. It was when they tried to get him to register for the draft in 1917 that his wife discovered that she had married a man of forty that long-ago sunny afternoon. It was too late then to make any difference. The old man always looked young. But she never forgave him. In the back of her mind was the nagging awareness that it had all started with a lie, and the Christian wonder if it might have been better if it hadn't. When furious, she would remind him, "If I had known how old you were then, I'd never of married you!" And he would wonder if war might not have been more peaceful.

He had on a suit in the photo sharper than any he ever owned after, complete with frock coat and white brocade vest with mother-of-pearl buttons, that was bound to make any little baker's Quaker creamy as that slick, rich cloth. Across the vest looped a heavy gold watch chain with a solid gold bear fob.

They went from the photograph to a sod house on a prairie homestead near Rocky Ford when life and dreams were twin and everything one needed was possible by hard work. They quickly had two children, a girl and a boy. But the house was still sod. Hard work hadn't produced board one.

Then Katie discovered a lump in her right breast. She was down to seventy-eight pounds before she admitted she could not cure the thing with hot packs and prayer. John found a woman doctor in town who was willing to try to cut the thing out. No one asked to see her credentials. There was only twilight-sleep for anesthetic. The woman did the cutting while Katie lay in her bridal bed with a rubber sheet under her and her wrists tied to the head of the bed. When the tumor was loose, the woman applied the mouth of a hot pint Mason jar over the place and drew the thing out. It filled the jar half full. Miraculously, the young woman lived. Her hair had been cropped short. She was little more than a skeleton. Most of the breast was gone. There was a hollow scar on her chest the size of a five-pound cannon ball. And ever afterward, she seemed constricted by some slight but gnawing pain. So she never fully straightened up again. Not like the proud, straight-backed young woman whose tits were melons in the photo. Only somebody after something ever called her beautiful again.

After that, without raising a permanent wall, they gave up home-steading to move back to Dodge, where John took a job as deputy U.S. marshal. Perhaps to change her luck, Mrs. Mac decided to switch churches and joined the Methodists. Mac would never join any church, though his people had been Presbyterians. (Later, when the Depression came, she converted again, going from the Methodists to The Church of Christ. Her excuse was centered on the discovery that nowhere in the New Testament was there any mention of instrumental music in the church, and the Methodists had a pipe organ. You could only go to heaven *a cappella,* it seemed. "Call *that* divine revelation!" MacDeramid said.)

Later they had run a cook shack on wheels, drawn by a four-up of mules, following the wheat harvest all the way to Canada to earn the money they had put down on a place in Wichita. It had never been easy.

Now it was all up to Roosevelt. "If he don't do something pretty quick, the jig's up with us," Mac was convinced.

And Roosevelt hadn't a notion in the world what it would take to save Mac.

# 4

THEY once made hay hooks out of steel fine enough for gun barrels—while the National Guard drilled with broomsticks for rifles. A hay hook was thick as a man's finger, as long as his forearm, with a D-ring handle bent into one end and a pointed hook the size of his loosely cupped hand at the other. It contained enough nickel that ordinary use was sufficient to keep it free of rust. The hooks were used to drag and stack dusty bales of hay that dropped out the back of a rattling old McCormick hay baler that was powered by MacDeramid's equally ancient, steel-wheeled Case tractor via a long slapping strap twisted between the flywheels of the machines.

For the boy guarding the burlaped gallon jug of cistern water beneath a fence-line sycamore, waiting to be summoned by one of the thirsty men, the scene was the initial circus. His Uncle Kenneth was up on the buckrake driving two mules, combing the field, rolling up a great, dusty curl of sweet, sneezy alfalfa, a dusty breaker of prickly weed.

The rake bucked and left the big roll of hay for the old man and Imo to pitch into the baler. Dust rose up around the clanking machines on visible waves of heat and flattened and hung there in the crystal sky, a cloud churning with bits of leaf and stem.

The bales dropped out a tattered canvas door at the back of the baler, slipped down a shiny galvanized ramp, square as a crate, tied neatly with new wire. Imo and a neighbor trading work hooked the bales at each end and threw them aboard the hayrack. They would go five, six, eight bales high. The neighbor would drive it in, a mere mortal standing way the hell up there on top in loose, faded blue biballs against the glaring, heat-bleached denim sky, with the thin black reins dipping down to the mules. The mules leaned into their collars, squatted, their leathery black assholes pooching out, and the whole shivering contraption moved! On *wheels!* As impressive to the boy as a full-rigged schooner. It was like the deck of a ship up there. The boy would leap up and wave his straw hat at the man and the man would wave back, clucking to the mules.

Awesome. Wonderful. The boy felt pulled right out through his eyes, so time skipped for several lost beats of his heart and could never be reclaimed, only remembered. To a child—so total the view!—not only the scene but also nuts, bolts, depth of flaking paint, granulated rust as interesting as the surface of the moon, the ooze of axle grease around a tortured hub, flecks of foam where the harness rubbed a mule, the green-gold back of a fly in its ear. Pure odors, high-fidelity sound, once and never again that perfect surrealistic view, from eye to brain to infinity for uncounted, selfless beats of the heart. Afterward, there was always the critical memory.

His grandfather raised his arm and motioned to the boy. He grabbed the jug in both hands and heaved it along on his leg down to where the men worked. He could see the old man's hands on the smooth pitchfork shaft. They could have grown on a tree. The dark hairs on his wrists and the backs of his hands were pasted down with sweat; the palms of his hands were smooth as a saddle seat—sure hands with tools, animals, a child, even more careful and less hurried than the women's hands. Thick gray hair stuck to his bumpy forehead beneath the brim of an ordinary felt hat sweated and dusted and faded to a neutral earthen shade. All the men, white and black, wore hats or caps of a common earth color. Hat or cap, gray chambray shirts or blue, their clothes were a distinct uniform that meant only manhood to the boy. And work. The future.

Sweat ran down the old man's big nose and dripped off the end. He lifted his hat and wiped his face on his sleeve. He had a horn like the handle of a Frontier Colt.

The men stopped and came to the water jug. Mac handed the jug first to his neighbor, who handed it to Kenneth, who passed it to his dad, who handed it to Imo. The old man then drank his fill, the water wetting his stubbled chin, dripping down his neck, dampening his shirt.

"You go in on the next rack, Son, and bring us another jug."

"I will, Grandpa," the boy promised.

The men smiled.

"That sure is a good little boy," Imo said.

"Sure looks like a Scandinoovian," the neighbor said. "His papa was, wasn't he?"

"That's right."

"He was an odd fellow," Kenneth put in.

"Really? I knew an Elk once and had an uncle who was a Woodman."

Mac and Kenneth were laughing. "No. He means he *was* odd. Even named Odd. Odd Andersen."

"Sure. Killed hisself or somethin a year or so back. Remember readin about it in the paper. I'm Irish, myself."

"Damn! This is a hell of time to let me know that. If I'd of been appraised of that, I'd of never let you near one of my mules. Don't want them contaminated by false prophecy."

"I ain't no Catholic Irishman. I'm a drunken Irishman!"

The men had their laugh and went back to work.

Riding in on the next load of hay, the boy climbed clear to the top, where it swayed so much he hung on tight, up where the leaves of trees brushed him when they went by.

The next morning he was out in the barn early to check on the new hay up in the loft. Though he had never climbed higher than the stanchions over the stalls, he had it in his mind to go clear up to the mow.

Nelly was there in her stall. She checked on him before poking her muzzle back into her box to nosh oats. Imo was around somewhere. The boy could hear him whistling. The cows, the mules, and the other horses were already outside. Harness hung along the front wall behind the stalls. Curry combs, cracked leather-backed grooming brushes with the bristles worn down to stubble, bottles of viscous liniments, tins of salves, leather dressing, all kinds of horsey stuff. But everything, harness, saddle, bridle, everything had been patched, wired, riveted, tacked, or sewn. There was nothing new on the place.

Hung near the door on a lateral stringer by their points were the hay hooks all in a row. The boy tipped one down. When it hit the floor,

Nelly jumped and grumbled in her oat box. Nelly was considered almost family, a sort of honorary aunt, who was quite aware of her position. He tiptoed the hook out of there.

Point down, with him astride, the hook was a jouncy plow scratching a furrow behind. It was the greatest fun until he plowed into something solid and damn near dehorned himself. The hurt made him very aware of his parts. He plowed around, then, content simply to drag the hook behind by hand, wondering at the difference between men and women.

He plowed over to the pig pen alongside the barn, where Imo was leaning on the fence looking up at the persimmon tree which grew so near the pen it had to be harvested at just the right moment or the hogs got half.

"Want a simmon, boy?" Imo asked him.

"Please thank you," he said all at once, rather the one before and the other after.

"Tween the old blackbirds and the hogs, they ain't *too* many simmons for folks." He climbed the fence and up into the tree.

They were not very ripe. The first bite about drew the boy wrong side out. Imo laughed just right rather than hee-heed the way he did if there was anyone around except the boy and his grandad. He tested the next one, taking a delicate bite with his crooked yellow teeth to make certain it was sweet before handing it to the boy.

It was warm from the sun, dusty and sweet, a wrinkled, measling persimmon the color of Imo's thumb. All flavor or all pucker, out of that Calvinistic soil they were absolutes. Imo liked them better than anyone except the boy and his granddad. Which somehow made them closer kin across the greater distance than all the uncles and aunts and cousins over the shorter. He climbed all over the tree one year tying bits of cloth to the branches to scare away the birds. It never worked. The gray little pennants still fluttered from some of the branches.

While the boy was lost in weighty consideration of his spiritual lineage, Imo ambled off and disappeared behind the barn.

Presently, the boy plowed after him.

Imo had been back there for a minute or two. The boy had all that machinery to cope with. He rounded the corner. There he was. The boy stopped. Imo was standing there facing the barn with his big black dick out, meditatively pissing on a dry cow chip. The prairie was open behind him all the way to Kechi. Everyone went to the privy. One of the first things Jacky had been taught was not to leak in the yard. But that wasn't it.

IT WAS BLACK!

Imo's pickle was black! He could not believe it.

"What's the matter, boy? You never seen a man taking a pee?"

"Sure. But . . ."

"What?"

"It's black!" He backed a few steps.

"What you spect it to be, red, white, and blue, boy? I'm black all over."

"Oh."

"Sure. An listen, it don't hurt the function none whatsoever. No. This one's just as good at makin hay as a white one. Some say it even better. Don know none about that. Never used no white one." He shook the last drops out of it and dropped it back into his shapeless biballs.

Makin hay?

Everyone turned stone silent that evening at supper when the boy told about seeing Imo's black pickle. Then the old man laughed. At the end of a sudden hush in which you could hear knife against plate and bugs flying blindly against the screens, the boy knew the laugh had saved him from a spanking. When the women laughed, they covered their mouths with their aprons.

"You stay out from back of barn. You're too little to start learnin about the conversations that go on there." The old man smiled.

"I swear it was that goat's milk we gave him as a baby," Mrs. Mac said.

"Jerry isn't like that," Elfie put in. "He's not nearly like Jacky was when he was that age." The intimation was there was something wrong with Jacky. He *had* tipped himself back in his high chair that time, hitting his head on the stove.

"Listen. He's smart as whip. He's just way and the hell ahead of everybody else, that's all. If he don't get hurt or beat to shit, that boy is going to be something." Mac shook his fork at the boy for emphasis. The boy glowed.

But it worried him about Imo. "Why don't Imo go to the privy, Grandpa?" he wondered.

"Well, because he's a black man. Now me, I don't care. It don't rub off, you know."

The boy had wondered about that.

"But the women, they are a little squeamish about sitting down after a black man."

And that somehow scared the boy more than before. The news had the quality of a ghost story with the dark camped out on the porches and bugs knocking blindly at the screens. It was his initial ghost story.

In his dreams he saw Imo turn red, white, and blue, striped like a barber pole, rotating slowly in a hay field.

Through his dream he heard the old man yell out the upstairs window:

*"Wilma, you and that sonofabitch going to sit out there in the drive makin hay all night?"*

The boy got up and looked out the window. There was just a car parked in the drive in the shadow of the elm. No one was making hay.

"It ain't no sonofabitch, Mister Mac. It's me, Clifford Scrovis."

"It's the same thing. Go home, Clifford. Wilma, get in here!"

The boy saw her get out of the car, settle her skirt around her hips. She sort of skipped, swinging her purse. She was very pretty.

"So long, W-w-w-wilma," Clifford stuttered.

She plucked a kiss from her lips, shot her hip, and slapped the kiss on her right buttock.

"H-h-hot tamale!" he cried and backed wildly out the drive.

# 5

MACDERAMID took a sitdown bath about three times a year. Between times he stood in a washtub in the kitchen and sponged himself with a rag.

Then he would get his wife to take one of the stiff old grooming brushes he used on the horses and curry his back. His back and shoulders were covered with dark hair. Naked, he appeared to wear a loose knit suit of hair longjohns. It ended as abruptly at his collar and ankles as if it were hemmed. The brushing turned the pale skin beneath as pink as a baby's. Then he curried his hairy belly, groin, and legs.

Next he put on clean underwear—longjohns in winter, BVD's in summer—and sat down to replace the heavy cotton twine he wore in single-stranded bracelets around his angles and wrists as charms against rheumatism: unless they were woven of red and white fibers like butcher's twine, which, because of their superior medicinal properties, he would wear until they rotted off.

He shaved with one of three straight razors that fitted in a case of scabrous leather. He had hones and a professional two-tongued strop to keep the razors sharp. Of all the men in the family only he could put a proper edge on anything.

He pared his thickened nails, hand and foot, with the extremely sharp small blade of his pocketknife, then dressed them with an ordinary mill bastard file. Something faulty in his system had caused his nails to grow thick, ridged and opaque as the nacreous keratin of a horn. Ordinary scissors would not cut them.

He took particular care of his feet, spending more time dressing them than an old infantry First Soldier railroaded into a twenty-mile hike. He could spend an hour dressing his feet. His grandson never missed a chance to watch.

"Grandpa sure cusses his shoes," he reported happily.

First the old man separated each toe with a pad of cotton. A flat, hand-shaped cotton pad went under the ball of each foot. Holding the pads in place somehow, he eased on and smoothed a coarse work sock with more care than a woman putting on her last pair of hose. If it did not feel just right when the shoe was on, off it all came amid a fury of swearing, and he would start all over.

One of his problems was he would wear anyone's half-decent castoffs he could get his feet into. When he had to *buy* a pair of shoes, he went to Sam Shusterman's Secondhand Shoe Store. If the pair he fancied at a price he cared to pay were a bit large, he cut cardboard insoles and packed a little cotton in the toes; too small, he relieved them over the bunion with little slits. Large or small, he never owned a pair of shoes during the entire Roosevelt administration that he did not cuss. And he was the bane of Sam Shusterman's life. Though Sam hadn't made a sawbuck off the old man in a quarter of a century, he got a hundred-dollar cussing every morning just as if *he* were the one who had singlehandedly screwed all the MacDeramids out of their little from day one.

However, beyond the pain and cussing, in the old man's memory there was a pair of $20 Johnston & Murphys of black kid as soft as the inside of a woman's thigh and strong as iron. With one of his high-top gunboats up on his own portable last gluing on a rubber half-sole with Iron Glue, he would tell the boy all about the Johnston & Murphys, and the boy would close his eyes and see those beautiful shoes. The old man laid half-sole upon half-sole, and heel upon worn-down heel, until his old work shoes weighed more than a lumberjack's calks and were inflexible as a wooden clog. He rubbed them with stinking tallow against the wet and polished them with blacking until they gleamed. Because he had once been a man who could buy a really good pair of shoes, he never forgot, even when everything was mended and the clothes he wore were patched as a coolie's, what a good pair was.

When he washed at the basin on the back porch, he cupped the water up to his face and snorted in it like a blown dray horse while vigorously splattering water all over hell. He was some kind of animal, his wife maintained. If he had known what "mystic" meant, he would have tried talking to bears.

Still, what gentleness the boy learned came from the old man. His mother, grandma, aunts, cousins played with him as if he were a doll, fooling with his hair and clothes, trying to fashion curls where a cowlick grew, or were too busy to do anything but relocate him for their greater efficiency. Only the old man talked to him straight. Everyone else acted like everything they had to say to one another was a great secret. For him they had a special, empty language he hated. He couldn't find out a damn thing from them. But his granddad could hold him in his lap, smoke a cigar, and read the whole newspaper to the boy while drawing full enjoyment from each activity. He would read about Roosevelt's latest pipe dream and ask the boy, "What do you think about a hare-brained goop like that?" When the boy was noncommittal, "Well, let me tell you, Mister Man, that sonofabitch is going to keep on until he cuts this country's throat forever!"

He knew what they all were. "Thieves, liars, and sonsabitches! All of them! The kings, the dukes, and the czars! The NRA and WPA. The VFW, CCC, AF of L, and the CIO! The goddamned Army and Navy and all the militarists. All the damn lodges and churches, Boy Scouts, Girl Scouts, Campfire Girls, and Uniformed Pullman Car Conductors. John D. Rockefeller, the Fords, the Mellons, the Carnegies, John Jacob Astor, the Pope, and the Great I Am. The Teapot Dome and Tammany Hall! The trusts and monopolies! The Wall Street Gang and the Pendergast Gang, the War Gang and the Three Straws Drawin Gang! *Greater thieves never had a gut!*" His enemies were an array as far-flung as the eye could sweep and deeper than intelligence could reach.

"Oh, I know em! I know em all!" he would ringingly assure the boy. "And I'm not afraid to tell em, neither. They can't shut *me* up!" As if they had all mobilized to try. "I don't play the whore to no man. I tell em what they are every chance I get. I'll keep on tellin em, too. And when you grow up, *you* tell em! The bastards want it all."

Then the old man spat out the soggy butt he had bitten off in his rage, turned the page, and calmly read the boy *The Katzenjammer Kids.* He was the only one who ever read the funnies to the boy without trying to make it some big deal. He simply read the words the way he read all words. The boy had eyes to see the pictures. "The End" or "Continued Tomorrow," it was all the same to them.

When it came time to vote, Mac scorned Roosevelt after having been fooled once and rejected Landon. He dutifully registered and voted, writing in the name of Dr. Francis E. Townsend for President.

With the alternatives offered by both major parties, he increasingly saw the nation's promise as a single bag with a tricky double-looped draw closure, like a Bull Durham sack. Whichever side you pulled, it was ultimately the same piece of string. So his futile recourse was to congregate with others like himself in from a little farm teetering on the verge of foreclosure, or already encamped in some Hoover's Orchard, in front of the Fourth National Bank at the height of the working day and cuss the world's governments roundly. When the bank bolted rows of spikes on its marble sills to deny the forum seats, the old man carried on standing while the others hunkered against the cool marble facing. The bank was located at the corner of Market and Douglass, a prime intersection, so the old man and the boy were centrally located, out early, and in a great spot should a parade come by.

The old man took the boy with him everywhere. Out to the stockyards where old-timers remembered when John MacDeramid walked the catwalks over the holding pens above a herd of his own cattle. The old man was always more generous when around his old friends, buying the boy an Orange Crush and a candy bar as if he did it every day.

Then, before grasshoppers came like a biblical plague, before dust blew away whatever the hoppers had left, Roosevelt sent a man to tell MacDeramid that the farmer's salvation depended upon his readiness to plow under his wheat, corn, oats, potatoes, sorghum, and truck, slaughter his livestock, and plant soybeans. Thereby stabilizing the market.

"SOYBEANS!" Mac bellowed, rattling windows in Wooten's greenhouse two blocks away. The notion was so ludicrous he immediately perceived the fellow was demented. He *looked* Jewish or Assyrian or something. But suggesting something like that with a straight face, he had to be loose in the canoodle. Mac could not contain his amusement. "And you say Mr. Roosevelt's going to buy my beans?"

"There will be a cash subsidy for all those participating in the program," the man assured him drily.

"Hmmmm." The old man studied. "Well, lookee here. . . ." He drew his hand casually over his land, which was planted from railroad right of way to fence line across the road and from beyond the barn to the horizon on the house side. A quarter of a section all abloom. A garden of truck was almost ready to harvest in a field near the house. All around, wheat roiled lazily like a yellow landlocked sea, heavy-headed Kaffir corn leaned in a zillion Reichian lolls, Burpee's Hybrid was as high as an elephant's eye. A half-dozen little Jersey cows chewed their cuds. Poland China hogs slept happily in the good black mud. A flock of Buff Orpingtons clucked peacefully, integrated with a family of brilliantly colored Bantams. Dragonflies dipped at the water trough. Bees buzzed Mrs. Mac's flowers. A dog slept under the front porch with two cats. Out front a neatly lettered sign offered the additional services of the proprietor:

GRADING
LANDSCAPING
BASEMENTS DUG

Inquire Within

"I reckon you better go back and tell Mr. Roosevelt John MacDeramid ain't going to be able to get at his bean scheme right away. You tell him just *thinkin* about all that plowin, burnin, choppin, and butcherin he wants me to do has made me so heartsick I'd just as leave butcher myself first. See, it's taken me a few years to build this little place up to how you see it today. Oh, I know it ain't much by some standards. But it's all we have. All we've worked for. I don't guess you'd understand that. You're from back East somewhere, ain't yuh? I don't reckon you've farmed much."

"No," the fellow cut in, impatient now. "But we at the Farm Security Administration have made studies, and I can tell you—"

"You can't tell me shit!" The old man leapt in. "Why goddamn it, man, them crazy Farm Administration cocksuckers ain't got sense enough to pound sand in a rat hole! Listen! I've been a farmer man and boy since the Civil War. I've plowed the steep where you had to blindfold your mules to get em to go. I've pulled stumps that would rupture a four-up of Percherons to clear a field to plant. If all the sod I've turned were laid end to end, it would cover the states of Kansas, Oklahoma, Nebraska, and run some up the side of Pike's Peak. And never, nowhere I've ever seen, Mister Man, have there been folks so little in need they could plow under their crops and call it getting ahead. Why, that's the most contradictory fuckin notion I ever heard. Ain't never anybody ever grown *too* much. If the goddamn system can't handle what the farmer grows while people are starvin in this country right before the politicians' eyes, then it's the system that ought to be plowed under. And something that makes sense tried. Man, you act like this depression is *my* fault!"

"But you will be remunerated. . . ." It was so simple. They just *would* not understand the workings of a market economy.

"Pay me? What good will the little money you're going to pay be when the farmers have plowed up all their stuff, killed off their livestock? Shit, man, you can't eat money! Why, a piece of meat will become so dear it won't be a short week before the only ones biting meat are goddamn millionaires. And *they* are the very sonsabitches that got us into this fix to start with! Why, hell, geniuses like them couldn't keep their goddamned banks from failing with everyone in cahoots and the power all on their side. Man, there's just got to be a lot of stealin goin on somewhere. And this soybean scheme sounds like a brainstorm from the same pissin source. Whose side are *you* on, anyhow?"

"It's obvious that since you have chosen to be an obstructionist, there is no reason to waste my time further here." He sucked back his spit and went prissily toward his business coupe, undoubtedly conscious of how womanly his posteriors were, pinching them tight to look more manly under the farmer's steady gaze. They simply would not try to understand. You could not help people like that, he was certain.

The old man spat tobacco juice onto the dry earth of the yard. It formed a damp ball in the dust.

"You come back here, you butter-assed little bastard, I'll just *show* you how goddamned obstructionist this Scotsman can be! Come around here again with your harebrained scheme and I'll plant *you* and *call* it soybeans!"

Wheat sold that fall for two cents a bushel. He fed corn to the hogs, then ate the hogs. The government bought up potatoes at near seed prices and dyed them blue so not even hogs would eat them. Thereby stabilizing the potato *and* hog markets, while people got in lines alongside the Wichita Forum to wait their turn to get a handout of something to eat. A little meal, potato flour, fried peas, powdered milk, lard, beans. On relief. But there was no relief from want. The stuff was handed out in the part of the Forum where the menagerie was stabled when the circus was in town; where the swine and sheep were penned for fat livestock shows; where the concrete floor was guttered so the place could be sluiced out with a fire hose when swine and sheep were gone. The line outside was bent by city police down the alley behind the building to keep its tattered numbers from offending the eyes of those who had not yet joined it. And everyone had to bring his own bag.

MacDeramid saw a specter of the relief line when he watched his horses and mules go at auction for $15 a head. When Nellie went, he wept without making a sound. She was so gentle the kids could climb all over her and play beneath her belly as safely as in their own beds.

He tried to let Imo go. He could no longer pay him.

"Mr. Mac, there *ain't* no place *to* go," Imo explained. And stayed until near the end, sharing hogs and garden with them until he could no longer bring himself to take from their dwindling provender. One evening he told Mac he had decided to go on relief. He had three kids to feed.

Even fools who had believed Roosevelt was the Second Coming marveled at the hollowness of the cures he offered. "It's just another way to skin the working man to the bone!" Mac insisted. "Hell, man, can't you see it? Forget them fucks who jumped out of Wall Street windows. They weren't nothin. The big boys are doin better right this minute than ever before. They just wiped out the penny-ante competition."

People said Mac was nuts.

He cursed the duplicity of his own kind. He railed at his own insignificance. He searched his wife's Bible for some parallel of mass insanity. Unable to find a suitable example, he told the boy when no one else would listen, "And, Son, it's going to get worse. By every crooked means known to man, this country has cut its throat forever."

His wife heard him and demanded to know what in the world he was putting in that child's head. The philosophy of generations of Protestants was being scorned by executive order, delivered by finky little bureaucrats from some alphabet office in Washington with an official sanctimony that made the virtues of a lifetime seem the most unredeemable sins of all. Rumor that help was on its way was greeted hopefully by men at the end of their rope, leaning with their ears against someone's radio for a word from Roosevelt that would make their soup less transparent, their children less thin. But the men Roosevelt sent came to enforce, not help. Help wasn't in it! These clowns *knew*. They were the way and the light. It had all been figured out. And in their self-righteous certainty, they cut the damn rope. Cut the world out from under thousands and then called the law to still angry men severed irrevocably from their little. Their most satisfying moment coming when some desperate cropper, ripe for the lens of Dorothea Lang, stood before his nearly bare-assed family on the porch of some rundown place with his baggage all around, turned his palms up helplessly, and squeezed out the words: "What are we going to do now?"

*Then* the government could help. Then Mrs. Roosevelt could show where her heart was.

"Pity and charity are the bitterest shit they make you swallow," Mac told anyone who would listen. "Tell em to do with it what the monkey did with the nut. All we want is our just deserts."

For no matter how helpful the government was, the bank got the farm. The WPA got the cropper, though it often only wanted him a day or two a week, and he was not the man when they got him, even for a day or two, he had been before. Nor the one he had hoped to be. Nor the one his wife had so counted on. The one his kids had thought they had known.

"You know," the old man confided to Imo, "face to face, all these fine friends of the working man don't like him at all."

"You're sure right there," he agreed. "They just like them friends of us folks come nosin round. They say 'Neegrow' so it make your back teef hurt. But you ast them in for some fatback and collard greens an fresh hot corn bread—shoot! They say, 'Thank you. We just et.' Then they go scribble in their little book. Nex thing I know, I read in the paper how much good they's doin me. They keep doin me good like that an I'm goin out some dark night wif a butcher knife an cut me some beefsteak off'n somebody's cow."

As good as his word, two weeks after he went on relief Imo and two of his neighbors slipped into a pasture of a dairy farmer named Hall, jumped on the back of a sleepy prize Holstein, and butchered her on the spot. They were stopped by a cop who was curious to see what it was they were hauling up Thirteenth in two coaster wagons and a rickety pram at 2 A.M. in the moonless morning.

"It just makes you want to fight!" MacDeramid declared. "And they are giving Imo and them boys two years at hard labor. And I'll bet anything he'd of brought us some of that meat. That's the kind of man he was. But nobody gives a shit. Everybody's so down and out and worthless themselves, afraid of losing what little they got left, all the spunk's gone out of them. Nobody's goin to do nothin to stop the fools from turnin this country into a banker's patch. We ought to take guns, pitchforks, axes, any goddamn thing we can lay hands on, and march on Washington and Wall Street. Turn those bastards out. One million people with as much craw as Imo and we could clean those cocksuckers out once and for all. Turn the country back to the people. This place was never meant to be the private perserve of a few. But everybody's just standin around scared, waitin in line for a chance to kiss the government's ass and say 'donkey shane' for what comes out. And the cruelest thing is, I ain't *that* much different! I don't know how to start. And I *know* what ought to be done. OH! GODDAMN SUCH A GODDAMN WAY OF DOING!" He lifted his moan to the skies.

This from a man who had never been a soldier and never wanted his son ever to have to be one. "I'll go right now! Tell em John MacDeramid's ready to go to Washington today."

There was no one to tell.

In a bag with a tricky double-loop draw that is all of a piece, it is not difficult to keep the struggle localized while controlling it centrally. So the warfare between the Caseworker and the Client Recipient was joined for keeps.

Mac took to shaking his head sadly like a stunned bear at the monstrous duplicity of man. But he never let up on those who so counted on it. "Counted, hell! They created the game!" And though he might damn a man for being a fool, there was more sorrow for the species in it than personal animosity.

Everyone noticed he had started talking to himself, sometimes quite loud.

# 6

HUMPTY DUMPTY was what the boy thought of when he looked at the new place on the laceless fringe of Niggertown. Four rooms drooping from a central spine, shored up at each corner by a concrete block. A former tenant had endeavored to keep the winter wind from whistling under the floor by tacking flattened cardboard boxes around. The boxes had weathered and failed, until a scared cat could shoot through like a streamliner taking a tunnel. The whole shebang sagged. The floors were at such diverse cants that a ball placed in the center of any room naturally came to rest against the wall. But it could be a different wall every time. The flooring was covered with unmatched, worn remnants of linoleum.

Mac had taken the $300 he had left from the farm and invested it with a man named Miller who owned the Coffee Cup Diner and a parking lot behind. Miller was a jakelegged bootlegger who had decided straight bootlegging was more profitable than plain home cooking. And his wife was tired of running the diner. He also gave Mac's son, Kenneth, a job running the parking lot. Mrs. Mac warned the boy not to get involved with selling whiskey. He promised he would just park cars and pump gas. What she didn't know wouldn't hurt her. The house was the best Mac could afford.

A few blocks away were the city produce market, a furniture auction, a fuel oil plant, Sante Fe freight tracks, Bond Bakery, Steffen's big dairy, flour mills, coal yards, refineries, the stockyards and slaughterhouses, Wichita Desiccating Plant & Serum Company, the new soybean plant, foundries, junk yards, bottling companies, hamburger and chili joints, beer joints. One smell trailed another, caught and merged with it until there was a single anthropologically perfect odor of the time, wafting between a transient deadfall up on Central everyone called the Cockroach Inn and the last doorless outdoor shithouse in Niggertown.

Kenneth and Elfie moved in with her mother, who had a similar rundown little house across town on the West Side. Somehow, even Niggertown seemed preferable to the boy than the distant West Side, where, across the Big Arkansas River, Jesse Chisholm, looking for a gold mine, laid out a ranch to tide him over and started a town. Where the Chisholm Trail crossed West Douglass, Big Nose Kate once ran a dance hall and whorehouse and dueled another madam in the street for the favor of a tubercular little rummy, Doc Holliday. Where Texans had camped when they brought cattle up to the railhead, it was Wyatt Earp's old turf and Bat Masterson's, and not a Texan was allowed east of Main. Wild Bill Hickock played high-stakes poker in the Last Chance Saloon, but not with his back to the door. Where the cowboys once camped on the river, a Hoover's Orchard now bloomed with wild sunflowers among shacks of scrounged tin and crates, cardboard and lath, and gutted car bodies and buses: freight-car ranch homes with the faded sign of their lines still on their sides. Where the Wichitas, Pawnees, Kiowas, Wacos, Caddos, Tonkaways, Kechis, and Osage once lit council fires before the lodges, a dog run shantytown winked to life in the flickering yellow glow of a thousand coal-oil lamps. Shades of cowboys and Indians alike were deposed by the crude, unskillful cookfires of their grandchildren, who had believed mass production was the whole answer—with prayer —to the problems of the earth. You could get scalped on the West Side when Billy Matthewson staked out his homestead around Cleveland and Central on the East Side. And you can get scalped over there yet. And left for dead behind the Cowboy Inn.

There was a beer-joint-rootbeer-stand shaped like a huge keg not two blocks from their new house where the boy could get a bowl of greasy red chili, a hamburger with everything on it, and a mug of root beer for twenty-five cents. Every major circus and carnival that came to town unloaded down on Central across from Steffen's and marched up in the early dawn to set up in Matthewson's Pasture. So, in spite of the dilapidated house and its location, everyone's hopes were running high.

They could get to the Coffee Cup on the bus. It was catty-cornered across from Western Union, equidistant from the YM and YWCA's. A good lunch spot that also did a decent breakfast and dinner trade from the Y's and night Western Union people. Mrs. Mac was chef. Mac was fry cook. Wilma was waitress. They would all clean up. That was the theory. Mac had *café-au-lait*-colored business cards struck in the shape of a cup and saucer, getting Maxwell House to underwrite half the printing expense in return for featuring their coffee and "Good to the last drop!" slogan on sign and menu.

Business did pick up for a time after they took over. The Millers hadn't cared what kind of slop they threw at their customers. And if Mrs. Mac was not one of the world's greatest cooks, neither were most women of her class, who had learned to feed a family on dandelion greens and make-do gravy. Her fare was what the customers were used to. There was always some half-starved Western Union boy in mustard breeches and jacket, all elbows, teeth, and Adam's apple, gushing, "Boy, Missus Mac! If my old lady could cook like you!"

"Nickel tippers and palm ticklers!" Wilma complained of the Western Union boys. She had herself rated for bigger game and found family enterprise very confining.

With everyone working to make a success of the diner, they had hired a girl to stay with the boy. A colored girl, fifteen, who lived near enough to walk was given charge of the boy from after breakfast until midafternoon, when his grandma came home for a nap before she went back for the supper trade. Then the girl came back and sat with him until after midnight, when everyone came home. He hardly ever saw his mother and grandfather except behind the counter of the café. He seemed destined to spend his life in the company of Vireena, who didn't seem to want to talk to him at all. She always said, "Hush! Be quiet! You botherin me, boy. Go play. Go play."

She had her housework to do, magazines to read, his mother's clothes to try on. His lunch was most often a piece of white bread with oleo and sugar on it. She also lied about everything.

Then one evening Wilma exploded. "I'm free, white, and twenty-one! I don't have to be treated like a child. If I want to go out and stay out all night, that's *my* business!"

"Not when you're too drunk and sick the next day to go to work," her mother told her. "You've been hotassing it around so much you ain't been worth beans at the place. You know it, too!"

"Fire me, then!" she challenged. "I can get a better job in a minute. Where the tips are good."

"Oh, sure! You'd like that. So you can just pick up and leave, park Jacky with us, and run around to your heart's content. Free as a bird."

"Listen," the old man put in. "I've heard enough from you, girl. You can't talk like that to us who raised you and bought your clothes and books and sent you to school to learn how to better yourself, while all you want is to lay around with some sonofabitch while we take care of your little mistake. It looks like you would have enough thanks in you to show a little consideration for your mama and me now when we are workin our guts out to make something out of the place."

"You've always worked your guts out to make something. And you never made nothing. God knows you've told Kenneth and me often enough about how hard you've worked all your life. Listening to that crap is worth *something*. If you know so damn much, why aren't we rich?" She arched a favorite question of the day.

*"Why, goddamn you, you smartass little whore!"* He rushed at her trembling with rage. *"You can't talk to me like that! I'm your father, goddamn it. Even if you ain't no good, you're still mine. You'll do goddamned what you're told or I'll break your back!"*

"Daddy," his wife warned.

"What do you know about what '*good*' is?" she sneered, lifting her dimpled chin. "There are some who say *I'm* the cat's meow."

"I'll break your fuckin neck!"

She scampered away, squealing, dodging the old man. She darted into the bedroom, hooked the door, got her coat, and crawled out the window onto the porch. "Ta! Ta!" she called to the old man through the screen.

He bellowed, *"Good riddance to bad rubbish! Go to hell, goddamn you. Don't think you're ever going to get this boy here, either! Don't you ever come back!"*

When the old man came in off the porch after seeing his daughter disappear around the corner, his wife said calmly, "What made you think she *wanted* to take the boy? Now that you've done it, you might as well get used to the idea we've got him to raise."

"I'll be damned!" the old man vowed. "We've raised one family."

"A damn fine job we did, too, wasn't it?"

"Well, I did my part. I always let them know the difference between right and wrong."

"But when you were always cussin and callin names, they never seen you go to church, what did you expect?"

"Aw, bull! That don't matter. I always taught them the Lord hates a thief and a liar and a sonofabitch. I showed them what real folks were made of."

"At least Kenny is reliable. You don't think he's peddling whiskey for Miller, do you?"

"You know how he is. He don't talk much. I don't think he'd get himself in trouble."

When they were in bed, Mac said, "Listen, if she ain't back here in a couple of days, I want you to find her and get her back here. Somethin bad could happen to her runnin around loose."

"Find her yourself," his wife told him.

Wilma returned in a few days in a cab to pick up a few clothes when everyone was gone but Vireena and the boy. She had a permanent, Vireena noticed, and was wearing lipstick and eye shadow. The boy noticed a gold anklet around her leg.

"A friend gave it to me," she explained.

The boy thought it a curious place to wear a bracelet.

"Can I come, too?" he asked her.

"No, not now. You be a good boy and mind your grandma and grandpa and Vireena, and maybe the next time Mama comes she will bring you a present."

"A toy?"

"Well, maybe a toy."

"Then can I go, too?"

"We'll see. Give me a big hug."

When she had gone, the boy said, "She's pretty, Vireena."

She snorted through her nose. "Yeh, she's pretty. Wush she had the care of you stead of me, is what I wush."

It was a long day for the boy with no one to play with but Vireena. She would lock him outside or lock him inside and go outside herself, for hours it seemed. She would tell him she was going to the store for something and be gone half the afternoon. If he got into things while she was gone or made a mess, the next time she would lock him in the big closet in the bedroom, where he would scream bloody murder and become hysterical, ultimately collapsing on the bundle of wash, sprinkled for ironing, that was always in there on the floor. Sleeping fitfully, sobbing in his sleep through the afternoon where the only light came from the crack under the door and the keyhole, he would eventually emerge, blinking, unsure of whether it was night or day but so happy to be free he would hug Vireena's legs when she let him out.

When he told his grandmother on Vireena, she denied it and swore the boy lied all the time. "He don't never tell the troof about nothin!" she exclaimed. "You sure there ain't somethin wrong wif him?" Mrs. Mac wondered.

One interminable day the girl went through all the bureau drawers. She dressed up in one of the dresses Wilma had left. She put on a pair of stockings, garters, a pair of Wilma's panties, high-heeled shoes, lipstick, hat and gloves. When she was all dressed up, she wanted the boy to play games. He was never quite able to get the drift of what she had in mind, but he tried.

"We is jus married an goin to a nice resturan for to have some supper," she explained. "You gotta take my arm and lead me like I might fall." He led her.

"Now you sposed to pull out my chair and sit me to the table," she went on. He seated her.

"Now you the waiter, see, and you bring us some menu. Use that magazine." He served her.

Then she led him into the bedroom for their honeymoon. She had him lie beside her, take off her gloves, and kiss her big, puckered red lips, feel her little titties, and touch her thing, which had short coarse black hair on it and a tight little slit. She took out his little penis and got him between her legs and rubbed herself against him until it hurt or scared him. But it was when they were on their honeymoon that she was always the nicest to him. When she was grouchy to him, he often suggested, "Vireena, let's be married."

It got so she dressed up every day. Sometimes she took a bubble bath with some stuff Wilma left and often let the boy get in with her. That way she would not have to wash him later. As long as they played marriage, everything was grand.

One day a neighbor boy so blue-black his mouth looked like a wound came over, went with Vireena into the bedroom, and stayed all morning, with the boy hooked out in the other room, dying with jealousy he could not understand.

"I'm goin to tell Grandma," he threatened when the boy had gone.

He caught a slap that flattened him. "Hush your mouth! You ain't

48

seen nothin! Understan!" She had a way of using terror and flat denial even while in the very act of doing something the boy could see with his own eyes; he often no longer knew what *was* true. She told him over and over, "You jus dreamin, boy." If he insisted—spang! on the ear. "See, boy, you jus dreamin. You don see none that. You run tell your granma a big lie like that, she goin to throw you out in the alley wif the trash, an the boogyman carry you off. An they'll feed you to *hogs!* An they *eat you all up!* . . . You want to be et by hogs?"

"No!"

"Then you learn to tell the troof round here. You keep your mouf off'n me. You don see nothin. You asleep all the time. You just dream up that stuff you tell your granma, unnerstan? You a crazy boy. Your granma goin to throw you away, she keep hearin you tell her stuff like that. Now you can have no sugarbread cause you such a dreamin, lyin boy."

Until he began to stammer a bit when he spoke, and spoke less and less.

One hot morning she sat the boy out in the backyard in a tub of water to keep him cool and out of her hair. Up the alley came a man leading a brown and white pony with a big wooden camera strapped on its back.

"Hey there, towhead! Your mama home?" he called to the boy.

"No. Just me and Vireena."

The man wore greasy boot pants with high, laced boots. He had on a ten-gallon hat and a red bandanna around his neck like a cowboy. His sleeves were rolled to his knobby elbows. He wiped his face on his arm. His shirt was rumpled and streaked with dark runs and patches of sweat. He had the least little line of a mustache, no more than a plucked eyebrow.

"Vireena! Come see the pony!" The boy raised a yell. "Maybe she's nappin," he confided to the man.

What if someone had sent him that pony? His Uncle Hans had sent him a toy birch bark canoe from a forestry camp up in Minnesota; why not a pony?

Vireena peeked through the dark screen door.

"Take a snapshot of the boy on the pony?" the man offered, touching the brim of his hat. "Only ten cents a snap, ma'am. Three for a quarter."

When Vireena stepped outside, the man said, "Hell! I thought you was a white woman."

"The missus ain't here right now. I just look after him."

"Surely there must be a dime around the house. Think how pleased the missus will be when she comes back and finds a nice picture of her boy."

"I don't know she be pleased or not," she replied.

The man derricked the boy out of the tub and plopped him bareass on the pony. "Lookee! Perfect! One shot, ten cents."

"Jacky, you get down off there right now!"

"No. No. You go look for a dime. I'll give him a little ride around the yard."

"Well, I don know. . . ."

"Sure. You go look. You want to ride the pony don't you, son?"

"Yeow!"

"Well. . . ." She edged back into the house. "Just so's it's only one dime."

"That's it, ten cents, one tenth of a dollar. A smile a minute."

Vireena returned with a dime. "Listen, I think you better let me put somethin on him. I don think they goin to want no picture of him on a pony buck naked like that."

"Maybe you're right," he conceded, looking her up and down as if measuring her for something. She had on Wilma's old Chinese teddy coat and a pair of sloppy high-heeled shoes. Her face was still made up from her morning's play. She had a pretty scarf with a picture of a stag up in the northwoods on it over her nappy hair. "I wonder if I could step inside for a glass of cool water while I'm waiting," the man wondered.

"Sho. Come right in."

He leaned against the door with the tumbler of water in his hand watching Vireena dress the boy in a yellow sunsuit. He had shoved his hat on the back of his head. The silk of her wrapper slid away from her legs as she squatted to button the boy's clothes. The man whistled softly between his teeth. Vireena hadn't anything on under the wrapper. The boy could look down her front and see her little chocolate titties.

The photographer said, "Honey, you'd be a beautiful dame if you got your hair straightened."

"Wha's that?"

"Sure. You got a good body on yuh. All legs and high little nigger hump. I take pictures of dames all the time. This stuff is just a sideline. You could be a model."

"You take pictures of colored girls, too?"

"Sure. I'll show you some pictures I took."

"I never seen no colored girls in ads an magazines an things. I never seen no colored movie star cept old folks, tap dancers, an the like. I can't dance."

"All you folks can dance," he assured her as if she had never tried. "A girl like you, with legs like yours and a can like yours, can go to New York and right into the chorus line of the Cotton Club."

"Wha's that?" she asked suspiciously. Her folks had told her *all* about cotton.

"It's a big jig nightclub up in Harlem."

"You been there? New York?"

"Hell, yes! I've been all over. Hollywood. Had my own studio. Worked on a few movies. Was makin it with the rich wife of this bigshot producer. He found out about it. I kicked his ass. He had me barred from every lot in town. I've seen them all. Harlow, Garbo, Swanson, all them dollies. Harlow. You know she's got a big spotted Great Dane trained to fuck her? Yeh! Lots of them rich bitches won't hardly look at a man once they tried dog. But she's done it all. She'll go to bed with a woman as quick as a man. Couples. Parties. She'd fuck the world if she could stuff it in her."

"Who she?"

*"You ain't heard of Jean Harlow?"*

"Well, maybe I heard of her. But I don go to shows much. I go mostly to park shows. They free. But they ain't much good. Mostly they all Krazy Kat and bout the WPA buildin toilets and roads. What that, uh, Harlow look like?"

"Oh, she's whiter than you are black. Her hair is like platinum. I got a picture here I don't sell for less than a dollar taken of her naked on the beach. See, her cunt hairs are black. But they say they are platinum now, too." He flashed a postcard photo in front of the girl's wide-open eyes. A beautiful blond woman stood with her arms lifted and entwined over her upraised face like a nymph. Even in the dim photo, she could see there was not a blemish on the lush woman's fair white skin. Flip! The man had sent it back to where it had been. Vireena had not seen where.

"I've got some more. Want to see?" He looked at her in a way that made her wish she were dressed. The boy was dressed. His cowlick was plastered down.

"I'd really like to take some shots of you," the man said. He lifted one side of her wrapper. She snatched it back.

"My mammy ain't about to pay for no picture of me on a pony!"

The man laughed. "Naw. I meant some art studies. Like this." From somewhere, out tumbled a deck of wallet-sized photos onto the table.

The boy could see they were pictures of naked women. There were some with naked men, too.

"Here, you stan away from there," Vireena ordered, pushing the boy back by putting her hand over his eyes. "Thass not for you to see."

The boy noticed the man had coal-black fingernails. He put his arm around Vireena's shoulders while she studied the pictures.

"Wha's that! Wha she call herself doin?" she squeaked.

"That's called doin it dog fashion. You never do that?"

"Nosir!"

"You ever do that?" He flipped before her two men taking one woman anally and orally while a second woman knelt below with her face shoved up into the other woman's sex.

"Whooeee! No!"

"Or this? Or this?" His hand was now making big circles on her back.

"Lemme see tha again. Whooo. . . . Tha's ug*leee!* Hey. You breathin in my ear."

"How about a little drink? The man of the house keep any booze around here?"

"There's some whiskey up the cabinet, but I don think you ought to touch it. Get me in trouble. This boy got *big* eyes and bigger ears."

"Just a drop. He'll never miss it." He came back with a water tumbler full of MacDeramid's scotch, the bottle which had lasted him into its second year. "Have a snort."

"I don like it."

"Listen. Let me take your picture and I'll give you five dollars."

"Five dollars! You kiddin?"

"No, I'm not."

"Gimme a drink." She took a belt, coughed, pounded her chest. "Whoo. Le's get this straight. You goin to give me five dollars to take my picture. How you wan to take it?"

"Stripped. Naked."

"I ain't about to do none tha dog-fashion stuff."

"No."

"Maybe. Hey! Watch your hans, man." She returned to the pictures.

"You ever done it with a white guy?" he asked in her ear.

"No."

"Then you got a treat comin."

"I ain't made you no promise bout *that!*"

"You ain't got nothin on under there have you, baby?"

"Look out," she breathed. "He sees everthing. He don miss nothin, him."

"You got the slickest little twat. I like a tight one. How old are you, anyway?"

"I eighteen," she lied.

"You do it a lot?"

"There's this boy. I oney done it ten-leven times."

"Vireena dresses up!" the boy blurted.

Vireena jumped away from the man. She whirled and gave him a slap. "I do not!"

"Them's my mama's shoes and robe," he insisted.

"They *not!* These my things!" she told the man. "He lies on me all time. He's a crazy boy!"

"I'm not! You keep callin me that, I'll tell my grandma! She let me see her pee!"

Pow! Down he went. Spang! when he tried to bounce up. "Now you ain't goin to get no sugarbread. You go outside and play."

"No, I won't."

"You go or I goin to know why, damn you!"

"Hey, listen. Why don't you give him a piece of bread an jelly or somethin and he'll go outside an eat it. You'd like to go out and see my pony, wouldn't you?" the man knelt down to ask.

The boy was no longer so certain. Something was up in there. But the pony. . . .

"Sure he does. See?"

"OK. I give you some sugarbread. Then you stay outside till I call you or you get a spankin, unnerstan?"

He nodded his head. She fixed him a piece of bread with oleo and sugar on it.

"Better make him two," the man suggested, rubbing against her backside. She made him another.

He ate the sugarbreads studying the pony, which was cropping grass all around a stunted old pear tree. When the bread was gone, it was time to ride. His idea was to move the pony over near a broken-down lawn chair, climb onto the chair, then onto its back. He put his shoulder into the pony's side, succeeding in budging it close to the chair. Before he could race around to mount, it moved. The next time he leaned into it, the pony kicked out with both hind legs, and the boy fell all over himself trying to get away. He had seen men move horses and mules around all the time. That was the way they did it.

He ran to the back door. It was hooked. He banged the screen, yelling as if the beast had torn a pound of meat off him. He knew Vireena was not about to come unhook the screen for a mere wail, so he screamed as if he were slowly being squashed under the wheels of a road grader.

She came wildly flip-flapping to the door, tugging Wilma's old wrapper around her brown shoulders. Barefoot, sweaty, angry, wild-eyed, she yanked the boy in onto the porch. She shook him until his teeth rattled. "I tole you I dint wan you botherin me. Now din I told you? You goin to get it! An get it good!" She slapped his face four times, flung him by one arm onto the floor, missing a roundhouse slap as he went down. Missing infuriated her. She began kicking the boy with her bare feet as he curled in a ball holding his head with both hands, howling blue murder.

*"Hush it! Hush it! Hush it!"* she commanded with every kick. "I beat you silly, you don stop! Little peepin round, sonofabitchin bastard. You jus askin for it! Come botherin me all the time." She flailed at him hand and foot.

He tried to stop screaming by stuffing his fist in his mouth so she would stop hitting him. He almost had it. Then a sob built up and blew his fist out.

"Slappin and kickin him like that ain't goin to make him stop," the man said disgustedly from inside.

"I snatch him bald, he keep on," she promised. "He gets like a crazy boy. He don listen to me. Ack like I don know nothin. Like I don have no feelins."

"Come on, leave him be. Let him cry it out." The man took her arm. He was naked, too, except for a sleeveless grimy undershirt, stinking gray boot socks, and the red bandanna around his neck. His legs were skinny, knobby, fish-belly white with sores on them. His thing, hanging out of thin russet hairs, was skinny and mottled-looking. He led the girl back inside.

She shook a warning finger at the boy. "You bother us once more an I'll just beat you deaf. *You hear me?"*

"Yes, Vireena," he sobbed.

"See you do!"

They went into the bedroom and hooked the door. The boy crept into the living room. He heard the bed moving in the other room. He could hear them grunt and slap the way it was when the neighbor boy came over sometimes.

"Hey, mister! You in the wrong place. There you go."

The bed began bouncing again. Then it stopped.

"You sure startin and stoppin a lot," she criticized.

"Makes it last longer," he puffed.

"I don like all that startin and stoppin."

The bed bounced furiously then, briefly, then slow for a little. And stopped.

"Wha's the matter?" she asked. "You done?"

"Just gotta rest for a second, scuse me."

"You sick er somethin?"

"Naw. Just gotta catch my breath."

"Vireena?" the boy called softly at the door.

"Now what you wan?"

"I got to pee."

"You know where it at."

"I got to do poopee, too."

"Can't you do it yoursef?"

"You got to, Vireena."

He heard her get off the bed. She opened the door. The robe was open down the front. There was something shining in her little hairs.

"What you and the man doin, Vireena?" he asked.

"We jus playin a game. None your business."

"Playin honeymoon, Vireena?"

"No we ain't playin *honeymoon, Vireena!* You do your dirty an be quick bout it!"

He couldn't do a thing.

"You jus foolin me? You jus call me out to bother me?"

"No, Vireena! No. I didn't. Please don't hit me, Vireena."

"I warned you. Now you really goin to get it! Now you really ast for it. Know what I'm goin to do wif you?"

"*Vireena!* I don't want to go in the closet."

"Yeh! Tha's where you goin. Goin in there in the dark where the spiders goin to get you if you make one sound. One peep an them ole black widda an brownie spiders goin to come crawl *all* over you! An you make another peep, they goin to bite you. An you'll *die!*"

"*No, Vireena! No, Vireena!*"

"You got it comin. You was tole." She dragged him kicking and yelling to the bedroom closet. The man sat up to watch. "Get in there!" She flung him inside on the bundle of wet wash. She slammed shut the door. Because the house slanted, the door had to be hooked from the outside to keep it shut.

It was pitch black in the closet. He wasn't really afraid of spiders. His cousin's family, they were afraid. They would not go into a cellar or outdoor privy if a spider, bee, or wasp was anywhere in sight. Still sobbing, he got up and peeked out the keyhole. He could see the man rubbing

Vireena's thing with his hand. He was kissing her, but she turned her face away. Then he got up and got between her legs and tried stuffing his thing into hers with his hand. She wiggled around until he told her, "Hold still a minute. Let me."

"There!" he breathed and settled onto her.

She went, "Ufff!"

Then they were bouncing up and down on the bed, him on top of her. She said, "You sure you in? I don feel nothin."

And he went faster and faster. It looked like his tongue was hanging out. Then he went, "Oooooh, gawd . . ." and went limp on her.

"Whooosh," she sighed. "We better get up now. Maybe somebody comin pretty soon. You goin to take my picture now?"

"Hunh? Oh, sure." He got off the far side of the bed, dressed, and came back with his camera and took several pictures of Vireena. He had her sit on the edge of the bed and open her legs wide and took a picture of her thing. When he was done, he folded up the legs of the tripod and flipped the girl a coin from his pocket.

"Wha's this?" she asked, holding up the coin as if she had never seen money. "You say you give me *five* dollars. You promise."

"Well, you ain't worth five. I thought you were, but you weren't. Who can screw anyhow with that kid interrupting all the time? Who the hell you know give you five bucks to use your pussy?"

"But you *promise*."

"Naw. That's what I give chincy dark meat. You're just a hick. You fuck like I swim, and I hate water."

"I was goin to get me some high heels an a new dress wif tha money." She began crying. "You quartergivin sonofabitch! Piss on your quarter! Piss on you! Piss in your mouf! Fuck your sister nex time! Fuck your mother nex time! Take their pitchers! OW!—"

He slapped her. "You shut your black mouth. You keep your nigger mouth off my mother. Don't you mention *my* mother!" He stood over the cringing girl on the bed with his fist raised over his head as if his fist held lightning. Then he was gone.

She was sniveling when she opened the door.

"What's the matter, Vireena?"

Her fist exploded in his face. He hadn't even seen it coming. He screamed once and saw stars. Then the door was slammed shut in his face.

"I was goin to get me some high heels an a dress wif tha money," he heard her say through the door.

The wet wash felt cool against his puffy face in the dark. He laid his cheek on it and cried himself to sleep.

He was awakened by his grandmother's voice demanding, *"Vireena, what in the world has been going on here today?"*

He sat bolt upright.

"Vireena, I'm asking you. *Wait!* Where's Jacky? Vireena, where's the boy?"

*"Grandma! Grandma! Here I am! Here I am!"* he yelled in the darkness.

Her work shoes were coming fast. The closet opened.

*"Grandma!"*

"There, there, now. Grandma's here. I want an explanation, Vireena. And what are you doing in Wilma's housecoat? Why aren't you dressed?"

"He peed on me. I had to take off my dress and dry it."

"He did?"

"On himself, tha's why he got on that sunsuit. An he got some on me."

"He hasn't wet his pants in a long time."

"He did today."

"Is that why you locked him in the closet? You know I won't have that."

"Well, he don mind me at all today. He messin inta everything. Don give me a minute to do my work. Gotta be after him all the time. I got this bad headache. Mus be sick er somethin. An he make me nervous, won't hush up. Keepin after me."

"That is what we hired you for, to look after him. The other is just if you have time."

"But I know how you look bad at me when the house ain't just spic an span. An he awful today. I jus put him the closet for a little to teach him a lesson."

"What's wrong with his eye? Vireena, what's wrong with his eye?"

"Oh, he fell. They was a man come wif a pony takin pictures and put him on an he fall off and hit his eye on somethin."

"I did not!" the boy protested. "She hit me. And hit and hit me. She put me in the closet—"

"He's just lyin. You can believe nothin he says. He lies all the time. Somethin goofy in his head. He *seein* things, Missus Mac!"

"An she and the pony man played honeymoon on the bed without no clothes on, too."

"SEE! SEE! See how he lies? Devil in that boy. The devil's got aholt uh him."

"Hush, Vireena. You're scaring him. I just want to know what was going on here today."

"I done tole you."

"*I* don't think you have."

"Then you kiss my black ass, too!"

"*Vireena!*"

"Yeh. You wanta take the word of a chile before mine, you can jus shove your fuckin job. I don work nowhere they take a crazy devil-chile's word fore mine. You come home early spyin on me. He jus dreamin tha stuff. Tell your granma you jus dream up tha stuff. Tell her the troof bout me!"

"I'm tellin the troof."

"Truth," his grandmother corrected. Vireena's eyes told the boy he would be garbage for hogs for certain. But he had to stick to his story. "I'm tellin the truth, Grandma. I *am!*"

"I ain't stayin here another minute," Vireena said. "I jus get on my clothes an go. An you can all kiss my ass."

"I want you to understand, I did not come home to spy on you. My hay fever is killing me. It was slow at the place, and Daddy says, 'Go on home and lay down.' You know Vireena we've always trusted you."

"No, you ain't. You ack like I ain't nothin. Like I don have no feelins. I don wanta be cooped up here wif some brat mos day and night. I wan to have some fun. See my frens. You goin to let me get dress, or you goin to watch to see I don steal nothin?"

"You know I don't think that way about you. I'll have a talk with your mother. Maybe we can work out something so you have some time for yourself."

"You leave my mother out of this! This between us!" Vireena spat. She leveled her little dark finger at the woman. "You go seein my mother, I fix you good! I fix you all! I double-damn promise you! You go botherin *my* mother."

Dressed, she came out of the bedroom as if she wore blinders, intending to walk out without a word or glance. Mrs. Mac intercepted her with some dollars folded lengthwise to be unobtrusive. She tried to put them in her hand.

"I wish you would think it over, Vireena. Anyway, here's what we owe you."

"Pfffft!" she half spat on the money, sailing out head high.

"OK. I'll just give it to your mother when I see her. I know she can use it. You earned it."

Vireena was back, pressed against the screen door. "I tole you. You go botherin my mother, I goin to kill you all. Set fire to you in your bed. I *triple*-damn promise you now."

When she had gone, the boy told his grandma everything. All the blocked things spewed out in a wild torrent of words. He told her how they played honeymoon. "She did what?" the old lady kept asking. "Now, are you sure that's so? I *can't* believe that." While he insisted he was telling the truth until she clapped her hand over his mouth. "That's enough! My head's splitting. I've got to lay down."

"Can I lay down with you?"

"If you lay still. And *don't* talk."

Her eyes teared and her nose reddened and ran from the middle of June until the first frost. Though she believed with all her heart that smoking was a mortal sin, she inhaled mentholated cigarettes in the closet under a blanket to try to open her head.

The boy followed her everywhere, afraid to let her out of his sight for fear Vireena would come back.

When the old man came home, she had the boy tell him all he had told her.

"You believe what he's sayin is the truth?" the old man asked.

"I don't know. You know how he stories. How much could he make up?"

"Well, it's a damn cinch he didn't make up that black eye. That eye's going to be ugly."

"I told you what she said."

"Is that so, Son? What Vireena said?"

"No! Vireena hit me and got in bed with the man and they did honeymoon and he hit her, and—"

"By god! I believe him! I ain't havin some black bitch knock that boy around. No call to do that. Say she locked him in the closet?"

"On the wash," the boy specified.

"I'm goin over there. I'm goin over there and get to the bottom of this or I ain't got a hair on my butt."

"Don't go."

"How's that?"

"I said I don't want you to go."

"And why the hell not? Don't you care what she was doin here all day? Don't you care if maybe she's been fuckin around with the boy all along?"

"NO! What good does it do to know? What good . . . ?" She was crying, and it was not the hay fever.

"I'll tear her black ass off!" the old man said. "I'll clean em out over there."

"No! You go out that door and I'll leave you! I *will!*" Her voice rose to high-pitched, constricted hysteria. *"I'll just go!"*

"Well. I'll be damned," the old man was amazed. He was pacing in circles around the room with a cold cigar butt between his teeth bobbing up and down like an assault gun on a half-track. He stopped and studied her a minute. "Well, I'm goin over there." He spun around and stomped out. The screen door banged behind him.

She burst into big racking sobs and dashed into the bedroom, throwing herself on the bed so hard she displaced a slat. It hit the floor like a shot. And she cried all the more.

"Everybody cried today cept Grandpa and the pony man." The boy offered an observation.

*"Shut up!"*

The old man came back calmer than he had left. "We're movin," he announced, as if they should leap up and begin packing.

"Did you go over there?"

"Unh."

"What happened?"

"Nothin."

"*Did* you go over there?"

"I said I was, didn't I?!"

But he never did say absolutely that he had gone. They talked a long time then about moving. There was an apartment in the old building across from the restaurant, next to the YWCA. They would look at it tomorrow. They guessed they could find someone to watch the boy. Or he could play behind the café where Kenny could keep an eye on him. They assured one another they would work something out.

"I sure hated this place," she said. "It never could seem like no home."

"Well, it ain't so *bad* a house," the old man said. "But I sure will be glad to get out of the neighborhood."

"Me, too," the boy called in from his bed on the couch in the other room.

"You're supposed to be asleep. Get there!"

"Maybe Vireena'll come back and burn us up. Can I sleep with you?"

"Oh, all right. Come on. Get in here."

He scampered with his shirttail flying, as if the girl could nail him between the couch and his grandparents' bed.

# 7

THE old man, his wife, and the boy moved into a three-room walkup across from the Coffee Cup Diner where the halls knew neither night nor day, running through brown-doored limbo where a 25-watt bulb burned the clock around.

The old man snorted and said, "Well we've finally made it to the Cockroach Inn."

The boy wondered if Cockroach Inns were a chain like Kroger's or Safeway Stores.

The others who lived behind the brown doors never just popped out whistling "Take Me Out to the Ball Game" the way the old man and the boy did. They all lived like people on the lam.

An old fat bird woman who wore her hennaed hair like a wig under a net and smelled like a cage lived behind a door that opened cautiously on a safety chain into a sleeping room she shared with a dozen roller canaries, a cocky cockatoo, and a very well-fed and contented tomcat. The boy learned what was in her room when she invited him in one day after her cat got out and made it downstairs to the street door before he caught it in a half nelson and dragged it back to the distraught fat lady, who could not have caught it in a million years if it had made the street.

She explained to him that she really should have that cat fixed, though it looked perfectly fine to him. She awarded him with half a Hershey bar so ancient it had turned white. He thanked her while casing her place. The canary bubbled brainlessly in a big cage set in front of the solitary window to catch the sun. Her day bed, settee, and cushioned wicker easy chair were all covered in printed cloth as wildly verdant as the Mato Grosso. So were the cat's box and the cupboard beneath the sink where her pans and tin oven for her gas plate were hidden. There was cat hair on everything. Over everything the fetid odor of a menagerie lay so thick even the old Hershey smelled like birds and cats. Yet the room was bright and spotlessly clean. The worn linoleum on the floor was cleaner than their own. The cages looked clean. The birds looked brand new. There were movie magazines and *True Confessions* all over the place. She had two bolts, a brass lock, and the chain on her door. Her window had two special bolts on it. The locks rather interested the boy. Until they moved there, they had never locked their house even when leaving for a weekend at Aunt Nellie's in Oklahoma. If the woman needed all those locks, how could he be certain they did not?

He thanked her for the candy bar but never ate it. Outside he flung it down the stairwell as if it were poisoned. He wasn't about to bite half of anything without some knowledge of who had bitten the other half. It was probably the lady. Or it could have been that shedding cat. Both possibilities were enough to make him gag.

Another neighbor on the floor was a short, round, rumpled cobbler with a thick foreign accent who wore baggy wool trousers which no longer closed at the top button, being secured by a loop of twine bridging the gap between hole and button. The system was suspended from frayed workingman's galluses. His frazzled shirts, grayer than the "before" picture on a box of Oxydol, had been laundered by hand in his cold-water sink, dried over the back of a straight chair, and worn without pressing. His black, high laced shoes bulged with eternally sore feet and had been repaired over repair.

He tried never to enter the hall if it was occupied, peeping repeatedly from the dark crack of his door until he was certain all was clear toward the stairs, then a quick look up the back hall with his whole head stuck perilously out. When he made a break for it, he came in a furtive rush as fast as his aching feet would propel him, with a look on his sweating porcine face that showed he was convinced it was only a matter of time before he was going to be caught in a withering crossfire between stairwell and hall donicker.

"Hi, man!" The boy trapped him once in the corridor when he peeked out after hearing the boy race a cast-iron model of Fred Frame's Indy race car the length of the hall bang up against the toilet door.

He eyed the boy carefully from the crack in his door before deciding he was not Immigration, Mafia, or Bolshevik terrorist, or whatever it was he constantly expected to find waiting for him outside. When he was absolutely certain it was not a trap, he said, "Liddle poy, don play in the hall! You get inna lodda trouble roun here. Shoo!"

The way simply had to be kept clear for his ever impending escape.

"You watch out for that goddamn Greek." The other tenant on the floor stopped to caution the boy a minute later.

Everyone knew everyone else's business at the Inn, though they did not know each other.

"That Greek try to touch ya or fool around with ya?" the man asked, looking the boy in the eye, which was no great trick for a man less than five feet tall. He spoke out of the side of his mouth and eyed the cobbler's closed door as if trying to stare it down.

The boy shook his head negatively. The midget was an incredible conundrum.

"Well, if he tries anything funny with ya, let me know, kiddo. I'll break his fat Greek neck."

The boy had the feeling he was trying to be friendly, though his words sounded mean. He gave the boy a wink from under the backstrap of his turned-around cap, striding away down the hall in child's laced knee boots that had a little knife pocket on the side. His whipcord boot pants were so greasy they looked like lead. A kid's brown leather jacket looked as if it had been flayed. Around his neck hung a pair of goggles. A pint-sized Lucky Lindy, he had half a dozen kids throwing newspapers for him, running the routes from an old square-tank Indian motorcycle with a sidecar.

Neither the Bird Lady nor the Greek ever had visitors as far as the boy could determine. But the prettiest lady he had ever seen often came down from the third floor to go in the midge's door. Even more often, he saw him climbing the stairs to three. She was blond and jiggly, always nice to the boy; she would touch his hair and tell him, "Honey, I know where you can get rich on your secret. A genuine brown-eyed blond." Twice she slipped him a nickel.

One evening the old man and the boy were going downstairs when she was coming up from the street. The stairs were narrow, so Mack turned sideways as they passed and nodded good day. She sort of brushed past the old man real slow, muttering something that made his face turn very red. She winked and jerked her head toward the top of the flight.

"Well, not right this minute." He chuckled.

"OK. Anytime, dad," she flipped happily back over her shoulder.

The old man watched her swing up the stairs. At the landing she leaned over the banister. "Shame on you! A great big ole man like you thinkin that about a little ole girl like me." She winked again.

Mac puffed his chest out a little bit and smiled happily to himself, his eyes very merry, and flicked the ash off his cigar, which had gone dead between his fingers.

They crossed the street and strode into the diner like King Edward and Son with a gracious "How-do" for the peasantry at trough. While the boy sat down in the kitchen to his bowl of potato soup, the old man was in no hurry to tie on an apron and finish rolling out the balls of hamburger to be mashed into patties upon order at the griddle. Mrs.

Mac was slicing big Bermuda onions to go with the burgers while tears coursed from her eyes, already inflamed by hay fever.

"Guess what just happened to me?" The old man grinned, edging over to josh her a bit.

"You joined the church," she sniffed.

"Hell, no! But I almost went down on my knees."

He pranced around a little to give the enigma time to work its way through the onion. He whistled softly while putting on his apron. A loose tuneless whistle with lots of air behind it.

"All right, I'll bite," she said resignedly. "What is it?"

"You know that woman who lives upstairs? She propositioned me on the stair. Gave me a wink." He showed her how she had acted and gave her a nudge in the short ribs that fussed her.

"Stop it! You act surprised. That's her business, ain't it? Maybe her business is as bad as ours. Or do you think it was your pretty gray eyes?"

"She didn't allow as to *what* it was. Next time I see her, I'll make it a point to ask."

"You do that. Ask her too does she take in boarders, while you're at it. Cause you can't come crawling back to me."

"Maybe I just wouldn't want to," he suggested smugly.

"Maybe," she conceded. "You and that midget ought to make a fine pair." She giggled.

"Now what the hell do you mean by that?" the old man demanded.

"Oh, nothing," she said airily. "Nothing."

"Hell yes you did, too! And you just know it's a damn lie!" It was as if she had slandered him before witnesses.

"Oh? *I* don't know a thing," she trilled on. "That's what you're always telling me. How dumb *I* am."

"Well, I sure made you cry calf rope often enough, didn't I?"

"Hmmmmmmmm?"

"You heard what I said. And it's a fact, too."

"Often enough for who? Why, I can't hardly remember." Slices of onion began falling neatly in a row as from an onion-slicing machine.

"Well, I'll by-god refresh your memory tonight!" the old man vowed. He looked angry, and his cigar had gone out again. It was down to a stub. He scorched his nose firing it up again.

"Oh, Daddy. . . ." She sighed and laughed aloud. "Talk's cheap." She wiped her fiery eyes and runny nose with the corner of her apron and looked happy for the first time since they had moved.

She scraped a carrot and sent the boy outside to play where his uncle in the parking lot could keep an eye on him.

He had to stay out of the drive and not venture across the sidewalk out front into the street, which left him a couple of square yards beneath an Orange Crush sign at the end of the diner from where he could watch traffic and see the Western Union boys come and go on their bikes across the street. Hopefully, he would catch them practicing between messages on the fabulous eight-man wheel they rode in parades. It was one long bike with eight seats and eight pairs of handlebars and pedals on a welded tubular frame between two wheels. Oh, it was a great bike!

It was a wondrous thing to see eight guys in their Western Union suits pumping that thing down the street. It was the Harvard crew for boys who were unsteady in a canoe. Eight pairs of legs, their toes in racing clips, stroking together like sixteen pistons on a silver chain drive. That wheel flew! Little kids raced it along the curbing and were fast eclipsed. Old ladies clutched their hearts when the thing zipped past. There simply wasn't a pretty girl of working people in town who would not jump up and down in her shoes and wave when it stroked powerfully by, the boys' visored brows low over the handlebars, their thin rears hoisted higher than their shoulders.

There was no question in the boy's mind. When he grew up, he was going with Western Union.

He was pal of all those guys. They always parked their individual wheels with him under the Orange Crush sign when they went in for lunch. He guarded them with his life, examining the skinny tires, the narrow saddle way up there at full extension of the post, the down-curving handlebars freshly taped. All the real guys rode Iver Johnson stiff-hub racers with caliper brakes. Occasionally some square would come along with a balloon-tired, coaster-brake job with upright steer-horn bars, which everyone called "German bikes," but those guys rarely lasted long enough to get a full Western Union uniform. The guys all worked strictly for tips and yet had to lay down a deposit for their suits out of their own pockets, thereby breeding self-reliance and free enter-prise in the young.

The name of the game was speed. Whenever there was a bike race in Matthewson's Pasture on a flat quarter-mile dirt, unbanked track, there was bound to be someone who rode for Western Union up front at the finish, running on Mrs. Mac's hamburgers with half a lemon strung around his neck for quick energy during the sprints. Then the winner, still in his smallclothes, would come into the diner with all the guys bearing the cup he had won, and everyone would have a high time drinking pop, eating pie à la mode or banana splits.

They often laid a penny, occasionally a nickel, on the boy for watching their bikes. Or for their greater pleasure, they bought a couple of ice cream cones on their way out to trade for the deck of scraped raw carrots with which his grandmother always loaded the boy. He *liked* carrots, but ice cream was fantastic.

Mrs. Mac did not approve of the guys giving the boy ice cream and candy. When they were apprised of that, he was buried in ice cream for awhile. Once he went nuts trying to handle three double dippers at the same time. He could not set them down, nor could he eat them fast enough to keep them from melting, though he nearly froze his nose trying, only to see half of his great windfall melt in the dirt beneath the sign.

Sometimes they would prop the boy on the crossbars of their bikes for a breathtaking ride up and down the street. Even when the guy came out with an onion breath that would pickle an egg, it was a hell of a way to go.

When the waitress disappeared, as waitresses often do, his Aunt Elfie volunteered to work until they found another, though she was beginning to show with another cousin. Then Jacky and his cousin Jerry were set out beneath the sign together, where Jerry's dad could see them. They dug in the dirt with spoons, played cars. After the lunch rush had passed, someone, usually the old man, took the boys across to the flat and put them down for naps. Though their grandmother or Elfie probably could have used the respite more, the truth was they tried to keep Mac out of the place as much as possible to prevent him from airing a political opinion. It was simply impossible for him to withhold his views in the face of opposing ones—even those merely overheard rather than directed to him. Four regulars inherited from the previous owners told Mrs. Mac they would regretfully have to eat elsewhere, for though the food had improved in both quality and quantity, it would not wash down so heavily sauced with Mac's insane slander of the President.

"Fuck em all" was how Mack felt about it. "We don't need to cater to such a lot of ass kissers, ignorant goody-goodies, and chumps. Good riddance!"

"Need? I'd welcome the business of a gorilla if he'd behave himself. How do you expect us to make it when we aren't now, if you drive away trade?"

"I don't give a goddamn! I wouldn't serve those mealy-mouthed, hare-brained goops, if they came back!"

"Listen! We're going broke! I'd be pleased as punch to see Roosevelt hisself come through that door right now."

The old man cut a quick look. You never knew.

"I'd say, 'Welcome, Mr. President, sit right down there, we have nice Swiss steak today and fresh, hot deep-dish apple pie!' "

"That just shows what *you* are. Besides, they got to push him around in a chair. They might *roll* him through that door. But you ain't going to see him walking. That shows how much *you* know."

"I don't give a good doggone if they mail him parcel post if it brings us good business."

Yet, as soon as he got the boys to sleep, he often slipped back over to help out until time for the boys to waken. She was not about to make *him* feel unwanted.

One afternoon he left before the boys were quite asleep. Jacky roused Jerry. He indicated they should get up, though suddenly with all that freedom there was very little unique to do. They could play cars anytime. There was nothing in the place to eat, neither candy nor cookies. While considering their next move, Jacky began idly bouncing on the old divan. Jerry laughed happily and began bouncing, too.

It was an absolutely forbidden sport. They bounced wildly, happily. Jerry gurgled like a fiend. Until a big spring or something popped and he went off on his head. He howled. It was terrible. He had a round, rather sullen face which Jacky truly disliked when he had to watch him bawl. His face clenched up like a baby's fist. His tears were copious. Further, he was wearing a new little Palm Beach hat backward and so deeply on his head it made his ears stick out. No amount of encouragement or logic could get him to shut up, spin that hat around, and look like something.

"Look! Look, Jerry!" Jacky was suddenly inspired. He put out his hand while sitting on the divan arm and stripped a string of glass beads from the fringe of a handy floor lamp. The beads hit the linoleum like small hail.

Ole Goggin shut up as if someone had pulled his plug.

Plick-plick-plick-plick-plick-plick—a dozen or more beads to the string. A jillion refracting surfaces spinning points of purple, rose, gold —fire colors. Water colors. All the colors of a prairie sunset. More! Each bead fell through silent space to kiss the floor with a jewel's quick kiss. Tiny cut-glass bombs falling faster than wildly beating hearts could meter the hits, they ricocheted away in all directions, the small sound like the echo of fabled thunder on storybook pages. Before the last tiny roll of a string died, Jacky started another on its way. Without a word Jerry climbed up on the divan and alternately, solemnly, happily, they stripped the lamp to the ultimate string. It was as if they had done nothing else all their lives. It was their work. There was not a cautioning thought in their heads, no measure of time other than that described by the beautiful flight and roll of the beads.

They could still hear the last string roll when their granddad came in. He was surprised to find them out of bed. One angry step into the room and his feet went everywhichway. He looked like a man trying to fly. If he could ever get his feet under himself again, he would kill them. Arms and legs aflap, an incredulous look on his face, he looked like a man full of chickens that had just had their necks wrung. The boys howled with delight and hysterical fear. One of the world's giants in their eyes was as helpless as a hog on ice.

"You goddamn boys," he gasped. It was both a threat and wonder at their treachery.

Then—BAM! Down he went on his prat. The whole house shook. It was very quiet afterward for a moment. Their laughter stopped.

"I'm just going to wear your damn backsides out," he vowed grimly. "What are these damn things, anyway?" He swept up some of the cut-glass beads in his big smooth palm. He saw the lamp.

"Well, I never heard of such a damn fool thing. Your grandma is just going to be sick. What made you take it into your heads to do a damn fool trick like that?"

"Dunno," they mumbled in unison.

"Pretty." Jerry tried for greater understanding.

"*Pretty!* Pretty damn lucky I didn't break my neck! This one of your brainstorms, Jacky?"

"Jerry, too," Jacky volunteered.

"Not me! It was him," Jerry insisted.

"Him, too!"

"Well, I'm just going to take the hides off you both. If I can get up here." He struggled a moment. The beads were everywhere. His face reddened again. He began swearing under his breath. Then as his efforts to get up increased, so did the volume of his curses. "Goddamn idiots! Leave you alone for a goddamn cryin minute and you tear the sonofabitchin place apart! I'LL TEAR YOU UP!"

From the floor he made a lunge and caught Jacky by the ankle, then improved his grip to his arm and jerked him off that couch as if the boy were hollow.

"No-no-no!" he screamed. "Don't whip me, Grandpa. I won't do it again! PLEASE!"

"I'll teach you to mess around here when I'm out. I'll teach you to tear up the place behind my back!"

The boy was across the old man's knees. Every heavy blow of his big hand was enough to make certain the boy would never strip a beaded lamp again. He could count on it. Not ever again. But it took a good ringing dozen to satisfy the old man's rage and restore his dignity. He was the hardest spanker in the world. He spanked so hard he invariably felt remorseful afterward and could not relax before being reassured by word or gesture that the boy, in spite of everything, knew he did indeed love him, though no one ever heard the old man ever use the word "love."

Right after the spankings they were hustled to bed with their butts still burning. Remorse hadn't yet set in. "Neither of you will get any supper, hear?" he promised, as in the other room he swept the beads about with a broom. He swore every time a too vigorous sweep destroyed the herd of those he had corralled and sent them zipping all over the hard linoleum.

"You stop that goddamn crying in there or I'll come give you some more, by God! Hear me?"

Jacky felt he had lain there in hungry dimness forever, while Jerry snoozed peacefully in his Palm Beach hat on the other pillow. Jacky's bones ached from having been so long in bed. The rosy warmth of the spanking had long since passed into whimpering doze, then to gentle restlessness. Now if he couldn't get out of that bed he would die of the aches.

He roused Jerry. "No. Grandpa come spank us," his cousin warned, ready to sleep there as he had been told until he starved to death. He closed his eyes, with no intention of opening them until given permission.

Jacky sat up, rolled over, wedged himself between bed and wall in search of coolness. He wished his grandma would come home.

When his grandma arrived, he sat bolt upright. It would only be a minute until she would come and tend to them and give them something good to eat.

"Now *why* would they go and do a thing like that?" she moaned.

"Beats me," the old man said dispassionately.

She moaned around about that lamp forever, trying to see how hard it would be to restring the beads.

"Well, it's just ruined. That's all," she sighed. "Can't keep a darn thing nice. Everything gets spoiled, broken, mildewed, or the bugs or mice get into it. It just ain't worth trying to keep things nice, make a decent place to live. I'm just going to quit trying." She plunked down on the divan, fully resolved, and the broken spring went thwang! "My land! They broke the divan, too!"

"I was going to mention that soon's you gave me a chance," the old man said.

"Well, *what* did you do about it?"

"I whipped them and put them to bed without their supper."

"They just tore up everything." She was about to cry. "Can't keep anything nice."

"Aw, listen," the old man said. "I can turn that couch over and put a board under the spring. It'll be all right. And I never liked that old lamp much, nohow."

"Well, *I* did! I've had that lamp almost twenty years."

"It wouldn't look so bad. Trim off them naked strings."

"Oh, drat! I just wish Wilma would do what's right. Do something to take care of her own child. *I* would of died before I'd of let *my* mother take her or Kenneth to raise. I'd of *died* first! I just can't do it no more. It's too much to ask a body."

"Oh, I reckon we'll manage. We've managed before."

"I'm tired of *managing!* I want someone else to do some managing for a change! *I want a little time for myself!* I've done for others all my life. I want someone to do for me."

"Now I suppose you mean me!" He had to put down his paper.

"It just looks like you could do *something* right once. All you had to do was sit here and read your paper and watch over them boys. You couldn't even do *that!*" She was angry and crying, too. "Where were you anyway while they were tearing the place up?"

"I had to step out for a minute."

"They didn't do this in a minute."

"I had to go to the closet, if you want to know. It took me a little."

"You sure you didn't just step upstairs for a little?" she sneered.

"Now *that's* the kind of cheap thinking I could expect from you."

"You've made me that way! We'll never have nothin! You move us from Niggertown to a whorehouse and call that getting ahead. I don't!"

"Then *move,* goddamnit! If you've got so much goddamn money, just *move!* If you're rich as Lady Astor, you find yourself some castle to your liking. You can have the whole shittin shebang. Just pack your duds and get out! See if I give a good fart."

"Oh, I *know* you don't! I've known *that* for a long time. You only stay with me because I'm goose enough to slave for you. But I want you to know if it wasn't for the kids, I'd of left you long ago! Put that in your pipe and smoke it!"

"Piss on you! The kids are grown. *Go!* Get your goddamn ass out if you want to. I say good riddance! *Go, goddamn you!"*

She was crying for certain then. On the ceiling of the dark room reflections from the lights of cars passing on the street below washed both ways.

No one ever left. Their arguments always came to the same frustrating inconclusion. So there was nothing left but the recriminations within their mutual entrapment. All their plans had always failed. All hope ultimately soured. Not for lack of industry but for want of ruthlessness. Not for want of magnanimous purpose but for being essentially truthful people as opposed to honest thieves, they never rose above working simply to acquire the necessities of life, never fully succeeding in even that. The status of things was as foreign to them as thoughts on the dark side of the moon. They grubbed all their lives in an infested trench of despair where the benefits of professional medicine were an unaffordable luxury, where walking wounded were the rule. And if Mac had allowed himself to worry about his children's teeth, his next move would have been to kill somebody.

Their argument rose and fell in the other room like a large hairy animal; sometimes loud, ripping like claws on concrete, then low and constant like a broad furry back being rubbed back and forth against bars.

"You want to go," Mac yelled. "You got such hot prospects. Go on! Don't let the door hit you in the butt on the way out."

"Not until I tell you what I think. If it wasn't for me that darn café would of been broke months ago. And you know it, too! But you don't care. Just as long as you can play big shot. Smoke them cigars. Go around cussing everybody out who don't agree with you. Then you're happy. Why do you think we let you take care of Jacky so much? To keep you from running off the trade we got left, that's why! You don't have no more business sense than a mule. That's the truth! You haven't made a go of a thing you started since I've known you. Everything you've touched has turned to nothin! Oh, I know, the bank got the farm. But maybe if you *had* done what they told you, we could have hung on."

"Hung on? Hung on and be told by some fuckhead who ain't never seen a farm how to starve in the heart of the land of plenty. I AIN'T NUTS!"

"What are you? *Just what are you?"*

"A man! That's all. Not a chump. A man. A saddle scamp who

tickled you twixt the legs when the Lord wasn't lookin, Mistress Christ Almighty!"

"Well, I never thought then things would turn out like this."

"Neither did I. . . . Neither did I. But no damn fool's going to tell me what to plant! I've been a farmer longer than them chumps been wearin britches!"

"*You're not going to!* You're not going to do *this*. You're not going to do *that!* But you'll let *me* do it! There's very little you won't let me do. I don't wonder you haven't let me do what that girl upstairs does."

"*Now-you-shut-your-goddamn-mouth-goddamn-you!*" His feet hit the floor. "I'm doing the best I can. I wasn't made to be no asskisser to some damn fool in pinchy-toed shoes who comes grinnin around about what a boon Roosevelt is when that sonofabitch is leadin this country to hell and damnation from which it will never recover. Our children and grandchildren and great-grandchildren will pay for this dope's pipe dreams. There's enough of everything in this world for everyone to go without want, but there ain't enough for the crooks who have brought on this depression and the rest of us, too. All Roosevelt is trying to do is get the goddamn crooks to be smart enough to give up just a little of what they might steal so's the people they are stealing from will go on making the money the crooks are stealing. They might steal from one another, but someone's got to steal it from the poor first. The working stiff. The crooks don't make no money. They make people old and dead before their time. They make the only evil on earth that man can rectify while your damn fool preachers rail about those things that are nobody's business but God's."

"But running off customers isn't going to change it. It's only taking bread out of our mouths."

"I told you! If you don't like the way things are run around here, get your ass out!"

"If you don't think I won't, *you're crazy!*"

The door flung open, and she stomped into where the boys were in bed, got a valise from the closet, and began throwing clothes from a chest of drawers into it.

Jerry was awake, too, now. Both boys played possum, watching their grandma from the barest slit in their eyelids. She clamped a hat on her head and tugged the suitcase off the chair on which it had been sitting.

"Where you goin, grandma?" Jacky asked from the covers.

She stopped. In the light from the other room they could see she was crying. "I don't know," she said. "No one cares where I go!"

"I do!" Jacky vowed.

"I do, too, Grandma," Jerry assured her.

"We do, Grandma," they chorused.

"You be good boys. Jerry, your mama and daddy will get you tomorrow."

"We're sorry about the lamp," Jacky said.

"Ooooooo. . . ." She ran from the room.

"Don't cry, Grandma!" Jerry begged, calling after her.

"Please don't go, Grandma," Jacky pleaded.

"Go on and get out, goddamn you, if you're goin!" the old man said. "Here! I'll show you the way!" He flung open the door into the hall. "Go on! Go on! I'll give you a kick in the ass to get you started."

"I HATE YOU!" From the hall.

"Go on! *Good Riddance!*"

Bang! the door slammed.

"Grandma! Grandma! Grandma! Come back! Come back!" the boys piped.

"Shut up in there!"

*"We want our grandma!"*

"Well, she ain't here now."

"Wah-wah-wah. . . ."

"Hush *up* now, I told you!"

"We want Grandma!"

"I'm hungry!" Jacky bawled.

The old man loomed in the lighted doorway.

"Listen here. If you two'll stop your damn howling, I'll go over to the restaurant and get you some cupcakes and milk."

They lay still as logs until the old man returned. There he was with two packets of Hostess cupcakes and two pint bottles of ice-cold milk. The cakes in their cellophane wrappers were a little mashed. Not bad. Just not perfect. The milk was so cold it hurt their teeth. The old man sat on the edge of the bed and watched them eat.

"Where did Grandma go, Grandpa?" Jacky asked when the edge was off his hunger.

"She went out for awhile."

"When she comin back?"

"She'll be back."

"When she comin back?"

"Will Grandma come back, Grandpa?" Jerry asked.

"She'll come back. Don't you worry about that."

The cake was gone. Jacky put the end of the cardboard on which the cakes had been packaged in his mouth and scraped the residue off with his lower teeth. He reversed it, did the same with the other end. Then for dessert he sucked the cellophane for the last essence of frosting.

"You going to eat the paper, too?" the old man wondered.

"I always do this."

"I do, too," Jerry piped and smeared the cake wrapper all over his mouth.

"You two are something." He stared at Jerry, who still wore his now battered new Palm Beach hat, and began laughing. He didn't laugh too loud, but the bed shook. There were tears in his eyes.

"You going to wear that damn hat forever?" he laughed.

Jerry nodded affirmatively.

He would, too. He was stubborn as his granddad.

The old man took the trash and empty bottles and started out of the room.

"Can we have the light on, please, Grandpa?" Jacky asked.

"You want the light on?"

"Yeow."

"OK. But don't make a habit of it."

He made himself a bed on the broken couch and lay down in his clothes.

Sometime toward morning, their grandpa and grandma carried the boys to the couch. Jacky was half awake. They put him at one end, Jerry at the other. The woman gently pried off the Palm Beach hat. There was a deep red line on Jerry's forehead. She brushed his dark hair back, putting his hat on the back of the couch where he would be certain to see it when he woke up.

"Goodnight, Grandma," Jacky said after she turned out the light and was almost in the other room.

"Oh, goodnight," she whispered.

"I'm sure glad you come back. We had cupcakes and milk."

"All right. Go back to sleep now. Good night."

"Good night."

Jacky heard her tell the old man, "Cupcakes and milk, huh? You spoil kids rotten. You always have."

"Now don't start up again. I've had enough quarreling for one night."

"So have I," she sighed. Then after a bit, "But you do."

# 8

IT WAS about eleven o'clock when the fight broke out upstairs. The MacDeramids had just gone to bed. The boy slept on the couch with only a sheet over him. There was an electric fan in the doorway between the rooms to stir a hot breeze. Curtains hung lifeless at the windows like empty ghosts.

Sometime during the afternoon the midget had brought a cowboy home with him from the White Way Pool Hall. He had found him playing poker on the back table with a lot of chips stacked in front of him and leaned up to whisper in his ear, "Pal, how'd you like to ride a real palomino who just loves to buck?"

The cowboy sized up the midget without actually turning his head to look at him and rapped to the other players he was checking.

"She a Shetland or full-grown horse?" he asked.

"Full size," the midget grudgingly replied.

"That's good," the cowboy drawled in no hurry.

"She's one of them *nymphomaniacs*," he whispered pronouncing every syllable. "She does it just as much for fun."

The midget was plainly feeling little pain. He had dropped out of a carnival once when it passed through town when he fell off the wagon and woke up in the drunk tank stark naked and being bitten all over by a hallucinatory gang of alley rats the size of tomcats. Every time he began yelling, they came and washed him down with a fire hose. When they let him out, he wandered around town bumming change for booze and a flop, waiting for a carnival to come through so he could get with it again. Then he made connections with the beautiful girl upstairs who straightened him out enough to pimp for her and set up his string of paper routes.

He could be found in the White Way every morning after delivering the papers to his carriers, drinking beer and kibbitzing the domino game. Occasionally he would play himself, though he was a rotten loser, particularly when potted. Then he would want to fight. Many a full-grown man took the midget's challenge too lightly and found himself being caught scoffing by a size four boot in the face and a bottle of Blatz across the skull, the midget's tactic being to leap squarely in the middle of the table and drop kick the daylights out of the citizen while he yet had the element of surprise on his side. If he could clamp his teeth on an ear or the end of one's nose, the citizen was due for plastic surgery. He once bit a gob out of a Fort Riley cavalryman's cheek that would have taken a size ten tire patch to close. Caught on the ground, he would go for the bigger man's groin with such unerring ferocity an old seaman-turned-bartender at the White Way who had seen India dubbed the midge "the Mongoose."

The cowboy found him amusing. "If a full-grown man is a pimp, what are you . . . a half-pimp?"

"Fuck you, Jack!" The midget spat on the cowboy's chips. He turned to go.

"Hold it! Hold on, little buddy." The cowboy caught him by the arm. "No hard feelins. I was just funnin ya. Come on, have a drink." He showed him a pint in a brown paper bag under the table.

The midget jerked his arm free. "I don't like wise guys."

"Have a drink. Forget it. I didn't mean nothin."

"OK. But watch your mouth." He took the bottle, tipped it up with his back to the street, and chased the long shot with a belt of beer. It left him hoarse.

"How much?" the cowboy asked.

"Five short time. Twenty all night. You lay an eye on her, I doubly guarantee you you'll want a party."

"Five? Man, I can get it for two at the Eaton Hotel and not have to leave my room."

"Yeow, if you want some scabby bag. I'm talking about a *baby*! Only nineteen. Looks like a college girl. White as plaster. Purely blond. Pud on her like a peach. Clean. Them nymphos, see, they take real pride in their selfs, ya canote?"

The cowboy looked at the other men at the table, locals. They nodded their heads sagely—you could count on the midge's every word.

The cowboy's balls crawled a bit on the seat of his chair.

"How far?"

"Not far. Just around the corner. Just a step."

"Guess it wouldn't hurt to look. . . ."

The men nodded that it certainly would not.

"But you come back to the game, hear?" a big loser growled. "You got all the dough *in* this game."

"Let him go, Irv. Don't you know it always changes a man's luck when he gets himself a little? Takes the edge off."

"I'd like to take his nuts off, the kind of fool luck he's been havin."

The cowboy had come up from the Panhandle on a cattle train. He'd been paid and was waiting for a train home. The White Way was directly across the street from the Union Station. But there was no special time he *had* to get back.

Still, he felt funny, being propositioned by a midget pimp. Though what could be safer than going upstairs behind a midget? Unless he was packing a gun, it wasn't likely he was going to jump you. So it simply had to be the creepiness of the thing. And yet in the juxtaposition between the runt and the vision he had conjured up, there was a horrible wonder, a creeping appeal that made the rider's thin ass tighten on his chair.

"Well, you got me interested, shorty," he decided. He signaled for the fat banker in a green celluloid eyeshade to cash his chips.

Gambling, like hard liquor, was outlawed, but only the WCTU raised a holy row about it *all* the time. The banker looked like he lived on beer. His nose was a porous florid blob. The cowboy got his cash under the table and counted his winnings surreptitiously under the skirt of the baize. He ordered a round of beer for the boys and thanked them for the game.

"Ready to ride, shorty?" he asked kindly.

"Don't call me shorty!" the midge warned.

"Man! You sure are a touchy lit—a touchy fella."

"Yeah. I don't like being called names."

"How you prefer bein called?"

"We call him the Mongoose," the banker said peering out humorlessly from the eyeshade.

The others around the table smiled little knowing hometown smiles.

"Call me Boots," the midget said.

"OK. Boots and his buddy." The cowboy tried to be jolly. He dropped a pink-shirted arm over the midge's shoulders as if they were posing for a photograph. And was immediately shrugged off.

"I don't like nobody pawin me!" he said narrowly.

"Well, hot damn!" The cowboy had about had enough of the midge's likes and dislikes. He was ready to tell him to go to hell.

But the runt had spun on his heel and was on his way toward the door. "C'mon," he grunted without even turning around to see if the cowboy was following.

How things had come to this pass was beyond the cowboy.

"Awright!" he said starting after the midget. "I'll take a look anyhow." Then trying to regain the upper hand before the others, he said, "Maybe if I don't like her looks, I'll give you five to watch you go."

No one laughed.

"That cowboy sure don't know nothin about midgets," the man next to the eyeshade observed to his cronies. They nodded their heads wisely and muttered agreement as the cards slithered around again.

The cowboy rubbernecked all the way to the apartment house, mentally blazing landmarks back to the depot for his return alone. The little man in front of him led him to a big Gothic frame rooming house with a dark porch as wide and deep as a dairy barn, the repository of the last coolness in town. Inside, the place was like a musty oven. The little man in front of him in child's boots went up the dim stairs like a mountain climber. He wondered how hard life must be for someone that size. He wondered why he wasn't in some kind of show. He had never seen a midget outside a show. He wondered about the midget's sex life.

"Call me Blondie because that's me all over," the pretty hooker explained when Boots steered the cowboy over her threshold. "What do they call you . . . Tex?"

"That's right. I'm originally from Forth Worth. That is, I was born there." He remembered his hat and quickly removed it. "I'm livin near Panhandle now. On a ranch. Just came up day before yesterday with a load of cows." The unexpected beauty of the girl made his tongue flap. She looked like a movie star.

"I knew a cowboy once from Beauregard, Louisiana. Know what they called him?"

"Louise!" the cowboy exclaimed, happy as a child.

"No, fool. *Beau!* Honey, he had one on him like *that!*" She measured off half her pale forearm and shook her little fist under his nose. She laughed like a schoolgirl. "Oh, you big long drink of water, comere." She put her hands on both sides of his head and stood on tippy toe to give him a monkey-lipped kiss that only chastely brushed his own.

"Hey! Didn't you bring a bottle?" She pushed him roughly away, searching him with her eyes, frowning as if he had made the dumbest mistake a man can make in a whorehouse.

"Well, I didn't figure on stayin—"

She wheeled on the midget. "Boots! I told you. I'm not takin no more quickies! If this guy ain't no sport, you can just take him back where you found him. You know how quickies leave me at loose ends."

Boots knew. He lived for those moments when some hurrying mark left Blondie prepared to beg him for relief. And he would berate and abuse her while she groped his crotch. She would eagerly unlace his little boots, take off his clothes. Lick him all over like a white mama cat. While he called her every vile thing he could think of, shouting things when words failed him like "mugger-hugger, doggie-dugger, shit-licker. . . ."

There was nothing she hadn't tried. A local woman, large in the art-park-historical-uplift circles—and big everywhere, standing six feet even in her brogans and weighing 200 pounds—came every Tuesday right after lunch to make it with Blondie before going to the nearby YWCA for a swim. "One of her tits must weigh forty pounds." The girl was amazed. "She ain't so bad. She's real clean. Her underwear is frumpy but nice. Her belly's hairy as a man's." What she liked best was a double-ended dildo 16 inches long with which she linked herself to the girl beneath her. "She fucks like a man." Blondie was awed.

She would lie in bed with the midget telling him everything she had done. When she would tell him how the young man she had married in high school left her so horny she started making it with their Chinese Chow, the midge would purely go out his little mind, throwing himself on her and banging her like a man trying to commit mayhem, feeling all the while that she was indestructible. How could a woman who looked so fragile, absolutely devoid of muscle one, be so unbeatable? was a question. After being trained by a squad of horse cavalry on a 90-degree afternoon that left her pale hair hanging like a wet mop and her face looking as if her brains had been pumped out, followed by a beating and bedding by the midge, she could take a bath and bounce back looking like a white tulip that had just taken dew.

Boots muttered something about the cowboy having to catch a train, but the cowboy was already digging for a pocket in his black pin-striped Western pants.

"Lookie, I'd be pleased to buy a bottle if you know where to get it!"

"Get a fifth," Blondie suggested, eyeing the wad Tex pried out of his pocket. Boots was right there, too, counting it from below. That Western fool had a couple of hundred there everywhichway like so many odd bits of paper.

"Leave me have a tenner," Boots said. "I'll get *good* stuff. Bonded. The best." He helped himself and was gone.

When he was out the door, Blondie leaned on the cowboy's shoulder and riffled his lettuce, laying her box a little this way and a little that on his lean left leg, promising, "Honey, I'm going to show you a *real* good time. I may keep you all week."

The kiss she gave him was more of what he had in mind and more of what he had been living for than any his wife had ever given him. Her tongue tasted better than any food. Her mouth seemed filled with some kind of angel's spit. She found a place in his mouth with her tongue that was on a direct wire with his prick. Yet the kiss was so soft and enfolding there was nothing in his experience to compare it with. His head swam. It was no chintzy whore's cold kiss.

For Blondie honestly never expected anyone to pay in a way that left a bitter hollow in them for something she held so cheaply herself. She might leave them broke; but their dissatisfaction with women would have to come from comparing others to herself, not from herself. For if men were truly ugly, hated things to her, as a Seventh-Day Adventist girl with terminal acne had once assured her while licking dry gray lips, unable to keep her eyes from trying to see through Blondie's teddies, then her own eyes lied.

"I love it," she whispered to the woozy cowboy, rubbing the hardening length in his pants. "Ummm, nice. . . . No! Don't play with my pussy. I'm wet already. We want to wait until Boots brings the bottle, don't we? Wouldn't want to be interrupted. But feel. I'm always a ready-teddy."

"Man, yeow!"

"Look out, it might snap at you." She laughed, taking his entire long chin into her mouth and gently chewing it.

He about blew five bucks right in his pants.

Blondie had met the midget in the Blue Lantern when he tried to sell her an afternoon *Beacon* he had rescued from a trash can toward making the price of a drink. Though she hadn't any other employment, she had not accepted the fact she was a whore. She was just looking for a break. In the meantime she had to eat. And she would be making it with whoever was nearest that had nerve enough to ask, anyway. It was both pity and curiosity that moved her to give him her last dollar for a half-pint of neutral grain spirits. She took him home with her out of a kind of childish maternalism and the same sort of crazy desire and wonder she had felt when she first knelt down beside her husband's Chow, took his woolly penis in her hand, and began gently jacking it. The midge on the tail end of a binge made that Chow look like a good catch.

It took two days for her to work the spirits out of him and build up his strength with canned soup, soda crackers, and ice cream to a point where he could do anything but lie on her and quiver like a baby. He cried out his whole miserable tale on her white breast. Then, to her surprise, she discovered midgets were just like other men when straightened out and full of soup. Nothing to write home about. Things *were* more or less in proportion. But he was big as midgets went. And he was an intense little bastard.

She let him become her pimp by simply closing her eyes and biting her lips while he slapped her silly to show her what he thought of inconstant bitches the first day he came home to find her door locked and a Syrian haberdasher in her sack. She explained how it was with her. He cornholed her dry to show her he was unforgiving. She bought him the red secondhand Indian motorcycle with a sidecar to prove she really cared. He organized his paper routes and rented a room downstairs. And it did take a lot of the risk out of hustling. Moreover, she could spend more time fixing up her room, hanging frothy tiers of white curtains on the windows, finding a good used Persian carpet for the floor, making things nice, the way she liked them.

What did it matter if some drunk or the midge in a fit wrecked the place every time she got it just the way she wanted it? That was part of it, too. She never stayed angry. She simply atomized perfume into the air and started over. It wasn't a bad life. Though she knew in her heart, and it made her sad, that someday someone was going to tear her up, too. Irrevocably.

In the meantime she was always on the alert for the first twinge in men who needed to hit her, turning quickly face down to protect her face and belly.

And good as her midge's word, she would do it all. Five bucks a hole. Twenty, blow your skull. With enough genuine soul kissing to confuse the guilty workadaddy who had only expected to get his ashes hauled and completely befuddle a country fool who had never been saddled with any urban illusion of love. The midge, looking to save something for himself, tried to get her to come on cold turkey like other hookers, no kisses, entombed emotions, wham, bam, thank you ma'am. But it was not her style. She tried. Lay there stiff and quivering until she couldn't stand it another second, jammed her tongue in some Okie's mouth, hooked her middle finger in his asshole, and raked his bare back with the nails of her free hand until he came like a length of dragchain being yanked out through his joint.

It was useless. So Boots dreamed boozy dreams of drilling a new hole in her someplace especially for himself. He was frightened of and hated dogs, particularly big dogs. And he was insanely jealous of her ex-husband's old Chow. He dreamed of her and that dog. In his frustration and anger he awakened in a cold sweat, his chest aching with tears that would not come.

After a few drinks the cowboy wanted to dance. He curled over Blondie's radio with his ear against the speaker grill, twisting the dial in search of some country music. The set was a good Atwater-Kent Boots had picked up for Blondie at auction. It had an ornate, inlaid veneer cabinet that looked like a portable cathedral. It sat on a clawfoot side table in front of the side window with the ground wire running outside and down three stories to a length of gas pipe the midge had driven into the earth beside the house. Even then, when there was a thunderstorm and he was with her, he would not let her play the radio for fear it would attract lightning.

When the cowboy found something with enough fiddles skirling to sponsor some ancestral urge, he turned for the girl, who was dubious but game. She clapped his rusty black Stetson on her short, silver fingerwave and cried, "*Yahooo!* Take me back to Texas, I'm too young to marry!"

He grabbed her around the waist, thrust her right arm out like a battering ram, and one-stepped her around the room so furiously it could have been a jerky life-or-death struggle in a penny arcade kinescope. *Doop-a-doop-a-doop.* She was curved into him like a bow. Her pink mules slapped her bare heels with every long, quick step. Her soft little hump bounced beneath her silk wrapper.

Boots poured himself a drink into a water tumbler from the cowboy's bottle. He drank, looking at nothing, seeing himself from a distance. Presently, he slammed the glass on the table, jumped up, and left the room. The door slammed.

"Looks like our little buddy left," the cowboy said.

"Honey, if you diddle like you dance, I'm goin to charge you double."

"Why, where I come from, I'm known as a *good* dancer."

"Where *I* come from they would hang warning lights on you."

"Might as well get to what I come for then."

"Might as well. You don't do *that* with your boots on, do you?"

"Don't do that with nothin on less I got to go to it standin. For the price I'm payin I feel like I ought to do it wrongside out."

"You feel free to suit yourself. I'd like to see someone come up with a really new way."

Going down the stairs, the midget heard her laugh. He went in his room and sat on the day bed staring at the diner across the street. He had parked his motorcycle in the lot behind the diner and thought for awhile about going over and working on it. Before he could move, he saw a beautiful young woman in a new yellow Nash roadster with whitewall tires pull into the lot. The young Honest Abe in overalls came over and waited on her. She smiled a completely certain smile that could have been an ad for Ipana.

The midget's head swelled with an instantaneous desire to rape her, to tear off her expensive, tasteful clothes, shove his thing right into her sweet clean pussy. As spontaneous as that. Do it. Put her through the whole thing. He could see the painful, pleading look on her pretty face, her eyes were wet with tears, her nostrils and throat fighting nausea. She speaks: *"Please."* It sounds like a strangled *"peas."* He busts her right in the perfect teeth with his fist.

She gave the young man some money. He went into the garage on the back of the lot, returned promptly, took something from his voluminous overalls and put it in the side compartment of her car. She smiled again, backed carefully out into the street, and drove off. The young man looked after her until she was gone. Then he leaned on the nearest fender and made himself a cigarette from a bag of Bull Durham and papers he took from his bib pocket. He put it carefully on his lip, struck a kitchen match on the seat of his pants, touched it to the cigarette, staring off in the direction the pretty young woman had gone.

All his life Boots had dreamed of fucking some beautiful, rich society woman, some movie star. At first his dreams were romantic fantasies in which he and the exquisite were linked in true love forever. Even the big dogs that roamed their California estate were willingly subservient to his every beck. Master of all he surveyed. Where kisses were ever sweet, the rain fell without lightning, dogs' eyes were like those of does, there was never a moment of killing heartache, and it lasted forever and ended in a magnificent funeral where hundreds of people he had never really seen before, yet who were his dearest fantasy friends, mourned him so sincerely it would have been cruel to return to them even if he could. He lay back on the day bed expiring with a smile on his lips. But the dreams bored him.

He sat up and opened the paper to the sports pages. There was a photo of a young Mrs. B. T. Evans and a couple of men in plus fours walking on the Wichita Country Club golf course. She smiled just like the girl in the roadster. "Nothin affects them broads," the midget assured himself. "They know so fucking much. Ain't life a cookie, though!" She was as tall as the men. She wore a cloche hat over her right eye, a belted sweater and white golfing skirt, spiked two-tone golf shoes. The huge unfettered tits under her sweater hung almost to her waist. If you looked real hard, he was sure you could see her nipples. He wished he had a magnifying glass. "Damn!" He threw the paper across the room. He felt like a bug. The room spun a little. In his midget mind he could hear Blondie's bed creaking.

"Big slimy cunt!" he cried out softly in agony. And threw himself over and began beating his pillow with his fists.

Which was as close as he ever came to actually telling anyone, "I love you."

When it was dark, he rolled off the bed out of his doze, roused as if he just remembered something he had to straighten out once and for all, and bolted out of his room still groggy, straight into his next-door neighbor, who was heading for the toilet with his suspenders down, a towel over his arm, a shaving mug and brush in one hand and a straight razor in the other. The little man hit him full force in the gut and bounced him solidly up against the wall.

"Whoooof!" the bigger man grunted.

"Whyn't you watch where you're goin?" the midge challenged.

"I watch," the fat man gasped. "You watch!"

"Pull a razor on me, hunh?" The midge put up his dukes.

"Hunh? I don pull nodding. I go toilet for shave."

"Yeh? Well, you just trying somethin with me, Clyde, an I'll break your fat Greek neck!" He took a couple of menacing steps forward and the fat man slid away, inching along the wall, holding his stuff in front of him.

"I don want no trouble wit you," he repeated twice. Then fled into the crapper and quickly hooked the door behind him.

He sat heavily on the stool, muttering, "Crazy peoples. Dot liddle tiny man." Then he sadly inventoried his own miseries until he wept silently and his fat feet went to sleep. When he tried to stand, the pain was maddening. He dropped his shaving mug, and it shattered on the lip of the scummy tub. He toppled to the floor like a big white hog that has just had its throat cut. He floundered there on his back unable to rise, his legs tingling painfully. He pounded his cobbler's fists on the floor and called, "Help! Anybody? Please help me!" Directly overhead on the ceiling a big brown cockroach was making its way upside down. He began to weep again. He wondered how painful it would be to cut his throat with his razor. He hated pain. He had left his home, his shop, his wife and four children out of fear of pain. He had never made enough to send for them. He had not heard from them in over ten years. He had felt bad all the time. He was full of gas. He couldn't even enjoy a good crap anymore.

MacDeramid heard his cries and came and pulled the screw eye and hook out of the door.

"I can do nodding no good no more," the man apologized, pulling his trousers up over his knees while Mac steadied him.

"A man gets on," Mac told him. "There's some things I don't do so good any more, either." He hoped to cheer him up.

"Nobody care if I live or die. Nobody." He babbled mournfully about all he had left in the old country. "Sure. I could die in my bed an nobody know until I stink. Eh? You bet. But I won die yet." He stiffened up. He got his trousers up. He hooked the string over the button that fastened the waistband. "I won die yet! They gotta put up with me. Shiddy ole man. I make them pay. Huh? Sure. They gotta *look* at me. They don get rid of me so easy," was his promise. His single victory. His inheritance. His legacy.

"No, sir," the old man said. "You stick in there."

While Boots had charged up the stairs and banged on Blondie's door.

"Who is it?" she asked groggily, obviously from the muffling island of bed.

"Boots. Open up!"

"What's wrong?" He never bothered her when she had a customer.

"Open up!"

He heard her quickly scuffing into her mules. The door opened a crack. Her face was glazed, smeary, her hair messed. "What is it!"

"I thought you might be hungry. I'd like something to eat. I'd like to talk to you."

"What's wrong, Boots?" She frowned. She had never seen him look so distant, strange. "I've got a guest, remember."

"Who's there?" the cowboy called from the bed. "That our little buddy?"

Boots pushed open the door. Blondie clutched her wrapper around herself.

"Hey-ya!" The cowboy waved and sat up, tousled and splotched, and dropped his skinny white legs over the side of the bed. His dirty feet, long pinched by tight, pointed boots, looked deformed, broken at the squeezed-together toes. He covered his loins with the tail of Blondie's fringed bedspread, grinned, and scratched his head.

"You sure wasn't just whistlin," he told the midget, nodding meaningfully toward the girl. "Yeowzer!" He patted his flat belly. "That palomino sure loves to buck!"

"Come on. Get your duds on and get out of here," Boots told the cowboy. "Something came up."

"Hold on there, I'm in for the night. That's how ya'll wanted it. Suits me jes fine. Ain't that so, girlie?"

"Beat it!" The midge jerked his thumb toward the door. "We got important business."

"I heard you say you was hungry. Well, so am I. Why don't you take some dough and duck over to that diner across the way and get us some fried chicken to go or somethin? Seems a shame to get all dressed now jest to go eat. How about it, girlie?"

"Get out of that bed," the midget ordered.

"Listen, little buddy, I told you. I'm paid up. I'm in for the party."

"You've had your party."

"Ain't how I figure it. I gave her twenty and bought that whiskey besides. I didn't ask you for no change from the ten, neither."

"Here's your change and what you got comin." He peeled a five off the roll he had in his boot pants and threw it on the carpet. "Now get out of here."

"Honey, this wasn't our agreement." He looked to Blondie.

The midget plainly had her puzzled. The cowboy was loaded. Why chase him so soon?

The cowboy sat stubbornly on the bed with no intention of moving at the request of a goddamn midget. His attitude was rigidly clear.

And Boots hesitated a beat too long before deciding he ought to jump him. The necessary, instinctive singleness of purpose never drew to an irrevocable spearhead.

Blondie said, "Listen. *Listen!* Let me talk to you." She wrapped her arms around the midget. "Come on." And he let her nudge him out into the hall until the brown door broke the unblinking tension between his and the cowboy's eyes.

She knelt and kissed his mouth. "Listen, baby—"

He shoved her roughly away. She fell backward asprawl, her kimono gaping. "Your mouth tastes like cock!"

"Shh. *Listen to me!*" She crawled back to him. Knelt again like a mother comforting a frustrated and angry child. "Honey, that guy's got a couple of hundred on him. We could get us a little secondhand car for that. A nice one. I don't like riding in that ole motorcycle sidecar, Boots. It's embarrassing. People laugh at us."

"You're nuts. I can't drive no car."

"I can learn. *I* can drive *you*. Please, Boots."

"I don't like this jasper. Somethin about him don't wash with me. I want you to get rid of him. I want him out of there."

"He ain't no different than anybody else. The only thing different about him is he's got that two hundred on him. I want that, Boots." She said the last in a way it was not a question. "For us, honey." She took the edge off it. "For our good time, baby. We can go out in the country. Take trips. You know you're the only one I care about."

"Shit! All you care about is yourself!" He plunged his hand in her kimono and grabbed a handful of pud and twisted until she bit her lip to keep from crying out. "Someday I'm going ta tear it right off ya! Crumby whore."

She slipped back into the room. "It's all right. He gets funny ideas sometimes. They are very high-strung and nervous." She stooped and retrieved the five Boots had thrown on the floor, and it disappeared as if by sleight of hand, and her without a pocket. "Now! Where were we?"

"You let that midget, don't you?" the cowboy asked.

"Ummhmmm."

"What's it like?"

She shrugged. "OK. You know. Only sometimes when he's bangin away down there, I feel sorta lonely. Out of it. There ain't all that much to hang onto with a midget. He likes it dogfashion best. I get up on a pillow on my knees and he can stand up back there and really throw it to me."

The cowboy rolled heavily on top of her, shoved his half-hard-on into her, and came before he was fully erect.

Chicken bones and a greasy paper bag from their dinner were on the card table she had set up. The coffee in the cardboard container had grown cold. It was getting on toward eleven. The fifth was almost empty. The cowboy stumbled around in the dark dressed only in his Stetson, found the bottle, held it up to the window, and measured the contents with his eyes.

"Only a couple of shots left. Want some?" he slurred.

"No, thanks," the girl said wearily.

She hoped he wasn't getting *too* drunk. She wondered if she could get him out. He had had it. There was little point in his hanging on. She had worked hard to get him as drunk as he was. She had his wad hidden safely away. She would like to sleep.

"How you feeling?" she asked.

"Wrung plumb dry. Never been wrung plumb dry by a woman before. Never seen a woman as prerry as you. Thass a fact. Prerriest woman I ever seen."

"Don't you think you ought to go back to your hotel now and get some sleep so you'll feel like catching that train tomorrow?"

"I'm in for the party," he slurred, weaving around, and tilted the bottle up to his mouth with his head back to let the stuff run down inside his neck. He drank. Then staggered toward the bed, talking to his dick. "Pete, you never had such a good time as this, have you? You ain't never been in somethin so plumb juicy fine in your life, and you ain't likely to again. I spect you get home and get a sniff of ole Sue you'll just duck your head tween my legs and hide." He slapped his flaccid member sharply once, twice. "Wake up, there! You gnarled-up sonofabitch. Wake up! Say something to the prerry lady. Stand now, bastard, if you never stand again!"

"Looks dead to me, cowboy," the girl sympathized.

"He's jes sleepin. Jes needs a lil res . . ." the cowboy said dreamily, turned like a big tree going down; the bottle slipped from his fingers, and he fell face down on the bed, stiff as a board, with a crash that almost broke a slat. He rolled over once and was out.

"Oh!" she gasped.

Boots got up from a chair in the shadows by the window where he had been sitting for the last quarter of an hour, having slipped in without the cowboy seeing him. Blondie had known he was there all the while. He walked straight to the bed. She put her arms around him, laid her face beside his. "We got it, baby."

He pushed her away, reaching between her legs.

"Take it easy, honey. I'm kinda sore. Ow! Don't be mean."

He crawled up on the bed, boots and all.

"Baby? Don't you think we ought to get rid of this first?" The cowboy snored softly, deep in his throat, through his slack, open mouth. He was out.

The midget didn't answer. He put the first three fingers of his left hand in her mouth and began unbuttoning his fly with the other. He stood astraddle her as she sat with her back against the brass headboard. She sucked his fingers as he slipped them back and forth in her mouth exactly as if it were her sex. As she became excited, he went faster. She pushed his own hand away from his fly and went to work on it herself with both hands. She dug out his dick and rolled it between her palms, skinning it back, groaning in her throat. She drew it toward her.

"You! I want you," she mumphed around his busy fingers.

She fastened on his little joint greedily. He grabbed her by the hair with both hands and shoved so deep in her mouth he repeatedly hit her soft palate and made her gag.

"Don! Let me. You choke me," she croaked.

He wanted to hurt her. The way he was doing it, she couldn't suck him. There was only his cruel pleasure. When he stopped and withdrew, she slumped over, gasping for breath.

"Why didn't you let me do you nice?" she asked sadly.

"*Nice?* He fuck you in the ass, too?"

She shook her head no.

"Roll over."

She obediently got up on her knees with her ass high, white in the light from the street below, her cheek pressed resignedly to her soggy pillow. He dropped his pants around the top of his boots.

"Get it up there!" He hit her a hard uppercut under the right cheek of her resignedly elevating ass. She moaned.

He spit in his hand, lubricated the end of his dick, and worked it into her little pink button. He held her by the soft flesh of her belly as if it were cloth while reaching between his own and her legs with his left hand and playing with her pussy. When she was wet, he could get all of his fingers and his thumb in up to the knuckles and roll the hard cone of her cervix in his fingers. He could feel dick and hand working in her through the warm living wall in her body.

The bed bounced furiously. She held on to the brass headboard with both hands. Beside them the cowboy's slack lower jaw clattered like a voiceless dummy's. Boots, on the verge of climax, tensely looked back and forth between the cowboy's defenseless face and the quivering white flesh into which he was plunged, slapping against her soft posteriors with his loins and belly, making them compress and expand like a breathing thing. Pouring it to her. Pouring it to her. Shorty! Fucking her up in the brown. A beauty. He stiffened, tried to force his whole hand into her box, strained her to him by the grip he had on her belly skin, shooting into her ass. She cried out, groaned, gently contracted, called him sweet words, and dutifully ground it out, aping ecstasy until the end of his paroxysm. Then he made the girl get up and wash his cock in a pan of warm water laced with purple pomegranate, just as if he were a customer.

It was their job then to get the cowboy out.

"Gotta sleep," he argued when they sat him up. And fell back heavily on the bed.

"No, honey. You gotta go. Listen. The cops are going to be here any minute. It's going to be a raid! You don't want to get caught."

"*Booooo,*" he groaned. He cracked one eye, peered around. "Wha cops?" He did not see any cops. "Sleep."

"No! No! You've got to go. You gotta get out of here *now!*"

"Gotta sleep now. Gonna way up an fuh tha prerry woman agin. Layer. Slee now. . . ."

"Let me get that fucker up." Boots cleared his sleeves for action. He went to the cowboy's head, plunged his thumbs in the hollows under his ears, and lifted, and that cowboy came up in the wide-eyed world like a man sputtering up out of four fathoms.

*"Hey! What the hell!"* was only one of the things he asked. He swung his elbows a few times, trying to connect with whoever it was that was derricking him so meanly out of slumber. The light was like a bat across his eyes.

"You've got to go, quickly," the girl insisted, talking into his face to impress him with the urgency. "The cops are coming to raid. You gotta go now."

He wasn't too clear. He stared at the girl as if trying to place her. The midge had let up, though he refused to let him lie back down. Then, as if noticing it for the first time, the cowboy shook the midget off angrily. "Stop that! Goddamn stupid shit!"

"Come on." Blondie put his shirt over his shoulders, tried to work his arms into the sleeves. He shook her off.

*"You must go,"* she said firmly.

*"Awrigh . . .* awrigh. Jus a minute. GIMME A MINUTE!" he yelled at the top of his voice.

The midget busted him right in the mouth. One-two.

"I'll give you, you drunk sonofabitch!" he said between clenched teeth. He hit him again.

Blondie stifled a cry. The cowboy's lips were split. Blood ran down his chin. He looked stunned. Together they got his pants on. Tugging and straining, they got them up and buckled, though not buttoned. Boots threw a pitcher of ice water on him. He slapped his face, got him to sit up again, piled his boots, shirt, underwear in his arms, put his hat securely on his head, got him on his feet, got him to take a step toward the door—one-two. He stopped.

"Somebody hit me," he realized.

"No. Nobody hit you, hon. You took a little fall," Blondie assured him. "Come on."

"No! Somebody hit me. Hit the shit outta me. WHO HIT ME?"

"Shh! You want to get us all in jail?"

"Wanna know who hit me." He shrugged Blondie away so hard she fell on the bed. He dropped his stuff and began circling around with his chin stuck out a mile and his fists up cycling. He spotted the midget. "You hit me, you little bastard?" Then answering his own question: "YOU HIT ME! Hit me while I wa'n lookin. . . ."

The midget hooked a digging left into the drunk's appendix, followed with a zinger right uppercut to the balls, and the cowboy folded over so stiff-legged his face kissed the floor before his knees buckled.

Blondie poured a bottle of ginger ale over him. They hoisted and heaved and got him totteringly on his feet again. He lurched this way and that. They kept turning him toward the door until he lurched up against the wall beside it. Again they packed his arms with his stuff. Blondie screwed his hat on his head. She had the door open and the cowboy leaning in the right direction when, in one of those moments of inexplicable drunken shrewdness, the cowboy fumbled his right hand into his pants pocket and painfully turned it out empty. He spun around, falling back to brace himself on something solid, hit the door, and caused it to close. Listing heavily to port, his stuff still cradled in his left arm, he tried erratically to draw a bead on the pair with an accusing forefinger.

"I had near two hunner in tha pocket," he slurred. "One you's got it."

"Oh, cowboy, honey. You are *mistaken!*" Blondie swore. "I swear, whatever you had in that ole pocket you must of spent or still got somewhere."

"Noooope." He shook his head. His lips were split. He was soaked with ginger ale and ice water; blood ran down his chin. "One you's got ma money." He leaned bent to the left like a right angle. He had to be seeing them upside down.

"Count it up!" she offered reasonably, willing to help. "Let's see. You gave me twenty for the party, then two ten-dollar tips for treating you so well. That's right." She could read the account as if it were right before her eyes. "*Three* or *four* bottles of whiskey. How many, Boots? Well, almost forty dollars, anyway. And that big fried chicken dinner they had to fix special for you. I told you hamburgers or meat loaf would be fine with me. But you wanted the best. And you must have given Boots something for doin all that running around for you. It all adds up, honey. It adds up. You *spent* your money. Wasn't no two hundred. But if you're broke, baby, you spent it."

"Don lak bein rolled. DON LAK IT!"

"Nobody rolled you, crumb!" Boots said. "Straighten up and get your ass outta here."

"*Doggone!* Jus spoils it all." Bam! He threw his boots on the floor. "Dirry, rorren, pimp trick ta mess up a man's goo time lie tha. GOD-DAMN SUCH A FUCKIN WAY OF DOIN A MAN!" He drew himself erect.

Before the cowboy could focus on the human bowling ball thundering across the carpet at him, it hit him head first in the pit of the stomach, plastering him against the wall. He heard his own breath rushing out, then there was only a distant ringing. Boots went after his nuts like a featherweight on a speed bag. The cowboy took it without a sound, without a breath to sponsor a sound. When the midge stepped back, the cowboy slid down the wall like something deflated. Crumpled limply at the bottom, he simply toppled over. Then the midget went after his head with his boots.

Blondie hissed: "*Stop it! Stop it,* Boots! You'll *kill* HIM!"

"Keep away from me, you stinkin slut! Dog-fucker!" He slugged her in the belly. He was a man at work.

"I've enough of your hittin me," she blubbered. And grabbed the ginger ale bottle, raising it over her head with both hands, fully intending to brain the midget with it. The cowboy's face was being kicked into a bloody glob.

"*You're just a mean little sonofabitchin monster!*" she screeched. "*Sick of you!* You're mean, Boots. MEAN! I'd *rather* fuck a dog than you. *Monster! Freak!*" She swung wildly and missed.

The midget felt the breeze of the bottle and wheeled just as she raised it again. She was muttering hysterically. He hit her left and right in the groin, the belly, her breasts. She flailed wildly, ineffectually at him with the bottle. He kept his head moving as he always did. The Mongoose. The bottle flew from her grasp.

"You had to want some, too, dint ya? Aw right. *Aw right!*" He stalked her. She tried to hold him off with her outstretched hands. She retreated.

He slapped her hands away, stepped in, wrapped his arms around her hips, and plunged his face into her crotch with his mouth wide open and snapped it shut, grinding his teeth into the hairy lips. She screamed. She screamed a second time. A third.

Someone with their head out their door down the hall asked tentatively: "What was that? Was that someone being hurt? Hello!" Very gently.

He tasted blood in his mouth. He bit harder. She clawed at his head, his face, with her nails, trying to find his eyes. He wrenched away, took a single step backward, her nails scoring his face, and leaped astride her like an angry orangutan, locking his legs around her hips. She was propelled backward onto the bed. He brushed her upraised arms away from her face. She was weak and utterly unable to defend herself.

"Please," she pleaded without hope. A tiny withered "please." Her arms were brushed aside like a rag doll's. "Please, Boots," she said again in a faint voice.

He tore loose her left eyelid with his fists, knocked her front teeth through her lips, smashed her nose, and bit off the entire nipple and aureole of her left breast before the police came through the door, stumbling over the cowboy, and pried him off her.

They were astounded at the havoc the little man had wrought. It would become a legend in the department. One of the cops retrieved the girl's nipple and kept it in a bottle of alcohol in the police lab for years.

People were all out in the hall when they brought them downstairs. It had been Mac who had run across the street to the diner and called the law. There was a pay phone in the hall, but Mac hadn't felt like spending the nickel. Only the Greek had remained in his room, the door tightly closed. It was not his problem. The bird lady was out in hairnet and a kimono as wildly verdant as her slipcovers. People from upstairs leaned over the balustrade. A young woman on four with sickly twins, swaybacked, broken-bellied, sunken-eyed already at twenty-four, said in a high querulous voice, "Serves a thing like that right!"

Jacky clung to his grandma's long cotton gown and craned around her to see.

The pretty woman half carried by a big policeman had her hands over her face and was crying, "Oh! Oh! My *God!* My *God!* Oh! Oh! . . ." all the way down the stairs. There were pink streaks of blood in her silver hair. A thin watery pink rivulet ran down each leg. She was wrapped in a bedspread, barefoot. It seemed the boy could hear her a long time after she went away in the police car downstairs.

The cowboy's stained pink shirt was just laid over his narrow shoulders. He was barefoot. His pants were open, gaping, twisted on his belt. You could see the hair on his belly. He hung between two cops like a bloody Jesus. The boy thought of the calendar in his grandparents' room from some mortuary that had a picture of Jesus nailed on a cross. One of the cops carried the cowboy's high-heeled boots.

The midget, handcuffed with his hands behind his back and with a tailor-made cigarette dangling from the corner of his mouth, plainly shot the boy a wink from under the shadowed peak of his cap when he passed.

He only did ninety days with time off for good behavior because the cowboy was from out of state and the girl was the kind of whore more than one cop on the force was secretly pleased to see defaced. Then, there was a kind of hometown pride in having such a cocky, roughy-tough midget on its streets.

But next Sunday the boy did not have to go to church with his grandma because the MacDeramids were moving again.

# 9

MAC moved them in with the bootlegger and his wife, from whom he had bought the diner and who rented a house a couple of blocks from the place. It was a regular house with a small front yard, a backyard, and a single big tree out front. They had two rooms and a kitchenette upstairs. The bootlegger and his wife had the downstairs. He had the jakeleg, the gouty consequence of drinking moonshine into which lead salts had been boiled from the solder of homemade stills. It was a social disease in their set, but a rung up from venereal. Nor was Mac's grandson certain it was not catching and steered a wide course around the man. The Millers used the front door. The Mac-Deramids came in by the back. Their second room was not truly a room, but rather a wide stair landing. A couple of heavy country patch-work quilts were folded to make the boy a pallet on some crates next to the stairwell. The Pullman kitchen was in a closet. Mac and his wife slept in the front room. There was no door between.

Miller and his wife went out every night and slept all morning. They were both short and fat and slept in a low bed with head and foot boards like black mirrors. They slept with a snubnosed .38 on the night table on his side of the bed and a box of Sampler chocolates on hers. The boy peeked in their window under the drawn shade one morning and saw them sleeping. He saw the gun. When he asked his granddad about it, the old man would not tell him but said, "Stay away from them folks. They don't cotton to kids." They both wore black masks without eye-holes while they slept. Every time the boy crawled across their porch to peek on them, his heart kicked in his chest like a pup scratching fleas. A funny thing was the woman was so fat, yet had little bitty titties just sort of sitting up there on her pale drum of a gut. He saw her get up in her nightgown and go to the toilet. The way her tits were put him off so much he did not care if he ever saw her thing.

They hadn't any children and trusted the boy not at all. They also told his grandmother they thought he was peeking in their window at them. That got him a spanking. They never left their shade up more than a crack. He had to wait until the breeze blowing in lifted it slightly for an instant to get a squint.

They had a Boston bulldog, black and white, and gouty as themselves. It was a kid-hater, too. Always grouchy, petulant, mean. No fun at all.

Though their name was Miller, that didn't tell you a thing. He lived deep behind a desperate business face, mopped his bald spot a lot with a handkerchief, and let his wife do most of the talking. She resembled a close relative of her dog. Slap smoked glasses on the mutt and it could have been mistaken for a replica of her. The heat bothered Mrs. Miller a lot. She fanned herself with a soggy little hanky in her left hand, the one with a jeweled watch on its wrist and three rings on its ring finger. On her other hand she wore a large dinner ring for breakfast and lunch, too. Her nails were long and lacquered a venous blood red. She could never pick up a dime off a counter. She had to sweep it off the edge into the other plump hand. Her wristwatch cord cut deep into her fleshy wrist. The watch was covered with diamond chips. She wore dark glasses day and night. Her face was actually more devoid of any trace of human sentiment, humor, anger, animal delight than that of her spayed bitch, both finding each day following night a sinister arrangement designed solely for their own discomfort. She never offered the boy a piece of candy, though she was always eating chocolates.

Her bulldog never treed a squirrel or flushed a robin. It made a dash for the security of the doormat in front of the door at the first sight of one of the hungry, narrow old cats who strayed in from the alley with beggary eyes and the cautious step and bearing of a lynx. From there it would bark its fool head off in a Boston bluff as phony as the big rough-cut jewels in its stud-dog collar. Yet the bitch would bite a kid or nip an old lady's ankle. It even foolishly growled at MacDeramid once and got a size 12½ boot in the ribs so hard it spent the rest of the day feeling sorry for itself under the front steps, puking its guts out.

Mrs. Miller's face was not so much a caricature of femininity as a standing rebuke to its essence. On its doughy surface a scarlet little mouth was painted which obscenely seemed to open inward when she spoke, as if the woman would eat herself. A common face devoid of all emotions save cruelty, greed, and fear, seen most often in close proximity to secondhand cash registers in greasy cafés with names like Dew Drop Inn where the specialty of the house is chicken-fried steak, or in cheerless bars where the passing of time is balefully blessed by the bending of silent mummers' elbows. That she used cosmetics and perfume and wore lingerie seemed the grossest sort of perversion. Her hair was sparse and dead, though dyed deeper than jet so even her scalp seemed stained. Her eyebrows were but single lines drawn unsteadily with a pencil. A face for Brueghel, Hogarth, Grosz. As an American standard, absolutely the flip side of Eleanor Roosevelt. A human boil.

Where do they go when they die? Dying in rented sidestreet rooms as stylelessly and miserably as they lived. A son in the Marines. A daughter who isn't speaking—like that. Where and how are they planted? With no pleasure in living greater than biting into a caramel-center bonbon and no dream more magnanimous than moving one day to Miami, they would seem more fit for desiccation than proper burial.

Out to skin with the skinners, yet too stupid and frightened to do anything more than chisel pettily, they fill the lesser courts with their chronic bankruptcies. Try something like the Bobby Greenlease kidnapping, they invariably panic, kill their hostage, and hope to get out with their expenses. The Millers had the faces of unsuccessful kidnappers, as asexual as the three globes over a hock shop, deadened by a basic perversion more directly traceable to the potato famine in Ireland and the Opium Wars than any prepuberty experience. Still, pity for them is squeezed from one by the weight of a sheriff's deputy closing a cheap suitcase somewhere on a quarter of a million in small bills. The case is closed and the perversion propagated. Faces for Brueghel and Hogarth and Grosz.

The Millers never actually kidnapped anyone. They ran a series of cheap establishments always in conjunction with retail bootlegging, punchboards, a location for a crap game, or a betting-slip drop for a bookie, until they saw tougher men move in and take over their dodge on a 60-40 split, then jobbing them out of most of their share in the daily audit until they found themselves going to a syndicate shark for a loan, only to go bankrupt simply paying the vigorish, hocking their place, car, furniture, *ready* to pull a kidnapping or ready to flee town whining for their very lives. So that wherever they went then, they needed drugs to sleep and nodded off every night afraid they would be slaughtered in their beds too doped up to wake up and fumble the snub-nosed .38 on the night table into action.

So perhaps it was only by dint of small courage and perhaps an absolute loathing of children that the Millers never tried to kidnap someone. But Jacky was convinced they were just waiting for the best chance to kidnap him. He could not sleep well on his pallet by that dark stairwell knowing they slept downstairs beside a real gun and usually found his way to the sofa in the other room after his grandpa and grandma were asleep.

Yet, only the front of the place was endowed with Millers' jakelegged spookiness for the boy. The nearly bald backyard and concrete alley was his garden of verse. A cocky robin pulling up an elastic worm and winging it away to a nest where bald-necked babies peeped. The life and metamorphosis of a fuzzy caterpillar to dusty yellow butterfly, leaving him its fragile cocoon and the memory of magic. Sunflowers, milkweed, uncultivated hollyhock ladies in blue petal gowns. Stick a bud on an inverted bloom with a toothpick and there she stood. Drowned pale grubs in puddles after a cloudburst. A place under the lip of the concrete from where after a rain he could mine gobs of pure gray clay. And all those lonely, lynx-looking cats.

The alley was paved when the telephone company built its automatic central exchange system on the corner to provide all-weather access to and from the garage for the repair trucks. His grandmother took him to the exchange's big open house. The whole building smelled of new linoleum, furniture polish, electricity, and wet cement. Its style was somewhere between Frank Lloyd Wright and the Wizard of Oz. A monster WPA-like mural in the lobby called *20th Century Ltd* depicted Trojan telephone linemen wiring the plains. Hero-workers with arms like oak tablelegs in spotless, skintight unionalls bringing word of the power of American Industry and Commerce, represented by a cubistic jumble of gears, levers, stacks and planes and trains and stuff, to an obscenely well-fed hero-farmer and his hero-wife who had some decorous how sired a couple of blue-eyed Aryan brats who waited patiently with their Dick and Jane readers as new and unbroken as their shoes under their heroic little arms for the linemen to put in their phone.

While the voice of Kate Smith came out of the woodwork singing:

> Whose alabaster beauty rise
> above the fruited plain. . . .
> *America! America!*
> God shed His grace on thee.
> And crown thy good with brotherhood
> From sea to shining sea.

Southwest Bell put on an open house without refreshments. All the telephone company sprang for were bell-shaped paper badges and a lot of pamphlets. When the boy had gone to the Bond Bakery open house with his grandmother's church group, they got paper bakers' hats, soda pop, and little loaves of Bond bread. He was ready to leave Southwest Bell, but his grandma had to see it all.

In the basement one could not talk for the generators' whine. Workers there seemingly swam through the noise like deepsea divers. But upstairs the building was spookily quiet, four stories of silently working machinery. Behind the lobby and offices and above the basement, the entire building was a vast bank of telephone circuits stacked tier upon tier with no real floors but open steel catwalks, so he could stand on the first level and see a guy four stories up against the skylight. A very scary building. And for years after it opened, cautious people found it prudent to walk on the other side of the street rather than pass a green enameled door on the side of the building that bore the warning:

DANGER HIGH VOLTAGE
DO NOT OPEN

No one ever did. The boy watched the thing for weeks, hoping someone would and naturally be struck dead on the spot by a visible bolt of electricity.

Not that he was above living a bit dangerously himself. He found a place on the sidewalk where he could stand and feel the turbine humming below through his feet. He discovered that by putting his ear to the concrete alley behind the building almost anywhere, he could hear all sorts of mysterious, electric sounds. Who knew what kind of invisible, debilitating rays he was absorbing? Certainly he was taking his life in his hands.

Coming up the alley to have lunch with his grandpa, with his crumby shoes eating the socks off his heels and his hair falling in his eyes, he had to pass the garage where S.W. Bell serviced its line trucks. They always walked to the diner for lunch. It was a four-block walk. Listening to the buried hum under the concrete always left him introspective, and rather on the frightened side of lonely.

So when the cackling voice of an honest to God witch screeched, "Fuckerfaster! Fuckerfaster!" his lank blond hair stood on end.

There in the open door of the garage in a sunlit corner sat a horny old green and yellow parrot chained by one leg to a T-bar perch.

"Fuckerfaster! Fuckerfaster!" he lilted brainlessly as a coprolaliac. "Wheet! How about a little, baby? Show me your ass." Looking the boy right in the eye, his head cocked to one side: "Hey Johnny! Johnny! Johnny Fuckerfaster! Wheet! Fuckerfaster!" Then in a strangely different voice: "If you can fuckerfaster, come fucker yourself!"

The unheroic-looking mechanics (if WPA murals were the standard) who kept the telephone company rolling looked up from their lunch boxes and put the laugh on him. Unheroic but dandy guys like his Uncle

Kenny, with their hair slicked back from a fire-break part with sta-comb and wave-set and chips on their shoulders. No biballs for those monkeys. Red-gored bell-bottoms, with nickel-studded belts, striped polo shirts with a pack of Camels in the pocket, sleeveless undershirts with a greasy palmprint like an expedient Legion of Merit, lowcuts with pointed toes and Cuban heels, thin clocked socks rolled to the ankles, caps shoved on the backs of their heads, cocked over one eye, silver skull and crossbones rings with rubies in the eye sockets. . . . Buccaneers too quixotic to be captured by a "social-realist" eye. The advance guard of a completely motorized age, out of gasoline alleys without high school diplomas, cutting a wide, stylish swath in the gap between Henry Ford and Jimmy Hoffa with the air of experts.

"It talks!"

"Sure it talks, keed. Say something to it," one of the guys encouraged.

"Polly. Pretty Polly."

"Fuck you, Jack! Fuck you!"

The guys roared.

"Polly wanna cracker?" he tried again.

"Up your ass! Up your ass!"

They really got a kick out of that.

The parrot had all the good lines.

"Fuck you, too!" he challenged happily. "Fuck you!" What did he know?

"Got the rag on! Got the rag on!" the bird piped.

The guys were rolling around on the concrete floor of the garage.

So for a quarter of an hour the boy stood trading obscenities with an unflappable poll parrot.

"Here, keedo," one of the guys with a skull ring said and flipped him a nickel.

"Stick it up your ass! Up your ass!" the parrot croaked.

He went skipping up the alley with the nickel, singing to himself, "Fuckerfaster. Fuckerfaster. Fuck-*er*-fast-*er*. . . ."

He skipped into the house and up the stairs to where his granddad was mending a pair of his old work trousers like a man wrestling an alligator.

"Fuckerfaster," was the boy's advice to him.

"*What?*"

"Fuckerfaster. Johnny Fuckerfaster. If you can fuckerfaster, fucker yourself."

Bam! He gave the boy a shot with his open hand beside the head that knocked him flat.

"Where did you pick up that shit?" he demanded.

"A parrot," the boy bawled.

"Who taught you that?"

"A poll parrot."

Pow! This time he stayed down.

"Stand there and lie to me!"

"I ain't lyin."

"You shut your goddamn filthy mouth! Come in here and tell me some crap like that!"

"I did! I did! An old poll parrot told me. Come on." He reached out and got hold of the old man's big forefinger and tried to drag him to be introduced.

He was reluctant to be led on so obvious a fool's errand. But he went. The boy towed him down the stairs, across the yard, up the alley by the finger. He followed reluctantly, feeling like a big goof, peering from side to side as if expecting an ambush.

The guys in the garage stopped eating as the old man and the boy approached. They were amused, vacant, expectant. There stood the bird.

Mac cleared his throat. "My grandson here tells me your parrot says a few things."

Someone chuckled in the garage.

The man who had given Jacky the nickel said, "Sure, dad. It talks. Say somethin to it."

"Well. . . ." He cleared his throat again, flicked his cigar a couple of times, choosing his opening. "Hello there, Polly. Pretty Polly wanta cracker?"

"Stick it up your ass! Stick it up your ass!"

"Sonofabitch!" The old man took a backward step.

The men laughed and slapped their legs.

"Hey, Polly!" One of the monkeys called. "What does Polly want?"

"Awwk! Polly wants some pussy! Polly wants some pussy!"

"Well, I'll swan!" the old man exclaimed in wonder. He explained, "The boy came home and told me he'd picked up some words from a parrot. I wouldn't take his word for it." He looked sheepish. "Must take something to train a bird like that."

The men laughed. Then one of them said, "Used to be my mother-in-law's. I'd sneak in and teach it dirty words. She's a real religious woman. About drove her nuts. Finally she asked me to get rid of it for her. She's a widow. Guy offered me fifty bucks for that bird in here a week ago. I wouldn't take a hundred. This is a damn smart bird." All the guys nodded in agreement.

On the way home Mac told the boy very seriously, "I don't want to hear you say that stuff no more. Mama would just have a fit if she heard you. Hear?"

"Yes."

"OK. Now, I mean it. If I hear you spoutin that crap again, I'll tan you good. Don't go wandering up there no more, neither. You play in the yard where you belong."

So when his grandma came home, he was playing an empty oatmeal can as drum and began scampering around beating time, singing, "Fuckerfaster, Fuckerfaster, Fuck-er-fast-er."

The old man looked at him pityingly and held up his big hands helplessly. "He picked it up from a parrot," he explained.

"I'll-wash-his-mouth-out-with-soap!" was her instinctive reaction. And she cast about in the frenzy of one trying to deal with a child who has inadvertently swallowed poison.

"You ain't going to do no such of a thing," Mac told her and got up to prevent her by force if necessary.

"What parrot?" she asked suddenly.

"The fellas up there at the telephone company garage got this parrot. Used to be one of the fellas' mother-in-law's. . . ." He launched into the story, obviously amused. "You ought to see it. Damndest bird you ever saw."

"No-thank-you! If it's all the same to you, I'll pass it up!"

"Suit yourself." He went back to his chair and paper.

"I still think I ought to wash his mouth out with soap."

"I whipped him. I don't hold with such meanness."

"Maybe if someone had washed *your* mouth with soap, you'd use the American language with a little more decency today."

"Like one of them mealy-mouthed palm-ticklin deacons and elders and psalm-singers at your goddamned come-to-Jesus-or-else church, I suppose you mean."

"I mean the way you swear around shows you don't have any respect for me anymore." She was near to tears.

"Horseshit. Don't show nothing of the sort."

"And it looks like you'd restrain yourself around the boy. The things he comes out with in public is just awful. You let him run wild all day. *I* can't be here to look after him and go out and make a living for us, too—"

"*There it is!* I knew you'd try and throw that up to me! Act as if I ain't made a living for you and ours all our life. Talk like I ain't nothin now. Like I ain't shit. Don't want me around the damn diner 'cause I upset the fuckin customers' delicate stomachs. I didn't ask for the government to screw us out of our place. I didn't tell this boy's mother to be no good and get herself knocked up and run around, never let us know what she's doin, or where she's at, leaving us with the issue! I've done my goddamned best all my life. If that ain't good enough, then you just find some *other* way of doin!"

"All I know is, that boy is picking up terrible language from you."

"You don't know shit about beans." He reached out and pulled the boy beside him. "Me and this boy get along just fine. Don't we, son?"

He nodded that they did. He knew then it wasn't going to be soap.

"Two of a kind," his grandmother muttered. She went into the kitchen, heated up a pot of water, poured it into a basin of Epsom salts on the floor, sat down on the boy's pallet, and soaked her weary feet.

She sighed when her feet were fully in the steaming water.

Mac thought again of the parrot and chuckled to himself.

# 10

THERE was not a day that the boy did not wish his mother would come and take him to live with her. He liked his grandad, but he was left a lot of time to be lonely. The old man spent most of the morning reading the paper, then sort of muttered around the rest of the day thinking about and quarreling with what he had read. He often became quite hot about whatever it was Roosevelt was trying to get away with. It was just Mrs. Mac and Elfie at the diner. The old man went over after closing and cleaned up. He puffed his two-for-a-nickel stogie like a steam donkey pulling a grade. When an anti-Roosevelt, anti-government fit was upon him, the boy was often his only audience.

From the morning paper on, Mac put forth the case of the Common Man in a fantasized convention of Congress where his inexorable logic and rustic metaphor exorcised a personal array of demons that extended in an unbroken line from Pontius Pilate to Colonel Parkhurst. The International Amalgamation of Thieves, Liars, and Sonsabitches would take a daily beating from Mac that left the world noticeably cooler from the breeze stirred up by the fanning of prison doors.

"Give me all the folks that are *in* prison and put all the politicians who are out in, and I'll give you a more honest, decent, fair government than this country has ever seen." He tacked down another plank of his platform.

He was all fairness and sagacity. He did not want to *kill* anyone, he assured the boy. He just wanted the scallywags out of office and in jail if necessary until they gave up their bad habits, namely, bilking the poor. How often he was hoisted in his daydreams on the shoulders of his fellow men and carried to the very gates of power, no one could know. But once there, he would have respectfully declined the honor on the grounds that he was a working man, too.

Ideologically he was a kind of Jacobean-Wobbly-Populist-Agnostic-Bullhead. His heroes, other than Lincoln, who was everyone's, were Jackson, Calhoun, Bryan, Huey Long, John L. Lewis, Pappy and Ma Ferguson, Will Rogers, and Dr. Francis E. Townsend. So between the ideal and real alternatives the old man was a rude mirror of the American voter's constant dilemma. When it was Roosevelt vs. Landon, the old man cried out, "How can we hope to go on when our choice is between such men? If this is the best our country can come up with, there's dim hope we will last out the century." Such was the state of hope for a man who had time to read between the lines of his newspaper every day. It was his unshakable conviction that a cooperative iron triangle of big business, rackets, and politics was formed out of the Crash.

Though he hadn't campaigned, his outspoken views earned him nomination for the presidency of Wichita Townsend Club No. 1, with an enthusiastic unanimity that assured his election over that of some petty politician named Frazee and a friend named McCabe. He respectfully declined in favor of his pal, yet ran so strong a third on the ballots of those who would draft him that his buddy lost. And both he and McCabe switched their affiliation to Club No. 4, clear over on the West Side.

"You should of taken the nomination," his wife declared. "You're always telling everybody what ought to be done, here might of been your chance to do something about it. At least we wouldn't be going clear across town. We'd of saved bus fare."

"That's the kind of small thinking I could expect of you," he charged. "I didn't want the damn thing. There's too much backbiting. I don't have the patience for it. McCabe has. The damn fools ought to have elected him."

"He's too quiet," was her opinion.

"That don't mean he ain't got more brains in his little finger than that pipsqueak Frazee's got in his whole teeny head."

"Well, I voted for you, anyway. Even if you said not to."

"Now, there you are! Goddamnit anyhow! Why don't you do what I tell you?" There was just no hope for an enlightened constituency anywhere.

"I figured you were the best man." She defended her vote simply. "And you are a lot better-looking, too." She giggled.

"Women should of never been given the vote," the old man sighed.

After that she and the boy did not go to the club with Mac as often. It was too far over to the West Side, and they could not get the old man to leave until the last dog was dead. The bus stopped running at eleven. The meeting rarely broke up before midnight. Unless they left Mac and went by themselves, it was a seven-mile hike through deserted city streets while the water trucks washed down the pavement.

Moreover, the club was rapidly degenerating into a purely social organization for old folks who just came to dance to the music of a three-piece band or play cards. The reading of minutes was dispensed with as quickly as possible, even while the fiddler was tuning up out in the hall and the sergeant at arms had already begun folding up the unoccupied chairs at the rear and stacking them against the wall.

No one any longer actually expected to see Dr. Townsend's plan for a two-cent sales tax on the dollar and a $200-a-month pension for everyone over sixty-five ever made a law. Yet, from beginning to end, Mac-Deramid alone continued to sport publicly a tiny photographic portrait of the doctor on his lapel, even in the face of ridicule and the smart money who had gone over to Roosevelt, box suppers, and bingo.

"Somewhere, because of the nature of the system, some poor sucker is starving to death or being shot to death for complaining about conditions," the old man argued. He had never read Karl Marx, but he understood. "It's *all* the people who make the world what it is. Not just this or that kind, this or that nation. It's *all* the people, *all* the time, over the generations who make it what it is, give it its quality. And I don't exactly mean traditions and religions and such shit. They're *part* of the trouble. I mean the underlying human quality of it all, the way it feels and goes. It ain't the uplifters and vested interests who define the way it really is. Never was. It's the people. And if the conditions are rotten, mean, frightening, then you're going to get rotten, mean, and frightened people. If nearly all the ways for them to be better than they are is shut to them, they're going to get worse and worse till like the frayed cuff on a pair of dress britches, they're going to show and make you wonder about your back seam while you're waltzin through your old traditional paces. You can only mend so much, then it's a raggedy-assed show from top to bottom. A new hat or an umbrella ain't going to make that much difference.

"It's the working people who make a dollar what it's worth. Their sweat and their dreams. It's the vested interests who feed off us, selling our sweat like so many old slavers, who pervert the values earned by sweat. They queer the whole country, drive up prices, skim off the cream, water the remaining milk, piss in the wells and springs and keep on in truly criminal ways until even the laws are criminal acts against folks. Eventually somewhere down the line, somewhere in the world, as a direct result of a corn share being traded in Chicago or a gold bond on Wall Street, a child starves to death, a woman trades her ass for a pinch of coffee and a crust of bread, a man is machine-gunned for complaining about conditions. That's how it works. That's how it's going to work until the world becomes like a lot of rats in the belly of a stricken cow or enough of us get together and stop it. Share and share alike!" was his simple view. Jesus' feeding of the multitude seemed less a miracle to him than a problem of getting a lot of strangers to take out their box lunches in front of each other. Reasoning: "Only a damn fool would set out for the day to hear a damn evangelist without a sandwich in his poke."

"What are *you* doing about it?" a skeptical reliefer demanded one afternoon while leaning on the front of the White Way Pool Hall in a puddle of sun.

"I'm telling them! I'm letting them know how *I* feel, every chance I get. I'm telling *you*. I'll tell the world! I'll tell you right now, if you want to get up off your ass and go do something about it, I'm ready to go with you."

"You and me?" The reliefer sized the old man up doubtfully. "Well, say we *could* do the job. What would you do when we had won?"

"Why hell, man, I'd take all the money that's in the world on a given day, set aside enough to keep things going, to make the necessary improvements, and just divide up the rest between every man, woman, and child in the world. There's enough for everyone. There always has been and always will be if folks are taught to use a little sense about things and think of their fellow man as a brother instead of an enemy. Them who tells you there ain't enough to go around are just trying to keep you scared, make you distrust your neighbor, get you looking in all directions so they can rob you from the blind side. When that don't work, they'll use a gun and call it 'law' or defendin their interests. You tell me why one man should have more than another when there's plenty for everyone, and I'll show you logic that justifies jack-rollin the blind."

"Yeow? But what about drunks and guys who don't want to work?"

That reliefer didn't want some bum getting a share as long as he had to work for his.

"Listen. If some sucker wants to take his share and drink himself to death, let him if he doesn't bother nobody. Makes more sense than prison or war. Would you drink up your share?"

"Hell, no!"

"Right. And neither would most folks. I suspect there'd be a lot who do now who'd quit. And there would be a law to protect the shares of wives and children and old folks."

"But nothin would get done. If nobody worked, we'd be broke in no time. Then our share wouldn't be worth beans." He was sure he had the old man there.

"Your reasoning there is that if you were starving and found yourself in an orchard, you wouldn't stir your ass to shake a tree."

"I would."

"But you think no one *else* would, is that right?"

"Lots wouldn't."

"Now, you don't believe that. The evidence doesn't support it. I've worked all my life, from one end of this country to the other, and I never met a man yet who wasn't beaten down by need who would sit by and starve to death, or let his loved ones starve to death, if there was anything at all he knew to do about it. A man *wants* to work. What else is there to do with his time? Oh, he doesn't want to slave his guts out for less than enough to keep body and soul together. He don't want to muck in a sewer, haul garbage, stuff like that. Wait! You're going to say, 'Well, somebody's got to do it,' ain't ya? Why do they? Who says garbage has got to be hauled? Give a man enough to live on and you might be surprised who'd come up with an idea for a mechanical goat you could keep right in the kitchen. That's work, too. The problem is and always has been: men are harnessed by one means or another to the desires of another man to make a personal profit greater than the first man's, instead of being set toward solving a specific problem that has to be solved to benefit us all.

"The way things are ain't the way things are going to be. It's really those who are gettin *more* than their share now, coupled with those who've been conned into believing they are likely to lose their little if they open their mouths, and the religious who are content to wait for their reward 'up there,' who insist things *have* to stay like they are— those who think the Lord looks like the president of the First Federal Savings and Loan Association. Forget them drunks and bums on Market and Main streets. It's keeping the rich in liquor and foreign vacations that's killing us. I've worked with too many kinds of men all my life not to have faith in my fellow man." He allowed himself a small smile at the beautiful simplicity of it.

Then sadly: "And if I'm wrong, it ain't going to matter much, because we'll all be dead and the United States of America'll hardly be a speck in history."

When the reliefer sneered and told the old man, "You talk like some kind of damn Red," Mac dropped him with as pretty a straight right hand as was ever thrown by someone over sixty-five, then dared the much younger man to get up.

"I'll bat your goddamned empty head over the Union Station with this stick if you even look like you want to rise," he vowed, shaking his heavy black cane under the man's bloody nose. "You've got to read the paper, man. Got to find out what's going on in the world. Think a little. Why, shitfire, you poor fuck, your vision is so dim you ain't hardly got lights enough to button yourself. I don't blame you, understand. I just want you to think before you start callin names until you know the nature of the title, and know then, too, you can't ever be one hundred percent certain you're ever right."

Over a split lip the patriot blubbered something about calling the law. "You're crazy! You ought to be locked up."

"Yeow? You call the law, you measly cocksucker, and then you keep to your kennel with your tail between your legs. Cause I'll knock you down every time I lay eyes on you. I'll knock you down if I have to cross the street to do it."

Feeling richer than Mrs. Astor's cat, the boy walked up the street beside the old man, who was really stepping them off. The old man must have felt pretty good, too, for as soon as they had gone under the viaduct they crossed the street to Popadopolis' Ice Cream Parlor, where he bought the boy a banana split and two King Edward cigars for himself.

Yet when the boy asked him why he knocked that man down, Mac said sadly, "Because it just looks like there ain't no hope in the world. It just looks like we're going to hell in a hand basket everywhere you look. Eat your ice cream. You don't understand. I shouldn't of hit that man. Hittin him won't make him no smarter."

"It won't?" Jacky held up his end of the conversation, shoveling in ice cream.

"Well, maybe a little," the old man said.

# 11

ALL over town, boys who couldn't catch on with Western Union or Southwest Bell sharpened butcher knives stolen from their mothers' kitchens and fashioned jimmies from old car springs, just waiting for the perfect moonless night to burgle their neighborhood grocery, and girls who scorned bandeaux beneath their middy blouses hung a Wings on their lip, rolled their stockings below their knees, and cocked a man's hat over one eye to go in and case the place for the boys. Boys AWOL from Scout meetings sawed the barrels and stocks off Iver Johnson single-shot .22's they had earned peddling seeds or magazines door to door while visions of tommy guns rattled in their heads. Roosevelt had nothing to tell them. Their heroes were John Dillinger, Pretty Boy Floyd, the Barkers, Bonnie Parker and Clyde Barrow, Alvin Karpis, and Homer Vanmeter.

When four kids armed with what were probably toy pistols and an ancient sawed-off, side-hammer shotgun knocked over a farmers' bank in Winfield, making their getaway in a stolen Model A coupe driven by a girl, everyone swore the Barrows had struck again.

There was somehow fateful honor in being robbed by the Barrows or the Barkers or Pretty Boy, akin to being wiped out by a twister, dispossessed, or other acts of God. It was as if everyone *preferred* being held up by the Barkers, the Barrows, or Pretty Boy. To concede the job to local talent would have been to be robbed of greater glory in a season of robbers.

And the bankers' terror was possibly the backwash of bad conscience over all those foreclosures. Surely there had to be *some* niggling question in their minds at such easily come by properties. And if Roosevelt —as had been initially feared—was not coming to punish them for their good fortune in a time of dire want, then perhaps through a mysterious system of natural selectivity the chosen were Pretty Boy, Bonnie and Clyde, or Ma Barker and her sainted boys.

A family in Chicago dined on their youngest child. A man in New York was arrested for marketing chops he harvested from cadavers freshly planted. Out of a season so desperate there flowered a bumper crop of young would-be desperadoes. From New York to Chicago, where the habit of holy patriarchal authority had been ground into the Catholic-Semite soul over generations, where the neighborhood was a nationality and salvation a birthright, the kids looked to get a leg up in the syndicated gangs, the political wards, the feudal businesses. But out on the Protestant plains sons of highlanders and lowlanders alike, whose daddies had discovered not everyone in the New World could be a shop-keeper and went ever westward changing their religions as often as their shirts, took to the public highway like so many nihilistic Robin Hoods.

*Rodeo, Stripped-down, Motordrome. Carnival. Indianapolis 500. On the run. Gunned down in cold blood. Shot in the face. Dead on arrival. Root hog or die!*

Compared to the boys back East who would sell denatured alcohol as drink to anyone desperate enough to ask for it and meats of unknown origin for pork and beef, boys and girls of the plains were total failures. Right from the start they billed themselves as bandits. They put the bankers on notice. Their ideology was as simple as a kid's going over someone's fence into an orchard. Their expectation: to take their best shot and check out; to be shot dead while shooting back. They did not view money in the bank as anything but trapped communal property, for they had never known anyone *personally* who had ever had an account. The bank was to money as an orchard is to a winesap. And cops were a species of doubly sold-out humanity who were content not only to carry a lunch pail but to bear the bankers' shield, as well.

So it was guerrilla warfare out on old U.S. 54 and up and down old 81, until it got so hot out on the prairie the bandits could not stop for a hamburger and Delaware Punch without holding half the population of the burg in which they rested hostage. Objects of the greatest manhunt in history, Public Enemies No. 1, chased by bounty hunters and hired guns in the employ of banks, ultimately riddled from ambush or captured in a military operation led by the FBI and of a magnitude sufficient to annex Cuba, they provided a lot of folks with the hope that, in the bleak years between 1929 and the Second World War, the people might get back their own. They continued to write their relatives while on the run, took snapshots like tourists, loved, suffered, laughed. And would risk it all to go in under fire for no more profit than the satisfaction of busting a pal out of jail.

While back East the question was ever, "What's the percentage?"

They said in Oklahoma that Pretty Boy Floyd's generosity with bankers' money did more in a single dusty season to save hard-up hardscrabble farmers from foreclosure than the Farm Security Administration did for them in its entire career. He could have led a little revolution if he had but known where to lead it. Ma Barker may have blasted her second husband and planted him in an Arkansas pea patch, but she was hell on her boys about attending church regularly. Then, Ma was a Fundamentalist who did not believe in divorce. Dillinger robbed banks with a flair worthy of the movies; and if he nabbed a payroll or three, he never nabbed it after it became the custody of the workers. There is the poetry that Bonnie wrote for Clyde out of a heart at least as full as Mrs. Browning's, from a point of view at least as true. Moreover, they say she could sing. Even though the music Clyde could coax from a saxophone was inferior to that which he could make with a BAR, he would have waded alone through ten legions of deputy sheriffs to free his Bonnie love from their hard rock tower. Karpis could draw your likeness. And Vanmeter? With a first name like Homer, could he ever have been a Capone?

Though it was a pointless rebellion of individuals not looking to be followed, with no hope other than to live fast, die young, and be a beautiful corpse, it was the only one they ever had between the Blue Ridge Mountains and Pike's old Peak.

A policeman came to the house Sunday while Mrs. MacDeramid was at church. He came first to the front of the house, scaring hell out of the Millers, rousing them from doped sleep under their twin eyeless black masks. They gratefully sent him around back.

"Are you the father of Wilma Wayne MacDeramid?" he asked the old man, reading the name from a small notebook.

"Why, yes. That's right," the old man admitted. "What's the trouble?"

"Well, we got her downtown. Picked her up with another couple this morning in the Allis Hotel."

"What the deuce did she do?" Mac asked a little breathlessly.

"Charged with accessory to a larceny. There's also a lot of stuff she charged at stores and some rubber checks. We been lookin for her for awhile. They'll fill you in downtown."

The boy padded out still in his sleepers. Mac told him to go back into the house. He retreated a couple of steps but remained close enough to see and hear. They were talking about his mom. The policeman was bigger than anyone he knew. He had on gleaming brown leather puttees, ice-cream-pink breeches, an olive tunic with a Sam Browne belt and a military-flapped holster holding a nickel-plated revolver with stag-horn grips. The belt had leather pouches for bullets, handcuffs, and blackjack. Both men stood straight up facing each other when they talked, with their hands hanging down quietly. He liked the cop. He hoped he would go to the front of the house and arrest the Millers. Yet he wondered if his mama was somehow hurt.

"Well, listen. I can't go right now," Mac said. "Mama's still at church, and I got this boy here. This is Wilma's boy, but we've looked after him almost since he was born."

The policeman looked at the boy and nodded as if he were no surprise to him.

"And we ain't got no money, you know," the old man went on.

"OK, pop. You come down when you can. I don't reckon she'll be going anywhere. We just wanted to let you know."

"I'm much obliged to you for coming by. We don't have no phone here. We got one down at the place, but not here. We run the Coffee Cup on Emporia."

"Sure. I've been in there."

"Best cuppa coffee in town," the old man said absently.

"Yeah," the cop replied indifferently. He flipped his notebook shut and put it in a little pocket inside his cap.

That was something! Only Western Union boys carried their messages in their caps. Cops, too. Maybe, Jacky thought, he'd become a cop.

"Say!" the old man called suddenly when the cop was almost around the corner of the house. "What do you reckon I ought to do?"

"I'd get a lawyer, pop."

"Well, we can't afford no lawyer."

The cop shrugged, looked at the boy, nodded sympathetically, and went on.

The old man's face looked lax, drained, stunned. It seemed to have shrunk beneath the gray stubble of his beard, leaving him looking suddenly very seedy. The boy had never seen him look helpless before. In his helplessness he sensed a personal loss of security and was ashamed of him, sorry for him, and mad at him and so scared he plotted simply to hang on and ride it out, hiding his panic until his grandmother got home. He was prepared to hold his breath that long. If for some reason she should never come, he would have to go find his mom.

The old man had him dressed except for shoes when his grandma came huffing up the stairs. The Sunday funnies were still unread, and he hadn't had breakfast, and his shoes had curled up overnight from having been wet the day before.

"She can just rot!" was Mrs. Mac's initial Christian council. "She got herself in this trouble without any help from me, let her get herself out the same way."

"Still, I reckon I ought to go down and find out what it's all about," Mac reasoned.

"Well, go if you want to. I'm washing my hands of it."

"Maybe it's a mistake."

"It's no *mistake*. She's mixed up in something. Lord knows we ain't got no money to put up bond or whatever they call it. I wouldn't know where to get it. I just *couldn't* go to one of our friends and ask them for it, for something like this. I won't do it. I *won't!*"

She would not lie. She was ever a kaleidoscope of moralistic shards, fundamental fragments of Christian dogma and recalled disappointments, a woman who believed the Lord had actually dictated the words set in red in her Bible to a secretary. Her philosophy could be recited while standing on one foot, but she never expected anyone to have to do for her as she knew she was going to be asked to do for them. Over a lifetime it worked out precisely that way.

The old man may have been more totally forgiving, more truly affectionate, yet it was Mrs. Mac who always came up with the necessary.

Without her, after 1932 the family would have disappeared with the first dusty chinook. Around her tenacity they knocked together the boards and tin for shelter, calked the cracks, and laid the fire with the certainty she would find something to cook over it. Her industry alone stitched together the rags, bags, and snippets of their lives to create whole cloth. An expedient crazy quilt without beauty or tradition, its sole remarkable characteristic was the durability of a strong hand-sewn seam. She could make a man's dress shirt out of an old coat lining, keep a little life insurance in force even while on relief, and create an edible gravy out of thin air.

No eight-foot-high pioneer earth-mother of impeccable posture peering stoically into the vasties, she was a touch over five foot two at full stretch but seemed shorter, for she always went in a crouch. She moved in a kind of squat like Groucho Marx's, which was the only way she could stay within hailing distance of her husband, who clicked the blocks off as if on the way to his inauguration as Man of the Hour. The boy went at a constant trot with a perpetual side ache, far to the rear. They always arrived at their destination in three sections.

Mrs. Mac's hair, which had been a luxuriant roan when she was a girl, was cropped and hennaed. She had a small, quick face with a jaw like a terrier. Her eyes were blue and could be merry, though most often they watered lifelessly behind rimless spectacles in cruelly inflamed flesh. Beneath hose that seldom quite matched, her ankles were raw with weeping eczema. Her coat, dress, shoes, and stockings were always someone's castoffs. Her chemise began life as a flour sack. And she would pin a paper flower or the skeleton of a rhinestone pin on anything she wore to dress it up a little, to look nice.

Courage and generosity were not virtues to her; they were nagging habits. Magnanimity was maybe a rhubarb pie at dinner. Yet, it was her courage that let them live. Only her lack of grace kept her from being adored.

She swore again her disinclination to do anything to spring her daughter from the can while her husband dressed to go downtown.

When it became clear the boy was not going to get to go along, he wheedled the old man, "Bring me a candy bar."

"He eats too much candy and not enough greens," Mrs. Mac said before the old man could consent.

"Then will you make me a beanie when you come home?" He was willing to compromise. He had been after his granddad to make him a slingshot for days. The big kids, seven and eight, in the alley called the slingshots "beanies," and they would pepper him and the stray cats with small stones when they got bored plinking cans and bottles and lusted for live game.

"Make me a beanie. You said you would."

"We'll see."

"Promise." The boy tugged his pant leg like a bell rope.

"No. Damn it! I said, 'We'll see!' " He shook him loose like a pup.

"We'll see" most often meant "probably not."

Out of every crisis the boy tried to extract something tangible for his own. Penny candy, a nickel, a top, a doll, some commitment had to be extracted.

In the uproar the boy cried, "Promise me!"

# 12

THE Calico Cat sat across the Harry Street Bridge no farther from the old 400 Club and the Dew Drop Inn than a drunk could heave an empty Falstaff bottle. Where else would a high-hipped young widow who some said looked a lot like a young Madge Evans look for work—Woolworth's?

"I'm no nickel and dime dolly. Gimme a fifty, you crumb, for the powder room" was a line from a movie she had seen that year.

She measured herself against the great beauties of the silver screen rather than those like herself who shoplifted their cosmetics from Kress' five and ten. She smoked but never inhaled, screwed but was not certain she had ever really come, worked hard but never made expenses.

She wore French pumps, black hose, and a short skirt that left her garters and a lot of creamy thigh exposed while she checked hats and coats at the Calico Cat. She had been switched from waiting table to checking hats because she bruised so easily. Waitresses had to make up and powder their thighs every night to hide the bruises from the customers' pinches. She had turned such a truly calico color between stocking-top and ruffled white panties that no amount of makeup would conceal it.

She worked strictly for tips. She had to pay for her meals and drinks, the maintenance of her costume, and carfare to and from work via taxi or else count on hooking a ride from the end of the bus line. She could take in ten or fifteen bucks on a busy night, but $20 a week was a big week. It was never enough for her rent and expenses. She was hiding from several department stores and owed the little grocer near her room $11. He had begun dunning her every time she came in, shyly leering the hint she could quickly take care of her debt in the back room.

She knew several girls who were willing to make a little extra on the side, arguing they might have gone with the guy anyway for nothing. She had so far refused to go along on one of their "dates," though she was offered the opportunity almost every night.

A drummer's way with the brushes might tickle her fancy, though. Or a crooner who doubled on Hawaiian guitar might elicit an electric shiver along her spine. Or perhaps it was a good-looking customer who had been places, on his way to Albuquerque. But she stubbornly refused to play the whore.

"I'm my father's daughter," she would say proudly, believing in complete freedom and equality for all while slipping into the back seat of the band bus.

Drummers were always slick guys with thin mustaches who could just as well have been cut-rate photographers, motordrome riders, carny spielers, or leading men in stag movies. The crooners were ever beefy boy-singer types with aging baby faces.

The customers who had been places came in all sizes and under all guises but with a commercial traveler's presumptuous habit of trying to tickle a girl's palm while tipping her a dime. "It's like they expect you to hop on the table and say, 'Let's go,' " Wilma complained. They were always after her to see Denver or Albuquerque, though they were very vague about where they went from there.

There were also all the bartenders, cooks, waiters, bus boys, guys who were ready to cut the crap and offer a slug from their own personal pint out back and borrow a car after work to drive up some lovers' lane where their breaths quickly fogged the isinglass and the only song was the slurpy gurgle of a finger stirring her insides. They would make small plans for the future, a show, a picnic, a party; then one crucial night he would be unable to borrow a car, or would come up broke, or she would have a better offer, and it would be all over. No hard feelings.

Wilma swore that as a group drummers were the best in bed but otherwise as undependable as a dollar watch. They would chisel a girl out of her tips for a backstage crap game and lose her forever to a clarinet player when her tips were gone. Yet they were somehow so forgivable. Crooners invariably fell into a jealous mope and threw such childish tantrums they ultimately had to be definitely and cleanly cut loose. With the trade it was mainly a tough, quick passing game for small stakes in pursuit of rumored gaudy thrills. Only the hired help were consistent as a lot, there after the band had gone and the customers had gone West, though individually they were as itinerant as gypsies.

*"And I got the scars to prove it!"* was the waitresses' universal cry.

So Wilma showed her pretty legs, curtsied to wives while flirting slyly with their husbands for a nice tip, came on brass to brass, lived on her tips as best she could, charged what she could not afford, moved often to avoid creditors, used phony names, slept with whom she pleased, and swore she would never become an alcoholic or a whore.

Then the club hired a slick new hostess named Rae to take the place of the blonde who had demanded that the Greek who owned the place give her a raise. She felt her personal relationship with the Greek gave her the right. There was some screaming the day she left. The Greek threatened to call the police and have her removed from the premises.

The hostess' post was near the door by the check room, so Rae and Wilma became friends. Rae was good. She greeted everyone who came in the door as if she had known them for years, steered them to the check room, led them to the table, lit their candle, and awarded them a menu. The atmosphere was pseudo-French *boîte,* but the *carte du jour* was purely Greco-ptomaine.

Rae wore a clinging long-sleeved black satin dress that depended from a starched white Puritan collar and was open in the back all the way to her dimpled coccyx, with obviously nothing worn beneath except sheer black hose. Rae was a few years older, more womanly, seemingly wiser, and curiously more revealing in her costume than were the French-ified young Scotch-Irishers flipping around with their bare thighs and red garters flashing. When a man followed Rae to a seat, he accepted the *carte* as if mesmerized and ordered something from it as if answering a summons.

"That girl, she makes em want to eat something!" the Greek observed gleefully. "That old Patty, all she make em want to do is chew her big titties. I know my business, hunh?"

Wilma and Rae became so inseparable the other girls stopped asking Wilma to go out with them, and she fast found her life completely arranged to suit the older woman's tempo and tastes.

Rae's husband was a hustler who had found it prudent to hustle the hell out of Kansas City, leaving most of their wardrobe behind, before all the women who had bought coupons for a two-bit permanent wave at a new, nonexistent Ritz Beauty Salon found him and put a permanent wave in him. They were on their way to Denver where Fred knew a guy who had a deal he was willing to share with a friend who could supply a little capital.

"A little gold mine in the West!" Fred enthused.

Though he was none too clear about particulars, Rae had to accept his enthusiasm as proof the deal was genuine, if no more than 10 percent as attractive as he would have her believe. There were a duck pin alley and miniature golf in it for the seasons. But the real deal was subsidiary and naturally very mysterious. Otherwise Fred would not have been interested.

"You don't catch me riding no bicycle and carryin my lunch," he bragged.

Anyway, he and Rae and Wilma played a lot of miniature golf for awhile. One brilliant Indian Summer afternoon they all went to the Mac-Deramids' in Fred's freewheeling Chevy coupe to take Wilma's son, Jacky, golfing with them. Fred tickled the boy in the ribs like an uncle, chucked his chin, and offered to fist-fight him before the boy had caught the man's name. Then he left the boy alone altogether when he wouldn't put up his dukes. He was all bravery. If the boy had been a hundred pounds heavier, he would have busted the clown's hawkish horn for him. He looked like a door-to-door hustler to the boy. A real picture-on-a-pony-man if there ever was one. Nor was his cause with the boy helped over the afternoon by the fact he never offered to buy him a thing.

"Gimme a nickel, please, man," the boy suggested straight away.

"Put up your dukes!" he countered, willing to fight him for it.

Rae, on the other hand, smothered Jacky between her nice soft boobs, gushing over his beauty, manliness, and intellect. She swore she would love to have a little boy just like him. In fact one of the first things she wanted when she and Fred were finally settled was a little girl, but if a lad like Jacky came along, she would not be disappointed. When his mother told her she had really wanted a girl, too, he was willing to make it known Rae could keep him. He stayed as close to her as possible all that day in hope she would get the idea. She just swept him off his heels the way he stood, straight to herself where she was soft and warm and bouncy. Her voice bubbled warmly inside her and was soft in her mouth and never turned phony just because he was a kid. That was probably the central difference. Nor was she careful about her dress and things because he might muss her. Instantly, it was just her and him heart to heart, so to speak, so she only smiled warmly when Fred began teasing her about her "new boyfriend." Sitting on his mom's lap in the coupe with both his bare knees digging Rae's thigh was the happiest moment the boy had had since moving to town. She let him play with her hand. Her palms were soft and damp, the fingers long and plump; her nails were long and glassy, enameled fire-engine red. Spit for old Nickel-keeping Fred. Jack needed neither ice cream nor candy.

Coming back that evening, Rae held the boy on her lap. Before he got out of the car, she kissed him on the mouth. He had never dreamed a kiss could be so large and soft. He clung to her neck, refusing to be parted. His mother had to tug him loose and give him over to his grandmother's gentle hammerlock. She scolded him for spoiling such a nice day by acting up at the end. He didn't give a damn. His grandmother told them, "Go on, I'll take care of him."

"Rae has that effect on all the boys," Fred said, not amused.

Rae asked her not to hurt the boy, laughing to show her she was not upset. She said he was just worn out from such a busy day. He could tell she was so sorry when he had to turn her loose. She threw him a kiss and waved out of the back window. Then he wanted to know why he could not live with his mom. "I don't like you and Grandpa no more," he insisted.

Fred and Rae had a room at the Traveler's Hotel, across from the M. K. & T. depot, where Fred hopefully waited for a card game with a pot big enough to take them to Denver. He also had a job printer run him off several hundred coupons good for permanent waves at a new Ritz Beauty Salon about to open in downtown Wichita.

He was willing to pass the time with any itinerant in a friendly game of poker, blackjack, gin, hearts, pinochle, or rummy, confident that his cards would always be more friendly to him than to the mark. If the game got serious and the guy suggested cracking a fresh deck, he had an arrangement with a bellhop or the desk clerk. If the mark insisted on using *his* cards, the game simply never got serious. Fred was no gambler, and the last thing he wanted to do was meet one.

Rae always kept every hustle very friendly, popping in and out, hanging around in a way that hinted at a good time without actually offering or promising a thing. So the hustle was always incidental to the good time and the inexplicit promise. Her presence in a hotel room where a bed and illegal booze were in plain sight was enough to make her most casual gesture deliciously illicit. The mark was never sure what kind of good time they were all headed for, but with Rae around he became increasingly confident it would be exceptional until it was over and his jaws ached from all the laughing and leering and he felt bloated like a man who had gulped air. Or discovered the whore he had wound up with was, in comparison to Rae, so commonly flat his use of her left him feeling defeated, worthless, and at fault. Or just got drunk. Whatever his morning-after feeling, he was certain to be lighter in the wallet than he had contemplated the evening before.

Yet, if the mark was still game worth bagging, Rae might chance to bump into him in the hall the next day or come rapping on his door in a state of pique and disappointment with her husband, seeking solace from the only kind face she knew in town. If the world only knew the *true* foul nature of her man! Not rushing into anything, you understand, merely allowing herself to be drawn in and comforted, a ripe, loving woman in need of understanding and sympathy, scorned by Fred in a drunken moment for some fictional floozy and beaten for protesting her rights. She could then be persuaded to take a drink to calm her nerves. Two made her so vindictive toward Fred and aching for revenge the mark could scarcely believe his good fortune. But just before he was about to have his good time at last, Fred would be at the door ready to raise a hundred-dollar holler in the hall. Inside he would have blood in his eye and a switchblade knife with a six-inch blade in his fist. He would cut them both open was his pledge.

"Give him some money!" Rae would shriek, cowering against the wall.

Fred never let the mark see his outrage was simply an act, even when he had the clown's last dollar in cash safely in his pouch and was hauling Rae by one arm out the door. It was this maintenance of illusion that made the dodge work, leaving the mark with a dignified public face although he knew in his heart he had been played for a chump. Fred instinctively understood that people do not want to be heroes. They'll take almost any properly staged debasement for the sake of avoiding trouble. He had never analyzed it. Yet he knew if he laughed in the mark's face, the guy would risk his reputation, his happy home, or even his life for the sake of a few bucks.

If the badger game seemed inappropriate, Rae might simply appeal to a well-feathered goose for help in fleeing that cruel, crazy Fred, permitting him to assume she was his as soon as she could get her possessions out of hock or paid some critical debt binding her to her husband. She had a knack of knowing what the traffic would bear.

If the guy was outstandingly well heeled, she might actually let him lay her (though she often avoided that extreme by showing up astraddle a sanitary napkin) with the assurance he would take her with him right then with only the clothes she had on her back or Fred would kill them both. Then while the mark slept the sleep of the drugged down the line, she would slip out with his wallet and all his negotiable goods and be whisked away in Fred's freewheeling coupe. They worked the game well. But it was not something they could do every week like piecework in some factory. Fred and Rae were wanted for some charge or other in fourteen states. Small forgeries were their most consistent method of getting walking-around money. An independent grocer, a deli, a hat store, a dress shop, a beauty parlor—papered from one end of the country to the other and none of it written for over $100. Towns in which they had been before were towns they approached cautiously again.

Rae told Wilma, "I don't want to be rich. I just want to live nice. No one in our family ever did. My kid sister married a fuckin farmer and looks old enough today to be my mother. Screw that!" All she truly wanted was Fred, a home where she could hang curtains and nurse a kid. At least, that is all she ever said she wanted.

They needed about $300 for Denver. Together they scanned the horizon for a convention of fools. And came up with Wilma.

Fred teased Wilma a lot, copping a feel, teasing her for a kiss in front of his wife, throwing back the covers when she came into their room before they were up to show her a standing hard-on and invite her to join them in bed. But alone with her he was about as much fun as a hat rack, scarcely looking up from his *Startling Detective Stories* when she sat on the bed and stripped her stockings and stretched out for a little nap while waiting for Rae. Business, not sex, was Fred's vice, though he was superbly equipped for the latter and not at all for the former.

"Stop waving that thing at her," Rae had laughed. "You'll turn her into a punkin or something."

Fred was hung. Of that Rae was proudly certain. The knowledge that she was equal to it was her single measurable advantage in a world where success was most often a matter of amount: a vanity more secure than mere beauty, like a certified high IQ or the ineffable joy in the ability to whistle up a taxi by putting thumb and little finger in your mouth and emitting a single knifing blast.

Wilma always remembered, "He had the longest one I ever saw."

And whatever was good enough for Rae was aces with her. Not that she had any designs on Fred or even found him personally appealing. It was simply a question of reach, a nagging wonder.

Fred called the nightclub and told Rae he had run into an old pal who was passing through town. He suggested she get Wilma and meet them for some barbecue after work. So certain had Fred been of Rae's ability to persuade the young woman to do anything, he borrowed five bucks from the guy he had just met that morning in the hotel lobby, putting up Wilma's ass for security. . . . Until he could cash a check.

Waiting until time to go get the girls, Fred played Dave a little gin in the room, using the five Dave had loaned him for fodder. He also sent the black bellboy out for a pint. When it arrived, Fred was down the hall in the can, so Dave shelled out again. He was a trifle suspicious but could not figure out how Fred could have known so precisely when the boy would get back unless he were psychic. Dave was a traveling salve salesman and naturally suspicious, a man who prided himself on being able to spot a phony.

"That better be some fine pussy," he warned the cards on the bed before him.

Fred was surprised the whiskey had arrived so soon. He gave Dave a couple of dollars that Dave had owned before.

Around midnight they went out to the club to sit around until the girls got off at two. Initially, Dave decided he was to be with Rae. It was she more than the other who fussed over him. On the way out it was Rae who clamped both arms around his left bicep, leaving his right free to go for his purse, and led him through the cold early-morning damp across the parking lot to a Packard touring car where a merchant mufflered and mittened for the long night's stand sold them a quart of Old Crow. With Rae shivering against him, not wearing underwear, her breath warm and visible before him, Dave was happy to pay. But then it was the other girl who sat on his lap once they were all in Fred's coupe, and he had to disassemble and reconstruct his entire thinking. It was no small task for Dave. He did not like being confused and fucked around. "I'm a low-pressure spieler and a four-square dealer" was *his* brag.

They went to Niggertown for barbecue at a dingy plain board backroom speakeasy known only as Chub's and not advertised at all. It was simply a rickety after-hours addition tacked onto the rear of an ordinary old nigger whorehouse on an unpaved deadfall called Moseley. Chub himself blocked the doorway with an imperious air like a great cannibal chieftain who dined on nothing but French *maître de*'s. When he moved into the room proper, he made it seem oppressively crowded. It was as if he compressed the greasy, sweet-spiced air, heavy with perfumes, sweat, and sweet peach pomade, with his bulk.

Jammed in one corner was a scarred upright piano, a taped-up bass, and a set of drums. Whenever a big band played town, some of the musicians could always be found after hours jamming at Chub's. There was a single huge round oak table on a claw-foot barrel pedestal in the center of the room, around which maybe a dozen people could crowd cheek to cheek on a squad of irregular chairs. That table had it all, had suffered every form of debasement that could be scratched, burned, or gouged into its surface, including poetry. There was also a smaller oilcloth-covered table up front for musicians, honored guests, and Niggertown officialdom. Along the walls were a couple of broken-down couches where you could wait for a shot at the table.

The ribs were served on a single huge railway platter set in the center of the table, from which you ate your fill with your fingers. There were no paper napkins, but periodically the little black potboy scampered around the room, and knowledgeable diners took the occasion to wipe their fingers on his woolly head. There were whiskey and beer available by the bottle and scalding chicory coffee by the cup. The bill was whatever Chub said it was.

"A hundred dollars," he'd tell someone who did not know the system in such a humorless way the always smaller man lived a moment of stark terror. When the tourist got the joke and laughed gratefully, he laughed alone. "Jes gimme some money, man," Chub said. If what he was given was not enough, he would say, "Gimme some more." When he had been given enough, he would say, "That's enough." He never thanked anyone, and he never gave a sign of being overpaid.

Every night after hours at least half a dozen cars and often a limousine or two were parked at careless angles under the old monster elms in the side yard.

Fred's party stood in the shivering damp on a plank thrown over the frosty mud outside Chub's door. It was a moment when they stood humbly before judgment. For as often as Chub would lift his hand and thumb them inside, he would silently shake his head no and shut the door, leaving them blinking in the sudden dark and every other place in town closed. There was no appeal. No bribery; Chub's standards for admission were as whimsically imperious as Nero's. Wilma said she once dreamed she saw God and he turned out on close inspection to be Chub.

Chub was six foot six, weighed over 300 pounds, was ugly, mean, antiwhite without being problack, and explained himself: "I don't respect nothin nor nobody. We's all shit for the catfish by and by." He didn't even like music. Yet, more than one local white society matron was willing to chew her way through a mountain of hog fat to find out what he was *really* like. If the initiation was best forgotten, the experience was at least as exclusive as membership in a secret society. None of them knew why they did it, least of all Chub.

"Bareass, all you white womans look just like scalded pork," Chub would tell some daughter of oil or wheat shrugging out of her old satin chemise. "That's why they call me the big pig-sticker round here." And then refuse to recognize a coffee merchant's fucked-up wife whom he had topped the night before on a whore's bed upstairs while all the little whores peeked in and giggled.

"Who you say you is?" He would squint vaguely at the shivering woman until she was forced to whisper recollection of the past night's shame. So he would peer closer. "Umm, you must be mistaken, lady. I don remember doin you. Musta been some other cat."

Yet there was no sign he took pleasure in the perverse game. It was a total point of view.

Wilma said, "I dreamed the gates of heaven was his after-hours doorway. He stood there with the light behind him, the smoke and steam swirling around him. I couldn't see his eyes. But he shook his head NO. And after that there was just no other place to go."

Her date was an unregenerate ten-cent tipper and a born palm-tickler. His favorite dirty jokes teemed with a fucking menagerie bordered by super-dung. Elephants he found particularly hilarious. He sold patent salves and tonics out of Cincinnati going West. Waving a dripping barbecue rib grandly, he told his store of dirty jokes like a man fulfilling some lodge brother's expectation, all the while kneading Wilma's leg above the knee with his free paw in quite the same dispassionate way calculating behind eyes that caught and held anything for only an instant how he would get Fred to start paying his fair share for their good time.

He did not mind paying his own share as long as he got what he wanted, but it was intolerable that he be stuck for anyone else's. His mind never slept. He always had an eye out. You had to get up early to beat Dave Hill. But there was never a morning on the road he did not awake in a hurry, afraid *that* morning was the one when he would be too late.

He pinched Wilma's tits and called them oranges. He appraised Rae's and proclaimed, "Grapefruits!" unable to bring his peripatetic lust to bear on the object he was plainly to have, wanting most that which was clearly Fred's. A man who had peddled worthless nostrums for two decades, he was bound to feel cheated at a free lunch. For who could really be sure what anything was worth anymore? There was always a chance it was being had somewhere else cheaper. Dave's central anxiety resided in the certainty that it was. There was ever that nagging doubt. He was even cheated in his dreams when there was no one but himself to cheat him.

They ate all the ribs they could hold, washed down with boilermakers, while a pockmarked ancient Negro played the upright piano decorated with a black boxwood "Feed the Kitty." When no one did, Chub took the box and levied the diners directly. When half a dozen musicians from the country club dance arrived, he tapped Fred's party and another couple to leave to make way for the newcomers.

In the coupe Dave tried to fight his pudgy fingers into Wilma's step-ins.

"Don't!" she hissed, clasping his wrist in both hands and locking her elbows to keep his crawling fingers just beyond their goal.

"Come on, girlie, you aren't being friendly," Dave argued. "Give us a kiss."

"Only if you'll keep your hands where they belong," she bargained. Her right breast was becoming sore from his constant, perfunctory rough caress. Her arms began to ache clear across her shoulders from wrestling his hand.

"OK," he agreed. His hand under her skirt clamped between her warm thighs relaxed for all the world to believe it was merely idly affectionate and harmless as a puppy.

She sighed, closed her eyes, and turned her face passively a quarter of the way toward him. He mugged her fully around with his chin and covered her mouth with his cigar-tasting lips. Coincidentally with trying to introduce his tongue into her mouth, he made a stab for her twat, getting two fingers under her panties and into the fur before she stiffened. His fingers roughly probed to get her started. She wrenched away from his thick tongue, sputtering that she didn't French!

"It's icky!" she told him, making an ugly face and quickly crossing her legs to trap his hand with his fingertips barely inside her slit.

He could not advance, nor could she force him to retreat. The cold air coming up her skirt from the floorboards made goose bumps on her legs. They strained against each other in the corner of the seat, she with her head wedged back and away against the cold glass to avoid his lips.

"You lied!" she accused him. "You promised you would be still if I gave you a kiss."

"I don't call what you gave me no kiss," he sneered.

"Then maybe you'll call this a slap in the face!"

She swung wildly, catching him a glancing blow on the off ear.

"Little bitch!" he hissed. "Prickteaser!"

Every bit of strength had been in her swing. When she had recovered, his hand owned her box. She shed a couple of tears in frustration at her helplessness. What was the use? What difference did it make?

Fred and Rae, who had silently ignored the war being waged beside them in the cramped front seat of the coupe, now produced the bottle that had nestled between them.

"Come on," Rae said. "Let's all have a drink and be friends." She nudged Wilma with the bottle. "Come on, Bill. Have a shot."

"Yeow. Take a good one, baby," Dave urged her. "Maybe it'll warm up your cold, cold ass." Though he was not willing to relinquish the gains he had made under her skirt to take a belt himself.

Wilma took a big drink and coughed. Dave slipped another finger into her. By the time they reached the hotel, Dave had her lipstick smeared from ear to ear and was bouncing her uterus so violently with his fingers her stomach felt queasy. But she was hot. Hating Dave, mentally divorced from what was going on inside her but wide open and hot and sopping wet, she stared at Fred's profile in the coming and going lights and wanted him. She closed her eyes and thought of other men.

In their room, Rae quickly started the bottle around again, arching herself and yawning meaningfully.

"Your baby's sleepy," she told Fred.

She did not ask anyone to sit down. They stood in the center of the room with their coats on, passing the bottle around like a quartet of winos on a street corner killing a communally sponsored jug before saying good night.

"I wish *you* were my date," Wilma boozily confided to Fred in front of everyone. She ran her right palm flat down his perpetually knotted tie and fingered his monogrammed belt buckle. She giggled. "I bet you could brand a girl with that little eff." She turned confidentially to Dave. "He's got the biggest *thing* you ever saw." She nodded assuredly and winked, which didn't make Dave feel any better.

"And it's all mine, honey," Rae added, moving to put both her arms around the trustee of her property.

"What's with her?" Dave wanted to know. He resented what he had assumed to be a closed deal tending to become renegotiable at the point of delivery. He'd invested a lot in this party.

"She just wants to be coaxed," Rae said. "She'll be all right. Won't you, sweetheart?"

"I don't think so," Wilma replied slowly, eyeing Dave carefully again.

"Oh, sure you will." Rae was enthusiastic.

"Well, hell, if she don't want to. . . ." Dave would have *some* sort of reckoning, however.

"She *wants* to!" Rae quickly gathered Wilma under her wing. "Come on, honey, we'll just take a little walk."

No one was about to take her home, that was plain enough. It was cold outside. She was tired.

She let herself be led unsteadily to the door. Rae jerked her head at Dave for him to come on, but Wilma wasn't being fooled. She knew what was happening. She was not as drunk as they supposed. She wondered how much Fred had gotten off Dave. She smiled to herself, saving the knowledge that at least she wasn't being conned. As if knowledge were a victory.

Dave took the opportunity to feel Rae's ass and confess he would even pay good money for a little.

"I won't say I wouldn't sell it," she said. "But you just don't look to me like a guy who could make that kind of investment."

"Oh, I'm always willing to pay for what I get, but I always intend to get what I pay for." He recited it as if the commandment swung on a little sign just behind his eyes.

"Are you willing to pay a hundred dollars?" she said as if teasing. Yet she wasn't teasing.

"A HUNDRED BUCKS!" He acted as though he would have to pay it out in installments. "What's it made of, *gold?*"

"Better. Sugar and spice and everything nice."

"You ought to see her puppy dog tail," Wilma put in.

"I wouldn't pay a hundred bucks to lay Mrs. Astor on the high seas!" Dave let them know where he stood.

"No? Mrs. Astor and the whole ocean don't have the snap and roll of this." She pasted a kiss on her ass with a slap and showed Dave a slow around the world that ended with a snap that would have yanked his joint out by the root had it been engaged.

"Twenty-five," Dave bid out of a throat gone suddenly dry.

"You're out of your mind. I got a husband who'll make it more worth my time than that. What do you think I am?"

He licked his lips.

"He's fat," Wilma observed, kneading the roll of suet over his belt.

"Naw, he's sweet. Just a little tight."

"Then you sleep with him. *I'll* go explain to Fred."

"Hold it!" Rae arrested her in midflight by one arm.

She fell back against the wall, giggling giddily. "But he *wants* you," she said.

"What do you mean, 'tight'?" Dave asked. "Listen, sister, don't think I was being fooled all night. I knew what your husband was doin. I been outfumbled by guys like him before. You can tell him I figure he owes me about fifteen bucks on the night. I wasn't goin to bring it up, you know, depending on how things went. But I don't like being called cheap nor played for a chump."

"No one was playing you for anything. Hell, buster, you don't think I'd actually go to bed with you for money, do you?"

He took out his old brown wallet, fumbled up a secret flap, and flicked out a new hundred-dollar bill as if it leapt like flame on his fingertips. He waved it under the woman's nose.

She followed it as if it were scented.

"Give us a little sample to prove you're worth it," he said slyly, slipping his other arm around her waist. He wafted the bill before her eyes hypnotically, moving in behind it to kiss her. The arm around her waist slid down over her hips, and his hand cupped the right cheek of her ass, his fingers parting the globes, shoving her clothes in the crack. She twisted loose and pivoted away from him.

"You should have put your money where your taste is earlier," she said breathlessly.

He put the bill carefully back into his wallet and buttoned it away in his trousers. "It's here if you want it."

"You aren't foolin, are you?"

"Only one way to find out."

"I couldn't get away from Fred. I'd have to get him drunk."

"Well, like I said, I'm always willing to pay for what I get." He took Wilma's arm. "I guess it's just you and me, girlie." He looked Rae up and down again. "If you get a chance to come join us, you know where we're at."

"Maybe I'll just do that. If I can."

In the room, Dave indicated the bed and told Wilma, "Hop in." It was cold. There was no heat after ten o'clock. She quickly slipped out of her clothes and hopped between the cold sheets, protesting, "I don't like this. I want you to know."

He slipped in beside her, rubbed the warm nose of his prick against her leg, and told her, "I ain't such a hard guy to like once you get to know me."

She pretended to be suddenly quite drunk. When he began finger-fucking her again, she would have had him believe she was too drunk to care. When he got between her legs, she muttered her dead husband's name to justify the ease with which she was entered.

"Odd?" she asked. "Oddie . . ." she sighed as old Dave shoved it home.

Yet she turned her mouth away from his kisses even while her body was responding to his heavy thrusts. He was hairy as hell, she realized. Hair all over. He was heavy and wide. But he had a big one and knew how to use it. Nothing fancy, he simply stuck with it, refusing to be rushed until she began moving her rear around in spite of herself. She hated herself, yet honestly wanted it more than any she had ever had.

"Thought you'd have a cuppa coffee, didn't ya?" he wheezed, pumping away, swelling larger inside her. "Figured me for a goddamn chump, didn't ya? I ain't no small-town hick, you know, girlie." He poured it to her. "I came to fuck, kiddo. No bitch cold-fishes on Dave Hill!"

"I'll say!" she puffed.

"I make em come. I made tough whores come. Tell me! You're about to come, ain't ya? *Tell me!*"

"*Yes!*" She grabbed his charging hairy butt with both hands and truly made it with a man for the first time in her life.

But when it was over, she hated herself. She hadn't even *liked* him. She was afraid she would get pregnant. He hadn't used anything to protect her. She reeled over to the wash basin and tried to swab herself out with a soapy washrag twisted tightly around and around. There was no bath in the room. She cried a little, more angry at herself than anything.

She just always let herself go along with somebody else's ideas when she knew she would hate herself after. She vowed to be stronger in the future, promising fate that if she was spared pregnancy on this occasion, she would never be so careless again.

"What's the matter?" Dave asked. "I hurt you?" There was a hopeful note in his inquiry.

"No."

"Then what's wrong?"

"I'm a whore. I didn't want it."

"Don't tell *me* you didn't like it."

"I *didn't!*"

"The hell!"

"But I *didn't* want it!"

"Forget it. You ain't no more a whore than any other woman in the world. What's your average wife anyway but a whore too lazy to hustle? Honey, the whole world's a whorehouse. Be glad you got that sweet face, them long good-lookin legs, and as pretty a pussy as I ever seen. You don't know much about it yet, but once you learn, you're really going to be something. Men like a woman with a pretty one. They like a perfect triangle of hair. Some of the things I've seen been so grizzly you feel like you ought to turn them with a stick." He studied her shivering in the darkness across the room, deciding how he would advance her education next. "I bet that Rae's got a great bush on her, ain't she? Hunh?"

"I don't know."

"You mean you ain't seen her?"

"I didn't look."

"I *know* she does. I can tell. But give you another five years and you'll put her in the shade." To reward her for her prospects he held open the covers, offering the warmth of his bed.

While she snuffled in the cold, he tried to initiate games.

"I don't go for that stuff," she protested, fighting to keep her head above the covers.

He was very strong. They wrestled silently for a few minutes. The only sound was the rickety bed complaining metallically and the huff-huff of their breaths in the cold air. He was willing to settle for her anus.

"DON'T!" she screamed. She bounced indignantly out of bed. "I said *no!*"

"Go on then and get your dumb ass out of here. And don't forget, I got about fifteen bucks coming to me."

"Not from me, mister! I don't know what they told you or promised you, but I haven't seen any of your dirty money. As far as I am concerned, what I owe you I'm still too much of a lady to do!"

He called her a "goddamn prickteasing snot!"

"Get out!" he commanded. "And tell your goddamn friends I got some money comin down here I intend to get or take out of somebody's ass."

"Tell them yourself."

"What happened?" Rae asked groggily. She stood in the door of her and Fred's room clutching her robe around her. "He pass out or something?"

"Hell, no. He wanted me to do a lot of dirty stuff. I told him I wasn't made that way, and he blew up."

"Oh, hell. Well, come in." Fred was asleep on his back, snoring like a man strangling to death. "Is he really pissed off?" Rae whispered.

"He ain't happy. He wants his fifteen bucks."

"What the hell? Didn't you give him some?"

"He screwed hell out of me." Wilma was suddenly near tears. "What did you get for me? I'd like to know what it's worth on the going market."

"Get off it. What the hell do you think? Sit down and have a drink. No one sold your precious ass. We were all out for a good time. You got your share. You weren't crying earlier."

"But I thought it was going to be fun!"

"Fun, grow up, for godsake. *Fun?*" She laughed. "What do you think fun is, some kind of girlish poem all pink, sunshine, and butterflies? Shit. Grow up, Bill. Fun is knowing you're alive and not that you just ain't dead. Fun is getting your ashes hauled, and laughing, and cryin, and fightin, and lovin. Fun can be being mean and hatin if that's how the world turns that day. But just feeling smug because you ain't dead yet like most folks do ain't *fun.*"

"But I just feel sick of myself. I feel like I've rolled in dirt."

"Aw, horseshit, honey. Who are you trying to kid? You weren't *that* drunk. You knew what was coming off. No one twisted your arm. What do you want from me?"

"I don't *know.* Nothing."

"Then wise up."

"I will," she decided firmly.

She accepted the drink Rae offered her and sat down in the only easy chair in the room and crossed her legs flippantly. Suddenly she remembered what it had been like to come. The recollection was a shock. She shuddered. A warm feeling flooded over her, making her feel almost cozy in the big chair. She couldn't wait to make it with someone she really liked. She felt empty and strong, clean, whorey, defiant, untouchable and undefeated.

"Here's how." She lifted the water tumbler and knocked back the fiery whiskey.

"That's the spirit!" Rae cheered. "Don't worry, kid. We'll take care of you." She went over and shook Fred awake.

"Shh . . ." she calmed him. "Listen. . . ." She leaned near his ear and whispered for some time.

"You're sure?" Fred demanded, full voice.

"I'm *sure!*" They fell to whispering again.

"Well, look," Fred said finally. "Why don't we just go tell him tryin to pull that on her has got her hysterical and that she's got to go to the hospital or something? Or like she's from this big local family, and they'll get the law after him?"

"Dumb. What's a society girl doing checking hats at a place like the Calico Cat?"

"Yeow. I ain't awake."

"Then wake up. He won't go for a lot of crap. He's been around. He's tighter than a tick. He isn't about to hand over dough on say-so. Remember Milwaukee?"

"Yeow."

"Well, this guy reminds me of him."

"Then let's just forget it. I don't want you takin no chances like that."

"OK. It's a shame, though, to let him get away with them hundred-dollar bills."

"How much do you think he has on him?"

She shrugged. "But a man with only one hundred dollars don't pack it around in a single C-note."

"That's right. Maybe, though, if you was able to use the dope. . . ."

"Want me to try?"

"Well, if you want to. I mean, it sounds like he might have just what we're looking for. We might be sittin pretty right on old Pike's Peak day after tomorrow."

"OK. Where'd you put the drops?"

"In one of my other shoes under the bureau."

She dropped down on her hands and knees and reached beneath the dresser. When she got up, she put something in her kimono pocket. She went to the basin and began touching up her hair and makeup.

"You be damn careful with that stuff," Fred cautioned, sitting in his underwear on the edge of the bed, vague and waxy, half awake.

"I will." She turned, snapping on a pair of step-ins under her robe.

"You and Miss Muffet get us packed while I'm gone. Don't fool around. When I get back, you better be ready to go."

"I will," Fred promised. "Now, you be careful."

"Yeah." She slipped out into the hall.

Between green enameled walls that were dull with a railroad patina, the hall runner was worn through the center like the track made by some kind of domestic herd following the same path morning and evening. Only along the walls was a grimy vestige of the purple and brown carpet discernible. Trodding the worn way, she viewed herself as bovine. The hall was no more distinguishable from halls she had gone down in Milwaukee, Peoria, Indianapolis, Springfield, Kansas City, Joplin, than one string of boxcars is from another. At the end of the dim passage near the fire escape under a bare red bulb a fire barrel filled with stagnant water, buckets hung around its brim, stood like the profane altar of some back-alley voodoo or store-front spiritualist sect. The barrel was a constant, impersonal, and blanket indictment of the rootless, like a midnight altar in any desolate parish where one's choices most often fall nearer the poles of complete abnegation of spirit or turning torch than any middle ground.

Turning her head from side to side, she clipped along, reading the numbers painted crudely on the doors behind which she heard the muffled snores of tired transient men.

"A goddamn number ought to have more meaning than that!" she thought. "A waste of mathematics. Counting crumby old men farting in their sleep. This way of living stinks."

Against satin, her haunches swung heavily beneath her robe. Her mules clapped her naked heels. The blue medicine bottle in her pocket gently nudged her thigh. She went quickly, as if the walls had eyes. As if the walls could care. Or remember.

Dave in a faded flannel robe and scuffed brown Romeo slippers slipped the latch on his door, rubbing his thin rug as if he had been awakened.

"I just dropped off. What can I do for you?" he asked to show her how cool he was.

"Fred's out like a light," she informed him, slipping into the room and shutting the door behind her. In the dark she snaked her left arm around his neck and pressed her body slowly against him to give him the full benefit of its several delicious parts. "Still want me?" she whispered, her lips brushing his.

For reply he tightened his arms around her and kissed her roughly. His hands roamed her body, squeezing and kneading her. He growled low in his throat like a dog. He stripped her robe off her left shoulder and covered her breast with his hand. He ground his flaccid parts against her lower belly. When she felt him start to stiffen, she pivoted away.

"Whew! Hey, let's have a little drink first. You're going too fast for me."

"Me, I don't need no more drinks. Besides, your husband kept the damn bottle," he sulked.

"I'll run and get it," she offered sprightly. "He shouldn't have kept the bottle. I guess he just assumed you'd have one."

"Forget it." He caught her wrist with his left hand and untied her kimono with his right, flipping back the flies as if he was unwrapping a bundle. "Yeow! Now that's what a woman ought to look like. Baby, I'm going to turn you every way but loose!"

She wanted to cover herself. He made her feel too naked and ugly. He licked his lips and pulled her panties down to her knees.

"That's eatin stuff," he proclaimed and went down on his knees, burying his face in her silky dark bush. She put her palms on either side of his face and stared down at his bald spot. A moment of tenderness swept over her. She worked it aside and tried to raise him.

He came up snapping at her tits, fumbling his dick out and shoving it into the damp where his mouth had been.

"I wish you had stayed from the beginning," he said crossly, regretting the energy he had wasted on Wilma. He wanted that edge on his desire back. "Let me look at you." He stripped off her robe and threw it on top of his clothes on the chair. She kicked out of her step-ins and stood for his inspection. "Turn around." She turned. She posed diffidently, cornily.

"Hey, hurry up. I'm getting icicles on it out here."

He pulled her to him again and covered her mouth with his. "Ummmmah!" He broke off the kiss. "Girlie, you may think you've had a hundred-dollar fuckin before, but you ain't seen nothin!" He pulled her left hand down and handed her his prick as if slipping her something he believed she had come truly seeking.

Almost an hour later she staggered from the bed, hooking her kimono from the chair and shrugging into it on the fly to the washbasin. She felt sticky with come from her chin to her knees. She stood on one leg astride the basin and turned on the taps. She urinated, holding her piss inside with her fingers for a douche until she was full, then let it spew out in a sizzling charge. She soaped a cloth and washed the stickiness from her breasts, washed her arms, belly, thighs, and bottom. She washed her face with her hands. Her toilet was made with her back to the man in the bed, her pink robe her only privacy.

"Wow! Man! This water is like *ice!* Would you like a glass?"

"Naw. I'll get it. I gotta get up and wash, too."

She simply had to get a Mickey into him somehow.

"Stay there and take it easy. I'll bring the cloth and wash you." She soaped it, all business and goodness. She quickly got the drops from her pocket, speaking over the shoulder on the opposite side to cover the move. "After all that exercise, you gotta be tired. Anyone ever tell you you could hurt yourself or kill some poor girl going at it like that?"

"There's the widow of a preacher in Joplin—nicest, quiet big woman you ever saw. You'd think she'd never seen a pecker. But lordhavemercy, that woman just inhales me. Calls me her Jersey bull."

"I'm sure."

"You doubt me?"

"No! Oh, no! I was just trying to think what you reminded *me* of."

She loaded the water tumbler close to her belly while the tap ran loudly, replaced the dropper—she hadn't been able to measure out any and had just splashed in almost half the bottle—and quickly got it back into her pocket. She filled the glass and picked up the washcloth.

"At your service, sir." She curtsied, handing him the water. She started to wash his parts, lifting his dick with thumb and forefinger by the skin like a girl examining a runover snake. Her face was puckered with distaste.

"What did you decide I reminded you of?" he asked.

"Oh? I don't know. I can't think of anything to which I could compare you. No animal *I* ever saw."

He wasn't certain whether he had been complimented or not. He took a sip of the ice-cold water.

*"Bleah!"* he exclaimed behind her as she bent to wash him. His right hand stopped running idly up and down between her legs.

"What's the matter?" She turned solicitously to him.

"I think you let this run *too* long." He held up the glass, peering through the tumbler against the light overhead.

"Oh, well, Kansas water is hard. You get used to it."

"This is hard enough to chisel." He smelled it. "Like medicine."

"Hold your nose!" She suddenly pounced on him, grabbed the tumbler from him, pinched shut his nose, and began slopping the water down his gullet. It was either swallow or drown where he lay.

She laughed. It was a joke. A big fun. A bit of roughhouse. And got almost all the stuff in him before he wrenched away, sputtering.

"You got some down my windpipe!" he barked, strangling. *"Jesus Christ! Cough-cough-cough!"*

She was laughing then for certain.

*I'd of got some of it in him if I'd of had to squirt it up his ass with the eye-dropper,* she told herself, giggling and thumping the jerk on his porky back.

When he straightened out, he started her fondling his limp machine. It did not respond. Still he insisted she continue.

"Keep on. Keep on," he encouraged.

"But honey, it's dead."

"Don't stop."

She shrugged, sighed, gave it a flip, a sharp pinch, then laying her head resignedly on his furry chest, continued kneading and jacking the flaccid tube. She had laid her head on his chest to escape his breath and prevent him kissing her. But the move was a mistake. He began gently nudging her head lower on his chest. When she stiffened in resistance, he urged harder. She pretended she did not know what he wanted her to do until he had her nose in the wool and she faced his penis eye to Cyclops eye.

She raised her head. "Look. You aren't going to do anything more. Why don't we just take a little snooze, and when you wake up you'll be ready to go again."

"It don't matter *what* I'm going to do or not do. We made a deal."

"But *rigor mortis* wouldn't raise him!"

"Then you just suck him until he wakes," he said as if deciding between the green beans or the corn on a blue plate special.

She hopefully thought she detected a slightly dreamy quality in his voice. She lifted his joint and stared at it head on with distaste for a moment, then sulkily introduced its cold head into her mouth and closed her eyes. He worked his fingers into her sex and played idly there.

After awhile he seemed to doze. She stopped and lay still, listening to him breathe. Just as she started to let the last little bit of his prick slip away from her, he stirred and shoved her back to work, busily beginning to churn her flue with his fingers. He showed signs of becoming aroused. She was fast being stirred by his busy hand and so more diligently tried to give him an erection. But before he became even partially erect, he lost interest, slowed down to an idle, then began snoring. She slid back from the slope up which his hand had been lifting her, angrily harboring the desire to flop over on the sleeping hulk with her cunt over his face like a goddamn oxygen mask and make it on his stupid face while suffocating him simultaneously. For fear of rousing him again, she let his penis slip away from her like a child losing a pacifier in sleep.

She shuddered involuntarily in the cold, fighting to get control of herself lest she wake him. She moved almost imperceptively with the utmost stealth, rising from the bed a single creak at a time. She knelt tensely on the edge of the bed, no longer touching his body, and reached for the floor with one foot. Slowly she transferred her weight from the bed to her foot gram by gram. She stared at his face for any sign of consciousness.

She stood frozen beside the bed until she was certain he did not miss her. She knelt for her robe. Both knees popped. She squatted there. The sound had seemed loud enough to bring the curious. She slipped into her robe, squatting beside the bed. He evidently was out pretty good. She was a bit bolder. She tiptoed to the chair where his trousers were and lifted them. They were wool, itchy, smelled bad. The first light was a chink of gray under the drawn shade. They would have to hurry. She was careful not to rattle the change in his pocket when she freed his wallet from its buttoned-down burrow. She did not take time to rifle it. She clutched the worn fat leather to her shivering breast, picked up her shoes, and slipped cautiously out of the room. Just taking what she had coming was a way to look at it.

In the hall she realized, "Damn! I left my pants."

She scooted on down the hall, cutting a quick glance back when she reached her door. She tapped softly with her fingers. Fred whispered, "Who is it?" It opened enough for her to duck in when she whispered back, "It's me!"

"What happened?" he demanded, his eyes shifting from her own to the wallet she held clutched in the bosom of her robe. "You got it? I was gettin worried. I was going to come down there in a minute if you didn't come on."

"Yeah? You'd of been too late," she said drily.

"What happened?"

She slapped the wallet in his outstretched hand. "You stupid sonofabitch! You kept the bastard's bottle."

He was busy digging through the wallet for the secret compartments where the ticket to their future was hidden. "Yeah?"

"So, you stupid fuck, I couldn't just slip him the Mickey."

"What the hell did you do?" He stopped counting the bills he found in the wallet. There was a shadow of panic behind his eyes.

"I fucked him to death," she spat. Then quickly grabbed him with both hands, framing his face to kiss him long and sloppily all over his mouth. "There! How's it feel to be a cocksucker by proxy?"

He shoved her away, wiping his mouth with the backs of both hands.

"*Awright!* I'm sorry! You're just trying to get my goat. We got to get out of here now. It's almost light."

"I'm not going anywhere until I brush my teeth." She strode to the washbasin, wheeled around aghast. *"You didn't pack my toothbrush!"* He had.

*"Oh, you diddle-dumb piece of shit!* I swear to God, Fred, this is it! This is the last motherfucking time you get me to do it. I *mean* it!"

"Never again! Never again, honey. I promise. This is it."

"Yeah. You promise. Until the next time. How much that fart have in there?"

"One sixty-seven."

*"Only—*? You mean— Can you *imagine* a fourflushing cheapskate like *that* gettin all his dough in a hundred-dollar bill to flash around? *God!"* The incomparable smallness of it was a maddening conundrum to her. "I hope he croaks!"

"Rae!" Wilma said, shocked.

"I *do!"* she insisted. "What the hell were you doin, Miss Frosty Pants, while I was coppin that old fart's joint? Oh, don't pull that hurt-look shit on me, sister. I know you ain't had nothin but big brown eyes for Fred ever since we've known you."

"I don't!" she protested. "Honest, Rae!"

"Bull!"

"Come on, you two. There's no time for that stuff. We've got to get out of here. It's nearly light now."

Rae hadn't let her bitterness keep her from dressing. She was about ready.

Fred said, "OK. You bring the bags down the fire escape, and I'll pull the car around in the alley and meet you. Give me a five-minute start, then come on." He left.

The fire escape was rimmed with frost. A cold wind whistled through the narrow alley and blew up the girls' thin coats. Rae had two large cardboard suitcases tied around with Fred's neckties. Wilma had a cardboard box tied with clothesline and a big laundry bag.

Behind them in the room were a pair of worn-out socks, a single laddered stocking, a broken cardboard belt, a nearly empty cold cream jar, a used-up lipstick, a broken comb, magazines, three days' newspapers, and a torn page of a letter from Rae's mother penciled on lined foolscap torn from a child's writing tablet.

Halfway down the steel stairs Wilma slipped and let the laundry bag go to clutch for the cold iron railing. The bag bumped down and took Rae right off her feet just as Wilma whispered, *"Look out!"*

Too busy to curse, Rae held high her two suitcases, riding the bag down a whole flight to the first-floor landing, each step an ass-breaking bump.

A light snapped on above, and an old switchman off a Katy caboose, a light-sleeping sparrow in long gray underwear, popped his knob out the window and piped toothlessly, "What's going on out there? What's the commotion?"

"Pull in your noodle, pop! It's an elopement," Rae called softly up.

"Heh? You say *fire?*"

"*Eeeee*loping," she stressed. "All the whores in the world are eloping with their Prince Charmings tonight."

"Heh?" He cupped his ear. "I don hear ya."

They began to giggle.

"Can't talk to you now, pop. See, here he comes." Fred's coupe turned into the alley. "If we don't hurry, he'll turn into an old punkin like you."

"Heh?"

"Go beat your meat, old man!"

"Do which?"

"Pull your stupid face in before it freezes that way!"

The retractable part of the escape ground and screamed when they rode it to the bricked alley.

Fred tossed the luggage into the rumble. Both girls were giggling insanely when they fell into the seat.

"Did you see his *face?*" Rae asked. They were set off again.

Fred cut over to Douglass, turned left past the big luxurious Broadview Hotel on the river, crossed the bridge, passed the marker on the old Chisholm Trail, turned left on Lawrence past the ball park, and the car began coughing. It died facing south just short of Waterman, with the river rolling blackly by on the left and the freight tracks not yet awake on the right, and not a filling station open within a five-mile radius.

"Boy! This is all I need," Rae exclaimed.

Fred came back from peering under the upraised hood.

"Well, what is it?"

"I don't know," he admitted thoughtfully. "I don't think it's anything real serious. Maybe it's the gasoline clogged up. Ice in the carburetor. Ain't the electric."

"What are we going to do?"

"We got to get it into a station where they can blow out the gasoline. I'll have to go find a phone and call an all-night wrecker."

"Great."

And off Fred hoofed into the predawn night.

There wasn't a car moving or a person stirring anywhere. Then, when Fred had been gone about fifteen minutes, a squad car passed on Waterman. It stopped on the bridge and backed up. Rae took Wilma's hand.

"Just act natural. Let me do the talking."

The black and white Ford crept slowly toward them. They hit the coupe with their spotlight, raked it over carefully to see why it was stopped on the parkway.

"What's the trouble, ladies?"

"We don't know. It just started coughing and quit. My husband went to call a wrecker."

"Nearest phone'll be at the Broadview. About a mile walk."

"He should be back any minute."

The cop on the other side of the driver got out and came toward them with his gloved hand resting on his pistol butt. His breath was visible in the air. He flashed the beam of his big six-cell flashlight in the window and around the passenger compartment. He went forward and shined it on the engine. He reached in and fiddled with something. "Try it."

Rae slid over under the wheel, switched on the ignition, and pressed down hard on the starter with her foot. The engine ground and ground without firing.

"OK. Hold it!" He came back shaking his head. "Sounds like it's either flooded or your gas line's plugged up."

"That's what Fred said. He always buys that cheap gas. It's happened before. I tell him. But he says if it will go on bust-head, he isn't buying it bottled-in-bond. I think once he tried to run it on kerosene."

The cop smiled. "I've used 'white gas' myself. You folks'er from Illinois, huh?" He nodded in the direction of the license tag.

"Oh . . . yeah. We're just on our way to Denver. My sister's getting married there next week."

"Congratulations." He leaned down for a better look. Wilma smiled, trying to look like a bride. "Lucky fella," he said. "But if you're goin to Denver, you ought to have stayed on Fifty-four. Back there." He shined his light in the direction which they had come.

"That Fred! I had a feeling he'd turned wrong."

"I hope we didn't scare you when we came up. Everybody's being careful. Got word the Barrow gang is in the state. Last seen in Blackwell, headed this way. So if you see any car lookin suspicious, you stop and tell the police in the next town. Don't stop to see if it's them, though. They'd as soon shoot you as look at you."

"Don't worry," Rae promised.

"I think here comes your husband."

"You be sure and warn him about those people. He's the kind who'll stop and help *anybody* beside the road. He's so darn good-hearted."

"I will. Hope you don't have any more trouble."

"Thanks."

He walked up and met Fred. They talked earnestly. Fred's head bobbed up and down like it was loose on its hinge. Then the cop got back into the car and waved to the girls. The car backed up and went away again on Waterman.

"What the hell was all that?" Fred asked, getting into the seat and rolling up the window.

"They thought we were Bonnie Parker and Clyde Barrow. When I told them who you *really* were, they weren't interested."

"Who'd you tell them I was?"

"None other than John Dillinger. Keep me warm." She took his arm and draped it around her.

The wrecker towed them into the all-night garage downtown next to the Allis Hotel. It was Sunday. The wrecker driver was the Sunday man. He was not the mechanic. But he promised to try to fix the car.

"I can't promise nothin," he said. "But I'll look at it. The regular man won't be in until Monday."

The hotel next door was one of the best in town, but even there the coffee shop was closed. It opened at five. They stood on the windy corner. The sky was almost fully light.

"Let's check into the hotel," Rae suggested.

"Are you nuts?"

"No, I'm not. But I'm tired. I feel like I've been dragged through a sewer backwards. I haven't even brushed my *teeth!* I don't want to go on until I can freshen up. You're dog tired. And look. That peapicker isn't going to get the car fixed. *I want a bath!*"

"You're nuts!"

"I don't care. I'm not going a step farther until I've taken care of myself, had a bath and a good breakfast."

"She's nuts," he told Wilma. Then asked Rae, "What about her?"

"She's with us, remember? She's my sister. She's getting married in Denver. Or didn't you get an invitation?"

"You know as soon as that guy back there comes to, he's going to start crying cop."

"Let him. They're all out looking for Bonnie and Clyde. They aren't going to put out no dragnet for small fry like us. They want that reward."

"I still don't like it."

"Then lump it. Aw, come on. Just for a few hours, hon. What the hell? Do you think we are less conspicuous standing around on a street corner?"

So the girls stepped into the lobby, where the doorman sized them up disdainfully while Fred went for their suitcase. When he came in, the doorman handed them over to an equally reluctant bellboy. He looked at the suitcase as if it had barked. It was something clearly to be handled with tongs.

"We broke down. . . ." Fred launched into a recitation of the whole yarn, including Wilma's impending marriage, and threw in a couple of new wrinkles of his own invention. While his wife harped, "You don't have to give him your life history. Just tell him to pick up the friggin bag."

The desk clerk was likewise fairly certain they had been misdirected.

"Hard travelin!" Fred offered by way of explanation.

"That will be ten-fifty in advance, please," the clerk informed him.

"Sure." And Fred could not resist flashing the corner of the C-note when he paid, just to let the snide ass know he wasn't some bum. What did a lousy desk clerk get a week, $15?

Their room was next to the elevator shaft, so they heard it every time it passed. When it stopped on their floor, they could hear people talking in it through the wall. It was weird. Fred thought he heard the elevator operator talking about them to the bellhop.

"Snooty bastards!" he groused. "I don't like these fancy damn hotels. They all treat you like you smell bad."

"I'm sure I do," Rae said agreeably. "It's wonderful! My own tub! I'm going to take a bath. Bill, call down see if they'll send up some bubble bath."

"It's five thirty in the morning!" Fred howled.

"I don't care." She turned both taps on full force and came out of the bathroom throwing off her clothes. "I want a bubble bath, and I'm going to have one." Naked except for her shoes, she went to the phone and picked it up.

"You're nuts," he said. "Really nuts."

She stuck out her tongue at him. "Room service? I'll give five bucks to the first person who gets up here with some bubble bath." She gave the room number. "Any kind. Thank you very much." She turned smugly, kissed her fingertips, and smacked the cheek of her bare butt in passing.

"Bubbles. You just don't know how to live, Fred."

When she finished bathing, it was broad daylight. Wilma was curled in the easy chair.

"You asleep?" Rae asked.

She did not answer.

Rae crawled nude and perfumed into bed beside her sleeping husband, laid her smooth leg across his body, and turned him into her as he awakened.

"I want it, honey. Wake up and pour it to me. I love you. . . . I guess I've certainly proved I'd do anything for you, haven't I? . . . Ummm. . . . Honey, you go clear to the bottom of me."

A little later Fred huffed seriously, "This sure is a good bed, ain't it?"

"Sure is," she agreed.

"Hey Bill!" Rae called from the covers where she and Fred lay whispering together. "You can quit playing possum now. Come on and lay down." She laughed. "You weren't asleep. I saw you. Come on. Hop in. Never been three in a bed before?"

Wilma feigned she had been asleep, stretched, yawned. "OK." She got up and stripped to her slip.

When Wilma lay clinging stiffly to the edge of the bed with Fred between them, Rae sighed. "I'll bet there isn't another woman in the world who gets any more satisfied than I do with Fred. He really straightens me out. Makes me feel sorta rich. Know what I mean?"

"Umhmm," Wilma said.

"No, you don't. And you know something else? I'd kill him before I let another woman have him. I mean, I *really* would."

"Hey!" Fred protested. But he was pleased. He took her in his arms, and they kissed for a long time.

"If you're going to do it again, I'm getting out of here!" Wilma blurted.

They laughed.

"Poor baby's little box is burning. Honey, I wish Fred was twins. I really do. That's how much I think of you."

"So do I," Wilma said in a small voice.

"Come on, let's get some sleep," Fred said. It was full daylight outside.

In her dreams Wilma heard a key being pushed into a lock. Then she was wide awake. Fred was sprawled across her, pinning her down with a leg and an arm over her. Her slip was raked up to her hips. Fred's hard penis lay on her bare thigh. Three men were coming through the open door with guns in their hands. Rae sat bolt upright in bed and screamed. Fred stirred and struggled up out of sleep, his hard-on making a tent of the sheet, demanding groggily, "What the hell's goin on?!"

"Just hold it right there and put up your hands. You too, girls."

"What is this?" Fred sleepily summoned indignation. "You got a warrant to come bustin in here?"

The old cop looked at him as if he were a child. The younger man went over and yanked open the bureau drawers. Finding nothing there, he went through the clothes hanging in the closet.

"Here we go," he said. He came out with Dave Hill's wallet.

"Well, we're much obliged to you, Sam," the old cop said to the heavy-set house dick guarding the door, just waiting for Rae to drop the sheet. She didn't have a stitch on.

"Yeow. Well they looked suspicious to me soon as I spotted them. Flashin around big money like that. I thought we'd caught the Barrow gang."

They both chuckled.

"Reckon if we shot them we could pass them off for the reward?"

"Hell, we might."

"I'd just like to know what this is all about," Rae fumed.

"You know, sister. Come on. One at a time, hie your asses out of that bed and get dressed. Let's go. You find a gun or anything?" he asked the young cop who was still searching the room.

"Naw. They're unarmed."

The two older men looked at Fred's long peter when he climbed out of the bed with his hands up. He wore only his undershirt. They looked at each other. The old one cracked, "If I didn't know better, I'd think we'd hooked John Dillinger. They say he's got the biggest cock on record. Look at this."

Fred tried to cover himself.

"Hands up, bastard!"

"Cut that thing up in regular ones and there'd be enough to piece out both of a couple of old crocks like us," the old cop told the house dick.

"No wonder it takes two women to take care of him."

"I'm just with them," Wilma said, getting dressed.

"I gotta pee *real* bad!" Rae groaned as if in pain.

"OK. Go with her, Hersh."

"What? He's not going to the can with me?"

"He is or you ain't."

"I'll go right here first!"

"You do and I'll rub your goddamn nose in it."

"Listen," Fred said. "We aren't bad folks. We're just tryin to get along. I don't know what you think we've done. We *found* that wallet in the hall over at the Traveler's Hotel when we were leaving this morning. Well, the truth is we were waltzing on the bill because we were busted. I'll admit it. We were waltzing. Then we found that wallet. We couldn't believe our eyes. Then our car broke down and had to be towed in next door. So we just decided to check in to a decent hotel, get some rest before going on. I'm going out to Denver to go in business with a guy. Miniature golf. Duck pins. You can check it."

"Come on. Get dressed."

"I'm tellin you the truth, Officer."

"Sure you are. I believe you. Everybody here believes you. On the other hand, the man you slipped the Mickey to before stealing his purse tells us you are not to be trusted. Get dressed!"

"Can I get my robe?" Rae asked, holding the tail of the bedspread around her. "I don't have anything on."

"I guess we know what she's been doin, don't we?" The house dick grinned.

"What I want to know is what part you play," the old cop asked Wilma.

"I'm just with them. She and I worked together."

"I wouldn't be surprised."

Rae wanted to get her robe. She *had* to get her robe.

The young cop followed her eyes. He went to the bathroom door. Her robe hung from a hook inside. "This what you want?" he asked.

She said, "Yes. Thank you." She put out her hand for the silk robe. She let the spread slip. The men looked at her. The young man's eyes were looking at her breasts. She let the spread slip to the floor. The young man opened the robe for her to step in. She turned and put her arms in the sleeves.

"Goddamn . . ." the old cop breathed.

"Thank you," she told the young cop again, looking for his eyes. They went to her pocket. He patted it.

"Hold it!"

He fished out the blue medicine bottle with its eye-dropper cap.

"What's this?"

"My nose drops," she said. "I got sinus."

"Oh?" He handed the bottle back to her.

"The peek at a little pussy scrambled your brains?" the old cop roared. "Gimme that shit!" He snatched the bottle from the woman.

"It's my sinus medicine!" she insisted.

"Sister, you got five minutes to piss and get dressed or I'm going to work you over until you wished you *had* just a sinus condition. *Move!*"

They took them down the freight elevator to avoid the lobby.

"That's them!" Old Dave identified them immediately at the station.

The chief of detectives had the incriminating little vial on his desk when he talked to Rae. "Chloral hydrate ain't good for sinus, honey," he told her. "Let's see your prescription."

"I was just with them," Wilma protested when it was her turn.

They held her on suspicion. By the end of the day she was charged with being an accomplice to grand larceny and hocking a fur coat taken from the check room at the Calico Cat more than a month earlier. Actually, the owner had left it and been too drunk to remember where she had been. Wilma had started to tell the Greek at the end of the shift, changed her mind, and stuffed it in a shopping bag she hid under the check room counter. When no one came for it after a few days, she carried the bag out with a sweater hiding the coat and, being afraid to wear it, hocked it for $35 at a pawn shop on East Douglass. It was worth seven times that. She had nearly $200 due on charge accounts at various stores. She was charged with illegal cohabitation when it could not be established she had ever actually taken money for her favors.

If she would plead guilty to lifting the coat and get someone to make good on what she owed the stores, they were willing to forget the rest.

She wouldn't even confess to her right name.

Faced in court with her father, she claimed, "I never saw him before in my life!"

She thought she was saving the old man from something.

He told the judge, "We'll try and clear up what she owes them stores if you'll give us a little time. If we can pay it off so much a week. See, we just ain't got that kind of money right now."

"*I don't want you to!*" she screamed. "Don't lower yourself in front of these people for my sake. Tell him what he can do with his damned old court! *I'm no criminal!*"

"Six months!" the judge said. And called the next case.

# 13

MACDERAMID'S friend McCabe drove over one morning in his two-door Model A sedan to plot some political action they were going to take at Townsend Club No. 4. They sat all morning in the backyard on McCabe's running board whittling sticks and planning their move. Jacky played around with their shavings and bugged them so much McCabe finally let him sit behind the wheel of his car if the boy promised not to touch anything or honk the horn. He drove that jesse to his Aunt Nellie's down in Oklahoma and back through a dust storm *and* a cloudburst.

They were still talking earnestly when McCabe had to go. They continued to go at it as he mounted the driver's seat, advanced the spark, and started up. They raised their voices to speak over the noise of the engine. The car barked with the beat of its little four-banger heart. Then MacDeramid quickly said, "Be seein ya!" And slammed the door on all four fingers of the boy's right hand. Jacky almost fainted. Then he yelled.

They were afraid his fingers were broken. They looked very funny in the middle. No matter how they tried to reassure him, their faces gave them away. His granddad gently tried each finger from knuckle to nail, saying softly all the while, "Steady, Son. Steady. I know it hurts like thunder. But it's going to be all right. Fight that hurt! That's the boy."

He told McCabe, "I don't think airy one's broken."

"We could run him to the hospital to make sure, Mac. I got the car."

"No. I can doctor it. I'd just as soon set my own bones than let them bastards out at the county hospital look at it!"

"Can't agree with you more there. It's a bitch to be poor, ain't it?"

"Sure as hell is!"

When McCabe saw he could do nothing to help, he left so Mac could tend to the boy.

The county hospital was something to be avoided. It was, even in the boy's young mind, a frightening adjunct to jail and the cemetery. No one he had known was ever cured of a thing there. The doctors were all interns, the nurses practical, and the diet kitchen on a par with the state penitentiary's. Consequently, it was never overcrowded even at the height of the Depression. It did a big business in the day clinics, but no one wanted to be kept overnight lest he not waken whole in this world again. The hospital was on the West Side, across the street from the Green Tree Inn, one of the wildest roadhouses in the county.

Mac rushed the boy into the house, holding his rapidly swelling hand in both of his like the seething head of a poisonous snake. There was very little bleeding, though already black wells of blood lay just beneath the puffed skin. Inside, he bundled him to bed and spent an hour plunging the hand into a pan of hot Epsom salts water. Ice would have been better, but heat was the family remedy for everything, including fever. He made the boy a hot toddy, though he could not drink much of it. When the water cooled, he laid the boy's hand in a towel on his knees and dried it carefully. It looked like a little blown-up rubber glove. He drenched it with turpentine, which burned like bloody murder.

"BLOW! BLOW! BLOW!" the boy yelled.

The old man dutifully huffed and puffed to blow away the sting.

He soaked some clean white rags in turp and wrapped the boy's hand in them. Then he wrapped it with more clean white rags and fashioned him a sling from a red bandanna. When the sting passed, the boy's hand lay in the sling throbbing warmly, while all sensation of fingers was lost in a ball of pain the size of a coconut. He napped fitfully, though his granddad kept wet cloths on his forehead to cool his brow. Whenever he awoke, the old man was sitting right there beside the bed on a kitchen chair reading his paper, smoking his cigar, ready to change the cloth on the boy's head and promise that his grandma would soon be home.

In the morning the hand only hurt if it touched something or hung down, which would make it begin to throb until Jacky wanted to dance. Mac adjusted the sling so it was carried just right. Mrs. Mac told Jacky to stay quiet that day and went off to open their diner. After breakfast his granddad came in where the boy was admiring his bandage in his grandma's mirror and said, "Come on. We've got some work to do."

He had about fifty feet of clothesline coiled in his left hand. He had on his overalls with a hatchet in the leg loop.

"What are we going to do?" Jacky wondered.

"You'll see."

"What?" They were going down the stairs.

"You said you wanted a slingshot like the other boys in the alley, didn't you?"

"Yeow!"

"Then we're going to get one."

"Oh, boy! A beanie! A beanie!"

"Shh. The Millers may still be asleep."

They sat quietly on Miller's front steps while Mac fashioned a proper slipknot in a bight of the rope to create a lariat.

"Is that how you did it when you were a cowboy?" the boy asked.

"Well, in principle. But we usually braided an eye in the end of the rope around a wood or horn grommet so it would slip good and throw straight. Had one once I picked up down in Laredo that was hand-braided leather. Fella offered me twenty-five dollars and a nearly new Remington double-action handgun for it up in Abilene when it was two year old. And I turned him down. That was a hell of a rope. A good rope's just like a good man. Takes some breakin in and workin. Then it's good for quite a little. Then one day when you're really comfortable with it, when it's changed and stretched about all it's ever going to— *snap!*"

Jacky heard it break.

Then the old man paused, took out his cigar, spat away a soggy bit of leaf, and offered the opinion: "If there *is* a God, it's a lead-pipe cinch he's in the opium or money trades."

The boy wondered what he meant by *that*.

He stood up and studied Miller's tree from all angles for just the fork he was looking for. Jacky hadn't dreamed making a beanie was so complicated. There was an awful lot between the desire and knocking over a tin can out in the alley. They had been an hour at it already.

Up the tree on the yard side at the end of the third major branch system Mac spotted the crotch he was looking for. On his first throw the noose peeled several coils off his hand, flirted with the branch, but closed before catching it and fell back around his ears like an Indian rope trick rebuked.

That was not the way either the old man or Jacky had envisioned his move. He carefully recoiled the rope in his left hand. His hair was mussed. He shook out his loop a little wider. He swung it round and round at a 45-degree angle to his own perpendicular. He launched it. It climbed into the air . . . and collapsed. The loop closed. It all came tumbling down. Mac stepped back this time to keep it from falling over his head and shoulders.

Some old cowboy. Boy! "Betcha Buck Jones could lasso that tree." The boy offered encouragement.

"If I had me a decent rope . . ." the old man grumbled. "Never have what I need for nothin! Make do. Make do." He angrily recoiled the rope, shook out the loop, sighted narrowly on the branch. No twirling fancy this time. He bent slightly at the knees, swung the rope back and forth alongside for a long time, then let it go with a quick, smooth underhand flip that sent the thing zizzing straight to the mark. It happened so quickly Jacky would have liked to see it again.

"*Gotcha, by god!*" the old man cried happily. He twisted and wrenched back on the rope as if he had caught a calf in full flight and had to set his loop on a living thing. The branch snapped neatly at the trunk like a shot. Mac fell hard on his left shoulder, wrapping himself fully in the coil of his lasso while trying to roll from under the twelve-foot branch of Miller's hibernating little elm which came ripping through the under branches and buried him, hatchet, lasso, and all.

Man, there was a big empty place in Miller's tree. The front yard was full of branches.

The boy peered in at his granddad. "You OK, Grandpa?"

He peered out. There were twigs and leaves in his hair. He began laughing. Jacky laughed. He picked his way out of the web of rope and cage of branches.

"By god, Son! We sure brought it down, didn't we!"

"*You* sure did." If Miller was listening, Jacky wanted him to know where the responsibility lay.

They laughed, but there was an awfully big hole in Miller's tree.

When Mac was free, he took the hatchet and began chopping away at the branches until out of it all he came away with a forked stick about two feet long. Then he chopped that down until the selected fork was no more than six inches from legs to butt. Out of all that wood! The boy was amazed. The old man laid the fork aside and set about dragging and piling the remainder of the wood neatly beneath its parent as if between it and tree something might be worked out before the city came and removed the wood, levying Miller for the service.

The old man coiled up his rope and hung it on his left shoulder. He placed the ax back in its loop alongside his leg. He brushed himself meticulously. He picked up the prize fork and carried it before him, sighting with one eye closed at its barky symmetry, seeing in it some perfection that completely escaped the boy. It seemed such a small souvenir for so much trouble.

They sat on the back steps while Mac took out his pocketknife, selected the proper blade for the job, stropped it on the side of his shoe, then professionally stripped the fork to white wood. He trimmed down the small knots, evened up the limbs, rounded off the handle, sighted on it with one eye again, and only then let Jack touch it for the first time.

*Zip! Zam! Pow!* He mentally drilled cans like a sharpshooter. He smelled and tasted the slick, moist wood where the bark had hidden next spring—sleeping there in the gray heart of late autumn.

Mac brushed shavings from his knees, and they went in to get ready to go to lunch at the diner. They entered by the back door.

On the way back after eating, Jacky with his unfinished slingshot in his good hand, they stopped at the Texaco station, where Mac bought a blown-out inner tube which the boy wore home over his shoulder like a bandolier.

On the back steps, then, Mac cut strips of rubber from the inner tube and lashed them to the ends of the fork with fishline. Then from his shoe repair box he selected a piece of boot tongue from which he cut the pocket for the missile and tied it securely to the free ends of the rubber slings. He smoothed the handle of the weapon with a bit of broken glass until it was cool and smooth as satin.

It was the middle of the afternoon, almost time for the boy's grandmother to come home for her nap, when they were ready to try out the beanie. Jacky set tin cans along the edge of the alley and went hunting small stones for ammo. He also found two half-inch steel ball bearings that the big kids prized so highly for shot.

The old man was a little rusty. He missed several times before zeroing in on the cans. He held the slingshot so Jacky could take a shot with his good hand. He did not hit anything. It was a two-handed art.

An old yellow cat peeked around Miller's shed, then sashayed across the alley with its tail crooked in the air over its little black button like an ignorant beckoning.

Mac let fly with one of the steelies. It kissed the pavement with an electric spark and ricocheted right into the cat's haughty ass. It left the ground with an awful yell, looking electrified. It landed clinging six feet up a chicken-wire fence.

It was a horrible sight.

Yet the old man smothered laughter, fought to control his amusement. Then man and boy they both howled. They bent double with laughter. That crazy cat dropped down off the wire and hit the concrete flying, its nails scraping to get leverage. ZOOOOOM!

"Don't-ever-do-a-thing-like-that-again!" the old man said, struggling to gain control of himself.

"*Me!*" the boy exclaimed. "*I* didn't do it! *You* did, Grandpa."

"I *know!*" he howled. "I *mean,* don't you ever do it."

"No!" No, he wouldn't.

"I didn't intend to hit it. Just scare it a little."

"You sure scared it, Grandpa," the boy acknowledged.

"I sure did, didn't I?" He erupted once more. Laughter bubbled out of him. "Did you see the look on that goddamned cat's face? Oh, Lord have mercy! Hoooooeeeee! *Man!* Hmmmm. Never seen anything like that since our old bull backed into Carty's electric fence."

The boy's grandmother came up the alley carrying her purse and a big bag of leftovers from the café for their supper.

"Now, what's going on here?" she asked by way of greeting.

"Grandpa made me a beanie," the boy explained. He and the old man giggled.

"Well, *that's* certainly something you needed." She looked pointedly at the boy's arm in the sling. "Then, I suppose if you was able to use it, I'd be payin for neighbors' windalights. And it's always good to see you're keeping yourself busy," she told the old man sarcastically.

She set down her bundles on the back steps and began gathering ice-cold flatwork and rags off the clothesline.

"Too busy, I guess, to of thought to take in the wash off the line before the damp. I work *my* fingers to the bone all day and would like just once to come home and relax a minute. Lord knows, *you* don't have so much to *doooooOOOO!* LOOKOUTTHERE!"

She almost outjumped the cat. She did not have hands enough to rub the place he had shot her. "That HURT, doggone it!" She rubbed furiously.

He went to her. He could not help laughing. He started to lift her hem to survey the extent of the damage—

"JUST YOU KEEP YOUR DARN HANDS OFF ME!" She slapped his paw away. She rubbed and limped into the house, leaving laundry, leftovers, and all in the yard.

She would not talk to either of them that evening. Supper was a very long time coming—stuff left in the pots, meat left on customers' plates. The boy hated eating a piece of meat someone else had bitten, a slice of bread half gnawed. No matter how good it tasted, he always ate it in spite of an internal cringing. Once Mac tried to lift her dress to see the place he had shot her. She cracked him on the knuckles with a big potato spoon.

"I just want to see the spot."

"You can go to blazes!"

Tucked into his blankets on the couch while the old man sat reading his paper by the gas heater, the boy felt dreamy and snug, with his sore hand on his chest and his beanie tucked safely away under his pillow.

"Grandpa?"

"What?"

"She sure did jump, didn't she?"

"She sure did." Absently from behind the paper. The paper shook a little.

"Jumped almost as high as that old cat, didn't she?"

The paper was shaking for sure then. "She jumped, all right."

"Sure made her mad, too."

"Sure did." Behind the paper, the old man shook with stifled laughter. Then his laugh broke and blew down the top of the paper. He clapped his hand over his mouth and rocked back and forth, stamping his foot, motioning that the boy should not laugh, all the time his eyes filled with tears.

"Oh, Son, we oughtn't laugh—" he choked.

Then they roared once more. The boy's side ached from laughing.

"All right in there. Both of you. If you think I'm going to forget this, you got another think coming," the old woman called in from the other room.

"I sure can't wait to shoot my beanie," the boy said.

"OK, now, that's enough. Get to sleep."

In the dark the boy was awakened.

"Is that where it hurts?" the old man whispered.

"*You'll* be lucky!" she snapped. "I mean it. You keep your darn hands to yourself. And I don't mean just for a day or two, neither."

The old man's muffled laughter shook their bed in the dark.

# 14

JUST when merely making ends meet at the Coffee Cup would have rivaled the loaves and fishes trick, the Millers presented MacDeramid with a new opportunity.

There was an old couple who had a café out on East Kellogg (U.S. 54) that would make a dandy truck-stop-café-beer-joint. The old couple were ready to slow down. The Coffee Cup could not have been slower. Miller engineered the trade. He reasoned to Mac: "If a man is drivin a truck, he's a man with money for food and drink, right?" And as the Depression wore on, the luncheon ladies became ever more tattered of hem and their dimes deeper in their long skinny purses. Men began taking their lunch in a bag from home when they had work to go to. "Mac, you just got to sell beer now or go under," Miller explained. Since the end of Prohibition, though Kansas remained dry, Miller's bootleg sale of whiskey was falling off. People were that broke.

Mac's wife absolutely refused to sell beer, though she did ultimately reason, "I may have to work where it's sold to keep from starving, but I'll starve before I sell it myself." So customers had to come around the counter and fish for their own beer in the cooler when Mrs. Mac was on duty alone, leaving their money in a dish beside the cash register. Most were amused at the little woman's obdurate refusal to be any part of the wicked transaction.

To refuse to touch 3.2 beer on esthetic grounds could have been understood, even championed, but to refuse to sell it *because* of its alcoholic content was extending the jurisdiction of sin beyond the territorial limits of reason. She would never ring up the change in the bowl beside the register, nor would she sell a punch on the punchboards that now lay openly on the counter. She would be no part of gambling. And if her son's brother-in-law Ray was selling Miller's whiskey out the back door, she did not want to know about it. "I put down a substantial meal of plain home cooking for a fair price. You can't go to hell for doing that," she thought.

The Millers ran the place at night. Mac and his wife ran it during the day. There was a trucker's hotel upstairs next door. The truckers took their meals downstairs at Mac's during the day and brought their women in to drink beer and play the jukebox at night. Mrs. Mac quit baking and started buying pies from the bakery. The sour smell of last night's beer and smokes when she opened the place in the morning killed her enthusiasm for baking.

Ray was permitted to live in the one room back of the place. His wife was supposed to help Mrs. Mac wait on customers while Ray washed dishes and looked after things when the Millers were alone at night. Because Miller had the jakeleg, he liked Ray around to hoist a case of beer or throw out a trucker bent on destruction. Then, because the MacDeramids' grandson would have to be transported from their apartment to the café via public transit at hours when he should be sleeping, it was decided the boy should sleep in a corner of the back room, too. Between washing dishes, hoisting a case of beer, bouncing drunks, and watching a snotty brat, Ray also found time to organize an unlicensed garage in the side yard where there was room enough for the big rigs to pull in and park. Ray had been a trucker and mechanic himself.

There was always an old car or truck up on blocks out there with its engine open or its transmission down. Ray, his kid brother, Roy, Kenny MacDeramid, and all their buddies were always hunkered down out there working on cars, drinking whiskey from a pint in a brown paper sack and beer from bottles, talking dirty, and smoking cigarettes. Kenny still rolled his own from a sack of Bull Durham, much to the amusement of Ray and Roy, who blasted Wings tailormades. They had never been farmers. It was beautiful. The boy never tired of watching and listening to them. The earth around their workplace was carbon black from crankcase oil. It smelled and felt oily. Car parts were strewn around, set in pans of gasoline, hung from the weathered porch pillars on nails. No grass grew where those machines were bled.

There was a two-hole double outhouse out there for men and women. On the men's side someone had carved the crude lifesize outline of a woman deeply into the door with a punched-out knothole for a gaping cunt. Mac regularly tacked flattened tin cans over the holes in the door and the wall between men's and women's, and just as regularly someone pried the patches off.

Young Roy Foster roared into the yard on a big red and black Indian Chief bike that had a suicide clutch. *Suicide clutch!* That was Jacky's new boogyman. He wondered if he would ever have the courage to straddle something with a suicide clutch. That young Roy arrived at all was a miracle in Jacky's eyes. They all lived dangerously.

Nor was there security to be found in turning to Ray's wife. She had all she could handle with Ray. They fought all the time. They would scream and swear at one another until Ray would end all debate by knocking her ass over the kitchen table. He was just as likely to give Jacky a shot, too, if he was handy. He had a cot in the corner and a chair at the table and was a major inconvenience to them anyplace he was put.

For openers, Jacky simply would not eat oatmeal. Ray's wife made a tacky, scummy, inedible glop from a can of Mother's Oats you could hang wallpaper with if you worked fast before it hardened. Cold, it would bounce. Let it sit on the table until it congealed and it could be sliced like liverwurst. They tried forcing it down him with a spoon by prying apart his clenched teeth. When it dribbled down his shirt, they clouted him on the head. At their wits' end, they turned his chair away from the table and made him sit there holding and staring at the bowl all day. *All day!* His feet nearly fell off. He ached in so many places he tried to eat the stuff and vomited. And sat there staring at a puddle of vomit *and* aching all over, learning forever that if instinct told him to resist, then resist totally.

Ray hated his guts, the boy was certain. He never touched the boy except to hit him. His wife was too hurried to try to comfort him. She slept, cooked, ate, washed, mated, and grew older each day in a single room with a mean, hard-drinking, out-of-work man who vowed: "I'm too damn proud to go get in line at dawn and wait around to kiss some WPA straw boss's ass at eight for a chance to chop wood."

Her only relief was the sobbing catharsis that came after being ringingly slapped face down on her rump-sprung old bed. Ray's, the boy guessed, came in the slapping. His was in dreamily digging his own world out of the hard-packed, oil-soaked yard with a spoon. But most of the time he simply hated. If he had been Ray's own, Ray would have killed him, he knew that in his heart. If he had been older, he would have cut Ray's head off with an ax. There was no question about it. They would have treated him right or he would have killed them both in their bed. They were nothing. And as long as he was in their care, neither was he. He felt he had been sidetracked, forgotten.

His bed was in the corner of Ray's back room, with a blue curtain hung around it to keep out the light. After his grandma and grandpa left, things swung around there until one or two in the morning. The light burned through the boy's curtain all night long, like a haze-eclipsed moon. Ray and his wife slept with the light on most of the time, collapsing in a sweaty, beer-soaked tangle on the never-made bed. From his cubbyhole he could hear the braying men making the shrill women laugh in the other room. He thought he heard his mother out there one night and went to find her. The air was sour with beer, blue with smoke.

"Oh! You're a little sweety pie!" He was swept off his feet into the great flaccid arms of a beer-joint Cleopatra whose bloated, massive face with its open, fetid mouth was like a dilapidated funhouse exit. The front of her housedress was wet with beer and sweat. Her cloudy little eyes did not quite track.

He struggled out of her grasp and hurried off with his flap down in the back.

"Lookee there. Ain't that just a cute little butt?" she cackled.

His mother was not to be seen. He searched every booth, checked every stool at the counter. He had been so certain it had been her voice. Maybe Ray, who hustled him back to bed, had hid her somewhere.

The boy went to sleep every night with the shrill, boozy laughter of women and the drunken bray of men in his ears, the sound of glassware against glassware, and the boom of the big juke pumping away on the other side of the wall. His dreams were often shattered on jagged threats which loomed suddenly like the shadow of Ray on his curtain. Though the threats were not directed at him, their implication was universal in the curtained night.

*"Charley, you're a goddamned liar."*

*"Call me a liar, you stinkin bitch!"*

*"Liar! Liar! Liar!"*

Bam!

*"Sure! Go on! Hit me, you dirty sonofabitch! Hit me! You'd hit a woman! That's what you like. To hit somebody!"*

Bam!

*"I don't care! You went to see her! You lied to me, Charley! I know you went to see her. My mother saw you. You went after you said you wouldn't! That's the last time you lie to me, Charley! The last time!"*

Bam!

"BEAT ME UP! HIT ME AGAIN. KNOCK MY TEETH OUT!"

Bam! Bam! Bam!

Screaming: "FUCK YOU, YOU DIRTY SONOFABITCH! FUCK HER! FUCK YOUR GODDAMNED KIDS! YOU WENT TO SEE THEM AGAIN, YOU LYIN BASTARD! DID YOU FUCK HER IN THE ASS, TOO? THAT'S ALL YOU LIKE, TO FUCK SOMEBODY IN THE ASS! THAT'S WHAT YOU LIKE!"

Bam! Bam! "Shut up! I'll break your ugly face!"

"GO ON! I DON'T CARE. YOU'VE BROKEN IT ALREADY! GO ON! . . . *Fuck your kids in the ass. . . .*"

Left-right-left. Left-right-left.

*"Hey!* What's going on back there?! *Hey!* Get offa that woman!"

"THE WHOLE FUCKING WORLD IS ONE BIG CORNHOLE!"

Feet running away on gravel.

A man tries to comfort the woman. His voice is a confidential mumble through the wall.

She snarls, "Getcher hands off'n me! Do I know you? I don't know you. Leave me alone."

He persuades in an indistinct mumble.

"I ain't goin nowhere with you. I don't *know* you," she says. Then after a little, "Where's the drink?"

Horns honk. Tires spin on gravel. A woman's voice moaning blue through the booze and smoke, rolling a skein of injustice into a neat damnable ball. A bottle explodes against the wall. The boy hears flesh being pounded, teeth being broken. Feet scuffle on the earth outside in a silent war of stags and boars. He listens hard for his mother's voice and hears a song on the jukebox:

> *Love, oh love, oh loveless love,*
> *Has set our hearts on goalless goals,*
> *From silkless silk and milkless milk,*
> *We are growing used to soulless souls. . . .*

Every night. All night long. Moreover, no one ever talked to him anymore. He hardly saw his grandpa and grandma. It was only a matter of time, as he saw it, before he was run over by a truck on the highway out front, killed in the nightly tug and maul, or strangled by Ray and his wife for not eating his oats. He felt awful. But he could not get anyone to hear his plaint.

Rule was he had to take a nap when the place was closed in the afternoon. But there was an early heat wave that year. It was hot and breezeless behind his curtain. Up front it was dim and cool. There was an awning over the front window that kept the sun off the plate glass. There were two big slow-turning overhead fans to circulate the air beneath the high stamped-metal ceiling. Flypaper curls hung from the fan hubs. The black corpses of flies were stuck in the tacky. On the back wall above the jukebox was a big print of *Custer's Last Stand* distributed by the Anheuser-Busch Brewing Company. It was a great picture with ponies wild-eyed and frothing in the dust of battle, ridden by howling Indians in warpaint, dropping, dragging, dying like flies all over it. And Custer, his hair like golden flypapers, golden mustachios, great white hat, fringed buckskin jacket, supported dying troopers around his knees, his pearl-handled six-guns blazing, mowing down Indians as if they were wheat. That dusty golden land was of the world the boy knew. He lived where Indians had walked. Where buffalo grazed. *Listen!* For the silent step. He could look at the picture for hours. Nuts to Western Union! When he grew up, he was going with the cavalry.

He also liked to draw and paint. The idea of making pictures could capture his full attention. An instant frozen, yet full of time. There was something very important, far-reaching, mysterious, and overwhelming about pictures for the boy. The frozen cry. The truth of a cry forever. He could hear those bloody Indians, smell the scene. His grandmother interpreted his desire and gave him pencil and pad often. It was the best way to keep him quiet, the *only* way to keep him quiet in church. And she would let him dab enamel on a chair or box she wanted painted.

"He'd rather paint than eat," she sighed, foreseeing a career for the boy as a housepainter or draftsman should he ever finish high school, which would have been a family first.

Barefoot, Jacky crept over the cool linoleum past the deep sink into the café. He left Ray and his wife sprawled in their underwear on the bed in a soggy, snoring tangle. He went straight to *Custer's Last Stand* and stood there until all spit ran down his throat and his mouth became so dry it might have stuck together if he closed it. He went behind the counter and fished a piece of ice out of the pop cooler and sat on the end stool at the counter sucking ice and spinning around until he got dizzy and began feeling a little sick. Off the stool, he ran up and down the line of stools like an antic plate spinner.

Within arm's reach all along the counter were setups of catsup, salt, pepper, a white ceramic mustard pot ranked on either side of a nickeled paper-napkin dispenser. In each mustard pot there was a small wooden paddle to spread the mustard on your sandwich. In the pot lid there was a notch for the paddle handle. He stirred a handy pot of mustard until it looked just like yellow paint. It was dreamy.

He just began painting stool tops with mustard and did not stop until every one was covered perfectly with a fresh yellow coat. It was no small task. There were a dozen stools. He used a lot of mustard. And he *knew* it was mustard, not paint.

He had barely finished when Ray's alarm clock went off. He was still beating the boy when his grandmother and grandfather came through the door. At first they were angry, too. Then they were fascinated. It was such an unthinkable thing.

"Land! He must of supposed it was paint!" his grandmother decided. There seemed no other explanation. "He'd rather paint than eat, you know."

He never told her he knew it was mustard. It was drying around the edges. You could see it wasn't going to be easy to get off.

Mac just shook his head. "I'll tell you. I've never seen the like. That boy's got too much imagination for his own good."

"You leave 'im with me long enough and I'll take it out of 'im!" Ray promised.

Jacky had no doubts.

It remained hot all spring. Easter, Aunt Inga Andersen, one of her brothers, and his wife came over in a little coupe with a rumble seat and took the boy for a picnic in Sims' Park. They had just started hunting eggs when a cold breeze like the ghost of winter blew their paper plates away and spilled their lemonade. Then the dust came stinging and getting into the boy's mouth while they tried to get everything bundled up in their picnic blanket. Inga held onto him to keep him from getting blown away. They could not see the car for the dust. They could not see ten feet. They groped for the road and followed it to the car. Inga and the boy piled into the rumble and closed the door over them as best they could, huddling on the floor in the gritty, suddenly hot air. On the road they crept along past cars with their lights on. Behind the initial cold passing blast that turned over the leaves of trees, there was a relentless Sahara wind deaf to prayer or curses. In the rumble dirty rivulets of sweat lined Inga's pretty face as she held her handkerchief over his mouth for a filter.

The dust blew into the night. No supper was without its seasoning of grit. No bed was not sandy. The dust got into everything. Beer and pop were the best things to drink, though it seemed as soon as a bottle or can of something was opened the grit was drawn in invisibly. Everyone felt itchy for days. There were little drifts of dust in the corners of the bathtub.

In May the castor beans hung like sleeping bats in the lop-eared trees. A shimmering river of asphalt oozed past the door. With a kitchen knife Jacky could dig up a chaw of butyl-tasting tar from the edge of the highway that would last all day. Men carried raffia fans in the street. Lemonade was consumed like air. Kids were set out in yards in tubs of water. No one wanted to go anywhere.

Jacky didn't have much of a birthday party. It was just sort of worked in right after the place closed in the afternoon. His mother was still away. None of his cousins attended. There was a cupcake with four candles that had been used before stuck in it and a dish of ice cream on the side. There were his grandpa, grandma, and Ray to see him blow out the candles. His grandmother sang "Happy Birthday." His granddad gave him a nickel. Ray gave him a hard swat on the ass to grow on. That was it.

# 15

THAT fall they went out of the truck stop business. Mrs. Mac found out about the bootlegging at night and learned that the Millers were paying off the police when she had thought they were only robbing the till. They always had some money. The MacDeramids never had any. They were paying off *and* robbing the till. When Mrs. Mac's trust in her partners failed, she simply could not continue.

"To heck with such a business! If I can't trust my partners, I'd just as soon be on relief," she said and stripped off her apron, satisfied that all she was going to get out of the place was a plaster of Paris horse with a clock in its belly that had been a punchboard prize a customer had given her rather than take with him. His taste was greater than his generosity.

But Mrs. Miller began screaming that the clock was hers. They argued about it, reliving the day the customer donated it from each of their points of view. Mrs. Mac had it in her arms and would not let it go.

Mrs. Miller threatened to slap her face.

"You just do that and I'll break this horse right over your dyed head!" Mrs. Mac promised. She sat down in a booth and vowed not to budge until it was agreed the clock was hers. Mrs. Miller placed herself in front of the door, vowing Mrs. Mac would leave with that clock only over her dead body. They were stalemated for nearly half an hour when Mr. Miller arrived to swear to his wife's right to the ugly thing.

Then Kenny MacDeramid and Mac himself arrived. "For godsake, Mom, give her the damn thing. It isn't worth anything," Kenny suggested.

"I don't *care*," she said, near tears, clutching the thing in both arms against the possibility Mr. Miller might make a dive for it from the side or he and his wife rush her at the same time. "It's mine and I want to keep it. They've done us out of every other darn thing we put in here. They've cheated and stole from us and lied all along. *This is my clock!*"

"You're crazy as hell, you psalm-singing old nag!" Miller replied. "We never touched a dime that was yours. You lousy farmers couldn't sell gold bricks for horse turds!"

Kenny busted him in the mouth. "You don't talk like that to her!"

The fat man went down and stayed down, with his eyeglasses twisted crazily on his brow. His nostrils showed blood. He blubbered about what a rat Kenny was for hitting a man who wore glasses and had a bum leg. He eyed the cash register.

Kenny knew Miller kept a gun there at night. Miller started to rise. His eyes gave away his thinking. Kenny gave him a little kick in the belly.

Mrs. Miller broke for the street, yelling for a cop.

Kenny was for taking the clock and making a break for it.

"We'll wait right here," his mother said calmly. "We're in the right."

Kenny was worried about what the law would think about him hitting a guy who wore glasses and had the jakeleg.

Mrs. Miller returned with the motorcycle cop who hid behind the Skelly station up on Kellogg to take off after speeders. He often had lunch in the place. She was banging his ear a mile a minute.

". . . and my husband is crippled. Why he just knocked him down for no reason at all. He hit him first. Yes, sir! . . ."

"Didn't even give me a chance to take off my glasses," Miller sniffed, heaving himself heavily to his feet.

The cop listened to charge and countercharge.

"It's my clock. Always before when she mentioned it, it was mine. She always teased me about my boyfriend who gave me the clock. She was jealous."

"Jealous! Of *what*? The clock was actually given to the place. It was just as much mine as yours. More so now, because we're keeping the place and you're sellin out."

"Selling! Whew! Where's the money? . . ."

". . . so I knew if that fatass could get his gun out of the cash register he might of hurt somebody."

Finally the cop raised his hand as if directing traffic. "Hold it! Why don't we go downtown, settle this in front of a judge. No? OK, then. Let's settle it here and be done with it."

No one wanted to go downtown.

"Now, the way I see it is this: I've never known Missus Mac to tell a lie, even if it hurt. I've never known of her going against her principles. I just don't know you folks that well. I don't say you aren't just as honest. I just don't know. If you want a judge to decide, it's fine with me. But it'll save you lot of trouble if you just let Mrs. Mac have the clock. I believe her."

Though it never kept the correct time, she prized the clock as tangible

*160*

reward of virtue until the gilt was all chipped away and the plaster of Paris underneath was revealed. She seemed to forget it had been a punchboard prize to begin with. It was as if in such a season of robbers even true virtue had the quality of bootleg goods.

# 16

THE West Side was old Wichita—cow town on the old Chisholm Trail astride the Big Arkansas River. The East Side was the Air Capital of the World. The East Side point of view was post-Lindbergh, ready to fly, wheeling, winging. East High athletes were called Aces. Across town at North High, which was actually West, they were called Redskins. While North had a class in canoeing, East mounted a flying club.

Where the Little Arkansas joined the Big River below North High, an authentic grass Wichita Indian Council Lodge two stories tall was maintained by the Parks Department in memory of a time when the many tribes held annual council on the island at the rivers' fork. Their ghosts still haunted the cool shadows beneath the trailing willows along banks as green in summer as Wisconsin. There was the feeling that had one been but a little quicker, he would have seen the moccasin print in the slick clayey mud.

The river ran down and curved through Riverside Park past the old great homes on wide lawns under ancient Indian trees, homes the men of cattle, rails, mills, and wheat built solidly to honor their achievement and sold out by sons who speculated in oil, natural gas, helium, aircraft, new wheat, and another breed of cattle; who banked their profits and built the sprawling ranch homes across town in Eastborough—a restricted community with no sidewalks and a private police force, with city bus service for the servants. On the West Side a kid could stroll past the old great homes on the way to the park in Levis, mocs, and a skivvy shirt. Try that in Eastborough and the cops would pick him up.

MacDeramid had always wished he had been rich enough to own the McClain Place on McClain Boulevard. It was a great old stone fortress with wide, deep verandas, glowing cherry paneling in the dining room, and a sweeping stair up from the foyer. It sat on about half an acre of land overlooking a bend in the river and an end of Riverside Park. Mac and his mules had graded the boulevard roadbed. He had helped landscape the park, dragging a hill up out of flat prairie to hide the city waterworks on the river below the dam. Jack always called the hill "Grandpa's Mountain."

Above the dam in the summer on holiday afternoons the smell of burning castor oil hung over the water, where little hydroplanes buzzing like angry wasps split the placid muddy water between the lolling banks in day-long boat races. Boys would dangle their feet in the water and cheer on their favorites and invariably, sometime before it was time to go, fall in the river and have a splash along the bank where it was shallow.

There were family picnics in the park with uncles, aunts, and cousins by the jalopy load.

On the East Side, where the prairie was a natural landing field for as far as the eye could see, Walter Beech snapped his staggered-wing biplane through a sparkling sky so perfect it might have been created in some vast crystal bell jar. In such winy air man's next thought was that he had to *fly. Or motorcar! Motorcycle! Speedboat! Race! Go! Cessna! Stearman! Beech! Ryan! Wiley Post! Amelia Earhart! Rrrrrrrrrrrrrrrrrr-rrrrrrrrrrrrrrOW! GOOOOOOoooo—LINDBERGH!*

Barnstormers, air circuses, wing-walkers, parachutists, dogfights, an Immelmann, the outside loop, autogyro, air races! Boys and girls alike in breeches and boots, leather flying jackets that had been traveled, lounging with an elbow on the wing strut of their planes smoking Camels, with their leather or canvas flying helmets unbuckled but never removed from their heads, sporting goggles shoved casually up like knightly vizards, with a view higher than any child's head. They wore white silk scarves looped around their throats and depending nearly to their knees. They talked toughly earnest in a foreign sky language—*aileron, strut, guy, fairing, filet, altimeter, wind sock*—words that leaped into the air of their own weight. And the ether of banana oil and airplane dope rode on the odor of alfalfa and August.

Being a child and beneath their sight line Jacky could observe them in detail unself-consciously. Gypsies of the air, sleeping in some farmer's field, giving the farmer a ride for a place at the farmer's table and enough gas to fly to the next town. Young men and women going somewhere more exciting than anyplace anyone else had ever gone before, kicking the family reunion thing forever. They shared an intimacy so magnetic the boy's heart thumped with longing to get in on it, to know whatever it was they knew, do whatever they did that gave them that sort of special sheen, that particular aura that graces mainly individuals, rarely teams—Grand Prix champions, climbers of Everest, some bullfighters, some great batting champions, a quarterback, milers, deep-sea divers. . . . He wanted their lofty satisfaction and confidence. It seemed a total sort of life. So the kid felt torn between the urge to play with himself and shout hurrah.

On the West Side there were memories and a few old-timers like MacDeramid who had actually seen the cattle drives and the cow towns and had, when the drives were long past, helped grade the runways for the new airport out East. But he would not take an offered free plane ride the day the field was dedicated. "If the Lord meant men to fly," etc., etc.

There was still a working blacksmith shop on the West Side a block or so off Waco, where it was cool and dark inside on a summer day in spite of the big hand-pumped forge in the middle of the place. The floor was earth. The walls were hung with millions of horseshoes. Huge shoes for dray horses, delicate thin shoes for high-stepping little mares, regular shoes for riding horses, baby shoes for ponies.

Every Saturday morning for one summer Mac and the boy would go there after they picked up their relief commodities at the Forum a few blocks away. Mac carried the stuff home in a clean gunny sack over his shoulder. He carried it on the bus and had hard eyes for anyone who stared at the poke. Before starting home, though, he would sit on a nail keg, and he and the smith would trade recollections and damn Roosevelt. The blacksmith was a member of Mac's Townsend Club. Jacky played with all the stuff around there and listened to history and civics real enough to raise his short hairs, real enough to fall close enough to the heart to matter. The blacksmith made Mac a stickpin from a horseshoe nail and made the boy a nail ring.

Then on Sunday they might take a lunch and catch a bus out to the airport and spend the day there watching the planes take off and come in.

Eventually they moved to the West Side so Mac would be near the WPA woodyard and be better able to line up for a day's work. The man who had graded McClain Boulevard and the runways for The Air Capital of the World took his own ax and got in line every morning at sunup in hope of earning a dollar a day chopping wood for the WPA.

# 17

ON the West Side they moved into a two-room basement flat in an old red-brick building on Waco near the Sante Fe Trailways bus barn that looked as though it had been imported brick by crumbling brick from Pittsburgh or someplace like that by a landlord with a great nostalgia for industrial slums or a particularly wide streak of mean. Mrs. Mac had a job fry-cooking in a tiny railway-car diner across from the bus barn. Mac was getting a couple of days' work just over the Big River Bridge at the WPA woodyard.

They got a sack of commodities every week from the relief: canned meat from which all essential juices had been squeezed by the processor to sell on the open market, thereby stretching one cow to the length of two—loaves and fishes! "Whew! Roosevelt must surely love the mechanics of it," Mac swore. (Or how one of the world's great bouillon makers got *his* start.) Mrs. Mac fried the remaining fibers in bacon drippings to give them some kind of flavor. Potato flour; dried beans and/or black-eyed peas, from which no mother nor all of her children could ever pick *all* the stones before starvation set in. (And relief dentistry was limited to filling or pulling or fitting full dentures. Break a tooth and either suffer or have it pulled. Have enough pulled and you got a $25 set of false teeth.) Uncolored oleo, which was not bad for greasing the wheels of a homemade scooter. Mrs. Mac was the only one the boy ever saw eat the stuff. But she would eat a tree—bark, roots, leaves, and pulp—his grandma. That oleo would ruin a piece of toast quicker than anything on earth. When she insisted *she* couldn't tell it from butter except by color, Mac said, "Shit," slammed away from the table, and blew the rest of his dollar's pay for that day at the woodyard down at the diner on smothered pork chops, biscuits and butter, and mashed potatoes and gravy. Mrs. Mac never tried selling him oleo again. Powdered milk was a new thing. It tasted burnt, bad. Beet sugar, dried fruit, which was the best thing they handed out; potato flour, beet sugar, water, oleo, powdered milk, and dried fruit, and you had a pie; dried fruit and a nickel's worth of longhorn cheese, a handful of crackers, and there was lunch; stewed with beet sugar and little powdered milk, and you had breakfast. A senator's wife who was never on relief discovered, just when everyone was starting to feel the least bit sorry for reliefers, "A person can live pretty good on that!" And made all the newsreels skarfing a piece of relief pie.

Then why was Jack hungry all the time?

He planted an orange seed in the ground beneath his swing under an elm and waited for oranges. When a twig with bright green leaves—a green completely foreign to Kansas—pushed up through the hard-packed earth under the swing, he gave up swinging in anticipation of oranges.

There were three girls ranging in age from five to eleven who lived with their mother in the basement flat next to theirs. Their mother worked three days a week in the WPA cannery on the river. On days when everyone was working, the oldest girl would look after the little ones. Big Sister taught them all, Jack included, what F-U-C-K was about. Even Middle Sister and Little Sister were way ahead of Jack on that score. When classes started, she treated him like some prize dummy. Little Sister, who was really a shrimp with a big head and fragile little limbs, nodded her head in a solemn, certain agreement while Big Sister straightened Jack out on what went where—exactly. But they called fucking "hitting" in ordinary conversation. To save their souls from eternal fire, Jack guessed. They were Evangelicals. Who *knew* what they could or could not discuss.

Jack was skeptical but game. He was just waiting around for his orange tree to bear fruit and school to start that fall. He was eager for school. He could already read a lot of words, count, do his letters. Big Sister often lined them up on chairs and played school. It was like real school, with books and everything. She even had a little blackboard on legs. Big Sister was a pretty good teacher, too.

All three sisters were emaciated, dirty-legged little blondes with common, big-eyed American faces that might have one day become pretty, or even decadently beautiful like Marilyn Monroe, but would more likely become haggard and gone to hell with booze and wrecked by violence before thirty. Their hair was fine, stringy, and dirty. Their clothing was thin faded cotton. Their underwear was tattered, grimy where they sat. They were most often barefoot, though they each had white strap sandals that hadn't been polished from one Easter to the next. Their daddy had run off with another woman, but their mother lived as if she expected him back tomorrow. She never had any boyfriend.

"But we seen Mama do it with Mister Lunsdorf," Big Sister confided.

They were all lolling on her mama's bed. There was a big picture of Jesus in a paper frame right over the bed. On the wall beside the bed there was a picture of The Last Supper, torn from a magazine and framed. There was a life-size, full-color cutout of a juicy black-haired woman in a red dress holding a bottle of hair tonic, which the girls had found in the alley and hung on the wall—a naughty barbershop madonna. Big Sister had her dress up to her armpits to let Jack play with her just-budding breasts. She had on a pair of her mother's cast-off pink rayon panties that were held up by gathering them at the hip in a knot and were laddered with a zillion runners. They made Sister's skin beneath them so silky he could have caressed her forever. She let him tickle her slit through her panties. That they were her mother's doubled the excitement and squared the pleasure for him.

"We seen her do it with Mister Lunsdorf twice," Middle Sister, who was the quiet one, reminded Big Sister dourly.

"On rent day," Big Sister explained. "Mister Lunsdorf comes in the evening right after Mama gets home from work, and Mama sends us out to play in the yard. But we kneeled down by the window and peeked through the crack in the blind, which don't look big enough to see nothin through until you get real close, and then you can see everything."

Little Sister's head wagged in agreement like some kind of nodding spastic. Her thumb, white and cold as a little corpse's, was stuffed in her sucking little mouth. *Num, num, num—yeah, yeh.* Whatever Big Sister said was aces with Little.

Mr. Lunsdorf was the landlord. He was Dutch, and Mrs. Mac said he was a Jew. He was shorter than the girls' ma, kinda fat, and sort of old. He had a new Plymouth two-door sedan. Whenever he came around, Jack ran around front to look at his car. It was the newest car he had ever seen.

Big Sister described in detail what they saw through the crack in the blind. Jack did not quite get it.

"How?" He wanted to know for certain.

He had to be sure of the way that tall thin woman with the dark brown hair actually did it. Her face was always sad, quiet. She never screamed at the girls and rarely spanked them. She always seemed so tired.

"First they did this." Big Sister dug out his little wienie. She jacked it between her thumb and forefinger and turned her head away to Jesus as if her eyes could not bear to see what her hand was doing. "Mister Lunsdorf's thing is big and fat and brown. He's got hair all over his

166

hands and tummy and back. Then he puts his fingers in Mom's thing." They tried to re-create the scene, Big Sister and Jack. "Mama's got a lot of hair on her thing, too. I asked her when I'd have some hair, and she told me soon."

If he looked real close, Jacky could see a little gold dusting of hair on Sister's thing even then. But when she spoke of her mom, he felt warm all over.

"Then she lays back like this, and you get on top of me." Big Sister lay back with her legs spread wide apart. "His thing goes right into her thing."

Little Sister nodded eager agreement around her thumb. Middle Sister studied the arrangement with a super-critical eye. "He's too little" was her considered judgment.

All Jack could do was his best.

Big Sister actually got his pickle stuffed into her thing. It was so hot in there that little way he recoiled in shock. But it had felt so electrically good he let her stuff him in again. Then she laid one arm across her eyes and began pitching around under him moaning like nothing he had ever heard before, and perhaps before his eyes she was almost transformed into her mother. He became frightened and bolted.

He looked back from the foot of the bed, his eyes wide.

"They do it for a long time. The bed gets going like this." She shook the bed back and forth until the head banged the sweating, calcimined concrete wall and Jesus danced overhead.

"Afterwards she gave us dimes for ice cream cones down at Greggs," Middle Sister added.

"Double-dippers," Little Sister said.

"Can I see?" he asked.

"Ummmm." Big Sister pondered the question. "Ummmm. I dunno. What'll you give me to let you?"

He shrugged. What did he have? He had a broken blue-eyed marble in his pocket. He proffered it to her.

"Naw." She wasn't interested in glass. "Will you play house the way I tell you forever and ever?" she bargained.

Now, he had to consider that. Big Sister liked to dress him up. And she liked a lot of love stuff, kissing, licking tongues, a lot of stuff Jack could live without, particularly when Big Sister tasted of old milk, and in spite of his curiosity about "hitting."

But, "OK." He didn't know how long it would be until rent day, when Mr. Lunsdorf came to see the sisters' mom, but he supposed he could live with the bargain that long.

To seal the deal Big Sister got her ma's wave set and a comb and pasted a big silly curl in the middle of Jacky's forehead.

"When he was good, he was berry-berry good. When he was bad, he was horrrrrrrrr—id!" she sang, leaning back to admire her artistry.

That night Jack complained to his grandma about sleeping alone. Big Sister slept with Little Sister, and Middle slept with their ma. Jack hoped to work out some kind of rotating sleeping arrangement among grandpa, grandma, and himself. He could close his eyes and see the girl's mother naked giving him a double-dipper ice cream cone and letting him somehow "hit" her, too.

Between their two rooms there was a tiny hallway about four feet square. In that hall on the far side Mac made a place to hang clothes behind a curtain. On the other side, the icebox was jammed up against a chest of drawers. The icebox was a front-loader. The boy's bed was a pallet made up atop the box and chest like an upper berth. It was snug and imaginative. He liked it. It was his private place. It was a great place when there were thunderstorms at night. No lightning would ever find him there. It was a ship, a covered wagon, a train, a tree house, a cave, a place to feed fantasy.

So, he lay there in the dark and schemed the whole thing. He wanted a brother or sister of his own, a permanent playmate, someone to sleep with like other kids.

His grandmother came in one afternoon and found him trying to roll up an old comforter to create a large doll to sleep with. When she perceived what he was about, she pitched in and helped. There is a way all grandmothers know how to roll and twist a handkerchief to form a crude puppet that is extremely useful for keeping grandchildren amused in church or at a funeral. She rolled the quilt just like a giant handkerchief doll complete with arms, legs, torso, and noggin. She bound it with cord to make it more durable.

It was a miracle! The thing was almost as tall as his grandma. It was bigger than Big Sister. It was really something to lug around. It seemed so possessed of life that Jacky found it sort of half alive. It gave him a feeling like that of placing one's palm against another's, fingers spread and extended tightly against opposing fingers, and stroking the facing fingers simultaneously with the thumb and forefinger of one's free hand. It was so real to him it made his head swim. It was his own creature. There was no sibling rivalry. That big baby was all his. He was its brains and its conscience.

That afternoon he boosted the doll up into his nook and clambered up the face of the icebox after it for his nap. In the cool basement niche he gently got between its legs like he had Big Sister and fucked hell out of it. It was the sisters' mama he was banging. His thing was going in her big hairy one like sixty. His heart was pounding until he was blind.

Every day was rent day for Jack until his grandma peeked in the nook early one morning and inquired in a hysterical screech that stopped clocks over in the bus barn, *"Jack! What do you think you are doing!"*

"Hitting my doll."

"Where'd you learn that?"

"Big Sister showed me." He told her everything. Along the way, he perceived he was not doing anyone any favor and, perhaps to take the heat off the girls, told her about Mr. Lunsdorf.

She told him never to do that again because God hated it. She said if he "hit" his doll anymore, God would send him to hell when he died. That nosey old God of his grandma's spoiled every good time he ever made up on his own.

There was no row or anything, but when he went down to the girls that evening, they could not come out and play with him. Nor could he go in, for their mother had come home from work with a sick headache.

When he went to go to bed that night, his "hitting doll" was flat as a pancake. His grandma had turned her back into a dank scratchy quilt that had been pieced out of old wool remnants. Jack knew enough not to ask why. He was wise enough to know he was skirting the edge of the biggest trouble he had been in yet. He heard his grandma telling his grandpa all about it in their bed that night.

The old man was amazed. "I wonder what gets into that boy's head," he said.

"The Devil, that's who." His grandma was adamant. God and the devil were more real to her in their heaven and hell than anything she confronted on the poor middle ground where she dwelt. They were at least as real to her as rent day. She gave God, Devil, and Landlord each their due and found the idea that the girls' quiet, industrious ma spread herself for Mr. Lunsdorf such a strain on her apprehension of reality that the real world seemed the wildest fantasy of all, while heaven and the hot place were more familiar ground.

"I'll be glad when Wilma comes home soon and can help look after him."

In his dark niche he lifted his head, his ears straining. Was she comin home? Did she say she was comin home?

"Grandma?" he called and lay rigid in the dark for a long time until she replied drily:

"What?"

"Is Mama comin home?"

"Yes. Now get to sleep."

"When?"

"In a week or so. Now get to sleep."

She was comin home.

For some reason, the next day he began biting his fingernails. He had seen Big Sister do it. She took them right down to the quick. Now he did it, too. He sometimes still ate buggers surreptitiously like Little Sister, but he was trying to kick the habit. His grandma told him it would give him worms.

When his mother came home and found him biting his nails, she painted them all with clear nail polish before she even unpacked. Everyone acted sort of funny around her because she had been in jail until she blew up and asked, "Jesus Christ! What are you lookin at? You expect your jailbird to have grown feathers?" She left the room.

"I don't want you swearing around here," her mother called piously after her.

In the other room Wilma sounded as if she had been stabbed. Jacky left the table and ran for her just in time to see her slipping on her jacket while going out the door. She did not return until late the next morning. That evening she and her mother quarreled for a long time, then they struck some kind of agreement that was a big relief for the boy because at one point his mom was threatening to move out and there was no mention of taking him.

She was different, there was no doubt. She talked differently, harder, faster. She acted tired all the time, rather angry most of the time. She got a job waiting table nights at the 400 Club and slept days. It worked out swell. His grandma and grandpa would get out of bed when his mom came home, and she would get in. They let Jacky stay up late at night on the theory he would sleep late and not bother his mother until noon at least. But as soon as his grandpa and grandma were out of the house, he would climb down from the pallet and crawl in with his mother. He was very careful not to wake her. He just lay there and looked at her sleeping.

She awoke and caught him looking at her.

"Well, hello there." She didn't sound hard at all. She sounded the way he thought she should.

She took him in her arms and pressed him against her warmth and softness and rocked him gently, crooning her sorrows and wishes.

"Why are you cryin?" he asked, fearing it was his fault.

"Because I missed you so much. Because where I was was an awful place to be. Because I wish we could have all just had a normal life together—your father, you, and me. If he had lived, it would have all been different." She said that often, but even she in her heart doubted it. "If this," "if that"—too many "if's." They were a family who might have done wonders "if. . . ." It scared the boy. He wanted to know about now.

She kissed his face and told him to stop looking like a worried little old man.

"*You're* my big man now. It's just you and me from now on."

"And Grandma and Grandpa," he hastily added. He wasn't sure he was ready for the kind of responsibility she was offering him.

She was softer and smelled nicer than anybody. She was so soft and smooth under her nightgown she made the sisters' mom seem old and ugly. He nuzzled right in there.

"Grandma says I've got the Devil in my head because I 'hit' my doll."

"You what?"

"Hit my doll." He explained, demonstrating what you did once you got between its legs by hunching her hip.

"Stop it! What do you call it?" She seemed almost as amused as she was concerned.

"Hitting."

"That's a new one on me." She snuggled him down with his cheek against her breast and told him why he must never do that again. It was what grown people did when they got married, and that was how they got babies.

A few days later he began fooling around, feeling her breasts very gently while she slept, inching up her slip to have a look at her. He touched the short hairs in her ass and she growled, slapping at his hand, "*For godsake leave me alone, will ya!* I gotta get my sleep." It was not her voice for the boy. It was her other, hard voice.

He slept with her every morning and saw her thing almost every day.

But his orange tree never produced orange one, though it grew until it got as high as his grandpa's knee.

# 18

THAT fall Jack began school at Emerson. Big Sister and Middle Sister walked him to school and back every day. He liked school and the Crayolas, really liked the big smooth building blocks with which he could construct things large enough to get inside. But he only lasted a few weeks. He went with his grandparents over to his Uncle Kenneth's for Thanksgiving dinner, and they all got quarantined with scarlet fever.

Kenneth and Elfie had a three-room shotgun kind of house on a dirt road across the river within walking distance, over the Second Street Bridge, of Mac's basement. Just over the bridge was the WPA woodyard, where Mac and his son sometimes got a day's work. It was fenced around with a cattle fence topped by three strands of barbed wire. When Jacky first heard of concentration camps later on, toward World War II, the woodyard was the model for his understanding. From the woodyard you could see the rusting mountain of junk piled in Kenny's side yard and the incredibly swaybacked, unpainted shanty in which he and his family lived. Behind it, nose to tail like two old boxcars on a siding, was an identical house in which another young couple with two kids lived. Jack never saw them except at their tightly closed wavery windows, for on their front door was a red and black placard in Frontier Gothic:

> KEEP OUT!
> SCARLET FEVER!
> > By order of The Kansas State Board
> > of Health
> > > signed (by somebody)

There was a brown paper seal like a sash pasted over the door.

His cousins and Jack gave that place a wide berth.

Kenny and a friend of his, Harry Shipley, junked. They would go around relieving people of stuff they wanted to throw away, buying out some old farmer's tool shed or barn for a few bucks. They had an old truck made from a big front-wheel-drive Willys car chassis. They dumped the crap in Kenny's yard and winnowed it for a salvageable motor, parts, a pot, a plumbing fixture, a pipe fitting, bottles, until there was only scrap metal to be sold and the growing mound of trash. Jack and his cousins, Jerry and Jimmy, got to help pick the unbroken bottles and jars out of the lot to return for deposit or resale. The heap was the greatest natural playground on earth.

There were old car bodies in which the boys could travel as far as imagination could roam. There were cans and pans and crates to set up a store, with a real burnt-out cash register on the counter. There were lots of broken toys: the bent barrel and receiver of a Daisy air rifle; wheelless, rusty little cast-iron and tin cars—midget copies of the full-size junkers all around—a toy junkyard within a junkyard; half an army of melted lead soldiers like casualties of an artillery attack—basket cases everywhere; dolls with their heads busted open, brainless, the counterbalance for their china eyes an obscene clacking little machine in their skulls, the pink fibrous flesh leached to white where it had lain in water, bloated, festering, cancerous to the touch—mutual, unspoken rejection of necrophilia by the boys. They were even reluctant to bury the bloated things, handling them with sticks. There were blue bottles with rubber stoppers for putting up secret elixirs; booze bottles for playing "uncle" and going on a toot. They would fill them full of water, drinking from them until they were reeling.

There were many things they were not supposed to find: bottles and tins of poisonous substances; old condoms like drowned monster grubs which the boys took for balloons and blew as big as beach balls, simply making Kenny's wife, Elfie, sick when she saw them from a window; and once Jack found a scorched .38 caliber revolver intact. His uncle's quick relieving him of it was a champion miscarriage of junkers' justice as far as the boy was concerned. He wouldn't stop nudging about the thing until his uncle gave him a whipping.

The cousins and Jack were certain they wanted to be junkers when they grew up.

At first everyone thought Jerry had ptomaine poisoning from the relief canned meat they had for Thanksgiving dinner. Then after a little, his grandmother knew he had the fever.

They were all quarantined. The men, though they did not get sick, were not permitted to go out and look for work. Grandmother Mac lost her job at the diner across from the Sante Fe bus barn. They had to give up their basement flat and move in with Kenny. Their stuff was stored somewhere. Wilma took a sleeping room or moved in with a girlfriend; her mother never could find exactly where she was. The commodities they were given by the relief without any special supplement because of their situation were truly minimal fare. Further, the men could not go out to get them. Harry or someone would have to get the stuff after a lot of red tape and hand it in through a window. Kenneth simply would not eat the relief food. He was too proud. There were days when dinner was a pot of beans and onions with used bacon rind in it for flavor and the illusion of meat. Breakfast and lunch the next day were the same pot of beans extended and "het" up.

The adults would sit around the table making fun of the sameness of the fare. "Umm, please pass the beans" would always get a chuckle.

Once Old Man Mac upon finishing dinner fished a toothpick from his vest pocket without thinking and absently began picking his teeth. Everyone almost fell on the floor.

"Yeow. You got to watch out for the bones, Dad," Kenny drawled.

Bawdy: "I don't think Dad ought to be allowed to smoke them cigars in the house anymore. I fear we'll explode."

Another: "When that health inspector comes back, he's going to rip that paper off the door and be blown all the way to Newton."

"Good-byyyyyyyyyyye. . . ."

Once, wanting to join in, Jacky said very solemnly, "Aunt Elfie, them's sure good beans." She jumped up from the table and ran to a corner and cried.

Sometimes there was corn bread, sometimes there was potato bread, often there was no bread at all. Just beans on a plate with sliced onions.

After Jerry, Jacky came down with the fever. Then Jimmy followed a few days later. Jerry and Jacky were bundled into the same bed. Days and nights became jumbled in a time of no season. During the night of crisis the boy's grandmother was there, and the others peered in through the fever tunnel from time to time. It was a night of near-death when, sweating under the mounds of blankets, the child instinctively fought all alone beyond the help of shanty medicine, beyond the solace of love, to live. Then the weak crawl back to full self, the solitary nut of self more truly one's own than before. At the very root, the only thing anyone can count on from someone else is concern.

"Hello there!" they say, peering in, but what they see then is not so much what they think they saw before.

A piece of ice to suck is nice.

Even after the quarantine was lifted, they were all stuck there until they could get a few dollars together. Kenny and Mac got an occasional day at the woodyard, an occasion on which everyone in earshot there and at home was informed by the old man what a rotten, no-good, ratbrained, chicken-livered, egg-sucking, weasel-mouthed, lying sonofa-bitch Roosevelt really was. He went on at such expressive length that his denunciation became a chanty accompanying the swing and split of the ax. *Swap!* Split-split. A quartered log. A hundred-dollar cussing per cord.

All over the lot men's breaths steamed from their mouths in the sunny, cold, dry air like combustion engines on the idle. From Mac the steam was like that from an engine lowering pressure.

"That old man is sure hell on Roosevelt," someone observed.

"They'll lock his crazy ass up one of these days, talking like that."

"But you listen. What he says is pretty near right, you know."

"Shit! His hollerin ain't no more than fartin in the breeze. Nothin's going to change nothin 'cept the one big union."

"Ain't goin to be no one big union. You think a white man's goin to be in some union with niggers and Chinamen and everything?"

"I meant for good folks."

The straw boss was getting red under the collar about Mac. He was a fat fink with his gut rolling over his belt, to which was hooked a beat-up holster containing an old .38 Police Positive worn in such a way that if the thing went off it would shoot off his dick. He had some kind of quasi-official badge pinned to his shirt to sponsor the gun. He was the kind of man Mac swore he would not hire to slop hogs. It was the straw boss, though, who decided who worked and who did not. He was full of his own importance as a personal representative of the New Deal to a bunch of lazy, down and out, beggary bastards who would have to toe the line in *his* woodyard, by god, if they wanted to come back.

"Listen, you!" He wheeled on MacDeramid. "You shut up that kind of talk in my yard. I ought to take you out and shoot you for talking that kind of treasonous crap. And I'm docking you fifteen minutes for malingering."

"*Shoot me! Dock me!* Why you pus-gutted cocksucker. I've known you and your goddamn brothers and goddamn folks too for over twenty years, and not a fucking one of you was worth the powder to blow you to hell. You ass-kissin sonofabitch, you're just like your old man, only worse, and for a farmer he couldn't raise cheese in the end of his dick! If any one of you fell in a pig pen, the hogs wouldn't eat you. You've never done an honest day's work in your life. And you inch your fucking fingers any nearer that goddamned pistol, you punk, and I'll split you right in two!"

The old man raised his ax over his head. The boss' right hand rested lightly on his belt a single grab from the gun. Could he get it out and fire before the old man came down with that ax? The other men nearby stopped chopping and moved aside. The cross-cut saws up in the corner stopped. The men's breaths rose straight up. The curious out-of-season chirp of a cricket in the log pile was the only sound. The men waited. It was a close thing.

Then Kenneth, coming on the run from the other end of the lot, broke the spell.

"Hey, *you!* You want to try somebody? You try *me!* Strip off that gun and badge and I'll bust your fat ass all over this lot!"

The straw boss weighed a good 200. Soaking wet, in bagging biballs, Kenny never weighed more than 135. But the boss never took off his gun or badge.

"All right," he said turning his back on both father and son. "Let's get back to work. Let's go. OK. Everybody back to work or I'll dock you all." He had to save something. He hurried away to give the cross-cut men hell.

The old man spat on the ground. "*Goddamn* such a goddamn way of doin! I ain't choppin another chop for such a fuckin system. I'll starve first! The rest of you can stay here like a bunch of chumps and take this shit, but John MacDeramid is walking off. And I ain't comin back."

"We'll lose the whole day, Dad," Kenneth reminded him. A man had to complete the day to get his dollar. If he got sick or fell over with hunger cramps, he didn't get a dime. It was that charitable aspect of relief that queered it from the word go.

"You're my son, but I won't tell you what to do. Me, I'm tellin you and that chump over there, all of you, Mister Roosevelt and the whole shittin shebang, once and *for all*—I QUIT!"

The men cheered. Someone shouted, *"You tell 'em, Mac!"*

He wiped the blade of his ax on his overalls and walked out of the barbed-wire gate. Men had to bring their own axes. Kenneth stayed and got his day. But he was never invited to get another.

Christmas came. Aunt Elfie did not want her mother-in-law to remind the boys to hang up their stockings.

"It'll be a disappointment, Mother." She was almost in tears. "There's nothing to put in them."

"Well, we'll find something. I've known hard times before, you know."

There was a little piece of Christmas tree hung with stuff cut from magazines and bits of cloth and yarn. There was a string of lights from somewhere. The boys hung up their long, tan relief stockings and went to bed hungry, all three boys in a bed.

In the morning their stockings bulged with spools strung on twine, clothespin dolls, a windfall pear each, an apple, a popcorn ball, and hard candy. Under the tree was a red coaster wagon for Jacky, a scooter for Jerry, and a little trike for Jim. That the wheels of their transportation were not mates was of little importance except in the case of Jim's trike, which because of oversize rear wheels always gave him a forward, downhill aspect.

There were beans for breakfast again Christmas morning, with a little fried side meat to honor the day. Elfie cried. Kenny slammed down his spoon and left the table.

"Where are you going, Son?" Mac asked.

"I'll be back," was all he promised.

Wilma came out in a car around noon with a man who did not get out and come in. She had color books and crayons for the boys, little gifts for the others. She could not stay. Soon the guy out in the car honked the horn. She quickly kissed everybody and trotted in her high heels out to the car. They backed out and drove away. She looked back from deep in the collar of her winter coat and waved.

"Guess she has *other* plans for Christmas dinner," her mother sniffed.

It was afternoon when Kenny came back with a big newspaper package under his arm. He looked sick.

"Here." He shoved the package at his mother and went into the front room.

She unrolled it. Two roasting-size hens tumbled out on the table. They'd had their heads wrung off. The bloody stalks of their necks hung over the edge of the table.

"Son? You didn't *take* these chickens, did you?" she asked out of an automatic, Fundamentalist sense of sin.

*"Mama!"* MacDeramid's voice cut like a sickle through the air. "Don't you say a goddamned word. You get a fire going and you cook them chickens and you smile like you're enjoying it and you eat em like they're the best you ever et and don't you open your mouth, otherwise, Christmas Day or not, I'll just rip you right to the ground."

She stood blinking at her man. "Well." She sighed at length. "I can't cook them with the feathers on."

Mac took the birds in the paper out behind the house with the boys trailing after him and plucked each one with no more than half a dozen moves of his big hand.

Kenny had a pint of bootleg whiskey. By the time the chickens were sizzling in two big iron skillets, he was pretty mellow. Mac took a drink with his son for Christmas, and they sat in the front room smoking, recalling other, better times and other hard times.

Mrs. Mac made biscuits of potato flour, and Elfie made a peppery giblet gravy.

Mrs. Mac was the first to say it at the table. "Son, this *is* good chicken." Then, because she couldn't resist it, "We ought to trade there more often."

Kenny did not eat much. He had hit the pint hard. He just sat there at the head of the table sort of grinning shyly. Jack liked him and his grandpa better than anybody.

"Well, one thing," Mrs. Mac said, staring out the window after dinner while she and Elfie did the dishes, "I'm glad we ain't had any snow this year. I just think that would of been the end if we'd of had snow."

# 19

MRS. MACDERAMID'S church found her a job caring for an old childless widower, Uncle Frank. That was his name. At least Jack never heard him called any other. Even Jack's granddad, who was as old, called him Uncle. He was a nice quiet little man like an old gray cat, who spent his summers in a rocker on the side porch and his winters curled in front of a baroque, cast-iron, potbellied ERIE coal stove. He was never any trouble. So between one winter and the next the MacDeramids took over the place and hooked up to gas.

But that first winter their tactic was simply to hang on, tough it out, while damn near freezing to death out on Uncle Frank's back porch. The joint was rented from attic to coal bin, and Uncle hadn't hired Mrs. Mac to sleep in, let alone provide room for her husband and grandson. But what could a Christian do? If it had just been her, he might have let her sleep inside, the two of them being of the same faith. Yet, when she tried to camp her family in the kitchen, Uncle insisted that would not be sanitary. Though he was no trouble, he was stubborn as hell. His all-time hero was Calvin Coolidge; Hoover was his second. There was nothing then but their mutual dislike of Roosevelt for him and Mac to talk about. When Mac began tacking flattened cardboard boxes and scrap lumber around Uncle's back porch to shelter their bed for winter, there was the look in Uncle's eyes of a citizen living in occupied territory. The old maid who lived next door, renting out her front rooms, peeked around the edge of her bedroom shade and wrote a letter to the city zoning board. The outside of Uncle's porch looked like the meanest shack in a *favela*. After the first cold rain had blistered the cardboard walls, it was a neighborhood scandal. Uncle really looked like he wanted to say something. But he just couldn't stir himself from in front of that roaring ERIE. No one had ever tended Uncle's fire so well as Mac and Jacky did that winter.

From the attic down, there were the Colemans—the doughboy who had been gassed in World War I, his wife, and their children, Wolford and Gladys; in the parlor was McCoy; the other two front rooms adjacent to the bathroom were Uncle's; and there was Curry on a cot in the unfinished basement down there with the coal. There was also the middle room with the space heater, a black leather settee where Uncle Frank took his naps under a gray and black afghan, a Zenith radio, and some chairs. Off that room was the big kitchen where the MacDeramids took their meals, after Uncle ate, at a large round oak table the pedestal of which rested on big glass balls clutched in talons as large as a woman's hand.

Uncle loved the way Mrs. Mac did his shirts. He seemed a little less anxious. She made a dollar or two a week taking in laundry. Her machine had been put together by her son, Kenneth, from parts cannibalized from other machines he picked up junking. It quaked like something trying to get off the ground and occasionally blew every fuse in the house and ate off everyone's buttons, but it was a Maytag at heart and ever owned a special place among machines in Mrs. Mac's own.

To the bed he set up out on the porch, Mac made a side extension from a narrow bench padded with quilts so the old man, his wife, and the boy all slept together under the same covers to share body heat. The boy's grandmother did her best to keep him covered all night the whole long winter through, yet he was awakened at the end of every hour when body heat had dwindled to only the thin, narrow puddle in which he actually lay. The cold sniffing around the bed, seeping up from below, was so strong there were nights when the boy truly slept not at all but only dozed. His grandmother clamped his limbs between her own to warm them, and his back froze. Their breaths iced the cardboard walls. He huddled there in that cold bed trying to conserve the thin strip of warmth directly under his body, his legs aching from immobility, dozing and waking and grumbling through the night. Daily his granddad cursed time and circumstance, seemingly on the edge of some desperate act. His grandmother grimly endured. And the boy prayed for Uncle Frank to die or something so they could move inside by the fire. He would keep that old ERIE red hot! He'd see that stove's bottom turn cherry! If he ran out of coal, he would stoke it with Curry. There was no guarantee Uncle's passing would result in such benefice; it was merely, without hearing of any superior grandparental plan, the boy's total hope.

Mrs. Mac got $3.50 a week from Uncle Frank and had the couple of bucks she got for the washing and ironing. The relief gave commodities. The WPA had a day's work for the old man every now and then. He did repairs around the place, hauled Uncle's coal in and his ashes out. He planned a backyard garden for spring and spent a lot of time trying to convince Uncle to let him raise a few chickens out off the alley. Most of the time, though, Mac spent his days playing pitch in McCoy's parlor with McCoy, Curry, and Coleman. Coleman got a pension for being gassed and never had to go to work. His wife was someone's housekeeper, his son was a Western Union boy after school, and Gladys clerked in a drug store. The boy wished his granddad had gone to the war and been gassed, too, if that was the kind of deal you got.

In summer, when it wasn't so easy to get up a game, Mac would walk down Third Street toward the City Produce Market to the Wichita Ice House, where he would spend the day letting the icemen know what was *really* wrong with the world. In summer the ice house was the best place to loaf there was. Jacky often went along with the old man, to loll there on the cool damp sawdust sucking on a long crystal of Wichita ice, content to let time bleed off the pointy end of that crystal drop by icy drop.

He was personally acquainted with the icemen, knew their horses' names, and could always hook a ride around the neighborhood on their wagons. Jack could tell less knowledgeable kids how they made ice and stacked it up in tiers of 200-pound blocks with sawdust between to keep the tiers from freezing together in a monster iceberg right in the heart of Kansas. The blocks were scored so the icemen could chip them up with their picks into the 10-, 15-, and 25-pound chunks the ordinary icebox owner bought. And they had a block of ice there that had a brindle pussycat frozen in it. The cat had fallen into the block in the freezing room when it was slush and had frozen as if caught in an eternal leap. Its mouth and eyes were wide open, its claws extended. They had kept the block there for several years.

Across the street from Uncle Frank's house was Azuni's Grocery, a white frame one-room store tacked on the front of a four-room house.

Mr. Azuni came from Lebanon and thought for two years that "Yes, We Have No Bananas" was the U.S. national anthem, for that was what the band was playing when he climbed off the boat. It was still his favorite song. It was the only one he hummed absently while sprucing up the lettuce or fluffing up the goose liver. He accepted food stamps from the relief when it was decided that direct distribution of commodities was unwieldy, but he was never totally convinced they were as good as gold. That money was even more wieldy than stamps evidently was never a consideration of the people in charge of relief. When someone outside the system was struck by such a revelation, the government patiently explained how they wouldn't be able to keep relievers from spending their dole on beer, tobacco, candy, and such frivolities if they used real money like real people. For Azuni's part, he would sell you anything in the store. He did not sell beer. He let everyone run a bill. At Kroger's and the Safeway, relievers were restricted to staples. They could buy oleo but not butter, cheese but not bacon—like that. No cakes, pies, or ice cream, no tobacco, beer, or pop, no candy. Azuni had special pads for everyone who ran a bill. The pads fit into an oblong Kraft cheese box which he kept under the counter.

Mrs. Azuni was a large sensual woman a head taller than Mister. She had the build and bearing of a mature belly dancer (the kind they keep at home for themselves) or an exportable lady politician from India. She had a large majestic nose, a plethora of blue-black hair, breasts like harem pillows, and blue feet. The latter was from soaking her feet in medicine that left them stained to the ankles. She had athlete's foot so badly it hurt her to walk. When she wasn't soaking her feet, she wore white cotton athletic socks and sandals.

Jacky gave her oldest son, George, who was a couple of years older than he, a lead Marine he demanded to let Jacky see some evening when she soaked her feet in a pan of that blue stuff. He hadn't *actually* seen that her feet were blue. He had it only on the say-so of her children. From flat on the floor in the doorway, pretending to be engrossed in a comic book, he saw her strip off those socks, and her feet *were* blue. She dipped her feet carefully into a big pan of the medicine and sighed deliciously, hiking up her hem to keep from staining her skirt. She read a Lebanese tabloid while she soaked. When she was done, she took each foot out and dried it in her lap in a big Turkish towel. He got a peek of her strong brown thighs and the thick black wool between. And wished George, Ted, and their sister, Jeanette, who was playing with paper dolls of the Dionne quints nearby would all fall through the floor so Mrs. A and he could be alone. She looked up and caught him looking and shoved her skirt quickly down between her legs. When the Azuni kids swapped sexual knowledge with Jacky, they withstood every blandishment, all threats, and swore to the end they had never seen their ma naked. Since Jacky had given them a description of his own mother and grandmother and thrown in a couple of aunts, cousins, and a lady his grandmother sometimes cleaned house for, he felt cheated by their own lack of perception, or figured more than likely they were collectively lying in their Lebanese teeth. At any rate he was happy to see Mrs. A had a nice big black one. If her own kids couldn't see it, they simply weren't looking. When he appraised them of what their mother had between her legs, they claimed *he* was lying. They looked at him as if he bore some mark on his head visible only to them.

Ted, who looked most like her, also had foot trouble. He was about Jack's age. He had to wear ugly, specially made corrective shoes, brown high-tops with steel braces inside the ankles. He had to wear them even in the hot summertime. It would make Jacky really hurt to watch him play ball or cowboy in those things.

There was nothing wrong with their sister Jeanette's feet. She could outrun either of her brothers, though there seemed no necessity she would ever have to do so. She was a skinny right fielder and no great beauty. With her black hair parted in the center as if with one of her dad's meat cleavers and warped into loopy braids over each outstanding ear, she was always a more believable Indian than she was Ken Maynard's girlfriend when they played guns. With a glazed little oilcloth glove that had absolutely no pocket at all, she was one of the all-time really bad right fielders. She never actually *caught* a ball in that little mitt of hers in three All-Star American League seasons behind the billboard on the corner of Cleveland and Second.

It was all related somehow in Jack's mind to the white goat's cheese they ate spread on unsalted bread almost every day for lunch. The stuff was wonderful. But they did not sell either the cheese or the bread in the store. Though their mother did not approve, they would trade Jacky a piece for a peanut butter and jelly sandwich. He got the idea the stuff had some kind of religious significance and was no little concerned it might change his faith, slight though it was.

The Azunis' success was due, according to Mrs. Mac, to "a natural head for business . . . like they all do." In her fundamental Protestant faith she was on uncertain ground if called upon to differentiate between an Arab and a Jew. In *her* Sunday school paper, God was blond, with china-blue eyes. If the Azunis hadn't killed Christ, they were at least somehow implicated in her mind.

"But they were *more* than fair to us," she always went to pains to insist.

They also had a couple of relatives in the wholesale grocery business. The Azunis were the first family on the block who bought a new car. It was a black Ford two-door sedan which Mr. Azuni operated using only second and reverse gears. Watching him start up and get under way was more fun than the Marx Brothers. He would tentatively let the clutch out, and that Ford would leapfrog forward in a series of neck-snapping bounds—*ruh!-ruh!-ruh!-ruh!*—like a camel with the hiccups for half a block until Mr. A finally got the clutch out to stay. His wife, with her hat on to go to town, would sit rigidly, grimly, staring straight ahead, trying to maintain hatted dignity. Mrs. Mac asked her son, Kenneth, to go over and show Mr. A how to use first and high. But Kenny, once seeing the performance, was so amazed and charmed he would not be a part of loosing Azuni on the world beyond that which he could take in second.

He never did find the other two holes. *Ruh!-ruh!-ruh!*

"*Heigh yo, Silver!*" The kids would yell tearing along the curb as he lurched down the street.

When fall came, it was time for the boy to take another shot at school. This time, for some reason, he did not want to go. He threw a tantrum on the steps, sat down, and refused to enter the building. Other kids were towed away from him by their mothers for fear his disaffection might be contagious. Ultimately his grandmother had to drag him kicking and screaming, with all pride blown, into Kindergarten 101. If the room had been on the second floor, she would have never made it. His rubber heels left a wavering double track on the waxed first-day-of-school floor.

Bereft of pride, angry and terrified, he did not want the other children to see him. Seeing him, he did not want them to suppose he was going to surrender. The teacher was a lavender horror. She had a pokey nose, one of those long lavender horns of strange subtle turns with a dimple on the very end, and she was always poking it into someone's business.

"*I don't want to stay!*" he yelled.

"You gotta go to school," his grandmother insisted.

"I don't give a fuck!" he maintained.

"Stop-that-kind-of-talk-right-now!" She raised her hand threateningly. She apologized to the teacher. "I can't understand it. He couldn't *wait* for school to begin. That's all he's talked about all week. He *wanted* to go." She had the boy pinned between her knees and the teacher's desk.

"Oh, I'm sure he'll be fine when he learns we won't bite him," the teacher soothed.

That's what *she* thought.

When his grandma cut out, Old Pokey Nose told the boy to sit on a little chair and be quiet.

He bawled, *"I want my grandma!"* He complained, "I don't want your goddamn school. I don't *want* to go to no school!"

She said he did not have to do anything but sit there and be quiet. She said everyone else was going to have graham crackers and milk pretty soon, and if he didn't shut up, he would not get any.

He wasn't about to shut up.

"Then you must go out in the hall and sit beside the door until you decide you can be quiet. The rest of us are going to have our graham crackers and milk."

Up your ole graham cracker ass, was his feeling.

"Out."

Gone! He made it home before noon. His grandmother hauled him back after lunch. He was worn out. He was tear-empty, emotionally exhausted. He sat on the little chair and kept his mouth shut and his eyes on his shoes. Neither paints nor crayons nor construction paper in every color you can name could bribe him to look up. No tiny voice tentative with friendship could cajole forth his name. Everyone else ran about with their names pinned on their shirts and dresses all day.

"Bet you can't write your name on this card for me, can you?" The teacher offered crayons and construction paper.

She would have lost, but he wasn't falling for something like *that*.

Some little prick with KEITH scrawled six inches high on the sign around his impertinent neck brayed snottily, "He can't write his name. *He* wears relief clothes."

*He'll break your little neck if you don't button your lip,* the boy thought. Because he had missed the first year with scarlet fever, he was older than most of the others.

The next day, because his grandmother had a washing to do, he was sent to school rather than taken. He had certainly learned the way, having fought for every inch of it relinquished to old struggling and shoving grandma. But he never made it.

Between the house and the school was Matthewson's Pasture: four square blocks of weeds, buffalo grass, and scars where carnivals, the circus, and tent revivals had set up and spread sawdust. His new school, Washington, occupied the most eastern block between Third Street and Central Avenue, with Hydraulic for its eastern shore. It was actually a fine school of red brick with white limestone cornices, a beautiful broad lawn out front, and a great playground behind that had swings, two slides, three chinning bars, a merry-go-round, giant strides, tether-ball poles, and room for two baseball games, a soccer match, folk dancing, and girl's relays to go full tilt at the same time. No one was permitted to leave the playground to go into the adjacent pasture or cross Hydraulic or Central. If a ball went over the fence, a designated monitor had to be found to chase it.

From nine o'clock, when he was supposed to be in school, until three thirty, when it let out, he lived in the weeds across the street in Matthewson's Pasture.

To an adult eye the pasture appeared a flat weedy meadow overgrown with milkweed and stinking ferns bordered by elm, oak, elder, silvery cottonwood, hedge apple, and clattering, poisonous castor bean. To a kid the place was a snaky jungle where rabbits still staked out their tribal patches, a sanctuary for stray dogs and cats. Bums and winos sometimes wandered up from the freight tracks or down from East Douglass to burrow out nests in the weeds. The islands of sawdust, whether from carnival, circus, or revival, were treasure troves. On a soggy sawdust beach on the shores of a fetid mudhole Jack found three four bitses, eight dimes, five nickels, and a seemingly limitless mine of pennies. Nearby he found a family of broken kewpie dolls, a slum circus whip minus the snapper, a lot of stuff like that.

In a depression in the ground where the tallest weeds grew he crawled himself out a room with a front and back passage and laid a cardboard floor. He brought cans and toys, paper, pencil, crayons, and weathered old magazines to the place. Under the floor he dug a hole where he could stash his stuff when it was time to go home.

When the kids across the street played on the school apparatus, he hid in the place and spied on them. When they had graham crackers and milk in the kindergarten room to which he had been assigned, he would have a Hershey and Orange Crush he had bought with money from his cache of coins. He kept the money buried in a special place in a Prince Albert tobacco can. When the kids across the way read, he perused the water-wrinkled old magazines he had gathered from the vacant lot and a Mother Goose book he had brought from home. He started a tinfoil ball of wrappers stripped from the inner wrappers of cigarette packs rescued from gutters. There was an old wildcat who often dropped by to see what he was up to. He also kept a garter snake in a Mason jar and some dead butterflies in a cigar box with some pretty stones, a chaw of wax, and fourteen different bottle caps. He was never bored. The only thing he really regretted was not being able to swing on all that schoolyard apparatus.

Then one lunch recess the temptation overcame good sense. He slipped out of the weeds and streaked across the street and got in line behind the smallest slippery slide. One of the girls from his class saw him. She was a pretty little white blonde with a Dutch-boy bob, whose name was Dolly Mae Sawyer.

"You been sick?" she inquired.

He ignored her.

"Don't you hear well?" she shouted.

He scrunched down a little in line. He hoped she would go away before she attracted attention.

"OK, stuckup, see if I care!" She flounced away. He saw her whisper to another girl—a pretty, dark-haired girl—who looked right at him. But they did not move to go tell anyone on him.

He came off the end of the slide right behind a kid named Bobby Walters, who turned and said, "Hey, you back now?"

He nodded affirmatively.

"You want to try the swings?"

He nodded again.

There was only one swing open. He let Jacky go first. When it was apparent that he did not know how to pump, the boy asked, "You want a push?"

Jacky nodded that he did.

He really got him going high. He was a hell of a nice guy.

He told Jacky on the way to the merry-go-round, "We made a train while you were gone. I'm the engineer for the whole week. It's big enough to get in and everything. Want to see it?"

"OK."

He led him over to a ground-level window. Jack cupped his hands around his eyes to see inside. It was his room. Only there were a lot of pictures the kids had made of trains and stuff tacked around the blackboards. And there along one wall and curving around the back of the room was a train made out of the big maple building blocks that he had seen stored in a big cabinet all along under the windows. There was an engine, a parlor car, and a caboose. God! It was a wonderful thing. The whole class could ride.

"I got a real engineer's hat to wear and a bandanna and a big oil can. But there ain't no oil in it. The conductor has a real conductor's hat, and Missus Parker lets him use her thing to punch tickets. And there's a switchman. We all take turns being something."

"Could I be something sometime?" Jack asked.

"Sure. Everybody gets to. And when you're something, you get a hat."

The bell rang. Everyone started running toward the school.

"Come on. We'll be late," the boy said.

Jack hung back.

"What's the matter?"

Jack shook his head.

Bobby was puzzled. Everyone was going around the corner. "I gotta go now."

Then Jacky was alone in the playground. The swing chains jangled in the breeze. In the silence the echo of the children seemed to rattle the apparatus. He tried the merry-go-round, the giant strides. The empty giant stride handles and chains banged the pole loudly. It wasn't much fun. From the top of the tallest slide, which was for fourth- and fifth- and sixth-graders only, he looked up at the building and saw a woman looking out of a second-floor window right at him.

*It was Mrs. Roosevelt!*

He shot down that slide and cut out. Zoom! He hit the gravel running and did not look back until he was deep into the weeds. She was gone from the window.

But it wasn't ten minutes until the custodian in overalls with a lot of keys on a leather belt came out of the basement door and walked right toward where the boy hid. He crossed the street and walked all along the gutter scanning the weeds for the boy. Once he seemed to look right at him without seeing him. After awhile he went back.

Jack always waited until he saw school let out before he headed for home.

That evening when he got there, his grandma asked him, "Well, what did you do in school today?"

"I have a friend. He pushed me on the swing. He's the engineer on the train."

"That's nice," she said, stirring something in a big bowl held in the crook of her left arm.

He told her all about the train; about how everyone got to take turns being things on it. "I'm the conductor. I get to wear a real conductor's hat. And the teacher lets me use her thing to punch tickets."

"That's nice."

He told her about all of the many activities at school. He told her about all the apparatus. He told her more than she ever wanted to know.

"My land!" she said finally. "You are certainly wound up this evening."

Monday he could hardly wait for recess, when he could slip over and play with his friend again.

He and Bobby were going around on the merry-go-round when he looked up and saw Mrs. Roosevelt in that window again. He panicked. She was looking at him. He scraped both knees getting off that thing on the fly. He looked up scrambling to his feet, and she was still there. The sound all around him was swimming. He felt sick.

"Hey! What's the matter?" Bobby asked.

It seemed like it took Jack forever to get his feet working.

Dolly Mae said, "He sure looks funny. Like he's about to throw up."

He began to run.

"Hey! Come back!" Bobby tried to stop the merry-go-round and follow him. His foot scraped the gravel.

Then the custodian came huffing out of the boiler room and was pumping after Jack. Bobby stopped on the curb at the boundary of the playground. Jacky plunged into the weeds. The custodian crashed in after him. The weeds were almost as high as the boy's head but nothing to the custodian. He made it to his place and flopped into it on his belly. But gasping for breath, he realized the man was right on top of him. He made another break for it. The man arrested him with a quick snatch at his biball suspenders. He was running in thin air.

"All right, sonny! All right! Just hold on, there. You're comin with me to see Miss Rebsteen. No use you kickin like that. No one's going to hurt you. Just be glad it wasn't old Dan Carrier the truant officer that caught you. Hold on there!"

He struggled to get away. The custodian improved his grip on the boy's arm and neck. His grip was too strong. Those pincers on Jack's neck took the pep out of him real quick. He howled and cursed at him.

"Sonofabitch!" he screamed at him. "Bastard!" The man high-stepped him through the weeds.

"Shut your filthy mouth!" he commanded and shook the boy by the neck.

"Fuck you!" he cried. "Fuck you!"

He dragged Jacky back across the street and hauled him into the building and up to the second floor, depositing him in the office at the end of the hall as if he were a cur.

"He's a wildcat," he informed the lady behind the desk. "Ought to be in reform school. He has some dirty mouth on him. Stand up there!" He yanked the boy onto his feet. "Been layin out there in Matthewson's Pasture like a cat. Got him a regular warren out there."

"Is that so?" She seemed interested but not angry or anything.

He peeked up and saw her leaning over her desk to get a better look at him. She wasn't Mrs. Roosevelt, after all, but she looked just like her —buck teeth, hairnet, flowered crepe dress over a big girdle, an old brooch, handkerchief tucked in her sleeve, everything.

"Have you had your lunch?" She smiled. "I'll bet you haven't." She didn't even wait for an answer. "Mr. Whiteside, see if there aren't some graham crackers and milk in the cafeteria for this little maverick."

The custodian left.

"You can sit if you like." She waved at a big wooden office chair with arms and sat back in the one behind her desk. The boy did not move.

"As you wish," she said, leafing through a little box of cards on her desk. "What is your name?"

*Puddin Tame. Ask me again and I'll tell you the same.* He didn't say a thing.

"No name? Maybe you really are a little maverick. Do you know what a maverick is?"

Let her find out for herself, was his thinking.

"Well," she began pleasantly, "a maverick is a little wild horse that runs free over the plains and lives in canyons and maybe he is very happy. But then maybe he isn't. For he never learns how to do anything except run and kick up his heels. He never gets a name and he never has a warm place to sleep in the winter."

"We near froze last winter," he blurted. "We had to sleep on the porch."

"That's really too bad. Don't you have a house?"

He shook his head that they did not. "We live with Uncle Frank on his back porch."

"But you *do* have a name, don't you?"

"Yeow."

"What is it?"

"Jacky."

"That's a nice name. Do you have any other names?"

"Sure. Jack Odd Andersen."

"Why, those are all very fine names. My name is Miss Rebsteen. So we both have names. So you really aren't a maverick, after all. Good. Well, perhaps somewhat a maverick." She reconsidered.

All the while she had been going through another of those card files on her desk. She pulled out a manila card with a tiny red tab on it. There were cards with tabs of blue and yellow, also. He knew the one she pulled with the red tab was his own. She laid it carefully on her blotter in front of her.

The custodian arrived with a plate of graham crackers and half a pint of cold milk and a straw. He set the stuff in front of Miss Rebsteen. She thanked him. He gave the boy a dirty look and left. She prized the foil cap off the bottle and shoved in the straw and offered it to him. She took a graham cracker from the plate and set it on the edge of her desk nearest him. With a gesture she invited him to eat.

"Why don't you have a bite while I study this a moment?" She meant the card. She nibbled her cracker while looking at it.

"Does your grandmother work, or is she at home?"

"She's at home." Her knowledge that he had a grandmother so took him by surprise he had answered in spite of himself. It was all the fault of that damn card there. After that finking thing there seemed no reason not to try the crackers and milk. He edged up on them.

"I like graham crackers and milk, don't you?" the woman said, still poring over the card. She turned it over. "I like them best just before bed. But I like them any old time, too."

He lifted one and tentatively nicked off just a corner. It was hard to swallow. His throat felt swollen. He felt like crying and did not know why. She made a note on the tablet. He washed down half the cracker with a pull at the milk. It was delicious! He hated the milk he got at home. It was made from a powder the relief gave out. It always tasted burnt. This milk was cold and sweet, with no little curds or anything floating in it. It took the swelling out of his throat instantly.

"Well! Do you have a nice place to hide across the street?"

He shrugged that it was OK.

"How long have you played there?"

He shrugged, sucking on the milk.

"Do you go there every day?"

He nodded that he did.

"Does your grandmother know?"

He lied, nodding his head that she did.

"Oh? And she doesn't care?"

"Naw."

"I'll bet if she really knew you were not coming to our nice school, she would be very sad. She wants you to come to school. There are so many nice children who would just love to get to know you."

"No, they wouldn't."

"They would, too! Why, I saw you playing with a very nice boy in the yard, and you were both having the best time. Wasn't he a nice boy?"

"Yeow," he admitted cautiously.

"Didn't you like him?"

He nodded that he liked him very much.

"Well, you will find there are a lot of little boys here just as nice who would be very happy to be your friends."

"The teacher don't like me."

"Oh! And what makes you think that?"

"The way she looks like I stink up her nose."

"Oh, I'm sure you are mistaken. I know if you got to know Miss Parker, you would see she likes you very much. You really didn't give her much of a chance, did you?"

Maybe. He wasn't committing himself.

"I see here you went to Emerson for nine weeks before here. They say you are a very intelligent, happy, and eager little fellow. Is that correct?"

He simply did not know. He could not answer.

"How about showing me your place in Matthewson's Pasture?"

Her request took him by surprise. She seemed truly interested.

"Will you take me over and show me?" She came around the desk with her hand out for him to take.

Just then another teacher from a room nearby came as if she had been summoned. He took Miss Rebsteen's hand.

"Miss Wells, please watch the office for a minute. My friend Jacky here is going to show me something."

Miss Wells smiled at the boy. She was plump, dark, younger than Miss Rebsteen. But they were out of the same mold. Their dresses were almost identical. He liked Miss Wells right away. If she were his teacher. . . .

He confided the thought to Miss Rebsteen when they were in the hall that if Miss Wells were his teacher, he would come to school like a shot.

"When you are in Two-A, if you are a good boy, Miss Wells *will* be your teacher."

Miss Rebsteen's hand was large and very smooth and soft, with nails painted as red as his mother's. He liked holding her hand. She didn't seem so old when he held her hand. Their hands were getting sweaty, but he hung on.

The custodian met them at the front door. Miss Rebsteen let the boy lead her by the hand to his place. The custodian grumbled along behind. She stood outside the small area he had cleared in the weeds, respecting its boundaries. He showed her his menagerie in the jars and cans, the cigar box, his book, the moldy magazines, his toys. Her hands made small motions toward the objects as he presented them without ever actually touching them. The things were pretty rank from the damp, smelled like stuff from an old damp cellar . . . still, he was very aware of her hands. He had bottles there to return for the deposit. He dug up his Prince Albert can and showed her his bank. She took custody of his savings, tying the coins in the corner of a handkerchief so he would see they were safe. He could tell she only half believed that he had found the money in the lot.

They went back up the crawlway to the place near the street where he lay to observe the school and the playground. Then she seemed to understand what he had been about and touched his head tenderly.

"He had his own school here," she explained to the man. "And not a half bad one it was, either."

But immediately he sensed something was queer in the sudden rush of tenderness that filled his chest. He looked up at her eyes and he was ashamed, though he could not tell anyone why. It wasn't going to be that easy. It wasn't going to be easy at all. He regretted that he had shown her his place. He was conscious and ashamed of the crumby relief biballs and shirt that clothed him, the goddamned run-over, cheap, tire-soled shoes the relief had given him. Yet it was more than clothes and hiding out that he was ashamed of.

"He's been hiding out here every day for two weeks," she told the custodian as if the boy hadn't ears. "Playing at school. Doesn't it just break your heart?"

It was in their eyes when they looked at him that he learned of his strangeness; in their pity he knew the tragedy that he was not more like them. Then he truly *felt* like a maverick for the first time.

"Kids!" the custodian growled. "Who knows what kids'll think of next to drive you bats?"

*Fuckem!* was how he suddenly felt. *Fuckem both!* Probably he was fucking old lady Rebsteen all the time. *Damn them.*

His grandmother had changed her dress and put on a hat to come see Miss Rebsteen, but her hands still looked boiled and drowned and her knuckles raw from the washing she had been doing when summoned.

"You'll just have to excuse my appearance." She giggled nervously, poking wisps of damp hair under her hat. "You caught me in the middle of a wash."

"I understand entirely." Miss Rebsteen sympathized. "We *do* seem to have a problem here. Jack doesn't think he likes our school."

"I just don't know what gets into that boy." She sighed. "We've had to move around a lot since he was born. Maybe that has something to do with it. But we try to do our best by him. Lord knows we've been up against it lately. But then so's most folks, ain't they?"

"I think the strangeness of a new environment certainly has a lot to do with it, of course. At Emerson, for the brief time he was there, he did exceptionally well."

"Well, maybe that was because his mother was home with us then. We had our own place. Now we live with this old gentleman brother of my church. The boy don't see his mama very often. She works nights and has to sleep days. She has her own room. . . ."

They blabbed on like that for awhile.

Then: "Well, young man, can we trust you to come to school in the future?" Miss Rebsteen asked.

"Oh, he'll come all right. Or I'll know the reason why," his grandma assured her.

Outside she pulled Jack's ear. "Now you listen here, young man. When we send you to school, we expect you to go there and nowhere else. You savvy? You know what happens to kids who play hooky? The truant officer comes and gets them and takes them to reform school."

They wore striped suits and balls and chains there, Jack just knew.

"So the very next time you gyp school, Dan Carrier's going to come get you."

That was the truant officer's name—Dan Carrier. Jack never saw him in his life, nor actually knew of anyone who had. But he was the one who came and took you to reform school. And his name was Dan Carrier. He had been the truant officer when Jack's mother and father were in school.

"They were making fun of my clothes," he protested.

"Who?"

"This kid. He sits on a chair funny with his butt sticking out. He's got *posture,* the teacher says. He does."

"Does what?"

"Makes fun!"

"What did he say?"

"He told everybody we was on relief cause I wore relief clothes."

"Well, we *are* on relief."

"I don't care. I don't like him making fun."

"Listen. When you left for school every morning you were clean, ironed, hair combed, and neck scrubbed. Now that's *all* in the world a person can expect. If that boy makes fun, it just shows his ignorance. You just ignore him. You don't ever have to take a back seat to no one when it comes to clean. There ain't a boy in that school no cleaner or starchier than you. We've always been clean. We can't help it if we're poor."

It was true. When Jacky put on clean overalls, they were starched so stiff the legs were stuck shut. It was fun to tear them open with his stocking feet, shoving them through the tubes, hearing them zip. When he walked, they crackled at the knees and went *woop-woop, woop-woop.* Yet they still came from the relief. Cut, cloth, and tailoring, they were as distinct from real clothes as margarine from butter. His plight was as publicly obvious as that of a prisoner of war.

Keith Dotson was the little wretch's name, a sissyboy who'd never taken that initial real shot in the kisser to know what he was. He sat *so* straight in his chair. No girl in the class had a posture so eagerly upright as Keith's. He had a fragile, exquisite nose and a supercilious lip. He always knew all the answers. Old Pokey Nose thought he was the real goods. But then she was a young spinster who took great offense at naptime when Jack pitched his rug where he could get a peep up her dress while she sat on one of the little chairs to read them some sleepy tale. For seven years she had been going with a CPA who wore a whole suit and drove a *Plymouth* coupe! She wore drawers and rolled her stockings on garters. Between biting stocking roll and peach trimless drawers you could see a span of plump frog-belly flesh.

"Dirty-little-boy!" she scolded Jacky, completely overlooking all of his grandma's scrubbing, starching, and ironing. From what Jack had seen in his lifetime, she hardly had any right to yell at all.

The worst thing was, Keith did the same thing. Only cagier, from a distance, more soulfully, without as great expectations. He was a kid who had his own room at home. Or perhaps it was just that his lashes were so long and full Miss Parker could not see his eyes.

At any rate, that afternoon when she let Jack out of the corner, he began negotiating with Keith to let him relieve him of his duties that day as conductor on the class train—so he could get the feel of it toward the time it was his turn.

Nothing doin! A rule was a rule to Keith. Impersonal authority being the mother of fascism, cowardice being the father, Keith was a potential Deputy Secretary of Defense.

"When I get to be conductor, I'll give *you* a chance," Jack haggled.

"Just for a little." He reached for Keith's cap. Keith was a railroad conductor like someone's kid sister was Bob Feller. Worse, he was mean. A little bully.

*"Miss Parker!"* he screamed. *"He's trying to take my hat!"* The only guy in the world who never dropped an i-n-g ending in his life.

Jack hit him. He plowed him. He smashed him. Keith screamed like a stuck pig. He bled like a boil. It was all over his nice stripedy polo shirt from Penney's. It was on his shorts and on his kneesies. Jack had never drawn blood in anger before. It was a heady moment. Keith screamed like a girl. He flipped his hands as if they were on fire but never raised them in defense of himself. Jacky hit him some more for all the hatred and terror in his eyes. He stumbled backward into the class engine, dislodging much of the boiler of old No. 101.

Miss Parker threw Jack away from the other boy and clapped her bare hand over Keith's lip to stanch the flow of blood from his nose.

The eyes of Jack's pal Bobby were interestedly noncritical, while Dolly Mae Sawyer's baby Dutch kisser just glowed. In that moment she became Jack's very first true "girl," his initial valentine love.

"You go straight to Miss Rebsteen's office and wait for me there!" Miss Pokey Nose commanded Jack with a tissue now firmly clamped on Keith's gushing horn to rush him to First Aid.

Not today! If he was going to reform school, he was going in a blaze of glory.

He picked up a three-foot length of sanded maple four-by-four from the wrecked engine and stove in the cab and tender. He laid waste the chair car. A spavined-looking relief child named Ferrer who wasn't ever about to be elected class president, either, grabbed a block in each hand and blitzed the caboose. Rose Marie Reid and her silent sister, Anna, who were always teased because they wore panties made from flour sacks, took a couple of ladylike shots at the train. And they were two kids who never volunteered to do anything, never spoke unless spoken to. Then others, the half-dozen or so relief kids in the class, stepped up to attack the train. Kids not on relief pitched in until the train was reduced to a rubble of blocks forever. That train would never rise again.

"We shouldn't of done it," Bobby said seriously after it was too late.

"I know," Jack told him. "I *know!*"

He walked out of the room, out of school, and went to hide again in the weeds across the street. No one came after him. He lay out there until school was out.

When Dolly Mae came out, she paralleled the pasture for a block before turning west on Central for two blocks where she lived with a lot of brothers and sisters in a big rickety house behind a Lucky Strike billboard on the corner. You could climb out any of the upstairs windows onto the framework behind the billboard and climb down to the ground or up to the top to look over. It was a great place to play, a castle, a perfect full-rigged pirate ship, that billboard.

"I love you; do you love me?" Jacky put it to her, popping out of the weeds.

"Yes!" she blurted, her face wide open with fright.

So he walked her all the way home. They said good-bye on her porch with lingering looks as full of love as greater knowledge and wider experience would ever sponsor.

His grandmother met Jack at the front door, shushed him, and sent him around back. He thought he had really bought it this time. There were a lot of grown-ups in the living room. There were two strange cars in the driveway. He steeled himself for the razor strop, for Dan Carrier, for reform school, the rock pile, a lifetime behind bars. He just knew they had oatmeal there every morning. He teetered on the brink of making a run for it, out through the alley and away forever. His grandma snatched him inside.

She whispered, "Uncle Frank passed away this afternoon."

Sure as hell! There he was in the parlor under the black and gray lap robe he always put over him when he napped on his leather settee. The people were from her and Uncle's church. Some of the ladies sniffed in little balled handkerchiefs. The old maid Willhite sisters from down the block were there with Brother Dykes, the preacher.

"He just lay down and went to sleep," Mrs. Mac recited in funereal tones to everyone who crept in for a last look.

"He had his lunch, said he felt tired today, and just lay down like always and slipped away peacefully in his sleep. When I tried to rouse him to take his medicine, I saw he was gone."

"Well, when you got to go, that's the way to go," some deacon said.

"He passed so peacefully."

"I understand he left this house and all to the church."

"He was never married, you know."

"Surely the Lord eased his way."

"Calling home his own."

"Praise the Lord."

"In his name."

"Amen."

*Hurrah!* was how Jack felt.

He went out onto the back porch.

Presently his grandmother appeared at the screen door. "What on earth are you doing?" she asked.

"Now we can move in off this old porch, can't we?" he said in explanation of all the stuff he was pulling out from under the makeshift bed.

She stepped out and knelt beside him. Cutting a look over her shoulder, she whispered, "Wait until the people are gone."

# 20

ONE of the first things MacDeramid did after Uncle Frank died, and the church to whom the place was deeded said he could stay on and manage it, was tear out the old potbellied coal stove and hook up to gas. He picked up an open-faced gas heater at auction and put it in the sitting room. The boy was branded at least once a winter for the four winters they were there on its metal grill, scorched the cat on it so badly the house had to be aired, cinderized countless marshmallows over its red-hot brimstones, and became almost asphyxiated snuggling up to it to stare rapt at the heat playing on the cherry fleece of the asbestos flocking of the reflector.

In the summer the old man disconnected the heater and capped the gas pipe for fear the thing would be turned on accidentally and, casually lighting a cigar, he would blow them to kingdom come. He also worried about electricity running out of empty light sockets inadvertently turned on.

Summer or winter, the thing the boy liked best was being allowed to sit up way past his bedtime to hear something special on the radio. His granddad and Coleman from upstairs always listened to the championship fights, the World Series, the *Grand Old Opry,* like that. The fights were the best. There was a tension in the room that was electrifying when the two big men took their chairs in front of the Zenith. Chicago, Detroit, New York's Madison Square Garden came alive and muscular in the room. The women sat in the kitchen around the table lamenting the folly of men. The men always grew bigger and heavier in their movements, rougher in their speech, on fight nights.

In June everybody's windows were open. The fight sounds blared from windows all over the neighborhood. Jack hurried in from the dark yard to hear Joe Louis fight Braddock for the heavyweight championship of the whole world.

MacDeramid had maintained from the beginning: "Louis will knock his block off."

Coleman would bet a million "no coon could cool James J."

Which was funny, because Jack's granddad was a Tennessee mountaineer with a cowboy upbringing and a Confederate suspicion of Federal authority, while Coleman was New York East Side with a doughboy point of view. So why was it Mac felt no threat in a black man being Champion of the World and Coleman did?

There had only been one other champ who had been black—Jack Johnson.

"You mean you don't care," Coleman railed during the prefight warmup, "if a dinge is champ?"

"Why should I?" Mac calmly wondered. "I ain't no boxer. I don't have to fight him."

"There ought to be *separate* championships," Coleman contended.

"Now what the hell would that prove?" Mac wondered. "Listen. I don't want to brag, but I always figured I could hold my own with any man ninety percent of the time or nine men out of ten *anytime,* whether it came to fist-fightin, fuckin, drinkin whiskey, choppin wood, pitchin hay, thinkin, talkin, singin, dancin, lyin, or tellin the truth, but I ain't never signified I'm champion of a thing. So if they have a world's championship for *all* them things and a nigger black as Natoby's ass takes the cake in them all, I don't count it as skin off mine. Power to him! I ain't discontent in any of them things. The only place I *always* feel a lack, Coleman, is in my pocketbook."

Coleman was a Roosevelt man, though he had always been a Republican. He always gave millionaires credit. He could not understand MacDeramid's obdurate disaffection.

"If you're so dead set against *our* way, why the hell don't you just leave the country?" Coleman challenged.

"Why, shitfire, man, it's as much *my* country as it's yours and Mr. Roosevelt's. And I reckon I done a damn sight more to build it up than that Eastern Shore caped cocksucker."

"They could shoot you for talking that way," Coleman warned, itching to be recalled to the colors for assignment to the firing squad.

"Shoot? Shoot *ME?* Man, I been shot at by experts. And not in no fuckin army, neither. Man to man. And I'll tell you one thing. Shooting me is the *only* way they'll ever shut me up. I'll tell them what they are from who-drawed-taw-to-who-played-the-chump. I ain't afraid of any of them. I'll tell em!"

"Yeow, while you're taking their handout on the relief line." Coleman felt smugly superior sitting there in his mustard Army pants, for even though he was also unemployed, he received a medical pension from the Army for having been gassed and did not, with his wife working as a housekeeper, need relief.

"Because I have to. I stand in that line with my gunny sack in hand like a goddamned beggar out in the street and the bile burning my craw so damn bad I can't speak for cussin and take their goddamned commodities because we got to live. We got a right to eat! We have our daughter's boy to take care of, feed, clothe, and send to school. People got a right to live, Coleman. You don't starve an animal just because it didn't work for you that day. Why, man, people like you act like eating's arbitrary. Why even old Roosevelt more or less accepts the fact that folks got to eat. Whether out of common decency or fear of revolution don't matter. What I'm arguing now is that making a man feel like a dog to get food for his family is going to turn this country into a nation of dogs who'll come waggin their stumpy little tails at a whistle, sit up and beg, and roll over and play dead on command. You must understand, Coleman, I've been around since right after the Civil War. I've been there and back, and I'll tell you, it looked for about fifteen minutes there between the end of Hoover and Roosevelt's first hundred days like this land was going to pull itself up and make itself into something so doggone fine and right it might on The Day of Judgment rise up whole and pass through the Pearly Gates intact. For about fifteen minutes there we probably had the best chance of any people in time of proving man was superior to the coyote. And muffed it. All those busy little hustlers back East hustled around to see what there was in poverty for them. And hustled first this, then that contract. Sent their sons into the bureaus until the business got on its feet. Never seen nor heard of an animal who'd treat their own kind so cruel as man . . . except maybe a goddamn rat or hyena. Pointing out the little differences between themselves and someone else to justify blue murder. Well, I voted for the sonofabitch. But I'll be the first Democrat to tell you I'd give my left nut to have my vote back. Not that Hoover would have been any better. That's the hell of it! What's a man and his vote worth when he's offered a cheese choice like that? But *Roosevelt!* He came on like a big friend of the working man. I don't know who got all the chicken, but I can show you who got the feathers! Why can't you see, man, what the big boys, the money interests, the kings, the dukes, the czars, the powerful few really think of you? You're a *commodity,* Coleman! They can buy and sell us. We ain't worth our salt the way things are unless some big shot can turn us into a profit. That ain't God's will, nor the will of any logical man. It costs the bosses less than two bits a day to keep us alive and in line and hungry enough to take any fuckin job they hold out. Then probably half of that is going to pay for the bureaucracy of the thing. *Goddamn* such a goddamn way of doin!"

"I still don't think a man has the right to bite the hand that feeds him," Coleman said piously.

"Well, see, you just never raised hogs. I'd rather step into a cage of grizzly bears than a pen of hogs that have been kept on swill too long. You slop men with swill *too* long and like hogs they'll go for you, you come too near—for a little taste of meat. Hogs'll not only bite your hand, they'll eat your whole arm off. Eat off your face. They'll devour a child in a minute. I mean literally and figuratively, Coleman, hogs *are* what you feed them. So's folks. You know, if it was just myself, I wish there wasn't no relief. See, then enough of us might become mad enough to do something about turning this country into a land of milk and honey. Them old Roosians had the right idea. They took over. Only our czars are smarter. Ours just say, 'Swill is the standard.' The Roosian Czar said, 'You're only *worth* swill.' *There's* the difference. *There's* the trick. That's the difference between tyranny and what Roosevelt calls democracy. By tossing in a handful of corn every now and then our people have been gulled by hope for better to accept anything. And they'll go on accepting. Until in the long run our czars will get ahold of all the guns and not even have to come around to rob you. They'll do it by an announcement in the newspaper naming some slicked-backed, rimless-glasses fuckhead to a new Cabinet post and call it progress. But believe me, Coleman, it's still mass murder somewhere. Maybe the Red Cavalry idea was the more humane. I don't know. I just know we'll take whatever the lyin bastards hand out just as long as they give us something and kiss their ass and say, 'Donkey shane and God bless, peace!' "

"I believe we get what we deserve," Coleman asserted, throwing out his chest.

"Is that a fact?" Mac replied dryly and spat a neat stream of tobacco juice into a Folger's coffee can near the radio.

Louis knocked out Braddock in the eighth round.

And Coleman went upstairs convinced the revolution had begun.

# 21

JACK had a kite string hooked into the Willhites' parlor screen with an open safety pin. He and Harold Lloyd Beers were on their bellies under a chinaberry bush in the old maids' yard, from where they could see the lighted double window. Harold Lloyd kept the string taut. Jack held the wet rag to squeak the end of the string. He crept up outside the lightfall to peek inside.

Old lady Willhite lived there with her three old-maid daughters, Opal, Pearl, and Ruby, in ascending pecking order. Ruby was a bookkeeper in an insurance office; Pearl ran the household; Opal hustled greeting cards, girdles, shoes, frocks, patent medicines, vitamins, cosmetics, needles and thread, stuff like that, door to door from two shopping bags and an enormous big black genuine leather purse. She had been in love with someone named Bob for years and years, but they never got married. Indeed, whether old Bob ever got into Opal's knickers was the source of much merry speculation. Jack's grandmother, who was Opal's best friend, swore it just wasn't possible. On the other hand, she could not swear he hadn't. Jack's Grandpa Mac couldn't see it.

"I look at her kisser and I can't even imagine her havin one. Anyway, not one you'd want to face up to on a full stomach. Ummmm. Man. Sir! Nope. Not me. Nosir." Mac rejected the possibility.

"But she's got a heart that's good as gold," Mrs. Mac always added.

It was her nose and the fact that kids made her nervous that put old Bob off, was the boy's best judgment.

Her nose was long and cold-looking and stretched so tight over its frame it looked as though it might split in the middle of her sales pitch to his grandma for Christmas cards.

"*Please!* Missus Mac. *Don't* let Jacky touch the cards."

"I'm sorry, Opal. He went and washed his hands. He likes to see, too."

Nothing on God's earth could get a little boy's hands clean enough for Opal. "*Please,* Missus Mac. I'm responsible for my samples." She whipped a red rubber-tipped pencil for writing up orders from her bun and vigorously erased some smudge visible only to her.

Her responsibility prohibited Jack from ever feeling any of the dress swatches and handling things from the incredible store she tricked out of her brown paper bags.

It was always: "If you can't keep your hands to yourself, you'll have to go play."

It was Opal who had sold his grandma on health foods—grass soup, bark teas, mock apple pie, mock chocolate cake, mock grapefruit, and such garbage—as well as the Original Vitamin Pill. The Original Vitamin Pill had the look and consistency of a squashed goat's turd, only, a goat's turd *smelled* better. And for taste it could not have been *that* far behind. Opal spotted the boy's heels one spring and convinced his grandma he was twenty-four hours removed from a terminal case of rickets or already silently suffering. So, from the same mystical source whence came the quarter for their insurance, money for the pills appeared. There was one of them beside his cereal bowl, or lurking in the depths of his powdered milk, or hidden in the warm heart of a biscuit every morning. He was now faced with the frantic breakfast task of ferreting it out and somehow getting it into the bib of his overalls without being caught by his grandma. At the absolute limit he would pop one in his mouth, chew like hell on nothing, and swallow, pocketing the thing in his cheek until she inevitably turned her back. "Man! Those things tasted brown!" he thought. And daily he visibly lost weight. Those pills so contaminated his breakfast that he was living on the peanut butter and jelly or baloney in his lunch sack and on the occasional candy bar he could chisel or steal.

In any case, Opal's mother and sisters picked on her unmercifully. Though only the old lady ever had any claim to beauty, Opal was treated just like Cinderella, only Bob never took her to a ball. For one thing, dancing was against her religion. It was against Jacky's grandma's, too. But his grandma had Granddad to contend with. Next to hating Roosevelt, dancing *was* his religion. So when he went fox-trotting off once or twice a week to the Townsend Club, she went along to take care of her best interest. She had more faith in God's mercy than did Opal. Opal leaned more toward his wrathful side.

Mrs. Mac said Opal lived on fifty cents a week. She often walked clear across town and back to save bus fare. She was known to faint from hunger in public places. As time passed, she made her calls on old customers and friends as much to catch a few winks in an easy chair as to make a sale. The police were always finding her asleep at odd hours in the city bus terminal, where she went to take care of her bookkeeping and correspondence at one of the free desks on the mezzanine. The police generally left her alone unless the station manager said something to them. Another of her spots was the ladies' lounge in Buck's Department Store. She would often set up a business appointment at one or the other places as if they were her property. She was a character whom only Mrs. Mac was able to genuinely love as well as pity.

"I don't care what you say about Opal, or make fun, she's as good a soul as there is on earth. She's honest to the penny. She's a Christian. She's never gone out of her way to hurt anyone in her life. And she's had a life with those *women* you wouldn't wish on a dog. I *like* Opal!"

The Willhite house was slowly moldering beneath its gingerbread, sinking inch by inch in a sea of flags, stinking ferns, tulips, hollyhocks, wisteria, creeping vines, night-blooming maneaters of all persuasions, and a pond of fat killer goldfish who would skarf your cat if it ever foolishly went fishing. The place was absolutely off limits to kids. They had the fastest line in town to the police department.

But it was Halloween, so naturally Jack and his pal were under the Willhites' chinaberry.

They had tossed a lighted bag of garbage on Azuni's front porch, rung the bell, and run. Then they fell on their heads laughing in Hawkins' yard when Mr. Azuni came out to stomp out the fire and kicked crap all over his porch, cursing all the while in Lebanese. They had caught a stray dog, tied a string of cans to its tail, and sent it clattering up Cleveland. They had chalked an anti-Catholic sentiment on O'Farrell's stoop.

It was about nine o'clock. Harold Lloyd was supposed to be home by nine. His old lady would step outside and give three blasts on a police whistle and Harold Lloyd would crumple, excuse himself, and hump on home. Man, he hated that whistle. Jack had no respect for someone who was called with a police whistle, but Harold Lloyd always ran home.

Sunday night was a big radio night. The old lady was in a padded rocker right in front of their big cyclopean Zenith console. Pearl and Ruby occupied a French provincial kind of settee at the side. Pearl and the old lady were sewing quilt blocks and Ruby was reading some magazine. Opal was out of the family circle, near the window in which the boy was peering, sitting at a lamp table, writing in the little fat black book she carried in her purse. The room was carpeted with an ancient Oriental rug and was choked with potted plants, bric-a-brac, old leather-bound books behind glass on shelves. Ruby was the official family radio tuner. Every family had one. Jack was tuner in his house. It was a gift. Only he could find the program everyone else wanted to hear.

The old man would try, give up in profane exasperation, and bellow, "Son! Come here and do this damn thing for me!"

Ruby tuned for the Willhites.

Jack dropped back through the shadows to the bush. There was a frosty smell to the air. The dirt under the bush where grass never grew for lack of sun was dry and dead-smelling like attic dust and old basement papers.

Harold Lloyd's whistle blew for him to come home.

"Wait!" Jack said. To scare the piss out of those old biddies was their collective intention.

Jack pulled the string until it was taut as he could make it without yanking the pin out of the screen. Slowly he wiped the wet rag along his end of the string, knowing that inside the room a rasping, moaning ghost was crying, URRR-AHHH! *Urrr-ahh*, UR-AH! UR-AH! UR-AH! If there *are* ghosts and they have voices, squeezing a wet rag along a kite string pinned to a screen is their cry. The women were on their feet in there. "Wait! . . . Now!" just as they resumed their seats. "Give them some more." *Urr-ah. Urr-ah*. Just a little. Then: URRRRRRRRRR-AHHHHHHHH! URRRRRRRRR-AHHHHHHH! UR-AH! UR-AH! UR-AH! UR-AH! On and on.

Then something happened.

There was a commotion inside. A lamp was knocked over. Opal ran howling from the house, beating her breast with both fists. Pearl yelled for her to get back in the house that instant. She too came out on the porch. Opal slipped making the turn at the walk and went sprawling. But she scrambled right up, hands prayerfully together, then cut out again. Suddenly all over town sirens were screaming.

"I gotta go home now," Harold Lloyd said back over his shoulder, his clumsy legs already pumping to gain momentum. "It was your idea." He took time to let Jack know how he was going to testify in court.

Pearl bellowed across the yard, "Opaaaaaaaaaaaaaaaaaal. . . ."

Opal was gone.

Jack gave the string a yank to jerk it loose from their screen, but he did not hang around to roll it up. Harold Lloyd was already at their back fence. Through a flag bed, a tulip plot, kicking the expensive darlings every which way, Jack vaulted a low hedge right into the killer goldfish pond, did not hesitate, came out of there with them snapping futilely at his soggy tenners, squishy, cold—every criminal step. Harold Lloyd was having trouble getting his fat ass over the fence. Jack hit it in the middle as if there were a step, made a grab for the top, and was over and gone. Fuck Harold Lloyd!

He flew up the alley, arriving at his own back porch just as Opal screamed into the front yard. Even in soaking wet sneakers, Jack was fast. Opal was about fifty with a low satchel ass the size of a Buick trunk and legs like porch pillars—so she had flown!

"*Missus Mac! Missus Mac! Pray to God! The Martians have landed!* In New York. Now!" She collapsed on the porch.

"Opal! What in the world?" Jack's grandmother rushed to help the woman.

Her first thought was Opal had been raped or something.

"*Martians,*" she moaned. "*It's the end of the world.*"

"Martin?" the old man said inside. "Martin who?"

"Opal, what are you talking about?"

"Our time has come, Missus Mac. Get ready to see God. Pray with me." She tried to pull the boy's grandmother down on the porch.

"I think she's slipped her traces," was Mac's opinion.

He had driven her stark raving mad, Jack thought; it was the end of him. He had really done it this time.

"Don't you have your radio on?" she asked.

"No."

"It's on the radio. The Martians have landed in New Jersey and are taking over New York."

"Oh, *Opal!*"

"Smell her breath," was Mac's advice.

"Daddy."

"Well, I thought maybe she's been tippling a little of that tonic she peddles."

"*They're coming!*" She begged their understanding. "*Please!* We heard a sound just when it started like a rocketship. Oh, Missus Mac, IT'S THE END!" She prostrated herself on the porch, racked with sobs.

"Maybe you ought to put the radio on," Mrs. Mac suggested calmly. "Opal. Listen. Get up, now. You can't carry on like that on the front porch." She scanned the neighborhood. They could hear sirens and fire bells. People were out in their yards looking up at the sky. A woman suddenly ran down the middle of the street like one about to breast a surf crying, "It's the end of the worrrrrrrrrrrrrrrrrrrrld. . . ."

"Put on the radio, Daddy."

He couldn't find the station.

"CBS," Opal offered distinctly and then threw herself over in a frenzy, writhing on the porch, tearing her hair, her blouse.

"Opal!"

"Son!" Mac called. "Where is that boy? Never around when you need him. SON! Come fix this sonofabitch!"

"They told you we needed an aerial and ground wire," Mrs. Mac reminded him.

"To hell with that!" The old man rejected the idea. "Draw lightning. SON!"

Jack had to go in. Just when Opal was about to tear off her blouse for sure.

The Colemans from upstairs came down. Gladys and Mrs. Coleman held each other and looked about to weep.

"What the deuce's going on?" the old man asked.

"This may be it, Mac," Coleman reported. "They've landed and are trying to take over the country. It looks bad. The Army and Air Corps are moving up. It's war."

"Who?"

"From *Mars!* Men from *Mars!*"

Mac's face split for an instant into a big grin. As quickly, it became a quizzical frown. "*Naw?* Aw?"

"*Yes!* Yes!" Coleman shoved the boy away from the radio. The knob came off in his hand. He handed it back. Gladys grabbed the boy by the hand. She already had hold of her mother and was circling on Mac to organize a prayer circle. Though basically an Evangelical Reformed, she was a student at Friends' U. She kept making grabs at everyone's hand to draw them together. Jack slipped her grasp.

"Pray now in the moment of divine retribution," she counseled, her homely face beatifically raised to the overhead 100-watt Mazda. "Pray for your eternal soul." She made another grab for the boy. His tenners squished away over the linoleum.

"How'd you get your feet wet?" his grandmother asked perfunctorily, hurrying through with a glass of water and a cold compress for Opal, not waiting for a reply.

"We are going to see Jesus!" Gladys was enthused. "See his face. Praise God." She caught the old man by the thumb.

"Hold on there a little, will ya, Gladys?" Mac wanted to help Coleman get the knob back on the radio.

"I got it!" Coleman cried.

"Gladys. Turn loose that," the old man said.

"They're engaging them with artillery, and bombers are on the way," the ex-doughboy reported, his ear next to the speaker.

"Turn it up, Son," Mac said to Jack. "Gladys. Look out, now."

Everyone was carrying on so, it was hard to hear the radio.

"I ain't goin down without a fight," Wolford Coleman proclaimed, having armed himself with a .22 single-shot Iver Johnson rifle and stuck a monstrous butcher knife in his belt. He wanted everyone to pile furniture up at the doors and windows, and he began shoving Mac's couch to lead the way. "Get mattresses and doors." He meant to rally them.

"Now hold on there, Wolford!" the old man cautioned. "You're going to knock off a leg like that. Gladys! *Will* you leave holt!" He could not shake her free. *"Mama!"*

"Rejoice!" Gladys cried. "Sing!" And launched into the hymn "Nearer My God To Thee."*A cappella.* "All sing!" she insisted.

*"Mama!"* The old man bellowed.

"Opal, listen now," Mrs. Mac told Opal on the porch. "There ain't no sense in carrying on like this. You're just making a spectacle of yourself. You just come indoors. Keep it up now and you're going to just feel like a prize fool tomorrow."

"Don't you understand? It's the end of the *world!* We are going to God."

"I don't care. I'd sure be ashamed of myself if I showed up with my blouse all out like you." Opal had been so lifted at the prospect of seeing Jesus she had virtually bared her not insignificant virginal chest for the occasion.

If Mac was going to meet his maker, it was going to be with his braces down and an insane girl permanently grafted to his left thumb. His specs were pushed up on the top of his head. He had been reading the evening paper. His trousers had slipped in the meantime until half the back fly in his BVD's was visible and might go any minute.

"Got a grip like a vise." He marveled at the tetched girl's strength. "Leave me *loose!*" He caught her fist with his free hand and had to prize his thumb free like a man pulling a cork.

Wolford had now barricaded Mrs. Mac and Opal out on the porch with the couch and was casting a glance at Mrs. Mac's Singer, clearly measuring it for a possible parapet.

"Get that thing away from there," the old man told him, putting action to word. "Give me that goddamn gun before you shoot somebody."

"Go cover the back door!" was Wolford's thinking. He hung on to his gun.

Coleman was relaying a minute-by-minute report from the battlefield, as it was far more strategic than turning up the volume. His wife was chiming, "Amen. Praise be," to every fool thing her nutty daughter, Gladys, prayed.

"JUST EVERYBODY HOLD ON A DAMN MINUTE!" the old

man bellowed loud enough to stay even Gladys' lyric climb to heaven. "Turn up the friggin box so we can *all* hear!" the old man demanded.

*. . . from the roof of Broadcasting Building, New York City. The bells you hear are ringing to warn people to evacuate the city as the Martians approach. Estimated in the last two hours three million people have moved out along the roads to the north. Hutchinson River Parkway still kept open for motor traffic. All communication with the Jersey Shore closed ten minutes ago. No more defenses. Our army wiped out. . . .*

"Wiped out! Did you hear that?" Coleman was beside himself.

The women began to wail again. Mrs. Mac had dragged Opal in off the porch.

"Shut that up!" the old man barked. "I want to *hear* this!"

Mrs. Mac came over and put her hand on his shoulder. They exchanged a look. Jack slid over, and his grandmother made a place for him at her side.

*. . . artillery, air force, everything wiped out. This may be the last broadcast. . . . People are holding services below us . . . in the cathedral.*
[VOICES SINGING HYMN]
*Now I look down the harbor. All manner of boats, overloaded with fleeing population, pulling out from the docks.*
[SOUND OF BOAT WHISTLES]
*Streets are all jammed. Noise in crowds like New Year's Eve in city. Wait a minute. . . . Enemy now in sight above Palisades. Five great machines. First one is crossing river. I can see it from here, wading the Hudson like a man wading through a brook. . . .*

"Oh, Gawd. . . ." Coleman fell to his knees beside the radio dressed in his Army pants and shoes and sleeveless undershirt. Down on his knees like a craven sinner.

It was clearly every man for himself on the road to eternity. And the boy remembered he hadn't even been baptized.

"What's happening, Grandma?" he asked.

"We don't know yet."

"Are we going to die?" When she did not answer right away, "Are we?"

"Everything's all right. Shush." She held the boy closer.

"You know. Maybe if the goddamn Army hadn't riled them up," Mac wondered aloud. "Did anybody stop to *ask* were they friendly? Fuckin Roosevelt can't do nothing right even at the end. This just takes the cake!" The old man wasn't going on his knees.

*. . . A bulletin's handed me. . . . Martian cylinders are falling all over the country. One outside Buffalo, one in Chicago, St. Louis . . . seem to be timed and spaced.*

"Well, they'll probably be awhile before they come looking for Wichita," the old man guessed.

*. . . Now the first machine reaches the shore. He stands watching, looking over the city. His steel, cowlish head is even with skyscrapers. He waits for the others. They rise like a line of new towers on the city's west side. . . .*

"How they know it's a he?" Mrs. Mac, the last of the Sabines, wondered.
"Yeow?" Jack chipped in.

*. . . Now they're lifting their metal hands. This is the end now.*

A collective gasp passed through those assembled in the room.

*Smoke comes . . . black smoke, drifting over the city. People in the streets see it now. They're running towards the East River . . . thousands of them, dropping in like rats. Now the smoke's spreading faster. It's reached Times Square. People trying to run away from it, but it's no use. They're falling like flies. Now the smoke's crossing Sixth Avenue . . . Fifth Avenue . . . a hundred yards away . . . it's fifty feet. . . .*
[ANOTHER VOICE]
*2X2L calling CQ . . .*
*2X2L calling CQ . . .*
*2X2L calling CQ . . . New York.*
*Isn't anyone on the air?*
*Isn't anyone . . .*
*2X2L—*

It was still in the room for a moment except for the women's sobbing. Opal was prostrated on the floor, resigned to her fate. Gladys was about home. Her arms reached out for her heavenly throne. Mrs. C seemed to have caught the vision. Wolford didn't see a thing, Jacky was sure, but he wasn't about to be left behind for want of reaching. Coleman, having repented all his sins as if the old Zenith were a two-way radio and God were tuned to its frequency, was now heavily launched on the Lord's Prayer for the eighth or ninth recitation. He'd even cited his war record and reminded God about his having been gassed in his closing argument.

Then Wilma and her new boyfriend, Bill, blew in, and everyone thought the Martians had come—in a Yellow cab. It was a good thing Wolford had put aside his .22 for the sake of grace or he might have plugged them. Wilma swept in and clasped her son to her, covering Jack's face with tears and wet kisses. She kissed him wet and warm on the mouth. Tears beaded her mascara.

Let 'em come was his feeling.

"My baby. My baby," she crooned.

The truth was, he just didn't *believe* in God and all that. He was scared, but whatever happened, he didn't think they were going anywhere. He knew his granddad felt the same way. The old man said he believed in God, but it was an equal sort of relationship. And Mac would have liked some sign from the other side *He* believed in *him*. Until then, Mac would light up a cigar.

Bill pulled a pint in a paper bag from his hip pocket, unscrewed the cap, and tilted it up right in front of God, Mrs. Mac, and everybody. If it was a miracle that God didn't strike him, it was a blue-eyed one that she left anything of him for the Martians. She saw him and said not a word. He was a little border jackal from along the Missouri line who wore a two-toned zipper jacket, a snap-brim hat, and asked everyone to call him Bill. He was a divorced alcoholic named Wild with a criminal record in more states than Jack could name the capitals of, one testicle left after a fall off the monkey board of an oil rig, and only the air-filled prospects of a border conneroo. So naturally Wilma loved him. That was not quite fair. On his side, he had learned to make dinner rings from toothbrush handles in prison, had beautiful clear blue eyes, a 7¾ hat size, and the second-longest pecker Wilma had ever seen. His knobby Adam's apple moved with the booze like a ball float in his neck. He cut it off neat, wiped his mouth with the back of his hand, extended the bottle toward the old man.

"Here, Mac. Have a snort," he croaked.

To everyone's surprise, he took one. He coughed.

"*Goddamn,* son! A man ought to face the end of the world with better whiskey than that."

"It's a blend."

"Of what?"

"I drink what I can get," was Bill's testament. Then to prove he was willing to stand on it, he knocked back the rest of the pint.

"Hold on, there!" the old man suddenly said and spun toward the set. "Everybody shut up for a minute! What'd he say, Coleman?"

The announcer had said:

*You are listening to a CBS presentation of Orson Welles and the Mercury Theatre on the Air in an original dramatization of War of the Worlds by H. G. Wells. The performance will continue after a brief intermission.*
*This is Columbia . . . Broadcasting System.*
*[FADE THEME 10 SECONDS]*
*KANS-Wichita*
*[ENTIRE BREAK 20 SECONDS]*
*War of the Worlds by H. G. Wells, starring Orson Welles and the Mercury Theatre on the Air. . . .*
*[MUSIC]*

"*It's a show!* It's all a goddamned show?" The old man was half mad, half elated, and altogether feeling foolish.

"*No! No!* That's just how it was before," Coleman explained. "They broke it on a show. There was music, and they broke in."

"Yeh. See. Like that stuff's just recorded. On a record," Wolford explained out of his more technical ninth-grade knowledge.

"I think it's just a show," the old man persisted.

"They why are all the police sirens and things going?" Mrs. Mac asked.

"Dad, people are running crazy through the streets all over on the way here," Wilma said. "The cab driver didn't know what was going on until we told him or he wouldn't of picked us up."

"Folks are breaking into stores," Bill added. "Bars wide open." He looked sorry he was missing the action. "Some guy caught one of the women from upstairs at the Eaton Hotel who came running down to the lobby almost naked and was trying to put it to her right in the lobby."

"Tryin, nothin!" Wilma said.

The radio was droning on:

*. . . I look down at my blackened hands, my torn shoes, my tattered clothes, and I try to connect them with a professor who lives at Princeton, and who on the night of October 20, glimpsed through his telescope an orange splash of light on a distant planet. My wife, my colleagues, my students, my books, my observatory . . . my world . . . where are they?*

"It's a show." Mac was certain. "Ain't it a show, Mama?"

"I don't know."

"Well, I think it's a show. I'm going out and take a look. Come on, Son."

Jack would just as soon stay there with his mom.

"Well, I'm going out and have a see."

"I'm with you, Mac," Bill volunteered. There wasn't anything worth stealing in there, that was plain.

Then the boy would go, too. Coleman was waiting inside. He did not have his gas mask.

Every house on the block was ablaze with light. People were out in their yards, some on their knees, others just standing looking up at the sky. The Hawkins boy had a pair of binoculars. Carey, the gouty land-lord from the stucco apartments next to Azuni's, had piled out with his 300-pound wife, stuffed her in their Chevy, and taken off for the country. Across Central over in Niggertown something was on fire. The Christian Scientists on the other side of Hawkins were tumbling about their lawn in their night clothes like a lot of Holy Rollers, while a total stranger skipped about among them yelling, "It was only a show! It wasn't real!" Getting an eyeful of Mrs. Cantrell's big snatch. She was fairly foaming at the mouth.

A man yelled across the neighborhood lawns, "MARION, IT WAS JUST A HOAX! COME BACK. MARION! MARION!" He kept yelling.

Her bubble burst, Gladys fainted from sheer exhaustion on the couch. Only old Opal hung in there. Only a word from Jesus himself could stay her now. She was going to God if she had to climb all the way. Mrs. Mac stepped over and shook her by both shoulders until her teeth clattered, her hair came down, and her eyes rolled back from staring at the inside of her head.

Coleman came up brushing his knees and hot enough to demand an investigation by the American Legion, the 40 and 8, all the Cooties, and their ladies' auxiliaries. "Damn station'd pull a stunt like that ought to be taken out and shot!" He swore he was through with CBS for the rest of his life.

The show was still running. People all over town continued to believe it was real. Sirens still rolled around the city.

"Well! Happy Halloween!" Mrs. Mac laughed. "I'd surely say the joke's on us."

"Didn't have *me* fooled," the old man said. "I just sensed something wasn't on the up and up." Then catching his wife's look, "Well, I didn't *think* it was real."

"I think I'll make some coffee," Mrs. Mac decided.

Wilma said, "Let me help you, Mom. I've got something to tell you."

Gladys came around feebly, but spirits of ammonia would not be required, she was quick to assure everyone.

Opal had buttoned her blouse, *and* her sweater, to boot. He had but been in her grasp. Verily. It was Opal's last shot. Afterward she was resigned to her shopping bags and never voiced hope of ever knowing better until the Lord took her away.

*Keep running, Jesus,* the boy thought.

If Wilma had picked any other night to announce she and Bill had got married, Mac might have killed them both.

Jack was thrilled.

"Go kiss your new daddy," was his mom's notion for his first move.

He went dutifully over. He put out his hand.

"Men don't kiss. They shake hands," Bill explained firmly. "Put 'er there!"

"See I'm going to have to toughen you up." He laughed grimly. He ground the bones in the boy's hands together.

Another one of *those.* But Jack had been so long without a real dad of his own, he would have given even one of those Martians every chance.

"What are your plans?" Mac wondered of the newlyweds.

They were going to leave for Albuquerque just as soon as Bill cleared up a couple of things in town. Wilma was sure Albuquerque was just the spot for her sinuses. Bill wanted her to have every advantage.

One thing she wanted was for the boy to be with them just as soon as possible.

Jack was ready to go that night.

"Just as soon as we get settled," she promised. "It will be *so* good to have a place of our own and all be together again. So I can take care of you and make you brownies like I've always dreamed."

He had done some dreaming, too. "Boy! Can I have a bike for Christmas?"

It had been a bit sudden. She hemmed; Bill coughed.

Then he said, "Sure, pal. Why not. One bike." With Bill anything suddenly seemed possible.

"Boy!"

"We'll see," his mother cautioned.

What Mrs. Mac wanted to see was their marriage license.

"Now, Mom," Wilma chided. But she was insulted.

So was Bill.

"Well! I *do!*" the woman insisted. "I want to see it." And ever after she claimed, "I'll believe it when I see it." She never did.

Wilma and Bill claimed they would not show it to her on principle.

Mrs. Mac said it was probably because they didn't have one to show.

Everyone toasted their happiness with coffee.

"But don't come crawling back here." Mac gave his daughter his blessing.

Jack couldn't understand what everyone was so unhappy about. Of all the guys his mother had brought around, Bill suited him fine. What if his real name was Wilburn? It had been only him and the old man who hadn't really been scared by the Martians.

# 22

WHEN Kenneth MacDeramid got a job painting Beech-crafts in 1939, everyone thought it was a sign the Depression was finally ending. But in case the sign was false, Kenny kept his job "parking cars" out at the Calico Cat at night. He hadn't actually parked anyone's car in years. Harry Shipley, his old junking partner, had a little three-room house on the corner adjacent to the nightclub, with a driveway that led from the club's parking lot straight past the little house's back door, then onto the public road. As at a filling station, customers pulled up in the drive and Kenny would come out and sell them a pint, fifth, or case.

Kansas was dry with the sober fury of Carry A. Nation, who was remembered locally not as some fanatic but as a heroine—somewhere there was a statue, and there were several plaques—out of a fundamental Protestant sense of sin in adulterating the natural human spirit with those neutral spirits of grain. Drunkenness was not being oneself, and being oneself was the essential pride. Old man MacDeramid's favorite saying he had taken from Popeye: "I yam what I yam and that's all I yam." No one expected life to be easy. Drunkenness was for Irishmen.

Sometimes the laughter of women, like the clinking of glasses, could be heard inside the little house on the corner, but Kenny, dressed in work clothes, had little to do with that. He mainly serviced the cars that pulled up in the drive with the air of a man about to ask leave to also check the oil. "Crime" was a mysterious evil, the sole property of "big shots" who lived in Chicago and New York, places where no right-thinking young Jayhawker ever wanted to go. Drinking was a sin, but selling booze was no real crime. And that as much as anything described the politics on which Kansas grew.

A case or two of booze was ever handy for raiding police officers to confiscate. Whenever there was a picture in the paper of cops ceremoniously breaking bottles of booze in a county toilet, wise guys knew how carefully the drama was staged.

Kenny's mother, with the look of Carry A. herself in her eye, never let him easily enjoy the profits of his enterprise. He would never come out and actually admit he was selling whiskey, so she would not accuse him directly. Yet, not a meeting passed between them that she did not inquire, "Still parkin cars nights, Son?" Or, "Looks like now you got a good job, you'd want to be home nights."

"Aw, Mom, shit." He would turn his face toward the pint of his own he then kept stashed not more than a step or two away.

He was paying for a four-room frame house he had bought on Hydraulic, not far from where his parents ran the rooming house, painting Beechcrafts by day and car-hopping booze for Harry at night. And if he was not a fifth-a-day drinker himself, it was because he did not need that much to maintain a cheerful, laconic glow.

For Christmas that year Kenny brought home great models of Beech's biplane and the Model 18 twin-engined transport for his sons. They were available only to employees. And his nephew, Jack, wondered when the Depression was going to end for him and his grandpa and grandma. In the face of his cousins' new riches, Jacky felt poorer than ever. An anxious craving for this or that thing grew to consume nearly all possible pleasure for the boy.

"Learn to enjoy what you got," was his grandmother's daily advice.

Then the church notified Mrs. MacDeramid they wanted the house where she was caretaker as a home for aged brothers and sisters. Old Man Mac found a finished but unimproved basement under the home of a hunchbacked tailor named Deffenbaugh who lived a couple of blocks away. But the boy did not want to live under some hunchback in another basement. He had no sooner come to think of 323 Cleveland as *his* home than suddenly it was no more his than was the moon. It made him ache too bad to cry. Whom could he fight? Whom blame? He wanted a real home with a front and back yard, a goat, a real black walnut tree that grew real black walnuts you could eat, a dog, and a little room for himself in which to hang model planes and pictures of things he treasured, like his cousins had.

They went ahead with their plan to move into Deffenbaugh's basement that winter. They would curtain it off into rooms. They had to go upstairs to use the bathroom. His granddad planned to use a slop jar at night. Jacky knew who would have to empty that. *God!* He didn't want to move. The loss in status was inestimable, but surely great. *Grandma and Grandpa didn't care,* he was sure. Status was never a consideration to them.

"You do your best and treat people fair, and if they don't appreciate it, that's their problem" was precisely how they lived. They never stole a cent from anyone.

The old man and Coleman argued over the war a lot. Jack could not make head or tail of it. Coleman said he was sure the country would be in the war, too, before long. The old man said if war came, he wasn't going. He hadn't gone before, and he wasn't going again. It did not matter, as his wife reminded him, that he had been too old then and so probably would not be called in the event of another unless the Hun was at the city limits.

The Germans again. It was the DuPonts, Rockefellers, Fords, Astors, and Roosevelt who were just as much to blame, according to Mac.

"Now that's just crazy, MacDeramid," Coleman said.

"Don't you call *me* crazy," the old man warned, getting to his feet.

Jack thought there was going to be a fight.

"You don't know enough about things, Coleman, to pound sand into a rat hole."

"And you're a stubborn mulely radical—uh-uh—— You just don't give nobody credit for knowin anything but you."

"The trouble with you, Coleman, you don't have no faith in your own kind. You let the rich fuckers tell you what's what. You can't see what's real when it's right before your nose. They tell you what's good for you, what to wear, what to think, where to set your chair. What the hell, Coleman, *do* you decide for yourself? Me? I'm sick of it. Me? I'll fight it any way I can until I die. And I'll teach my kids to fight it. Oh, Son, he don't have no political interest. And, Daughter, she just runs around. But this boy, he listens." He put his big hand flat on Jack's head.

Coleman saw no revolutionary in the boy's face. All he saw for certain was a towhead in need of shears and a snaggletooth like a broken fence picket.

"Don't underestimate this boy," Mac said, looking down, not so confident, it seemed, as before. "He's a lot smarter than he looks."

The boy felt proud as a pup.

Coleman went upstairs, and he and Mac did not play cards for a week.

The boy's mother had been sending long folders of picture postcards from all the wonderful places she and Bill had been since leaving Wichita—Albuquerque, Denver, San Antonio, New Orleans. Places where not a scrap of paper littered the streets, apparently; where skies were bluer than Kansas, grass geener, water softer.

"Guess the sonofabitch can't keep a job nowhere," was the old man's judgment.

Secretly Jack wrote his mother a letter:

Please let me come live with you becus we got to move and I dont want to live in Defenbas basment. Writ me soon and tell me I can come live with you soon. Pleas tell me soon as you can when I can come becus I sure dont want to live here nomore. I sure do want to come live with you real bad sted of in a basment agin. Please writ me when you receve this and tell if its OK. I love you and want to come live with you from now on. With love. Your Son Jack

P.S. I am anksus to hear from you. Love. Your Son Jack

He sneaked the letter out of the house and got a stamp from Mr. Azuni at the grocery, telling him to put it on their bill.

"One postal stamp?"

"Yeow." What was wrong with that?

Azuni thought the boy was nuts anyway.

He walked all the way up to Douglass where there was a *big* mailbox, rather than trust so vital a message to the dinky job on the corner that was stuck on a pole. He wanted every chance.

That afternoon he found a gallon of crankcase oil in the corner of the garage where everyone worked on their bikes. Harold Lloyd was at Y camp. The Azunis were off with the Boy Scouts. There wasn't anyone to play with. Crawling up behind him was Curly, his box turtle. He had named the turtle Curly, though he was obviously bald as a brick. He couldn't recall why. Curly crawled through the old shed in a shaft of sunlight, leaving a strange primeval track. Sometimes Jack felt the thing knew him.

He lugged the can of oil out into the yard and reached for the bunch of kitchen matches that he always carried in his pocket. He could throw a kitchen match the way you throw a knife so it would hit head first against the sidewalk and light. Throwing matches was his specialty, but matches would not light the oil. He collected sticks from the alley, set the can up on two bricks, and built a fire under it. The paint on the outside of the can stank when it burned off. He touched the oil with his finger to see how it was. It was hotter than hell! There would be a blister there. What would it be like to be boiled in oil? he wondered. Bad! He opted for the firing squad any day. The oil began to smoke. It smelled awful.

Here came old Curly, crawling through the heat waves of the drive, coming as if he had been called, in that weird wide-tracking turtle way.

Jack picked him up. He had brought him all the way from a dirt road out by an abandoned Indian reservation school on Twenty-first Street in his shirt on the College Hill bus. But Curly wasn't much of a turtle.

Not wanting to, but wanting to know what would happen even more, he dropped Curly into the smoking oil. He sank to the bottom without a fight. What the hell. He hadn't learned a thing. Curly was gone. He fished frantically for him with a stick. He could not get him out of there. He hadn't wanted to do that. The stick caught fire. The flame leaped to the top of the oil. A column of black acrid smoke rose from the can. The breath of the flame touched the boy's face. His cowlick and eyebrows were singed. The smoke was high as the house.

"Jacky! What in the world are you doing out there?" his grandmother called from the kitchen window. "What are you burning?"

"Nothing!" he called back.

"Put it out this instant or your grandpa will tend to you when he gets home. Do you want to burn the place down?"

He batted the can over with the flaming stick. Curly tumbled out onto his back, covered by a fur of blue flame that turned yellow and died. His limbs and head hung out seared and shiny black. A sweet oily stench hung over the yard. A long oil slick made the grass ugly.

He picked up a piece of cement block from under the pear tree, carried it over, lifted it high over his head, and flung it down on Curly. It made the turtle jump a foot and seem for a moment to be alive. He cracked like a walnut, but nothing popped out. Inside he was white, like chicken. Nothing had been as the boy had expected. It was just a sad mess. He was disgusted with himself—everything. In death Curly had no dignity. It was pathetic. Jack almost puked.

He got two sticks and rolled and carried Curly to the shady side of the shed, scratched a hole, and buried him.

He burned himself again picking up the blackened can. It hadn't looked hot.

He awoke that night in a sweat. Curly had grown in death and come back blackened, still cracked down to the white stuff, to pay him back. Though he could see it was not a giant next to his bed as he had dreamed, he was not sure the turtle wasn't alive in the dark on the floor —under the bed.

"GRANDMA!" he hollered.

"What in the land?" She came in a rush, sleepy and barefoot in her homemade cotton gown. "What is it, Son?"

"I don't know. I had a bad dream."

"Well, there's nothing to be afraid of. Go back to sleep."

"Can I have a light on?"

"Why, you're a big boy now. Big boys don't sleep with a light on."

"Just for tonight?"

"No. Now, you just snuggle down there and go to sleep."

"Uncle Frank died on this couch."

"All right. I'll put on this lamp. But we aren't going to make a habit of it."

It was probably punishment for all the trouble he had gotten into that caused a thing like a soft wart or long mole to grow right where the part began in his hair. He could not comb his hair without hitting the damn thing, raking it with the comb. Kids who would overlook a snaggletooth began to avoid him. When avoidance was impossible, they stared at the thing as if it might be catching. No one wanted to share a seat with him.

Bobby Walters wondered: "You let a doctor see it?"

Dolly Mae jilted him for the first time since kindergarten. She began playing the field. She was Keith Brandon's girl. Then Bucky White's. When Jack saw her holding hands in assembly with Bobby Walters, his best friend, he felt like running away from home. He had never felt uglier. He felt like he had a worm growing out of his head.

His grandmother called it a tumor and spoke in low solemn tones about it.

Her friend Opal insisted the boy see a doctor immediately. But there was no money for a doctor. Neighbors offered home remedies. The thing was all Jack thought about.

"Why don't you have that thing taken off that boy's head?" his granddad snapped one evening at the table. "It looks like hell."

"I can take it off if he'll let me," Mrs. Mac said mysteriously.

"Don't cut it!" Jack was ready to bolt.

"Don't have to cut it"—as if she might witch it off.

"How?" the old man asked.

"Tie a clean linen thread around it and leave it alone, and it'll fall off."

"Then why don't you do it?"

"Because he screams every time I try to look at it."

"I'm afraid it will hurt."

"It won't hurt," she promised.

"That's what you always say."

"Then you'll have to live with it."

"Do it," the old man commanded. "I'm sick of seeing it."

Jack was terrified. It wasn't like a sore or scab or something. It was alive and *moley*. A growth on his head! *God!*

There was no debate. The old man held the boy captive between his legs and pinned his arms to his side while Mrs. Mac made a little loop in the end of a thread and drew it tightly around the base of the growth. It actually only hurt a little, though the boy screamed bloody murder. She took a few more loops, drawing each tight as possible. She tied them securely. There was a moment of sheer panic when she produced her sharp little sewing shears to snip the ends of the thread. He was certain all had been mere prelude to the real operation, which she was about to perform. She was wont to do such things. But it was only thread she cut.

"Now, aren't you ashamed of yourself?" she chided as if she had never lanced a blister or boil on the pretext of just examining it.

The thing felt engorged in its tiny way, rather numb, nothing more. Kids laughed about the thread around it at first. Then Jack forgot about it.

A few weeks later he was wrestling with George Azuni in the yard when, escaping from a headlock, he knocked the thing off. George looked scared. A rivulet of blood fell into Jack's right eye. He really bled. He ran into the house, trying to stanch the flow with the tail of his shirt.

Mrs. Mac held the boy's head under the cold water tap until it had almost stopped bleeding. She was very pleased with herself. There was only a tiny spot where it had been, pink and smooth. She touched the place with merthiolate. It stung. George went home. The next day Dolly Mae had lunch with Jacky.

His grandmother promised the thing would never come back.

Around Thanksgiving a letter came from the boy's mother saying she would be coming soon to take him to live with her. It was news to the MacDeramids.

Mrs. Mac and the old man had long talks about it. They wanted to do what was best.

"Can we believe anything she says?" Mrs. Mac constantly asked herself.

"Well, he *is* hers by rights, though we've raised him." The boy's granddad made a point. "I don't guess we could stop her legally. We ain't gettin no younger, neither. Maybe it would be best for all concerned. We raised one family. What does *he* say?"

"*He* wrote a letter all by himself asking to go live with them."

"Is that so? I'll swan. I didn't know that." There was a note of both pride and wonder. "I reckon then we ought to let him go."

"I'm just afraid."

"Well, what else can you do?"

Jack could hear them talking about it in bed at night.

But he was going to go. He knew he was going to go. He had only to lie low and keep his mouth shut. He was going to go.

# 23

THE bike was red and cream. It was a brand new Schwinn. Jack's mom had put a down payment on it at Goodrich Silvertown, and he had ridden it home, falling only once at an intersection, twisting the handlebars a little. He was certain everyone seeing him going on home with whopper-jawed handlebars was laughing at him. They could not have cared less. He had forgotten how invisible kids are. The bike was easily fixed by his granddad once he was safely home. On Christmas Eve he insisted that they let him bring the bike in and set it up near the skinny little Christmas tree just as if it were a surprise. He shined it until it was almost good as new except for the scab on the handlebar where the chrome had been scraped away.

Wilma had come home to spend Christmas with her parents and take the boy back to Mississippi, where Bill had a good job in a shipyard. Right after she and Bill had got married, they had gone to Albuquerque, where the climate was good for Wilma's sinuses; then there was a long folder of scenic views of Denver, where she was working in a drugstore;

then Galveston, New Orleans, Biloxi, and finally Pascagoula. It was always difficult for Bill to get or keep a good job. Everyone liked him. He was a good worker when he wasn't drinking heavily, but he had never learned to drink light. Although he'd drink stuff you could barely stir with a stick, he considered hopheads and dope fiends perverted. He had his standards. But it was his criminal record that most stood in his way of finding a good job somewhere and settling down. As soon as they found out he was an ex-con, out he would go. That's how he explained his nomadic drift. Yet this time it was different. The shipyard knew he was an ex-con when they hired him. So maybe Pascagoula was the spot.

Jack was proud of his new stepdad. It had been a real drawback among his school chums, not having a dad. So, of course, he gave Bill all the best of it until he had done everything but *actually* win the heavyweight championship of the world and fly the Atlantic solo. If he was but one-tenth the man Jack said he was, his old man made everyone else's old man an oyster.

He cherished all the long technicolor scenic folders his mother had sent from all the places she and Bill had been. He took them to school to show around. In his mind, because they had seen Buffalo Bill's grave, so had he—sorta. He had a tiny pearl-handled pistol from Pike's Peak, a pecan-man doll from New Orleans, and a team of dried sea horses from Galveston. Soon he was going to go live with them and be off relief forever.

Mac put up a full bed in the parlor for Wilma and the boy.

It was the happiest night of Jack's life. The bike gleamed beautifully in the moonlight, its shadow a monster bike on the wall all the way up to the ceiling. It was cold. A wispy, wind-swirled snow had begun falling in the afternoon, giving hope for a white Christmas. It was still falling, though it gave no sign of thickening up and sticking. It would be frosty dust in the frozen tan grass the next morning, scurrying little snow buds along the edges of the walks.

Snug in the covers, the boy whispered once more, "Can we really go swimming in the Gulf even in winter?"

"Yes." She let him snuggle with his head on her bare shoulder, cradled in the curve of her left arm. The arm was the one with the scarred little tunnel in the crook of the elbow where she was burned with an iron when she was about fifteen. The tissue had healed so there was a tiny cave there into which he could just insert the tip of his little finger, though she hated him to do it. Her body radiated warmth under the heavy winter covers that flooded over him, wrapped him. Her nightgown was silver satin. All of his grandma's night clothes were coarse cotton, often flour sacking. Under his mom's satin gown her stomach was rather puckered, twisted, and uncommonly soft, because he had stretched her so much when he was a baby in her.

"Did it hurt much when I was a baby in you?" he inquired for the god-knows-how-often time. He did not know what else to ask to get so close.

"No. Not exactly. You were a *big* boy. And your head was awfully hard." She laughed. "Like all the men in this family. When you came, it hurt. If I had been in a hospital, it probably would have been easier."

"Why weren't you?"

"Well, your daddy was away, and we didn't have any money."

"Can I have a brother or sister when we get to Mississippi?"

She laughed. "I'd certainly like to have another. I've always wanted a cute little girl to take care of. We'll just have to see, I guess."

"I'd rather have a brother."

"You'd like a little sister, too. There is a boy in Pascagoula you can be friends with. I told him all about you. He can't wait to meet you. His name is Allen."

"Allen." That was a good name. Sort of sissy, maybe, but not really. He made her describe the boy to the best of her ability. As her voice became drowsy, he snuggled closer. Ice had formed on the windows along the bottom frame. He put his arm over her. His elbow brushed the place where her hairs lifted her gown ever so lightly. She took his wrist and moved his arm to a nice neutral place across her middle and tacked it there with a couple of gentle pats.

"Let's be still now," she said, as if sleep were a deep kiss.

"I'm sure happy, Mom."

"Me too. *Now go to sleep.*"

She rolled over on her side with her back to him, arranging his arm again neatly across her waist, holding his hand, chapped from winter, cracked from throwing ice balls without gloves, cradled in her own soft, lotioned, manicured hand, curved under her soft, breathing belly. The satin was like another warm skin. In turning, a warm breath of Evening in Paris came from the cozy depths of the bed. It made the boy drunk. He felt as if he had been spun, twirled, rocked, and sunk. The only reality now beyond the bed was the shadow of his new bike—a promise of elegant entertainments. It was almost too much to have at one time. The bike or the bed? He would have preferred taking them one at a time. How much room *was* there in a boy's head?

Her hip rose beyond his arm like a small, warm, sleeping mountain. His breathing became synchronized with hers. Then whether by the action of breathing or the willful lift and fall of his arm over her waist, the sleek, heavy satin of her gown began crawling up the long slope of her thigh and sliding down the steeper side of her hip until it was bunched at her waist and her hem was slanted across her bare buttocks. Blood pounded in his head. From the tip of his rigid little thing, sticking straight out, hurting in its hardness, he seemed to be drawn by an even greater wash of heat from the radiant center of where she was bare. Before the very point of him actually touched her, there was a tactile awareness that dizzied him. The room was spinning so fast he felt as if he were being pulled away even as he was drawn forward. Then the head of his thing was just nosing the great soft halves of her bottom. The heat radiating with the throb of a single heart was like the first instants of a deep soul kiss.

*Did she move?* To get away. Yet—

There, in one blinding moment, his prick was deep between the unbelievably dear globes into the hot heart of them. His heart stopped. He was near death or disintegration. Breath, heart, sight, and hearing, caught on a single beat, paralyzed. Surely death would have been a gift. Her hand came back fumbling, then firmly pushing.

*"Stop it!"*

What else did she say? He could not understand. *Mumble-mumble.* Then her gown was yanked down purposefully as a window blind. He cowered in the glow of his own fever, amazed at his daring. And having dared, became the secret pirate of the night, who might never sleep again.

When her breath was once more steady, he slipped over inch by inch until he was again within her radiant warmth. Gently, ever gently, his arm aching as if he had been pitching ball all day, he snuck it over the valley of her waist. Where his knees touched her thighs she was bare. He fell asleep in the still hour of night when even cats crawl under parked cars to sleep and milkmen are an hour from rousing, with his hand cradling the soft curve of her belly.

He had to be called twice to the Christmas tree. The place where she had lain on the other side of the bed was a shallow depression filled with the disquieting memory of the night before. Yet he felt no fear of reprisal.

From that time on, night would ever come to him in the form of a woman, whether spreading lazily, lushly over the land, or furiously stripping trees, lashing dark seas. Lying soggily in his own sweat in stifling transient summer rooms in cities where a breeze never moved the curtains; or raining spring tears for the joy of a young girl's legs *and* some young heart's *tristesse;* or buttoned to the eyes in an ice storm with the sleet slanting out of a streetlight peppering his face; or groaning on rented bed for more and more while the bed springs once again impersonally sounded like the clockworks of soul—night would be a woman. Though the memory of Christmas Eve receded in the bright boyhood of Christmas Day, that *had* to be how being rich felt. Satisfaction was all around the boy to the degree of not wanting another thing. It was the first day he had ever lived that had not begun with a pang of anxiety.

FREEWHEELIN BOB! was a phrase that sprang to his mind for no reason and stuck like a refrain on each turn of the black balloon tires. He was certain he would grow up, get rich now, and marry little June Carter of *The Carter Family* from the radio and live happily ever after —freewheelin.

They were going to have their own house in Mississippi. "What kind of house, Mama?" he asked again.

"Oh, just a nice little house, Son." She looked away to see it better and describe the curtains in the kitchen, the stove on which she would make them fudge and in which she would bake brownies, and all the things there were to eat when you were off relief.

"Welch rabbit!" he ordered ahead. She had made that once in the little kitchenette apartment she and Bill rented for a few weeks before they left for Albuquerque. Because his mom's cooking was no more sophisticated or extensive than it had been when she was a Campfire Girl, it suited Jack just fine. Brownies were her specialty.

She laughed. "Anything you want."

"Boy! We'll never go on relief, will we?"

*"No!"*

Mrs. Mac's back stiffened while she stood at the kitchen sink cleaning the chicken for Christmas dinner. The boy was watching her back.

She sniffed. "We can't help it we're on relief. It ain't our fault. If Daddy hadn't had to sell everything or let the bank get it. . . . How we do seems good enough to you when you ain't got no better. You have to make do." She said it without turning around. Chop! She split a chicken with one whack of her butcher knife. She went after a chicken like a surgeon performing an operation for the ten-thousandth time.

"Well, it doesn't seem good enough to me," Wilma said, examining her perfectly manicured nails. "I always *hated* it. I just couldn't *ever* get used to it." Her nails clicked nervously together like ruby beetles kissing.

"You think we *like* it?"

"Well, I don't have to do it. I've got a choice."

"Yeow. Let's hope your choice ain't just another of you-know-who's pipe dreams."

She meant Bill. Jack always knew everything she tried to keep from him by talking that indirect way.

"Don't *you* worry about it!" Wilma snapped.

"Oh, I don't worry about it. You made your bed and you can lie in it. I hope you're happy. But you never have showed me your marriage license. Why, I don't know if you're married or not. If someone asked me, I'd have to tell them, 'Don't ask me.' "

"Oh, *Mother!*"

"Well, I don't *care!* Never mind. If you don't give a darn what folks think, I don't. No, ma'am. What worries *me* is who's going to keep up the payments on that new bike Jacky just *had* to have."

"It won't be you!" Wilma vowed. "I guarantee you that! I'd steal first before I'd let you pay a cent."

"I don't put it past you. But we'll just see who has to pay off that wheel," she sang smugly. She had cosigned with Wilma. There was still $20 to be paid off at $5 per week.

"We don't have to stay here another minute if that's how you feel," Wilma said.

"Oh, don't get up on your high horse. It's Christmas Day. I didn't start it, though." Mrs. Mac always had to lay the blame.

"The first thing I'm going to do when I get to Mississippi is swim in the ocean, Grandma. I can go every day if I want," the boy said.

"I guess they don't have school in Mississippi."

*"Now, there you go again!"* Wilma jumped up. "Of course they have school. I told him he could almost *any* day, not *every* day. You just won't give Bill or me a chance, will you?"

" 'N' them kids there won't know I was a reliefer," Jack went on. "I'll be just like them! Boy!" It was too much.

Wilma put her arm over his shoulder, and they went out of the kitchen. They wouldn't let grandma pay off that bike now even if she wanted to.

His mom was beautiful. When he wasn't showing off his new bike around the block, he could spend an hour just watching her. She made his grandma seem so old, and even his Aunt Elfie didn't shave her legs. His mom seemed to grow out of her high heels, while Elfie seemed perched on hers.

In Wilma's suitcase were lotions, creams, mascara, eyebrow pencils, lash curlers like weird pliers, lipsticks, astringents, a perfume atomizer, powder and puff, nail buff, emery boards, orange sticks, nail polish like molten jewels; and with them she washed, sprayed, manicured, creamed, polished, and shined herself. She would sit on the bed after her bath with her robe stuffed down between her thighs, one leg cocked up on the bed, to paint her toenails a deep ruby red. In the tub she pumiced all the hair off her legs and laved them with lotion so they were smoother than any living thing on earth. She was very proud of her legs. She was what her mother called "short-waisted," which meant she had long legs. They were of a shape the boy had seen only in the hosiery section of the Monkey Ward's catalog, and she made him feel how he did looking at the underwear ads.

Then she stood with her back to him, her robe open, and spritzed herself from head to toe with Evening in Paris. The bottle was frosted royal blue with tiny stars on it so it looked like a tiny bottle of night. The atomizer ball wore a silver snood. The nozzle was like the head of a tiny silver prick. The smell gave Jack a hard-on. She sprayed the back of her neck, all around her front, lifting each breast to spray underneath in turn. Spraddling a little, however stylishly, she sprayed the deep auburn bush that was such a perfect upside-down triangle under her soft, scarred belly.

"Hey. Haven't you anything better to do, young man?" Still with her back to the boy.

"Hunh-uh."

"Well, I wish you would find something. Why don't you go out and ride your bike?"

He shook his head. Then, realizing she hadn't seen, "Naw. I'd just as soon stay here."

"I'll bet you don't hang around your grandmother when she's getting dressed."

Who'd want to. He shrugged. "I've seen her."

"It isn't good for you, you know?"

No, he didn't, though he certainly suspected anything that made him feel so good had to be bad. "Why?"

"Well, it just isn't. Might put bad thoughts in your head."

"Like what?"

"Oh, you know. . . . Don't you? . . . Well, I'll bet other boys you know don't hang around watching their mothers dress, do they?"

"Sometimes. They try."

She laughed a little.

"Except the Azunis. The Azunis never look at their ma."

"You aren't going to call me 'Ma,' are you? I hate that. Call me 'Mother' or just 'Mom.' "

He had thought about that. When he looked at her she was not like any of those things. She was all new to him. It was as if she had changed in the few days just past from the distant primary notion of "Mom" into a real flesh and blood woman of a dimension and depth that exploded his baby view right in his face. There was suddenly so much of her. Yet he was as tall as her chin. So though he usually called her "Mom," she was also in his mind as "Wilma," while between the two something that was neither was growing.

"I never seen no one as pretty as you," he confessed and turned red.

She laughed and said, "Why, thank you very much, kind sir. That's the nicest thing anyone's said to me in days. Come here."

It was true. None of the guys had as pretty a mom as he.

She wrapped her robe around her tight and sat on the edge of the bed. "Oh! You're too big a boy to sit on my lap. But you don't mind if I baby you just a little bit. For all the times I missed."

She laughed throatily and kissed his lips by just nipping them with her own. Yet he could taste her lipstick, smell the sweet warmth of her breath. She lay back on the bed with his head on her shoulder, holding her right hand palm to palm against his left, overhead, measuring. "You'll have nice hands for a man. They are almost as big as mine. Your father had nice artistic hands." She laced her fingers in his and, squeezing tight, hugged his hand to her breast. She closed her eyes and talked about how much she had missed him all those years and how nice everything was going to be now that they were together. They would remain together until he grew up and was ready to go out into the world on his own. It was a promise. It was nice there. His grandma was in the back of the house. The door was closed, the shades pulled.

He asked very softly, "Can I touch your titty?"

"Jacky! For goodness sake . . . why?"

"I just want to, to see how it feels."

"You never have?"

"No."

"Well, I don't know—I don't approve. . . ."

"Please."

"Well, just a little," she said.

Shaking, he slipped his hand in the top of her robe while she muttered about how she *knew* it had not been a good idea for him to be in the room while she was dressing, and how from then on she would see that he wasn't.

*Yeah, yeah. . . .* He could not cover it with his hand. It spread and slipped around. . . . *So damn soft. Softer than a kitten, a rabbit.* So different from either. The nipple was warm like a little nose in his palm. Then it stiffened until it felt like a warm mulberry, soft from the sun. He tried to gather her breast up, but it was like trying to pick up a balloon filled with water.

"That's enough, now," she said gently. She playfully extracted his hand. "Out of there!"

"It's so soft like."

"Um."

"How does it feel to you?" he wondered.

"OK."

"Does it feel bad or good?"

"Listen, you're just getting much too inquisitive. You wait and ask your girlfriend someday."

If he had to wait until Dolly Mae grew tits, he would sure as hell have outgrown his bike.

"Now let me up. I've got to get dressed. And you go comb your hair."

"I combed it."

"It needs it again."

Somehow it was all in the way she said "bath," like it was spelled "baaath," that made it so much more than just a wash.

She was dressing for the long bus trip. He had on his new blue cotton gabardine slack suit and shined shoes. His hair, water-combed down, was beginning to leap up fore and aft.

"You need a haircut. Bill likes a kid to keep a neat haircut," she observed.

OK. . . . He would make a concession.

She snagged her garter belt from the open suitcase, a silver satin harness which she fastened at her waist in front, then spun around so the fastener was in back. The nickeled garters on their elastics danced around her thighs. She bent to step into her panties. They had lace around the legs and over the diamond-shaped place where her pussy went. She flipped her robe up in back as she drew on her panties. For a second Jack saw her smooth white bottom framed between her garter belt and panties. The elastic caught under the shimmering cheeks, squashed them upward until they dimpled—then they snapped into the satin so forcibly he blinked. She wiggled, walking in place without lifting her toes until everything was properly adjusted. Her robe dropped. She bent forward to lift her breasts one by one into the shiny satin cups of her brassiere. When she wheeled around—hurrying now—the garters were dancing out of the legs of her panties like elastic snakes, their little nickeled jaws with their rubber teeth clicking together. There was a shiny, shadowed dimple in her panties over her belly button, then smooth over the unique roundness of female belly down to where lace framed the shadowed crush of her bush. She sat down quickly, crossing right leg over left knee, to start on her stockings, which she had gathered in a soft beige cloud in both hands and which flowed carefully up her leg toward the rubber-toothed snakes lurking in her lap and under her thigh. She hooked the front garter, rolled her extended leg to straighten the seam, fishing the while under her butt for the other garter, finding it, stretching it out, losing it. When it snapped back, she made a prim face, found it again, hooked it up.

*"Fuck"* lay on Jack's tongue like a large butterscotch lozenge.

She stood up and stepped into brown pumps. Her stockings were a gleaming tan sheen up her legs to the pale hairless white bulge of thigh indented by the tensed garters. Her back looked so soft he thought he might lift it like the skin of a big pussy cat. She had one small mole near the left corner of her mouth and another she would not say where. Otherwise, except for the scar in the bend of her left arm, she showed not a freckle. Her teeth were large and white, her lips soft and generous, her eyes dreamily myopic when she removed her glasses, huge bright and liquid brown when she had on the thick rimless glasses that were so strong they made her temples appear notched when one peered through them at her.

"Mama?"

"Ummhmm?" Peering in the mirror, tugging at the corner of her right eye delicately with the tip of her little finger.

"I sure love you."

"I sure love you, too." Sort of garbled. Inspecting her teeth.

"I'm sure glad we're going to Mississippi."

"So am I."

"When I'm grown up, how old will you be?"

"Well, when you were two, I was twenty-two. You figure it out. Why?"

"I just wondered."

"Monkey."

Then they were very busy. Everything had to go into the suitcase. She checked her watch. It had been a present from Bill. She had one large suitcase and one smaller one she would carry on the bus. He had a new big black cardboard suitcase his granddad had bought at a hock shop for a dollar and a half. The old man had strapped an ancient piece of harness he once used for a belt around it just in case. Jack took the closed suitcases into the other room.

"Please don't forget to send my bike, Grandpa," he said.

"Box it up right today," the old man promised. Behind the shy Mac-Deramid grin he looked sorry to see the boy go. He was embarrassed.

No one in the family ever learned how to say good-bye. Leavetaking was accompanied by a litany of dire warnings against the dangers of travel, the season, and one's personal failings, all recited in the emphatic, unvarying tone and form of religious responses, all totems against the unseemly sorrow that burned in the MacDeramid breast.

Then inevitably: "Don't take any wooden nickels."

"I won't," Jack fervently promised as if the world were overrun with a nutty horde of wooden-nickel pushers. Frankly, if he had been offered one, he would have snatched it like a shot.

His grandmother carefully buttoned his blue melton relief coat just like the ones state prisoners wore, brushed the hair out of his eyes, quickly gave him a cold, stiff little kiss. Her breath was bad. She needed to have all her teeth pulled and get dentures.

"Now, you be a good boy. And remember how we taught you to do. I guess you'll just get to Mississippi and forget all about your old grandma and grandpa." She tried to make it a joke, but her resentment was so plain she was near tears.

"No, I won't, Grandma." He was hurt that she would think such a thing.

"Well, you be sure to write and let us know how you're gettin along," the old man said in a tone he used with equals.

Jack felt proud. And for the first time his feelings were mixed about going. They always had done everything for him they knew how. He suddenly realized he was leaving his grandma's biscuits and peppery flour gravy forever; that when it came to whittling something for a kid, or fixing up his shoes, clothes, toys, or a hurt, the old man had no peer. And his mom was the world's worst cook when it came to the main things. And Bill was pretty mean sometimes. But then he thought of the cold winter out on the back porch where he had slept the first year they were on Cleveland. He thought of the days he waited all day in a commodity line with the old man with hunger and the first fever of some childhood disease making him sicker than hell. It seemed like everything he caught, from chicken pox to measles, began on the relief commodity line. He had to go. The church was trying to sell the house. His grandma and grandpa would have to move soon, anyway. He didn't want to be cold anymore—*ever!* Sorry. There was a real house waiting. *His own room!* It was thus decided. There was his mother.

Why was it when his grandma said "Mississippi," there was in her voice every nuance of scorn she harbored for "the Hot Place," though she hadn't personally seen either. If anything good ever came out of Mississippi, it would be news to her.

"If for any reason you want to come home, we'll always make a place for you, Son," she said in a rush as if it were something she just had to get out.

*"Mother!"*

*"Well?* I'm sorry. But I mean it. I hope everything you've told us is the truth. But if it isn't, I want the boy to know he's got a place here. That's all I'm going to say. But I just had to say it."

"Well!—"

"Go on," the old man cut in. "Go. Your cab's waitin. We'll be all right. . . . Take care now, hear?"

"Bye, Grandma. Bye, Grandpa."

Why in the hell couldn't they ever do *something* like Dick and Jane? the boy wondered. When *they* went somewhere, there wasn't all that heartache.

He wiped it out. They were in a Black and White cab and off relief. He was happy.

As soon as they were really on their way, he wanted to throw himself on the pretty lady beside him and convey to her his happiness at being off relief, which was beyond his power to articulate. But she had changed slightly. She seemed suddenly sad. He realized she was pretty much a stranger. It was as if a cloud had come in front of the sun. He became anxious. She was staring straight ahead. Her mouth was set in a determined way. It was cold and bright outside. The familiar streets, houses, curbings, and trees of Wichita seemed only remotely familiar, as a place occasionally passed through, but not in any way any longer home.

"Mama?"

"What?"

"What's wrong?"

"Wrong? *Nothing.* Why?"

"You look sorta sad."

"I do? Well, I don't mean to." She smiled and took his hand and squeezed it. "I'm just so happy we are all going to be together, I guess I can't hardly believe it. Pinch me." But her eyes were sad.

He smiled. There was a riddle they played when he was just a tad:

*232*

*Three kitties went for a sail. Flopsy, Mopsy, and Pinch Me. Flopsy and Mopsy fell overboard. Who was left?*

And serious, literal little kid that he was, he was a furious, frustrated pinchee for a lot longer than one of his intelligence ought to have been, much to the delight of everyone whom he had trusted so completely.

He pinched her.

"It's just that your grandma always has to *say* something. She can't let well enough alone. She has to get *her* two cents in."

"Yeow, she always says whatever's on her mind. That's for sure."

"Well, I'm not going to let it get me down!" Wilma decided brightly. He was with her.

"To hell with them all!" she said with a flick of her gloved hand.

He wasn't going to go that far. But when she laced her long fingers in their tight brown leather gloves in his and pressed his ungloved fingers against her thigh, he was willing to condemn all else to hell in a handbasket. When she crossed one leg over the other, her stockings zizzed.

"Sonny boy, you're sure lucky having such a pretty-lookin sister," the cab driver said, leering shyly at Wilma, setting their bags on the curb in front of the Trailways Bus Depot.

"She ain't my sister. She's my ma," he said.

"Sure don't look old enough to have such a big boy," he wowed.

She just smiled and gave him a dime tip.

"Why did you do that?" Jack wanted to know, thinking of all the better employments he could arrange for that ten cents.

"You're supposed to tip cabbies when they help you with your bags."

He thought that over. "It's sure great going first class, ain't it, Mom?" he decided, repeating what his granddad said on those infrequent occasions when he traveled by car or cab.

She laughed aloud and hugged his head against her, caring not a damn about his haircomb. "You betcha!" she said.

When they had checked their baggage through to Pascagoula except for the one they were going to carry, she suggested, "Let's have a Coke."

A Coke! Just like that. No nagging. No waiting until later. Life was improving too fast. There were the little distinctive Coke glasses full of shaved ice. If you ordered a limeade or a "400" you got it in a Coke glass. Jack wondered if Coke cared. It only seemed fair the others get *their* own glasses. He had lime; she had cherry.

"Don't eat the *ice*," she warned, as if it were contaminated.

"I always eat the ice," he protested.

"You don't eat the ice in public. It's not nice. It's annoying."

If you didn't eat Coke ice in public, just where else would you have the opportunity? was what he would have liked to know. Wealth had its less attractive responsibilities.

Still, when she let him buy a brand new comic book *and* a Mr. Goodbar for when they were on the bus, he was so jaded he no longer begrudged the cab man the dime tip. *Thank you, my good man. I'm gettin mine!* was how he felt about it then.

The wondrous names of all the places people were going rolled through the station from the flatulently honking loudspeakers: "*. . . boarding now at Dock One Sante Fe Trailways to Dodge City, Liberal, Guymon, Borger, Tucumcari, and Albuquerqueeeeee. . . .*" The voice was like Ned Sparks', bored, capable of calling destinations through eternity. "*Continental Trailways Cimarron Special loading on Dock Two for Ponca City, Enid, Stillwater, and Oklahoma City. Change for Ada, Ardmore, Denton, and Forth Worth. All aboard.*"

"That's us." She took his hand.

The driver punched a bunch of holes in the first of their long string of tickets, winked at the boy, and offered Wilma a hand up. He had a neat uniform and a cap canted rakishly over his right ear. Jack wanted to sit in front where he could see the road, but Wilma led him back to the middle. It was all right once they were in their seats. It was like being in their own little room down between the high seat backs. She let him have the window seat.

"We're moving." The big engine way back in the rear whistled, and the driver ground it into gear. She took his hand. "Here we go." Jack was braced as if about to be airborne.

"Relax. We have a long ride ahead of us. Happy?"

"Yes!"

"Love me?"

"Sure!"

"And from now on we'll stay together no matter what, right?"

*What was that?* They were pulling out of the station, turning out on Market. "Yeow. Sure."

"Through thick and thin?"

"You bet. Thick and thin."

"Monkey." She squeezed his hand.

He was up on the edge of his seat, eyes glued to the window so he wouldn't miss a thing. He always tried to get his money's worth. *Happy? Yeow.* He had never been so happy. There was little to compare it with. He hoped he was happy enough. Cokes, comics, candy, everything coming before he even formed a desire for it. It was too much. How happy was he supposed to be? He hoped he wasn't missing any of it. He *did* wish they had taken those front seats.

Wichita dwindled away into a shantytown out across Harry Street. Then the bus slowed and came to a stop at a railroad crossing. Outside the window a little girl in a dirty, ragged dress under an adult's sweater that was riddled with holes stood at the mouth of an impromptu road that led back to a shanty camp of tattered tents, cardboard and tin-sided shacks. Her face was beautiful, though very sad. It was as if she had never laughed. Stringy, dirty blond hair blew around her face like the snakes of Medusa. If he had a sister, her face would have looked like that. And Jack suddenly loved the girl more than anything or anyone in his life, more than himself, more than his mother, more than anything! He wanted to quickly take her everything she needed. He wanted to keep anyone from ever hurting her. He would certainly never hurt her himself. He would gladly die for her—no question. She carried an empty old bucket in her left hand. Maybe she was going for water. He wanted to take her with them to their new house where she could take a hot bath, wash her hair and tie it with a ribbon, where they would both wear nice new Dick and Jane clothes and never feel any heartache. She had on a pair of boys' tennis shoes many sizes too large for her. Her poor, beautiful thin legs looked so cold. He waved. She lifted her thin right arm and waved back as if under water, so solemnly it stirred waves of sweet pity around in him until he was aware of an everlasting ache no amount of riches could ever dispel.

"What-is-your-name?" he mouthed so near the cold pane his breath fogged the glass.

She smiled slightly and shook her head, not understanding.

"What-is-your-name?"

She smiled the more sweetly and shrugged.

Then a freight train like a cyclone blew past in front of the bus. There was no way to make her hear. The train rumbled away. The bus' air brakes let go—*chhhhh.* . . . The bus began to roll. He pressed his forehead against the cold glass to look back. He saw her turn away from the road, swinging her bucket. God, but her sweater was full of holes.

His mother hadn't even noticed. She was leafing through a *Woman's Home Companion* idly, her mind on something else. He said nothing to her about the girl. But from then on, he could close his eyes and always see her.

"Tell me again about our house," he asked when they were out of town, fully on the road.

"Oh, *Jack.*" She was annoyed.

"Can I have bunk beds in my room so I can have friends stay over the night?"

"Now, that's enough!"

"Well, I just like to talk about it."

"We've talked enough about it. You'll make me tired of it before we get it."

"What do you mean?"

"What do you mean what do I mean?"

"You said *before* we get it. Don't we have no house?"

"Yes. Of course. It's just that we have to work out a couple of things."

"What do you mean?"

"I mean Bill has to take care of some things."

That was news to Jack. "But you said—"

"*All right!* Now, that's enough! There are things you just wouldn't understand, things that are just not a little boy's business. Now everything is going to be just fine, if you will shut up about it and leave me alone."

So there was the catch again. The entire success of the world hinged on his silence and deportment.

"Hey! Don't look so glum. Don't you trust your old mom?"

"Yeow. . . ."

"You've just been around your grandma too long. That's what's wrong with you. Wait until you've been with me awhile. Come here and give me a kiss. I'll fix you up."

She could. She would. She did. Certainly something like a house was no simple thing. There almost *had* to be problems. He understood. Though a desperate fundamental angel suddenly a long way from home whispered in his window ear: *Obey your instincts. . . .*

She turned her lips out to kiss him with the wet pink part inside her lipstick and so save her makeup.

There is nothing on wheels more illicit than a cross-country bus. There are forty people or so locked in together day and night at sixty miles per hour. No train or plane is as intimate. People who travel by bus live more viscerally than those who fly or go by rail. A bus trip is not an event but merely life in transit. Even those taking a bus vacation were traveling on a shoestring. Their mementos were all so alike each had to be boldly inscribed SOUVENIR OF . . . lest someone think they got it elsewhere. Early in 1940 there were few vacationers on the American trailways. It was as if those who went by bus lived lives in which the expense of a ticket was such an extravagance it could not be bought without guilt, no matter how necessary the trip. And there were more servicemen traveling around. Every bus seemed to have a soldier, sailor, or little lost Marine. Up front talking to the driver was a pretty lady in a fur jacket and high platform shoes who was going to visit her husband at the Norman Naval Station. At each rest stop she and the driver had coffee together.

"Don't *they* look chummy?" Wilma asked the boy.

The pounding of the big tires over the joints in the highway became so a part of the boy that the rest stops became the unnatural experience. He blinked forth in someplace like another place, groping unsteadily through the sunlight or floodlit night toward a lunch counter where the wax-paper-wrapped sandwiches were a continental common denominator along with Coke, Orange Crush, Dr. Pepper, 7-Up, Nehi, and Delaware Punch. Root beer might be any weird brand at any stop. People repeated the name of the place where they stopped as if saying it meant they were aware of being somewhere. The toilets, lunchroom, souvenir counter were touchstones assuring them they were properly routed, surely bound, on their way. By bus.

In the night, signs, fences, lone farm houses, towns slipped past. Sometimes the bus passed under keening overhead powerlines. An occasional car was overtaken and left falling behind. They raced a freight through the night—highballin.

In Oklahoma the air smelled of oil. On the lawns of homes pumps like giant grasshoppers sucked oil from subterranean pools in what was once the world of dinosaurs, going up and down like insane cocksuckers in a relentless rhythm. Everywhere there was the bobbing, bobbing: insatiable insects pumping oil out of the heart of the earth day and night.

"I hate those things," Wilma said. She did not explain.

Snuggled down under her coat in the darkened bus at night, isolated from the others by the high seat backs, protected from the world rushing past by safety glass, she and the boy were truly alone together for the first time in his memory. He pressed against her back, and she snuggled into him, trapping his hand just beneath the place where he sensed the weight of her breasts. They slept. His backside froze while his front was warm as toast. But it was too good a deal to risk for greater comfort.

He awoke feeling stuffy, rumpled beyond repair; his mouth tasted of brass, his eyes burned. She took a tiny handkerchief and cleared sleep from the corners of his eyes with her cool spit. She tried to comb his hair with the rat-tail comb she carried in her purse, succeeding only in electrifying it into a wild whisk.

"This is Denton, Texas," the driver announced. "We will be here one hour for breakfast."

"Where are we?" some sleepy man asked.

"Denton. Denton, Texas," the driver said again. "We will have an hour here for breakfast. Lunchroom on your left. Restrooms to your right. One hour."

Everyone was anxious to get off and stretch his legs. Jack could not get his shoes on. His feet had swollen during the night. *That* had never happened before. Man! They were tighter than new when he finally got them on. He walked off the bus like a Frankenstein's monster. Wilma's tan and brown two-toned gabardine suit was very wrinkled. His own clothes were worse. They looked like something dragged out of the dirty clothes hamper and put on. Nor did he have anything else in the hand baggage to change into. It had been an oversight. She seemed embarrassed to be seen with him. He tried to pull some of the wrinkles out with his hands. The suit had been the first new-bought clothing he'd had in years. He had been so proud of it when it was new, but it was just another cheap damn thing that looked like shit now. *You can't count on nothin,* he reminded himself.

He wanted a ham salad sandwich and an Orange Crush. She wanted him to eat some eggs. Then, to compromise, "Have a ham and egg sandwich."

"I hate ham and egg sandwiches."

He got the ham salad. What was the difference how you had your ham? was his thinking.

"It's just baloney ground up," she hissed.

"Must be why it's so good." He had always wondered how they got ham to taste so delicious.

"Monkey."

She had only a donut and coffee. Nor could he get another comic, or a souvenir horse for a dollar. He really wanted that horse.

"Later," she promised as if they were in a hurry.

"Why can't I just get another funny book, then?" he pleaded.

"You couldn't have read all the other one yet."

"Yes, I have."

"Then read it again."

She was not much fun between Denton and Fort Worth. She seemed to be concentrating on something, anxious about something. He wondered if she was getting sick.

"No. I'm all right. I just have a little headache." She did not want him to bother her. She would not make small talk.

"Read your funny book."

"I read it."

238

"Read it again."

"I *did* read it again."

"Then take a nap or something. Let me be. I have to figure something out."

In the big Fort Worth bus depot where everything was grimier, busier, noisier, and more cowboy by far than Wichita, he could hardly hear the buses called or understand half of the destinations. Wilma planted the boy on a bench and told him not to move until she came back. She said she was going to go call Bill. They had to change buses. There was a three-hour layover. Jack was hungry.

He could see her in the phone booth. It was strange thinking of that pretty young woman over there as his own, that they were really part of one another. She looked more like a big sister or aunt. She wasn't like anyone else's mom that he knew. A mom was tired, old, smelling of food and soap, damp from washing something and had nagging complaints that might wipe her out at any minute. His was sure a good one, he congratulated himself. He didn't want to lose her, certainly not in such a loud dirty place as Fort Worth. There was the stuffed head of a longhorn steer on the wall up near the ceiling. The horns, tip to tip, were wider than he was tall. When he looked back to the booth, she was gone. He spun around on the bench. There were so many people, moving around, sitting. If by the power of his will he could only make them all stop for a minute, he could spot her. Where had she gone? Then there she was back in the phone booth, rummaging in her purse in that characteristic, almost-with-her-nose-in-it way she had. Maybe she had to get change or something. He sighed and sat back. He would not take his eyes off her again.

She was talking pretty good at someone on the other end of the line. She looked mad. He could almost hear her: "OK! OK!" Then there was less agitated talk, and she hung up. She fished casually for the return of her dime. When it was not forthcoming, she gave the box a ladylike shot and clearly said, "Damn!"

"What's wrong, Mama? Did you talk to Bill?"

"Yes, I talked to Bill," she said, barely able to pry apart her teeth to let words pass.

"What's wrong, then?"

"We've run a little short. I spent more at home than I'd expected. And I'd be damned if I was going to ask Mother for anything after the way she talked."

Jack felt sorry his grandma had blown her big chance to lend them some money. Poor Grandma, she would never learn.

"But Bill's wiring us some right away. It should be here in the hour."

"I'm hungry." He thought she ought to know.

"Well, you'll just have to wait until we hear from Bill."

"Can I get just a candy bar?"

"No. It would just ruin your appetite."

A whole box of Snickers would not have curbed the animal in him.

"We'll just have to sit tight," she said more kindly. "I'm hungry, too. You don't hear me carrying on. Be a little man. Buck up."

If that money did not get there pretty quick, he would be too weak to chew, let alone buck. At least around his grandma's there was something to snap. Not anything good, but *something* to fill a hole in you: a dried prune or two, a brown banana, sugarbread, burnt toast—*something!* The memory of his last ham salad sandwich made the back of his jaws ache, made him salivate until he had to swallow. He was too hungry to talk. She, too, was anxious. She shredded a Kleenex. They sat looking in opposite directions for time to pass until they could go get the wire.

Western Union was about four blocks away. They walked it so quickly his side began to hurt. Fort Worth wasn't so sunny, either. In fact, it was colder there than it was in Kansas. The ocean where it was always summer seemed so far away Jack began to fear it might be a lie.

There was no message for them. The woman went through the sheaf of telegrams twice.

"Nope. Sorry."

Then because of their obvious anxiety, she checked the string of tape hanging out of the printer in case it had come in the last few minutes. "It could come in the next hour or so," she said. "Could be there was a delay at the Pascagoula key. Never know, those little places." But Jack knew she did not believe it. "Check back in an hour."

He was starving. Wilma could see it in his upturned face.

"Listen. I hate to have to ask you this." She stared at her knuckles gripping the locked mouth of her purse. The lady stiffened visibly. "We really are flat broke. I *know* that money is going to get here. But we haven't eaten since early this morning, and the boy is about to have a fit if I don't get something in him soon. I wonder—"

"I'm sorry. I'd like to help you out. But I just can't. It's against company policy. And I just don't have it to spare, besides."

"Just a dollar until the money order comes."

"I'm sorry."

"But it's just a loan. My husband said he was going right down and *send* it. Can I help it if Western Union gets their wires crossed or something? Fifty cents, then. A quarter to get the boy a sandwich."

She shook her head gently no. "I really *am* sorry. I just can't. If I loaned two bits to everyone who came in here lookin for money orders that never come, I'd be broke every week."

"But mine *is* coming."

"Honey, if I was you, I'd give your husband another call."

"Hell, I don't even have a *dime*."

"Oh, here!" The woman dug ten cents out of her smock. She looked right at the boy, shook her head, and went back to her ticker.

"Thanks," Wilma said. Then, muttering as they went out the door, "Hope she can spare it."

Jack did not understand. He thought it had been a generous thing, the lady giving them a dime.

"Lousy bullbitch!" his mother muttered.

He had a lot to learn. He was still looking back to see why she was so angry with the woman when she yanked him by the arm.

"Come on!"

"What are you mad at me for?" he wondered.

"I'm not!"

"Can we get something now?"

"No! I've got to call Bill again."

"I'm *hungry*."

"I *know* you are hungry! There is nothing I can do about it until we get some money. You'll just have to tough it out. You can *thank* your Daddy Bill when you see him."

She tugged him along for blocks. They were on a street where winos slept in dusty doorways on little piles of litter wrapped in raggedy overcoats or freezing in short jackets, curled like children in the cold, the clear glass pint empties, sticky from cheap wine, near to hand or head. There was one whose scabby bare feet Jack could see through the soles of his shoes. He felt sorry for, afraid for the doorway men. A drunken Negro, tattered as a scarecrow and bearded under his shapeless felt hat, stumbled out of a doorway toward them yammering incoherently, his arms open as if to embrace them. His eyes were bright red. Slobbers glistened in his whiskers. Snot dripped from his flaring nostrils. Jack clung to his mom's waist. She sidestepped the drunk's awkward lunge. He stumbled past, tripped, fell headlong into the gutter and lay there blubbering. They turned a windy corner that plastered Wilma's short skirt against her legs. They leaned into the wind. Up ahead were the three tarnished gold globes of a hock shop.

It was warm and snug inside, with stuff hanging from all the walls, the ceiling, cramming the small room as if it were a great treasure chest. He could have spent a day there just looking at the things. There were guns and guns and guns. Pearl-handled six-guns, police and Army guns. Musical instruments to arm a marching band and orchestra. Gold. Silver. Old stuff. New stuff. Radios, irons, tools. Sporting equipment. God! All that stuff there in the heart of skid row. The man was in a wire cage where there was a cash register, safe, and watch repair counter. Wilma shoved her watch through the gate in the cage.

The man picked it up as if it might bite him. He grunted. He screwed a jeweler's loop into his right eye and held the watch up to it. He pushed the watch back through the gate, unscrewed the thing from his eye, pulled his mouth down at both corners, closed his eyes, and shook his head no.

"What's wrong with it?" she demanded. "It's a good watch. Cost thirty-nine fifty. I know. It's an Elgin."

"I don't need."

"But what will you give me?"

"Let me see."

She pushed the watch back through the gate in the wire.

He picked it up and looked it all over again. Plainly he did not like her watch. Jack wanted to bust his fat lip for insulting her watch. *What the hell did he know about her watch? It was an Elgin. He had read it right on the face. Seventeen jewels.*

"Four dollars, no more." He put down the watch and became busy in the back of a big gold railroader's turnip off to one side. He did not look at them.

"No!" she said. "Let me have ten."

The man picked up the watch again. "No." It only took a glance. "I give you four. No more. Take it or leave it. I don't need. You need."

"No," she said. She retrieved her watch.

The man had forgotten them before they were out of the store.

They tried two other pawnshops. One offered four dollars; the other would only go for three-fifty. "Nobody needs no Elgins," the boy said.

Back in the bus station, they crowded into the phone booth together to call Bill. She talked to someone, but it wasn't Bill. She was mad. She slammed the receiver back onto its fork. The machine again would not cough up their dime. She swore and stamped her foot. She looked like she was about to cry.

"Why don't you call Grandma?" he suggested.

"*No!*"

"What are we going to do, then?"

"I'll just have to see if I can cash a check," she told him.

That they had a bank account was a surprise to Jack. It was a family first. There was something very wrong about Bill and his mom and checks, he seemed to recall. *Hot checks,* that was what his grandma called them. He wasn't sure what it meant or how you heated them, but he knew it could get you in jail.

"Don't cash no hot ones," he pleaded.

She looked at him sharply. Then, "Don't worry."

She led him to a bench.

"I won't be long. You wait right here and watch our suitcase."

"Can we eat then?"

"Yes." She touched his hair. "I'll hurry. But if it takes me a little, you wait right here. OK?"

"But hurry."

"I promise."

Then he saw her again about fifteen minutes later out back on the loading ramp, talking earnestly to a tall man in a tan cowboy hat, wearing a belted hip-length leather surcoat. She clutched the sleeve of his coat. He carried a leather Gladstone bag. *What was she doing? Was she crying? She was!* He got up and started toward the swinging doors out to the ramp. There was a crowd of people rushing for a bus suddenly between them. When he had weaved through them, she and the man were gone. He ran to the end of the ramp. He looked both ways up and down the dingy street. Nothing. He tugged the coat of a man who was trying to get some gum from a wall-mounted machine.

"Did you see my mom? She was right here a minute ago, talking to a cowboy in a leather jacket. Did you see her?"

"No. No, I didn't see nobody, sonny."

He had *seen* her! It hadn't been a mirage. His stomach felt even emptier. It ached constantly. *She don't care. She don't care about me. Fuck her! Dirty, stinking bitch. All she cares about is her fucking own self. I don't even care if someone does steal her damn suitcase!* He took all the time possible walking back to his seat and waited until his butt was surely as red as a baboon's from that hard Texas bench. She had been gone for *hours!* He left her stinking bag to look out for itself and went prowling the depot.

The magazine rack was a treasure trove. He leafed through the detective magazines like those his Uncle Kenny always read. *Amazing. Startling. True.* All had screaming good-lookers on their covers having their clothes torn off by some tough guy. Their dresses were up over their stockings, showing a slice of thigh and a frosting of black lace. Their big squashy knockers bulged painfully out of their brassieres.

Their screams, ripped from such creamy throats, reverberated in his private ear. His face throbbed.

"Hey, little boy!"

*Me?*

"Yeh, *you.* Can't you read? No pawin the magazines unless you're going to buy." It was the lunchroom cashier. She looked ready to come out from behind her cash register for him.

*Boy! People sure got excited over things.* He carefully returned the magazines.

"Nobody wants to buy a book with some kid's sticky prints all over it." She wouldn't let up. "Unless you're goin to buy somethin, you got to sit in the waiting room." She ran a tight newsstand.

NO SOLICITING! NO CHECKS CASHED! NO LOITERING! NO BROWSING! NO FREE WARMUPS! NO CREDIT! Signs were everywhere. Texas wasn't giving an inch.

The frigging suitcase was still there. A fat woman was sitting beside it, paying it no attention, reading an *Amazing Love Stories,* eating a Mounds. She poked half of one of the little twins into her butt-like mouth and tore it cruelly in two as if the bar had bones. The pure white coconut in its dark chocolate robe made his mouth water. She skarfed the other baby and nibbled the chocolate off her fingertips.

He went to the men's room. He stood at one of the squad of urinals. The place smelled so strongly of pine disinfectant it burned his eyes.

He became aware of a guy at the washbasins looking at him.

"Hi," the guy said. "Taking a trip?"

He seemed friendly enough. Though he was not a big man, he gave the impression of being weighted down. He was neither young nor old, though younger than older. Beneath his rather puffy face his beard already showed like black grease, though he had certainly shaved not too long ago. His clothes were heavy, needed pressing.

"Me and my mom's going to live in Mississippi." Jack shook the dew off his wienie and zipped it back into his rumpled new slacks.

"How'd you like to earn a fast quarter!"

"A quarter?" It was as if Jack had forgotten what that was. *Hell, yes!* "How?"

"You ever jack off?"

"Hunh?" Had he heard right?

"You know. You ever play with your prick?" He pointed at Jack's fly. *Sure. But what business was that of his?*

"If you will play with mine, I'll give you a quarter." He had buttons on the fly of his baggy trousers. He had a Pocket Book in his overcoat pocket. He fumbled his dick out. It looked dark, fat, and wrinkled up in a collar of inflamed skin. It looked ridiculous in his clumsy fingers. He was jacking it gently.

*Play with your own!* was Jack's thinking. "Naw."

"Come on. I won't hurt you." He reached with his free hand toward one of the free toilets.

"Naw." Who'd want to do something like that. Oh, sure he and his cousins had played with each other's. And he had played with Harold Lloyd's ugly pickle in return for Harold's playing with his own beauty, but he didn't like it. In fact, if he hadn't been such an ethical guy, he would have reneged on the deal. The head of Harold Lloyd's miserable stub was in the raw fleshy roll of his chopped-off foreskin like a pale nut in some poisonous fruit. Then they had both tried to fuck Danny King in the ass one afternoon when he got them over to his garage on the pretext of seeing a show and they found Danny dressed up in his old lady's clothes with a black lace mantilla over his red hair and his face made up so like a woman's they had to keep looking real close to make sure it was Danny. . . .

*Keep your fast quarter, slow man.*

He always had a suspicion all that handwashing after taking a leak was queer. After all, *he* hardly ever pissed on his fingers. And since it spent most of its life in his pants, he figured his prick had to be cleaner than his paws. If you *were* nuts about washing your hands, why didn't you do it first? was his thinking.

The fat lady was gone. The suitcase was still there. It was beginning to take on the look of a permanent landmark. A porter had come by swishing muddy scrubs reeking of Pine-Sol and left the case untouched, a rock in a muddy, painted sea. Jack began counting to ten in the belief that when he had run out the very next string, she would BE THERE! His confidence held for almost an hour. *Goddamn her! Why couldn't that bastard in the donicker just of given him that quarter?* Tears blurred the clock. He blinked. He tried to watch both doors. FUCK HER! He wanted to scream it out. He resumed counting to ten. Each digit was an ache in his chest above the pangs in his belly. He no longer had any faith in the system. If she didn't turn up pretty soon, he would go find a cop. It was only a matter of time. She wasn't coming back.

They were calling their bus. "First call Trailways Gulf Coast Special for Cleburne, Corsicana, Waco, Temple, Austin, Houston, Galveston, Corpus Christi, Harlingen, Brownsville. Change at Houston for Port Arthur, Baton Rouge, New Orleans, Gulfport, Biloxi, and Mobile. Loading Dock Four. Thirty minutes. Please check your luggage."

Well, now they were going to miss the damn bus! *That bitch!* He hated her. He hoped she was being killed, punched, stomped, cut up like all those women on the detective magazines. *No! I'm sorry. I didn't mean that.* In fact, if she showed up by the time he counted ten three more times, he would forgive her everything. He counted slowly. Nothing.

*OK. That's it. I give up.* And suddenly all anxiety lifted. So he was hungry? He would get a cop, call Grandma; she would send him some money. He'd go home. It would be tough, after all the bragging he had done. The kids back in Wichita would never believe him again. He had described his house to them as if he had seen photographs. He should have known, though, it was all a lot of crap. Nothing she ever did, no matter how well-intentioned, ever ended up any way but hurting somebody. Nothing she ever promised ever came true. So that was that. *To hell with her.* She was on her own. He was beginning to feel *good* when she blew up, out of breath but looking so beautiful to Jack it was as if the sun had come out.

"Whew! Think I was never gettin back?"

*"Yes!"* His chest ached so he could hardly speak. He wanted to hit her or something. He felt guilty for feeling so bad. That was *just* what he had thought.

She fussed with her hair, which was now pulled back off her face and caught with her scarf. It was a little damp at the temples. Her eyes were bright. She looked as if she had washed her face and put on fresh makeup.

He peeked in her purse when she opened it. There were several dollars in her fat wallet. Her breath smelled of whiskey. She gave him a dollar.

"Quick, get something for yourself to take on the bus. I've got to go to the restroom before we board." She said she wasn't hungry.

"Bill sent the money?" he asked.

"Yes."

It made him resentful to think of her eating in some restaurant while he was waiting there with his guts gnawing his insides. He blew eighty cents out of the dollar. He ate one sandwich standing right there, wolfing it down so fast he got the hiccups. He got on the bus with two ham salads, one pimento cheese on whole wheat, two chocolate donuts, an orange drink, a Hershey, *and* a Mounds.

He left Fort Worth with his belly gloriously full, warm and cozy once more. Sucking his orange drink through a straw, he asked, "Who was that man?"

"What man?"

"The one I saw you talking to in the cowboy hat."

She hadn't been aware he had seen them.

"Oh! *That* man. Oh, he's an old friend. . . . An old friend of Bill's. We had a drink for old times' sake."

In the dark on the road out of Austin after midnight he snuggled up under her coat against her bottom. As soon as he actually touched her, she jumped a little and reached back to push him firmly away.

"You roll over there toward the window, OK?"

"I'm cold."

She adjusted her coat over him and gave him a pat that said he was expected to stay right there. He didn't like Texas for shit. When did it start to always be summer?

They were nearly broke again in New Orleans. They had to watch their pennies. She went out to cash another check. She was gone a couple of hours and had a few dollars when she came back. But she was real grumpy, even though she'd had more to drink in New Orleans than she had in Fort Worth.

In the bus that night when she was asleep, he put his hand up her skirt under the coat and played with her legs up where they were warm and soft for a long time until he just brushed her crotch. She woke up angrily, smacking ineffectually at his hand beneath the coat.

*"Just stop that crap!"* she hissed.

He guessed *that* stuff was over, then. He was a little relieved. It simplified his life, actually. From then on he could concentrate on the scenery.

They crossed into Mississippi one morning. It had indeed been warm since New Orleans. Mornings were all like spring. Fields were green.

"Is our house like that one?" he asked while oozing through Gulfport.

"Oh, no, not exactly."

"I can hardly wait. Boy, it's going to be so great having my own room and everything. . . ."

"I wish you would shut up about that for awhile. I *told* you there were some things we had to take care of."

"What things?"

"I don't want to discuss it. It's none of your business. You wouldn't understand," was her explanation. "I've got a lot on my mind," was her excuse.

They passed many nice little houses coming into Pascagoula, none of them theirs. It was just a little place. The main street was barely paved.

The bus stopped in front of a restaurant-store-bus-depot. They got down into the dusty street. Dust like brown talc covered their shoes. There was a colored man on a wagon box hauled by two mules parked against the wooden sidewalk. His granddad would have loved to see those mules. He loved good mules. He made a mental note to find a picture postcard and send it to him. The bus door whooshed shut. The bus pulled away. Dust blew up off the street from the engine in back. Their main baggage was on another bus.

No question about it, it was like summer there. The sunlight was as if reflected off water. It made Jack squint. There was no taxi. Wilma was disgusted Bill had not met them. They went inside so she could telephone. The people in there who were sort of sprawled around looked the woman and the boy over. One redneck said something behind her back while she was on the phone. The man he said it to laughed and slapped his thigh. Both men wore bell-bottom dungarees and unpressed work shirts. Both chewed tobacco. Both looked her bare legs up and down and grinned. Her stockings had given out in New Orleans.

"Someone is coming to get us," she said.

Presently, a dusty black, dented, however new 1940 Plymouth two-door sedan pinged up to the porch. A fat man in a white shirt and rumpled white cotton trousers held up with both workmen's suspenders and an old black belt with a monogram buckle heaved himself out of the car and lifted his yellow straw Panama in greeting. He looked sort of Indian. His black hair was slicked straight back from his low, flat brow. He had what the boy took to be a locust on his right cheek right by his ear. Then it looked like a leech.

"Uncle Willy, this is Jacky, my sonny boy. Jack, this is Uncle Willy Best, who's been awful good to us since we've been here."

The man put out his strangely narrow hand. His little finger was missing. His hand was stiff. He was not a good man with his hands. It was as if something soaked up the impulses from his brain before they reached his mitts. That thing near his ear was a molelike, slightly pendulous growth out of which grew dozens of wiry black and gray hairs. It made Jack want to gag. His gut was like a pillow out front. He was tall, yet stooped slightly, as if suffering from a bad back or actually trying to shoulder his big flat ass. The way he wore his trousers hiked up high under his tie, caught in the crack of his butt, enhanced the illusion.

"Ah'm right pleased to meetcha, suh," he drawled.

"*Hunh?*"

"I guess the cat's got his tongue," Wilma explained, clearly ashamed of Jack's Yankee manners. It was that "suh" that threw him.

Uncle Willy Best and the boy were not going to be the best of friends. Everything else being equal, there was still that thing by his ear. Before he started the car, he plucked a Tums for his tummy from a roll and slipped it too daintily into his thin-lipped slit. He wore black high-top police shoes that looked so tight his ankles bulged out the top as if he had a touch of elephantiasis. His socks were white for sanitary reasons, for the eczema that inflamed his gouty ankles. With the engine pinging merrily away up front, he took time to lay his pinkyless hand on Wilma's bare knee—pat it, pinch it, rub it—and teasingly made as if to run his hand up higher. She stopped him, patted his hand.

"*Now, now,* Uncle Willy. . . ."

"A woman pretty as you gives me ideas."

What gave him gas? was a question in the boy's mind.

"Wouldn't want to get me all hot and bothered, now, would you?" Wilma sparred.

He sniggered dirtily, slipped the dusty, untuned Plymouth into low, and rode the clutch, criminally letting it out. Some uncle.

The road out front was dirt. The drive was dirt. There was no garage. Uncle Willy parked the Plymouth under a spreading hickory tree where the woodpeckers could shit on it. There was a dull-looking, rather malnutritioned boy lounging on the front steps barefoot, his dungarees rolled to his knees. He got up when the car turned into the drive and waved languidly. That would be Allen, whom his mom had assured him would be his friend. Allen was fourteen but not very big. Coming out on the porch was a fat little biscuit of a girl about fifteen and another about seventeen with black hair braided in tiny braids wound around her head. The latter was by far the prettier. But both girls were big and flat in the butt like their father, with heavy, shapeless legs. Their legs made Jack think of the Goons in *Popeye*.

The house was a two-story frame monster that would have been a farm house in Kansas. Next door was a vacant lot fenced with barbed wire in which four cows nuzzled the sparse grass. On one corner of the broad front porch there had been added a rough board extra room that looked like a large crate rather than a habitation. Across the dirt drive under the tree, near where the car slept, was a one-room clapboard shack only slightly larger than a rough dollhouse. Jack thought it was for play. It was like the cabins at the YMCA free camp for poor kids they had out on the Ninascaw River one summer, except this one was unpainted. The green boards were beginning to warp and pull their nails. Out back of the big house, off in the side yard, was a woodpile near a burned-off place where a big iron pot like the kind cannibals cook missionaries in was turned upside down on a couple of cement blocks.

The cabin was where Wilma and Bill lived. When Jack saw the dead army of Calvert bottles abandoned under the shack, he knew, with a sinking in his heart that went beyond despair, disappointment, anger to touch some ironic, funny chord that made him smile even while water blurred his sight, *We are home.*

After all, how else could it have been? Had he really expected all that other? No. He had only half believed her from the start, though truly *wanting* to believe. To make his grandma be wrong. Make his fears foolish . . . *just once!*

*But look at her! Great God!* It was as if she had delivered him to his vision.

*Was she blind?*

"This is only temporary," she said.

# 24

IF there was to be applause for reuniting a doting mother with her son, Bill was willing to rise for it. And Wilma and the boy *believed* that it was not he who had left them stranded in Fort Worth without lunch money. In spite of all evidence to the contrary, he had to be given every doubt while Western Union got hooked with the blame. For how else could they live with him? When the boy's bike arrived by express from his grandparents, that too was Bill's gift.

Yet Jacky felt a constant nagging inside his chest. He *knew* his grandmother had signed the paper for that bike. He *knew* his mother had tried to hock her watch in Fort Worth. He had dined on stuff paid for by money she had somehow hustled. Still, in the face of Bill's energetic generosity and Wilma's cow-comfortable acceptance of the charade, he did not dare spoil the party.

After only one night in the little cabin under the hickory tree in Pascagoula, with a pint of Calvert to toast her return, Wilma was apologizing to Bill for having ever doubted him about the money order she never received. Two weeks later the boy was telling anyone who asked that

Bill had gotten him that red Schwinn for Christmas and was happy to do it, though the knot in his chest would not let go. Neither Wilma nor Jack could tell each other why.

They were sprawled on the bed in the cabin one muggy afternoon. There was no chair. There was no room for a chair. There was a pipe across one corner on which they hung their clothes. There was a chest of drawers. There was the double bed with peeling, enameled iron stead. The open horizontal two-by-fours framing the simple cabin were shelves of chance.

"Bill didn't really get me my bike . . . did he?" the boy asked.

She rolled over onto her back and held her magazine overhead. She wore only a slip. Her hair was up in curlers under a snood. The magazine was *Horoscope*.

"Did he?"

"Well, Bill and me."

"Oh."

She put down her book, brushed back his cowlick, tweaked his nose.

"Don't worry so much about things. Makes you look like a little old grump."

"I don't."

When she uncrossed her smooth legs, it seemed he could hear one warm thigh peel itself from the other.

Was it because their lies were so vulnerable it would have been a pity to shoot them down? Was it because even to the sensibilities of a young boy most of his fellow citizens appeared so stupidly unquestioning that bullshit became common currency whether in the service of history, crime, business, or romance? If so, a charming conneroo of your own was ever preferable to some sincere stranger striving to sell you a miracle solvent or drag you down on your knees beside him to make some fateful decision for Christ. Then there was the practical fact—he did not have a return ticket.

Everyone liked Bill. Though he personally viewed everyone out of prison as peapickers, hoosiers, hayseeds, or clodhoppers, chumps who rode a bicycle or carried their lunch, he could light up a beer-sour bar on any skid row, spinning the fabric of a new, portentous day out of nothing at all but energy and every man's yellowed dreams, which, like cotton candy, were all sugar and air. But for beer-sour men the taste was tooth-sucking rare. When he had gone he was missed and asked for when he was not there, welcomed when he arrived as something more than a brother. He often took the boy with him and he sat at the bar beside him, instructing him confidentially: "Just watch me operate." And he'd turn the joint on, though Jack could never be certain quite why. All afternoon it seemed as if they were all about to go somewhere else known only to Bill, not too far from Big Rock Candy Mountain, which existed in the boy's mind as a real place in the Ozarks where all the drunks and down-and-outers of the earth were going to get them a little place one day and raise chickens. Through the twilight afternoons in a bar, departure seemed ever more imminent. But they never went anywhere, except eventually home, the bartender ultimately taking Bill's personal check in spite of the sign over the register proclaiming:

In God We Trust
Others Pay Cash

Bill was supremely confident he could out-think anyone in stir or out. He was most proud of his great hat size. He would do a little shuffle, click his heels, slash his palms together as if about to receive money, and throw the boy a conspiratorial wink.

"Cop a mope," was his advice to Jack. "It's a hard life if you don't weaken," was his philosophy, which never made any sense to the boy.

He always had to be best man in the room, the center of all concern. It was always that way. He would absolutely organize the immediate lives of any crowd he was in. And he *was* Wilma's and Jack's. So in spite of Jack's regret that no one wanted to take him swimming in the Gulf—those picture postcards hadn't shown the waters teeming with sharks and stingarees—his dad was better than your dad, whoever you were. He decided to take Bill's advice and "tough it out. Tough it out." It always seemed something more exciting and fine than anything he could imagine was just out of sight beyond the rise.

Once he accepted that "our home" had been a fiction constructed to shelter his mother's pride when she came to take him with her, he was able to scale down his aspirations to having a bed of his own. At first he shared the bed in the cabin, sleeping against the rough boards of the wall on the other side of Wilma. But after reaching for her soft ass when half-full of Calvert, overreaching himself and snagging Jack's gristly little hump, Bill shooed the boy into the main house to share a sagging double bed in the parlor with the landlord's son, Allen.

The first night, Allen was so excited about it all he pissed the bed. Jack was awakened by the warm flood. He could not imagine what it was. It was not a situation in which he had expected to find himself while sharing a bed with a fourteen-year-old boy. He figured it was some monstrous Southern slime in which he would dissolve and so raised an unholy holler that awakened every boarder on the place including Red Shorty Jones, who slept in a big packing box on the front porch.

When Jack realized by the odor what it truly was, he was more aghast than if it *had* been some Mississippi quickslime. Allen just grinned sheepishly.

"I shoulda warned you about that," Uncle Willy Best chuckled, shuffling in wearing a cotton nightshirt and felt slippers. He couldn't have been more amused if his old blind black dog had pissed on Jacky's leg mistaking it for a favorite tree. The dog had somehow been blinded by lye water.

Allen's problem Jack subsequently related to the dollar-sized ringworm whorl on the ball of his right foot. Nobody suggested changing the sheets. Clinging for his life then to the combing of that sagging old sogger, Jack came to the conclusion that people in Mississippi were more than a mite funny but not at all laughable, decidedly, if not clinically, weird.

However, by daylight it was Jacky who was the strange one. Ringworm, incontinence, moley growths, waters full of stingarees, woods full of cottonmouth snakes, and fried baloney and grits for breakfast were the standard.

Allen, who was in ninth grade, read as if tracing each letter in stone with his forefinger. Jack felt sorry for him, while it was Allen who more truly pitied Jacky. Poor, backward Yankee who had never gigged a flounder or frog; never bitten the bony buffalo fish, skarfed Mama Best's muddy shrimps, or swallowed a "rawor yoyster"; never whipped the head off'n a black snake or plugged a gar; never heard a painter back in the piney woods cry like a lost baby; never milked; never trapped a flying squirrel high in a pecan tree; never really chopped kindling or laid a proper fire; never sucked an egg; never fucked a cow.

The old lady cooked on a monster cast-iron wood stove in a long room that paralleled the back porch. All the boarders ate there at a homemade pine table. Uncle Willy sat at the head and dealt to Doc, the young shipyard medic who lived in the best room off the parlor, Bill and Wilma, Mrs. Best, or one of the daughters at the foot, then Red Shorty Jones, the other daughter, Allen, and Jack. One of the girls always waited table after everything was dished up. When it was hotcakes, eggs, and stuff like that, the old lady and one girl never sat down.

Doc was courting Mary, the older and prettier of the two. She was seventeen. When she was eighteen, she and Doc would get married. Bill teased them about it so bad, Mary often left the room rather than suffer the embarrassment. The other girl was a fat, short, slab-assed thing who always looked painfully chapped between the thighs for all her slow-witted cheerfulness. She was perpetually splotched by some subcutaneous inflammation. All the Best women were so thick of ass and ankle they looked as though they had settled in a loose mold. Wilma tried to help them look better. She did their hair and gave them makeup, only to have their ma make them comb out their hair and rebraid it the way it had been, wash their faces, and return the half-used lipsticks and rouge. The old lady was angry for days. In fact, she was always angry about something. She never chatted with anyone, never reminisced. She was always in the kitchen, even when everyone else was in the parlor listening to the radio. She trusted Yankees not at all. Of the three, Mary was most likely to be wearing shoes around the house.

Jack would watch the old lady frying baloney in spitting-hot lard on that iron, wood-gobbling stove and almost feel in anticipation the sting of hot grease splattering her bare, broken-down instep—but it never happened. She sliced up half a baloney and fried it for breakfast as if it were ham, with no notion she owed those to whom she served it an explanation, to say nothing of an apology. The boy's expressed preference for his baloney to be served "raw" on white bread with lettuce and mayonnaise was dismissed as a Yankee barbarism. "Raw" baloney was a way to get worms. So it was fried baloney and eggs like rubber novelties, grits and gravy for breakfast, raw whole milk from the Bests' four cows, complete with curds and whey and an occasional cow hair and never cold enough to kill the smell. After Allen showed one night how he fucked the cow with the bent horn called Moon and swore he'd caught his old man doing the same, at which time they made a pact never to tell, Jack passed when it came to milk around there altogether. He figured, what could you get from something like that?

He was hungry *all* the time, if he stopped to think about it. Even the candy bars around that town were mostly odd, molasses-based types out of New Orleans, Atlanta, Chattanooga, or Memphis. Only the New Orleans bottled Cokes were superior to any he had tasted elsewhere, sharper. He decided he might survive on Cokes and windfall pecans.

"Coke's the worst thing for you on earth," Uncle Willy informed him then, less concerned for his Yankee health than in showing up yet another Northern ignorance. "I catch Allen drinkin one uh them things, I'll take a hoe handle to 'im. Eat chore guts right out, boy. Fella down at the co-op put a hound's tooth in a bottle of Coke, stoppered it with a rag, and set it on a shelf down there, and it plumb *dee*-solved." He popped a Tums for his tummy into his lipless mouth and reared back in his rope-bottomed chair, spreading his thin, weak thighs and adjusting his balls by hand beneath the burgeoning weight of his belly.

When Uncle smoked, he puffed little black Mississippi Crooks cigars. When he didn't smoke, he stoked his lower lip with a finger of Copenhagen snuff. So did the old lady. *That* was why she never talked! And so did Allen and the older girl from time to time. Jacky tried it while everyone watched amusedly. It was awful. It was hot. His lips were numb for an hour. The taste was with him for days.

Delaware Punch and Dr. Pepper were acceptable, as well as the local fruit "so-dees," but Cokes were definitely deadly. Every time Jack snuck one at the bus station or a back street café, he felt like a fiend. Most of the time he went around like all the other kids with his mouth stained blue from Delaware Punch, which made him at first glance "one of the boys" when he reported for Pee Wee Football practice at his public school. If you went out for the team, you got out of school at two thirty in the afternoon, an hour before everyone else. Unless you wore a brace or actually played a musical instrument, it was impossible to retain any teacher's respect or catch the heart of a pretty girl if you did not try out for the team.

The team suited up in a dirt-floored room under the stands where there was an unheated shower bath, a puddle of cold dope to keep you from getting athlete's foot, metal lockers without locks, and uniforms that smelled as if they hadn't been laundered from one season to the next. But the uniforms *were* real: shoulder and hip pads, canvas pants with thigh pads, red jerseys, white leather helmets, and some shoes. If a boy could not get a perfect fit in shoes, he had the option of playing barefoot. Jacky would trot out onto the stickery Bermuda sans shoes, indelibly blue-mouthed from months of Delaware Punches, ready to do or die for Pascagoula. The entire team subsisted on fried baloney and pop.

On the first day of practice he forgot to call the coach "suh" and was never trusted near the actual ball ever afterward. Though he could run faster shod or barefoot than any white Mississippian in fourth, fifth, or sixth grade, the coach put him down for a tackle. Jack explained to him he hadn't *expected* to play quarterback right off, what with his being a new boy and all, and since fullback was cinched by a twelve-year-old who had failed back in second and third grades, he would be happy to hold down right half, or even left, if that more suited his style, or even an end. But forgot again to say "suh" and so found himself a second-string tackle, first down the field, last in the hearts of his countrymen.

The first game against Biloxi, he sat on the end of the bench in his reeking pads and red jersey, full of fried baloney, ready to snap out a

"Yes, suh!" at the first nod in his direction, clap on his battered white leather helmet, and go do or die for Pascagoula. He had understood how the coach simply could not take a chance starting a Yankee who had not absolutely proven his loyalty, but he began feeling anxious when the score mounted in the third period to 38 to 6 in favor of Biloxi. His side was stinging and snapping more at one another than at the enemy. The No. 1 quarterback had been benched in ignominious disgrace, but not even then did the coach look down the bench and yell, *"You! Nigger-lover, get yo ass up in there and hold 'em!"*

Oh, Jacky would have bit and clawed, snapped and barked—bulldog *and* stingaree! What he would have done for Pascagoula that night under the dim lights if only it had called upon him.

Bill said he was ashamed of him. The only damn kid on the team who didn't get into the game. He chalked it up to Jack's being some kind of obvious sissy. Jack knew it was sheer blind ignorance on the part of the coach, but being a kid confronted by superior adult wisdom, he could not be absolutely sure.

Jack played exactly five minutes all season, other than when Pascagoula kicked off—a rare experience—for which the coach liked to employ him because he could get downfield at least as quickly as the ball. The other five were when he mistook Jacky for another kid who also played without shoes.

The coach also taught a version of American history in which he called a spade a spade, or more precisely, a Nigra a Nigra. So did Jack's homeroom teacher, pretty Mrs. Kearns. The first time she opened her wide rose petal mouth and said "Nigra" and Jack knew she was not referring to the falls up by Canada, the short hairs on the back of his neck honestly raised. When *he* said in replying to a question, "Negro," she looked at him as if he had done something unspeakably dirty.

"You mean Nigra, boy?" she inquired.

"I mean a colored person," he elucidated.

"What color uh person you referrin to?"

"Uh, brown, you know. Negro."

The class tittered.

"You got a lot to learn around here, boy. Don't he, class?"

"Yessss Maaaam!" they chorused.

"You mean Nigra in Mississippi, *suh.* I recommend you don't forget it."

Jack nodded OK.

"What's that?"

"I didn't say nothin."

"You didn't say nothin, what?"

"Ma'am."

"One thing we *do* teach in Mississippi is manners."

In spite of that, he could get a hard-on just sitting there dreaming on her bare legs. She never wore hose. She shaved her legs, like his mom, until they shone. They were long and shapely from foot to knee. You could see she was proud of her small feet. She always wore high-heeled strap sandals. They were never run-down or scuffed. On hot days she hiked her full cotton skirt up above her knees beneath her desk, carefully adjusting the hem repeatedly between comfort and modesty, never dead certain of the line. She was nothing like all the old-maid teachers they had back in Kansas. She was more like someone's big sister, aunt, or mother. Her husband was a big, slowfooted country boy who had played football for State and now had the town's used car lot. He always picked her up after school in a different car. Or almost always. It was a game to try to guess what make he would arrive in next. Jack could kill half a day just dreaming about her and that big guy doing it. She didn't even come up to his shoulder. *Boy! I bet he makes her grunt,* he dreamed. And he sat there with a peewee hard-on, secretly mashing it, skinning it back through his dungarees, squeezing it tight, while she raved on about Nigras and Yankees and the War Between the States. He did not dare call it the Civil War. She hadn't heard of that one.

Nothing he did ever pleased her. When he read, he read too fast. "We don't need no show-offs around here. Ah cain't understan a dang word yer sayin. J. C. Y'all read that passage, please, suh."

"Yessum!" J. C. would hop to it, putting his finger right on it to pin it down and proceeding to stammer and drawl his way through the recitation.

While bees buzzed in and out the open windows, Gulf breezes wafted the scent of magnolia and fresh-cut grass, touching the old moss-hung trees as if they were daughters. Outside, a "Nigra" handyman mowed the school lawn. It looked so cool and shady under the bordering willows. . . . The whole afternoon stretched beyond the drone of some kid's voice like the moo of a cow. It was all Jack could do to hold his seat when the school was adrift on waves of summer. Ole left eye already gone to sleep, righty about to follow.

He concocted an elaborate scheme to get into Mrs. Kearns' attic and bore a peep hole above her bed so he could lie up there and watch her and her husband fuck. More boys dropped their pencils in her class to try to look under her skirt than any he had ever been in.

Then one day during fire drill he realized she was standing on the second-floor landing of the steel grate escape talking to Mr. J. T. Gates, the principal. He simply dropped out of line under the iron steps and looked up. Great God! There it was! He felt swarming faint. White panties caught in the crack of her ass, the bulging cheeks, the fringe of russet hair. She shifted her weight to one foot; there was the whole dark bulge of her pud. His knees felt liquid. But Christ! Her butt was covered with a rash of angry little red bumps. And her panties were not that clean, either. He felt he had been fooled again. He was disgusted with himself.

Across the way rising above the trees on the roof of a cartage company was a huge sign:

M-👁-ss-👁-ss-👁-pp-👁

Back in line, he whispered to Elizabeth Sue Gowen, the prettiest girl in the class, who lived in the fancy part of town along the Gulf Road, "Be my girl."

"Ah cain't be the girl of no damn Yankee."

So he never asked another in Mississippi.

# 25

AFTER supper Red got out his guitar and sat on the steps, chording. Uncle Willy sprawled in a dilapidated, overstuffed parlor chair that had been demoted to porch furniture. Weathered and worn to the color of unpainted pine, small game made a home in its mildewed horsehair innards. Jack would never sit in it. *What kind of thing could you catch from something like that?* A canvas-covered pillow kept the springs poking through the cushion from biting Uncle's butt. Inside the house, the women were heard in the kitchen doing the supper dishes. Wilma was in the cabin. Doc was in his room, reading. Bill slouched on the other side of the steps urging Red to play "Troubled in Mind," a song Red claimed to have written. Uncle opted for "Great Speckled Bird."

Red sang mournfully, nasally, soulfully, so you could appreciate the distance involved:

> Oh, I'm dreaming tonight of my blue eyes
> who is sailing far over the sea. . . .

He sang:

> From the broad Atlantic Ocean
> To the wide Pacific shore
> She's coming down from Birmingham
> On the Wabash Cannonball.
> Oh, she's long, she's tall, she's handsome
> And known by one and all
> As the greatest combination
> On the Wabash Cannonball.

His guitar was the drivers of that great train, his voice its lonesome call.

Light faded. Evening came to the land reflected off the Gulf in such a more suspenseful way than evening which creeps over the prairie. It hung between memory and tomorrow, where the great trains of all time run between lonely thoughts of blue eyes and nostalgically purified notions of home.

Though they were both drunks, Bill had no respect for Red beyond the possibility he actually *had* written "Troubled in Mind." Bill swore he could quit drinking if he wanted to. Red said, "Booze cost me my wife, my two little girls, my good times. I know it. But I just can't leave it alone. Oh, hit's a hell of a note. Don't ever let whiskey get aholt uh yuh. It don't want to let go."

"I won't," the boy promised solemnly.

He could be on the *Grand Ole Opry*. Everyone said so. He played a full-sized guitar, though he was hardly bigger than a boy.

> I was born in East Carolina
> But West Virginy is my home . . .

Bill passed Red the bottle. Red was yet a few songs from tears. The night was young.

> What a beautiful thought I am thinking
> Concerning that Great Speckled Bird.

Remember her name is recorded
On pages of pure shining gold.
All the other birds flocking around her
And she is not loved by the squad.
But the Great Speckled Bird in the Bible
Represents the Great Church of God.

Out in the road Jack was showing off on his bike. Since Allen's old Hawthorne from Monkey Ward's hadn't fenders, Jack had stripped down his own, lest he be thought ostentatious. He then killed his casual diffidence by coming down the road standing on the seat, no hands. Allen nearly killed himself trying that one. Jacky could sit on the handlebars riding the thing backward. He was master of the Russian Cavalry drag, where he stood on one pedal, both feet, at about a 45-degree angle to the bike and plucked a dandelion or handkerchief from the ground. Moreover, he could link all the stunts together in a continuous program. Everyone said he ought to be in a circus.

Bill and Red, high and happy, borrowed the boys' bikes—two wobbly, unsteady old clowns in work clothes and work shoes. They touched wheels, veered off, touched again, and crashed in a jumble of arms, curses, broken spokes, barked shins, and twisted handlebars. Emerging from the wreckage at the end of Bill's arm was the pint of Calvert Special—intact. They had a drink to celebrate their survival before trying to extricate themselves from the tangled bikes.

Bill wanted Jacky to wrestle Allen. He could beat the older boy in a foot race at any distance. Allen couldn't run. His old man said he had "shortness of breath."

Bill warned the bigger boy, "Son's pretty good. Quick as a cat." He figured Jack could out-quick the bigger boy.

"Watch 'im, boy," Uncle Willy cautioned.

Full of Bill's confidence in him, Jack went for Allen's legs for a quick takedown. But he was just not strong enough to hold him or pin him. He could take him down easily and escape with only a little more difficulty, but in the end, Allen's size and superior leverage had to prevail.

Bill bet Uncle a dollar on Jack after the first takedown. After a quarter of an hour, no fall, Uncle asked him if he'd like to make it two.

"Hell, yes. I'm no piker," Bill said.

When Jack fell into a scissors between Allen's knobby knees, he felt as if his head were in a vise, and Bill sensed he was overmatched.

"Is that a legal hold?" Bill inquired.

Jack could actually feel his cranium being compressed, squeezing the stuff inside. A pain shot through his brain front to back. His head hurt so bad he could not think what to do. Grass and dirt made his face itch intolerably.

"Calf rope?" Uncle Willy asked.

How could he even reply?

"He ain't crying calf rope or he ain't no son of mine," Bill reported from his forward vantage point. "Get out of that," he commanded.

"Had enough?" Allen inquired under great strain. His legs quivered from the tension.

"No." Muffled. Not if he crushed his skull. Jack could imagine it cracking like a melon, the way the kid's head looked who had been swept off a freight-car ladder by the Safeway warehouse siding and fallen under the wheels the summer before, back in Wichita. Bobby Walters and he were right there. They had hopped the car ahead of the kid. They knew the kid, Danny Troost, a quiet, unathletic boy on relief. They hopped freights going through the yards all the time. Rode them from Central down to Douglass to go to the movies on Saturday. But who would have thought Danny would try? Then he was lying there on the tracks near the Third Street crossing, his head squashed flat, his face like a bloody, blown-out ball. All the things were there, eyes, nose, mouth, but empty. And everything from inside had popped out the top in a great spew—brains, blood, sense, like the insides of an exploded pup—bits of red meat and gray stuff. His old lady had it all put back together by a mortician so that when they paraded by his casket, there he was, looking like a cheap hand-tinted photograph. Jacky and Bobby had taken up a collection in class and door-to-door in the neighborhood to buy flowers. They returned to the spot on the tracks where Danny had been crushed every Saturday on the way to the movies until they began arguing over exactly which tie marked the spot.

Jack kicked with both legs the way real wrestlers do to get free. He could not escape Allen's scissors. He turned his head slightly and sank his teeth into Allen's leg just above the knee.

"Ow! Goddamn you!" Allen howled.

Jack was free. He rolled away from the slashing blow Allen let go at his seemingly much narrower head. A new pain shot through his skull as pressure forced it back to its normal shape. He was blinded for an instant, though both eyes were wide open. Allen did not know he could not see.

"Not *fair*, Pa! He bit me lak some ole girl!"

"He didn't pin 'im," Bill insisted. "Got to pin to win."

"My boy says he bit 'im," Uncle said.

"Hell, if we counted takedowns and escapes like they do in the AAU, my boy would be way ahead on points."

"Don't know about that," Uncle studied.

"That ole snaggletooth of his'n goes right through you to your nerve." Allen sulked, rubbing his knee vigorously to illustrate his claim.

Jack didn't say a thing. He just stood ready, determined that if they were joined again, it was going to be no holds barred. He would have to do all the damage he could as fast as he could and hope that it was enough.

"I call it a draw, before someone gets hurt," Bill offered.

"I reckon we know who that'd be," Uncle grumbled.

"Well, what we have here is the example of a good big dog versus a good little one," Bill soothed cheerfully, pointing toward the moment he could conclude, "All bets off."

"Shake and make up," he urged, coming off the steps and dragging the boys together by the right wrists.

"He didn't have no call to bite me," Allen sulked.

"Well, you're bigger than me." Jack put forth his side.

"Come on, you hoosiers, or I'll take you both on."

"Oh, yeah?" Allen squinted.

"You think you two sissies can handle me, huh?"

With a yell they both leapt on him. Allen went high, Jacky went low. They took the man down. Then Allen was flung ass over breakfast off him, leaving Jack trying to pin his legs. He simply gave a heave with both legs that sent the boy straight up, flat out, about four feet in the air. He came down, splat, in a belly-buster on the ground. He was winded. Allen might have a broken arm.

Wilma wandered over from the cabin to survey the carnage. Bikes were broken in one corner. Allen was crying and holding his arm as if he had found it apart from himself. Her son lay flat as a cow patty, trying to catch his breath.

When Jack could get to his knees, Wilma approached and brushed dirt, grass, and his hair from his face.

"What in the world?" she wondered.

"Don't baby him," Bill warned.

"He *is* just a boy, Bill. You could hurt him."

"I didn't hurt him. Cop a mope, for chrissake. Want to keep him on a sugar tit all his life? I'll make a man out of him. Let him alone. He's all right. Aren't you, Son?"

Jack brushed his mother's hand away. "Yeow," he agreed readily, but still not ready to gain his feet.

Wilma went over to the steps. She did not like rough play. When she sat down, you could see up her dress until she tucked her skirt modestly under her thighs.

Bill had another drink, offered Red, Uncle, Wilma one. All accepted. Wilma took hers quickly, glancing around to make sure no one but those on the porch could see. Even then she felt guilty about taking a drink in front of Jack and Allen. She refused another. Uncle always looked at her in a way he never looked at any of his own women. He never bossed her around the way he did them. He was always asking *could* he do this or that, *would* she like something or another. She made him laugh, smile, act foolish, as no one else on the place did.

"Hey!" Bill crowed, leaping up. "Can anyone step through a broom?"

No one volunteered to know what he was talking about. Wilma knew, having seen about all of Bill's tricks by then, but she kept still, smiling knowingly.

"Get me a broom."

Jack ran back through the house to fetch it. "Bill's going to step through a broom," he told the unimpressed women in the kitchen. They were all barefoot, smelling of the homemade lye soap they boiled up in the big black kettle in the side yard, damp from doing dishes. They dried their hands on their aprons. Curious in spite of themselves, they followed the boy out onto the front porch. What was it? They shyly arranged themselves along the wall at the back of the porch. They would not take seats. They could not stay long.

"He ain't going to break my new broom, is he?" the old lady grumbled.

Bill held the broom horizontally before him between his knees and belt, one hand along the bristles and one hand at the tip of the handle. He visibly concentrated on the feat, exaggeratedly measuring the distance between his hands, seeming to judge the angle of evening light, direction and velocity of the wind, and rotation of the earth, calculating the phase of the moon, time of tides, and deflection of his dangle; all in a contorted, conniving conneroo's crouch. . . . Until Wilma said, "For *godsake,* Bill, get *on* with it."

He stepped neatly over the space between his hands and the broom handle with his left foot as if his life depended upon it. More calculation, drama, agonizing; he stepped over with his right, grimacing as if in great pain. The broom handle was now held behind his knees. The corded muscles of his forearms looked like great tense ropes. The tattooed heart with his first wife's name on the ribbon of it on the inside of his left arm looked like a brand on cordage. Up he rotated the broom perpendicular to his spine, then over his head.

He had stepped through the broom. There was a smattering of applause. The old lady sniffed and went back inside without further comment. She looked cheated to Jack. No one ever called her "Auntie," though Wilma had tried a couple of times. It just didn't work.

"You get in here and hep me now, Dulcie," she called.

Mary remained outside. She was close enough to her wedding to be more independent.

"Who's going to try?" Bill held out the broom.

"I can do it!" the boy cried. He had watched closely.

After a couple of false starts, Jack could do the thing in almost a single motion, virtually jumping through the trick. Bill hadn't had to go through all that stuff. He was funny.

Allen could do it after a couple of tries.

"Let's see Wilma do it," Uncle Willy suggested. "Bet she can't do it."

"Bet I can," she retorted. "I will if you will."

"Show 'er, Pa," Allen encouraged the gouty fat man.

He chuckled. "Y'all think I'm too old and fat, do yuh? Gimme that broom. Now stand back."

"Pa?" His oldest daughter had her doubts.

"Show them damn Yankees, Pa." Allen was on all fours and beside himself.

"This how?" Uncle grunted his swollen left foot over the broom so he was astride the handle. Unsteady, trying to gain his balance, he sort of hopped around the yard like a clumsy giant baby astride a stick horse. Trying to get his right foot on the same side of the handle as his left, he turned and fell over on his side. He went down loosing an airy grunt like an elephant lying down to rest. He had to call on both Allen and Jacky to help him up. He huffed back to his seat, fumbling a roll of Tums for a lozenge to relieve the indigestion all that exertion had stirred up inside him.

Wilma's turn. She got one leg over, modestly tucking her skirt in under, but not before everyone had a good look at her legs. Suddenly Jack realized that was what Uncle had in mind all along. She was clearly not dressed for stepping through a broom.

"Hey, let me go change into slacks and I can do it," she suggested.

"Nosiree!" Uncle protested. "Ah didn't change." He brushed the stained leg of his white cotton trousers.

"Aw, go ahead, Bill," Bill encouraged her. "Show these peapickers this whole dang family can wheel, wrestle, run, hold their liquor, and step through a broom with the best of 'em."

Put that way, how could she refuse? Modesty be damned. It was them versus the peapickin world.

Jack saw the shadow of her thing through her panties when right leg followed left. Uncle gave a soft appreciative grunt. Allen saw, too. The boys were both flat on their bellies in the yard, pressed tight against the grass. Only Red seemed not to look. Bill didn't seem to give a damn.

"Ah! Ah! You switched your grip," he challenged her, engrossed in the sheer athletics of the feat. He liked to show her off, anyway. He'd get a little high and start pinching her tits and flipping up her skirt in front of other men to tease her. "Best goddamn piece inna world!" he'd brag.

Then she was twisting the broom up toward her head. Between jacket and skirt a few inches of bare skin was exposed. Jack didn't like Uncle and Allen looking anymore. He could not understand why Bill did not stop her.

But she could not do it. There was the sound of a tiny tear. She let go one end of the broom.

"I can do it," she insisted. "I'm very limber. I was just afraid I would tear my sleeve."

"Want to try it, Mary?" Bill offered the girl the broom.

She demurred, shyly shaking her head no, pressing against the wall.

When Wilma sat on the steps beside Jack while Red was doing the trick, she idly arranged his hair, pulled his ear, fingered the hair on the back of his neck.

"You need a haircut, Sonny boy," she observed.

"Leave him the hell alone, will yuh?" Bill protested. "Just determined to make a goddamned sissy out of 'im, ain't yuh?"

"All I said was he needs a haircut."

"Needs a good ass-kickin. Needs to learn how to use his dukes. I'm just the Puke to teach 'im, too. Come on, keed. Put 'em up." He began sliding around the dusty yard, cycling with his open hands, thumbing his nose like some punk Mick kid. "Open palms." He showed them all his weapons. "You use your fists," he told the boy.

"Now you be careful, Bill," Wilma cautioned.

"Dummy up!" He danced in. "Here it is, baby boy. Let's see you tag it." He hung his chin out like a lantern.

*Swish!* Jack didn't graze a whisker. *Swish!* He took another cut. Nothing. Bill grinned at the boy. *Splat!* The flat of his hand made Jack's left ear ring.

"Don't lead with your right. Keep your guard up." He bobbed and weaved in and out on the boy, offering his chin.

*Whoosh! Whoosh!* Two roundhouse haymakers. Nothing. *Splat! Splat!* Both ears rang. Tears filled Jack's eyes.

"Bill," Wilma cautioned.

"Dummy up. I know what I'm doin."

*Whoosh! Splat!* This for that. Jack was getting afraid to swing. He was having trouble seeing through his tears. Allen was rolling on the ground with delight.

Bill dropped his guard. "OK, kid, hit me in the gut as hard as you can." He yanked open his shirt to offer his skinny bare belly, ridged with muscle like Roman armor.

"Be careful," Wilma warned.

"Don't worry. Like iron," he said through clenched teeth. "Give it all you got, kid."

"I didn't mean *you*," she explained.

*Pow! Pow! Pow! Pow!* The sound of the boy's fists thumping Bill's belly was like that of pummeling a leather sofa. Pain shot from both hands to Jack's shoulders. Bill only smiled, braced with legs slightly apart.

"Like iron," he said. Danced back, *Splat! Splat! Splat!* exacting his fee. Jacky's face felt on fire. He was silently crying.

"That's enough now, Bill," Wilma suggested.

"Shut up! This is important. Make a man of him or a girl."

*"Girl, you, you sonofabitch!"* Jack yelled.

*Splat! Splat!* He took two sharp slaps for his impertinence. There was the coppery taste of blood in his mouth.

"Come on! Want to talk like a man, do yuh? Show us what you got, tiger. Put some muscle where your mouth is. Hit the old man and win a cigar."

Jack hated him. He could hardly see him for tears. He could hear Allen laughing; the rest was a roar.

Jacky started to throw a right and held it, perhaps out of fear of a quick return slap. Bill feinted left. Jacky caught him with a left-hand flush on the button that snapped his teeth together. Accident or instinct, he heard the liquid china click of Bill's teeth. And zinged him again with a right. Bill was blinking and backing, bobbing and weaving. He wasn't set to slap back. Jack popped him again, eagerly, too eagerly, high on his right cheek.

"Hey!" he heard the man say. Bobbing and weaving, leaning forward in a crouch.

He was a windmill, a dervish, coming at him from all sides. Bill wrapped his head in his arms. "Hey!" Jacky was whipping them in more than punching then.

"*Sock him!*" his mother squealed delightedly, clapping like a little girl, stamping her feet. "That'll teach him to show off."

Jack set himself for a genuine uppercut in under Bill's guard that found his face.

"Calf rope!" Bill called.

"Your ass." Jack pounded his arms.

"*Calf rope!*" Bill cried joyously. And swept the boy off his feet into his arms, pinning his arms to his sides.

"What are you bawling about?" he demanded.

"*I don't know!*" Jack yelled back right in Bill's face.

Then Bill was laughing, and Jack began to smile even while tears rolled down his cheeks. He set the boy down and rubbed his jaw tenderly, working it around exaggeratedly. "He really laid a couple on me, had me seeing stars, you know," he told Wilma.

The boy had never made him that happy before.

"Serves you right," Wilma said. "The winner gets a big kiss."

"Naw. . . ." Jack hung back.

"Let's have a drink on it, pal." Bill held out the bottle to the boy.

"Bill!"

"Hell, he's had a drink before. Ain't you, kiddoo?"

"Yeow." Jack had had a taste more than once.

He took the bottle and wiped the mouth carefully with his left hand the way he had seen men do. He tilted back the bottle and took a big slug. It was only the smell that got him and the tendency to gag on the aftertaste. A man among men. He was more Bill's then than his mom's.

It was fully dark. Night birds piped in the trees. The cows in the field beyond were huddled under an old pecan at the far end of the field near their shed. An owl swept down from over the house, snatched a mouse from the pasture, and swooped up in a gliding sweet climb into a high tree, bearing its prey in its talons.

"Why don't we cop a walk?" Bill asked Wilma.

"OK," she said in a very soft way.

When they had gone, each with an arm around the other's waist, Mary went inside to unplait her hair and put on her long-sleeved cotton nightgown. Uncle Willy got up, belched, and went inside, too. Soon Jack could hear him tuning in the Carter Family's show on the radio. "You come along d'rectly," Willy instructed Allen.

"OK, Pa."

Red leaned against the porch pillar, chording his guitar.

"Man alive! I sure miss my old lady and them little girls tonight."

"Where are they?" Jack asked.

"They're in Galveston. She married this fella with a shrimp boat."

"How come you got divorced?" He knew all about that stuff. Bill had two daughters older than Jack by a previous marriage. That was one reason Jack's grandma had been so against Bill. That and because he drank. She did not believe in divorce.

"Oh, it's the same old story," Red claimed. "I was doin good. Feelin cocky. Writin songs. Had me a good little sign-paintin business goin. Had me a partner. Began drinkin. Let it get the best of me. Started livin just to drink. Next thing I know, I come home one night from a singin trip, about three sheets to the wind, and she'd moved my things out on the porch, and my partner's moved his'n in. But he wasn't no better than me in the long run. He drank the business up in the end. She says she's got her a *good* lovin man now. Goes right out on that boat with him. Don't want no drunk shorty lak me. Stay away from it, son. That's my good advice. Makes a man old before his time. Makes 'im so's he ain't no good for a woman, you know what I mean? Makes you neglec your kids. No good. For nobody. Get to feelin so bad thinkin about it, you just got to have another drink to make you forget."

"Hey, Jacky, want to go down to the cow shed with me?" Allen whispered in the dark.

"OK. I guess."

The boys drifted off to the side of the yard. Red sang:

> Goin' to lay my head on some lonesome railroad track
> And let that Midnight Special ease my troubled in mind.
> Troubled in mind, I'm blue. But I won't be blue always.
> Cause the sun's going to shine in my backdoor someday.

They ducked through the fence and cut through the rocky field, watching their step. Down by the shed Allen drove old Moon inside with a stick he had picked up off the ground. He put her head in a stanchion, threw a quart of bran in the trough. He got a milking stool from against the far wall and set it behind the small spotted cow. He dropped his trousers and began jacking his dick to get it hard. He never wore shorts. In the winter he wore BVD's. When he was hard, he got up on the stool, lifted old Moon's tail aside with his left hand, and introduced his thing into her big black-lipped cunt with his right. He began hunching her pretty fast. She mooed and tried to look back. She bowed her back a little. He hunched her real fast for a couple of minutes, sort of went weak in the knees, and stopped. He no sooner jumped off the stool than she pissed a stream.

"Mangy old bitch!" he snarled and kicked her in the side so hard she mooed again. "She shit all over me, onc't."

"Try it," he offered.

"Naw. I don't want to," Jack decided.

"Pretty good stuff. Better'n some ole girls. Better'n an old Yankee girl, I'll bet."

"You ever did it to a girl?" Jack wondered. Allen *did* have those sisters.

"Naw. Not exactly. We used to have an ole cross-eyed handygirl around here just before you came. She let me try onc't. But she was scared. Ma caught Pa pluggin her early one Sunday mornin 'fore anybody was up and was goin to get a divorce and everythin. Then Pa gets rid of that girl. An Ma cools down. Ma still don't leave him have none, though. So he'll come visit ole Moon onc't in awhile. And they's a nigger place up the river I know he goes to sometime."

"We better go."

"OK. I guess you're too young to do much good nohow."

It was sad being too young. It made Jack feel so alone. Red had made him sad. The cow had looked so sad. Jack didn't want to go into the house. Allen headed around back to wash up. He smelled like a cow. Across the yard, the light was yellow and cozy behind the flowered curtains in the cabin. Jack could hear his mother's portable tuned to dance music rather than hillbilly. The door was open, but a curtain covered the middle of the door for privacy. Jack wondered what a cow knew. Did it remember?

Approaching the cabin, he heard his mother giggle and say, "Bill! Don't be so rough. Why are you *always* so rough?" Then she giggled again.

He knocked on the screen door, calling, "Mama?"

There was a sudden silent moment. The bed springs squeaked the way they do when someone sits on the edge of the bed.

"Yes?"

"Can I come in?"

"Now?"

"Yeow."

A moment passed.

"I thought you were going to bed."

"I don't want to go in there with Allen."

"Well, it's pretty late."

The boy didn't say anything.

"Aw, let 'im in," Bill growled.

There was a rustling around for a couple of minutes. She came and unhooked the screen door. Bill sat on the edge of the bed in his undershirt and trousers, barefoot. Wilma had on her tan and brown two-toned gabardine skirt and jacket. She was rumpled and undone. She fussed self-consciously at wisps of hair, raising both arms to pin them up, exposing her bare midriff. She had on her brown and white spectator pumps. She was bare-legged. Bill held a pint of Calvert between his knees. His belt was unfastened.

"We were just havin a little party," he explained. "Your old lady and me."

She smiled crookedly over private knowledge. She wasn't wearing her glasses, which made her eyes look bleary, soft, unfocusing. There was something particularly vulnerable about her without her rimless bifocals. "Don't tease him, Bill," she said softly.

"Am I teasing him?"

"No, but—"

"Then dummy up."

It was hot in the cabin. No breeze stirred the cheap flowered curtains at the single window in the back wall. Overhead, bugs blew the naked 60-watt bulb. Wilma and Bill looked at each other in a way that made the boy feel like an intruder. Then they both looked at him and chuckled. He felt as if they were making fun of him.

"What do you think me and your mama were fixin to do?" Bill asked.

*"Bill!"*

"I dunno." He looked around.

"Have a drink."

*"Bill,"* Wilma said again.

"OK."

Jack closed his nose to the sweet-rotten smell, tilted back the bottle, and really took a belt to impress them, swallowing four times.

"Hey! Not it all!" Bill pulled down the bottle. "Kid's a rumdumb."

The whiskey burned in his throat. His eyes watered. It flooded warm and sickeningly through his belly. He fought back nausea.

"You OK?" Wilma asked. "Want a chaser?"

When he spoke his voice was a croak. "Smooth."

They laughed. She hugged his head to her bosom. Her breasts were soft and loose under her jacket.

"Reg'lar little alligator, ain't he? Hang one on the old man, drink up his booze, next thing he'll be wantin to get into your pants."

"*Bill!*"

"What? You think he wouldn't give his left nut to stick his little dingus in you? Look at him, for chrissake!"

She looked at the boy and blushed.

He felt very warm, a bit dizzy—great!

"Don't kid yourself. Year or two and I'll have to kick his ass to keep him off you. Ain't that right, keed? You'd like to get into your old lady, wouldn't you?"

Jack wasn't talking.

"Bill, I don't like that kind of talk in front of him."

"Bullshit! Time he knew. What do you think men are? You spend six months or a year in stir sometime, you'll learn what people are. Tell the goddamn truth, Son, no one'll hurt yuh. You'd *like* to do it with your old lady, wouldn't you?"

He nodded his head affirmatively. His mother's face softened until he thought she might cry. Looking right at him, she blushed. His face was aflame. His focus narrowed.

"There you are," Bill said smugly. He took a drink and passed the bottle to Wilma. She absently took a swallow. Bill handed the bottle to the boy. He took another belt.

"He'll get drunk," he heard his mother warn.

"You know me and your mama was fixin to get us a little when you came and knocked on the door, didn't yuh?" Bill asked.

His ears buzzed. "I don't know," Jack said.

"Sure you did! Can't stand bein left out. You feel bad 'cause she lets me and don't let you, don't you, boy?"

"Bill."

"He knows a hell of a lot more than you think or he'll let on. Ain't that right?"

Jack shrugged. He could not see what Bill was building, but on the off chance it was to culminate in an invitation to the party, the boy was not about to jeopardize his chances by popping off.

"You know how a man and woman do it, don't you?" he asked.

Jack wasn't certain he was not compromising his rights, but he admitted he had some rudimentary knowledge.

"You've seen what a man and woman's things look like?" Bill bore on.

"Yeow. Well, *sorta*."

"What do you mean?"

"You know. Not really."

"Haven't you seen your mama's or your grandma's?"

"Yeow, sorta."

"What do you mean?" his mother said. "You've seen me in the bath."

"Yeow, but I was afraid to really look."

"You've seen your grandpa's?" Bill asked.

"Yeow."

"It look like this?" He whipped out his whang. "Come here." He pulled Wilma down beside him on the bed. He put her left hand around his thing.

"Bill, please," she protested. "I don't think this is healthy."

"Dummy up."

She moved her hand gently on his prick, the movements slight, as if she were trying to hide them. It grew long in her hand. She looked away, neither at him nor the boy nor it. Jack had never seen one like Bill's. It was bigger than anyone's, longer. Her hand looked so girlish around it. The idea of that going into her thing made Jack's head swim.

"Show him yours," Bill said and whipped up her skirt.

"I don't want to." She tried to get up.

He toppled her back on the bed, driving his left arm under her knees and rolling her backward.

*"Bill!"* she shrieked, trying to haul her skirt down over her exposed bottom and thighs. She looked so broad that way. "This isn't funny now!" she hissed. *"Bill!* I don't *like* this!"

"Dummy up! You see. My prong goes right in there." He held her legs aloft with his right arm wrapped around her knees, pointing quite medically, it seemed, with his left forefinger at the peach-sized ball of dark auburn hair that fluffed out in the diamond-shaped juncture of her upraised thighs and exposed bottom. His two first fingers tickled into the hair, parted the fold in there slightly.

"BILL!" she shrieked. Her legs from the knees up scissored so violently they were a blur. *"I mean it!"* she screamed.

He could not hold her. She rolled upright, whipping down her skirt. "DAMN YOU!" she spat.

"Just showing him how babies are made," Bill said innocently.

"Don't you know how helpless and ugly a woman feels when she's exposed like that?"

"Aw, come on, have a snort. Cheer up. Listen, you said yourself, when you came down with him, he was getting so curious you wanted me to have a talk with him."

"*Well!* I didn't think you were going to invite him to have a ringside seat while we . . ."

"Shit, he's been slippin around peepin since I married you. That time he stayed with us on Matthewson for a few days. Why do you think I said get on the floor? Think he was asleep? Let him have a little feel. Satisfy his curiosity."

She wasn't certain of his logic. "Bill?" she said, sliding off the bed when he grasped the boy's left wrist and dragged him toward her, clearly intending to stick it under her skirt.

"*No! Bill?* Now. . . ." Wilma retreated toward the corner. Bill stalked her from a crouch, his head no higher than her breasts, carrying the boy's hand low beside his knee, Jack straggled out behind. He feinted at her box with the boy's hand as if he held a snake, flipped up the back of her skirt with his right, and stabbed at the quivering bare globes of her ass with Jack's hand. The back of the boy's hand was rammed into a cool resilient cheek of her buttocks.

She shrieked, "BILL!" and curled her near leg up and over her other protectively, cowering against the rough boards, laughing in spite of herself. "Quit it, now!" she said so Jack could hear every letter. "*Bill!*"

He smacked her bare bottom hard, and she cried, "*Ouch!* Damn it! *Don't, now!*" She turned her back more toward the wall.

He ran the boy's hand up her front, grazing the bush of hair up into the soft curve of her belly, driving it in hard, not as a blow but a relentless push. Her words came breathlessly. "Bill, you're hurting me." The skin of her belly felt loose, soft, like gathered satin or layers of thin silk with something underneath it.

He dragged Jack's hand down and ground his knuckles into the soft flesh under the wedge of hair just above her tightly clamped thighs. His corded left arm leading the boy's thin arm under her skirt writhed like the neck of a great snake, grinding Jack's loose fist into her sex. His face shifted from evil merriment to almost brutal purpose.

"Bill-you-are-hurting-me," she said calmly but definitely. She quit struggling. Jacky looked up. She was staring blankly across the room. She glanced down. Their eyes met. Her look was not saying, "Son," yet it was not unkind. She looked at the top of Bill's head. "Whenever-you've-had-your-fun," she said coldly.

"OK. Smartness! Want to run your fucking mouth." He yanked open her jacket. Her bare breasts leaped out. The nipples drew up into big raspberries.

"Is this how your father taught *you* the facts of life?" she asked archly.

For an answer he reared up and roughly covered her mouth with his. Jack heard her head hit the wall. She was thrown back. Her belly came up. He had plunged the boy's hand between her thighs. Then he vigorously rubbed it roughly back and forth along the fold of her thing. The boy could feel the long hairs being pulled by his fingers. Bill's mouth muffled Wilma's protests. The boy didn't want to hurt her. Yet . . . *yet!* Until that moment, he had been more Bill's than hers. She beat the back of Bill's head with her fists. He held her pinned to the wall. Then suddenly Jack's fingers were between the long lips of her sex. It was slick, and they moved easily back and forth along the length of it. She fought all the harder. The boy tried to pull his hand away. He didn't want to. Bill was hurting her.

Suddenly Bill let go of Jack, reached up behind Wilma with his right hand, and grabbed her by the hair, yanking her head back and over onto her left shoulder. Like an enraged cow's, her big liquid eyes rolled down and her gaze fell on her son. It seemed she wanted help. Before Jack could decide how to help her, Bill threw her onto the bed by her hair.

"OHHHH!" she cried out.

Jack could see everything. Her legs were flung apart for a moment as she struggled to get back up. Her pussy was like the tail of a lovely dark red squirrel between her legs. Bill shoved her back down. He dropped his trousers.

"Bill!—for-godsakes-not-in-front-of-*him!*" She was looking right at Jack. Her eyes and face were pained. "Please, Bill. *Make him go!*"

Looking right at him, *"Please make him go."*

"Cop a walk, kid!" Bill turned and said out of the corner of his mouth, jerking his head toward the door.

Wilma smiled weakly then, begging the boy's understanding.

*Fuck 'er!* He wouldn't give her the satisfaction of understanding.

Bill's prick stood out like a spear. There had been a moment when Jack's hand was on her big warm box and Bill was grinding it in. Then nothing had so made him feel singularly himself, so unqualifiedly important, or given him such absolute ambition. While his hand was on her, he was older than Allen *and* his cow-humping old man. He was older than Bill. He could not explain it, but he had felt it. And he would never be scared of the dark again.

He backed out of the room. His mother's dippy smile was trying to say good night.

When the door was closed in his face, he heard her say, "Bill, you're awful!"

"And you love it, don't yuh?" he asked.

"*Unnh!*" she grunted sharply. "*Why* do you have to be so rough? You know I like you to be gentle. *Unnnh!* . . . Damn it!"

The light went out. There was a string tied to the head of the bed and the light cord. Jack lifted his fingers to his nose and could smell her on them, a hint of Evening in Paris and something more bitter, something else, her own scent. He wanted never to lose it.

Inside the bed creaked unrhythmically. They were sort of thrashing around. He could not see under the curtain across the door. There was nothing he would not dare. He really was quite high. Without fear, everything he knew seemed to fall into place.

"That's it," he distinctly heard her say.

Behind the cabin, an unpainted picket fence separated Best's property from the town jailer's vegetable garden. The jailer had a lot of time for gardening, since there were hardly ever more than one or two citizens in the local two-story brick pokey. Jack climbed the fence, balancing between sharp, splintery pickets, leaning over against the rough, unfinished boards of the cabin with his head even with the window sill. Gnats blew his sweaty face, making him flinch and puff at them. Behind him, around him, the heavy Mississippi Gulf night dripped, cracked, piped, and buzzed.

He could see only the bulk of the bed in dark shadow. The low shaft of light from the bottom half of the curtained door fell on his mother's two-toned spectator pumps. The sound of the bed had become slow and rhythmical. *Unnnnnh;* the springs would go down and stay for one, two, three, four, five, six beats of the heart; then, *aaaah.* And *unnnnnh.* Every time they would go down, she would say, "*Unnh.*" When they came up, she went, "*Ahh.*"

Bill muttered something from time to time. "Come on, Bill, honeyfuck," he heard Bill say to her. They called each other Bill. "This one's for our pretty little blue-eyed blonde-haired girl, baby."

"Oh, Bill, I wish." She wanted a baby.

"Give it to me!"

The bed began moving faster. She made those "unnh-ahh" sounds in time with the blood beating in Jack's temples. Then:

"*Bill!* I think he's at the window watching us."

"Take it!"

"Bill, he's out there!"

"Fuck, damn you!"

"*Uh-uh-uh,*" she began panting. On and on.

The bed sang. The cabin shook. The boy had sensed her eyes looking at him in the dark. Now he sensed they were closed. The sound of the bed became a pounding in his head. *"Enough! For chrissakes!"* he wanted to cry. How could she *do* it so much? They were grunting and snorting at each other, grabbing and pulling. Then Bill groaned like a man hit in the small of the back with a bat. *Bam! Bam! Bam! Bam!* that bed smacked the back wall.

"You make it?" he growled.

"Um-hmmm," she murmured.

"The hell you did."

"It was fine. I told you, *he's* right outside."

"Piss on him! You were about there."

"Bill."

Jack dropped over the far side of the fence into the jailer's garden. Perhaps Bill would come looking for him. He cut down between monster rows of sticky beet leaves. On the boardinghouse front porch Red was singing at the sliver of moon:

> She is spreading her wings for a journey
> That she's going to make by and by
> And when the trumpet shall sound in the morning
> She will rise up and go in the sky.

There was no lonelier little boy on earth than Jacky.

The small two-story red-brick jail sat between four huge, moss-dripping shade trees. It might have once been the schoolhouse.

"Hey, boy, would you have some tobacco on yuh?"

Jack about jumped out of his skin. It was the voice of a black prisoner he could hardly see in the dark, tall, barred window.

"Nosir," he stammered.

The prisoner chuckled to himself. "You don't got to call me no *suh*. Where you from, boy?"

"Kansas."

"You a long way from home. What cha doin here?"

"I live over there. My stepdad works at the shipyard."

"That a fac? What was you doin peepin in that winda yonder?"

"Nothin."

"Nothin? Betcha you was trying to see someone gettum a little, wa'nt yuh?"

He didn't answer.

"What's that Kansas like?"

"Well, it's the air and wheat capital of the world," the boy remembered.

276

"Is that a fac?"

"Yeow. It's a free state." He thought he might like to know that.

"What's that mean?"

"Well, it came into the Union against slavery." His teacher at school seemed to blame Jack personally for that.

"Is it true colored folks can live where they want to in Kansas, and sit in the front of the bus, and anywhere in the picture show?"

"Well, uh, mostly they live in Niggertown and sit in the balcony. But they sit in the front of the bus if there ain't no seat in the back. Nobody says nothin. They go to high school with everybody else."

"That's what I figured. Sure you ain't got no tobacco?"

"Nope."

"Got an extra nickel on yuh? I can buy me some Bull Durham."

"No." Jack shook his pockets for him.

"Where you headed?"

"River, I guess."

"Yeh. Good night to go to the river. Too hot to sleep. Lak to be out there now in an ole skiff wif a good light, a jug, and gig me a mess uh frogs. Man, man, I'd lak me a mess uh frog legs."

Jack had never had the delicacy, though his mother said they were delicious.

"How come you're in jail?"

He laughed. "Well, I gets a little looped up las week an the old lady say I was bustin her up some. So they puts me here until she say I can come out. Mos the time, I'm jus as nice uh hard-workin sawmill man you'd ever see. Then now an then I got to get me a little drunked up. An they say I get mean. Sometime, there ain't nothin I *see* don mak me mad. They afraid I kill somebody someday. . . . Maybe they right."

"Well, good luck."

He laughed. "Better you look out, peepin in them windas, yuh'll wind up in here wif me."

Jack cut down to the foot of the main drag to where a Coast Guard river patrol boat was moored at its special dock. Down the wide river toward the Gulf the lights of the shipyard glittered like a large amusement park. The skeleton of a ship was strung with electric bulbs like incandescent beads along every deck.

Up the dock, three men were unloading a battered fishing trawler. Nearby, an old Negro sat on an overturned bucket beside a bushel basket and a pile of oyster shells, shucking oysters from the basket into a second bucket held between his knees. He would stab between the halves of the oyster shell with a strong, short-bladed knife, prize the shell open, and flip the oyster into the bucket, checking to see if he had found a pearl, all in one motion. He could shuck a dozen almost as fast as Jack could count to twelve. To reward himself he flipped every thirteenth oyster into his mouth rather than the bucket. He would chew a couple of times to let it know where it was, then swallow the thing down like a goose. Every few dozen, he'd wash the oyster down with a nip from a bottle of bay rum.

He caught Jack's eye, smacked his lips, and winked. He offered the boy an oyster, gray and snotty-looking, on the end of his knife.

Jack declined, "No, thanks."

"Naw? Don lak rawor yoysters, boy? What's the matter you?" He guffawed, flipped the oyster in the air, snapping it on the fly like a dog. He was a little off. A bit of it hung out the corner of his mouth. He sucked it in noisily, chewed twice, down it went. He opened his mouth wide, gesturing around his toothless gums with the tip of his oyster knife. He said something.

"What?"

"Jus lak yo mama's pussy," he said.

Hunh? Had he heard right?

The next oyster hit the boy flush in the face, cold, wet, snotty. He turned away fast. The Negro cackled like an old crone.

One of the men unloading fish said, "Better look out for that old fart. He'll try to suck your dick."

Jack kept going fast. The old man's swart, toothless laughter barked him down the dock.

The Coast Guard boat was getting ready to pull out. The sailors moved about smartly. The lights in the wheelhouse were all red. The men inside were in tones of red. Everything looked shipshape, important.

"Why aren't you home in bed?" one in a visored cap called to the boy.

"Too hot to sleep."

"Your folks know where you are?"

"Sure."

"How'd you like a ride?"

"You mean on there?"

"Sure."

"Yeow! Boy!"

"Come aboard. Gangway, guys, here comes the commander."

Jack leaped from the dock onto the deck with the man's hand to steady him. Instantly Jack felt himself afloat. The entire big gray boat moved gently beneath him. It was great.

"What's your name?"

"Jack."

"No bull! Hey! So's mine."

"Really?" Wow.

"You stick with me, pal. We're getting under way now." His hand rested lightly on the boy's shoulder.

"Cast off fore and aft."

What Jacky couldn't figure out was why the sailors' hats were dark blue instead of white. He could feel the engines accelerate somewhere down deep inside the boat. A boat was so much more than a house could ever be, and everything a house ever was, except maybe home.

"Let's go forward." The sailor led him up to the front of the boat. "You hungry?"

"I could eat something," Jack admitted.

"Kemper, get the kid a horsecock and cheese sandwich and some moo juice."

Suddenly he was afraid it was going to be oysters all over again. *Horsecock and cheese.* He had been conned into tasting some headcheese his grandma had made once when his grandpa had butchered a pig. The memory could make him gag.

But it was just lunch meat and longhorn on white bread. Moo juice, of course, was ice-cold milk in a white cup that was made without a handle. It was great to be aboard.

A big fish jumped four feet out of the water dead ahead.

"Gar!" the chief called. "Stop engines!"

The boat slowed, drifted. "Get me the oh-three," he commanded.

A sailor ran inside and ran back out with an Army rifle.

The chief slipped his left arm into the rifle's leather sling, aimed it ahead at the water. Jack could hear the gars croaking across the water like alligators. "Give me the light!" he called out. A big spotlight on top of the cabin zoomed a yard-wide smoky blue hole in the night and threw a big searching circle onto the water.

The gar broached again to the right of the boat. The chief swung over and fired as if the rifle were a shotgun. The explosion nearly deafened the boy. Jack had never heard so large a rifle fired. It was the ringing of a terrible bell, and the ring hung in the air long after the blinding flash had sunk into the center of his eye. He hadn't seen a thing except the long, twisting brown flash of the fish.

"I think you got him, Chief," the sailor said.

The boat circled slowly while a man played the light over the water.

"There he is!" the sailor called.

He grappled over the side with a boathook. Another sailor came with a gaff. They hoisted the gar up over the gunwale and flopped it onto the deck. Jack had never seen so large a fish. It was about four feet long. The long gatorlike snout opened and closed in gasps. Its eye, the size of an overcoat button, was staring and seemed to the boy very angry.

"He's still alive," the sailor said. "You got him right through the gills."

The chief stepped over, raised the rifle a little, and brought the butt down on the fish's skull. It quit gasping. The sailor lashed it to a cleat, just in case.

"Hate them ugly bastards. Ain't no good for nothing. Can't eat 'em. They'll take your bait, steal your catch. Hate things like that."

Looking at it, the boy agreed. "Me, too."

"Good boy."

The boat ran up to the shipyard. *Lord!* Jack hadn't realized a ship was *that* big. He had never been so close to one before. When he looked up, the stern rose high as a seven- or eight-story building above them. He could see the workers up there on the scaffolding that went all around it like a giant basket strung with electric lights. Bill worked on that ship. Men looked like toys up on the catwalks. They wore hard helmets like Bill had with his name on it. The boy imagined him up there in his work clothes. It was not easy being a man. Working. There was more to it than just growing up, Jack suspected. He could hear Bill: "It's a hard life if you don't weaken," and it still did not make sense, but thinking of Bill and his mom in the cabin, he began to understand.

He could see the spark sprays of the welders spit into the night, hear the rat-tat-tat of the chippers and riveters. Overhead, cranes swung great steel plates from yard to ship.

"Going to work in the shipyard when you grow up?" the chief asked.

"Naw. I want to be a sailor."

"A Coast Guardsman," he corrected.

"Yeow."

He laughed.

When they got back to the dock, he gave Jack the hat from Kemper's head.

"Why is it blue instead of white?" the boy wondered.

"So the enemy can't see it so well. Camouflage."

"Oh."

He thanked them for the ride and the cap.

"You can come down and ride anytime," the chief said. "You're our official mascot now."

Well! You couldn't beat that. He marched back up the street at a stiff attention worthy of a U.S. Coast Guard Mascot. And whoever the enemy was who could not see him because his hat was blue instead of white, he was not afraid. They had tommy guns and everything on that boat. He had to remember to tell his mom when she asked what he wanted for lunch next time: "horsecock and cheese." After that night, if he wasn't a man already, he had a bead on what it was like.

It was after midnight when he climbed back into the yard. A few spatters of rain plunked in the dust around him. He carefully tried the cabin door. He wasn't sleeping with Allen anymore. That was final. Man, would *he* envy him his sailor hat! The door was not locked. He carefully crawled inside and made a pillow of his arm on the bare board floor. He fell asleep scorning all the damn old granddaddy long legs and brownie spiders he knew roamed the floor at night. He feared nothing anymore.

When he awoke, he was in bed beside his mother, who was snoring softly. A dull, all-day rain was drumming on the shingles overhead. Bill had left for work. In her sleep his mother smelled warm and of her perfume and last night's whiskey. Her near breast had slipped from the loose lace bodice of her gown, so soft, white, inviting. He snuggled down with his face next to it, the rose nipple not an inch from his eye. She muttered softly in her sleep, turned, making a pillow for his head of the inside of her arm.

"Hello, Sonny boy," she said groggily.

He told her all about where he had gone the night before.

"You shouldn't roam around like that so late," she said sleepily.

When his knees touched her beneath the single sheet that covered them, her thighs were bare. He pressed closer. Her slip was rucked up and twisted around her waist. She gave up trying to get it down. His thighs lay against her bare hip. He laid his arm across her soft, naked belly. The rain dripped unremittingly from the cabin eaves, making bubbles in the trench they had dug below. A constant drip hit a whiskey bottle that had not found its way under the floor into the cemetery of dead soldiers there; the sound was like the continuous ringing of a dull glass bell. He took the nipple of her breast into his mouth. She made an agreeable sound. He had *known* she would. *Hadn't he?* He pressed close to her. Whatever maternal illusion she held, he was more his own then than hers or anyone's. They were adrift alone on the river, cozy, safe, far from either shore.

# 26

WHEN summer came, the days had a new exotic division. Wilma and the boy lay abed after the men left for work, their relationship too complex, too Yankee weird, for bayou comprehension.

"Surely the boy must be feelin poorly," everyone thought.

Beneath a sheet as damp as if it had been left out all night, it a thin opaque tent over his head, he slipped down the shoulder straps of her gown and gently unpacked her breasts.

"Sonny boy, listen. . . ." Half protest, half too indolently curious to care. He knew in his anxious heart she wanted him to—if not as eagerly —as surely as himself. "I shouldn't have let this get started," she would murmur.

He explored the substance of her breasts with the total dedication of a child for whom time unfolds slowly as a flower. Fondling her bare breast, feeling it swell mysteriously under his hand until only both of his own might contain it, lifting the nipple of her more flaccid near breast with his tongue, sucking it into his mouth, it too swelling then, her right hand gently stroking the back of his head—prayer wasn't in it. The Judeo-Christian God would not look upon such scenes. Man forbade it. Man and God, they will not look. To think of such a thing makes them want to kill.

They would have tarred and feathered the woman and the boy, had they known. The Klan.

Jack and Bill had gone with Uncle Willy Best to a meeting of the Klan one moonless night. They drove out in his dusty Plymouth. It was in a field. About half of the people wore sheets over themselves with holes cut for eyes. They had an insignia that looked suspiciously Catholic to Jack, but Uncle Willy assured the boy that the Klan hated "Papist rapists and fishy-eyed Jews even more'n niggers." Jack had thought it was going to be a picnic. There was nothing at all to eat. Everyone stood around in a big circle in a lumpy field slapping mosquitoes, holding pitch torches, and singing "Rock of Ages." Kids like Jack played tag between the parked cars and trucks, chirping through the dark. Back in the black piney woods figures of daring Negroes darted silently over the carpet of needles like strange barkless hunting dogs. Everyone knew they were there. Big boys said, "Let's go get us some niggers," and bragged elaborately what they would do when they got them. Allen's face in the flickering pitch fires was crazed the way one sees the faces of stupid men about to see God or gangbang the local pushover.

The man on the little stage up front threw back his hood. *Wow!* It was the rich dentist-doctor to whom everyone deferred when he came around. Jack had seen him at school. The principal always went around with him like a pup dog. His rimless glasses glinted and flickered in the firelight. He held a Bible in one hand and a copperhead snake aloft in the other. Some others came up shaking snakes. *Man!* Jack wanted out of there. The place could be crawling with them. His very ankles cringed. Allen got hold of someone's snake and began dancing around the bonfire in the middle of the circle, waving the thing overhead with both hands.

"Bill, let's get out of here," the boy suggested to his stepfather.

"You ever see such a goddamned bunch of lunatics?" he whispered back.

The doctor was launched on a breathless evangelical tirade that made no sense whatsoever. Allen looked as if he were having a fit. So did some others. The big cross made of railroad ties set up in the center of the bonfire, which was being stoked by four men in sheets, finally caught fire and blazed all cherry and yellow. A collective moan lifted from the circle. "Amen!" "Praise the Lord!" was called out.

A tall gaunt man in work clothes, with a face like a beardless Abe Lincoln, jerked past in a kind of St. Vitus' dance, letting snakes coil all over his head. Another man like an insane concessionaire jerked by with both arms coiled with snakes, offering them to all believers, his own tongue puffed in his mouth like a damn cottonmouth. Right before the boy's eyes a middle-aged woman in a cotton housedress, her hose rolled down to her ankles above a beat-up pair of men's oxfords, with two little blond daughters clinging to her heavy thighs, took the head of her snake into her mouth and sucked it like a popsicle. Jack got in Uncle Willy's car, rolled up the windows in spite of the steamy heat, and locked the doors.

And getting into his mom's deep white tit, he scorned such foolish angry men and antic gods.

"Does that feel nice?" he inquired.

"Umhumm," she hummed.

"How? Tell me."

"Oh, like when you were a baby." So maternal. So wistful.

"Just like?"

"Umm?" She shifted her body heavily, more comfortably into the boy. "Not exactly."

He was stretched out along the length of her. He went back to the now erect, cool nipple. *I knew it,* he thought. It was something else.

"That one's getting a little tender, love." No other instructions.

He rose up to lie across her to get at the other. She turned a bit toward him as if she were going to go that way anyway rather than to make it easier for him. She stretched and relaxed. The other breast rolled heavily toward him. When she breathed, her belly brushed his hard little penis, tightly packed in his jockey briefs. She gently stroked his back with just the soft tips of her fingers, then lightly with her nails, then the soft pads. All the way down his spine. It made him shiver. She laughed warmly. He did the same to her. When he made her shiver, she would say, *"Ou! Ou!"* and shiver closer to him still.

"You're so *gentle,*" she purred. "Just like your father."

That meant Bill, off building a ship like a chump, wasn't as gentle. One for their side.

"Can I tickle your legs, too?" he asked.

"Oh, if you want to."

He did. He carefully slid up her gown until he could stroke her bare thigh along its entire length. Turned toward him, her left leg lay over her right. He stroked the smooth length of her thigh as far toward her knee as he could reach without losing her breast. Up the back of her long thigh he tickled, just grazing the softer, cool globe of her butt, then daring to go on up full over the great feathery swell of fantastic meat to the top, where hips and spine and pelvis converge. Over the top of her hip, across the gentle valley of her waist, around into the warm powder stuff of her velvet belly; his head reeled with his daring. Her belly contracted involuntarily—once—twice—three times—four—she giggled.

"Hey!"

"Can I touch your thing?" he croaked, his throat dry.

"Jack-*eee.*" Low, her exasperation tipped with the humor of recognizing the expected. For what else had she expected—really?

"Can I?" he insisted.

Silence, though she did not in any way move away from him. There it was. His fingers already grazed the uppermost perimeter of hair.

"Please can I?"

No answer.

It was up to him.

284

Her eyes were closed. From her expression, her thoughts seemed to be sailing far away. She looked neither happy nor unhappy, though she seemed to suffer some slight inner pain. His fingers crawled deeper into the thick, most fantastic of all hair.

"I wish you wouldn't," she said softly.

"I want to."

"I know, dear, but it isn't good. It isn't right."

"Why?"

"It just isn't."

"I *have* to." The hair clung to his fingers. It felt as if the dense bush grew from a damp loose web of hair woven over the plump underlying flesh by a crazed spider.

"Munh—" more a breath in the top of her throat than a vocal sound. "Please be good."

"*No.* I've got to."

She straightened her left leg, falling more onto her back. She laid her left forearm over her eyes. And there was three times more of it. Rushing out. A palpably alive strawberry-roan cloud entwined his fingers. A zillion minute points of sensation—teasing the down on the back of his hand, tickling his moist palm.

"Can you feel anything?" he wanted her to tell him after a few minutes.

"*Ummm.*" Her voice small, dusty.

Up and down, over and around, almost tentatively, just grazing the fluffy bush with his palm, then down into the thicket with his fingers, combing it with his outstretched fingers. Her belly visibly did little jumps.

"Does it tickle?"

"Kind of."

"How?"

"Nice."

"But how?"

"*Shh!* You ask too many questions. It feels good."

"Boy! I could do this forever."

She sort of laughed. "Do you like me?"

"Boy! Yeow. Do I!"

She laughed. "I'll take your word for it."

"I *love* you."

"I love you, too." But her mood changed. She seemed sort of sad like. "Do you love me because I let you . . . do this? Or because I'm, uh, your mother?"

It was a trappy kind of question. He thought for a minute. She really did look sad.

"Well, see, I'd love you because I do *anyway*. You know. I mean you're so pretty and nice and all. But golly, I'd rather touch your thing and kiss your titties than anything. You're the most beautiful woman in the world."

"You're a monkey." She hugged his head to her breast. "And a *terrible* flatterer."

"I *mean* it!"

"I *know!*" She kissed his mouth hard, quickly, wetly.

Her hairs were more sweaty, sticky, something, thicker.

"I'm just afraid someday you will hate me for this."

"No, I won't. *Ever!*" he swore. How could she imagine such a thing? He kissed her cheeks, her eyes, where single tears clung to the corners. "I love you more than anything." It was true.

"I love you, too. I just hope when you're all grown up and married to some sweet girl, you will love me still."

"I *will*," he insisted.

"Hug me tight."

"Why are you crying?"

She held him fiercely against her; his hand was pressed deep and hard against her thing; she stretched and arched herself around, making pleasant, lazy, surprised little sounds, sort of wrestling him playfully, yet always pressed tight against his hand caught between her squeezing thighs.

"*Oh!* . . . Maybe because I'm happy," she finally drawled, stretching back deliciously.

Her hairs were wet and sticky. "That's silly."

"Women *are* silly, darling." Then suddenly shifting gears, she definitely extracted his hand from between her legs. "That's enough now." She patted it like a pet. Another hug. "OK. I think it's time you got up and went to see what Allen's doing while I get dressed. It's almost noon. We ought to be ashamed. Such lazybones."

He could have stayed there until the dawning of the year 2000. No single boyish delight could have pried him from that bed. If Bullet Bob Feller was pitching to Joltin' Joe DiMaggio in Uncle Willy Best's driveway, he wouldn't have cracked the curtain. But he knew there was yet something to do in the bed, and knowing would leave him ruffled, edgy and unsatisfied. Still, to stay there forever, melting into a buttery blob on the sheet, his hand on the forested warm mound of her thing, would have been ideal. Who needed muscles and legs when where you were at was so mixed up you couldn't separate out the feelings you felt by hand from those swarming inside you—so that touching was being touched, and loving was more real than promises, hope, envy, and fear, which had been until then the most real of all?

Poor boy? Yeow. Yet no boy had more than he.

Could he really fuck her? The idea made his head swim.

He vowed to himself he would die if he did not try.

# 27

DOC brought Bill home in the middle of the afternoon in a company pickup. Bill was ashen, too weak to stand without help.

"Think he took a bad shock," Doc explained.

Allen and Jack helped get Bill into Uncle Willy's parlor and onto the double bed there, where he would be close to Doc during the night. Jack carried Bill's lunch pail. He hadn't eaten a thing.

Bill was shaking. He smiled wanly at the boy. "Hit was a hell of a jolt, Son," he said. "I feel like a burned-out bulb." He was shaking so badly he couldn't hold the little glass of clear medicine Doc poured for him. It smelled like rubbing alcohol. Doc held the back of Bill's neck as if he were an infant and poured the contents of the glass over his white lips.

"*Oooooooh,* Christ! That's awful stuff," Bill moaned and fell back onto the bed, curling into a tight fetal position. His skinny, almost hairless legs looked weak and vulnerable. His gray briefs were stretched and loose about his bony ass. His single large testicle was a soft purple nut caught between his shivering thighs. Doc covered him with a sheet and a blanket.

Wilma came running in from the cabin.

"Goddamn peapicker on a crane set a plate down across an arc-welder's cord where I was workin," Bill stammeringly explained. "Knocked me clean across the ship. Said my hair stood up on end. I'll never take a drink again."

"Oh, Bill baby," she crooned. If only she could count on that. Jack could see the hope forming in his mother's eyes. Then she tucked Bill's covers up under his shivering chin and tried to stroke his sweaty brow. He shrugged her away.

"Looks just like he's havin the D.T.'s," Uncle Willy observed drily from the doorway.

"That's how a peapicker like you would think," Bill stammered. He was in real misery.

"Doc, can't you give me something to make me sleep?"

"I can put you out so you'll rest if you'll trust me," Doc said.

"My brother Ned had the D.T.'s. Looked just like that," Uncle said.

"He doesn't have D.T.'s, and he never has had them," Wilma said angrily. No one ever gave an ex-con the benefit of the doubt.

Doc did not bat an eye. If Bill's story of near-electrocution was a lie, Doc was not going to compromise his professional ethics by saying so.

He sat beside Bill on the bed, placed his hands on either side of his head, back of his jaw, near his ears. "Just relax," he said. Then he pressed hard, very hard, or pinched. It was hard to tell. "Relax. Sleep," Doc said. Old Bill arched up under the pressure, then relaxed back. "Count backwards from twenty," he ordered.

Jack counted to himself along with Bill and Doc, who said, "Twenty, nineteen, eighteen, seventeen. . . ." Bill's gray face turned very red. The veins at his temples and in his forehead swelled enormously. "Ten, nine, eight, seven. . . ." Very faint, constricted. Then Bill gagged: "*Aggghhhhhh . . .*" like a man dying in a movie and went completely limp. Soon he was snoring like a man drowning in his own throat.

"He should sleep until after dark now," Doc said. "I'll be back then. He may be restless. Just keep him in bed, and there isn't much more you can do."

"Will he be all right?" Wilma asked.

"Oh, sure. But you really should get him to cut down on his drinking."

"I try," she said hopelessly.

Doc was a very serious young man. He was an intern. He went to the back of the house to say hello to his fiancée before returning the truck to the shipyard. She poured him a glass of lemonade. They just stood there in the kitchen looking at each other and sort of grinning. He called her "honey" when he left, but he didn't kiss her or anything because Allen and the boy would have teased them.

Bill acted as though he were having nightmares. He pitched around in the bed, lashing out with his fists, throwing punches, muttering and yammering. He would cry out and curl up with his arms wrapped around his head, whimpering like a whipped pup. *"No! Please. Don't do that. Don't do that to me. Don't do that to me,"* the boy heard him distinctly say.

"It's all right, Bill. It's all right, darling." Wilma tried to comfort him.

His pillow was yellow where it was not stained with sweat. Jack could see the striped ticking of the mattress through the sweat-soaked sheet beneath his body. When Wilma tried to wipe Bill's brow with a damp cloth, he slapped her hand away.

"Honey, it's me, Wilma, your wife. I just want to help you."

Whimpering pitifully, he tried to crawl under his pillow.

"You kids stay away from there," Uncle Willy said. "Go on, get outside." He hovered around the room all afternoon.

Jack wore Bill's silver hard hat. It was so big it rocked around his noggin like a pot. But the sweat-blackened leather suspension system inside was smooth and cool on his brow. He sat on the porch and went through Bill's lunch box. A wormy little windfall apple was all that was fit to eat. His sandwich was cold fried egg and baloney on white bread. Even that had butter and salt and pepper rather than lettuce and mayonnaise. Allen would eat it. Allen would eat snot.

Allen chunked windfall pecans at Jack's hard hat until the constant *plunk* was making him mad.

"Cut it out now, Allen," he warned.

*Plunk.* And that Mississippi cat-eatin-shit grin. "Make me if y'all don lak it." *Plunk.* He had gathered another handful of squirrel-nibbled nuts. *Plunk.*

Jack took off the damn hat. *Thonk.* "Ow!" On his bare skull.

Allen laughed and retreated a few feet. "*Yah! Yah! Yah!* Yankee Bill's drunk to the gills! Yankee Bill's looped to the gills!"

"You shut your mouth, Allen."

"He's got the shivers, got the shakes, seein little green men, seein snakes."

"I mean it, Allen." He was just jealous because Jack had Bill's hat to wear. They hadn't been such good friends, either, since Jack no longer slept with him, preferring to camp on a cot on the porch until Bill left for work, when he could go pile in with Wilma until about ten, rather than risk getting pissed on by Allen. He acted like he never wet the bed at all. It was as if someone else had done the deed.

"*Bedwetter!* Allen wets the bed!" It was something Jack had promised his mom *and* Uncle Willy he would not tease Allen about. But he was saying all that shit about Bill.

*Thup!* A pecan hit Jack on the shoulder. "Your ma's uh ole whore."

*"Sonofabitch!"* Jack scooped up a handful of nuts from around his feet. He ran across the yard at him, Allen retreating, sharpshooting Jack with well-aimed pecans. Jack charged in the teeth of his fire. He snarled and growled. Running right at him, from not more than four feet away, he flung a salvo of nuts full force in Allen's face. One nut hit him squarely between his piggly eyes. That was the shot that crazed him. The boys came together like wild dogs. Jack swung Bill's helmet a glancing, ringing shot off Allen's skull. He busted Jack fair in the mouth with a fist full of big country knuckles. Jack's lips were numb. He could taste blood.

"Here! Doggone you boys, you stop that fightin out there!" Uncle Willy came to the front to yell. "Ain't we got enough trouble around here today without that?"

"He started it," Allen said.

"I did not. He wouldn't stop chunkin pecans at me."

"He called me a sonofabitch."

"You called my mom a whore."

"Now if there's any more I'll tan you both. I won't have that kind of talk around here, neither." He was getting mad.

"But if he don't leave me be, Pa, I'll throb his dang knob."

"*Yeh?* You and who's army?"

"That's enough!" He'd taken a step down the porch. "You go around back until you cool off," he told Allen.

Once around the corner of the house, Allen gave Jack the finger. Jack gave it right back to him.

An hour later Allen came up and asked Jack, "Wanta pitch washers?"

Jack's mouth felt the way a Ubangi's looked. "OK," he agreed.

In the bald dirt drive, some twenty feet apart, Alan had dug two holes the size of number-two cans and half as deep. They took turns pitching ten two-inch steel washers between the holes. Every washer in the hole was a point. It was Allen's sport. Jack could rarely beat him at it. After the first warm-up game, he suggested they contest for the right to wear Bill's hat. Allen wore it all afternoon.

Bill dozed fitfully through dinner. Mrs. Best despaired of ever getting the sheets on that bed white again. It was lucky there was the rubber sheet under him that was always there for Allen, but no one said that.

Bill awakened about nine, so dry he could hardly speak. But it wasn't water he wanted.

"No liquor," Doc said and measured him out another double shot of paraldehyde. He acted like he was drunk for awhile, then conked off again in fitful sleep.

Wilma stayed there with him all night. Allen went to a pallet some-where else. Jack had the cabin to himself. He could see a light in the parlor window of the main house throughout the night.

It was late, but he could not sleep. He hugged his mother's pillow to him and pretended it was she. It smelled of her perfume and hair. Her nightgown was underneath it. He took it out and dressed the pillow in her gown. He could stroke it and imagine it was she. Beneath the tattered lace bodice, he sucked dry titties filled with dusty feathers. He slowly eased up her gown and carefully got between her imaginary bare legs. He took his dick out of his briefs and fed it into the big, dry, feather-filled cunt. He fucked it like a fiend, the mental bedstead whomp-ing the wall like a champion. Pouring it to her, he called her "Wilma," not "Mom." She took it, loving it, murmuring, *"Fuck me, darling. Fuck me, Jacky!"* He could smell her warm breath, taste the flavor of her lip-stick, feel her soft, wet lips along his cheek, panting toward a climax that never came, all of it running out maddeningly until he was empty and the hollow filled with aching regret. It was all so grubbily shameful, artificial as the dry cunt in the pillow that had rubbed the head of his prick raw.

WHY CAN'T I KNOW! He railed at the way of things.

What kind of cruel, unfeeling punishment was it that kids had to go through? It was worse than cold, if you weren't actually freezing. Worse than hunger, if you could still remember the taste of food. It was cruel enough to make him almost believe in God.

*"Boy! If Bill died,"* he told himself, breathing the words. *"It would just be me and Mama then."* He had nothing against Bill, except he was a little rough, but man, if it was just the two of them. . . . But she would probably find someone else. Better stick with what he had, he de-cided. *OK. Bill could live.*

It was awful, being too young to come. *Fuck some old Church of Christ God who'd make such a miserly world,* he remorsed.

*"Pussy! Pussy! Pussy!"* he muttered, as if calling a cat. *"Got cunt on the brain, boy,"* he acknowledged. *"Want some! Want some! Got to get some. Fuck ole Mom, man! Fuck her good . . . one day."*

*Please let her come sleep with me.* He waited and fell asleep under the naked overhead light.

He awoke with a headache, hot and sweaty. It was daylight. What had happened? What had he missed?

"Sonny? What's this?" she asked. She was standing by the bed, staring down at the pillow dressed in her nightgown. She wasn't angry or any-thing, just sort of sad.

"Aw, I just was lonely," he muttered. "I just sorta pretended it was you."

She made a strange soft cry in her throat and dropped onto the bed, wrapping her arms tight around him. "Poor baby, my *poor, poor* darling. So lonely so long." She looked awfully tired. Her eyes were dark around, her face puffy.

Hell, it wasn't all *that* bad. "I'm not a baby," he reminded her.

"I know you aren't, darling. You're a big man. And I love you so." She was afraid there was something wrong with him. He could see the doubt in her eyes. It scared him.

"You're tired, ain't yuh?" he asked.

"Yes, I am. Very. I didn't sleep two winks all night. Bill was so restless." She stood up and began taking off her blouse. "You hop out of there and let me get some shuteye."

"I could sleep some more, too. I couldn't get to sleep until late. I got a bad headache," he said.

"No, you don't! I've *got* to get some *rest*. Go take a couple of aspirin."

There was always a big bottle of aspirins next to her toilet articles on the chest of drawers.

In the middle of the morning, Bill awakened wanting a drink.

"No liquor, Doc said," Uncle Willy told him. "Have some milk, a little fried bread. Get something on your stomach."

What Bill wanted on his stomach he could consume right there in bed and never drop a crumb.

"Christ! What the hell do you people think I'm made of? I'm damn near killed, and all I get around here is a lot of Prohibitionist static."

"If you want a drink, it'll have to be someone else gets it for you," Uncle Willy said.

"OK. *OK!* Where's Wilma?"

"She's sleepin," the boy informed him.

"She was up with you most the night," Uncle Willy said.

"Go get her, willya, Jacky? I gotta get out of here."

She came at a trot. "What's the matter?"

"I can't stay here. I gotta get up and go see a man."

"You don't have to see anybody. Doc said you were to stay there until he saw you tonight."

"Now, are you goin to give me a lot of static, too? I'm getting up."

He almost fell. He grabbed his head. Even his arms, which were muscled like a calf's leg, looked weak. He looked like he had lost a lot of weight. His belly was concave to such a degree his grimy jockey shorts hung loosely on his hips. "Help me get on my pants, Son."

Wilma steadied him while Jack slipped his trousers on over his crusty feet, hoisted them to his waist. His hands were shaking so badly he couldn't immediately button them. Jack buttoned his fly and fastened his belt. Bill was annoyed the boy had to. He slipped into his beat-up shoes; the pair he wore to work was also his best.

"Sweat all that good booze out of you," Uncle said, looking down at the sheets. "Run these through a little branch water and you'd have enough to stay drunk a month."

"Wise guy," Bill said, using Wilma and the boy for crutches. "He's been around. You can tell by his asshole."

"Bill!" Wilma warned.

Uncle snorted. *He* didn't have to be carried around by a woman and a boy.

"You *know* I'm always on your side, love—" She reached out a tender hand to soothe.

He slapped it away hard. "Keep your mitts off me. You're no different than they are. You're a fucking clodhopper from the word go, and you won't ever be anything else. You're never there when I really need you for something. Always give me a lot of noise. I don't know what the hell I'm doin dragging around with you and that snotnosed brat of yours, anyhow."

"You don't have to!" Jack blurted. "We don't need you!"

"Listen to that. Who pulled your chain, twirp. I'd swat you like a fly, but I'd break your *mama's* heart."

"Go outside, Jacky," she said. "This is none of your business."

"Yeh. Come back later and you and your *mama* can go beddy-by together and she'll give you some sugar-tit and tell you what a great big boy you are."

"*Bill!*"

Jack's face burned. *How did he know? Did he know?* He hadn't thought Bill knew anything. *Did his mom tell him?* He hated them both.

"Are you going to get it or not?" Bill asked again.

"Bill, I don't want to. Maybe it would hurt you bad. Anyway, I don't have any money."

"There's some in my pants."

Not wanting to, she went through his pockets. "There's only some change. Forty-two cents." She seemed relieved. That wasn't enough for the kind of booze he drank. He had never gone the cheap wine route yet.

"There's more there."

"No, there isn't."

"Someone took it. You always got something stashed away. I know you. Come on, quit holding out on me."

"No, I *don't*. BILL! Stop it! You're *hurting* me. You're hurting my wrist."

"You miserable no good fucking bitch!" He slapped her. Jack heard. He didn't care. Kill her, for all he cared. She didn't care about him. He no longer cared about her. *Fuckem both!* was his feeling.

"You can get it," he began confidentially. "Ask Uncle Willy for it. *He'd* give *you* anything for just a little smile."

"I don't want to, Bill. Please don't ask me. Every time I have to ask him a favor, I feel his eyes are licking me."

*"You don't want to do this. Too good to do that."* He mimicked her. "I can nearly kill myself for you, but you can't do anything for me. When I'm dying for a little drink. Treat me like I'm some wet-eared kid."

"Oh, Bill, I've done everything for you a woman can do, and you know I have. I've done things for you few others would. You *know* what I mean."

"Listen, no one was holding a gun to your head. Don't throw *that* crap up to me. You were no vested virgin."

"No. I'm just the dope who loves you. And you're too blind to see it."

"Be yourself. Act your age."

"I just don't want you to hurt yourself."

"Hey, you ever known me not to know what I was doin?" Kindly then.

"No."

"You bet. Everyone thinks *I'm* crazy. I'm crazy like a fox. Go ask him."

"OK. But I bet he won't do it."

She was right. She trudged back to the cabin after Uncle refused to loan her a couple of bucks. She looked vulnerable. Her ungirdled butt jiggled when she went back across the yard. Uncle stood on the porch, his left hand in his back pocket over his wallet, sucking a toothpick, watching her go.

"Then send Jacky to find Red."

"Red's painting a sign."

"Send the boy. Give him a note."

Jack went on his bike. Red stood in the sun and read the note. He

294

shook his head sadly. "I don't have it. I just don't. But tell him I'll bring him something in an hour or so."

Jack wheeled back to the cabin and delivered Red's message to Bill.

"Nobody ever does anything right. If you don't do it yourself, forget it. Can't depend on anyone. Not you, Red, *nobody!* Got to make it yourself or fuck you, you can die."

"Bill, that's not so. Everyone is trying to help you," Wilma said.

"Nobody wants to help me. They just want to run their own bullshit. I'm a drunk. A goddamn geek. I need a drink. Get me one or cop the hell out. That's the only way you can help me."

"I tried."

"*Tried, shit!*"

"I *did!*"

"Listen, you coulda had that old cock creamin himself tryin to let you take a couple of bucks. If you'd *tried,* you'd of got it."

"Bill, you're not *fair.*"

"Get out! I'm tired of lookin at your stupid face."

"Bill. . . ."

"*Out!* You don't give a shit about me. Nobody gives a damn about how I feel."

There was nothing to do but wait. Wilma and the boy sat on Uncle Willy's front porch, she on the top step, he below, keeping watch on the cabin.

Bill moaned like a man being tortured. He yelled curses. Something glass crashed against the wall. The sounds he made were like those of a newly caged wild animal. He was throwing everything around in there. Uncle Willy came onto the porch to study the small cabin set on cement blocks under the big hickory.

"He hadn't better be breakin up my furbishins," he grumped.

What furbishings? A sagging old bed and a crummy chest? Five bucks tops. The whole damn structure *with* his furbishings hadn't cost him a hundred.

"If it was me, I'd call the law," he said.

"He'll be all right," Wilma said.

"Not worried about him. I'm concerned for my property."

Doc should have left him some paral but probably figured he would take it all at once. And there was really no one there strong enough to keep it from him if he wanted it.

Around three in the afternoon, Red scurried into the yard.

"Got here as soon as I could. Had to tap a couple of guys to get up the scratch. How is he?"

"He's been quiet for awhile. I've been afraid to go to the cabin to find out," Wilma said.

They walked over, coming up on the shack as if it might explode at any minute.

"Bill?" Wilma called softly through the screen.

"Yeh?" as if he had a throat full of broken glass.

"Red's here. He's got something for you."

"Red?"

"Yeow, Bill?" Red said.

"Man, I need a drink."

"Got it, pardner."

"Well, it ain't doin no good in your pocket."

Red opened the door. The place was a wreck. He had to step on the mattress, which Bill had thrown off the bed. The curtain on the window hung like a flag of ultimate defeat, bunched on its rod that hung by only one end. Bill lay on the quilt pad over the bare springs. He wore only his shorts. He might have weighed 125 pounds, and five of that was pecker. Or so it appeared.

"Red, old buddy, you're a gentleman and a scholar," he croaked, reaching eagerly for the brown-paper-sack-wrapped pint. Red broke the seal for him and unscrewed the top. He had to help him hold the bottle to his lips, where Bill went after it like a hungry infant.

"Oh! *God!* I needed that," he sighed and fell back onto the springs. He capped the bottle and nestled it against his chest.

"It was the best I could get," Red apologized. "I had to scratch around to get it. I know you would do the same for me," the jock-sized sign painter said solemnly, his paint-spattered white overalls rolled to their natural knees in great wads, from which peeked just the toes of his tiny spattered cowboy boots.

"You know I would," Bill agreed, the alcohol soothing his raging veins all the way to his toes. What had been conduits for madness were now piping unbonded Kentucky balm—*a blend.*

Bill had himself another deep dose before offering Red a snort.

"Just a taste, thanks," Red said to be sociable. He didn't want to deprive his buddy of that which he so sorely needed.

Wilma's clothes Bill had ripped from the hangers on the bar in the corner and thrown to all corners. Many things were torn to shreds. Bits of clothing hung from the bare overhead rafters.

She sifted the rags like a scavenger. "Oh! My new blouse. *Bill!*"

"Dummy up! I'll get you a new blouse. A whole new wardrobe. Give you a hundred bucks, go buy anything you want. I was tired of looking at that old stuff, anyway."

"I wish you'd given me the hundred *before* you started ripping. You'll probably get a lot tireder of looking at what I'm wearing before I get new," she muttered, holding up two halves of a peasant blouse, seeing if it could be repaired, throwing it back down as hopeless.

"Listen, we aren't going to stay in this jerkwater joint, anyway. We're goin to Mobile, where I can get a *real* job. Where there's a *real* town."

"My *perfume!*" she cried. She held the empty bottle upside down. Not a drop fell out. She did not see where it had spilled.

Had he drunk it? Was that what calmed him while waiting for Red? Jack read her thought. Bill was happy, jovial. He'd get the world back on the track now. You could see he was impatient to get going. Just as soon as he finished that bottle and caught a little shuteye he would be up and movin.

"Double up and catch up," he promised, giving Red a wink and hoisting his pint in a toast to Wilma. "You know, that's the finest woman a man ever had," he told Red, who turned to look. Bill hadn't shaved in two days. The boy was amazed his whiskers were sprinkled with gray. It seemed beneath the sourness and whiskeyness of his breath, the boy detected the scent of Evening in Paris.

Bill never went back to the shipyard. He got up and shaved the third morning after his accident, found a clean shirt and socks, and spent the better part of the day scurrying around getting together a bottle. He promoted himself a fifth of Calvert and never did tell Wilma how he came by it.

She had spent all day getting the cabin back into some sort of livable order. Other than the clothes she had on and some blouses and underwear she had in a drawer and the things she had in a laundry bag, everything she owned was torn. She sewed a skirt and a couple of other things which she could wear in a pinch.

Bill only owned two changes of work clothes and a pair of baggy, brown gabardine dress slacks, a couple of white shirts, and a limp Panama straw hat blocked with a tightly pinched peak in front—it was a Mississippi classic, except Bill never looked like a man who owned an acre, hatted or bareheaded. He never wore a tie. Made him think about hanging, he said.

After supper that night, Uncle Willy hit Bill up for three weeks' board he was behind.

"Yes, sir. Just as soon as I get my money from the shipyard. Be ready

Friday, I guess. In the meantime, I was wondering, could you let me have ten on account? There's this fella I know in Mobile who tells me I can get on at the yard there. Just got to go in and apply. Thought I would run over there in the morning. If you could let me have ten until Friday. . . ." Bill talked fast.

And to everyone's surprise, the old moley man grudgingly derricked out the fat old purse from his hip pocket, in which he carried it carefully buttoned, and thumbed Bill out a single ten-spot. "That's thirty now you owe me," he reminded Bill narrowly.

"Yes, sir. You'll get back every penny with interest." Bill bobbed up and down. He could not take his eyes off the old man's fat black wallet.

"I don't give a damn about no interest. I just want my money back." He had never talked so tough to Bill before.

"You'll get it. You've got my word." Bill raised his hand as if taking an oath.

Uncle grunted.

Jack heard Uncle's wife ask him in the kitchen as they walked away, "Did you loan him some more money?"

"I'll take care of my business," he told her.

"I don't know sometimes where your brains'er at."

Bill left the next morning. He packed a lunch. He said he was going to hitchhike. He carried a two-tone tan and brown sport jacket flung over one shoulder when he strode out of the yard. In the inside jacket pocket was a pint of Calvert Special bought with some of Uncle's ten. The rest was in his pocket except for fifty cents which he had given Wilma for some personal necessity.

That night, Jack spent the better part of an hour working her gown up over her bottom. Then, overcome with the possibilities of the whole night which stretched before him, he essayed to introduce his rigid little wienie into the puff of dark hair jutting from the hollow of her thighs. She jumped a foot at first touch, yanked her gown down viciously, and tucked it between her legs to forestall any further probes while she slept.

"What's the matter?" he inquired solicitously.

"There's going to be no more of *that*," she promised firmly.

His heart died. "*Why?* You said—"

"No! I was just kidding you along . . . to see what you would do."

*Did he believe her?* "But . . . but—"

"No buts. It's final."

He didn't want to live.

"Are you crying?"

"Yeow. A little," he confessed.

"Well, cut it out. There's no sense in it. A boy just can't do that with his mother. It isn't right. It's against the law. That's just all there is to it. You must put it out of your mind."

"It isn't *in* my mind!" he tried to explain.

She laughed and rolled toward him. She embraced him maternally. "Now, just be nice. You must love me like a mother, not a girlfriend. I'm Bill's wife. And your mother. I love you. But it's different than I love Bill. And it must be that way. Do you understand?"

"Yeow," he grudgingly admitted.

"Monkey." She hugged him hard, but being careful to keep her belly back so it would not touch him. "Now, here's a kiss. Then go to sleep." She gave him a tightly pursed peck and a pat that said, "Be a good little boy."

When she was breathing the way she did in sleep, he once more snuck up her gown, inch by inch. She was more on her back than her side. When the hem of her gown slipped over her hairs, she jerked both arms and legs and sat bolt upright.

"*All right! Now-if-you-don't-roll-over-there-and-leave-me-alone-you-can-just-go-sleep-in-the-house.* Now, I mean it, Jack. I think I'm about to get my period, and I don't like to be fooled with."

He scooched over to his side of the bed. Finally, he slept. Yet when he awoke the next morning, he was jammed tight against her bare bottom, his arm over her waist, his hand cradling her left breast. The sweat running along the weld of their bodies in the ovenlike cabin was what awakened them. Neither felt rested. Both professed headaches.

"Boy, I'd like to get out of here. I hope Bill finds something." She yawned, standing beside the bed, stretching. "Is it only ten in the morning?" She peeled her gown from her skin and fanned it to cool her skin. She put on her underwear beneath and her slip over her gown before removing it in front of him.

The second night Bill was gone was the same—she wouldn't let him lay a finger on her in any save the most modest places. She would clap his hand there under her own, warning Jack, "Be good, now. Let's not have a scene."

Nothing he could do would crack her will. *Some big chance.*

They had missed breakfast for the second day. At least she was getting a lot of rest.

"Can I have a nickel?" he wheedled.

"I don't have a nickel."

"Bill left you some money."

"Fifty cents! I need it."

"Uncle Willy will give you some."

"Listen! I get enough of that from Bill."

"Please. I'm hungry."

"I don't like you living on candy bars."

"I won't get no candy."

"What then?"

"A Fudgsicle."

"Oh, *that's* different." She shook her head. "I don't know about you." But she gave him the coin.

"Why, I'm just a growin boy," he said cheerily.

"Yes-you-are!" she agreed sarcastically. "Scat!"

He was halfway home when he discovered he had a FREE stick. Sometimes one of the Fudgsicle sticks had FREE on it. He turned around and marched back to the little store immediately to redeem the stick for another 'sicle. You never knew when a good deal like that might be withdrawn without a moment's notice in Mississippi.

When he came into the front yard licking his second ice cream, his mother and Uncle Willy were close in the shade of the main house, engaged in earnest conversation. When she started to turn away, he gripped her high around the arm, letting his fingers slide down and squeeze her hand.

"What was that?" Jack mumped around his Fudgsicle.

"What? Oh, Uncle Willy and I had to get something straight."

"Um. I got a free Fudgsicle."

"You'll turn into one."

That was OK with him. Better a cold Fudgsicle than a fried baloney, was his thinking. His mom believed a person was what they ate.

That afternoon she said, "We're going to take a ride."

"I was goin ridin on our bikes down to the beach with Allen."

"You know I don't like you going there alone."

"I wasn't goin to go alone. I was goin with Allen."

"I want you to come with me. I need you to look out for me. Will you do that?"

He did not understand.

"You just come with us, keep your mouth shut and eyes and ears open. I don't want to be alone with Uncle. OK?"

"OK." He still wasn't sure what was expected of him.

When they went to get in the car, Uncle was already behind the wheel with the motor running, as if he wanted to make a getaway.

"What's he comin along for?" Uncle demanded rather surlily, meaning Jack.

If that's how he felt, Jack would be perfectly happy to go riding with Allen.

"He wanted to go for a ride, too, won't take no for an answer," she said.

"Oh, I think he would." Uncle looked about to offer the boy a bribe. She gave Jack a slight surreptitious nudge to remind him of his duty.

"Actually, it's a good thing he's coming along. Your wife's watching from the screen door," she said.

He flipped down the left-hand seat so the boy could climb in back. Wilma slipped in the front. Uncle took off before the door was securely closed. He leaned heavily across Wilma to close it. Jack didn't see Old Lady Best behind the screen door. He saw better than she did. Uncle was sweating. He took off his straw hat, mopped his brow, dropped it in back beside Jack on the seat.

"It sure is *hot* this time of year," Wilma whewed, flipping her skirt up and down over her bare legs to create a breeze. Uncle kept glancing down at her legs. Jack could see his eyes in the rear-view mirror. "Aren't you hot?" she asked, looking right at him, tucking her skirt way up over her knees.

"I'm gittin that way, daughter," he breathed. He reached out and stroked her left knee with his hairy paw, the one with the pinky missing.

"Now, now." She patted his hand. "What I wanted to talk to you about was the possibility of making some sort of arrangement on what we owe you. If we could send it to you as soon as we get settled. . . ."

She shifted in her seat again, then again. Uncle was rather straining toward her, reaching with his arm. He could hardly keep his eyes on the road.

"I sure don't know about that," he muttered, the words coming hard. "It . . . ain't . . . I don't . . . trust . . . you . . . you understand. It's just I got . . . this-uh . . . uh . . . uh . . . policy— great God, honey, you make me feel like a boy. Yore legs is like sweet butter."

She frowned and shook her head, jerking toward the back seat. "Little pitchers have big ears," she warned him.

And eyes. Was he touchin her pussy? Jack wondered. The idea made his ears ring.

She was sitting more toward the division in the seats than the window. She put her left hand on Uncle's leg.

He was only doing about twenty—all over the road.

"We could give you a note."

"Yuh . . . you . . . could . . . give . . . me . . . a note."

"Why are you sittin so close?" Jack demanded, leaning on the back of her seat. His creepy mitt held a gob of her thigh, inside, up high. Her hand stroked his leg playfully, raking her nails along his quivering, dilapidated old thigh, coming within a few inches of the wad of cock and cods under the bulge of his big belly. A braided leather watch chain looped from his belt to the big Ingersoll in his watch pocket. Jack wanted to hit him.

"It's all right," she explained levelly. "We are just being friendly. Sit back and enjoy your ride."

"Don't see why you had to bring him along," Uncle sulked.

In reply she scooted closer. Presently Uncle turned that Plymouth off the road onto a lane that ran down through some pine woods to an abandoned clearing where a sawmill was rusting under its tin canopy.

He tried to kiss her, puckering up clear across the car and reaching for her. She gave him a peck and turned her face toward the back seat. She made a little mouth as if to kiss Jack and gave him a wink over Uncle's shoulder.

"Hey, wait! Hold it!" she said. "If you want me to be good to you, you got to be good to us."

His full weight toppled her over against the door. Just the top of her head appeared above the seat back. "Oh, honey!" he puffed.

She laughed.

He sat back. "Damn! You should of *tole* me you were sick. Get me all hot and bothered like that."

"I didn't promise you anything, now."

"Not in so many words."

"Not *nohow*. I just wanted to ask you as a favor if you could trust us for what we owed you for a little. You be good to us, I'll be good to you."

"When?"

"When you take care of us."

"How I know you will?"

"You'll have to trust me. Think I'd try and fool you?"

"I don't know. Get me all het up, I'm supposed to cool down just lak that. Looks lak you'd have the decency to do *somethin!*"

"Decency? What do you mean?"

He picked up her hand and plopped it in his lap.

She quickly withdrew it. She looked angry. "In front of him?" she said as if she couldn't believe it. "You better take us home right now, Mister Best, or we will walk."

He looked like a man who thought he was being robbed but was not certain how.

"Oh, don't look so sour." She plucked his underlip playfully. He jerked back. "I told you what I'd do, OK? It isn't as if I don't like you," she said very confidentially.

Jack would kill him at a word from her. She didn't have to be nice to him.

"Sit back, there!" he commanded, giving the boy a shove back in the seat as the car began rolling.

Jack came up with his right cocked to bust him on the ugly big mole by his right ear.

He slammed on the brakes and whirled around as if to slap the boy, madder than hell. *"Draw back to hit me, you little bastard!"*

Wilma threw herself between them.

They drove back to the house in silence.

As soon as they pulled to a stop in the drive, Wilma was out, yanking Jacky after her and yelling like hell.

*Man! What was it all about?* Jack looked around. It was embarrassing, her carrying on like that. He wished she would keep it down. *What was it?*

*Uncle? Yeow. But, Christ, here comes everybody.* He wanted to tug her skirt and tell her to can it.

"We came to you and asked for help like you were our own and you treat me like I was-was-*was*—RIGHT IN FRONT OF MY OWN SON!"

Red and the girls were out on the porch to see what the commotion was. Allen lurked at the corner of the house. Then the old lady came to the screen door armed with a big wooden spoon.

"You wait until Bill gets back and hears about this," Wilma warned.

The old lady busted right out onto the porch. She feared nothing. You could tell she was also neutral, as if the title to everything were in her name.

"What's this all about?" she demanded, the spoon cocked up on one hip.

"You ask your husband," Wilma said archly.

"I'm askin *you*, Missus. I'll ask him, too." She had a sparse goatee of white and black whiskers, some about an inch long. Her chin never quavered.

"Well, you'll *have* to ask him. I'm not going to stand in the yard and discuss it. I'm not saying anything until Bill gets here." She gave the impression she felt outnumbered.

"She's just tryin to badger me, that's all she's doin," Uncle said. But he was not on all that secure a footing.

"I want to know what this is all about, and I don't mean maybe," the old lady said. She didn't trust Yankees at all, but she didn't trust Uncle, either.

"She's just tryin to pull a fast one," Uncle insisted.

"Yeh? I have a witness," Wilma retorted. "Jacky was right there. He saw it all."

Jack assumed a pose more consistent with his new importance. Yet he wasn't at all certain what the hell he was supposed to be mad about. He wanted to say hi to Allen but sensed somehow it was all over, their being friends. It was as if everything he had done there in Mississippi had been written in chalk, and now an eraser had obliterated all the words, all the times. It was as if months of his life had been wiped out. He had never felt so rootless before.

Uncle hadn't hurt her. She wasn't carrying on about him fooling around with her, was she? Hell, she'd sort of asked for it. . . . *Hadn't* she?

"Bullshit!" Uncle said.

"Well, you'll see what's what tomorrow," she said in a way that included Uncle's whole family. "Come on, Son." She turned on her heel and marched into the cabin. Her rump went solidly *chunk-chunk* with each step.

Jack sneaked a look back. They hadn't moved. They looked frozen, elongated, diminished, yet unchanged, unchanging. They were nearer kin to the cows in the lot behind them than they were to himself, he thought.

Red came over to the cabin after supper. Wilma and the boy hadn't gone to table.

"What happened?" he asked.

"Oh, you know, Red. I just asked him if he would let us send him what we owe him when we were settled in Mobile. If he had just hit me up—but he started grabbing me. Pawing me. He tried to *kiss* me. Pushed me down on the seat. Put his hand clear up my dress. If I hadn't been sick, I don't know what he'd of done. And Son was right there in the back *all the time*." She drew the boy to her and hugged him against her. "He was so brave. Trying to protect his mama. He was going to hit him, weren't you, Sonny?"

He nodded enthusiastically. But he knew she was faking anger and shock. He could tell inside she was dead as hell.

In the meantime, he was getting hungry.

"Mom, can I have some money to get a hamburger or somethin?"

"Honey, I don't have anything. Bill didn't leave us any."

"I'm hungry."

"I know you are. But we can't go to the kitchen now after what happened, can we?"

"But I'm starvin."

"Red?"

"Oh? Yeow. Sure. Let me see." He dug into a pocket in his slacks. He came up with a single crumpled dollar and some change. "Here." He handed Wilma the bill.

"No. I don't want to strap you," she protested.

"Take it. I'd only drink it up, anyway. Take it."

She sent Jack to the Rainbow Café with instructions to bring her an American cheese on whole wheat toast and a chocolate shake. He had a hamburger there and a Coke. The hamburger tasted like it was part pork. It was fried to a black crisp, yet it was greasy.

Fortunately it turned cool, for Wilma insisted on closing and locking the cabin door that night. A breeze that smelled of fall back in the Midwest lifted the curtain on the window and drove them under sheet and bedspread. It was as if summer had gone so abruptly it might never come back. Wilma said there was a big storm out in the Gulf.

Jack awoke to the sound of his mom and someone talking earnestly in the dark.

Bill was home.

"Hey. We wake you?" he asked cheerfully.

It was four in the morning. He could smell booze on Bill.

"Your old lady was tellin me how you stuck up for her when old fart-hammer over there got fresh with her. I'm real proud of you, Son. Put 'er there." He wanted to shake the boy's hand. "Nobody can mess around with our gal, right?"

"Yessir."

"You bet. Well, everything's copasetic." He rubbed his hands together happily.

"You get a job?" Jack asked groggily.

"It's all set."

That could mean anything. He rolled over toward the wall.

"Go back to sleep, honey," his mother said.

They whispered together in the dark. The flare of Bill's cigarette lit the room when he took a drag like the light of a great firefly.

Jack awoke again when Bill's rough hand insinuated itself between his backside and Wilma's to pull her toward his side of the bed. He was dragging up her gown. He did it quickly, like he owned it, not stealthily the way Jack did.

"Bill, I really am sick."

There was the snap of elastic against her bare skin.

"Ow!"

They stifled giggles. They nuzzled together, kissing, hunching around.

"Don't wake Jacky," she whispered.

Soon all was quiet except for Bill's snores.

Before leaving the cabin, Bill squatted, holding Jack by both shoulders and peering into his eyes. He said sort of out of the corner of his mouth, "Now, you just follow my lead, kid. Just remember to tell what you saw when I call on you. How he tried to get into her pants. Right?"

"Right."

At the back of the house, the woodpile was a potential ambush, the great cast-iron laundry pot bottom up on its charred stones some anti-Yankee mine. The benign family banana tree by the back stoop which only grew bitter, inedible green finger bananas was a tattered symbol of the place to Jacky. A place of Klans and snake worshipers, where foxes were run to ground by possum hounds and clubbed to death by men in biballs and khakis.

He followed Bill up the steps, one step back, off his left hand. The boards in the porch squeaked familiarly. Jack still did not know what was expected of him. They were going in to face Uncle. He could not have explained why, precisely. Yet it was a showdown of great portent. . . . Why? Only a few days before, Mississippi had been it. It had been where they were going to make a good new life. Even though he was a Yankee, Jack was as much a part of the boardinghouse family as a stray dog. Hadn't he been? Just what *did* he mean to these people? was a question that bothered the boy as they went across the porch. The possibility that he meant nothing at all was a sudden, frightening prospect. Still, what did it matter?

"I want to talk to your husband," Bill told the old lady roughly after Dulcie let him into the kitchen.

"Go get your father, Allen," she said. No one else spoke.

The women were all barefoot. They were damp from doing the breakfast dishes. Though the night had been very cool, the morning sun was hot. The heavy white crockery was stacked neatly on the table, where the girls would cover it with dish towels until time to serve supper.

"I understand y'allud have a word with me," Uncle said filling the doorway.

"You know damn well what I want to talk to you about," Bill said very toughly, glaring at the man, tensed, turned a little with his left shoulder forward.

Jack sort of grinned at Allen. They weren't mad at each other. But Allen wasn't grinning back.

"Let's us step outside," Uncle suggested.

"Hell, no! I'll say what I have to say right here. You didn't think twice about the boy when you went for Wilma."

The girls gasped.

"You children get out of here," Uncle ordered. They scooted. "Looks lak you'd be a man about this," Uncle said.

Bill exploded: "Man me! You pus-gutted old fart! I'll *show* you. I'm not the kind of man whose wife you can't go drivin out into the woods with and make a dive for her pants just because we're a little down on our luck." He made a menacing move toward Uncle that made the man jump and put up his dukes in a pathetic, old-fashioned stance. Bill would kill him.

Then Bill had a better thought. The click of his switchblade knife was like a rattler's warning in the steamy morning kitchen.

"I'm going to call the sheriff," Mrs. Best announced. She went to the ring phone on the wall.

"You *do* that!" Bill encouraged her. "I'm sure the sheriff would like to hear the details of what your old man was trying to do out in the woods yesterday with my wife."

"What *were* you doin?" Mrs. B. asked. Her hand rested on the receiver.

"Aw, you better ask Mr. Bill here. *He* cooked it all up. *He* knows better than me," Uncle said.

*"Don't try to fuck me around, old man!"* Bill yelled. "I'll open you up like a scalded hog."

"You don't scare me one little bit," Uncle claimed, backing, side-stepping. Then he had his own big wooden-handled Barlow knife in his mitt. He held it in his pinkyless right hand and prized open the blade with his left. "I gotta knife, too."

Bill crouched like a cat about to spring. They both moved on their feet, circling a bit. Uncle squatted like a Sumo wrestler with bad knees, but he looked a hell of a lot more formidable with that ole Barlow in his hand than he did ready to go to fist city.

Jack saw the old lady just in time. "BILL, LOOK OUT!"

The old lady split crockery with a meat cleaver that would have made two of Bill sure as hell. Jack's hair felt like it was standing on end. Uncle moved quicker than the boy had ever seen him and caught the woman's wrist in both hands before she could take another shot. Bill was backing —fast. He damn near backed over the boy.

Suddenly he shifted gears. How could you read the guy? One minute he was going to cut open Uncle sure. Then he's got that hanging, apologetic conneroo's look in his eye. It made Jack wonder if he had been mad at all. There was that same deadness he had sensed in his mother.

"Listen, I guess I just lost my temper there," Bill said. "I never in this world would want to hurt you folks. Why, Missus reminds me so much of my own mother—I've told her a hundred times—"

"I would never have been mother of one like you," she told him. "*You're* the devil. I told him when you first came here, 'That man's the devil incarnate.' Look what you have driven us to," she demanded.

"I didn't mean to cause you any trouble, Missus. Believe me. It's just Wilma told me this, uh, and the kid backed her up. I didn't know what to believe. Uncle Willy would do the same if it was you."

"He'd-never-have-cause. *That's* the difference." But she had put down the cleaver and turned her back so as no longer to have to look at him.

"Maybe Wilma was a little excited and imagined a lot *more* was going on than actually was." He'd snuck the knife into his back pocket. "It was her time," he confided low, so ingratiatingly he could have worked the family room of a funeral.

*Chameleon! That's what he was.* Jack had a chameleon once. Bill changed faster. Jack felt giddy but was also now angry with Bill.

"So maybe it wasn't what she thought at all," he went on. "She's been so upset since I had my accident an all. Why, hell!" He stepped toward Uncle. "We've always been friends, ain't we? We've always been able to trust one another. I'm willing to go on record here and now as saying I trust Uncle one hundred percent in this. If he says nothin happened, then Bill Wild agrees nothin happened. And here's my hand."

Uncle just looked at it.

"I say let's shake on it."

"On what?"

"On trust."

"I wouldn't trust you to fetch water if your shirttail was afire," Uncle said.

"*Why, goddamn you!*"

"Nosir! I've heard enough swearin by you in my house. I've had enough of you tryin to gull me, badger me like some hillbilly chump. Who the hell you think you are?" He turned and walked out of the room.

"Listen, I got a good job in Mobile. I gotta be there Monday morning," Bill pleaded. "I swear, I'll send you everything I owe you just as soon as we get it."

Uncle came back with an old Winchester pump shotgun.

"You come in my house swearin in front of my kids, pullin a knife on me, accusin me in front of my wife of somethin you know more about than me. Then you want to shake hands. Want to be friends and get me to *trust* you for three and a half weeks' board and thirty dollars I was fool enough to trust you for before. I'll give you one hour to clear up what you owe me and get out here, or I'm callin the sheriff."

"Hey, listen, you know I can't raise that kind of money in an hour. You got to give me a chance. You don't know how tough it is for an ex-con—sure I've done time, I admit it—to get a break. I *swear* to you on my mother's grave, you'll get your money. Look! Let me leave our stuff—Wilma's watch. It's an Elgin. Seventeen jewels—the boy's bike. Keep her iron and toaster. She's hardly used the toaster."

"What would we do with all that stuff?" the old lady sneered.

Uncle thought a minute. "OK. You get it here and clear out in one hour."

Bill banged into the cabin cussing a blue streak. "Lousy no good redneck cracker sonofabitch! Pulled a shotgun on me. Said if we aren't out of here in a hour, he'll call the sheriff."

"You said it would work," Wilma protested.

"Dummy the hell up. Gimme your watch."

"Why?"

"Gimme it!" He started to yank it off her arm.

She slipped the clasp for him and handed it to him. "I knew when you gave it to me I'd never get to keep it."

"Act your age, for Chrissake. If *he'd* of done his part, it would of worked. He just stood there grinnin like he was going to a wienie roast."

"*Who, me?*" Jack asked.

He jerked his head at the boy. "Get him. Dumbest damn Swede I've ever seen. *I bane a car-painter from Minn-e-sota,*" he mimicked.

"If he had just followed my lead. I had that old fart scared shitless. But he let me down."

Jack thought he had saved Bill's life.

"I guess I better get packed," Wilma said.

"I'll pack this." Bill hauled out Jack's big old cardboard suitcase. He threw her iron, the toaster, some of the raggedy clothes from the pole across the corner. "Take only what you need," he told her.

"I *need* my iron."

"Naw. Naw. Just take the handbag. Forget it. When I've had a pay day, we'll send for the rest of the stuff."

He banged out the screen door. He was wheeling Jack's bike over to the house. Jack busted out after him.

Wilma called after the boy, "Jack! Wait!"

"Where you takin my bike?" Jack wanted to know.

"We're just goin to store it here with Uncle until we can send for it," he said kindly, not rough at all. Who could figure him?

"Will Allen ride it?"

"Aw, naw. They'll just hold it for us. You couldn't take it on the bus, could you?"

"No."

"So. Here, give me a hand."

Jack wheeled the bike to the back porch. Uncle and Allen came out. Uncle took Wilma's watch, looked at it, held it to his ear to be certain it worked, dropped it into his pocket. He took the grip and Wilma's winter coat with a real fur collar. Allen came down and hoisted the wheel up the steps. He didn't even look at Jack. But there was a look of Christmas in his eyes.

"You won't let Allen ride it, will yuh?" Jack asked Uncle.

He didn't answer.

"Dummy up, Son," Bill said. "They'll take good care of it. This is only until I can send you what I owe you," Bill said loudly.

Uncle continued to the door. He turned, fished the watch out of his pocket, looked at it, and said, "You got about forty more minutes."

Hands in pockets, Bill hunched back around to the cabin.

Wilma was throwing her underwear and some clothes from the chest of drawers into a zipper overnight bag.

"Hurry it up," Bill said.

"What's the rush?"

"I want to be out of here right now. Before I go over there and do something to that sonofabitch I'll be sorry for. That's all I need, a bad rap like that. They'd throw away the key. Shake it."

"I am as fast as I can." She wrapped her cosmetics in a bath towel, putting in a wash cloth, her travel alarm that had a busted sliding door but kept good time. She looked around for her portable radio.

"Now, why would you want to lug it on the bus?" Bill asked as if she were feebleminded.

"Well, I'll never see that again, either."

"Here!" He hipped her out of the way. "I'll show you how to pack."

He began shoving her stuff into the little bag. When he zipped it and the cuff of one of her blouses hung out, he ripped off the cuff.

"There! That's neat." He banged the bag into Jack's chest, catching him unaware, knocking the wind out of him and damn near bowling him over.

"Sometimes I hate you," the woman hissed between clenched teeth.

"Yeh, and sometime you love me." He gave her a goose that made her furious.

*"Stop that!"*

"As we bid farewell to beautiful Pascagoula, home of sunshine, jumbo shrimp, and sonsabitches." He bowed.

She was not amused. Crossing the yard, Red came groggily from his carton room.

"Keep your cock up, pardner!" Bill called gaily. "You better come, too, before you get mossy and moldy like the rest of these figs."

"Luck to you," Red called. "Luck to y'all."

"He's a nice little guy, Red," she said.

"Fuck 'im," was all Bill said.

They told Bill good-bye across from the bus depot. They had only enough for a ticket for Wilma and the boy. Bill would hitch.

"See you in Mobile," Bill said.

"See you," Wilma said.

They didn't kiss. He did not tell the boy good-bye. Jack guessed if he hadn't been there, Bill could have ridden.

She had on her brown and tan gabardine suit and her spectator pumps. She hadn't any hose. Jack wore his only pair of dungarees and a chambray shirt. He had on black tenners, worn out and too small. He had grown so fast. All the stuff he had arrived in he had outgrown. In Mississippi a boy only needed dungarees and a shirt to put on when he was called to eat. Jack had a couple of polo shirts in the bag and maybe an extra pair of pants. His mother carried a light spring coat.

The bus pulled in just before dark. They had had nothing to eat all day except a Mr. Goodbar and a bottle of Dr. Pepper. She would not get him a sandwich for the bus. The bus was packed with soldiers and sailors and women traveling to visit their husbands in service. Jack had never seen so many servicemen at one time before. There was a whole new, exciting atmosphere on the bus. Everyone was talking loud. Women laughed. Young men laughed. The bus was old. It was not air-conditioned. The seats did not recline. But there were little jump seats on the aisle. Wilma and the boy had to sit on the jumps.

Then at Gulfport a whole bunch of sailors got on. There was a sailor standing in the aisle between each jump seat.

"He looks like he's going to fall off that," Jack heard a young man say as dark telephone poles moved by in the night. He was falling asleep on the jump seat, catching himself just before he fell on the floor.

"Yes, poor little fella. He's had a rough day," she said.

"Got just the place to stow you, pal," he said. He scooped the boy up and deposited him in the luggage tray above the seats.

"Is it all right?" she wondered.

"Could the driver get back here to stop us?" the sailor said.

"I guess you're right." She laughed a little.

"My name's Chet." The sailor introduced himself.

"Mine's Wilma, but all my friends call me Bill," she said.

"Sure don't look like no Bill I ever knew," Chet said.

Man, it was great being around a lot of sailors. Jack wished he were one. He hoped the country *did* go to war and it lasted forever. It sure as hell would beat being poor.

He awoke during the night. He was freezing. There was an air vent up there, and it was blowing right on him. The bus was less crowded. Hardly anyone sat on the jump seats then. He panicked. *Had she gotten off and forgotten him? Had she just left him?*

"*Mama!*" In his head he screamed it. But his throat was so constricted with terror he had only croaked. Some people below him were startled. They evidently hadn't known he was traveling Pullman. "Mom!"

"Honey! What?" she whispered up out of a coat covering her and the sailor across the aisle. Her head had been on his shoulder. His arm had been around her. He sat up and lit a cigarette, a dark shape against the window. She whispered to the boy, "What is it?"

"I'm cold."

She felt his hands. "You're like ice. Let me cover you with this." She tucked her coat in all around him. It smelled of her perfume.

"Get some sleep," she said. She patted his head.

He imagined he was on a great battleship, breasting great seas, like in the newsreels. His grandmother had written that Wolford Coleman had come home from the CCC's, lied about his age, and enlisted in the Marines. He was only fifteen. David Noonen had joined the Navy the same way. He was only sixteen and was on corvettes escorting English ships. His ship had already been sunk once.

Jack peeked over the lip of the tray. The sailor was kissing his mother on the mouth, moving her head around and round. His left hand disappeared under her right arm.

*Well, so long as it's a sailor,* he decided.

In Mobile she rushed him off the bus.

"I'll be lookin for that letter, Bill," the sailor called down the aisle. Wilma threw him a smile.

She quickly dragged the boy through the station. They virtually trotted a couple of blocks after rounding the corner, then cut over to the left for a block and then back to the right. He was getting a stitch in his side. It was cool in Mobile, cloudy. He was chilly. They ducked into a narrow chili parlor where the window was steamed over and the smell of spices made his belly roll.

*Surprise of surprises!* She asked him what he would like to eat.

"Can I have a bowl a chili *and* a hamburger?" he asked.

"It's ten in the morning. I'd rather you had ham and eggs or something wholesome."

*In a chili parlor?* She was nuts.

*She* had breakfast: cereal, two eggs sunny side up, toast, jelly, juice, and coffee. His chili floated oyster crackers in the ruby grease on top. It was fantastic. He had never been so hungry. The guy who ran the place was a Greek. They made better chili for Jack's money than Mexicans. But the Greek was close with a second bowl of crackers.

Wilma blotted her lips daintily with a coarse paper napkin. She opened her purse and thumbed two dollars out of a fat black wallet in there that had a gold anchor embossed on it.

"What's that?" the boy asked.

She almost snapped his fingers in her purse.

"Curiosity killed the cat," she reminded him.

She dawdled over a second cup of coffee. They had been about an hour in the chili parlor.

Then they went back to the station to look for Bill.

# 28

THE woman and the boy waited near the newsstand in the bus station. She pretended to read a newspaper while he was on the lookout for Bill. When Bill came up behind them, unnoticed, and caught Wilma by the elbow, her knees buckled. Her face turned white.

"What's up?" he wondered.

"Don't ever do that. How would *you* feel if I came up on you like that?"

She slipped the wallet she had taken from the sailor on the bus from her purse and dropped it into his left pants pocket.

He put his hand in, grinned, gave her a kiss on the lips. "Good girl."

"Let's get out of here," she said, peering around, still not certain the sailor hadn't discovered his loss and jumped off his bus.

The boy carried their single bag. He was proud to be entrusted.

A couple of blocks away Bill snuck the sailor's wallet from his pocket and riffed the contents.

"Sixteen bucks?" he asked.

"We had breakfast," Wilma explained.

Clearly a man ought to travel with more on him than that. That Bill had thumbed to Mobile with traveling money he could jingle was not to be construed as a cultural standard. His poverty was accidental and only temporary; the sailor's was obstinate, dumb, and un-American. There was something about letting yourself get rolled on the open highway for $16 that was unpatriotic to Bill. That Wilma had not cased her man better was equally unforgivable.

"Well, it will help," she argued, hurt that her effort wasn't more appreciated. "It's sixteen bucks more than we had."

"You sure you ain't ratholed some for yourself?"

She did not even answer.

Bill hiked along as if he knew where he was going. Jacky was hard put to keep up. Even his mother seemed to flag a bit. It was cold in Mobile. The boy figured the cold was temporary. Mobile was still the sunny South, wasn't it? In the meantime his teeth were chattering. He hadn't even an undershirt on under his chambray.

"Tough it out, kid," was Bill's advice.

He bowled on across the last street before coming to the river. Running down to the docks was a wide street of small, half-dead shops, a café, and buildings boarded up for warehouses. The river was wide enough and deep enough for ships to sail in and tie up at the docks at the foot of the street. Across the river the monstrous steel cranes of the shipyard moved like gigantic birds constructing nests of beams and plates on the river bank. There was a far-off, wavery, constant pecking of rivet gun and chipping hammer. In the cold haze there were deep-sky star points of welders' torches.

On the corner, across the street next to a dinky corner grocery with stuff heaped helter-skelter in the window to the top as though the place were a simple bin, was a dimly lit stair going up under a painted glass sign in which just a single bulb burned:

THE STAR HOTEL
day, week, month

On the other side of the stair was a nameless barber shop displaying in its dirty window only bottles of bay rum stacked in a pyramid, around which a summer's army of dead flies lay on faded butcher's paper.

Wilma followed Bill up the creaky stair. The boy was close behind her.

A man wearing an undershirt under a tattered gray cardigan came out sucking on a stub of a cigar in answer to a push on the buzzer beside the door labeled MANAGER. He hadn't shaved that day, perhaps not the day before. He dug his trousers out of his fat ass and waited.

"How much?" Bill asked.

"Dollar uh day, six uh week," he growled as if the effort was almost too much.

Bill gave him a five. "Just for tonight. Maybe we'll stay later."

The man grunted, took Bill's five inside, and closed the door. By and by he returned and gave Bill a skeleton key with a grimy paper tag in a tin grommet tied to it on which was penciled the number 6. He gave Bill four singles that were so old they were limp as cloth.

"You ever see money so damn used?" he asked, showing Wilma the limp bills. "I bet he's got a mattress full of green like that in there."

Jacky had a vision of a literal mattress stuffed with dollars.

There were eight rooms on the floor above a patio. Overhead the sun seeped feebly through a big skylight that was opaque with years of accumulated grime and streams of gull shit. An ornamental iron railing ran around the inside balcony.

"This was once an elegant place," Wilma observed.

"Fanciest cathouse in Mobile in its day," Bill said.

"*Bill.*"

"Was. Now it ain't so fancy."

There were at least five truckloads of trash and junk heaped in the patio below. A rusted-out boiler, leprous couches and overstuffed chairs, an extension table with a broken back, two bathtubs, sinks, a stove, iceboxes. In the dirt-filled basin of a cracked fountain, a brown-stained toilet bowl leaned at the knee of a water-pouring nymph sheared off on the bias from the part in her hair to her left knee. Jacky often daydreamed of carving himself a beautiful, glassy marble statue and devising some kind of rubber cunt for her he could actually fuck. *And you*

315

*could get real hair to paste on her, couldn't you?* he thought. The boy fell in love with statues everywhere, bringing them to life in his dreams, where they were delighted to be his slaves. They thanked him for every cruelty, suffered to assuage his every tantrum.

There were mattresses in the patio below that looked like rotting slabs of meat flayed from some mastodon. One mattress had a hole burnt through it the size of a washtub. The smell that came up from below was one of mold and decay that had gone beyond stink. Drifts of yellowed newspapers, abandoned garments, bags of garbage disposed of via "parachute," garbage *sans* bag, tin cans, beat-up aluminum cookware, chipped enamel basins, and the fatal rusty chancre surrounding a hole you could waggle your fingers through—a running inventory of life's nonenduring necessities rose layer upon layer around the nymph's basin until it was only where someone had removed something large that the once bright-blue-and-white-tile patio could be seen. After dark, rats and cats contested for dominance of the heap.

Two 40-watt bulbs were the only illumination on the balcony. When the sun was down, musty old ghosts seeped up out of the blackness below. And Jack would piss in the sink rather than risk a trek out there to the donicker across the hall. After dark the courtyard below was dark as a mine and filled with creaks, rustles, pops, and sometimes a bang. The screams of combat between cat and rat were frequently hair-raising. The eyes of a cat prowling down there could make one's heart stop.

From across the hall, next to the can, there was the constant sound of a baby crying at full siren. It hurt the boy to hear a baby cry like that. A girl's voice screamed at the unremitting wail:

"SHUT UP! SHUT UP! SHUT UP, GODDAMN YOU! PLEASE, PLEASE, PLEASE STOP CRYING . . . baby."

But the baby cried all the time like a crazy runaway anger pump.

In their high, large room there was a fireplace between two windows overlooking the women's jail across the street. The stones had been sooted so long they looked like iron. The windows of the room hadn't been washed in a generation. There was an iron bed, a sink, a rickety common little table, a coat tree, a closet without a hanger, and a single painted blue pine chair that could never put all its legs on the floor at the same time. The only source of heat was the fireplace. There was neither bucket nor coal. No wood. No tongs.

Bill went out for a pint and their dinner of cold hamburgers and coffee. When they had eaten, it was cold in the room. Bill took the boy to scrounge the block for something to burn. They found an apple crate in the alley and a bunch of newspapers in a trash can. They burned the crate. Bill showed Jack how to make kindling of newspaper balls and logs of newspaper rolls.

There was no blanket on the bed. When the fire went out, Jacky shivered under the sheet and thin spread. His mother said, "For goodness' sake, lay still."

Bill had Wilma and the pint to keep him warm. Jack had only her back. Moreover, he was on the window side of the bed. Sleeping cold turned him killer. Either the sonofabitch produced a blanket or a big bucket of coal by tomorrow night or it was curtains for him, the boy promised himself, staring at the high ceiling awash with eddies of light and shadow from the street below.

Across the street, women in the jail were singing the blues. Others at the windows called to men scurrying along the cold street.

"Getcher hands out of your pockets, old man. Somebody think you playin wif yoursef."

"Could I get to you, darlin, I'd *light* your fire."

"Hey, you! Yeh, *you!* You longlegged-lookin drinka water. You uglier than shit, baby, but my hot pussy is blind."

"Betchoo I gots what you lak."

To men black and white they called from their jail with greater freedom than they had ever known outside.

"Hey, mister. What's your name? I *love* you!"

The next morning Jack lay shivering in bed, seeing his breath in the air. It had got colder overnight.

"Hey, Son, haul your ass out of there and go rustle up some boxes for a fire," Bill suggested.

Haul your own, was Jack's feeling.

"Go on. When I was your age I had to lay a fire every damn morning when you had to knock frozen logs loose from the pile with the back of your ax. If there wasn't a fire roaring when my old man got up, he would take a piece of stove wood to my back hisself."

*That* was why he was so damn mean, the boy thought.

"Get movin!"

The linoleum floor was like a rink. Jack jumped into his pants. He had slept in his shorts and shirt. His teeth were chattering.

"Cut that out!" Bill ordered.

"Wh-wh-wh-wh-wha?" he chattered.

"That phony damn chattering. Get rough!" He dug his pint from under his pillow, uncapped it, and had breakfast lying there cozy, with the covers up to his chin, on the most radiant side of the boy's mother.

Jack leaped into his cold tenners. In their single bag he found a short-sleeved summer polo shirt that he put on over his shirt. His teeth only stopped chattering when the motor gave out. Inside he was still silently quaking so badly his side ached.

Before he was out the door, his mother whispered something to Bill and slid her leg over his. Jack noticed Bill's dick raised the covers like a little tent.

There were rims of ice on the staved-in tops of garbage cans. There was frost on metal sills where the rays of an overcast sun had not reached. An old boobatch slept in the doorway of the bay rum barber shop curled tightly around himself, his blackened hands thrust between his wasted thighs. His sockless feet in mismatched cast-off shoes stuck out on the sidewalk, more corpse than transportation. He was dying by degrees from the skin in. Jack felt there was only a thin trickle of him left inside. He was less man than alcoholic snake. Near his head was an empty bay rum bottle.

In those sadass bums the boy sensed his own mortality. And so felt pity for them that was pity for himself in the face of such human possibility. He vowed *he* would never end up like that. Yet, he never intentionally hurt or scorned a bum, just in case . . . just in case.

He made it down to the dock, where fog hung over the river. The water was warmer than the air. At the corner of an ornate, cast-iron warehouse he spotted three cardboard boxes.

A soldier shivering in khakis in spite of the warm wool sweater peeping out of his cuffs came marching down the dock.

"Halt," he said in a strange tentative way, more question than command. But he snapped his '03 down to port arms in a very businesslike way. The naked bayonet on the end was as long as a sword.

Jack had just stepped onto the dock proper. "Me?"

"Who goes there?" he asked in that strange, hollow way.

"Jack Andersen."

"That's not the password, kid."

"What is?"

"I can't tell you. It's a secret."

"Can I get them three boxes over there?"

"What for?"

"To burn."

"Burn?"

"For heat."

"Where do you live?"

"Up there." He pointed in the direction of the hotel.

"You *live* there?"

"It's only temporary until my stepdad gets a payday."

"Well, I ain't supposed to let anyone on the dock."

"Them boxes are just *cryin* to be taken."

"How do I know you ain't a spy?" he asked.

"I ain't no *spy*."

"How do I know?"

"I'm too *little*."

"Maybe you're half a spy?"

"Naw."

"Maybe you're a midget."

"Naw." He was just fooling around.

"Well, I gotta walk my post now." He snapped the rifle back up on his shoulder. "If when I pass them boxes and go up there to the other end of that far building and they ain't there when I come back, I'll just figure some spy tookum."

"Thanks."

He winked and said out of the corner of his mouth, "Stay out of the Army."

"I'm going to be a sailor," Jacky said proudly.

"Yeh. Now that's usin your old bean." He marched off with a big grin on his face under the eaves of his steel hat.

The rummy was awake in the doorway when Jack went back. He was sitting up beating himself on the arms like an old pelican the boy once saw bogged up to his ass in a puddle of pitch.

The unearthly sound "gaack-gaaack-gaaack" went through his mind.

"Hey, boy, give me them boxes," he croaked.

"No."

He stirred and reached out but did not rise, as if it were that easy or his maximum effort were a frail reaching. The boy skittered across the sidewalk.

"Give me one uh them boxes. I'm about froze."

No, he shook his head. Jack was sorry. But, no. He broke into a run. He felt like a rattletrap car with the boxes flapping and bouncing.

When he turned up the stairs, the old bum was heaving himself up hand over hand up the wall. He stood like an infant with a load in his pants. He was hardly making it. Jack went up.

Bill and his mother jumped apart when Jack rumbled through the door, boxes banging both sides.

"I told you to hook the door," she whined as if the boy hadn't ears.

"Yeh, yeh."

Bill's dick still made a little tent under the covers. He raised a leg to hide it.

"Why don't you run get yourself some breakfast?" Jack's mother suggested.

"Yeh. Cop a walk for a bit, kid. Your mom and me got something we want to get straight between us."

"You." She gave Bill a poke on his skinny, freckled shoulder.

"Give me some money." Jack knew why they wanted him out of the way.

"Bring me my pants."

He lifted Bill's trousers off the back of the chair as if they would snap. They seemed irrevocably formed to his character. Jack would have known them if they had been pressed and hung in a rummage window. He found a cold two bits in there for the boy.

His mother smiled maternally. "Get something good for you."

*Same to you,* he thought.

He trotted down three blocks to a King Orange. They had an outside service window, but he went inside. There were free fat red-jacket peanuts in wooden bowls on the counter. There was the smell of coney islands and chili. Like glassine chocks, the sandwiches were ranked in neat triangular packages, labeled, and visibly so tasty they made his stomach growl—whole wheat and white, in every kind. Or was it the chili smell? They made the greatest coney islands in the world. On a soft, warm hot-dog bun they laid a grilled wiener, spooned on chili con carne with beans, and sprinkled it with chopped onion—10¢ each, two for 15¢. A big orange and two coneys—25¢. Jack always felt he could eat a dozen. There were desk-chairs like those in schoolrooms, painted bright orange, with a little cup of free red-jackets at each desk.

Sitting there, with the steam rising from the grill and table where the chili was kept warm in a deep stainless pot and moisture beaded the window, he was warm for the first time since hitting Mobile. He felt drowsy and snug. He could have stayed there skarfing coneys and nuts forever. A middle-aged woman with a shopping bag munched an early lunch across the room. One short, plump leg was crossed over the other. He could see pounds of dimpled fat, very white thigh above her brown stocking-top. Her hair was jet, probably dyed. Her face was broad, sullen, her mouth loose and wide. Her teeth were short and chunky, biting into a soft egg-salad sandwich. He thought he could hear her chewing the greenish egg stuff. She never adjusted her dress. Maybe she never saw him, though they were the only two customers in the place. Maybe she thought he hadn't eyes.

320

Two girls gypping school giggled in, silly with guilt and freedom. They wore identical boys' melton jackets with the name "St. James" on the backs in raised felt letters. There was an elaborate monogram on the left breast. The jackets were much too large for them. Barely six inches of plaid skirt showed below the edges of their coats. Heavy white athletic socks were rolled down around their ankles above scuffed saddle shoes. Like the egg-salad lady across the way, they did not seem to notice Jack. He was, at his size and age, simply of no possible consequence to middle-aged ladies with dyed hair and teen-age girls.

He would have liked to have had one of those girls' coats. They were off to an early matinee. That would be nice, too. A bag of warm popcorn, snuggled down in a seat in an almost empty theater, the place like a palace. All his for the day. It didn't matter what crummy movie they were showing. He just went to the picture show . . . because it was there.

He was down to where the orange was thin and watery in the cone of his Dixie cup. There were three red-jackets left in the nut cup. Anticipation of leaving the place for the street chilled him. A cold blast from the door when a bus driver came in made him shiver. He *needed* a coat. There had never been a time before when he had been aware of *that* need. Winter came, and he found himself layered in old sweaters that poured in from relatives and friends and encased in *some* kind of heavy winter outer coat until he was better fit for moon exploration than ambling along to school. He particularly recalled a stinky, inherited, sheepskin-lined corduroy job that was the warmest but smelled like a dead rat after a day shut in the school cloakroom. He even longed for the reprocessed wool and cotton job the relief had given him—a prison coat—left back in Pascagoula—security against their debt. Other people came in the King Orange. It was about 11 A.M.

The guy from behind the counter came to mop the tables and set out fresh nut cups. He stopped beside Jack's seat.

"You done, kid?"

"I'm waitin for my mom. She said to meet her here."

"Yeh? Well, you been here more'n an hour. You can't occupy a seat unless you're eatin. You wait for your mama outside."

Jack's knees creaked when he got up, he had been sitting so long.

If his mom and Bill weren't through yet, they would send him away again. He didn't want to make them mad. Give them time. He didn't want to go back while Bill was there. He would have him scuffling around trying to find something to burn. Where could he go?

No sun ever touched the walls of that street. Storekeepers burned their neon the clock around. There was a cold invisible fog in the air that went right through him. A window full of musical instruments drew him to the glass. Golden trumpets, silver cornets, weird brass trombones, great farting sousaphones, big beautiful guitars, a pearlized set of drums, reptilian woodwinds, a hunky-looking family of accordians, sized octarinas like something Latin and edible.

*"Learn to play an instrument and you'll never be without what to eat or want for a friend."* An adage of his grandfather's sounded in his mind like the voice of God in some movie. The old man played a little mountain fiddle cocked on his left knee and picked a bit of mandolin and always regretted he hadn't done more with it. Jack wished he played somethin. But no one ever suggested he take lessons. He saw himself a great singing cowboy, grown up and married to little Junie Carter of *The Carter Family,* who had naturally grown up, too.

Then a uniform shop with a pair of bell-bottom blues on a stiffly grinning landlubbery mannequin that was clearly in the wrong neighborhood, but too damn grinning ignorant to realize what danger a faggy cat like himself was in around there. Man, those blues and his pea coat looked good. That was how he was going to go, breasting the waves on the prow of a cutter, staring into the torrential night.

He ducked into a penny arcade that was just opening. The owner, still in his overcoat and hat, cranked back the steel grill that enclosed his entrance at night.

Jack hadn't a cent. He turned the crank of the Giant Claw machine, swinging the claw on its derrick over the camera and wrist watch and pearl-handled Derringer, wanting the penny to drop it on riches of his heart's cold longing. He aimed all the guns that fired beams of light and pulled the dead triggers. He peered into the inky blackness of a peepshow and spun the crank so "The Sultan's Delight" and "Frenchie" did their stuff in total darkness.

"You dere, kid. You vant me to get arrested? Don you read da sign? Dere, see, *No Minors.* Dot's you. No peeps."

"I didn't put in no money," Jack explained.

"Den why you lookin in da peeper? You can't see nodding. You vant you should vere it oudt?" He bent over "The Sultan's Delight," spun the crank. "You can't see nodding. Why you vant to look at nodding, boy? Hey, you got money? Show me your money."

"I hadda dime when I came in, but I musta lost it." He looked around the floor.

"Yah-yah." He put his hands on the boy's shoulders and turned him toward the door. "Yah. You go finda dime. *Den* you come back. But no peeps! Dere for da pig dummies. Good-bye."

Liquor stores along there carried a lot of stuff like sloe gin, cheap wine, clear grain neutral spirits under a label that sported a shock of wheat, booze in little shot bottles for customers who didn't have the price of half a pint.

On the corner in front of a brightly lit, steamy ham-and-egger, a cop wearing a blue winter mackinaw and gloves chatted with a strapping, tall, black-haired whore perched on a pair of white patent skyscraper sandals. Her ass and thighs were squeezed into a black and white polka-dot skirt topped by a short, mangy muskrat jacket. Her heavy wicked legs wore black fishnet hose. Her towering upsweep was capped by a little black satin topper wound with a fuchsia ribbon that trailed down the back. Her white patent shoulder bag matched her shoes. Jack knew a whore when he saw one. With the shipyard working a night shift, whores, like the neon in the sunless street, were turned on the clock around. The cop held his billy by the thong about badge-high. The stick swung like a lazy pendulum between them, its tip gently tapping the woman between the legs.

Blowing around the corner in a whirlwind of grit and petty trash was a legless old newsie strapped on a platform that had three-inch steel ball bearings for wheels. He rowed and braked the careening ball-bearing mother with two treaded rubber pads—one in each hand—sectioned from an automobile tire. Jack skipped out of his path as a vision of being sliced off at the ankles himself reared before his eyes. The man carried papers in a canvas bag hung around his neck. He had a nickled changemaker on a leather belt around his loins like a sporran. Two leather straps lashed his stumps to the board. He hollered headlines at full cry from first paper to last, rain or shine, and not a word he howled was intelligible. Yet when he rolled up on steel bearings under the carry-out window of the King Orange and banged the tin sign below with his quarter until the guy inside leaned out and took his order, he talked like a whole man.

A big skinny dog came from across the street and sniffed up to where the newsie crouched under the carry-out window eating a coney island and holding a big orange in the other hand.

"Git! Go on! Beat it!" He faced the dog on a level of animal equality unknown to whole men. "Beat it!" He tried to keep from spilling his orange by cradling it against his chest while lashing out in a shooing motion at the mutt. The dog backed a step and bowed his back, growled. *"Beat it, you fuckin mutt! Beat it!"*

The counterman leaned out to see what was going on. He broke into a grin. The cop and whore where Jack stood turned and saw the sawed-off man backed against the King Orange sign by the dog, and they laughed.

"Sic 'em, boy! Gitim!" a spidery Negro newsboy about Jack's age and just as coatless hissed, dancing out of nowhere to encourage the dog.

The little man knew better than to seek help from his fellows. He never even looked to them. He never took his eyes off the ribby mutt. What fascinated Jack was how such a sadass, woebegone-looking dog could find it in himself to turn so mean. He looked more like a spavined, drowned sheep than a wolf. But he was for Shorty's hot dog or would know the reason why. He came on, back bristling, head down and growling.

*"Take it, yuh goddamn crumb!"* the man screamed as if at an equal and flung his frank at the dog, hitting him on the nose. "I hope yuh choke yuh!" Then he flung his big orange at the dog, too. The mutt did not even look up from skarfing the coney island from the sidewalk—meat, bun, chili, onions, and all. The newsie wheeled away in a swirl of candy wrappers and dust, his ball bearings on the sidewalk sounding like canvas ripping, scattering citizens left and right. Yet even he had a jacket—a red and black blanket plaid job. And he wore a kid's imitation leather aviator's helmet with the flaps down.

Jack could see his breath. His nose was runny. He wiped it on his cold sleeve.

*I don't give a damn! I'm going home and get warm!* he vowed to himself.

He bounded up the stairs. He was on the attack now. He yanked open the screen door and nearly fell. He had expected it to be hooked. He was more careful shouldering through the door. Bill wasn't there. His mother had her light coat on over her slip. Her feet in her pumps looked blue. She was rinsing out her underwear and hose in cold water at the sink. She had a bar of Camay soap she had brought in the bag. The boxes Jack had scrounged were just warm black ash in the fireplace.

"I'm colder'n hell!" he announced.

"Don't talk that way. You know I don't like it."

"I don't give a fuck! I'm freezin. I want a fire and a coat." He was near tears. It seemed little enough to ask.

"I *won't* have you talk to me like *that.*"

*"Fuck you! Fuck you!* I'm *cold,* goddamn it!" he yelled.

"Well, *so am I!* This water is like ice. Be a man, can't you?"

"No! If I was a man, I wouldn't be freezin here. I'd have a goddamn coat. And if *I* had a boy, *he'd* have a coat!"

"Oh, *you* would do wonders, *you* would. We're doin what we can. You'll just have to tough it out like the rest of us."

"Yeow." His chest ached so badly, just crying could not possibly be enough. "*Bill* can buy whiskey, though. . . ." Then the tears came.

She came over, dried her hands on the bedspread, put them beside his face—they were like ice. "I know it's rough right now, baby. But it's going to be better. Bill went to the shipyard today. You're a big boy. Show your mama you can take it."

"I'm cold."

"Hop into bed." She began stripping off his tennis shoes. His dungarees were a sight. She unlatched his belt and tugged them off. She whipped back the thin covers. "In with you!"

He lay there chattering between the cold sheets. "I'm freezing," he stammered.

"It'll warm up in a minute."

"No it won't. Get me warm, Mom."

"I haven't time."

*What in hell has she to do?* he wondered. She had washed her lingerie. There was nothing to eat. "Why?" They hadn't even a magazine to read.

"I have to do my nails," it occurred to her.

"I'm freezing to death."

"Well, just for a minute."

She crawled in, coat and all. "You *are* like ice! Poor old fella."

She hoisted her slip over her belly and held his icy hands in hers, nestled between her breasts. She trapped his feet and legs between her own. Soon he felt feverish. His skin burned. Then he fell asleep.

He awakened when he heard his mother say, "I think he's coming down with something. God, if he gets sick now. . . ."

"Maybe you ought to wire your mother and send him back," Bill suggested.

"I told you from the start. From now on we leave her out of this. I'm not going to go begging to *her!*"

There was a rough hand on Jack's brow. "Hell! He ain't got no fever. He's just connin yuh. Ain't yuh?" Bill cracked the boy on the forehead with a single knuckle, like thumping a watermelon to see if it is ripe. The pain was like an electric shock right through him down to his toes.

"Bill! He's half frozen. Poor little kid, hasn't even an undershirt. He *needs* a coat or he's going to catch pneumonia."

"People in hell need ice water, too. Seems to me if he was so damn cold, he'd haul his ass around and find something to burn in the fireplace instead of crying in there freezing to death like a goddamn punk." He slipped a pint from his pocket, still wrapped in a little paper sack, peeled it to expose the cap, and broke the seal. He had a long belt, wiped his mouth with the back of his hand. He started to put the bottle back in his pocket, had a thought, offered it to the boy. Jack took it, uncapped it, and tossed down as big a belt as Bill had.

"*Bill.*" The boy's mother shook her head.

"That'll warm you up," he said.

As cold as the liquor was, it burned all the way down. Yet he hardly gagged at all. Soon he did feel a lot better. He no longer felt abandoned or sunk in self-pity.

"How'd it go?" Wilma asked Bill.

"Poco-poco. You know."

"Did you get on?"

"*Of course I got on.*" He mocked her tone. "That's what we came here for, ain't it?"

"When do you start?"

"Next Monday."

"You can't start tomorrow?" There was a desperate ring in her voice.

"I start Monday. All right? Now get the hell off my back."

The unspoken question in her eyes made Monday seem a season away.

He asked if she had found anything. She shook her head. "After Jacky got to sleep, I tried the Katz, and they said maybe something later. Rexall liked my experience and wanted me to check back in a day or two."

Jack hadn't anything to eat since morning. "If I had a coat, I could sell newspapers," he suggested.

They both looked at him.

"Come on," Bill said. He flipped the covers off the boy.

"Where?"

"Going to get you a jacket."

"*Boy!*"

"Bill?" Wilma looked worried.

"Dummy up. He needs a coat. I'll get him a coat."

"Don't do anything dumb, Bill."

He jerked his thumb at her for the boy to look. "Get her. A featherbrain like that worrying about a couple of slickers like us."

"Yeh!" Jack was totally on his stepfather's side again.

Sears Roebuck, five blocks away, was lit up like a party ship. The store was open until 9 P.M. out of respect for first-shift, second-shift, swing-shift money.

They marched through the main floor to the back left-hand corner, where hundreds of jackets hung on the racks. He could not recall the last time he had gone shopping for something new. He had *never* gone shopping for an item of clothing as rich as a leather jacket. It cost nearly $20!

"Can I have a leather jacket?" he asked in disbelief.

"Might as well go first class."

Hell, yes! "I'm with you." He grinned up at Bill. He loved him more that moment than anything on earth. Bill winked back. He was enjoying himself, too.

"What size are you?" Bill led the boy to a rack in the center of the floor, positioning him between the rack and those on the wall.

"I don't know." But Jack felt warm already. *Shopping with my dad,* he thought. *Buying leather jackets.* The smell of new leather made him drunk. It was like a dream.

"Try this." He held up a brown capeskin job Jack had seen in the old Sears wishbook at his grandma's. Inside it was gold quilted satin. He slid into it as if it had been made for him. When he bent, it creaked deliciously. The new-leather smell was now his own scent. He felt lifted an entire social level. And suddenly he was determined never to sink back.

"Can I help you?" a motherly woman wearing glasses and carrying an order pad inquired sweetly.

"Well, ma'am, we're just lookin right now. We want to find the boy and myself a couple of leather coats. But I want his mama to see them before we decide. She's lookin at dresses or somethin. She'll meet us here. What's your name? I'll be sure and ask for you when we decide so you'll get the sale."

"Missus Ryun—"

"Ryun! Wouldja be Irish, now?"

"Sure and I would." She giggled.

"So are we, now. Fitzgerald." He put out his hand. "And me mither came from Ireland."

"Pleased to meetcha, Mr. Fitzgerald."

"We just moved here recently. The shipyard."

"Yes. It certainly has been a boon around here. Particularly the last year. I sure hope we ain't goin to war. But since they put on the night shift, it's sure been a boon. I was just stayin home keeping house. My old man can't do nothin but night watchman. He's got a bad heart. So, I says, I can clerk in a store. Why not?"

"Indeed. An extra tater in the pot is always welcome, me old mither always said." Bill nudged her elbow.

She giggled. Then very seriously, "I don't think Mr. Roosevelt is going to let us get mixed up in a war, do you?"

"Of course not. But it's no skin off ours what the Germans and the Limeys do to one another, is it? And if it builds ships, givin honest men work, they can fight each other forever for all I care. Just so's they leave us Irish alone, right?"

"Yessir."

"We'll be sure to see you get the sale," he assured her again.

"Thank you. That's our best model the boy has on," she said.

He turned his back on her and began looking at the men's coats along the wall. She drifted away.

"You gettin a coat, too, Bill?" Jacky asked.

"Sure. Double up and catch up."

"Wow!"

Bill was a great guy when he wanted to be. He slipped on a black belted horsehide surcoat. It cost nearly $50! He looked great. But Jack looked great, too. He liked the brown best.

"Zip it up," Bill said, "if you like it." Then zipped it for the boy. When he took his hand away, he had snapped the sales tag off the zipper pull in the same motion.

"When I say so, I want you to turn around and walk straight out the door. Just the way we came in. Don't look around. But don't hurry. Just walk out."

"Why?"

"Don't be a dummy. Do what I say."

"Are we buying this jacket?"

"Sure. Sure. Just do what I say. You trust me, don't you?"

"Yeow. . . ."

They were hidden by the rack of coats. He was crouched down as if adjusting the boy's coat, checking it.

"OK, then."

"I don't want to steal it."

"Don't be a fool, kid. We aren't stealing it. I know what I'm doing. Trust me. Just do what I say. You want the thing, don't you?"

"Yeow, but—" He was scared.

"OK, go!" He turned him toward the door. Mrs. Ryun was two counters away, waiting on someone else. *"Go!"*

Jack felt large and awkward as a giraffe walking toward the distant door. He looked straight ahead, never taking his eyes off the door. The new jacket creaked like a rusty wagon. He *knew* he was stealing that coat. Yet, in spite of his fear and certainty, he trusted Bill to save him if it came to that. Bill always had an angle. The world was organized in a series of loops which guys like him used to skirt the bog in which all the peapickers, clerks, and night watchmen were trapped. Maybe this was his way of buying a coat at Sears. At 100 percent off. Then Jack was out the door onto the street. He was aware he was sweating. He had to fight the temptation to run. Every footstep behind him was the tread of a pursuing floorwalker.

"*A goddamn floorwalker is lower than a cop.*" He recalled one of Bill's adages.

At the corner he risked a quick glance. *Was that Bill?* A small hunched figure in a beat-up hat with his hands in his pockets, wearing a leather surcoat, was scurrying off in the opposite direction. He did not risk staring too long. He put his hands in the jacket pockets and found them in warm cotton fleece. *God!* He was warm all the way through. He had never felt so goddamned perfect in his life. Not bundled in layers, but right and ready in quilt-lined capeskin. Brand new!

He sauntered on past the street on which the hotel was located, whistling in the cold damp air. He crossed the dark street and cut along beside the jail.

"Hey, baby, how'd you like to lick my black pussy?" a woman called from a window.

He stopped dead in his tracks. Man, how much time he had wasted before he wore leather!

"He's just a baby, Jazz."

"How old'er you, boy?"

"Twelve," he lied.

"That's *about* old enough," the first one said. "How you like to kiss my black titty, then?" They both broke into giggles.

"You come back in a year or two, honey, we show you a *good* time."

"Yeh, baby, you come back. We'll likely be here." They broke into high laughter.

"Not me," the first reconsidered. "I be here no year, I start fuckin *your* ugly face."

"You wanta *try* somethin, you oughta be here when Sister Sue's here wif them hard ice-cream-cone tits. Some say it feel better'n mos' men." They continued in an ordinary conversational tone.

"Hey! You better run home and tell your mama she wants you," the first one called.

Jack felt he could live on the street in that jacket. There was a soul comfort in it that went deeper than mere warmth. Fear lifted. The cold dark street, dark women, dim stairs no longer held any terror for him. To prove it he went up the back stair that was lighted by a lousy 25-watt bulb and had only been constructed to give someone a 50-50 chance in case of fire or whatever. There were four crates outside the store next door. He hauled them up, being careful not to scratch his jacket.

Wilma was alone. He told her what had happened. She wanted to say that what Bill and he had done was wrong, but she really did admire the coat. "That will certainly keep you warm."

He was reluctant to take it off indoors. Then he built a roaring fire in the fireplace to surprise Bill.

When the second crate had burned to ash, it was after ten.

"Maybe he stopped someplace and met somebody," she suggested. "We better go to bed."

They put his new jacket and her coat over the spread and clung tight together, sharing body heat.

Jack awoke the next morning when his mother groggily ran her bare thigh up over his legs murmuring, "Billllll. . . ." Then she was wide awake, too.

They had left the door unlatched, but Bill had not been there.

# 29

JACK was certain his stepfather had been caught stealing a leather jacket for himself. He told his mother he thought he had seen Bill walking away from Sears in a black coat like one he had been looking at. He was going in the opposite direction, so Jack could not be sure.

The boy felt lucky. The jacket Bill had zipped him into before telling him to cop a walk was spread over the thin covers of the bed, and he was snuggled underneath with his mother like "two bugs in a rug," as she liked to say. For the first night since the boy had arrived in Mobile, he had slept warm, slept deep. They could see their breath in the room that morning. His pillow was a warm, perfumed shoulder. Her breast rose gently against his cheek.

"Ohhh!" She yawned and stretched, arching her back. "It's so nice I hate to think about getting up."

"Let's stay in bed all day," he suggested, turning toward her, burying his face in her breast, slipping his arm across her waist. He stretched against her.

"Wouldn't *that* be cute when Bill came home and found us sloughing off."

"I bet he ain't comin home," the boy guessed.

"Don't say that! You were mistaken. He just ran into somebody he knew. They started drinking. Or they hit on some deal. What makes you think you stole that coat, anyway?"

"Huh?" Was she nuts?

"You just imagine things sometimes. Bill knows more ways to skin a cat than you would dream of."

"How?" His voice was hysterical with disbelief. "This coat cost twenty bucks."

"Well, he could of got it on time. There are more ways to skin a cat than one, smarty pants."

What was the use of saying anything? He snuck his right hand up and cradled her left breast. She didn't say anything until he gave it a little squeeze.

"Now, now. None of that." She removed his hand to a neutral site and shifted his face back onto her shoulder. "Come on, you. Let's up and at 'em."

"Who?"

"Us. You. Me. I've gotta get a job. And weren't you going to get a paper route or something just as soon as you had a warm coat? Or didn't I hear right?"

"Yeow."

She flipped down the covers. "Ooooou. . . ." She flipped them right back, shivering down. "This must be some kind of record cold for Mobile."

"There's still a couple of crates. I'll light a crate and warm up the room a little."

"That's a good boy," she chattered.

He hopped out of bed as if making a parachute jump. The cold was a total, all-over shock that routed all memory of warmth. He shook uncontrollably, barking, "Whoo! Whoo! Whoo!"

He wadded some newspaper balls and tossed them on the pile of black ash in the fireplace. Then carefully slanted a crate in the blackened maw. It gave off more heat and lasted longer when burned whole than when busted up into kindling. One crate would take the chill off the room. When it had caught, he dove back into bed.

"Wow! You're like an *icicle!*" she squealed, engulfing him, chafing whatever she reached to warm him. She caught his bare knees between her thighs, which felt feverishly hot to his quaking shanks. "Oooh, you'll take care of your mommy, won't you?"

"Yes," he stammered. He was proud it had been his idea—the fire.

Her belly was like a warm, satin-covered, down-filled pillow into which he pressed long after he ceased to be chilled. There was nothing between her curly bush and him but her thin slip and his raggedy shorts.

Pretty soon she said, "I think you're warmed up enough now." She moved to release him from between her legs. Their skins peeled apart. In two quick motions she tugged down her slip over her butt and front.

"I love you, Mom," he told her. He hoped they'd thrown away the key on ole Bill.

"Umhmmm. But we've got to get up now, no joke. Come on, last one out is an Irishman!" It was one of Granddad's sayings.

"I'll count to three," she said.

"OK."

"One . . . two . . . three!"

Neither of them moved. She laughed.

"*Ho!* OK. *You!* I'll get you up." She pounced, her nails like ruby-backed beetles scampering over his belly and ribs, boring in under his arms. The tickling went clear through him until the sensation on one side touched the other in some central liquid core of himself and he was as helpless as a frying spider. He was jerking, hysterical, giggling jelly, too weak to pick lint. He was out on the cold linoleum with shivers rising up over his ribs, drowning the giggles of that silvered, delightful pain. She leaned out of bed and kissed him quickly, hard, on the chattering lips. Then she flipped over—flashing white thighs, bare buttocks, jumping tits—bounding out of bed. She snatched her coat around her, dancing on the icy floor, fumbling her feet into her pumps. He could see the goose bumps on her pale calves. She shivered and dressed quickly in front of the fire.

"We want to come home today with jobs to surprise Bill tonight," she said.

Well, maybe she *did* know something he didn't. Studying her optimistic, bland expression, he began to believe that Bill would be there when he returned. She read horoscopes. You never knew.

"I'm hungry," he said. Of that he was certain.

She dug through her purse and found a nickel and dime that felt and smelled of face powder. He put them in his jacket pocket. He did not ask what her plans were for breakfast. A hot dog and a five-cent orange at the King Orange were his. Lunch hinged on the optimistic belief they would both be gainfully employed by then and have earned enough to dine.

She was about at the bottom of her lipstick. Her compact and perfume were also running low. She carefully filled in her lower lip with the tip of her little finger. When she kissed him good-bye, she was careful not to spoil her lips. She squeezed the heavy, soft leather of his jacket between her fingers.

"It's really nice, isn't it? I love the smell of new leather."

"Yeow. Me, too. I always wanted a real leather jacket."

"You want to be sure and let Bill know how much you appreciate it."

"Yeow. OK." There it was again. He bounded down the stairs, she calling after him to be careful. Yeh. She was wild. She simply would not see the jacket had been got any differently from jackets on kids in magazines. It wasn't that she fooled herself exactly. It was just that once the thing was on his back, with his face sticking out the top, there was no way to *know* they hadn't a sales slip. She could introduce him to anyone and they would say, "What a fine jacket," and think how generous his folks must be. There was no sign over Jack's head that his coat had been stolen.

After eating, he went down the street, passing on the side opposite Sears—just in case.

Yet he had more respect for places called things like The Hub or Freddy's, where they nailed everything down to the counter and chained everything to the rack. With stores like that the lines were defined. They were out to cheat you blind before you kypped half their store. They were men who actually would lie awake at night if they hadn't screwed somebody a little bit that day. *"That's a genuine lamb's wool!"* Yeah, it was the lamb that was reprocessed. There was no bullshit. With Sears it was all "Aunt Nelly" clerks upstairs with their little pads and "Uncle Walt" in the basement with the tools, sporting a little Craftsman hammer or plane tie clip for long and loyal service. And you got your money back if not absolutely satisfied. Jack had never known anyone who could spend $20 for a jacket, so what good was the guarantee? Like his ancestors he traded where the prices were always pegged a bit higher, the quality was a bit lower, and credit was based on a character judgment across the width of a counter when credit was given at all. Satisfaction was never guaranteed, but it was occasionally negotiable.

He asked a brown newsboy wearing earmuffs and a man's suit coat how you got to sell papers.

"You gotta go to the newspaper and get your papers." He looked Jack over. "You can't sell no papers here, though. This is my corner. My street up to there." He pointed up to where the lights of a grind house stuck out. "Catch your ass sellin papers round here, I kick the shit out of you."

No nigger had ever talked to Jack like that. He meant it. He wasn't mad at Jack or nothin. He was just lettin him know how it would be if he *got* mad. "I won't," Jack promised sincerely.

"See you don't. Then you go on up here six block an' you see the place on this side. You go round back an' get your papers."

"Thanks."

He grunted. Then a final warning. "Jus' don't you forget what I said."

"I won't."

"Don't."

The building looked like an armory or something to the boy. There was an American flag on top. He went inside. It was all clatter and bustle. There was a kind of lobby formed by counters on three sides, behind which girls were taking ads and selling subscriptions.

"What do you want, little boy?" a pretty girl in an apricot sweater, with pointed tits and with a new pencil stuck in her honey-colored hair, asked impatiently.

"Who do I see about peddling papers?"

"Jerry." She had already dismissed him. She was riffing through a stack of slips busily. "Go around to the back."

Eight kids were down on their hands and knees just off the wooden chute where the newspapers came down as fast as they could be gathered. A dozen others lounged around the filthy, scarred, and graffiti-illuminated walls.

Jack asked a kid in an earflap cap whom he had to see about selling papers.

"You getcher papers and see Jerry." He dove into line on his knees off the end of the chute. "Come on!" He was a tough kid.

Jack dropped down beside him. He stacked up a pile about a foot high. It was all he could get under his arm. Jack followed the other boy over to a little open-fronted office and watched him flop his papers down on a table. A fat guy counted them and wrote something by his name. "See ya," he shot back over his shoulder, bent way the hell over to his right to balance the papers under his left arm.

The fat guy counted Jack's papers, then looked at him for the first time. "Who're you?"

"Hunh?"

"What's your name. I ain't seen you before, have I?"

"I'm just startin."

"OK. Gimme one-twenty."

"Hunh?"

"One-twenty. You got forty papers."

"I didn't know I had to pay."

"Sure. Unless I know you."

"I don't have it."

"How much you got?"

"Nothin."

"Look, you're holdin up progress."

"I thought you just brought the money back."

"Dink tell you that, hunh?"

"Yeow." Whoever the hell *that* was.

"Well, OK, since you know Dink, I'll let you take the forty. But if you crap on me, I'll take it out of *his* ass. Whatcher name?" He licked the end of his pencil preparatory to putting Jack's name on one of the cardboard lists.

Jack walked out the door with his forty under his left arm, but he could not immediately bring himself to holler, *"Getcha red-hot newspaper here!"* the way everyone else did. They hollered all the way to the places they had staked out for themselves.

Jack slipped along the street a block over from where he had encountered the black newsboy. "News. Get your newspaper here." He tried it out. *"Hey, getcher red-hot newspaper here!"* He let 'er rip coming up on a more populated corner. *"Latest news. Hot off the press. Getcher Paaaaaaaaapah!"* When he realized that no one really looked at him, he sang out.

"Paper, boy!" A man hurrying away, about to cross the street, called, a nickel in his hand. Jack fumbled the flick-fold he had observed others doing neatly, taking the nickel in the same hand. He handed the news to the man flat, and he had to take it before dropping the coin. "Thanks," Jack mumbled to his back. *"Hey! Paper here! Getcher red-hot newspaper!"*

He sold half by noon and bought a Mr. Goodbar and an Orange Crush at a stand. He cut over to the bus station and haunted the doors, catching people before they hit the big newsstands inside. He had sold out by three o'clock. He headed back to the paper. It had begun to rain a little mixed with sleet. He paid Jerry his $1.20, which left him with 70¢.

"Want some more, kid?"

He wasn't sure. "I better get home."

"You did good. Take ten, you'll sell them on the way home. It's starting to rain. People buy them to put over their hats. I guarantee you'll get rid of ten."

So Jack sprang for the 30¢. At first he wasn't so sure. He had gone two blocks without making a sale. It was sleeting and spitting pretty good. Then there was a gob of people in Sears' doorway. They bought three. He got rid of two at the other entrance. A lady trying to hail a cab bought one, clapping it overhead, handed him a quarter. A cab pulled up while he was digging for her change. She piled in. It pulled away. He saw it stop and her gesturing in the foggy back window. He turned away. The cab wasn't going to back up. It was his first tip.

By the time he had hit the docks, he had only the paper he was saving for himself. His mother would be proud. He was $1.10 ahead on the day. His granddad and Uncle Kenneth had talked about working for a dollar a day. He had done as good as they. Better.

No one was home. The door was locked. He hadn't a key. He went back down and scrounged around three blocks for crates to burn. He found an apple crate, the pedestal of an oak table that must have weighed twenty or thirty pounds, and an egg crate full of cardboard egg separators. By the time he had horsed all that back to the hotel, his tenners were soaked through. His feet felt frozen. He camped on the stuff outside the door, waiting for his mother.

A tall Negro woman came up the stairs flicking water from a big shiny black parasol. She had on a good black coat with a fox pelt wrapped around her neck. Her hair was swept back from her haughty, wide face. Big hoop earrings swung from her ears. She looked at the boy sitting on his junk like something that smelled bad. She unlocked her door, then looked at him again. "You locked out?"

"Yes, ma'am."

She sort of cringed. She looked at the puddle around his feet.

"I'm waitin for my mom," he explained.

"You want to wait in here where it's warm?"

"She should be along any minute."

"Suit yourself." She went inside and closed her door.

Then he remembered the sounds that they had heard through the wall. How Bill and his mom had looked at each other when they heard them. After counting to thirteen thirteen times, he got up and rapped tentatively on her door.

"What is it?" from the other side.

"It's me. I guess she ain't comin right away."

She opened the door. Her door had two other kinds of locks besides the one under the knob. Her room was like his own, but stuffed with furniture. There was a little French settee before the fireplace in which real logs burned. There was a whole box of them alongside. There were dark Oriental carpets on the floor. A potted palm shaded the settee. A jungle of plants spilled off the walls, crept from every cranny. Her windows were closed with heavy double draperies that gathered generously on the floor. Her bed was almost chest high to the boy, a great mound of a feather bed covered with some kind of fringed Spanish gold and white cover pretty enough to wear. An albino cat with a little collar like a pup's slept curled in an easy great dimple on that angel-food bed. The stead was gleaming brass. The room was so warm he was quickly sweating in his jacket.

"Sit by the fire and dry your feet," she said. "How come you were out running the streets like that?"

"I was selling papers."

"Yeh? How'd you do?"

"OK." He had almost told her what he had made.

"That's good. You'll excuse me?"

"Yessum." She looked at Jack real sharp again.

She had her own bathroom. There was an electric heater in there. He saw it when she opened the door. When she came out, she was wearing a long yellow satin housecoat that had yellow feathers around the top and cuffs and bottom. She carried a steaming café mug.

"Here. Drink this." She bent down and handed him the mug. She was taller than Bill by half a foot. She had the longest fingers Jack had ever seen. Her skin looked soft and was sweet-chocolate-colored. Her hair had all the frizz stretched out in a severe sweep that left her ears bare the way he never saw women's ears. It was caught in back by elastic bands covered by the tiny gold hand of a woman. Then it exploded in a great ball of hair. In the black were gray strands like steel. Everything about her was big. Her face, above the longest neck he had ever seen, was broad, with a sort of Indian nose, huge eyes. . . . He could not stop looking at her mouth. It was so wide, her teeth so large. Her tongue was once again as large as his mother's. Her thighs were twice the size of his mom's. Tremendous pressures and weights came into play when she moved, walked, sat and crossed her legs in the chair across from him. It seemed her leg from foot to knee was longer than his whole leg. Her feet were bigger than Bill's. He would think of her as a man for a sec, then notice the fineness of her wrists and ankles. She was not a bit fat, and everything was so in proportion that she was awesome rather than startling. He could not have covered one of her tits with both his hands and a helper.

"That's cinnamon tea. You like it?"

"Umm!" He nodded over the cup. He had never liked it before. She offered him a tin of crescent-shaped cookies that tasted of almonds.

"What's your name?"

"Jack, ma'am."

"Ma'am! You keep callin me *ma'am*. Where you from?"

"Wichita, Kansas."

"Whichawhatchee? Well, I guess that explains it. Hey. Get out of them wet shoes. Set them by the fire."

He looked for someplace to put his cup. She dropped to her knees before he could make a decision and began ripping at his wet laces.

"You don't have to do that."

"I got a boy," she said. "He's all grown up and in the Navy."

God, she was big! She took his bare foot in her lap, kneading it in her long, beautiful hands. Her robe fell open a bit. Her thigh looked polished and hairless as a statue's. She caught his look and dropped his foot. She got up, leaving him to take off his other shoe. She went to a dresser and dug out a chromo-colored studio photo of a very serious young black man in Navy dress blues sporting a pancake-flat wool hat instead of white. There was a little quarter-moon on his uniform arm.

"I'm joining the Navy when I grow up," he informed her.

"He's been to China, everywhere. He's a cook." This last she did not say very proudly. "I never et anything he ever cooked, and I sure don't want to." She put it back in the drawer. "I hear from him ever now and then." She gestured at some exotic bric-a-brac. "He sent them things from all over."

"How tall are you?" he suddenly asked.

"How's that?"

"How tall are you?"

"Me? I never measured. But the only man that ever made me *feel* small was six foot six and weighed two hundred and fifty *bee*utiful pounds. Drink that tea. Keep you well."

"You're ah . . . uh . . . pretty." He was going to say for a Negro. But that was not what he meant. She was fantastic! She made his dick feel like the end of his little finger. When she shifted her weight, you could feel a change in atmosphere.

"Thank you." She bowed her head.

He sat there sipping cinnamon tea and told her everything about himself and his family and everything else that was on his mind until it had gotten dark. She had gone about her business, saying, "Uhunh," every now and then, letting him ramble on.

"Say. I think I hear your mama next door." She stopped him in midramble.

It was. He knew her sound. "Well, I better go, then."

"Nice havin somebody to talk to." She laughed, recalling all the talking *he* had done.

"Thank you for the tea and everything."

"That's all right."

He was in his shoes and had his jacket. He was on the way to the door. "Hey? You want to leave me a paper every night?" she asked.

"Sure! . . . But you can get a regular delivery. It's less."

"I don't want no regular delivery. I want a *special* delivery. You."

He beamed. "Hey?"

"What?"

"What's your name?"

She thought a long time, looking him in the eyes. "Jocylyn. And don't you ever call me *Joy. You* call me Jocylyn."

"Yessum."

"Say it so I know you got it right."

"Jossuhlyn."

She gave him a thumb and forefinger OK.

"Where have you been?" his mother asked rising from the fireplace where she had burned a couple of paper balls but had only singed the crate she was trying to light. She rubbed her arms to show how cold she was. Her hair was stringy and wet. Her clothes were soaked.

"I was next door at Jocylyn's," he said casually, going to build a fire. "Boy! Has she got a neat room!"

"*Next door?*"

"Yeow."

"How'd you get *next door?*"

"I got home early and couldn't get in, and she came up and asked me in to wait. She's real nice. *She's six feet tall!* But regular, you know?"

She did not know at all.

"I don't want you going over there! She's uh . . . uh . . . she sees men for money."

"You and Bill said she's a whore."

"That's what I *meant*. And she's uh-uh-uh nigger, besides."

"Yeow." That was right, she was. "Anyway, she's my first customer."

"For *what!*"

"For a paper. She wants me to leave her a paper every day."

"What's her name?"

"Jocylyn."

"Well, I don't want you going into her room."

"Why?"

"It isn't good for you. I just *don't*. I mean it. I'll get you a key."

"She made me cinnamon tea."

"You *hate* cinnamon tea."

"Hers I don't."

"I *mean* it, young man. You stay away from there. You could catch a disease."

"A disease? How?"

"Never mind. Just you stay away from her room."

"You get a job?"

"Don't change the subject. No."

"I made a dollar-ten."

"Really? That's wonderful." She came over and gave him a hug. "I'm so *proud* of you!"

He regretted he had told her how much exactly. He could have kept some for himself. Well, tomorrow. There would be other days.

He got a crate going good in the fireplace and carefully laid on the big table pedestal. Soon the varnish began to melt. Little rills of flame leapt along the flow. Then the wood began to catch. The oak burned at a much lower flame—blue, almost invisible—though it was a lot hotter than a crate. He had to step back.

Their clothes hung over the little line she always carried and had strung between bedpost and the rickety table.

"My feet are *blue!*" she exclaimed, extending them toward the fire, waggling her toes. "Rub them for me a little, please, Jacky."

He caught her left foot in his hands.

"They're so cold they hurt!"

Thin steam began rising from her coat over the line.

"Oh, that's *nice,*" she sighed.

He shifted to the right one. She flopped back on the bed with her left arm over her eyes. She had stripped to the skin, putting on one of Bill's sleeveless ribbed undershirts for a chemise and then wrapping the bed-spread around her.

"You just don't know what a miserable day I've had. I walked a million miles. 'Nothing now. Leave your name and call back.' Um, that feels nice. You know, that's how your father and I, uh. . . . That's how we got together. We'd gone sledding on College Hill. My feet and legs got so cold he was afraid I'd gotten frostbite. We went to his buddy's house. He washed my feet in snow."

"And *that* got you warm?"

She smiled knowingly up at the ceiling. "It sure did. You know how Swedes are."

"What do you mean?"

She raised her head to look down over her breasts at him kneeling on the floor. She wove her fingers in his hair. "You will. You're *so* much like him. You both have a great gentle touch. Come here to me, you!" She hauled him up beside her by the hair and gave him a big kiss and a hug. "If we had a pan and some tea or coffee, that would be nice," she mused. "It's really nice and cozy in here now."

It was almost *too* warm. That oak piece really put out the heat. The humidity of their drying clothes steamed the windows. There was a minor iridescence on the greasy, fogged panes that made it seem more isolated, snug.

She sat up, stretching Bill's shirt girlishly over her knees.

"Darn. If we had a deck of cards, I'd beat you in a game of Hollywood rummy."

"I'd beat you!"

"Ha! That'll be the day."

"I've done it."

"Just an accident. Let's make cards!" She bounded up. Bill's shirt just covered her bottom. The thin straps caught her nipples. When she moved, her tits looked like they would jump right out. They bounced and swung deliciously, unself-consciously. She fastened on the thin cardboard egg separators in the last crate. "These will do." When she bent over with her back to him, he could see a puff of her dark bush under the inverted valentine of her bottom.

"You help me. You draw on the deuces to the tens in each suit." With her manicure scissors she carefully cut the thin board into about 1½- by 2-inch rectangles. The cards were dark blue on one side, regular cardboard gray on the other. On the gray side he drew the spots and numbers, stacking them in suits. Then they made face cards.

"We need a Joker," he suggested when they had done.

"Not for rummy."

"Maybe we'll play poker or pitch sometime." He drew a devil on a card drinking a bottle of whiskey. Then wrote "BILL" under it.

"That's not nice," she said. She threw the thing in the fire. "We don't need any more Jokers around here as long as we have you, young man. Come on, let's play."

She sat cross-legged in the center of the bed. He could never see how she could sit that way for *hours*. He couldn't do it. It killed his knees and made strings hurt inside his thighs. She stuffed the tail of Bill's shirt down in front so nothing showed.

"I don't see how you can sit like that," he said.

"Women are more limber than men. Their hips and thighs are different than men's. So they can have babies." She sat bolt upright and extended her legs out stiffly astraddle the width of the bed in a virtual split. She held the tail of her shirt over her thing with both hands. "See. I am very limber." She could also kick higher than her head. Bill liked to show her off, holding his hat higher than her head and getting her to kick it. She had beautiful legs. She was very proud of them. Everyone told her they looked just like Betty Grable's. In fact, Bill insisted she would look just like Betty Grable if she would bleach her hair blond. But she wouldn't do it. "I'll never dye my hair for any man," she vowed. "If you want a blonde, buster, you should have married one. I think peroxided blondes look cheap."

Jack always assured her, "*I* like auburn best. With hazel eyes."

She insisted her eyes were hazel but they looked just brown to him. He went along on things like that with her.

"And don't call me 'Red'!" she constantly warned everyone, to no avail.

They played three games of rummy. He won one game, and they realized they were starving.

"Why don't you get dressed and run downstairs and get a loaf of bread with your dollar, and some lunch meat, and a quart of milk?" she suggested.

The little store under the corner of the hotel stayed open until about nine. It was a single bin of a room with boxes of vegetables beside a box of work gloves, tins of tobacco, and tins of nuts. The round little man with a white goatee and floor-length apron had either to clamber over a lot of crap to get at something or reach it via a pincers on the end of a long pole. The place smelled good, spicy, and in the center of the six feet or so of clear floor stood a one-arm bandit.

The man weighed the few slices of lunch meat fifteen cents would buy as if they were gold, squinting one eye at the fly-blown scale. He handled groceries with a slow preciousness that set Jack's teeth on edge. It was as if he were selling favored possessions of great value.

Jack punched a nickel into the one-arm bandit, yanked the handle. Three plums tripped into place. *Tick-tick-tick.* There was a cascade of nickels.

*Wow!* God, there were at least twenty!

"Hey, liddle boy. Dot ting is fer grown-ops. Nod fer you. Dey put me in chail." He eyed Jack's nickels. Jack stuffed them away in his jacket, ready to bolt if the man made a move to come for him. "You vant something else?"

"Yeow. A little box of Lipton's tea bags. And . . . these." He laid a package of chocolate Hostess cupcakes beside his original order. It all came to seventy-five cents. He left the store richer than he came in.

"I hit the jackpot!" he announced, happy to display all the stuff that he had in his mind gotten for nothing.

She was amazed and delighted with the tea. "You really *are* a darling, thoughtful fella, Jacky. You really are." Her eyes behind her thick glasses looked large and loving. "You'd take care of me good, wouldn't you, if you had to? I know you would. That makes me feel very proud. Gimme a kiss."

Her sincerity was a bit embarrassing. Her kiss was wet and full.

"I love you, you know," she said into his ear. "Hey! Now all we need is a pan or something to heat water in."

"I'll find one." He was on his way. At the end of the hall there was a big trash barrel, overflowing and stacked around with sacks of rubbish. He found a new two-pound coffee can.

His mother washed the can carefully and filled it about a quarter full of water. She sat it carefully in the edge of the fire, squatting before the fireplace on her heels, leaning back from the heat. They were in their own cave. Looking at her made his dick tickle. The tickle rose in him until he shuddered uncontrollably a sec and broke out in goose bumps. When she stood up, her bush made a puff under Bill's undershirt.

They had cups, a chipped, egg-colored, handleless thing he had found in the room and a café mug Bill had kypped from a café the first day they were in town.

She used Jack's shirt for a pot holder when the water was steaming in the blackened can, but she burned her finger pouring the water into the cups. She popped her forefinger into her mouth like a little girl to suck away the pain. She dunked the tea bags with her other hand. She had laid out the sandwiches on Kleenex from the five-cent packet she always carried in her purse, slicing them neatly with her nail file. There was a cupcake at each place. It made Jack feel like a regular citizen, and although he really did not like tea, he drank it. It made him feel calm and cozy.

She kept saying, "Isn't this nice! Isn't this cozy. I think we're going to get by just fine from now on, don't you?"

When they were in bed, he lay with his hand on her shoulder. While they both watched the flicker of flames on the ceiling, she asked, "How you doin?"

"You know what?"

"What?"

"Sometimes I think we're better off *than* when Bill's around."

"Well, *I* don't."

"I can take care of you, you know?"

"You sure can!" She hugged him with the arm that was around him. "But you must understand. I love Bill. And I don't like a minute he is away from me."

"Not even if I'm here?"

"Well, it's not the same. I mean, I love *you,* too. But a woman likes to have her man around."

"I can be your man." The words hardly squeaked out of his throat. He wasn't certain what he was suggesting.

"Yes, darling, I know," she said very tenderly. "But it isn't quite the same. One day you will understand. . . . When you meet some nice girl and fall in love. You won't want to be away from her, either."

"I love you."

"Don't you know that is a different kind of love?"

"No."

"Well, it is."

"Do you love Bill more than me?"

She sighed, somewhat exasperated. She knew he knew what she meant. "Of course I don't love Bill *more* than you. Just differently."

"How differently?"

"Oh, I can't explain it now. I'm sleepy. I had a rough day. Now let's go to sleep."

"Mom?"

"What?"

"Mom. . . ."

"*What?*"

"Can I please kiss your titties?"

"Jack-*eeee*. . . ."

344

"Well I want to."

"What am I going to do with you? I will sure be glad when you have a bed of your own."

He was no longer as enthusiastic about such a possibility.

"Probably if you had had one, this would never have gotten started," she mused.

"Well, it wasn't my fault. You told Grandma you had a house and everything."

"*I did not!*"

"You *did!* I heard."

"You misunderstood. You always misunderstand."

"Not so much."

"Yes, you do. Now go to sleep."

"Please can I?"

"No!" She was sulky because he had reminded her of the lie she had told everybody when she came to his grandma's to take him with her.

"Please, I got to!"

"You don't *got* to."

"Yes, I do."

"It isn't good for you."

"Why? Yes it is."

"No, it isn't."

"You let me before."

"Well, I was wrong. I was half asleep. I didn't know what I was doing. I'd had too much to drink the night before."

"You liked it *then*."

"It doesn't do you any good, Jacky. It just gets you all worked up and nervous."

"I won't get all worked up and nervous," he promised.

"Oh, you won't?" She smiled in the flickering light. Her voice, so suddenly sly, skeptical, reached through him down between his legs.

He began to stammer. "N-n-n-no. I p-p-promise."

"Well, if you *promise*." Her voice was still that warm honey liquor that made him feel afloat on his own vibrations. She pulled him toward her. With her left hand she was reaching across to slip the strap off her right breast. She held it for him until his searching mouth found the erect nipple. She said softly, stroking the back of his head, "Just gentle. Not hard. I'm kind of sore."

She was asleep in ten minutes.

Asleep. He felt her body had been abandoned to him. Boldly, he stripped her to the waist, kneading her left breast while skarfing the other one. He lifted his head to see how she was doing. Her mouth was slightly parted. Her front teeth gleamed between her lips. He scooched up and kissed her mouth lighter than a feather. She went, "Brrr," a bit, tossed a little, but did not awaken. Soon she was snoring very softly, just a rustle of air between her lips.

He moved his right hand down very carefully along her body, lifting the covers with the back of his hand so as not to brush her and wake her up. Soon he was touching her left hip below the hem of her shirt. Her skin was so smooth, so warm. She told him women were softer than men because they had a thin extra layer of fat under their skins so they could stretch better to have babies. It also made them better able to stand cold weather. That was why she and his grandma always swore ladies' hose were really warm, when you could see right through them. He moved his hand over her hip onto her loin. He let it lie there, dead, feeling her breathe until he knew sweat was forming between her skin and his palm. His palm itched. He lifted the hem of her shirt and millimeter by millimeter eased it up over her belly until it was just a wad around her waist. Peeking under the covers, he could see her flat on her back, her dark bush rising at the bottom of the soft shirred slope of her belly. He touched the ever loose skin around, below her puckered navel. It was the softest texture on earth. It always felt like talc or fur more than skin; yet it was living. An infinite softness beyond compare, lightly dusted with fine blond hair. A slight golden trail down into the rich dark *maleza* rushing up between her pale thighs.

He let each breath she took ease his hand a micro-inch at a time down the slope of her belly. When she exhaled, he merely lifted his hand and let it slide a bit lower until his pinky just grazed her electric hairs. After a time of letting his fingers prowl the perimeter of her little forest, he lifted his hand and carried it over the crest, just grazing the topmost tendrils. The springy hair must have risen two and a half or three inches above her skin. His wrist ached, then began to go numb. The pain shifted to his shoulder, back, neck. He slowly lowered his hand, careful to apply pressure gradually. She stirred a little and said, *"Ummuh? Mumble-mumble. Smack-smack."* She licked her lips in her sleep. Her legs were left slightly parted. She scooted her ass around for a few seconds, then her breathing became normal. Through it all he held his hand dead, in place.

He became bolder. With his palm parallel to the space between her legs, he tediously worked his forefinger down into the thicker, longer hairs between her legs. When she moved a bit or sighed, he stopped dead still until she resumed normal breathing. When he was down to where the warmth was radiant, it seemed to liquefy, and his finger felt as if it had been in warm water too long. Longer, and the feeling was one of slight pain. The heat and liquid sensation did not diminish. There was an opening between her legs as long as his finger, gaping slightly, and hot as liquid fire. His head was swimming. He felt almost totally liquid himself. There was no turning back, even if death were to strike in the next wave of desire. The lips under the hair were liquid flesh. It was a human night-blooming flower, compelling, hypnotic in depth, softly carnivorous. Open. Enormous.

"*Um! Um!*" She barked without warning. Her hips jerked forward, back, around, wildly. The bed exploded for four, five, six seconds. His fingers were deep in her gaping hot pie. Her knees were drawn up, flung wide. Her right leg pinned him underneath. Her heels thumped the bed. "*Uh! Uh! Uh!*" she grunted, throwing her hips upward. Her lower lip was caught between her teeth. Her hands and arms were raised, trying to clasp someone to her. Her belly jerked convulsively. He jerked his hand away. He was speechless with fright. He had no notion of what he had done.

She was wide awake, bolt upright, blinking in the flickering light. "*Ohhhhhhh . . .*" she groaned, pressing her temples as if she had a headache. She sounded sad, angry, disappointed, tired, all in a single expression. She briskly adjusted her straps on her shoulders, yanked Bill's undershirt down around her so viciously he heard threads snap. "*Oooh, Christ!*" She sighed again, turning to her left with her back to him and pounding her pillow with her fist. He lay still as a stone boy, playing possum.

"It's just impossible to get a decent night's sleep around here, I guess." She got up, grabbed her coat and slipped into her pumps and slammed out the door.

When she came back, she was shivering.

"Mom, I'm sorry," he said, trying to put his arm over her to warm her up. She flounced over with her back to him.

"No! You stay on your side of the bed. I knew if I let you get started, you wouldn't stop. . . . You're all alike."

"Who?"

"Men. Go to sleep."

"Do you love me? I *love* you."

"*Yes* . . . GO TO SLEEP!"

"OK." He felt not quite bad enough to cry. He also felt rather mean.

# 30

DINK always took the boxer with black enamel hair and red trunks. Jack got the blond in light blue. There was a two-penny plunger on each side of the glassed-in penny arcade ring next to the pistol grip with which you moved your fighter. The manager of the down pug put in his entry fee, pushed in his plunger, raising his man to a cast-iron stance in the center of the ring to challenge the champ. Each pistol grip had a double set of triggers which loosed left and right uppercuts. Each fighter could be moved left and right and back and forth. Each pug had a little pin sticking out of his chin. Connect with an uppercut on the pin, and down went the man.

The blond never seemed to move as well as the other, so Dink always took the other. He was a good guy, a couple of years older than Jack though not that much bigger. When he was going good, Dink's tiger could rush across the ring and take Jack's guy out with one punch before he could get left or right up to block.

"Your guy's got bad reflexions," Dink analyzed. The big honky lay there on his back with his little pin pushed in and his hands up on either side like a stiff.

They looked in the peep shows. There was a blond stripper called "Venus with Arms" and the biggest natural tits Jack had ever seen. He turned her crank real slow to make it last and played with himself through his pocket. He loved her. There was also a cute little brunette called "Frenchie LaTour" in black stockings, who held a special fast-working place in his heart. The pair could have fulfilled his every desire. Dink looked, but he did not act as if he liked them. "Dirty who-ores," he called them. And kept his hands out of his pockets.

Dink was Catholic.

They drifted down to the docks, where men were unloading a banana boat. The ship was black-hulled, rusty, listing over the dock toward the warehouse. Men with split gunny sacks over their heads like monks' hoods, down over their shoulders and backs, pissanted stalks of green bananas out a door in the side of the ship into the warehouse. They called to each other in a foreign language.

"What are they?" Dink asked.

"Mexicans er something."

"*Mira! Mira!*" one began yelling. It sounded like *"Meata! Meata!"*

"*Aye! Aye! Aye!*" the man before him, who had fallen on the gangway, piped over and over, thrashing about, holding the back of his neck. He rolled down onto the dock.

"*Mamba! Mamba!*" The man behind began yelling, pointing at the man's dropped stalk of bananas.

"*Mamba!*" all the others chorused.

One muscled like a little horse ran up with a piece of board and began beating hell out of the bananas the man had dropped. Others crowded around the fallen man. He seemed to be praying. He looked very sad, very scared. Many hands picked him up and bore him aloft shoulder high. They were all speaking to him. Like a many-legged, spastic centipede, they shuffled off with him bouncing limply overhead, staring up at a clear china-blue sky. Spread-eagled, his limbs and head bobbed crazily as they picked up speed. They were running. The military guard stepped out into the center of the dock at port arms as if to stop them, but chattering wildly, they surged around him. His cry of "Halt! Halt!" was engulfed, swarmed under. In the van came the one muscled like a little horse, swinging at arm's length the slender, long, banana-green corpse of the snake.

Jack shivered in his clothes. As much as he loved bananas, he was not certain he would ever eat one again for fear of being poisoned.

Having run way up the dock toward some distant First Aid they did not find, the men laid their compatriot on the boards and stood around. One knelt over him performing what Dink called "Stream Unction." When he was through, men began breaking away and strolling back toward the ship in twos and threes.

"He must be dead," Dink said.

It did look that way.

A Chris-Craft with two men and two women aboard bubbled rapidly along on the river. A very pretty woman with her hair streaming back like a pennant smiled at the boys and waved. Jack could see her white teeth. He waved back. The others on the boat looked, but they did not wave. They held drinks in their hands. One of the men took the woman's arm and turned her attention to himself. Up the dock, only two banana handlers and the military guard now stood over the body of the dead man. It was a chilly day for all the clear sky. The Chris-Craft was the only pleasure boat on the river. A chain of barges went past. A guy way out on the end waved. The boys waved, then turned and went away.

Where the stairs to the Star Hotel went up between the bay rum barber shop and the no name grocery, Jack told Dink, "See yuh tomorrow."

"Wha—?" He took a step back. "You live *here?*"

"Yeow. . . ."

"Whoo-*eee!* You live *here?*"

"Yeh."

There was a look of shocked amazement in his eyes that melted to sly amusement. "Your old man works at the shipyard, huh?" he sneered.

"Yeow."

"Then how come you live in a cathouse?"

"Hunh?"

"How come you live in a cathouse?"

"A what?"

"A cathouse! You *deaf?*"

Jack stared up at the old building out of another time with its deep-set big windows, wavery panes, ornate blackened cornices. He had surely heard the term before, but it had never registered, really. When he looked back, Dink was halfway across the street. His shoulders visibly shook with laughter. On the other side he turned and looked at Jack and laughed again. Jack waved. Dink waved once in a gesture dismissing Jack from the human race. Then he was lost in the pedestrians hurrying along after work.

Jack left Jocylyn's paper in her screen door. To his left, from the room next to the manager's, the thin young woman who had the baby that always cried slipped out and sort of jumped when she saw him, then hurried on to her room on the other side of the courtyard balustrade, stuffing her blouse into a faded cotton print skirt with her right hand. In her left hand she held a couple of dollars. Her face was thin, with haunted, black-rimmed eyes. She was only nineteen, his mom had said, always adding, "Poor baby."

Jack's mother was not at home. He let himself in with his key. Sun falling through the windows had warmed the room, so he did not need to build a fire right away. He had laid in a good supply of stuff to burn —crates, three oak table leaves, a broken kitchen chair, boards from a heavy packing crate. He had made a dozen newspaper logs and a heap of kindling paper balls. They were pretty well set. When his mom got a job, they could buy charcoal by the peck from the little store downstairs. And they were going to buy an electric hot plate so they could do a little cooking.

Jack was bringing home six bits to a dollar every day. So though they were hungry, they were not visibly starving like the young woman across the hall.

His mom came right in and flopped face down on the bed in her coat. There were big holes in the bottoms of both shoes. She made cardboard insoles every day to cover the holes. When she came home, the cardboard was always ragged and worn through. She had spent some money for a pair of stockings. A woman could not look for work in winter bare-legged. She handled the stockings as if they were glass. Lying on her back, she reached down and undid them from her garters lest they pop a runner from undue strain. She kicked off her shoes. Jack caught her left foot and began massaging it. *"Ummm,"* she sighed. "Oh, that feels nice. I really walked my butt off today. Everywhere! Nothing. Everyone says with the shipyard going on three shifts things will be picking up, but no one will give me a job." She took her pocket mirror out of her purse and held it aloft to see herself. "It isn't hard to see why, is it? I look terrible! My hair looks like a rat's nest. I need a facial and new makeup. My clothes!"

"I think you're pretty," he insisted.

"Got a job for me?"

"Nope."

"See?"

"Want me to take off your stockings?"

"No. I'm afraid you'll snag them. Wait." Without getting up, she lifted first one leg then the other aloft, bent it at the knee, and stripped off her stockings. He could see her panties, butt, everything. There were red marks on her legs from her garters. She rubbed the places as if they itched. She rolled onto her stomach, kicking her bare feet for him to rub. She read the paper he had brought home, turning quickly to the inside. She never read the front page much. It wasn't anything but war news, which neither of them could understand. Roosevelt had promised they weren't going to war, and that was good enough for them, in spite of the fact that his granddad had always said Roosevelt was a "thief, liar and sonofabitch of the first magnitude." Granddad was nuts, Bill said.

Jack massaged each foot and leg. When he worked up too high above the knee, she would kick her foot once and say, "Uh-uh! Watch it." When on the second leg he went quickly all the way up over the soft buttery top of her thigh and grazed her tightly encased sex, she said, *"You* are *incorrigible!"* She stuffed her skirt down between her legs in back.

"What's that mean? Miss Rebsteen said that to me once."

"It means you won't take *no* for an answer."

"Oh."

"Yeow. You just keep your hands where they belong."

"Want me to rub them in front?"

"Never mind." She sat up. "I guess we better think about something to eat."

They had a shoe box with some lunch meat and stuff out on the fire escape, with the lid tied on to keep the pigeons and sparrows from getting at it. They also had half a quart of milk out there. She sent him downstairs for a can of Campbell's tomato soup. They had a packet of crackers. They ate soup and crackers, a sandwich, milk and cupcakes.

"You should buy an apple or something instead of those cupcakes," she advised him.

"His apples are mushy."

"I like a mealy apple."

"I hateum!"

She would not let him fool around with her that night.

"Just keep your hands where they belong, young man," she warned.

"Tomorrow," she mumbled, "I *must* find something." And began snoring softly.

There were definitely crystals of snow in the air. The Good Eats Café had a plaster of Paris turkey and a beat-up celluloid Santa Claus in its window. Jack realized they had missed Thanksgiving. Men were stringing decorations across the street. Two-faced cardboard Santas topped every light pole. Sears' windows were crammed full of toys, bikes, sporting goods, guns, archery sets, boots and saddles, cowboy and Indian suits, roller skates, everything. *How many days is it until Xmas?* a sign winked in his mind.

When he went in to get his papers, someone said, "Hey, Dink, look who's here," and leaned back, grinning at Jack.

The colored paper boys were gathered in one corner, down on their knees getting their papers together. The one who had first told Jack on the street where to go to get papers dropped his eyes as soon as Jack caught him looking at him. His name was Evans or something.

"Hi," Jack said.

No one answered. Dink just looked him up and down. "Beat it," he said finally.

"Hunh?"

"You heard me. We don't want no whoreson workin here."

"No what?"

"You heard me. Want to make somethin out of it?"

Jack did not understand. But he sort of understood.

"Dink says you live in a whorehouse. Is that right?" someone said gleefully.

He hadn't realized he was among such a group of citizens, such a bunch of picayune JayCee-ers.

"Your old lady a whore?" someone else called.

"No!" he protested.

"Sure she is. His ma sells her ass for money."

"No, she don't!"

"Bull! How come you live in a whorehouse, then?" Dink bore in.

"It isn't. I don't know. It's just where my stepdad took us."

"What stepdad? You ain't got no stepdad working at the shipyard," Dink sneered. "I *checked* on *you*."

*What?* What was he saying? *Checked!* Jack felt trapped, naked, caught out completely, though he wasn't sure why. *Dink had checked on him.*

"I seen her, too. Your old lady. Got a ratty little ole reddish coat. She comes out like this." He lifted his right arm up, limp-wristed like Jack's mom, and nanced around in front of the guys. Jack could see her there, exposed, vulnerable. He had *checked* on them. Secretly. *When?* Who would do something like that? *Goddamn catlicker sonofabitch!*

"You're a dirty, stinkin liar!" The words hurt Jack's throat.

"*You're* the liar! You can't call *me* a liar and get away with it."

He was coming for Jack. He saw it coming. He stuck out his left inside Dink's right, so it glanced off his eye while Jack connected next to Dink's mouth. But Dink was punching. Jack's arms felt leaden, slow. He was terrified. He was angry. He was hurt.

A kid dropped silently down on all fours behind Jack. Dink's fist busted his mouth like a thrown rock. He went backward over the kid and came down hard on his tail. Before he could get up, Dink kicked him twice in the ribs. Jack's breath was gone.

"Give him a chanc't," someone suggested calmly.

"Yeow, let him get up."

Dink waited with his hands high, a grim set to his face, his head cocked purposely behind his left shoulder. Like his cast-iron, penny-arcade pug, he came straight for Jack before Jack felt steady, winging left and right hands. His fists were like rocks. Jack had never been hit so hard, so relentlessly. After the shock of the first couple of real shots, his whole head felt numb. He tried to hit back, sticking a left ineffectually inside Dink's hooks, connecting too, but his punches were only pushes. He hadn't strength to pull the trigger. He was just trying to

**353**

keep him off. Every punch Dink threw was a shot. Everything was a whirl of lights, grinning faces, a roar of sound that made Jack think of a YMCA gym on a Saturday morning, the yelps of boys. And the big rocky fists of Dink coming at him out of the swarming background like trains out of a tunnel.

*"Fight back! Fight back, yuh yelluh!"* There was encouragement. Jack was down a dozen times. The loose newsprint underfoot was treacherous as ice. Yet Dink seemed solidly anchored, as if he moved on steel glides. He really wound up. Jack saw it coming with one eye. He leaned back. Someone pushed him forward. Dink was grinning evilly, aiming at the point of Jack's chin as if he saw a pin hanging out there. Jack saw it. Then he saw stars. His knees buckled. But he didn't go down. Then Dink hit him some more, and he went down. He was inside the midnight globe of an astronomer. Then the lights went out.

He came to outside in the cold, down against a wall. There was a big scrape along the left arm of his new leather jacket where he had rubbed against brick or something. His left eye had swelled shut. His lips felt so puffed he fumbled with fingers four inches away trying to touch them. Something plugged his nose. Still, he hadn't felt so warm and cozy since arriving in Mobile. Except for the ache and throb, which were sort of remote, he felt very comfortable inside himself. He had never been less afraid, less anxious than he was at that moment. Beyond vanity, where fear of pain had been numbed, he was quite content.

Someone slipped a hand under his right arm.

"You OK?" It was Evans.

"Yeow. I think so." It sounded like "Fink so," his lips were so puffed. There was the coppery taste of blood and there were a lot of loose teeth in his mouth.

"You sho do got some lotta knots on yuh head. He sho kick the livin' shit out of yuh."

"He sure did."

When he saw Jack could stand, Evans let go of him as if he had something that might be catching. He walked along beside Jack. His hands were stuffed straight down into the pockets of the man's coat he wore.

"I had a fren once who did me lak that. For nuthin, yuh unnerstan. Jes gets his head all set to whip my ass and comes on me. I goes down. But I comes up wif a big rock. I break his kinky head. I knock him cold*ee!* He don fuck wif me no more. An' he never tell me why he come on me that way. You get yuhsef a rock tomorrow, er a piece of iron er somethin."

There wasn't going to be any tomorrow. Jack wasn't going back there. Dink had *checked* on him—*checked on him!* That creeping Jesus sonofabitch! Nobody Jack had ever known went around *checking* on somebody. *Fuck that!*

At Jocylyn's door he stopped. He had to tell her he wouldn't be delivering her paper anymore. He rapped on the frame of her screen door. The sound echoed in the hollow hotel. Maybe she was not at home. All of a sudden he felt sick to his stomach, faint. He *wanted* her to be home. His mother wasn't home. He really banged the door.

"*All right! All right!* For godsake! Don't knock the door down." She appeared above the modesty panel. "*Wha*—My lan'! What? You hit by a car? Come in. Come in. Gah, I ain't together, boy. Come in. Sit down. Give me a minute, will yuh?"

Her hair was frizzed out on either side of her puffy, lax face like a wild witch's bush. She brushed imaginary cobwebs from before her face. Her eyes were bleary, devoid of whites, wet. She wore only a stained quilted housecoat that had burst beneath each arm.

"Lay down. Lay down. God. I got to get myself together. You look awful." She led the boy to her bed and leaned him across it backwards. "Get a towel and a cloff." She stumbled away. Then she was back, putting a towel beneath his head, folding a wet cloth, carrying it to put over his eyes. As she leaned toward him, her huge breasts swung out of her open housecoat in a heavy, liquid way. Her face was haggard and old-looking. Jack noticed a gold eyetooth. When she wasn't beautiful, she was *ugly!* It was a shock. *Ugly!* The cloth coming over his eyes. He kept seeing her bending toward him, as in slow motion, over and over, her enormous brown breasts swinging toward him again and again.

He lifted the cloth. Where had she gone? He saw her upside down through the open bathroom door standing in three-quarter profile in front of the bathroom sink. Her robe hung from her shoulders. He saw the big sexy slope of her brown belly. And the glistening tight black patch below. She was holding a hypodermic up to the light. Then she lifted her left breast up, craned her head down, and stuck the needle in where the weight of her big tit folded the skin. Her lower lip was caught in her teeth. Her belly jumped a couple of times. Her right leg, which was raised slightly at the heel, trembled; the long powerful muscle in her thigh quivered. She laid the needle on the sink and rubbed the place it had gone in as if it itched. Then dropped her breast. Jack lowered the cloth.

She returned presently and sat on the bed. There was a weight on his forehead on top of the cloth. A cold weight.

"Icebag, honey. Ice take that swelling out of your pore head. What happened to you?"

Jack stammered out his story.

"Well, that was one dumb boy," she said softly. She held the bag on the other side of his head. "Folks in cathouses ain't no different than other folks. Some are a damn sight better. Like me and you, huh? Forget that dumb boy. It looks like you got a broken tooth there in front."

"That one already was."

"Ain't *you* lucky. I never noticed before."

He could see in her eyes how badly out of shape his head was.

"You just rest there until your mama comes home. You want a little tea. It relax you."

He didn't want tea.

When he awoke, she was dressed in her yellow robe with the feathers. Her hair was slicked back and shiny. She looked just the way she had the first time he saw her. Beautiful. He could discern the murky whites of her eyes. Above, her lashes were long, sweeping, like tiny bird's wings. It was amazing. Her face was so clear, so soft.

"Hi." She looked up from her book.

"You're so pretty."

"Hey. How about that? Don't want to come on me without warning. Catch me on my witch side."

"Are you a whore?"

"Hunh? . . . Now, why you want to mention that?"

"I don't know."

"I do what I do. Call it whore. Call it anything."

"Men give you money to letum fuck you?"

"Thassit." She looked old again behind her makeup.

"Anybody?"

"Yeh, anybody." She was not liking the talk. "I guess you take a beating like that for livin in a cathouse, you got a right to ast a couple of questions."

"Can I?"

"Can you what?" She was looking down her nose. Her eyes were haughty, suspicious slits.

"Do it to you?"

"*You?* You too little."

"I could try."

"You're just a baby, honey. You shouldn't be thinkin about such things."

"If I brought money, would you let me try?"

"You'd just be wastin your time and money. How old you say you was?"

"Ten and a half."

"*Whoo.* . . . I could get arrested jus talkin like this to you."

"But *could* I?"

"You don't want to think about somethin like that, son."

"Yes, I do."

"Waste your five dollars."

*That was what it cost!* It seemed a lot.

"What's the matter?"

"I never had five dollars."

She laughed. "Well, when you big enough to spend five dollars, *then* we'll talk." She was happy again. "How about some tea?" When she stood up, she altered the perspective of the whole wobbling world.

"Ten-and-a-half-years-old," she muttered, shaking her head. She jabbed him on the heart with her long brown forefinger. "You're a rascal. Yeh. *You* are a *real* rascal."

After the tea, she asked him if he felt good enough to go to his own room. She looked at her watch and said she had an appointment.

It was getting dark. He built a fire in the fireplace. Through the wall Jack heard the muted sounds from Jocylyn's big feather bed. He scooted up and put his ear to the wall to hear better. Her bed did not squeak like theirs, but it did bump a little. Then he couldn't hear anything. Then he heard her voice and a man's voice just muttering regular talk.

He was asleep in the dark when his mother came in. When she put on the light and saw his face, she screamed. When she learned what had happened, she wept and said, "I should never have brought you to this. Can you ever forgive me?"

Jack assured her he did not blame her. If anyone was responsible, he blamed Bill. Some dad.

"We have to stick together, don't we?" she sniffed.

"Yes."

"You and I against the world, right?" She wiped her eyes with her knuckles. She gave him a touch on the chin with her fist. Even a touch made him wince. She threw her arms around him kissing his bruises, washing his cheeks with her tears.

"You'll never leave me, will you, darling?" she asked, hanging on his neck.

"No."

"Promise?"

"Promise."

"I *do* love you so."

He slipped his right hand in her jacket over her breast. She lay back, pulling the string to put out the light. They dozed that way until the fire had about flickered out and cold crept again around the bed.

The next morning he could barely work his jaw. The numbness had been replaced by stiffness and pain. He could not have bitten Jello. Milk, cold from the fire escape with ice crystals floating in it, was wonderful. Even his throat behind his Adam's apple hurt.

"I guess you'll be home today," she guessed.

"I'm not ever going back there," he told her.

"Oh? You think it's that bad?"

"I'd have to get a knife or something."

"Well, if you think it's that serious. I'll just bet, though, if you went back it would all be forgotten."

*Was she nuts?* "You don't *know* those guys! They ain't like *little* kids! They never liked me anyhow."

"Maybe you acted smartass or something to get them after you."

"*No I didn't! What?* Do you want me to go back there?" He couldn't believe it.

"No. It's just—I haven't found anything yet. . . ."

"Then find something!" he said cruelly, turning away and throwing himself on the bed.

She finished dressing without a word and spoke only when she was at the door. "I don't know when I'll be back. See you."

"See you."

"I hope you feel better when I get back."

"I feel better."

"OK. Bye."

Later, he read the paper he had brought home the night before. The Germans were sinking lots of ships in the Atlantic. German armies were sweeping through everything. Lindbergh said he thought the Germans could conquer Europe easily. *Blizkrieg! Stuka! Air Power. Junkers.* He didn't understand. Roosevelt promised mothers in Washington he would not send their sons to fight a foreign war. The women looked reassured.

The baby from across the court sounded as if it was right outside Jack's door screaming bloody murder. That was *all* he needed, a baby abandoned on his doorstep. Jack peeked out.

The young woman had the baby hanging limply, howling, in the crook of her arm. She was pecking at the door next to the manager's. It opened a crack. The face of the welder on the night shift at the shipyard appeared in the dark opening, then his shoulders, his chest. He had on a sleeveless undershirt. His arms were pale, beefy, freckled. He was not happy about being awakened. He went away. Then he came back and shoved a couple of dollar bills out to the young woman. The baby's screams pumped one after another, as relentless as a long-distance siren. She turned away from the closed door. Her eyes were dull, dark-rimmed, yet desperate in their dead depths.

"Oh! Hey! Little boy. Please. Help me." She came toward the door. "Please, will you go down to the store and get me two cans of Pet Milk for my baby?"

"Sure."

She handed Jack a dollar. "Hurry. Oh, thank you."

Their room was actually a slanted trunk closet under a boarded-up stair that once led to a roof garden. The right wall was like a lean-to, and the boy felt slightly tipped to the left just inside the door. Four dingy diapers hung on a cord over the two-burner hot plate under the slant. A pan of water bubbled on the plate. A grown man could have stood in the center of the place and touched each wall with his out-stretched hands. A single bare bulb in the center of the place cast wavering shadows and made the place seem unstable as a boat. One could not pass the light without grazing the cord, setting it to swaying. On one side of the bulb they had tied a piece of cardboard to deflect the light from the bed which filled the back of the cave. You had to crawl in over the end. When Jack saw the skin and bones on the bed, he froze with his mouth open.

"Is that your, uh, old man?" he whispered.

"He isn't well," she explained over the howls of the babe in her arms. The baby was just a skeleton itself.

"Your baby sure cries a lot."

"Yes, I don't know why. Just hungry. I had to stop nursing. I never had enough milk. She doesn't take this very well. I don't know."

*He wasn't asleep back there! He was just lying back there with his eyes open, looking at nothing. He lay on a bare mattress that had a big burn hole in it. He lay there in jeans and dingy plaid shirt, barefoot. His bony long feet looked crusty. His nails curled over the end of his toes.*

The young woman was pouring hot water and Pet Milk into a baby bottle. "Can you do this?" She indicated the nipple. She could not manage it one-handed.

Jack slipped the rubber nipple over the neck of the bottle. The woman tested it on her arm, and gave it to the baby, who sucked greedily for a few seconds, broke off, howled doubly, then spewed out all it had taken. Its cries were deafening. Jack could not stand it.

"I just don't know *what to do,*" the woman moaned. "Come on, baby, please, *please,* take it."

He felt bad about the baby all afternoon. It never stopped crying. It cried as if it would burst itself.

*There was his mom!* Down in the street, walking along searching hell out of the bottom of her purse, a frown on her face, annoyed she could not find what she was looking for, her nose practically in the thing, her short skirt whipping around her legs. She looked pretty good. A guy with a reflex camera hung around his neck leapt off the curb in front of her and took her picture, handing her a coupon with which she could claim her image.

When she came in, Jack told her, "I saw you get your picture took."

She looked at the window. "Oh. I don't like someone jumping out taking my picture like that without my knowing it."

"You going to get it?"

"I don't think so."

"Please. I'd like it."

"Well, we'll see." She put the coupon in her purse.

He told her about the baby. She told him the man in there was the *baby's* father, not the young woman's old man, as he had assumed.

"But he's a thousand years old!"

"No. He's a dope fiend."

"What's that?" He had heard the term but had never had occasion before to examine its implications.

"He takes dope. They both do. Only he's completely shot. She can at least sell herself to keep them in the stuff."

"She lets men do it to her for money, too?"

"Umhmm."

"Looks like the guys were right about beating me up at the newspaper for living in a cathouse."

"Well, they had no right to pick on you. Beat you up like that. Kids are cruel, sometimes."

"Yeow? So are adults."

"But not like kids."

"Bill is."

"No, he isn't."

That would get them nowhere. "How do dope fiends do it?"

"What?"

"Whatever they do."

"Oh. Take it? Well, they shoot it into them with a needle."

360

"And it makes them drunk like Bill?"

"*No.* Not like Bill. Bill is an alco—*Bill* drinks, that's all. Dopes can't stop. Once they start, they can't stop it. They have to have more and more until that's all they crave, all that matters. *Bill* can stop drinking any time he wants to."

"And he wants to every day."

"That's something smart you got from your grandma, isn't it?"

He didn't say a thing. He wondered if his big friend next door was taking dope when she shot that needle under her big brown tit. But she wasn't like the people across the hall. He could not be sure about what his mother said all the time.

"Do you have any money?" she asked.

"No." That reminded him. "You get a job?"

"Maybe," she mumbled. "I'll know tomorrow."

"Where?"

"Oh. A place. A drugstore."

"What one?"

"Oh! Look at *this!* My stockings! Both ruined. I can't even darn them. *Look at them!*" She flung them into the fire where they burst into two bright, brief puffs of flame, and were whisked up the flue.

"How can I go looking for work looking like this?" She plucked at her one outfit. "My shoes!" She threw herself face down on the bed, sobbing so hard it shook. Her back bucked in deep racking sobs.

"Don't cry, Mama. Something will turn up. It always does, don't it? Please don't cry, Mom. It makes me want to cry, too."

"Oh, my big man!" She rolled onto her back, pulling his bruised face down into hers where there was the salty taste of tears mingled with the perfume of her powder and the flowers of her lipstick. "Hold me! Hold me tight! *Tighter!*" she implored.

He squeezed her as hard as he could. Until she sighed. "Now I feel better. Whoo, you almost squeezed the life out of me. You're really getting strong. And *tall.* Stand up." They measured. He was higher than her chin.

In bed that night she let him kiss her breasts for having gone to bed hungry, and tickle her all over. Finally he touched her pussy.

"You know, what you don't realize is how it isn't good for me, either, to let you do this."

"Why?"

"It leaves me dissatisfied and grouchy."

"But you said it feels good."

"Well, it still isn't good for me. Or *you!* And we really *must* stop it. It's getting to be a habit with you. That's enough, now."

"No, it isn't. It ain't no habit. I could stop . . . anytime."

"*You are a devil!* You *really* are. *Jack!* Don't, now! That's enough! I don't like you to do that. No, now, please. . . ." She flung her legs open wide and began fucking the three fingers in her. Then he slipped in four, then his thumb, his hand driven in her up to the knuckles. "NO!" She clutched his wrist with both hands, shoving it from her, trying to crawl up out the top of the bed. "STOP IT!" Her legs clapped shut audibly. *"No more!* Never again. I *mean* it!"

From what old Harold Lloyd Beers had told him that time, he knew she had been about to come. He would have liked to have got his whole fist in there. It was like liquid velvet. He smelled his fingers. They smelled like sweat, piss, the greening earth, and the ocean. Where his nails were bitten to the quick there was a tiny burning.

The next morning she took him with her to the welder's door to borrow a couple of bucks to tide them over. He let them in and went and reclined on his unmade bed in his old flannel bathrobe. His calves were monstrously heavy-looking. He had a big gut that rolled over his belt. On the old overstuffed chair beside his bed there was his welder's mask and rawhide gauntlets, his holster of welding rods and torch-starter on a thong, all on a heavy leather belt. Hung on the head of his bed was the rough hide jacket and leather biballs he wore to work. Below were his safety toe boots and tin hat. The stuff smelled of burnt metal. He smelled like a foundry. On the footrail of his bed hung a pair of woman's pink panties.

"Not yours, I trust?" Wilma said like a movie star.

"What do you think?" He patted the bed for her to sit.

She sat carefully on the edge, crossed her legs at the knee, took the cigarette he offered.

"Hey, Mom, you don't smoke!" Jack reminded her.

"You don't know *all* I do," she purred, looking at the guy. She blew smoke out her nose. Only he noticed her eyes watered behind her glasses.

"We would just like to ask you if you could let us have five or so for a week. My husband will be back then—Jack! Leave that alone."

He had picked up the welder's mask.

"That's all right. He can't hurt it."

"I've always told you to ask before you touch," she reminded him.

He put on the mask and strolled over to see himself in the dresser mirror. The black glass window was almost impossible to see through.

He flipped it up and looked through the clear. It was dirty and pocked by tears of molten metal, but he could see himself. There were pictures of women around the frame of the welder's mirror. Most of them were naked. He could see everything on them. A lot of them had been taken right there in that room. They all seemed posed the same way. On his bed, sitting up with their legs apart, pulling their pussies open and smiling like they were riding on a park swing. Some, though, were not smiling. A couple had their faces turned away. *There was the young woman that had the squalling baby.* Her titties were small and hung down. You could see her ribs. Her pussy was thin. You could see through her hairs all except the very center. In the corner was a closet with a sign on the door: DARKROOM. Wilma turned to see what Jack was doing.

"I took all those," the welder said matter-of-factly, a trace of boast under his words.

"You always take trophies?"

"Yeh. Sort of my own garden of memories."

"You keep busy."

"It's developing the pictures that takes the time."

"Yeow. I can see how that could kill a weekend. Can you help us out or not?" she asked.

He smiled and stretched his hands apart about a yard. "You see how it is. Come back by yourself. Maybe we can work out something. I'd let you have five."

"*Thanks.* Come on, Son." She derricked the mask off the boy, skinning his ears. She carefully returned it to the chair.

"Any time," he cracked, grinning.

They were in the room about half an hour. Jack was hungry.

"I know you are. So am I," she said.

"Can't you get some money? Why didn't he give us some money? If I don't get something to eat pretty soon, I'm going to die."

"You'll not die!"

"Well, I feel like it! Can't you get some money somewhere?"

"Oh, shut up!"

But he would not shut up. Finally she got up. "All right! I'll feed you!"

"Where are you going?"

"None of your business!"

"Are you going to the welder?"

"No! If you want something to eat, you stay right here until I get back. Don't you leave this room."

She was going to the welder. He knew how she was going to get the money. He knew when he was begging her, that was what she would do. They would do it. He went to the door. He saw her tap on the welder's door. He opened it. He was not grinning. She went in.

He hated her. He hated him. She was pulling her thing open for him to take a picture. He threw himself on the bed and buried his head under the pillow. *He wanted to do it to her!* He wanted to more than he wanted food. And he had driven her to the welder! He had knowingly driven her to him. He was so hungry he hurt. He took out his little dingus and skinned it back and forth until he really began to feel something. *What was it? Was this it?* OH-OH-OH-WOW! *Yeow! She was getting it and so am I! So am I.* . . . There was a clear tear on the end of his prick. OH, WOW! *Boy! How great.* His knees had kicked and feet jerked, and his vision had focused down to a tunnel, racing a gauntlet of all the welder's naked women into the liquid, hot velvet heart of *her* big cunt. He felt faint afterward. He felt like he had been kicked in the small of the back. He sort of ached all over. But he did not worry. It was great! He rolled the clear, tacky tear between thumb and forefinger.

But then, suddenly, he was jealous of the welder. *Why hadn't she gotten back? What was taking her so long?*

He had counted to thirteen hundreds of times before she came through the door. It was dark.

"OK. You're so hungry, go eat." She flung a dollar down on the bed.

"Aren't you coming with me?" he asked.

"No. I don't feel like eating."

"You said you were hungry before."

"I've got a headache."

"Well, maybe if you had something to eat?"

"Oh, leave me *alone!*"

"I'm sorry, Mama. I just want you to be happy."

"Oh, all right."

They had hot turkey sandwiches at the Good Eats Café on the corner. She had apple pie with a slice of cheese on it for dessert. He had his à la mode.

"Feel better?" he asked after.

"No."

When she was asleep he played with himself again, and though she stirred fitfully and grumbled, she did not fully awaken. When he felt the swelling inner tickle, he touched the tip to feel the tiny tear. Just a drop.

From then on, she went out every evening, returned around midnight or after, and they always had a little money. They had enough to eat and get her some few clothes. She said she got the job at the drugstore, but she would not let him come have dinner with her at the fountain. She really acted like she was ashamed of him most of the time. He began staying away. He would leave during the day so she could sleep, roam the streets, docks, penny arcade, go to the movies and jack off under his jacket when the girls went into their dance.

He got a *Tillie the Toiler* fuck book from the geek who sold them and jerked off over it until his prick was raw. Tillie did remind him some of his mom. "Give it to me, big boy! Hot and greasy!" "I'm going to fuck you in your flue!" "Oh! It's so big! I'm afraid you will tear out my partition!" "I'll remodel your whole garage, baby!" "Here today! And hot Tamale!" He ran the streets crying wildly in his heart. He feared nothing. He stole the stores blind and sailed a toy fleet on the rumpled counterpane.

Monday, the sun fell in fine big rectangles in the room for the first time in weeks. It was warm on the bed in the puddle of sun. His mother had gone to the bathroom. Sunday night she did not work, so she was up early. Jack was stalking a fleet of battleships with a little blue plastic submarine just out of sight behind a chenille wave, just in torpedo range.

"Looks like we have so little money, you wouldn't spend it on stuff like that." He hadn't heard her come in.

"I didn't spend nothin for them."

"What did you do—steal them?"

"Yeow. I took them."

"Don't you know I don't want you to steal?"

*Why didn't she come off it?* He just shrugged.

"I mean it! I don't want you to grow up thinking you can just take whatever you want, young man. We have to work for what we get."

"Like you and Bill?"

"What do you mean by *that?*"

"Nothin."

"You are just getting too smart for your britches."

He went to his jacket and came back and laid a gold compact on the bed.

"What's that?"

"It's your shade."

"It *is!* Oh, you're so thoughtful. You really do love your old mom, don't you? I'm sorry. I'm just on edge lately. The, uh, work is all I can take."

"Un-hunh."

"This is just wonderful."

"I can get you anything you want. Lipstick, powder, stockings, you name it."

"Aren't you afraid of getting caught?"

"Naw. That's the funny thing. I thought I would be scared. I wasn't scared at all. I feel like I'm invisible. Nobody even looks at me hardly. I just pick it up and walk out."

"Really?"

"Sure. Want me to show you?"

"Well. OK. But just so I can see how you do it. And I could use some lipstick and cologne." She giggled.

"Mom?"

"What?"

"Sometimes you make me feel older, and you like a little girl."

She gave him a hug. "We'll stick together. Through thick and thin."

"I've seen the thin, when do we get the thick?" He recalled one of his granddad's lines. They both laughed.

There was a tiny triangular park across from Woolworth's. Old men fed pigeons peanuts. Jack envied the birds. He would have kept the nuts for himself. Winos expropriated an entire bench in spite of the cold stares of sober citizens. The big trees were a skeletal arbor overhead. The sun made lacy shadows on the pigeon-striped walks.

*What was that headline?*

WAR!

Jack scurried after the paper. Then they heard the newsboys. They came boiling down both streets that forked off at the base of the triangle. No one could understand a word they were saying. WAR! That was all. They all cried the news in their own way. Men in the park pricked up, stood, cupped their hands to their ears.

"What is it? What do they say?" they asked one another.

"What is it, Mom?"

"I don't know."

The newsreel theater across the street at the base of the park came to life. Its marquee flashed on in neon stutters. Then, over tinny loudspeakers hung under the eaves of the marquee, the voice of President Roosevelt raised goose bumps along Jack's spine. The faces of old men became helpless as the faces of little boys. Old women wept into balled handkerchiefs. Middle-aged men became grim, determined. They moved heavily, turning their shoulders. The winos never stirred. They might not know until day after next, next week, or never in this world at all:

Yesterday, December seventh, 1941—a date which will live in infamy—the United States of America was suddenly and deliberately attacked by naval and air forces of the Empire of Japan. . . .

Everyone was acting brave. Everyone looked at one another in the park for the first time. Old men looked at the woman and the boy. They looked at the other people. Everyone seemed about to say something. A woman crying in her handkerchief asked Wilma, "How old is he?"

"Ten and a half."

"My boy is nineteen."

"Let's hope it's over soon."

"Mom?"

"What?"

"I hope it lasts until I'm old enough to get in it."

"Well, I don't!"

"I want to."

She measured the boy again with her eyes. He was still as high as her chin.

# 31

JACK lay for a long time in the sun-splashed Monday morning bed. His mother slept softly beside him. Her perfume, warmed by the sun, made the bed smell of night flowers and warm musk. They were going to look at another place to live. There had been a blackout the night before. The girls in the jail across the street got in trouble for striking matches in the dark, barred windows. Jack wondered if they wanted to be bombed. Everyone knew that a bomber could see a lighted match from 10,000 feet.

His mother stretched luxuriously and smiled before opening her eyes. They had gone to a movie Sunday and had dinner in a café. She was wearing the black nightgown he had stolen for her from J. C. Penney's. It came boxed with a matching peignoir—$5.95! He had simply hooked the box under his left arm and walked out with it, stopping to browse the nut counter near the front door like a Christmas shopper. A Penny's

Santa who wore cheap black oilcloth leggings over his scuffed brown shoes rather than real boots offered him saltwater taffy.

"And what can Santa bring you for Christmas, young man?"

Jack shook his head. Did he think *he* went for that crap?

"Ho-ho-ho. And a *Merry* Christmas!" Santa went looking for an easier mark. "Visit Sant's toyland in the basement. Ho-ho-ho!"

*I will,* Jack silently promised. *Ho-ho-ho.*

But he could not wait until Christmas to give his mom the gown. She said it was too "sexy" for a boy to give his mother, though she wore it anyway.

"Hi, Puddin Tame," she husked sleepily.

"Do you hear something?" he asked.

"What?" She lifted her head to listen.

"That baby ain't cryin."

"You're right. Isn't that wonderful?"

"Sure seems funny not hearin it cry all the time."

"The poor little thing has been so miserable."

He could see her pale breasts through the black bodice of her gown.

"A mother's heart just goes out when she hears a baby crying like that." She hugged him to herself. "I never let you cry like that. I'd find some way to feed you and make you feel better."

He slipped his right hand up and cradled her left breast. She trapped his hand there.

"Please, Sonny. Now, that isn't going to do you any good. You'll just make yourself feel frustrated."

"It just feels so nice to me. I like it."

"But it isn't *good* for you. And you know, you, uh, really should watch it, and not play with yourself too much, dear. You could hurt yourself."

*How did she know? What did she mean, "too much"?* "How?" he asked. He had skinned his thing raw, but there never appeared to be any damage that lasted longer than a day. Once he doused it with her perfume to make it smell nice and nearly burned it off. Not cold water, soap, talcum—nothing could stop that burning.

"Well, it just isn't good for growing boys to play with themselves so much. It can make them soft in the head." She giggled at some private joke that made him ask, "What?"

"Nothing. You'll understand when you are older. Nothing." She smiled. "Anyway watch it, OK?"

"OK." *Man! There was always a catch to everything. What was too much?* He did it at least once a day. Would that make him soft-headed?

He had a fast vision of himself stashed away on a funny farm, like his grand-uncle Mervin, forty-five years old, dressed in the state's overalls, pounding his meat like a fiend.

"Maybe I should take you to see a doctor . . ." she said, thinking out loud.

"I don't want to go to no doctor. I won't go."

"Then you're just going to have to stop this." She removed his hand from her breast. "There's some medicine they can give you to make you not feel this way."

"I won't take it!" His eyes filled with tears. "If it's so bad, why don't I feel bad?"

"Because you just don't know any better. The Bible says: 'Honor your father and your mother.' "

"I *do!*" he insisted.

"Well, not if you want to do *that* to me!"

He did not see why not. "Why? Bill does."

"But I'm his wife. We are supposed to. That's why people get married."

But that did not stop his wanting. "Then kids should get married, too. Sometimes I just can't think of nothing else."

"Well, you must try. You really should have a bed of your own."

"You *said* I'd have my own room."

"Well, it just didn't work out that way. In any case, you must think of me as your mother, Bill's wife. Understand?"

"No."

"Yes, you do. Hey! Come on, now. Buck up. Let's get up and go see the new place. I hope it's nice. Don't be glum, chum, you have lots of time. Enjoy being a boy while you can. Being a man is a longtime thing. Then you can never ever really be a little boy again. And a handsome fella like you, you're going to meet a lot of nicer and prettier girls than me."

"Not prettier er nicer than you."

"Well, you might. There's a slight chance." She laughed. "Out!"

There were soldiers and sailors all over Mobile. Down near the docks a drunken soldier staggered past the few citizens dressed for church. His Sam Browne belt hung through one blouse epaulet, his garrison cap slung by its chin strap through the other, his jacket open, his shirttail half out, he swam through the sunshine toward some far-from-home dream of fulfilling his lonely heart's desire around the next corner.

"Hey, soldier-honey, you lookin for me?" a frowzy redhead with scabs on her ankles called to the boy.

He turned as if he had been hooked around the neck with a crook. There stood his heart's desire in a houndstooth box jacket, a slouch hat over one eye, a big plaid skirt of uneven hem, teetering on a pair of two-inch, tricolored, ankle-strap platform sandals. From a nearby saloon there was the music of a Glenn Miller tune. She popped her gum and asked low, "Honey, you got any money?"

Jacky and his mother walked on. He whistled under his breath. He wondered how his mom did it. *"Honey, you got any money?"* he heard his mother's voice ask in a midnight shadow where Glenn Miller played the whole night through.

ALL-OUT WAR!—the way Roosevelt said it, it sounded like *"waa-ah"*—while behind blackout curtains people who had been broke yesterday were having the time of their lives. Three shifts. And everyone was on overtime! Across the river the rivet guns and chipping hammers rapped steadily on another ship for the convoys. All he hoped was it lasted long enough for him to get in on it. Man! They were giving everything away free to soldiers, sailors, and Marines at those stage-door canteens. Pretty, jiving girls like daughters of women for whom his grandmother did laundry were just dying for a chance to wrap their bare, patriotic legs around some far-from-home Marine.

The house was an old yellow frame bungalow with a front and side porch, turned porch pillars, and a touch of gingerbread at the corners. It was located in a working-class residential neighborhood from which the more steadily employed had since moved, leaving the street to pensioners, transients, and war workers. There the third-shifters lived by night, their houses ablaze with light, jumping with laughter during parties that lasted past dawn. The shades were drawn when Jack and his mother went up the porch. She talked to a woman who answered her knock at the side door through a crack. The woman obviously was not dressed. She handed a key through the crack. The woman and his mother seemed acquainted.

"They work nights," his mother explained. "Actually, that's ideal, isn't it, because I do, too." She was happy as a clam.

They went around back. There was a room and a screened-in porch with a door that opened at the side of the house. In the room there was a big bed with a good soft mattress and a chenille spread. There was a gas heater. There was a real bathroom. And a nice closet. Out on the porch part, which was reached through a door that locked, there was a kitchen and a table and four chairs, a double sink. The porch was insulated and warm, with the big shutters down. They took it. They would move in that night.

Jack had forgotten how convenient was a gas heater, a stove on which to cook, a bath with hot water. The place was no more luxurious than a AAA-ignored motel cabin in the Ozarks, but its bright linoleum homeliness tripled the world's possibilities in the boy's mind instantly. There was still in his dreams a little house of their own like everyone else's, a room of his own, a sunny, calm, well-dressed, well-fed kind of reality, where instead of being an All-American back like Brown of Minnesota, he would become the Navy's air equivalent of Colin P. Kelly—only *survive* to receive the medal . . . singing:

> Praise the Lord and pass the ammunition!
> Praise the Lord and pass the ammunition!
> Praise the Lord and pass the ammunition!
> And we'll all stay freeeeeeee. . . .

SLAP THE JAP! STUN THE HUN! SHHHHHH! TOJO IS LISTENING.

The boy believed it all. He could not wait until his mother could hang a blue star in her window for him.

There was a police car and an ambulance in front of the hotel when they got back.

"What's happening?" Wilma asked of one of the cops on the stairs.

He shrugged as if he hadn't a clue.

Going up the stairs, Jack was afraid something had happened to Jocylyn. But she was out in the hall in her ugly robe, not her nice one, holding herself together with both arms, shivering in the cold hallway.

A cop came from the little slanty room under the stair that no longer went anywhere carrying a little bundle wrapped in a blanket in his arms. Wilma and Jocylyn gasped. The tall brown woman hid her face in her hands, moaning, "Oh no, Lor! Oh, noooo. . . ." The cop just shook his head sadly.

Then two ambulance men came out with the baby's mother under a blanket on a stretcher. She seemed so much slighter than before.

"Is she dead?" Jack asked.

"Yes," his mother whispered.

He was sorry she was dead. Yet, he wondered if it was possible to do it to someone after they were dead. They certainly couldn't stop you, was a notion.

"She killed herself and the kid," the welder volunteered, a note of scorn and self-righteousness in his voice. Jacky remembered the photo of the dead girl stuck in the welder's looking glass.

"Smothered the kid and shot herself full of Clorox," one of the ambulance guys offered.

"Ummmm-ummm," Jocylyn crooned.

Then the cops came up with another stretcher, went in under the nowhere stair, and came out with the husband. He was a living skeleton. He lay on the stretcher on his side, his head cradled on one arm, his eyes staring blankly—pale blue eyes, as innocent as a Sunday-school picture card of Christ. He never blinked.

"Here's the spook she shoulda done in," a big cop proclaimed. "Just look at this sad sonofabitch. He don't know if he's here or gone." He lifted the man's emaciated arm as if displaying a dead rattlesnake. Inside the elbow it was infected, festered, a seeping sore. "Shot enough shit through him to put his little family on easy street. And his little baby starvin to death!" He flung back the man's arm as if throwing it away. It flopped down as if devoid of bone and muscle. The cop stared at them all there in the hall—the satyric welder with the bloated, degenerate face; the gigantic, beautiful ugly chocolate whore; the manager, a petty miser, a saver of snot; and the woman the cop had never seen before, with a kid that ought to be in school. "What a goddamn menagerie," he muttered to himself and turned away. Then he turned and spoke to Wilma. "What are you doing in a place like this?"

"My husband went out a couple of days after we got here to look for a job and never came back."

"This is the best you can do?"

"No. I got a job. We're movin today. Right now."

"Humph. Good idea." He turned again and went down the stairs.

Wilma made up the bed in the room with just the spread, packing the worn, yellowed sheets in a shopping bag. They had arrived with a single handbag. They were leaving with the handbag stuffed and two shopping bags. On the curb out front they hailed a cab. In the car, Jack remembered he hadn't said good-bye to Jocylyn, he had been so happy to be leaving. Well, what did it matter? he decided. But when he got five dollars to spare he was coming back to do it to her. He promised himself.

They made the bed in the new place. Wilma put away their things in cupboard and drawer. They would need linens, dishes, cookware, so many things. Jack was eager for the morning to arrive so he could begin kypping stuff for their new home. They went to a nearby store where

Wilma bought a pound of hamburger and some bread, while Jack lifted four cans of tuna, a jar of artichoke hearts, and a bag of caramels. He hadn't the vaguest idea what an artichoke heart was, but they were expensive. His mother loved them.

After dinner he took a bath. Then his mother scrubbed out the tub, ran hot water until the bathroom was like a steam cabinet, and took a bath that lasted hours. When she came out, she had on a new lime green and black lace slip she had bought for herself, which she was going to wear in honor of the new bed. The green caught the light and shimmered over her body of so many feminine curves and gentle planes. It slipped up over her butt when she hopped into the clean, soft bed.

"Ooooooh. . . ." she sighed and stretched beneath the covers. "How nice."

"You look like a little girl, sort of, in your face," he told her.

"I feel like a new person. I only wish Bill were here. . . ." She snapped out the lamp.

When Jack eased her slip up over her bottom after he was sure she was asleep, she shifted a little, but the movement left her thing even more exposed than it had been. Nor did she stir when he touched the long soft hair. He played in the hair for a long time. It began to feel sweaty. She shifted again, and he felt the long velvet lips beneath the hair against his fingers. She had drawn her legs up, curling, with her bottom stuck out toward him. He eased his fingers in where all was liquid fire and clinging softness. Two, three fingers probed the velvet folds. She shifted slightly again, and her inside was open to his fingers. He had never felt so way back in her before. There was a tough little cone with a hole in the end of it in there—tough, but wrapped in softness. *What a cave!* He was amazed. His ears ringing, his face aflame, he felt free to do anything with her. He did not question why or how. He moved his hand around and around and jammed it in, trying to get his whole hand in; a vision of making a fist in her played in his mind. He tried snapping his fingers. She was full of warm paste. She moved from time to time but only provided him with a new purchase, an infinitesimal extra millimeter. He scooted down deep into the bed. Keeping his fingers inside her, he fumbled his stiff little penis from his shorts—*This is it!* he told himself wondrously—and fed it to the fire. He did not move. He lay there pressed against her soft bottom, his little thing throbbing in her big hot inside. Then she made some kind of noise in her throat—tender and something else new to Jack—moved back against him, slowly, then down and around. His tongue swelled in his throat, dots bounced before his eyes in the dark. He started to pull away. Her hand came back over him in the dark, pressed against his bottom, pressing him against her. She began making larger movements. Pressing him tight against her. Holding him inside her. She felt enormous inside. His lap felt sticky. She began moving around against him more rapidly. The bed sounded like it did when she and Bill did it.

"Mom?" he croaked. His teeth were chattering as if he were freezing. He felt on fire. She still held him tight against her, moving purposefully, almost desperately, around him, trying—he wondered if she knew it was he. Then she shook, too, from head to toe; shook as if she were having a fit.

"*Mom?*"

She never answered. When she quit shaking, she jumped out of bed and ran into the bathroom. There was a lot of water running for a long time. Then she came back and flopped in bed as if she were very angry.

"Mom?"

She did not answer. He touched her shoulder. "Mom?"

"Don't."

"What's wrong?" He felt on the verge of tears.

"Oh! God!" She buried her head under the pillow. Her back shook as if she were crying.

"Don't cry, Mama," he pleaded.

"You can't stay with me anymore," she blubbered under the pillow.

"I want to. Don't send me to Grandma's. I won't do it no more, if you say so. I promise. I don't want to live with Grandpa and Grandma in no basement and be on relief. I *want* to stay with you. Please don't cry. I'm sorry." It all seemed so totally over, so quickly in the past. Had it happened at all? What *had* happened? Had *that* been it? He did not think so. But. . . . "Please don't send me away, I love you more than anyone. I love you more than God. I love you." Didn't that make anything all right?

She threw off the pillow and snatched him to her, kissing his face and neck, burying his face in her soft neck where her tears wet his cheeks, rocking him, crooning, "Oh, darling, I'm *so* sorry! So *damn* sorry. We're some pair, aren't we? I love you, too. If only Bill was here where he belonged. . . . If we could only live like everyone else. . . . If you could have grown up like a son should. . . . Gypsying around the country. . . . Seeing so much—damn it! You *should* have a room of your own. Go to school. A decent life." She kissed his mouth. Her lips were warm and wet and salty with her tears. "I don't blame you, darling. It was just I was asleep. You must never do something like that when someone's asleep. It isn't fair."

He thought about that. He would have to concede she was right. But it still seemed like an excuse.

It was as if then she figuratively pinched herself. The world hadn't come to an end. In the corner, the gas heater glowed happily. The room was warm and snug. In such a room you could comfortably go naked. She sighed and shuddered like a child recovering from a tantrum.

"Promise me you will keep your hands to yourself when I am asleep," she demanded kindly.

"I promise."

"Good. Now let's go to sleep."

He snuggled against her, his arm respectfully across her waist, his feeling as romantic and pure as a valentine. He had never felt happier. Then the swarming memory of her hand covering his bottom, pressing him into her, the warmth, the heart-pounding blindness. . . . In his sleep he hunched her soft hip, his erect little penis nudging her insistently. She made him turn over, cuddling his back into her warm belly, her hand flat, fingers extended, on his naked chest.

"Be still, now," she mumbled. "We've got to get you your own bed."

# 32

BILL got home at 3 P.M. the day before Christmas. They had let him out of jail at noon, but he had found some way to get a pint on the way home. Before he arrived he had broken the seal and taken a few drinks. So he showed up aglow, though shivering in the odd suit jacket several sizes too large the city had provided him in lieu of the new black leather job he had on when the floorwalker nailed him outside Sears.

"Looks like you've grown a foot since I saw you last," he greeted the boy cheerfully. "How's it goin?" He was looking past the boy.

"OK."

"Who's there?" the boy's mother called from the bathroom.

"Who the hell you reckon? Never saw a woman who spent as much time in the donicker in my life—"

"BILL!" She blew out of the bath in a cloud of steam, wrapped in her new rose-colored chenille robe. Her hair, up in pins, bobbed in myriad damp tendrils around her face, which glistened with cold cream. Damp splotches formed on the back and thighs of the robe. She had leaped from her bath dripping. "Bill. . . ." She kissed him. Only his arms around her kept the robe from slipping to the floor. "I missed you so!" she whispered huskily.

Jack studied the linoleum, tracing the pattern with the toe of his tennis shoe.

"Miss me?" she asked.

"What do you think?" he kissed her again. They stumbled a little, caught themselves, laughing. He sat down heavily on the bed. She perched on his lap, tucking the damp robe around herself.

"You didn't come straight home," she pouted.

"Want me to go and try it again?"

"*No!*"

He glanced around the room. "Hmm. You ain't doin so bad."

In the corner was a tiny two-bit artificial Christmas tree. It was flocked with a hard, white plastic substance that was supposed to resemble snow. On it Jack had strung a string of lights he had stolen from Western Auto.

"Sorry I won't be givin you a present this Christmas. Have to take my marker."

"Just having you home is the best present I could get."

"You too, sport," he said to the boy. "I'll have to make it up to you later."

"I got presents," Jack said, happy to be acknowledged again. He dived under the bed and began dragging out all the stuff he had secretly stashed there, intending to put it under the tree after his mom was asleep.

There were cosmetics, perfume, bubble bath, lingerie, hosiery, gloves, a purse, an electric clock, a steam iron, a portable radio, stainless steel silverware for four, a box of plastic dinnerware for four in a box 24 inches by 36 inches which he had carried out of Montgomery Ward's basement, costume jewelry, a pair of red pumps—5 AAA—and a pair of sexy silver mules with feather trim. Nor had Bill been forgotten. There followed an electric drill, a set of Craftsman box-end wrenches, a really good pair of sheet-metal shears, drill bits, ball peen and carpenter's hammers, a set of ratchets, a ratchet screwdriver, a small set of dies, an electric razor, after-shave lotion, a cigarette lighter, and a leather-covered pocket flask.

Bill kept saying, "I'll be goddamned," over and over, as the stuff began piling up around the tree. The boy's mother made astonished sounds and then began giggling. They looked to the boy like amazed children.

For himself Jack had got a Daisy Red Ryder air rifle, roller skates, a Mickey Mouse watch, a Scout knife and a sheath hunting knife, a leatherette aviator cap with plastic goggles, and a pair of black cowboy boots with red stars inset that had been on a sale table at Penney's.

"Would you look at that!" Bill hooted. "Would you look at all that crap! Boy, I take my hat off to you. You're the best I ever seen." He put his battered wide-brim felt on and ceremoniously doffed it.

The boy's mother just shook her head in happy disbelief. "Come here to us, you rascal." She offered an arm to enfold him in their family group. Tears welled up in her eyes. "I'm just so happy to have us together again."

Out of respect for the emotionalism of the moment the boy tried not to be aware she was bare beneath her damp chenille robe. He would be happy to put all that out of his mind, now that Bill was home. He felt a tremendous relief, as if his chest had been unstrapped from bindings that had held him all these days. How long had he been gone? It seemed in reflection to the boy like a year. There had been so many days, each with its terror, hunger, crisis. The little boy he had been the year before seemed as remote to him as a cousin. He felt washing through him a wave of homesickness for all the poor Christmases past, vaguely wondering against his mother's soft breast, with the familiar whiskey breath of his stepdad enriching the air, why in view of riches he had never known he felt so suddenly lonely, so strangely frightened that there were no backs or sides or reality to all the stuff he had kypped for their Merry Christmas. What if they were all nonworking copies of the real things? The recalled exhilaration of the successful thefts flushed his face, made his breathing quicken. There was a hell of a lot of stuff, but there was no feel at all of Christmas.

"I wanted to get a real tree, but I didn't know how to manage it. Those guys ain't like stores. They watch their trees."

"By God, you want a real tree, we'll *get* a real tree!" Bill promised. "Get dressed, Bill," he told Wilma. "We're going for a tree."

"Bill, be careful, now." She got up.

"Don't worry. Get your coat, keed." Then low, out of the corner of his mouth, "Got any dough?"

"A little."

"Let's have it."

She gave him five. "That's about all I have. I knocked off early today, because of the holiday."

He did not want to hear about that. He pocketed the fiver. "Try and make yourself look nice for when we get back."

"I will," she promised.

They had a drink to toast the going after the Christmas tree. She threw her arms around his neck and cried again. "I'm so happy to see you. I missed you so damn much," she mumbled into his chest.

"Well, I'm home now. We'll double up and catch up."

"Yeh, honey. I'm your girl."

"I know no matter what, you're always true blue."

"You can always say that."

"Come on. We gotta get this tiger a tree."

Going up the sidewalk, he dropped his arm over the boy's shoulders. "Your mom said in her letters how you was having a pretty rough way to go for a while."

"Yeow." What else was there to say. He was surprised to learn his mother and Bill had been in communication. She hadn't said a thing to Jack, and he saw no point in telling Bill about how he thought she was making money. He guessed he probably knew.

Up on the end of the main drag where it ran down toward the docks there were stores of all kinds—hardware, fruit, clothing—that spilled outside onto the sidewalk. Christmas Eve or not, all the stores were open, selling identical Yule decorations behind hastily carded 50% OFF signs. A man with half a dozen trees at the fruit stand warmed himself at an oil drum in which trimmings and culls from his stock blazed with a pine-yellow glow, snapping sparks into the air, making the night smell cozy and scented of distant snows and northern fires.

Bill got a tree the man assured him was worth $4 for 75¢ and a drink of Calvert to toast the season. Then Jack had to hold the tree outside a bar while Bill went in and bought another pint for the long winter's night ahead.

At a hardware store they stopped again. Bill bought a canvas-bottomed camp cot that had been stored too long for around a dollar and a quarter.

Then they went home. Bill with the cot on his shoulder and the pint tugging down his bum's coat even more pathetically, Jack as mere legs under a six-foot Christmas tree.

The boy curled on the cot in the kitchen. Fire in the open oven left on to keep him warm beneath a single blanket flickered on the table and chairs and along the dark floor. The door into their room was closed. But he could hear them.

"There you go," she said encouragingly. Then, "*Oh. . . .*"

"Goddam it!" Bill swore. "Wouldn't you know I'd have this kind of luck."

"It's all right, honey. Maybe you just drank too much."

"You know that ain't never been a problem with me."

"Yes! There . . . unnh . . . here. Let me. . . . Uh! Rats! I'm sorry."

"But goddamn it, when I think of all the lousy bastards that was gettin in you while I'm locked ass up, up there."

"Don't. Shhhh. You know there has never been anyone for me really but you. You're all there will ever be this way for me. No one else ever meant a thing to me. No one else ever will. It's you, honey. It's you, all the way, all the way. Oh, yes. *Yes!* Now you got it. Now you're there. Oh, baby, I've wanted this for so long. You don't know. . . ."

"I know. All them other guys gettin in you. . . ."

"Just *you*, Bill. No one was there. You know that. You know."

"Yeh, I know."

The bed began rocking rhythmically. Then it was quickly over. They went to the bathroom. Then in the hush when they were back in bed, she said happily, "My, it's nice having you home. Jack has been a handful. We need a man around this house."

Jack hoped again it would work out. Maybe they would live like regular people yet. There seemed no reason why they could not. He, for one, made a Christmas promise to himself to really try.

The next morning, the only presents under the tree were those he had put there himself. She hadn't gotten him a thing.

Both his mother and Bill rose up in bed, tousled. She held the sheet in front of her breasts. Her gown was a satin puff on the floor on her side of the bed. His shorts were a wad on the other.

"Merry Christmas!" they chorused and giggled together over some private joke.

"Hand me my gown, will you, honey?" she asked Jack. "And turn your back for a minute."

He turned and stared at the tree, decorated with a single string of stolen lights.

# 33

BILL went out and came back and said there was no way he could get work in Mobile. Not on first, second, or third shifts. He said it was his record. He took all the negotiable presents Jack had lifted for their Christmas and turned them into cash; everything except what they could wear went in hock, never to be redeemed. Bill did not even save the pawn tickets. There was enough money to buy a couple of cardboard valises, a melton zip jacket for Bill, a pint of Calvert Special, and bus tickets to Pensacola. Wilma also had a few dollars tucked away for emergencies. When Bill was around, every day was an emergency.

It was cold in Pensacola. Even the gulls and pelicans looked cold, hunched on dock and piling, their heads pulled down into their shoulders. Sailors from the naval air station wore winter blues and pea jackets in town. Air cadets wore long bridge coats and gloves—saluting each other and everything that moved from bus drivers to CAP colonels, just to be on the safe side.

The sound of the Mighty Wurlitzer seeped out of side-street saloons and main-street cocktail lounges and crept along palm-planted boulevards and out into rented rooms with hastily erected beaverboard walls, like a guy come to town to dance up all the daughters and no one daring to ask how long he intends to stay. The burg and everyone in it would never be the same, never so innocent again. It left everyone with a nagging taste for jazz from which the children of the land never recovered, hooked for keeps, hooked ultimately by sounds and circumstances that occurred before they were born. Night and day the mighty jukes throbbed. For the duration and then forevermore.

The house stood alone, unpainted, two blocks off the main drag where it ran down beyond the bus station toward the bay, where supermarkets and radio repair shops, cut-rate drugstores and shoe-repair parlors bloomed. On the side streets, hard up against silvered, gingerbread monstrosities where rooms were rented by the week, small industries subcontracting war work blossomed in old garages where the previous signs could be made out beneath the new enamel. The house sat on a corner next to a vacant lot, in the way of someone's dream of putting up a small factory on a cost-plus basis and subcontracting a fortune. It was owned by a Gothic widow in her lavender dress and purple lisle stockings of a thousand little mends. She inhabited the downstairs parlor, sharing her kitchen with the wife of a civilian instructor in aircraft mechanics and the bride of a second-class torpedoman. Upstairs there were three one-room kitchenette housekeeping rooms, and a bathroom at the back of the hall. They were lucky in getting the room next to the bath, which had a door to it off their own—$7 per week.

The double bed filled the space between the wall and the single window, with just enough space at the foot of it to fit in a cupboard, sink, gas plate, drop-leaf table, and two straight chairs. Next to the window was a tall, narrow, standing wardrobe, then Jack's cot wedged in like a berth against the wall adjacent to the bathroom door. The light was a single 100-watt bulb in an overhead drop with a four-way socket so they could plug in toaster, iron, and radio.

Bill did not immediately catch on in Pensacola, either. He would drink about half a pint of Calvert every morning and go look. One morning he rousted the boy out of bed, shouldered his toolbox, and hiked up the alley four blocks to a side-street sheet-metal shop where four men were busy bending huge sheets of galvanized into ducts for central air-conditioning. It was as if Bill and the boss, a tall man about Bill's age, had known each other forever, though they had met only that day. The man wanted to help Bill. He stared silently in his eyes for a long time.

Then he decided, flatly, "Can't use you right now. I'll be honest with you. I could maybe use you soon. We're gettin all the work we want. They're puttin up a new NCO club at the base. . . . But I just can't take on no drinkers. I don't doubt you're every bit as good as you say you are." He appreciated Bill's heavy toolbox. "But I promised myself when I started this—no drinkers."

"Look, I promise, it'll never get in the way of my work. You'll never lose a nickel on account of Bill Wild."

"I sure as hell won't if I don't take the risk."

"I'll work a week, if you ain't satisfied you don't owe me nothin," Bill offered.

"Naw." Now it was too much like begging.

Jack could smell the booze on Bill's breath and realized he had probably never seen him completely sober.

"Check with me in a couple of weeks," the man said. He no longer looked at Bill.

"Let me leave my tools with you for a few days while I'm looking around," Bill suggested.

"Take your tools. Don't leave them here. I don't want to be responsible."

Bill shouldered the heavy metal box of tools. They trudged back up the alley. After a block, Bill and the boy carried the box between them. It was all the boy could do to hold up his end. The unpadded metal handle blistered his palm instantly. The weight was a pain all along his arm. He could feel a slight, sickening, sucking sensation in his shoulder socket with each weighted step. Yet he wanted Bill to be proud of him, so he gritted his teeth and toughed it out. They turned out of the alley onto their street.

"Bill, lookee there. In that car."

"Yeh. Keep walkin. Case it later."

"It ain't locked."

"You sure? Keep walkin. Don't look back."

They could see the two-door '38 Pontiac sedan parked at the curb from their window. There were radios or something in the back seat. A lot of stuff.

Jack put on his roller skates and went downstairs to skate back and forth along the sidewalk. The thing wasn't locked. Jack was so excited he could not skate fast enough to tell Bill.

If they waited until dark, it might be gone.

They went down the back stairs, around the block, to come up on the car from the direction of town. Bill went straight to it, opened the door, and handed out the stuff as if it were his own. There were an electric guitar with amplifier and mike and three guns in canvas cases. Jack carried the guns like cordwood; Bill struggled with the guitar and big amplifier. They went past the house, around the corner, and up the back stairs. Once inside, they locked the door; Bill stashed the stuff in the wardrobe and told the boy to go with him for a walk.

He followed Bill through a couple of bars where Bill claimed he was looking for a man and only took a couple of drinks with a glass of beer at each place to ease his disappointment in not finding him. They arrived back at the house around dark. The car was still there. About eight o'clock Jack saw a man come to the car. He put his hands on his hips and stared at it angrily for a few minutes, then stomped off in the direction of the main street. Soon he was back, waiting beside the car until a police car pulled up and two cops got out. The man was young, wore a cowboy hat and fringed jacket.

"Probably with a band," Bill guessed.

That was good. That meant that he would be moving on soon, Bill explained.

When the police left, the man got in his car, slammed the door, and drove off very fast.

They looked at the wardrobe. Bill took the stuff out. There was a worn slide-action 12-gauge shotgun in one case, an over-and-under .22-410 and a nearly new Winchester .30-30 carbine in the other two cases.

"Can we keep the guns?" Jack felt he ought to have some say. He had spotted the stuff, had cased it and helped kyp it. "We can go hunting." There was the shotgun for Bill. It was as long as Jack. The over-under for his mom; and the carbine fit him just fine.

"Look out there! That thing might be loaded." Bill ducked away. Then, "See, you don't know how to handle guns. A kid can't be trusted with a rifle like that."

"I'll be careful. I won't never put no bullets in it. I just want it, Bill. Please."

"Honey, I don't feel safe with guns around," his mother said. "They make me nervous. Even unloaded ones."

"I saw it first," Jack complained. "You didn't give me nothin for Christmas. You gave away my bike. I just *want* it. I always wanted a real gun like that."

"Knock it off. I won't have none of that baby shit. Just proves you ain't ready for a gun like that. When you prove you're man enough to handle one sensibly, then you can have one. Now, are you going to well up and bawl? Mama's big boy want a real gun to go bang-bang?" he mocked.

The boy stifled the sniffles. The first thing next morning he was going to Sears and steal himself a Red Ryder air rifle just like the one Bill had hocked on him in Mobile. He wasn't interested in the electric guitar or the microphone. Bill plugged it in and got a hell of a noise before blowing every fuse on the floor. He quickly stashed the stuff back in the wardrobe.

When the lights came back on, Bill explained, "We'll let that stuff cool awhile in there. Ought to be worth three-four hundred. That's a good rig. They'll be watchin for it for awhile. Catch us with that stuff and it's hard-rock city."

"Can't we please keep the guns, Bill?"

"Well, maybe that ain't such a bad idea at that. Might be easier to trace them than anything."

"If we do, can I have that carbine?"

"Yeh."

"Boy!" He threw his arms around Bill's neck. "Come on. Don't be a baby. Act like a man."

Three days later Jack opened the wardrobe, and the stuff was gone. Bill said he had met a man who was willing to take it off his hands. With money in his pocket, he was too busy looking for important contacts he had to make in bars to seek work. His toolbox sat day after day by the door, too heavy for the boy or his mother to move very far alone. Together one day they shoved it under the bed. When Bill came weaving home, he demanded to know where the hell it was.

"We just put it out of the way so we wouldn't trip over it," Wilma explained.

"Smart-aleck goddamned thing to do. Suppose that means you don't think I'm lookin for a job. Well, that just shows what a couple of dumb peapickin pieces of shit you two are. I got a deal on. 'S goin to make plenty. Goin to get me a right sort of partner and set up a shop and bid on some of this construction that's goin on around here. Now's the time to start. No way you can lose. *No* way. Get a little place started. Get a defense contract. Got it made. Guys 'er doin it all over. This is my big chance. Chance to become somethin. Just need a couple of partners with a little capital. Could be in business next week. You think I'm just drinkin around. Well, that shows how damn small you are." He tapped his head. "They gotta get up early to beat Bill Wild. This is it. It's now er never. I gotta get around and see a couple of people. I can put this together if you'll stay off my back."

Which was why Wilma and the boy never saw any of the money he got for the guitar and guns except a single at a time. Jack and his mother continued to steal a dollar's worth at the A & P for every dollar they spent. Nothing changed in their life except Bill, who became more distant, quarrelsome, and mean.

A constant row centered around their diet. Bill decreed that oats and eggs were the most nutritious of breakfasts. That Jack could not swallow either without gagging was taken as a personal criticism by Bill, or at least a sissy trick that could be overcome by threats, cuffings, determination, and fasting. When the boy and his mother brought home a box of Rice Krispies as an alternative, Bill threw them in the trash and stomped them down with his foot. It was eat oats and eggs or go without. Jack preferred to starve, at least until he could cut out of the house and forage the city for himself. Nor did the prospect of a piece of meat for dinner hold any appeal for the boy, for if the piece had a rim of fat, he was expected to eat the fat and swab the plate clean with a torn slice of bread, either of which made him want to puke. Instead he lived on little stolen packets of crackers and a can of tuna opened and eaten with a Scout knife in the alley, a bottle of pop, candy, a big King Orange and bought sandwich and nickel cup of nuts. In his mind's eye he would see Bill bite a rubbery, cold, boiled egg and know what a dumb bastard and loser *he* truly was.

Everything Jack did was wrong according to Bill. Jack felt Bill hated him. He called him all kinds of names all the time: twirp, punk, shit, mama's boy, sissyboy, Mortimer Snerd, bastard, sonofabitch, creep, jerk, dummy, and combinations thereof, until knowledge of Bill's existence somewhere on earth weighed a constant ton in the boy's heart. When Bill was around, the boy was braced for a slap, poke, or jibe every second. Nothing the boy did pleased Bill: not the way he looked, acted, talked, moved, failed to move—it was as if his very breathing angered the man. How it got that way, he was at a loss to know. He was reluctant to look in a mirror and went days at a time without getting a glimpse of himself. Coming on his reflection by chance in a plate-glass window was like bumping into an old acquaintance. He was getting pretty tall. He was getting skinny, too. His face seemed bonier. He felt his jowls for flesh. The sleeves of the jacket he had stolen a scant two months before in Mobile just reached his wrists. His dungarees cleared the tops of his tenners by three inches. His lank blond hair fell across his brow, and he sort of tipped his head toward his left shoulder to keep it out of his eye; it feathered over his ears. Maybe that was what annoyed Bill. That business with his head. Bill liked a kid to keep a neat haircut.

Jack took a dime into the nearest Barber College and bought himself a butch, a real Army job, a crew cut that left a quarter-inch of stubble on his pale scalp. When he went home, his mother cried and wanted him to wear a cap so she wouldn't have to see his naked head. His cap was two sizes too large. It rested on his suddenly very visible ears.

Bill came home and said, "You can go without supper. I can't eat and look at it."

Nothing he did was right. He curled up on his bed with a funny book, thinking if things didn't change around there pretty soon, he was going to run off and go to his grandma's.

Bill also became very suspicious of what Jack did all day. Even when he brought in something he had stolen that Bill could use or sell, Bill took it as something expected. If a few days went by and Jack did not turn up with something of value, Bill began picking on him until his rage was sufficiently stimulated and he could properly hit the boy. The boy's every private moment, thought, dream was an unspoken affront.

Jack stayed out of the room from early morning until ten or so at night, running the streets, hanging around the library, the bus station, stores, and as it got a bit warmer, haunting the park that ran down the center of the main drag, looking to see some sailor reach under his girlfriend's dress. Once even hiding under a bush while a sailor put it to a drunk woman right on a bench while traffic moved along the street not fifteen feet away. Then the sailor got up, buttoned up all the buttons in the front of his pants, and swaggered away, setting his cap, leaving the woman sprawled on the bench, slowly coming to realize her rider had gone. Jack crawled out from under the bush and drifted over on the off chance he might take the sailor's place.

She wore a perforated rubber girdle from which the crotch had been unsnapped. Her snotty russet bush looked like a runover squirrel between her beefy thighs. Jack smelled the sour booze smell of her and decided to pass the possibility of taking the sailor's place.

"Where'd he go?" she asked blearily, unsure of when he had disappeared.

"He left," the boy told her.

"Rotten sonofabitch'n bastard. Goddamn swab jockey. Never trust a fuckin sailor. Only myself to blame. I goddamn ought to know. Been married to one for eight years. Who're you?"

"Jack Andersen."

"I knew a Jack Andersen once. Fuggin gunner's mate on the *Wichita*. You ain't no relation, are you?"

"I was *born* in Wichita," Jack offered.

"Ain't it a small world?"

She hoisted herself up, spilling her purse out from where it had pillowed her head. Her hat, with a long, broken pheasant's tail feather, hung from her loose pompadour over her right eye. She tugged down her skirt, not bothering to try to hook her crotch piece. Jack dove under the bench for her purse. He tossed her coin purse deftly under the nearby bush. He handed her the stuff and the purse. She fumbled it back together, dropping half the stuff all over again. She turned with her back to the streetlight to see how she looked in her mirror. She pushed futilely at her hair and hat. Her blouse was undone, and her loose bra was tugged up over her flabby breasts. Jack reached out and squeezed one.

"Hey, what the hell you doin? Hey! You little fart. Leave that alone." She got lipstick unsteadily all over her mouth, belched, and said, "Fuggit. . . . Hey, kid, leave my tit alone." She slapped his hand, slipped

386

back on the bench, and her face disappeared under her hat and the dinky fur collar of her cloth coat.

He reached up between her warm beefy thighs and pushed his hand between them until he felt the long slit under hairs that felt stiff as mattress stuffing. She sort of spread herself.

*"Hey, you! What the hell you doin?"*

Jack broke in the opposite direction of the voice. Fast. God, he could sprint! He was gone. He circled around.

"Man, lookee here, Ace. What we found here?"

"Finders keepers, losers weepers, buddy."

"Hey, you two sonsabitches know a gunner's mate off the *Wichita* name of Jack Andersen?"

"We sure do, honey. He said as soon as we got ashore to look you up."

"And here we are."

One on each arm, they hoisted the drunken woman up and between them dragged her over into the shadow of a dark bush.

"Listen, one you guys got a drink on yuh?" she asked when they let her down on the ground.

"Sure, honey. Sure." But neither produced a bottle.

When the first was between her legs and began hunching her, she mused, "You don't know Jack Andersen at all."

When the second had done with her and buttoned his pants and both had walked out of the park together, leaving her sitting drunkenly in the dark of the bush, the damp beginning to come down, the chill seeping along the ground, she cried out, *"What kind of dirty bastards are yuh, leavin a woman here all alone without a drink or shit?* Rotten goddamn swab jockeys. Fug 'em every damn one! Fug 'em all! Fug 'em all!" She collapsed on her back, her right leg bent under her, her crotch bare to the cold night dew.

Jack slipped from one shadow to another and got her coin purse from the bush. Across the street from the park and a block from where he left the woman, he went up to a cop.

"There's a drunk woman back there in the park passed out under a bush. Someone might hurt her."

"Thanks, sonny. You oughta stay out of there after dark. Lot of stuff goin on in there not fit for a lad to see. It's the war."

Jack went on. There were three dollars and change in the woman's purse. And a rosary with brown wooden beads. He threw away the beads lest they put some kind of curse on him.

Bill demanded to know where the hell he had been. He turned over the purse less one dollar, telling Bill he had found it. Bill did not even say thanks. His mother warned him about staying out so late.

The worst thing was the way Bill began waking Jack in the morning by thumping him on the head. It was like being awakened with a hammer; like being roused with electric shock. It was torture that in a split instant ripped through any deep boyish dream to some maddening nerve complex deep within the marrow. He was completely aware of the pain long before he was able to rouse himself to react to it sufficiently to cause Bill to stop. Though the entire torture might last no longer than it took to count to three, it was ultimate and all the boy could stand. He was awakened every morning cursing, weeping, flailing ineffectually, and if he cursed Bill aloud or inadvertently took a swing at him, he got beaten.

Once he connected in flailing protest with Bill's whiskery face. "Hit *me,* you goddamned mama's boy, sugar-tit, ass-kissin little whiney punk! Sleep there all damn day if I let yuh! Too fuckin good to eat what I eat, do what I do. Got to have *tuna fish,* and milk shakes. I'll tear your goddam ass off, goddamn you!"

Jack still did not understand what Bill was so mad about, nor why *he* had to leap up every morning when they weren't going anywhere. Bill was still working on his deal, the problems of which seemed to make him all the meaner. He'd come home drunk, quarrel with Wilma or Jack, slap them around. Then he'd send Jack outside so he could screw Wilma with the lights on. Otherwise, he'd screw her in the dark in spite of her whispered pleas to please wait until Jack was asleep, while Jack lay staring at the dark shapes humping in the bed six feet away, hearing their flesh slap, sensing the friction between them there in the dark.

"Little creep's playin possum!" Bill cried and pounced from the big bed. His long, partially erect cock swung between his scrawny legs in a silhouette against the window.

*Thonk! Thonk! Thonk!* came the raps on his skull. "Piss call, you little shit!" Bill cackled cruelly. "Get up and piss, the world's on fire!"

"I'LL KILL YOU, GODDAMN YOU!" the boy screamed, throwing himself up and at his hard-muscled, bandy-legged tormentor. Snapping to bite his face, reaching to claw pieces off him.

"Kill me, you miserable punk? I'll show you what it's all about. *Kill me?* Take a better man than you." He busted the boy with a right hook that knocked him flat against the wall like a thrown dog. He hit him again coming off the wall with a ripping uppercut in the side. Face down

388

on the bed, the boy was only partially aware of the man beating his head and back with his fists.

"Tell me you'll kill me, you goddamn twirp. I'll break your goddamn back."

Somewhere his mother was shrieking for Bill to stop it. She had yanked on the light, breaking the string to the pull. She stood in her slip in the bed, bouncing up and down like a hysterical child, shrieking that Bill was killing the boy.

Someone in the hall bellowed, *"If you don't knock that off in there, I'm calling the cops."*

Bill and Wilma shut up as if someone had pulled their plug. She leaped to the boy's side. She got a wet cloth to staunch the blood, cradled his beaten face against her breast. He heard her tell Bill, "Damn you! If you have hurt him permanently, I'll leave you. And I won't come back. Goddamn drunken— How could you do something like this?"

"Aw dummy up," sleepily, drunkenly, from the covers. "He'll be all right. Think that's something? Ought to seen what my old man did to me the time me and my brother, Paul, burned down the chicken coop sneaking a smoke. Took a whiffletree to us. Seen him knock a mule cold with a whiffletree. We couldn't walk straight all summer."

"You're so damn tough. Well, it didn't take no bravery to beat up on this boy. You better get ahold of yourself or you're going to wake up and find yourself in a nuthatch one day."

"Is that so?" He rolled over and pulled her onto the bed.

"Let me *go!* I got to tend to him. Now. . . . Stop it, Bill. I'm certainly not in the mood."

There was no way to turn out the light without standing on the bed. He would not let her up. While Jack cried inside, curled in a warm cocoon of pain, she took it on her side, facing the boy, her eyes closed.

"Please, not like this. Not with the light on, Bill."

He reached across her and took a heavy glass ashtray from the window sill and scored a bull's-eye on the bulb, which exploded the room into darkness.

He rolled her over and got on top, catching back her left leg in the crook of his arm. When he was about to come and felt she had held back to spite him, he punched her face with his free hand. She did not cry out but merely cursed him quietly and cried herself to sleep.

The next morning it was all a bad joke on old Bill. He was happily soused by the time Jack awoke, wanting to examine the bruise that covered the left side of his face, in which his eye was somewhere locked in a pocket of pus. He could see in his mother's eyes how hideous he looked. He did not want Bill to touch him.

"Come on, Son, I won't hurt you. I promise. Let me look at it. You know if I was myself, I wouldn't do something like that to you for the world. Somebody must of slipped me some bad stuff. Made me crazy like that."

Since Wilma seemed so ready to accept the explanation, Jack found it difficult to shore up the hatred of the night before.

"Look, Sonny, I'd do anything to make it up to you. Don't you know that? It hurts me as much as you." Then when Jack looked skeptical, "Lay one on me if it'll make you feel better. Lay one right on my button." He indicated the spot with his forefinger, sticking his chin out a mile.

Jack hit. Without warning or change of expression, he swung his right fist with all his might, aiming with his good eye for the point of Bill's chin. The shot stunned Bill. It sat him back in his chair. He couldn't speak for a minute. Tears filled his eyes. Then he said huskily, "I had that comin. OK. Put 'er there, pal. Even-steven." He offered to shake hands. Jack shook warily. "Think you chipped a tooth." He spit a particle onto the floor. He rubbed the knot growing on his jaw.

He fished a dollar from his pocket and gave it to the boy. "Go to the store and get a piece of liver big enough to cover that side of your face. Keep the change for yourself."

When Jack returned, Bill tenderly dressed the terrible bruise. Jack could see even he was worried about it. There was a blood vessel ruptured in there. Both Bill and Wilma knew it and were afraid to mention it in front of the boy.

"I'm worried about the eye," she whispered when the boy was in the bathroom.

"Dummy up. Don't worry about it. You want him to hear?"

When Bill had gone, the boy told his mother, "If he's knocked out my eye, I'm going to kill him."

"Don't talk like that," she shushed him.

"I mean it, Mom."

"It's going to be all right."

"I just wanted you to know."

"Rest now." She lay down beside him in the big bed, and his pillow smelled like Bill. He slept until noon.

In a couple of days, when he felt like going out into the street, people stared at the bruised side of his face. He could see light as a bloody glow through the slit of his left eye. He knew he wasn't going to be blind on that side.

Amazingly, many people looked back at him as if they thought he must somehow have deserved the injury—or why else would he have it? As often as there were looks of pity and concern, there was that prim self-righteous rejection of anybody who would get himself in such a scrape.

He leaned against the corner of the bus station watching the girls in their short dresses and chunky platform shoes trot by, hurrying home from work to get ready to go out. The first wave of sailors swarmed out of the station. He flitted among their hurrying legs, plucking at a sleeve here and there.

"Sailor, can you give me a dime or somethin? I lost my money and I can't get home."

He collected fifty cents in less than fifteen minutes. He wondered why Bill was so proud he had never panhandled.

The sailors washed out of the station onto the town, hailing every taxi in sight, piling in by threes and fours. The neon began stuttering on. Someone turned up the Mighty Wurlitzer. The streetlights all along the boulevard parkway came on like a great string of pearls.

# 34

HIS mother told him to wait across the street while she went over into the Brass Hat Bar & Grill. Her plan was to cop a sailor's wallet and slip it out to the boy, who would run it home to Bill. In all the bars he haunted, Bill hadn't found the perfect partner with whom he could open a shop. They were broke again.

For the first hour the boy waited, he examined the cars parked at the new meters along the curb. He wished they had a car. On his side of the street there was a colored café in what had once been a store, the plate-glass windows unshaded, the interior lit brightly as a bus station. Inside, men in two-tone, dagger-toed shoes and drape trousers with a reet-pleat twirled four-foot watch chains, jiving the chicks in their fuzzy plaid skirts and tight little Lana Turner sweaters—zoot!

Old colored men in overalls and work shoes did a little careful jiving standing outside, looking in the windows, grinning toothlessly at one another, jogging their recollections while the desire to be young again danced in their rheumy eyes.

The war was something remote the white man cooked up. It was his business. But if it gave black men better jobs and a little fun. . . .

Two colored mess cooks in tailormade dress blues held the center floor, jitterbugging with two tall girls who were all elbows, knees, and pickaninny hairdos. It looked as if one girl was thrown through the other. The old men clapped hands and stamped their feet to a more basic rhythm which they heard somewhere deep in themselves, way beyond the saxophones. When the sailors tossed the chicks overhead, Jack could see their white panties. The sailors' hair was cut like the porter's on a box of Cream of Wheat, while the zoot-suiters' hair beneath their flat porkpie hats with the six-inch brims looked like crinkled black patent leather. Still, in a strange way the drape-shapes seemed more uniformed than the mess cooks.

A police car slowed almost to a stop in the street. The two white faces in the front seat cased the action in the well-lit café. One said something to the other. They both laughed. They drove off.

Across the street, the door to the Brass Hat opened into a tiny, deep-blue-lit alcove between the door and a heavy curtain. Behind the neon wheel in the narrow, horizontal front window a similar curtain closed the bar's interior to the eyes of the passersby.

Two colored shoeshine boys eyed the white boy solemnly, their eyes flat behind films of suspicion. Then they seemingly blanked him from their minds after deciding he was no trouble. It made Jack feel invisible. After awhile he went inside to buy a Coke.

"Sorry, this is a *colored* café," the tall man behind the counter said. "We don't serve white folks in here."

Jack wanted to explain he didn't consider himself "white folks" but did not know how to begin. Some people turned blank, staring, somewhat annoyed faces toward him.

"I didn't know," he said, taking back his dime.

The man resumed a conversation with a boy and girl at the counter as if Jack had already gone, giving the place where the dime had lain an absent flick with his cloth. Jack felt he was clearly on the wrong side of the street.

He crossed over to sit on the fender of a Terraplane and watch the door. An hour passed. Two sailors went inside and came right back out. One said, "Fuckin brass-asses."

Hanging on the arm of an officer, a woman wearing a box jacket, a snap-brim felt hat with long feathers and woodsy stuff bulging from the crown, and a flowered crepe dress whipping above her knees turned into the dim bar. Her shoes had soles an inch thick and straps around her ankles. A thin gold ankle bracelet caught the light under her sheer, dark hose. A brown bag hung from her left shoulder. Her high, wide hips accidentally bumped the officer in the blue entrance, then she bumped him again on purpose, and they laughed in each other's faces, happy. They hadn't even noticed the boy when they passed.

A clock in a jewelry store down the block told him he had been waiting over an hour. He would give her thirty more minutes, then he was going in. The door glowed like an illuminated blue bottle. When someone was inside, between door and curtain, they seemed bottled medicinally. He stared at the door as if by the power of will he could draw his mother forth. His gorge felt knotted with hatred. *She's so goddamned selfish!* he told himself. *Goddamn her! I ain't waitin out here all night.* He had a vision of her in trouble in there. The movie version of a waterfront deadfall came to life in his stare that penetrated the silent walls.

He hopped off the fender and went through the forbidding door as if packing a gun, on the verge of tears. He slipped through the inner curtain. It was a moment before he could see, the place was so dim.

People were three deep at the bar, a forest of long blue serge legs masking rayon-sheathed knees on the stools. Three levels of sound circled one another like dogs. Under it all, the constant blue poop-poop of the juke was the catalyst melding the high shriek of women for whom tomorrow is as distant as old age with the cracked "old boy" baritones of college frat houses. The bar was Officers' Territory, not by fiat but through possession. When anyone in bell-bottoms wandered in, no one had to tell him to leave. Though an occasional chief petty officer, part of a flying P-boat team, or a pilot himself would not be unwelcome, the lowest-ranking cocks in the pit were naval air cadets, who could only drink while wearing their caps backward. The boy stood there blinking in the dim light.

"Hey! No kids allowed in here." The bartender spotted him through the pack at the bar. "You can't sell papers in here." He didn't have any papers.

"I gotta see my ma."

"*Wanda!*" the bartender called.

"Here, you, little boy, you can't come in here." A dark-haired waitress trying to grow the world's tallest pompadour bustled up. "No kids allowed."

"I gotta see my mom a minute."

"Your mom ain't here," she assured the boy in a perfunctory way. Her eyes swept over him, plucking the skinned-up leather jacket, his faded Penney's polo shirt, the faded knee-popped dungarees as if seeing something obscene. "Out!"

He was braced in case she tried to rush him. Tears blurred his vision. Cadets with frozen fraternal smiles began to sense his presence as an intrusion on their good time. They smiled because he was a boy. But their eyes had the look they had for dogs. "I gotta see 'er." He shouldered past the waitress.

"Here! Come back here!" the bartender honked. He moved along behind the bar.

The boy shoved through the clot at the end of the narrow room where the bar jutted onto the dance floor. There was just enough room for the dancers to wiggle. The juke was playing "The Pompton Turnpike," a long, wavering, honky blues that brought the dancers' bellies together. The boy jostled his way among the dancers, searching for a female shape as subtly different from the other women in their short skirts and square, padded shoulders as one officer was from another. The soft rubbery bottom of a woman bumped him. She missed a step and turned to glare at the incredible urchin wandering in a tin-pan dead end, a place of no lasting memory or deep regret, a way station on the way to war. The thin red smoke of cigarettes hung like the glow of technicolor fire.

"Mama!" There she was belly to belly with a tall dark-haired officer with a tired young businessman's face. He tugged her sleeve.

"Hey, what the hell's this?" the officer barked, looking down. "Is this yours?"

Such a good-time smile faded from her face. "No," small. Her eyes were bleary, blank. "I never saw him before." She looked at him as if he were trash.

He was crushed. The knot inside him tightened until the words were squeezed out in a hoarse, tortured croak. "I'm your son, goddamn it! What are you tryin to do?"

"Is that right?" the officer asked. "Is that right?"

"No! He's nuts. I never saw him before in my life." She tried to talk to Jacky with her eyes, warning him not to queer the setup.

He knew what she was doing. He didn't give a damn. She had been in there all that time drinking and belly-rubbing with that fuck while he waited outside like some crumby pup. "You are *too* my mom!" he croaked loudly, tears again filling his eyes. He hung on to her.

394

"I'll have him thrown out." The officer looked around. He had been drinking.

"*Let go!*" she hissed. "Run along and be a good boy. Why don't you give him some money and maybe he will go away?" she suggested, dragging her partner over to their upholstered booth.

"Hunh? What?"

"Give him something and he'll go away." She spoke as if the boy were a Mexican beggar who did not understand English. "Give him something, honey, he's embarrassing me. Give him a couple of dollars and he'll go away."

The officer slid four bits to the edge of the table.

"You are so my mama," Jack blubbered, the tears finally breaking through. "*I hate you!* You stinkin slut!"

"Here there, you little bastard! You can't talk like that!" He was coming up in his seat. The woman hung onto his right arm for dear life.

"No. No. Give him something and get rid of him," she insisted. Then she had his wallet in her hand. "Here!" She threw the boy two bills. "Now get lost!" Her eyes softened to a plea after her hard words.

"What the hell did you give him there?" The officer tried to see over the lip of the table.

There was a ten and a fiver on the dance floor at the boy's feet. He scooped them up and slipped them in his pocket. He turned and slid away. Fifteen was a lot.

"Hold on there!" the officer called.

"Let him go. Good riddance. I've seen things like that before. They'll stick to you like a leech, call out the awfulest things about you in public. Just want you to give them some money to go away. Kiss me. Umm." The crowd closed behind him.

"Don't you ever come back in here again," the bartender warned. The waitress glared at him as though she wanted to spit. He slipped between the curtains, hardly disturbing them, into the blue entrance, out onto the street. "Fuck 'er," he hissed aloud to himself. He spat a tiny bullet as if trying to get rid of a bad taste. His mouth felt dry.

Bill was stretched out on the bed in his trousers, socks, and undershirt with a pillow wadded at his back for a prop, reading a *True Detective* under the bare overhead light. A cigarette with a long, dangling ash hung from the corner of his mouth. When the boy laid the tenspot and the five on his belly, the ash fell down his neck. He brushed it into a gunmetal blaze on the front of his undershirt.

"That's it?" he asked. He wasn't as happy as the boy had expected, after all.

Jacky told him how he had got tired of hanging around outside and gone in to see what was happening and that she had given him the dough to get him to go. Bill grinned. He clapped the boy on the shoulder. He folded the bills together, swung his feet off the bed, and began to put on his shoes and socks.

"Where you goin?" the boy asked.

"Gotta go see a man. Be back."

Bill came in about midnight, his eyes lit by Calvert Special, moving neatly as if the floor were a deck and he were on a cruise. His speech was never slurred until he was just about gone. He spoke carefully. "Your mother hasn't come back yet, hunh?"

"No."

"Well, I guess she'll be along directly." He sat heavily on the bed and began pulling off his shoes. "Might as well hit the sack, pardner. It's a hard life if you don't weaken. And tomorrow's another day. No sense in us just waitin up for her." Sitting on the edge of the sagging bed in his underwear, he tilted up his pint. Before he capped it he offered the bottle to the boy, who shook his head no thanks. Bill set the bottle on the floor where it would be handy during the night. "Turn out the light will you, Son?" he asked. The boy dutifully pulled the light string and hopped back into his cot.

He had dozed off and awakened and dozed off. It seemed something blocked him from the true depths of sleep. Bill snored loudly in the big bed. He dozed and roused again. At first he thought it was an electric barrier in his mind again that had barred him from sleep.

"Mama!" He lay tense, straining to hear, listening to the swarming darkness. There was a car door slammed. Then another. *That was his mother's laughter!* There were the voices of two men.

*"No you don't, goddamn you!"* one called.

*"Hey, baby . . ."* the other called.

*"I gotta go in, fellas,"* his mother's voice wheedled drunkenly. *"You've had your fun, come on now."*

*"Hey! Stop her. That bitch's got my wallet."*

There was the sound of feet on the downstairs porch.

*"No! Leave me alone! OW! OW!"* Those were slaps.

The boy spoke. "Bill?"

"Yeh?" He wasn't asleep.

"That sounds like Mom."

"Naw. That can't be her. That's a bunch of rumdumbs on a toot."

The sounds of scuffling went off the porch. *"No, don't! I don't want to go! Leave me alone!"* Two car doors slammed. *"BILL!"* she cried out. Then the car roared off. The boy leaped to the window. He saw a dark turtleback sedan careen around a corner. He could see the shadows of two heads in the back seat. In his heart he knew one was his mother.

"That was Mom, Bill," he told the figure on the bed staring into the dark.

"Naw, I don't think so, kid. Don't you worry about that girl. She's been there and back. If anyone can take care of herself, it's her. If she ain't back by morning, we'll go find her."

The boy was crying quietly. He felt guilty for all the mean things he had thought about her while waiting outside the bar. What if she never came back?

"Hey, come on, dummy up, little buddy." Bill rose on one arm and reached between the beds to touch the boy. "She'll be all right. She's too smart for some peapicker to hurt her. Tryin to pin her down when she don't want to be pinned is like tryin to pick up mercury. You don't know your old lady very well, but she and me been in scrapes that would scare the nuts off a brass monkey. And she's cool as a safe-cracker. Don't you worry about her."

"But I do," the boy blubbered.

"Why, don't you think if I was worried I wouldn't go right now and bring her back?"

"Yeow. . . ."

"Well, then? Come on and have a little snort." He lifted up the bottle. The boy took a sip. The man tipped it for him. He took a real drink. It burned, but he no longer gagged from the taste. "Atta boy. Get roughy-tough." Bill nearly finished the bottle, leaning there in the dark. "We gotta stick together, you and me. Oh, I know your grandma and grandpa set your head against me like I'm some kind of bum cause I take a drink. But when I'm workin, there ain't a better master sheet-metal mechanic anywhere than Bill Wild. Hunh?" When the boy had remained silent, he gave him a nudge with his elbow. "You know that. Don't you know that?"

"Yeow," the boy responded.

"Hell, yes. . . . Hey, come on, buck up. Step on your lip." He roughly plucked the boy's lower lip in a motion as if to tear it off. When the boy jerked away, he laughed. The rotten-sweet smell of his boozy breath made the boy feel drunker. "You know, I always *wanted* a son. Your mom would like a little girl, you know. Too bad. Looks like she can't have no more kids. We tried. And nothin. It ain't me, I know that. But I want to tell you somethin. Listen, I wouldn't have married your mom if I hadn't seen right from the start what a regular fella you were goin to be. I mean to tell you, if you had been some cringin, sissy kind of kid, I'd of just thrown my hat out the door and gone after it."

"You're always tellin me how I'm just a dumb Swede and ain't no good for nothin and call me all those names," the boy said with some heat underlying his sulkiness.

"Yeh, well, you don't want to take seriously everything I say. I say a lot of stuff I wouldn't if I stopped to think. I'm a tense guy. That's why I take a drink or two, to relax me, so I can think an operate. You just want to know, I always think you're one of the best damn kids I ever knew. Put 'er there, Son." He wanted to shake on it. Jack shook.

"From now on, things are going to be different. I'm goin to be a *real* father to you, see you get all the things I never had. If you will, I'd like you to call me Dad." He gripped the boy's left bicep. "How about it?"

"OK," the boy agreed hollowly, without enthusiasm.

"You just think I'm talkin. But you'll see. I promise yuh. May I be struck dead on the spot if I'm lyin. Hunh? Is it a deal, Son?"

He was drinking, but he seemed so damn sincere. There was no doubt Bill *could* turn the world around if he really wanted to. He had put out his hand again. In the dark the boy could see the pleading look on the man's face. If only it was so. . . . He let his heart out a length when it wanted to leap miles. He took Bill's hand again.

"Come on, Son, crawl in here with ole Daddy Bill till your mama comes home." He flung back the sheet.

Jacky crawled over him to where his mother usually slept next to the wall and lay rigidly on his back staring up at the dark ceiling.

"Come on, don't be so unfriendly. We can be pals." Bill slipped his arm under the boy's head and cradled it roughly against his shoulder. "When I get me my shop, I'll teach you all I know. An' when I get old, it'll be yours."

"Can I go to school when it starts again?"

"Hell, yes! And in style. You'll have as good clothes as the rest of the kids. And all the advantages I never had. I had to work after school to help support our family. I want you to play ball and enjoy yourself. Do all them things I never got to do. Jazz them little hotass cheerleaders, hunh?" He leered in the dark and gave the boy a jog on his shoulder. "Bet you'd like that, check?"

"Yeow."

"Betcher ass. I know how boys are. Better'n your mama. She don't know how us guys are, really. She asked me to have a talk with you. Said you were bother'n around her about it, yuh know what I mean? Hell, I understand that. We all go through that. 'Member when I made her let you have a feel of her business?"

The boy nodded that he did.

"How'd that make yuh feel?"

"Funny."

"How?"

"Well, sorta good."

"She says you play with yourself a lot. Is that so?"

"Well, not an awful lot."

"Would you like to feel what mine feels like?" He reached for the boy's hand, catching his left wrist.

"Naw, I don't think so. . . ." He resisted slightly.

Bill just pulled his hand over and wrapped it around his long, upstanding penis. It made a tent under the sheet. He tried to get the boy to jack it, but Jacky wasn't jacking anybody's but his own. He tugged free.

"I just thought you'd like to see. OK. Let's cop a snooze."

The boy rolled over away from the man to face the wall. When Bill's breathing became regular, the boy permitted himself to slip into the shallows of sleep.

He sensed it before he was awake. Then he was wide awake. Bill held him cradled in his right arm with barely breathing space against the wall. "*I'll* be your Daddy," he heard Bill mutter. His big rigid penis was between Jack's legs from behind. Bill had him clamped in the position by the curl of his own body. He was slipping down the boy's shorts with his left hand.

"*Bill!*" When the man only grumbled, Jack began to fight, flinging back his sharp left elbow repeatedly, spitting like a cat. It stopped the downward crawl of his jockey shorts.

"Come on, Wilma," the man said thickly.

"*I ain't Wilma!*" Jack let him know. His elbow caught Bill's chin. There was a wet china click.

"Hey . . ." the man said, rolling heavily over, his erection already dying.

The boy clambered over the man, who now lay with his forearm over his eyes. "Where you goin?" Bill asked.

"To my own bed."

"Listen, don't get the wrong idea, kid. I mistook you for your old lady." He laughed cruelly. " 'Fraid I was goin to make a punk uh yuh? You crazy fuckin Swedish peapicker, crawlin your little ass out of bed actin like I was some kind of queer. '*I bane a Swede from Minny-sota.* I bane a *car-painter,*' " he mocked the boy.

Jack was done with tears.

"What do you think I was tryin to do to you, boy?" Bill raised up and demanded in the dark. The boy lay silent, warily watching the dark figure in the other bed. "Answer me, damn it!" He hit the boy with his wadded pillow as if it were a club.

"I don't know," the boy said.

"Well, it wasn't what you think. I was asleep. I thought you was your ma. That's all. An if you think anything else, you're nuts. You got that?" After a silence. "Hunh? You got that? I asked yuh."

"Yeh," grudgingly.

"You better damn sure had, boy . . . hunh?"

"I said yeah."

"Punk! You'll never amount to a damn! . . ." He drifted off.

When Bill was snoring softly, bubbling, muttering in his sleep, the boy stealthily got up and tiptoed to his trousers, from the pocket of which he took his Scout knife. He opened the big blade, and cradling the rough horn grip in his palm beneath his pillow, tiptoed into sleep.

For the first time since they had been in Pensacola, Bill did not wake the boy by thumping him on the head. Fully dressed, shaved, he shook the boy by the shoulder, not gently, but it was a remarkable improvement over being thonked. He indicated the knife that had slipped from under the boy's pillow. "If there ever comes a time, Son, when you pull one of those on me, be sure you're ready to use it."

"I just don't want you ever thumpin me on the head no more."

"That's a deal," but he didn't offer to shake. "Get up now. We gotta go look for your ma."

Jack leaped into his dungarees and sneakers, his shirt, splashed water on his face in the bathroom, and was ready to go.

"Don't you want somethin to eat?" Bill looked ready to fix something.

"No. I wanta find Mom."

"Yeh. Me, too. Come on." He dropped his arm over the boy's shoulders as they went out into the hall. "You gotta understand, kid, I don't know what all I'm sayin and only half of what I'm up to when I'm three sheets in the wind. OK?"

"Yeh."

"OK. I'm sorry."

"Yeh. So am I."

It had rained during the night. The sky was still dripping. The sidewalks were wet. It was cold. Bill said, "The whole damn city looks the color of chicken shit."

The jail was a red-brick fortress with arched doorways and a dirty octagon-tiled floor. A bench like a church pew ran along the wall on their left as they entered. A desk higher than the boy's head extended along his right to a barred gate like a cell door. Behind the desk a short hallway went back to where there was another barred door. A clock like those in schoolrooms clucked relentlessly back and forth—clock-clock, clock-clock.

"I was wonderin, Captain, you find a woman last night, Wilma Wild?"

"You lose one?"

"Yeow."

"That her *real* name?"

"Yeow."

"Who are you?"

"I'm her husband. This is her son."

The captain glanced at the boy. He turned and called back to the turnkey, "They bring in a woman named Wilma Wild last night?"

"Brought in a wild one all right. Bout kicked out Perk's eye. Name wasn't that, though."

"She's got auburn hair, about five-two, weighs about one-fifteen," Bill called back.

"Sounds like. What was she wearin?"

"Kinda uh brown suit, white blouse, brown and white shoes, a sorta little hat over one eye, like, with a feather on it."

"She wear glasses?"

"Yeow! Bifocals. Them rimless ones."

"That's her," the turnkey told the captain. "Name she gave was Mac-Deramid."

The captain went through the night arrest slips on the desk. "Wilma MacDeramid, white, twenty-eight, unmarried, 323 Cleveland Avenue. . . ."

She had given an old address in Wichita.

"Bring 'er down," the captain told the turnkey.

"What are the charges against her, sir?" Bill asked.

The captain scanned the sheet. "Plain drunk is all there is here. The officers found her wandering around out on the highway."

There was the sound of clanking back in the hallway. Jack heard his mother's voice shouting drunkenly, "Take your paws off me, you bastard! I know what you're after. You're like the rest uh them! I ain't takin *on* no more. Lousy, cheap Navy bastards."

"Hush up. Your husband and little boy are out there."

"Ain't got no goddamn husband. Ain't got no goddamn little boy. Ain't got nobody. Broke my goddamn glasses un everything, you bunch lousy crumbs, treatin a girl thisaway."

She came limping like a bird that has lost a foot, one shoe on, one shoe gone. Her face was puffed worse than it had been when she'd had all four wisdom teeth extracted the same day. Her left eye was completely closed, both eyes were discolored, all the buttons had been ripped off her blouse, her bra was ripped loose, one sleeve of her jacket was loose so the shoulder padding showed, her skirt was stained and ripped, one stocking was a sodden tangled web around her ankle, the other was held up by the scab drying on her left knee.

"This man says he's your husband and that your name is Wilma Wild," the captain explained.

"My name is MacDeramid, and I never saw this sonofabitch in my life. Never been Wild."

"The boys say it was pretty wild around here when they brought you in." The captain couldn't resist the joke.

"Screw you, *too,* buster."

"Mama!" Jack cried. "It's me. Don't you recognize me?"

"Oh! It's you. You look like some kind of Swedish peapicker to me," she said drunkenly. "To hell with both of you! I don't know these two, Captain, and I wouldn't admit it if I did. You ever see two more worthless types? If that's what's runnin around out there, I want to stay in here." She leaned on the desk on her elbow, slipped. "Oops."

"You want to pay ten dollars and sign her out?" the captain asked Bill.

"Yeow." He fished for ten Jack had brought in the night before.

"I won't go!" Wilma screeched.

"Mama, please," the boy begged.

"I ain't your mama! Never been your mama. Get him out of here!" she insisted to the captain. "I don't want him to see me like this. Don't any of you have no decency? Go *away* and leave me alone. I *like* it in here. I want to stay."

The turnkey led her to the gate, while the captain returned her property, purse, and glasses broken at the bridge, one lens chipped. "I'll get them soldered," Bill promised.

"Fuck you! I don't *want* to go!" she insisted when the captain buzzed open the door. It was the only time Jack had heard her use that word. "They don't care about me. They're the ones got me here. *Why don't you leave me be?*" she moaned at both of them. "*No!* Don't touch me."

402

She yanked her arm away from Bill on one side, then the boy on the other. "I can walk. I'll show you I can walk. Keep your hands off me from now on." She limped toward the door, one shoe on, one shoe gone. Her hips humped crazily in her twisted skirt. She held her battered face high, chin tilted challengingly to all who would look her way. Nor would she let Bill and the boy walk with her. They had to follow behind or she balked and would not go.

In the room she fell onto the bed, breathing through her mouth. Her nostrils were clogged with blood. A gurgling sound came from her throat. Jack removed her shoe and the remnants of her stockings. He brought a pan and water to wash her feet. Bill unzipped her skirt and tugged it down over her hips. "Please, no more . . . fellas. . . ." she whimpered. Her panties and girdle were gone. Her sex looked matted. Bill got off her jacket and blouse. There were dozens of bruises on her body and limbs. She bruised easily, and the things were purple and orange. Bill gave her a sponge bath with the washcloth, but even to touch her face gently with it made her stir in pain. They put a gown on her and tucked her beneath the covers.

She slept until after dark that night, wakened, was sick and had to be helped to the bathroom.

When she was back in bed, Jack bent over to tell her good night. She reached up and touched his face with the palm of her hand. "Don't look at me, honey," she said. "Your mama's a mess."

She slept until nearly noon the next day and took a little tomato soup with lemon in it for lunch. "Bastards slipped me something," she explained to Bill. "I called for you. Didn't you hear me?"

"It was too late," he said.

"Honey, I feel like I been cut open. I'd like to get a warm bath in the worst way."

"Later. You rest now."

"I just feel awful. I hurt all over. I hope they didn't bust something inside."

"Shh. You rest now."

Jack went out the next morning when she got up so Bill could help her bathe and get cleaned up. When he returned, she was sitting up in bed, looking in a hand mirror, combing rats out of her wet hair. Her face looked like hell. She was certain her nose was broken. Bill assured her it was not, but from then on it always looked a little flattened to Jack.

When she was once more asleep, Bill dumped the contents of her purse onto the table and searched it for coin. There wasn't a cent. The sailors had rolled *her*. Stuck down in the lining of a narrow compartment was a badge. Bill dug it out. Its clasp had snagged the lining.

"What's that?" the boy asked.

"Pair of wings." He tossed them on the table. "I gotta go see a man. I ain't even got dough enough for smokes. You got anything?"

"No."

When Bill went out, the boy plucked the wings of gold from the stuff on the table. He polished the face powder off them against his shirt and pinned them to the left breast of his jacket.

# 35

JACKY saw the man stagger into the park spilling cigarettes from a pack, trying to get one to his mouth. Where he leaned in the light of a bus station window, the cicadas flew headlong into the plate glass and fell dead into a windrow heaped against the building. Along buildings all over town the bugs died in heaps. People went about with their teeth set against the constant crunch of bugs underfoot. Summer had come, and was going. The nights were cool with a breeze off the Gulf. Jacky shoved off from where he lounged against the window and followed the drunk into the park, his fists plunged into the pockets of his beat-up leather jacket.

The man slumped onto a park bench. It was after eleven. The air smelled like the Gulf. It was humid. The man's chin fell onto his chest; his lighted cigarette dropped into his lap. He wore a dark suit and a lightweight black raincoat. The boy approached and lifted the cigarette from his lap and threw it away. "Hey, mister?" he called gently, shaking the man cautiously by the shoulder. "You all right? Mister?"

"Hunh? Who're you?" The man stirred blearily.

"I just saw you. You almost burned yourself up with a cigarette. I put it out for you."

"Hunh? Thanks." He made as if to lie down on the bench. The boy tugged his right arm to keep him upright. "Wanta sleep," he insisted.

"Not here," the boy said. "You wanta go home. Let me get you a cab?"

"Hunh? Let me sleep."

"No. Let me get you a cab. Come on, mister. You don't want to sleep in the park."

"Who the hell are you?" The man sat up and tried to focus on the boy.

"Let me get you a cab so you can go home."

"OK. You get me a cab." He slumped back over.

It was only a few yards to the street. The boy sprinted across to the taxi stand in front of the bus depot. He piled in the back of a Yellow cab standing there. He told the driver, "There's a guy in the park asked me to get a cab for him. He's drunk and wants to go home."

"He got the money to pay for it?" the driver asked before starting up.

"Yeow."

"OK, kid, show me where."

Jack had him pull up at the curb on a drive that went through the park and told him to wait and he would bring the fare. He found the guy still slumped on the bench, snoring. He roused him by shaking him roughly by the shoulder. He had him boozily upright on the bench when it began to sprinkle. The driver called from the street, "Hey, you comin?"

"Yeow. Hang on," the boy called back.

"Where we goin?" the drunk wondered while the boy tried to get his shoulder under the man's right arm and help him to the taxi.

"You're goin home," the boy told him. "It's startin to rain. You don't want to sleep out here in the wet."

The man put out his hand to feel the raindrops. He staggered up, leaning heavily on the boy. "You're a gentleman and a scholar, young man," he slurred.

The driver hopped out and helped the boy get the man in the cab. As soon as he was inside, the man slumped over in the corner, his chin on his chest, and muttered toward sleep. The boy piled in, too.

"Where to?" the driver asked.

"Where do you live?" Jacky shook the man.

"Don live here, jus visitin. . . ."

"Where are you staying?" He shook him again.

He mumbled something. The driver said, "I know that."

"Listen." Jack shook the man. "The driver wants to be paid before he takes you. He wants to be sure you have the money."

"I got the money."

"He wants it now."

The man fumbled at his back pocket. Jack moved quickly to help him. He got the man's thick black wallet out and asked the driver, "How much?"

"Be about three bucks, I guess." The driver craned his young canine face around to see what the boy had there. He gave the driver a ten.

"That cover it?"

"You bet, sonny."

"What's the holdup?" the drunk demanded.

"I paid the driver and gave him a little tip. Is it all right if I take a couple of bucks for my trouble?"

"Sure. Sure. Let's get this show on the road."

Jack extracted everything in the man's wallet except a five-dollar bill. The driver saw and was amazed. He just sat there silently staring in his rearview mirror. Jack returned the man's wallet to his pocket and got out. "You'll see he gets home all right, won't yuh?" he asked the driver.

"Yeh. Sure." Across his amazement a doggy grin spread.

Under a street light Jacky saw he had a twenty, two tens, and a five. He ratholed the fiver in his left-hand pocket for himself and tucked the rest in his right-hand pocket for Bill and his mother.

He wasn't sure how much he was bringing in every week, but it was more than he would have made peddling papers. He left the house before noon every day and stole something that could be hocked for at least $5 before returning at night. Tools and portable radios were his specialty; electric irons were good. Sears, Ward's, Grant's, Western Auto, Penney's, Kress, the big superdrugs—a different store every day, and never on the same day of the week. He moved beneath the sightline of adults, a common, guileless face beneath a shock of blond hair; he always moved in a store as if he were on an errand, never loitering or standing long before the thing he would steal. He would go to the item he was after, having cased it on a previous trip, lift it, and carry it out of the store in his hands. He never tried to conceal anything on his person, not even an item he might have hidden in a pocket. He carried everything out in his hands as if it were his right. Clerks had seen him go, and only a fleeting question crossed their minds.

Once he was stopped by a male clerk on the second floor of Sears with an electric iron in a box in his hands, half a counter's length from where he had found it. "Where are you going with that, sonny?" the clerk wanted to know.

"I'm just taking it to show my mother," the boy explained. "She needs one."

"Where's your mother?" the clerk inquired.

"That's her over there." He pointed out a heavyset woman in a dark coat fingering a cascade of flowered oilcloth.

"Well, you leave the iron here and ask your mother to come over and see it."

"OK."

The woman was muttering to herself, "An I told *her,* and she *heard* me tell her, I said, 'Laura, you gotta ack right now.' But nobody listens to me. . . ."

"Excuse me, lady." Jack plucked her sleeve. "That clerk over there wants to talk to you."

"Hunh? What's that? What's that?"

"He wants to talk to you." He pointed her in the right direction, saw her launched, and cut out down the stairs without ever looking back.

He went to a matinee almost every day. He would make his lunch of popcorn and a couple of candy bars in the dark theater. Whether the movie was crowded or not, he often stumbled into a seat beside a woman as if, just coming in from the streets, he could not see. Often the woman would huff at his intrusion and move away. When she did not move, he let his elbow on the arm slip over until it nudged her tit or allowed a dead hand to fall gentle as a whisper against her thigh. If she changed seats, he went back to the lobby and came in again to stumble into a seat by another.

"I've been watching you," one matron hissed. "Touch me, you little creep, and I'll call an usher."

Another dramatically plucked his hand up and dropped it back in his lap, saying, "I think you lost this." She changed seats. He troubled another woman for a light for his cigarette. He didn't inhale, but it made him look older. It didn't matter too much what the film was about, or that he had seen it before, perhaps several times before. It was the intimate atmosphere of the theater, where the ceiling was a starry night sky over a Mediterranean town, the curtains a cascade of gold, and everyone there for the matinee shared a midday loneliness. There were few men there. "Leave me alone, you little sonofabitch!" one woman cried out loud enough to cause those near to turn and stare. "My husband just shipped out, and I don't need a jerk like you!" Another, wearing her husband's wings bent into a bracelet around her wrist and smelling of whiskey, squinted through the balcony haze at him as his hand climbed over her stocking top, crawling between her hot, fat thighs, and asked, "Hey, how in the shit old are you anyway?"

"Fourteen," he croaked, advancing his age three years.

"The hell you are!" She recoiled. She was quite indignant at having been fooled. "You ought to be put away!"

Another day down front in the fourth row on the left side, he dropped his arm over the back of his seat between the legs of a teen-ager who sat scrunched down beside her girlfriend, both chewing Milk Duds. Instead of pulling away, as almost always happened, the girl scooted her tight little crotch in reach of his inching dead hand. He had two fingers in her until it felt his shoulder socket was on fire. All the while the girls spoke and giggled quietly together, watching the movie. Once the other girl peeked over the seat to see what he looked like. When he removed his fingers from the girl and got up, intending to move back beside them and continue, the girl whooped and covered her face with her hands. Leaping up, the other girl giggling right behind her, she raced up the aisle. They were fifteen or sixteen.

Once one of the ushers collared him moving from one side of the balcony to the other and warned, "I've been watching you. You light in a seat and stay there or I'm calling a cop."

Yet none of them would believe that he was anything more than a nuisance or, at worst, trying to steal some woman's purse. Down in a matinee seat all alone in a dark empty row, his jacket over his lap, throwing it to Ann Miller, Betty Grable, Alice Faye, Dorothy Lamour, he loved them all. Their big shivering thighs made his heart skip with desire. He'd jerk his wienie until the electric shudder shook him, then feel the tip with his thumb for the thin, clear smear. He would wipe the thumb on the worsted seat, unwrap a Black Cow sucker, and sit back to laugh at the cartoons with pure boyish innocence and delight.

War—as soon as he was old enough to join up he would be free of loneliness, pain, and being poor forever. The war seemed the greatest break in the world to Jacky. No other career any longer mattered. Laughing at Tom and Jerry as recruits, he found more hope for himself in a war that never ended than in any official promise of peace. In a war he had a chance. In the way things had been, even a smart guy like Bill ended up tapped out, his victories measured by the pint but ultimately paid for in time done by the yard. He was thirty-eight years old and had spent nearly half his life in jail. It was curious; Bill always thought of himself as an ex-con. Jacky, for all his daily thefts and unspeakable longings, did not think of himself as a criminal. He would join the Boy Scouts tomorrow if they would give him a bed, something to eat, and a suit.

It was a bright day. The smell of the Gulf lay over the streets. With the gold Navy flier's wings on his leather jacket, Jacky felt confident and well-routed. He dropped into Western Auto, drifting along the narrow aisle to the very back of the store, where the radios were. It was just after noon. There was a single clerk on the floor and another in the glassed-in office near the radios. There were two other customers. He picked up a two-toned gray plastic portable Motorola about the size of a loaf of bread and carried it by the handle down the other aisle and out of the store. He felt he had been seen. He felt spooky about how it had gone. Western Auto wasn't like one of the big stores. Had the clerk passed a signal to the guy in the booth? Maybe he was just getting jumpy. He had begun to be afraid of getting caught. There wasn't a store he hadn't been in at least twice. That was the second time for Western Auto. He looked over his shoulder, in spite of Bill's warning, *"Never look back. Keep walking."*

He went up the back stairs. "I think they saw me," he told Bill breathlessly, handing him the radio.

"Yeah? What makes you think so?" He slid up the roll-top door of the radio and turned it to some music, then a ball game.

"I just felt like someone was following me."

His mother clutched her robe at the throat. "I knew it! I knew this was going to happen," she told the man.

"Take it easy. Easy." He quieted them like the conductor of an orchestra. "Probably just his imagination. But we'll stash this stuff somewhere just in case." He prowled the single room looking for a place. He went into the bathroom. He came back to take two large portable radios from the wardrobe and stash them under the tub. The new thin one he slid down behind the tub in the corner.

It was a move they would look back on later as guided by Lady Luck or the best damn fool stroke Bill ever made, for it wasn't a quarter of an hour before there were cops at the downstairs door. Bill picked up on them right away.

*"Get him into the tub quick!"* He twirled the taps to fill the tub. "Get your clothes off," he told the boy.

His mother yanked off his tee shirt. *"Quick! Quick!"* She helped him into the tub, which now held about four inches of water. She shut down the taps, ducked him, and began vigorously soaping his hair.

"Open this door; police officers."

"What is it, Officers?" Bill asked solicitously.

"There a boy live here, about twelve or thirteen, blond?"

"I've a son, but he's only nine."

"Where was he about half an hour ago?"

"Why, right here. He didn't feel good this morning. His mother's giving him a bath. What's the trouble?"

"Mind if we step in and look around?"

"Sure. OK. I just wish you'd tell me what this is all about."

The two shouldered into the room, one looking to the left, one to the right. They eyed the boy's cot. One opened the wardrobe and peered inside. The door to the bath was open; one looked in, stared at the boy in the tub, the woman on her knees beside it soaping the boy's hair until it was a cap of white lather.

"What is this?" she demanded indignantly.

"How old are you, son?" the officer asked.

"Eleven."

"I thought you said he was nine?" He turned to Bill.

Wilma quickly explained, "He's nine and a half. You know how kids like to seem older."

He was really ten and a half.

"You let him run around town alone?"

"No!" As if that were the last thing on earth she would do. "He has strict orders not to cross any street. Listen, what is this all about, anyway?"

He did not answer. Turning to Bill, he took out a pad and a pencil. "What's your name?"

"Bill Wild. Listen, I've got the right of a citizen for an explanation. You can't come in here and—"

"Where do you work?"

"Well, uh, I work for Hahn Sheet Metal."

"Where's that?"

"Four eight three Peachtree."

"I never heard of that. There a 483 Peachtree?" he asked the other cop.

He hadn't heard of that one, either. "Why ain't you at work?"

"I work night shift."

"Yeh? Check him out on the box," he told the other, who then left to go call on the car radio.

"Listen here. You got a warrant?"

"No address like that," the other officer reported, hollering up the stair.

"All right, mister, let's just you and me go downtown and check you out." He reached to take Bill's arm. "Hold it! Lacy, come help me."

The other cop hurried up.

"You can't do this to me. You haven't any warrant for me."

"You come quietly or we'll take you out in cuffs."

"I'll sue you for false arrest!" Bill protested, being led out the door. "What do you think I am?"

"We know what you are. Provin it may take a little. You lousy Fagin."

When the police had left, Wilma got the boy out of the tub. They quickly dressed.

"Where are we going?" the boy asked.

"Just do what I tell you and don't ask questions."

They took nothing, in case the house was being watched. On the porch, the woman said loudly, "Now don't forget, be sure I get two quarts of milk, a loaf of bread, and something for tomorrow."

At the corner they caught a bus that took them to the bus station. They went inside, around, and quickly out the side entrance, where the woman jumped into a cab and pulled the boy after her. "Take us to the Dixie Travel Agency."

"Right." It was a thirty-five-cent drop.

The agency was a single room behind a store front on a side street, where those with cars looking to defray travel expense could pick up paying passengers bound in the same direction. A leering, side-street romeo in sideburns and a ten-gallon hat sat behind the desk.

The first destination was Shreveport, Louisiana, at 6 P.M. with room for one passenger.

"I can hold him on my lap," she argued.

"He's a little big to hold on your lap," the dispatcher argued.

"We've just got to get to Shreveport tonight. My mother died."

"Well, you can hang around and ask the driver if he can squeeze you in if a single don't show up by six."

"Pray no one comes," she told the boy. He prayed.

The man who owned the car, a '40 Mercury sedan, looked the woman and boy over carefully before he decided. "If you don't mind squeezing in the front between me and my brother, I guess we can carry you." They were two young workers in leather jackets and khakis. There was a solemn young couple already wedged in the back of the sedan with a common paper sack of clothing, another cheap soft bag, a dirty-faced little baby asleep on their laps, and on their faces the look of people who have just tapped out.

On the highway, the brother who was not driving took out a bottle and had a drink. He insisted Wilma, who sat between them, have one. She took one to oblige. The brother behind the wheel asked those in back, "Mind if I take a snort? I promise I won't put you in the ditch."

"Go ahead," the young man said distractedly.

Jack curled in the corner in the back the best he could and fell asleep.

# 36

SHREVEPORT was just waking up when the Merc rolled in through the morning mist while water trucks washed the downtown streets. They let the couple with the baby out at the bus station and drove the boy and his mother to the local branch of the Dixie Travel Agency, a store-front office down by the river. The office wasn't open. The men pulled into an alley beside the place. The woman gave the boy in the back seat fifty cents and told him to go buy himself some breakfast.

"You don't want to eat?" he asked. The two big men in the front seat, between whom she sat, stared silently ahead up the dirty alley.

"No. I'm not hungry. And if I'm not here when you get back, don't worry. Just wait for me. I'm going to send Bill a wire."

"I want to go, too," the boy said.

"No. I want you to wait here."

"Why?"

"I just do. I've got to take care of a couple of things. You would be in the way."

One of the men snorted as if stifling a laugh.

"I want to go with you," the boy insisted.

"No. Now, you can't. Do what I tell you."

He got out of the car. She looked small between the two men. The brother on the boy's side winked at him and said, "Take it easy, pal. We'll see your mama gets back all right."

He turned away to the street. They backed out of the alley and drove away. He knew where they were going. They were taking her someplace to fuck her. He knew it in his bones, and his bones felt old. Suddenly he didn't care. The smell of the river came up to him with the fragrance of pitch and jute, of wood and moist earth. Somewhere someone was frying bacon. Negroes on boxes hunkered against the walls of stores and offices all along covered sidewalks, sipping cups of hot, black chicory coffee, eating big ham and egg sandwiches, loading their cheeks with the morning's first chaw of tobacco. The boy went along with his hands in the pockets of his zipped-up jacket, the only white face in sight. But his difference was no longer important, for he was no longer afraid. His old lady was humping a couple of big guys somewhere for their fare, he was walking down a street of black men he had never walked before, and he felt safely at home for the first time in his memory. The certainty that at that very moment one of the brothers who had driven them there was fucking his mom was a matter of objective speculation rather than a source of maddening jealousy. He loved her none the less; he was merely no longer anxious about anything. *He would get by,* of that he was certain. Time suddenly became his thing, rather than the other way around. It was then just as important to him how the black men along the street looked to *him* as it was how *he* looked to them. He turned into a corner café.

On a stool at the counter he ordered. "A bowl of chili and a Coke."

The beefy red-faced woman with arms like hams wasn't sure. "For breakfast?"

Before, the hour might have intimidated him into corn flakes and milk. No more. "Yeow. And plenty of crackers, please."

The woman shrugged. She stirred the constant pot of chili on the steam table with the big ladle to break the red scum on the top and dredged up a bowlful plump with beans and hot in its peppery red grease.

"Kids run around loose now like so many stray dogs," the woman confided to an old river rat at the end of the counter, nodding at the boy hunched over the steaming bowl. "I don't know what the world's comin to."

"Always been the same. I was on the river when I wan't no older than that 'un. And doin a man's work, too. Folks got some funny idea most kids'er like some Christian plan. Hell, my experience's been—and I been all over the world, yuh know—most kids gotta scuffle to live, right from little 'uns on. Kids'er uh lot more than folks like tuh think." He waved a fork of fried mush around and landed it in his mouth.

They got a ride out of Shreveport that afternoon for Houston. Wilma had sent a letter to Bill in care of General Delivery, Pensacola, to tell him they would wait for him in Houston. It seemed the majority of the population of Shreveport was black. That meant low wages. She thought Houston would be the place to wait. The man who took them was about fifty, heavyset, though not fat. He was an oil driller. He said he thought he had heard of Bill Wild. "In Oklahoma, thirty-seven or so I think it was."

"He was there," the woman said. "He was a rig-builder then."

"Yeow, it seems I heard of him. But I just can't place him."

They were the man's only passengers. He said he had two boys, one in the Air Corps and one still in high school. Along in the afternoon the boy got sleepy and crawled over into the back for a nap where there were the man's tin hat and muddy driller's boots with a beat-up brown leather gladstone bag. Jack liked the man a lot. He was a comfortable, easygoing man. He could tell his mom liked him, too. He said his wife was sickly and didn't follow him around the fields any longer.

When they got to Houston, the man insisted on getting them a room at a small three-story hotel near the bus station. It was no flophouse. There was a desk and clerk, keys on plaques, carpeting in the halls, phones in the rooms; and most rooms had baths. The bed was pressed metal painted to resemble wood and the furniture was pine, but it was a real hotel. His mother, near tears, told the man, "We can't thank you enough."

"Well, this ought to hold you until your husband comes." He glanced again around the small room.

The woman said, "Wait." And took a dollar from her purse and gave it to the boy. "Why don't you run out and see a movie? There's one just around the corner. I want to talk a little business with Mr. Harris."

A whole buck? The boy leaped at the chance. Going out, he heard the man say, "You know, you don't have to do this."

"I know," Wilma said. "I *want* to."

Jack didn't care. He liked Mr. Harris, too. He wished Bill were like that.

When he and his mother were alone in the room that evening, as she prepared to luxuriate in the hotel tub and Jack lay on the bed amidst four comic books, he said, "I wish Mr. Harris was my stepdad instead of Bill."

"That's not a nice thing to say." Then upon reflection, she straightened, smiled to herself, and admitted, "He wouldn't be bad."

Bill blew in around suppertime the day before the week Mr. Harris had paid for was up. He made a place for Jack in the bathtub that night so he and the boy's mother could have the bed. Lying in there in the tub with the door closed, he heard them doing it in the room. The old jealousy rose in him toward Bill. Then he caught himself. It didn't matter.

The next day, Bill found them a single room in a ramshackle old Victorian house in the poorest part of town. It was cold in Houston after dark. There was no heat. The room was long and narrow and had four tall windows. In better times it had probably been a study or smoker or sun room. The windows rattled in the frames. One entire pane had been replaced by a piece of cardboard. The only furniture was an iron bedstead with a thin, bare, hair-stuffed mattress on springs and a straight-backed chair. The windows had only decrepit roller shades to keep out the draft. The floor was filthy bare boards. Yellowed newspapers were wadded and thrown in one corner. The place hadn't been swept or dusted in years. The crone who showed it to them demanded $3 a week. "Rooms are scarce now," she twittered, palsy shaking her hands. She lived in a sealed-off parlor, wrapped in shawls, huddled before a little electric heater. "The bathroom's upstairs. Be sure to jiggle the handle when you're through, or the commode will run. I don't like to have to climb the stairs to take care of it. I'm eighty-three years old, you know." When she took their money, Jack noticed she wore string gloves that left the tips of her old gray fingers bare.

Bill put newspapers between the mattress and the springs to keep out the cold. They covered themselves with their coats and newspapers, shivering in their clothes. Only Bill really slept, and then only because of the whiskey he had bought with Wilma's last few dollars.

The boy lay there in the dark, his nose cold, his breath visible in the night air, and was tempted to run off, but he was not too clear about where Houston was. It seemed such a long way from anywhere when he was so alone.

The next morning Bill took the boy with him to do something he swore he would never do—panhandle.

"Never look them in the eyes," he coached the boy. "Look at their bellies or hands." He braced a passing businessman in the winter shadow of the Gulf Building. "Pardon me, mister, can you spare me and my boy a dime for something to eat? I'm down on my luck an— Thank you, sir." He slipped across the walk to another. "Pardon me, sir, can you spare me and the boy here a quarter for something to eat— Thank you, sir." An older man with a briefcase, puffing a cigar. "Pardon me—"

"Beat it! Get a job and work for your goddamn money like the rest of us."

Two out of ten would give them something. In a couple of hours they had enough for lunch in a bar, where Bill took his neat, standing up, with a beer chaser. Though it was work that depressed Bill, Jack thought it was more lucrative than stealing. He tried it on his own after lunch and bummed $4.85, most of it when the offices let out at five. He did not hit everyone in sight the way Bill did. A lady lectured him. A man said he ought to be in reform school. He picked up Bill back at the bar and turned over his take to him. Bill bought a pint. Then they went to a secondhand store where he purchased a big red coaster wagon for a dollar and a half. He got a couple of throw pillows for two bits each at a nearby place and begged an orange crate from a fruit stand.

Back in the room Bill built a little platform to fit in the wagon, using a beer bottle for a hammer and nails prized from the crate with the boy's Scout knife. Then he got Wilma to kneel in the wagon on one of the throw pillows.

"What is this?" she wondered.

"You'll see." He placed the platform behind her over her calves and feet. On it he put the other cushion. "Now sit back." When she was so mounted, he tucked her coat over her lap and knees and said to the boy, "Pull her around a little."

The boy happily towed her up and down the narrow room while Bill studied his creation with his big head cocked toward his right shoulder, his lips pursed. "What we need is a lap robe," he decided. "Be right back." He was back in ten minutes, giggling to himself, carrying a fringed tapestry tablecloth he had filched from the old lady's room, virtually right from under her nose. She still was not certain what he had been after. Bill tucked it around Wilma in the wagon. "Pull her again, Son." He wanted to see the new effect. "Yeh. Looks perfect."

"Hurry up, it's getting me in the knees," Wilma complained.

"Want you to get used to it. Can't have you poppin up downtown during rush hour."

"What the dickens are you talking about, Bill?"

"I got this idea today, see. The boy and me were bummin, and I saw this. See, he can pull you around town. I'll get a tin cup and make a sign. An—"

"*The hell he will!* Nobody's pullin *me* around town in a little red wagon. I'll do a lot of things, but I ain't being pulled around in a little red wagon with a tin cup. And *that's* final. Go pull yourself." She was off there, and a court order could not have got her back on the contraption.

"I'll do it," Jack offered. What could be easier than riding?

"OK. Then Wilma, you pull."

"I won't do it! I told you, pull yourself."

"Naw. It wouldn't be the same, me pullin him. It don't look right. Don't have the same effect."

"Well, I'm not having anything to do with that wagon, not as passenger or horse, and nothing you can say or do will change my mind." It was plain to Jack the whole thing was up to him and Bill. She moved behind the newspaper, tucking her legs under her on the filthy bare mattress. She would do a lot of things, but that wasn't one of them.

The next morning Jacky towed Bill in the wagon toward town. He sat in the wagon behind Wilma's smoked glasses, his hat brim turned down all around, a tin cup held on his stumps, a dime in it to rattle, and a sign on cardboard around his neck:

GOD BLESS YOU!
FOR HELPING MY DADDY.
FROM AN OIL DERRICK HE FELL
TO LIVE IN THIS LEGLESS HELL.

Thank You!

Going up and down curbs was the hardest part. When there was a driveway near the corner, the boy wheeled the man out into the street, across the intersection, and up a driveway in the next block. Going off a curb right in front of the First Black American Baptist Church of the Living Word while a wedding party was coming down the steps, Jacky spilled Bill out onto the street. The blacks on the church steps whooped when they saw the legless man pick up his pillows and cloth and trot, Bill yelling, *"Goddamn it! Can't you do anything right!"* They pointed their fingers and stamped their feet.
"Pick up thy bed and walk!" a deep, swart voice commanded. The crowd broke into giggles.
Downtown, he just wheeled Bill around and around the block the Gulf Building was on. They had over $10 before lunch. People just dropped money in Bill's cup without looking. Once in awhile some lady would mutter, "God bless you, brother. God bless you, son." One dear soul with tears in her eyes touched Jack's shaggy yellow hair and said, "You poor brave little boy," and dropped two bucks in Bill's lap.
"Bless you, mother," he crooned.
A whore with a face like a nicked blade beneath her thick cascade of sotty dyed hair but swinging a champion ass still, on a pair of legs like a marathon runner, snarled in passing, "You fuggin creep. Makin a little kid tow yer around." She spat in his cup. "Bless that!"
"Up your rusty, bitch!" he snarled back after her. "If you had as many stickin out of you as you had stuck in yuh, you'd look like a porkypine."
"It's an *honest* livin, creep-o!"

After that he had to go have a drink. Jack wheeled him into a little shopping arcade so he could dig his bottle from under his seat.

They were home by dark with $34 and change. Jack and his mother sat on the edge of the bed and counted it, stacking the coins in proper piles, smoothing out the bills, while Bill got stupidly drunk pacing the tiny room, complaining he thought he would never sit again.

"You know how much you got here?" Wilma asked incredulously. "This is more than I could make in a week . . . in a drugstore."

The next morning Bill had half a pint before he mounted the wagon, while Wilma made plans to go shopping for bedding and some kind of heater. When Jacky towed the old man in that night so full of Calvert he was happy to ride all the way home, he found the floor had been swept and mopped. An electric heater glowed pleasantly, and there were sheets and two blankets on the bed.

Sleeping in his underwear for the first time in about a week, Jack was awakened by his mother whispering loudly to Bill, "You'll wake Son."

"I wanta lil," Bill persisted drunkenly.

"Honey, you've had too much to drink. Wait until tomorrow."

"Wanta lil now. And I'm gonna have a lil now." He was awkwardly trying to get up, over and between her legs. She was gently trying to frustrate his efforts.

"You'll wake Jacky," she said again, perfectly aware then that the boy beside her was wide awake.

Bill mounted her. The boy felt him fumbling to get his thing in her until she had to reach down between them and do it for him. He went at her without talking, just rumph-rumph-rumph. Her bare thigh was upraised and lay slightly over the boy. He reached up and ran his hand along it from buttocks to knee. She found his hand with her own and clasped it tight down between them where Bill could not know. In the dark the boy could see her face turned toward him on the pillow. Her eyes were open. She squeezed his hand tight to let him know it was all right. She smiled and winked. When the pace quickened, she closed her eyes and squeezed tighter. The boy sang in his mind, "Hang on tight. Hang on tight," in time with the groaning iron bed. But at the end, his hand was forgotten in hers. Only the insistence of his own held hers captive. That goddamn Bill had won again.

Jacky towed Bill out of October and into November. They had a cot for the boy then and a lot of new clothes. Bill bought Calvert by the fifth and stayed high all season. His only nagging problem was how to do so well without being towed around like a cripple in the wagon. Jack had stolen Bill a pair of basketball knee guards to make the riding even eas- ier, but he did not seem that much happier. He began cutting down their forays to two days and one night a week. Saturday night was good for $30-$50 easy. They had more money than they'd had since Bill lost his job at the shipyard. Even more, since it was tax free. Bill stayed drunk and schemed with Wilma about a fleet of franchised beggars in little red coaster wagons while Bill sat in an office in California and got receipts by mail.

Then one Saturday night the boy was towing Bill past a theater that was letting out when four big kids in college jackets came out and bumped the wagon. "Gee, I'm sorry!" one cried. The others tried to catch the toppling wagon. Too late. Bill spilled out. He fumbled with the robe as if he had some notion to cover his fraud. His bottle rolled lazily into the street. Women gasped. Men cursed.

"*Look! He has legs!*" some woman shrieked.

Laughter and catcalls rose among the curses of outrage. "*Run!*" Bill yelled to the boy. His own poor cramped pins were too slow getting him going. One of the college boys collared him, crying, "You damn fake!" He busted Bill right in the mouth. Blood dripped from his split lip.

"*Run, Son, run!*" Bill glared at the boy, oblivious of what would hap- pen to himself. "*Run!*"

"Call a policeman!" a man in a tie and suit shouted.

"Somebody get a cop!" a woman echoed. "A thief and a cheat like that ought to be locked up. Goin around preyin on folks' good natures."

The boy bolted from the grasp of one of the college boys and was away through the crowd. Bill had about $50 on him. The boy hadn't a dime. He ran through downtown alleys until he was sure no one fol- lowed him. Then he made his way back to the room.

In the institutional marble halls of the courthouse it smelled like a public toilet, the dim, high catacombs reeking of pine disinfectant. On narrow benches along both sides of the corridor men and women— disproportionately black and Mexican-American—sat in shadows of their own desolation, whether waiting to pay a fine, swear out a com- plaint, answer a charge, or get married. Children played finger games, scrap games, wedged between the adults on the scarred benches set up to accommodate the overflow from courtrooms. The benches had been raised to a fine common polish by contact with the rough clothes of the poor. They all looked up to stare blankly at the randy-looking little sparrow with a scab on his lower lip being led in handcuffs by a tall Texas deputy who was towing a little red wagon. As the men moved to the head of the line and right into the court, the silence of those on the benches reflected the ultimate satisfaction that no matter what their problems were, they were not handcuffed.

Judge Garza presided in a venerable gunmetal suit as institutional as the walls. He was a heavy, short man whose little asphalt-blue necktie looked to have been tied by a Thugee. With fingers like sausages and the loudest sound in the room his labored breathing and the rush of water through unseen overhead pipes from higher court flushings, he riffed Bill's sheet.

"You got an attorney? No? OK. You are charged with vagrancy, begging in a public place, fraud for the purpose of illegally obtaining money, and contributing to the delinquency of an unnamed minor. You want a lawyer?"

Bill shook his head he did not.

"Then how you plead, guilty or not guilty?"

"Guilty."

"Then I'm going to sentence you to jail for thirty days on each of the first three counts and one year on the last one."

"Why so much, your Honor?"

"Because you are a bad man." He lifted the top sheet in the folder before him and read: "Five years, Kansas State Penitentiary, Lansing, for forgery; a year in New Mexico, same thing; six months in Missouri, stolen car; a year in Missouri reformatory, attempted armed robbery of a gas station—"

"That was a wrong one. Me and a friend was goin huntin and scared the old guy a little with our guns. They weren't loaded."

"That's why only a year. If they had been loaded, you would have gotten at least five. You been in jail for something most of your life, from here to California and back. Thirty, thirty, ninety, ninety, ninety, thirty, fifteen, ten days." He riffled the folder. "I could go on."

"I always got off for good behavior," Bill reminded him.

"Yes. That's so. You are such a good prisoner maybe we ought to keep you in jail all the time. Anyway, you are a three-time loser as an adult now. You take one more big fall and they're going to hit you with twenty to life someplace. How you like that?" When the man remained silent, the judge said, "You better straighten yourself out. Your life's running out. You wanta say something?"

"Naw."

"OK. Credit him with time served," he instructed a court stenographer. "Sentence to start immediately. There's just one thing I want to know." He turned back to the prisoner. "What's it feel like, a grown man like you, being pulled around the streets in a kid's coaster wagon?"

The man with the oversize head looked at the fat little *empanada* above the high bench out of blue eyes like broken glass. They studied each other for a few seconds, then Bill held out his cuffed wrists and said to the deputy, "Let's go."

They went out with the deputy dragging the wagon along behind them. The people on the benches looked up again to watch them into the elevator that went only to jail.

# 37

TERROR was often Wilma's alarm clock. Too often she could not readily remember the name of the cheap hotel, or even the city, in which she awakened. The vague morning light falling through windows opaque with grime made the season ever a lonesome mystery. What was the year? By whom had she slept? Under what alias?

The tousled dirty blond head on the pillow next to hers was her son's. So she concluded she had to be herself. Her identity finally established, her history sorted, she had next to know if she had time for a good stretch in bed or needed to make her next move quickly before another dreaded knock on the door.

The doors everywhere were always thickly enameled over scars and had for so long closed upon desperate lives that failure permeated the rooms until they were cancer houses of two-bit schemes and petty fantasts' dreams. Out of flowered wallpapers brittle with age and rot, repulsive to the touch as the bodies of slobbering old bums, seeped a root sickness that could only be hidden, though never removed, by war.

When the boy laid his leg across her lap and cuddled her left breast, Wilma stretched lazily and thought of the alternatives when there was only seventy-five cents in her purse and the rent on their room was past due. When the boy became more daring, she stopped his hand and removed it, saying, "Now, now." She slipped deftly from under the covers, hooking on her faded rose chenille robe as she arose. She went out and down the hall to the bathroom.

When she returned, the boy sat up in bed with his chin on his knees to watch her in her slip before the portable magnifying mirror on the rickety table where her cosmetics were ranked with the condiments of their window-sill larder.

She was still pretty. But there was a thickened, broad look beginning underneath the prettiness that made her resemble at times—particularly in the morning and when she came in drunk—the old bags he saw in bars that had names like Mom's, The Shamrock, Lone Star, Tough's & Min's, The Dew Drop Inn—women who always wanted to hear "The Waltz You Saved for Me" or some such when they were so drunk they could hardly stand, let alone dance, and who found it so poignant to sleep with a regularly employed man who was not tattooed they might dare to think once again of a house on a regular street and recall the recipes they had been saving to cook for someone. She wasn't *that* bad. The boy felt guilty in making the comparison. It was mainly her nose. It had definitely been flattened. Where it had been pert and straight before Pensacola, it was now broad and soft-looking like a young boxer's, emphasizing the flat myopia of her dark eyes and the fullness of her lips.

"What are you staring at?" she asked, looking at him in her mirror.

"Just you."

"I'm not much to look at anymore, am I?"

"You look all right."

"Just all right?"

"Well, you don't have your makeup and stuff on."

"Love me anyway?"

"Yeow," he said. But he saw in the mirror her doubting eyes and doubted his own words while they echoed in his ears. *Do you love her?* a voice like God's demanded. *No, sir,* he confessed. *Do you hate her? . . . No, sir,* he admitted honestly. *. . . Like her, then? . . . Yes, sir.* Yeow, that was it. He liked her. Just thinking that made his cock stiff as he watched her put on lipstick.

"You love me?" he asked.

"Of course I do," she mumphed, carefully drawing in the corners of her mouth. Only the prettiest women, for Jack's money, ran their lipstick so fully into the corners. She blotted her lips on Kleenex and turned to ask, "Better?"

"Yeow."

"Think I'm pretty?"

"Yeow."

She looked again in the mirror. "I guess I'll do. What are you up to today?"

422

"Going down to the beach and sell ice cream."

"That's good. Sometime try to sell more than you eat." She tweaked his nose on the way to sitting on the edge of the bed to put on her hose.

"You know my birthday's tomorrow?" he said.

"I hadn't forgotten, but I'd hoped you had. I'm afraid you're going to have to take a rain check, honey."

"Like last year."

"All right! I'm sorry. I'll do what I can. OK?"

"Sure," he said gloomily.

They had moved to Corpus Christi as soon as Bill had been sentenced, Wilma arguing that in Corpus it was never winter and therefore she would save the cost of a new coat. They had been there nearly a year.

The boy hawked ice cream along the nearly deserted beach from an insulated cardboard box slung from a shoulder.

"Hey, ice cream!" a tanned woman who had twin girls with bouncing black Dutch bobs signaled from her beach blanket.

"I wanta orange Popsicle!"

"I wanta Fudgsicle!"

"Nen I wanta Fudgsicle, too!"

"All right, make up your minds." She organized the twins, swarming to peek into the steaming box Jack opened on the sand.

The woman was so deeply tanned under her coating of oil there was a blackness in the creases and folds of her skin. When she sat up yogalike to distribute the ice cream and pay, he saw the shockingly pale contrast of her skin just below the perimeter of her striped lime and orange, wool-knit two-piece suit. There was a fringe of long, shiny black hairs against the pale hollow of her right thigh that made him feel he was in the roaring of a sea shell. She was so rich she didn't care what she showed, was a thought. She had a diamond ring and broad wedding band on her beautifully manicured fingers. Her kids' sneakers were brand new. Only a woman who was rich would be so smilingly casual about how her long heavy breasts nearly fell out when she leaned over to extract a dollar from her wallet, fat with photos and maybe money.

She smiled at him when she handed him the dollar. She didn't give a damn what he saw. She smiled again when he carefully counted her change into her pale, upturned palm. She peeled and snapped her cold lime Popsicle into its twin batons, tentatively licked the end of one, then introduced the frozen tip into her mouth, closing her glazed red lips around it and delicately sucking. "Umm!" she told the girls. "Ummm!" they chorused.

The boy hoisted his box and went on. She probably lived in one of the big white houses down the beach that towered on pilings above the force of the tide. Or maybe she was staying at one of the fancy hotels along the angel-food-cake beach.

All the big houses were closed, both because it was not the season and because of the war. Since the German sub had tried to land men down the coast near Brownsville, the National Guard had intensified its Gulf watch. Not a glimmer of light was permitted along the beach at night. No few Mexicans were startled to have a party of armed guardsmen swoop down on them just as they were about to turn their redfish on their small fires. The great houses sat up there storm-shuttered and silent.

Business was lousy. He always denied himself the pleasure of a swim until his ice cream was gone. Then a family of Mexicans bought seven bars and he decided to knock off for lunch. He had a Fudgsicle and a Creamsicle, which didn't sell well, anyway.

He doubled back under the boardwalk where it was cool amongst the litter of newspapers, soft-drink cups, beer bottles, and the carcasses of a jillion little crabs, the occasional small skeleton of a sand shark, the rotting corpse of a hammerhead; where the smell of the sea was strong and fishy, challenging all the natural instincts of man; not a voluptuous place in the sun for a basking lady who did not care what she showed. He was directly above the woman, whose twins were making a sand castle down near the rising tide. She lay on her belly with her halter undone to bare her back. She rose up as if she had decided that was enough sun on that side, holding her halter against her breasts with one hand, and rolled over, rearranging her halter to just cover her nipples. He dropped his trousers and shirt onto his ice cream box and dashed down into the water in the pale blue trunks he always wore under his dungarees.

He swam in the piss-warm shallows where he could look up at the glistening brown woman on the beach. Tiny minnows inside the bar nipped the fine hairs on his legs. When she lifted both knees as if giving herself to the sun, he slipped down the front of his trunks and jerked off under water, imagining he was between her long oily thighs.

She lifted her sunglasses and smiled at him when he sauntered past again on the way to his clothes.

"How's the water?" she asked, rising on one elbow, squinting in the sun, holding her halter against herself with one beautiful hand cupping her left breast.

"It's OK. Sorta tepid. Lots of little minnows biting on you."

"I don't think I'll go in, then. I hate that."

Man! Would he like to fuck her! He bet she did it like someone in a fuck book. He imagined her husband was a big dark guy with a real big one, dark and circumcised, making her crawl the walls. That was why she didn't give a damn what she showed him, he decided. He envied her husband. That was how he wanted it to be when he was grown up. And they would live happily ever after. Then there was the sudden fear, almost like another Godly voice in his head—that he might never grow up; that he would just get older and be some kind of weird snaggle-toothed monster. He made a promise to stop bothering his mother and jerk off but twice a week, and only when he could not stand it any longer. He would start exercising to build himself up. He would send a coupon off the back of a funny book to Charles Atlas, who could make him a new man in just fifteen minutes a day.

When he was dressed, he went up the beach past a sign marked PRIVATE BEACH NO TRESPASSING to where a great white frame house with porches like the decks of a river boat sat on pilings fifteen feet above the sand. The windows were battened with solid wooden shutters that had steel drop bars across the outside. The boy went under the house where a skiff was stored keel up beside a padlocked shed of some kind. A plain open wooden stair went up to a back porch. Because the back of the house faced the highway, the porches on that side were screened by decorative lattices like the galleries of a sultan's palace. He stood on his ice cream box to lift the drop bar of a window. He just wanted to see what was inside. But the window only looked in on a small, plain room with a three-quarter-size bed—a maid's room. So with the butt of his Scout knife he tapped the glass along the sill next to the latch. Then he tapped it sharply and knocked out a fist-sized piece of glass, through which he could reach and unlatch the window. He raised the window and rolled over the sill into the closeness of the shuttered house. Off the hallway outside the maid's room were a laundry room, a pantry full of canned goods. The kitchen was equipped better than any café in which his mother had ever worked. There was a walk-in cold storage, open and empty, smelling like an old icebox. There was a huge living-dining room like a big hotel lobby, all divided by furniture into areas for different functions. The furniture was mostly white woven raffia with verdantly flowered cushions. Hawaiian decorations, coconut masks, grass skirts, spears were all over the place. The bar was a little grass shack in one corner, completely stocked and just waiting for the luau. The half-dozen bar stools were made from bamboo. There were bamboo-and-glass coffee tables, bamboo tumblers on the bar. There were copies of fancy magazines on the tables. There were games set up at little tables along the wall: chess, backgammon, cards. A wall of books seemed awesome to the boy. It was like a library. He pocketed lighters, knickknacks as he went along.

Upstairs were a big bedroom and three smaller ones. The big room had a dressing room and a bathroom with two sinks and two toilets. But one toilet didn't have a seat and had some strange-looking plumbing on it. The medicine cabinets were only about a third full. He could tell stuff had been taken away. He turned one of the taps shaped like a dolphin, and aerated water bubbled from the faucet like champagne. The rugs on the floor were like huge sheepskins. He tried the lights. Nothing.

In the dressing room the closets were about half full of summer clothes. The man's stuff was too big for him. It would be too big for Bill. The guy had a size 13 shoe. But the woman's stuff looked about his mother's size. He found a soft Panama straw suitcase with the initials M. H. G. on the leather fittings and packed it with a blue blazer and white pleated skirt, white pumps, some gabardine dresses that buttoned all the way up the front. The dresser drawers were full of underwear, hosiery, cosmetics, perfume. In the man's side there was a leather cup full of change, some gold cufflinks, a Shriner's lapel pin that looked as if it had a diamond in it, a silver Ronson lighter. He packed the case. From the woman's dresser he took a pair of black lace panties like something for a movie queen. He pressed them to his face. They smelled of an Oriental perfume, woody, musky, of deep purple flowers and China. He quickly skinned out of his trousers and trunks and stepped into the panties. He stood before a full-length mirror in the dressing room, clamped his penis down between his legs, and tried to see himself as a girl. His butt was too skinny. He put on a pair of the woman's high heels. It was grotesque, his poses more the mockery of woman than desirable, dumb show.

"Creep!" He challenged his image in the mirror. Then he quickly dressed, tossing the panties back into the suitcase.

Down the hall he found a boy's room. A teen-ager's room, with great model planes on wires from the ceiling, an air rifle, a ball glove, a football, a million things, sweaters, shirts, a pair of cowboy boots only a little too big for him. Gabardine Western pants, a genuine 3-X beaver Stetson hat. He dumped the dry ice and loaded up his ice cream box.

On the porch he stood on the box to carefully replace the drop bar. Then he went down under the house and quickly away through the dunes where side-going little green fiddler crabs scuttled out of his path.

He ducked under the boardwalk and followed it as far as it went, back deep in the shadow.

Wilma shifted from one leg to the other, her arms crossed under her breasts, her brown shoulder bag on her hip. A high-hipped woman in a short seersucker suit, she could have been waiting for a bus but for the fact she was half a block from a stop. She waited near the alley in front of the Airway Recreation at half past four in the afternoon in anticipation of men getting off work.

Presently, two sailors in whites came up from the subterranean pool hall and looked first one way then the other, on liberty, bound purely by whim to any direction at all. The woman drifted near.

"You boys looking for a good time?" she inquired so softly it did not immediately register. Then they looked at each other inquiringly, examined the woman more closely, stifled grins.

"How much?" asked the shorter one, who had a nasty pug face beneath his elaborate Jello-mold pomp. He puffed up his chest a bit, preparing to transact business.

"Five apiece and two dollars for the room," she said.

"You take both of us?" the sailor asked.

She nodded that she would. The tall one sort of hunched into his shoulders as if wishing he had pockets for his large, knobby country hands. When he had first looked at her, a shy smile had played at his thin lips. Then when the proposition was made, his eyes never again climbed higher than her knees. For her part, she had to calculate quickly if they might be trouble or a fast ten bucks. She was $13 in arrears in her rent and needed a little more to get her and the boy through another couple of days.

"OK?" She linked her arms through theirs and started up the street. "Where are you boys from?"

"I'm from Nutley, New Jersey," the short one said as if that was something in his favor.

"Indianapolis," the tall one mumbled.

They turned the corner. "Wanta flip to see who goes first?" Nutley asked.

"You can," the tall one said.

Nutley reached across the woman and squeezed her tit.

"Watch it!" she cautioned. "Don't handle the merchandise." She smiled to take off the sting. The tall one looked away.

"Just wanted to see if they're real," Nutley said smartly.

"I'm all real," she said wearily.

"And a foot deep, probably," he cracked, snorting at his wit.

She led them into the Lone Star Hotel that had hot and cold water in every room by the day, week, or month. There were four dusty plastic and chrome chairs in the small lobby. They were mended, seat and back, by long strips of dirty, wide adhesive tape. Scummy, acrid spittoons were next to each chair. In a rack on the wall were yesterday's Corpus Christi *Caller* on a wooden wand and year-old copies of *Life, National Geographic,* and *True Detective,* the magazines all branded with the stamp of the secondhand magazine store that had resold them. The ferret-faced young man, with an enflamed, seeping complexion that wanted sandblasting, took the woman's two dollars and gave her a key on a plastic plaque. The sailor from Nutley hovered near the stair, tugging down the front of his jumper nervously, trying to look indifferent. His buddy sat in one of the greasy chairs and flipped through a tattered copy of *National Geographic.*

The corridors were so dim she never saw the dust that always made her sneeze. "Excuse me!" she apologized. Sometimes she was not certain if it was the dust or going to bed with a stranger that made her sinuses load up. No matter how many times she'd been the whore, there was always an anxiousness and anticipation that was not like the casual indifference other girls claimed to feel when they did it. Going down the hall, she found it impossible not to be a little curious about the man who was going to come into her body. Even when the guy was like the little fellow beside her, mean and unsure of himself, who seemed always to try and pump some curious salvation or peace from her cunt, she wondered what they might be like when they were just being themselves. Then, there were all the things they said . . . their dishonesties . . . the excuses they made . . . an army of men with faces like dead soldiers.

She turned the skeleton key in the lock and opened the door on a musty cubicle as nondescript as the universal, washable bedspread—a nubby tan field striped by coarser brown and white yarns. She had dreams of opening a door in some ultimate promised land, and there would be her bed covered with such a spread.

"Whew! Get undressed while I get some air in here," she told the sailor, stirring the stale air immediately before her face with her hand. "Oh, first." She put out her hand, palm up. "I almost forgot." She smiled as if the joke were on her. He fumbled a black wallet from the waist of his trousers and, holding the opening cautiously toward himself, handed her five. "And for the room?" she added.

A Gulf breeze lifted the shade lazily, freshening the air. The afternoon sunlight on the ancient shade made the room slightly golden. She stripped to her slip, removed her panties, laid her clothes neatly on the room's single chair. The young sailor stripped to his socks and floppy issue drawers that had the name R. D. Huffman stenciled on the waistband. He sneaked glances at the woman, who undressed with an unexpectedly modest air. Then she flipped up the back of her slip and sat on the edge of the bed, patting the place beside her, smiling in a friendly way. Her dark bush just peeped beneath the hem of her slip, which was across her lap. "How long you been in?" she asked like a hostess at a USO while digging his short penis from his shorts.

"Uh, about a year," he replied distractedly. He sat there with his hands at his sides.

"Like it?"

"Hunh? Yeah. It's OK."

As soon as he showed a sign of life, she lay back, spreading her legs, and spat on her hand to lubricate his penis and inserted it in herself. She had to work to keep him in. He kept popping out whenever he got serious. So she finally had to lock him in place with both legs and hold him there, doing the work herself until he stiffened and discharged in her.

She whipped a handy hand towel between her legs even as he rolled off, holding it there while going to the sink, where she stood on one leg to wash herself over the small basin. She tossed him a towel of his own and indicated he could wash himself.

He dressed with his back to her and slumped out of the door, even less happy than when he had come in.

"Good luck," she called after him.

"Yeah," he growled.

It was such a timid knock on the door, she was smiling when she called, "Come in." The tall young sailor entered cautiously, head first, craning his long neck around the door like a turkey.

He stood in the center of the room waiting to be told what to do, rooted, turning his head back and forth while she moved about. "You ever been with a woman?" she asked.

"Well, sure. But not no, uh—"

"Whore?"

"Naw. I wasn't thinking that. I meant no grown-up woman. Just some old girls back home."

"How old are you?"

"Eighteen."

"Got five dollars?"

"Oh! Yeow. Sure. Here." He dug out his billfold.

"Don't be nervous. I won't bite," she assured him. "It'll only take a minute," she teased him. "Put your clothes on the chair." She flipped her slip and sat on the bed as she had before, while he intently concentrated on his buttons. He folded every stitch neatly as he took his clothes off. He laid his socks in his shoes as her father always had done every night before getting into bed. Naked, he looked like a stork. But the long skinny whang hanging down and curved slightly to the left between his almost hairless, bird's legs made her quietly gasp. He just stood there looking like someone about to be hurt, totally at a loss without pockets. She got up and went toward him, lifting her slip over her head, peeling it off and dropping it on the chair. He watched her, his Adam's apple working. She pressed her soft belly against his hip, her breasts divided by his ribs, her head resting on his bony collarbone, her right arm around his waist. She lifted his penis, weighing it in her hand, testing its length. She playfully led him by it to the bed.

She trained him, taught him how. "Take it easy. There's no hurry, is there?"

At the end she shot her legs straight in a wide, tense, quivering vee, dilating so completely he felt lost in her, then clamped and nearly broken as she came down on him and ground out her excruciating pleasure.

"Never was like that before," he confessed with obvious awe as she washed him at the sink and dried him with the towel. He dressed while she stood at the sink taking care of herself.

"You're sure a pretty woman," he told her.

"Thank you."

"How come you do this?"

"Need the money."

"Can't you get a job?"

"It's a long story, sailor."

"I'm feelin kinda like goin again," he mumbled, looking at the floor. And in spite of the prospect of easy money, she did not want to spoil what had for a moment been good, so shook her head no. Then when he looked hurt, she quickly assured him, "Only because I really like you."

"You ain't like that with everybody?"

"No. You just happen to have the kind I like. My husband's been away for awhile."

"You got a husband?"

"Yes. And a little boy. And I take vitamin pills and even go to church once in awhile."

"I didn't mean . . ."

"I know."

"I sure wanta thank you, ma'am," he said, leaning back in the door.

"Thank *you*. And call again," she cracked.

"I will!" he promised.

*I'll never be a good whore,* she criticized herself.

The desk clerk looked up from his *True Confessions* when she came down. "Ain't seen you around much in the last couple of weeks. Thought you'd left town."

It made her cringe to look at him. A string of yellow pus had congealed between a scarlet fester on his neck and his shirt collar. I had a job for awhile," she said.

"You want to keep that room?"

"Sure. I have it aired out now. Let me have some more towels, though."

"Check."

She noticed he always stared at her as if he wanted to proposition her himself. Thank God he never had, she thought. Maybe he thought no one would take him on, oozing like that. Or maybe he was a queer, she thought. Poor guy, she pitied him.

She had dinner in a Chinese restaurant. She also bought a pack of Chesterfields. She only smoked when she was hustling. She hardly inhaled. But she often wondered why she wanted only then to smoke.

A large man in an expensive but baggy light suit sitting at one of the tables between her booth and the counter eyed her with every forkful of chow mein he hoisted to his mouth. He openly looked at her legs, took a pull of iced tea, and smacked his lips. He finished his meal and picked his teeth with a flat toothpick while she made up her mouth. They signaled the waiter at the same time. They met at the cash register. He paid, flashing a wallet full of dough. She was so close he brushed her with his elbow when stepping back. He tipped his straw hat and said, "Pardon me, honey."

"My fault," she confessed.

He dawdled outside the door until she emerged, putting her wallet back into her cluttered shoulder purse. He touched his hat again respectfully and said, " 'Scuse me again, honey, but I'm just in town for the night. I was wondering if you could tell me where I could have a good time."

"I might," she admitted coyly.

"How much?" He came right to the point.

"How much of a good time do you want?"

"That depends." He rolled the toothpick with his tongue from one side of his mouth to the other and back. "If I like what I'm doin, the sky's the limit with me."

"That's how I am," she said, hooking her arm through his. "But it's five for a short time. There are lots who say how they want to fly but never get off the ground."

"Your place near here?"

"Just a step."

"Let's go." And she was towed off on his arm. He seemed sincere enough, but much too weighty to be a flier. He was a good six feet three inches and had to weigh over 250.

"I've never been with a man as big as you," she said.

"I'll take it easy on you. Big night?"

"No. You're the first tonight," she lied. "Actually, I don't do this regularly. My husband's away and I lost my job. I was working in a drugstore. Little snotty manager said I stole some cosmetics and canned me."

"And you were perfectly innocent, right?"

"No. I took them. But if the bastard had paid me enough to live on, I could have afforded my cosmetics. What do you do?"

"I do a sort of survey, you might say, for my outfit. A little missionary work. Public relations. Goodwill ambassador."

"That sounds interesting," she said uninterestedly. "Here we are." She led him in past the desk. The desk clerk looked up with a strange expression when he saw them. She chalked it up to the man's imposing size.

He looked around the room as if preparing to sublet for the season. He peeked into the empty closet. "Don't like to be disturbed," he explained, closing the closet door.

"You can trust me," she assured him.

"Yeow. Well?"

"What?"

"Strip."

"You, too."

"Come on. I wanta see what the hell I'm gettin into, honey."

She didn't like undressing while someone simply stood watching. She began to feel she had made a mistake. Whatever he was there for, it wasn't to have a good time. If it wasn't fun, why the hell did they all do it? she wondered once again. He was about fifty, with thin, gray-black hair combed straight back. There was a roll of suet over his collar at the back of his neck. "Bet you played football," she said, making small talk while stepping out of her clothes.

"Naw. Swimming."

"Oh." He had a pinky ring on his right hand, a blue stone flanked by diamonds, cutting into his large fleshy finger; his nails were filed to neat

432

shallow points and lacquered with clear polish. She had never seen a man in Texas with his nails so neatly manicured. And she found that particularly repulsive in a big man. He watched jadedly while she stripped before him. He hooked his thumbs in his belt, a wide piece of exotic ostrich or elephant hide with a monogram buckle—COP. Her heart fluttered inside her for a moment.

"Your buckle spells 'cop,' " she pointed out to him.

"Yeah?" He never took his eyes off her.

"What I need is some music," she said in her slip, kicking off first one shoe, then the other. "Take it off, take it off, cried the boys in the rear," she sang, sliding her panties down under her slip, whirling them around on one finger while doing a very unprofessional grind. Then, aiming them at the guy, she shot them like a rubber band. He stepped back, re-coiling, even as they floated to the floor well short of their mark.

"Come on," he snapped.

She lifted her slip by the hem, turning it wrong side out over her head. She flung it on the chair with a "Ta-ta!" freezing with her right arm overhead, hand cocked like Betty Boop, her hip jutted. "That's all there is, there ain't no more." She stuck out her palm for his five and two for the room. He backhanded her in the mouth with his left, giving her such a shot she was sent spinning across the room head first into the base of the far wall, trailing a truly surprised scream. He kicked her viciously in the ass with the toe of his professionally shined shoe. He dragged her up by the hair and slapped her face back and forth, hissing, "Shut your filthy mouth, you rotten, whorin bitch! Shut your damn mouth!"

She fought to control herself, like a hysterical child. He shoved some sort of badge under her nose. "Sister, when I'm done with you, you ain't goin to be able to sit on your ass, let alone peddle it."

"Please," she begged. "I've got a little boy. Do you think I'd go to a room with someone like— Do you think I *like* this?"

"Why ain't you home where you belong, then?"

"Let me go. I won't do it anymore. Please. Don't hurt me. I'll treat you right. For free. Anything."

"How many tricks you turn tonight?"

"Just two, honest."

"Where's the dough?"

"I'll get it." He released her so she could get the money from her purse. She handed it over with shaking hands. "My rent's due tomorrow. I was going to pay it with that. But take it. Just give me a break, please."

"Yeah, all you bags got a story. I'll break your butt."

"Don't. Let me take care of you. I'll treat you right." She put out her hand.

He took it, twisted it cruelly up behind her back until he had spun her around with her head bent lower than her bottom. "I wouldn't stick my dick in your stinkin cunt, sister. I'd as lief stick it in the head of a cottonmouth moccasin." He booted her with his knee face down across the bed. When she tried to get away, he caught her by the left ankle, stripping off his belt. He turned her loose long enough to scoop her panties off the floor and stuff them in her mouth for a gag. Then he lashed her with his belt. Each bite made her jump as if touched with an electric wire, crying out behind the gag. The sounds of the bed and his labored breathing could have been mistaken for the sounds of violent love. The toothpick was erect as a miniature bowsprit between his gnashing front teeth. "Lousy whore! Stinkin bitch!" He cursed her with every rip. Her gagged sobs were coming like a hysterical, exhausted child's. He threw down his belt and yanked her off the bed by her hair, holding her limply before him, studying her streaming face. Her hair was wet and limp, as if she had been in a steam room. Sweat coursed off her splotched body in sheets. Where she had lain on the bed there was a dark outline. He let her sink to her knees before him. Holding her face up by her hair, he dug the gag unceremoniously from her mouth with a forefinger. As matter-of-factly, he unzipped his trousers and fumbled out his prick. "Bite me, you bitch, and I'll kill you," he warned.

"Swallow it, you goddamn garbage can!" he commanded a moment later, threatening her with his upraised hand. He let her fall to the floor. He wiped his penis on her panties and threw them at her as if that could hurt her more. He stepped back to rethread his belt in his trousers. "There's houses for pigs like you. We don't want a bunch of syphy old bags around infectin our boys in service. You get your ass in a house where you can be checked or you haul ass out of town. I see you runnin loose again and I'll have you sealed up with a red-hot poker. You hear me?" He nudged her with his toe.

She nodded she had heard.

"Then let this be a lesson to the wise."

When he had gone, she wept until no more tears would come. She threw up on the far side of the bed. Then she struggled to the basin. She saw her face in the mirror and gasped. She touched her face with her fingertips. *That wasn't what she looked like! Was that how she really looked?* She looked like some tough, broken-nosed old bag in any skid row bar. "NO!" she screamed aloud. She dashed the water tumbler in the basin. But it bounced and did not break. In a hysterical frenzy she repeatedly threw the tumbler into the sink, but it would not break. *"It's goddamn plastic!"* she cried aloud, flinging it across the room, and collapsed on the bed. "Plastic. I can't even cut my wrists right." After a time she dozed.

The room was fully dark when she was awakened by a tapping on the door. There was a moment when she did not know where she was or why she was so sore. "You OK?" It was the desk clerk hissing at the door.

"Yeah— Ow! Yeow. Listen, do you have a drink?"

"I can get you one."

"I don't have any money."

"That's all right." She heard him go away. Her back felt encrusted, so every movement seemed a painful cracking. She was amazed when, looking over her shoulder in the mirror, the skin was not actually broken, though every purple stripe would be an even uglier bruise the next day. She gingerly dressed. The clerk returned with two double-shot bottles of Four Roses. She opened one and drained it with tap water for a chaser. Then she drank the other.

"Maybe I'll make it," she decided.

"I wanted to warn you. Everyone knows what he's like. He's everybody's daddy. He hit a black girl once so hard it knocked out her left eye. He's made people I know not want to live anymore."

"That's him. . . . Here, give me a hand." He helped her to her feet and steadied her until she got used to walking again.

"Let me get you a cab."

"He took everything I had."

"Take a cab. I'll take a dollar out of the cash register."

"Thanks."

"Oh, you're welcome. I always liked you, you know. You were never tough and mean like a lot of the women who come in. I thought you had moved away. I've been going to move away a lot of times. But I like Corpus. It's so balmy."

"Yeow. But it's sure been spoiled for me."

"I'll bet."


The boy met her at the door to her room. "Missus Means was up here three times for her rent. She says she wants her rent tonight and we gotta be out tonight because someone else is moving in in the morning."

"I wish I was dead," she sighed.

"You got the money you owe me?" the woman asked, huffing up the stairs.

"I'm getting it."

"When?"

"Soon."

"*Soon* ain't soon enough. *Now!* I want you out of here, *now*. You owe me thirteen dollars. I want my money or you don't move out your stuff."

"All right, give me an hour." She thought about going back to the hotel and asking the desk clerk. She cast about the room, looking for something to hock.

"One hour," the woman said firmly, huffing back down the stars.

Wilma noticed the fancy, soft straw suitcase on the bed. "What's that?" Jack flung it open to show her the stuff he had taken from the house on the beach. She went through it. "If there is something we can hock . . ." she thought aloud.

"How about this?" He held out the diamond Shriner's pin.

"Is it real?" She snatched it and scratched a water glass with it. "Baby! You may have saved our lives!" She dug the stone from the setting with a nail file. It bounced away under the bed. The boy crawled after it. "For godsake let's not lose it," his mother prayed. He lit one of the lighters he had in his pocket. The stone winked at him.

Thirty minutes later she was back, limping stiffly, not happy, but ready to make her next move. She had paid the woman what they owed and had $12 left over. She was bitter because she was certain she should have gotten the fifty she had fantasized for the stone. "Pack up," she ordered.

The boy dutifully packed their two suitcases and a cardboard box. With his stomach growling with hunger, he dragged from the back of the closet another big cardboard box that had been the only thing his mother had redeemed from the landlord they had left their things with in Mississippi. It was a Wheaties carton that had in shipment and transshipment become almost rounded. It was pasted with stickers and oft stamped, tied with clothesline, and he hadn't the vaguest notion what was in the heavy damn thing. He more often rolled the thing than carried it.

She came back looking much better. She had washed her hair and combed it straight back, covering her wet locks with a scarf. Her face was puffy but clean.

"Mom, what's in this old box?"

"Oh, just some stuff of mine. Personal things."

"You never open it."

"Well, I will someday. It's things I want to keep."

When they were packed, he went to call a cab. They took all the stuff to the bus station, checked everything but a suitcase each which they would carry. When they were settled, they would send for the stuff, and it would be shipped to them by bus. They had a snack at the bus station counter. They took a cab to the edge of the town on the highway toward San Antonio and walked along the shoulder. When a car passed, they both turned and stuck up their thumbs. It was hard, hitching at night. They never knew when the approaching lights might be a patrolman. The boy was dressed like a dude cowboy in the clothes he had stolen from the house on the beach. She wore her suit and had a sweater over her shoulders. She held the boy's free arm to help her walk along the uneven shoulder. He was as tall as she. A semi loaded with drill pipe stopped way down the road, the driver braking his full load carefully with the air brakes. On the door which the boy helped his mother reach was the warning: POSITIVELY NO RIDERS!

"Where are you headed?" the driver asked.

"Where are you going?" the woman asked.

"Goliad."

"That's fine," she said.

He let go the air brakes, which went *chhh!*, working the heavily loaded rig through gears. Very soon, in spite of trying to be grateful company, Wilma nodded over on her son's shoulder and slept fitfully, making anguished faces in her dreams.

"She's plumb tuckered out, ain't she?" the man observed in a whisper.

"Yeow. She's had a tough day," the boy said.

"I see that."

They drove then in silence, the boy watching the road until sleepiness had passed. The concrete was being eaten up by the truck, and he vowed to himself not to sleep until he saw her safely to a bed.

# 38

WHEN the rigbuilders left, the roughnecks moved in, and the girls in the house out on Mile Road managed the transition without missing a beat. There were the same tin hats on the chair and the same muddy boots beside the bed. The men who got over Wilma were as alike as an army. The roughnecks worked seven days a week, the girls six. Wilma got every Sunday off so she could be with her son.

She had gone to Goliad's only drugstore the second day she was in town to see if they had a job. She had been to both cafés without any luck. It was a dusty, dun-colored little town. The sign on the railroad stop said the population was 1,446. The main street was wide enough for cars and trucks to park nose to the curbing. From the cool, cracked marble bar of the drugstore fountain, heat waves off the parked cars made the entire street seem a mirage. She sipped a cherry Coke through a straw, wondering if she could just get up and walk out of there, leaving the boy in the room she had rented, leaving Bill in jail, and simply disappear forever. She could find some steady guy, start all over. . . . *To hell with guys!* she told herself. There were no alternatives in the common world that did not lead to the same end—a guy, a kid—getting on her back for a guy to provide for herself and the kid. *How did I get in something like this?* she wondered, truly curious. For suddenly she saw what had been her life was no prologue to better days to come. What had been was the pattern of what was to be. She wished for a moment that she was a Catholic so she could become a nun, longing for the quiet protected walks and routine of an imagined nunnery. *If I could only get away for a couple of weeks,* she dreamed wearily. Goliad was it. She hadn't money, energy, or idea of going any farther.

So when a tall woman in sunglasses, silk dress, and wide-brimmed straw hat finished buying a quart of expensive *friction pour le bain* and took the stool next to hers, Wilma turned to smile out of spontaneous camaraderie, though she was then, as always in such cases, certain her instincts were wrong. Only this time she was both gratified and disappointed when she knew they were sisters under the skin.

"You with the drilling crew?" the woman asked, her eyes completely hidden behind her dark glasses. She lit a long cigarette with a lighter, and Wilma knew she did not work with her hands. Her hands were almost as large as a man's though beautifully groomed.

"Not exactly. We—my boy and I—came here to wait for my husband to, uh, join us. I came ahead to look for a place and get things set up. But I need a job. I can do almost anything in the sales line, or fountain, waitress, anything."

"Umm. What's he in for?"

"Hunh?"

"Your husband?"

"What do you mean?"

"If I'm going to help you out, you got to be honest with me. What's your name?"

"Wilma."

"I'm Vera. Come out to my place. Maybe we can work something out."

She had a DeSoto club coupe. Sinking back in the seat, Wilma felt so suddenly relieved of a crushing burden she could have dozed. She felt as cozy as she had supposed she might be in a nunnery. She dropped her head back and shook out her hair, sighed, closed her eyes and smiled. The woman glanced at her and smiled, too.

The house was a two-story farm house fenced from the surrounding land by ranks of shivering tall cottonwoods under the command of a mighty live oak. The house was ramshackle, silvered beyond the memory of paint outside, the porch sagging, held up by cement blocks standing on end. Inside, the place was plainly functional, with linoleum on all the floors, a Sears Roebuck oil heater in the living room, second-hand couches and furniture that were of a style that could be ordered from a catalog. The place *could* have been a common residence, except for the two girls in kimonos who sat in the parlor with their knees crossed, doing their nails.

"This is Rusty, and that is Rita. This is Wilma."

"Hi." "Hiya." They acknowledged her without any of the ordinary cattiness of two females sizing up the new girl.

"Anybody want a beer or lemonade, a drink?" Vera asked.

She went back through the house. Rusty, a tall redhead, held up her nails to examine her work, blowing to dry them. Neither girl felt it necessary to make conversation. Wilma felt self-conscious because of her appearance. She touched her stringy hair and wanted to have it washed and set. She was aware that the left lens of her prescription sunglasses was cracked. She felt cheap and dirty before the cool girls doing their nails in the parlor where the shades were always drawn. The electric fan on the floor washed a cool breeze back and forth across her calves.

"Here we are." Vera returned with a tray of beers and glasses, trailed by a heavy old black woman with steel-wool hair and a cloudy left eye who bore a plate of dainty pimento cheese and liverwurst sandwiches from which the crusts had been trimmed. The woman always turned her head slightly to get a more head-on view with her good eye and consequently talked out of the side of her mouth.

"This is Sugar." Vera introduced the woman. When she had left, Vera explained, "She just looks like an old one-eyed mammy, don't she? Well, that woman once ran the goingest house in Galveston when Galveston was *wide* open."

"I thought it was now."

She waved that away with a dainty sandwich. "She caught her husband with a little high yella and shot him dead right on top of her. One bullet went through him and nicked the girl, too. They closed her place and convicted her of illegally discharging a firearm. Then when she was sixty-three, she did in her fourth husband, a man of thirty-two who she claimed was trying to inject her with something while she slept so he could get her money and run off with another woman."

"She did that one in with an ax!" Rita exclaimed, her eyes wide with wonder.

"Yeah. She's a tough old girl. Seventy-five now, but she flattened a tough little roughneck here just a couple weeks ago with one sweep of the side of her hand. We don't need no man around with her. But you treat her right and she'll do anything for you. Couple times a year she goes away for a week and won't tell us where beyond saying, 'I gots my needs.' The girls figure she has her a young sugar baby somewhere she spends her money on."

"We each give her a couple of bucks every day. And if you miss a day, don't think she's going to forget. You might, but she never will."

"We're an up and up place. The citizens know we're here and consider us a public service. We're unaffiliated. The sheriff takes his little *mordita,* but he ain't goin to get rich on it. Believe me, I been on the big wheel and I been on the little wheel, and this is better. If they ever try to organize me, I'll shut up and open a beauty parlor. That's why I haven't had the place painted. Now with the wildcat coming in I need another girl, sort of part-time. If they strike oil, this could become a boom town, and the organizers would move in and I'd have to move on. But as long as it's just this bunch, another girl will do."

So Wilma turned out that night, turned four tricks, and went back to her room with $12 net. From each $5 she earned, Vera took $2. She took half or more of what the other girls earned for their room and board.

She operated in one of the slopey little bedrooms upstairs on a chenille-covered bed that had no footboard. It was a clean place, with a linoleum floor and throw rugs and lights with pink bulbs set no higher than her waist. When some lonely roughneck sought love, she chided him pleasantly, "I'm here to take care of the needy, not the greedy." But she was so naturally kind the guys began calling her Sears Roebuck, and one pasted a slogan on the headboard of her bed: *Satisfaction guaranteed or your money back!*

"She's a right regular kind of girl," they agreed.

The other girls were glad to have her help out. They each had their steady clientele—Rusty was very popular with guys who read erotic books and sought to try out their fancy ideas. She got a lot of married men, many who wore suits and ties. "She could sell a half-and-half to a Seventh-Day Adventist," was Vera's judgment. Rita was a small, bubble-breasted, bleached blonde who Rusty claimed was not quite right. Rusty claimed Rita hated men, but what else was there to ball without messing up her head? While Rita admitted she had never had an orgasm except when she was in jail, the sweetheart of a beautiful Mexican bulldike. But even then she hadn't been in love. That was the source of a quiet sadness. "Tell me what it *feels* like when you're in love." She pumped Wilma, soliciting yet another opinion. Listening hard for a word in the platitudes that would prove once and for all "love" actually existed. If it did, then something was definitely wrong with her. If it did not, and no one had so far convinced her it did, then perhaps she was the straightest of all.

"Maybe," Wilma said, "it's just getting up every day and going to work because there are people you care about who are also trying to make a little niceness, do a little better."

"But if that's it, then we all got it," Rita argued. "So what's all the bullshit about?"

"I often wonder that myself," Wilma admitted.

A black '40 Chevy coupe crept up the gravel drive and hid behind the house. The man, in an expensive tropical worsted suit, Palm Beach hat, and rimless glasses, came in through the back door. He stopped in the kitchen to tease Sugar. Wilma figured him for a traveling salesman or hot-shot local booster. "One of these days I'm going to take *you* upstairs," he laughingly promised the black woman, slipping his arm around her.

"Don do me no favors, Deacon. I never been with no white man ever, an I don never want to be. Thass why I was a madam, if you wants to know."

And he had thought he was being kind.

"Preacher man's here!" she bellowed to the girls. He always came early in the afternoon before anyone had shown up. The girls dutifully came down the stairs in shorts and halters, Rusty, Rita, and Wilma.

"Well, well, what have we here, a new addition." He appraised Wilma with his lodge brother's leer, such a phony his reality could be totally expressed in a one-color Chamber of Commerce pocket pamphlet. "New blood in the old corral." He selected his metaphors carefully, his grin making his mouth appear to be wired. A man ought to be more ashamed of his teeth than that, was Wilma's initial thought. They were long and muley beneath a Thomas E. Dewey mustache. His thin, dark hair was combed straight back to best hide his bald spot. He wore two-toned, tan-and-brown perforated shoes and clocked tan rayon socks. "I choose you."

"Lucky you," Rusty drawled. "Come on, Rita, let's go cry over what we missed."

"They are a couple of great girls," the man laughed, slipping his arm around Wilma's waist, sneaking up on her tit, the smile excruciatingly fixed. Nothing dampened his enthusiasm. A real positive thinker. He threw off his clothes, hopping and strutting about as if he were the only man in the world with a peter, or so sublimely ignorant of the world he was certain he had nothing to be ashamed of. "How that?" he asked, as if she should applaud.

She glanced at him. "I've seen better and I've seen worse." He was quite ordinary. And for beauty, considerably below her standard. Her father had the most beautiful equipment she had ever seen, her husband the second most formidable. The man posing before her was not even in their class. She washed him in a pan of warm pink permanganate, hoping futilely he would come in the pan. He was no boy, though.

Staring at her beautiful bush, he offered her a ten. "I always get a half-and-half." It was the first time she had been called on to perform so there. He was particularly distasteful to her that way. She had already lubricated herself. He sprawled on the bed with his hands behind his head. She sat down facing him, leaned down, and took his pudgy, flaccid joint in her mouth.

When he moved his hand up her thigh, she caught his wrist and took time to tell him, "Don't play with me."

After fifteen minutes, when he hadn't come, she stopped and looked up at his still-grinning face. "I always get my money's worth," he informed her.

"Pig!" she muttered to herself, rolling over beside him, laying her leg over him, taking his penis in her hand to keep it from getting cold and so lose the advantage she had gained. She got him quickly into her and tried to drive immediately to a finish, while he was back there somewhere trying to excite her.

"Come on," she encouraged him. "Ten bucks doesn't buy an eternal relationship."

"I don't like to be hurried." He hoisted her ass with his hands, trying by movement and variance of rhythm to get her going, until she finally gave up, turned her face away, shot her legs out in a vee, gripping the spread with both hands, dilating until he was lost inside her, and never really feeling him again until he very quickly came, leaving her unfinished and disgusted with them both.

"Where the hell did you go?" he asked wonderingly.

"I was there. Where were you?"

"Never had one just open up on me like that," he muttered. "You made it, didn'tcha?"

"Oh, yeow. But don't tell anybody, see. I ain't supposed to. Get me in a lot of trouble."

"Sure. I understand. I don't feel right unless I give pleasure, too."

"Noble. More men should feel like that."

"Well, a woman is more than a vessel for our lust."

"She is?"

"You're making fun of me now."

"No, I'm not. I'm all ears. Your wife must be happy with you."

"Sherrill Lee doesn't have the desire I do. She's a fine woman. But a cool woman. Don't get me wrong. God never made a more pious, true woman and natural mother. But me, I got to wrestle with the Devil." He struck a fighting pose as if Lucifer were in the corner behind the chair. "Got to go to the mat with him and fight the sin that's in my soul." If it was two falls out of three, Wilma was putting her dough on Satan. "Well, you're a real nice little screw," he told her, tarrying a moment, expecting her to return the compliment. She lowered her eyes modestly. She took his arm and led him back downstairs. He tipped his hat to the others and promised he would see them soon. "Keep up the good work!" he called cheerfully.

"And to you, Reverend," Rusty cracked.

"Sweet girls," he told Vera, reaching to feel hers on the way through the hall. "How about me and you sometime?" He leered at her.

"Sure, lover, bring a hundred for the night. I don't go for a short time." She gave him back his hand as if it had died.

"Why do you call him Reverend?" Wilma wondered.

"Oh, he preaches at some little Godforsaken church here. He's a creep."

"Roughnecks, railroaders, the old one-legged Jew tailor who comes every Thursday afternoon, none of them make me feel dirty. But that guy does," Rita said. "He tell you about his wife?"

"Yeow."

"I've the biggest notion to follow him sometime and see what she's like, where he lives, you know?"

"And leave a stick a dynamite inside the door," Rusty added. "The fuckin creepo!"

It was his insistence that they accept him as a citizen they resented the most, his need to involve them in the fact he was alive. Others came and went, and the girls hoped only they would be decent and kind. But they were men who knew where they were and how to act. Even the young boys who came in packs, a hard-on in every pocket, so unsure of themselves out of inexperience, so beautifully solid and with themselves in their youth, were preferable in their callousness and self-conscious crudity to guys like the Reverend.

"Those guys are the *real* nuts, you know," Rusty observed.

"I'm never at ease when one is in the house," Vera agreed.

"I mean, you hand an ass like that a mirror and he's going to take it as a compliment."

"I don't think he'll be asking for me again," Wilma said.

"Don't believe it!" Rita exclaimed. "Rusty's his favorite, and she insults him like any other man would kick her ass."

"I tell him he's got the ugliest little dong I ever saw, and he thinks I'm just joshing him. I tell him how much more of a man everyone else who comes here is, and he thinks I'm just trying to get his goat. Nothing. At first I acted like I couldn't remember him from one week to the next. I think what he'd really like is to be whipped and crapped on or something. There's a lot of that in him, don't you think, Rita?"

"Yeow, I do."

"Yeow, see, maybe he's goin to come on like the way he does until we can't take it no more, snatch him bald, and rub his nose in it. That's what he *really* wants!" Rusty proudly sat back, admiring her theory.

"She's probably right," Vera agreed. "There are guys who get their kicks being obnoxious."

"The world's full of weirdos," Rita agreed.

"Sometimes," Wilma said, "I wonder about Presidents and kings and the like. I mean, who knows more about men than us?"

"Yeow?"

"Then why should we think our leaders are any different than regular men?"

"They ain't, honey," Vera assured her as if she knew. "Every politician I ever knew either wants to whip or be whipped, one way or the other. They're all a bunch of nuts. That's why my only allegiance is to myself. I mean, I'd rather be doin it for a bunch of American boys than German or Japanese. But I'd bet if you closed your eyes among all the generals and politicians on either side, there wouldn't be a nickel's worth of difference. From my point of view, Hitler and Mussolini, Tojo, Roosevelt, Churchill, and Joe Stalin are the kind of a party you got to worry about getting out of with your skin."

"Roosevelt's paralyzed," Rita reminded her.

"Maybe it's just his legs," Rusty speculated. "There was this rich spastic kid in Kansas City when I was just startin. His mother sent a big Lincoln car around for a girl once a week, every Saturday, and it took you to this big mansion, and you went in the side door and upstairs and did the guy, who lay flat on his back tryin to tell you how happy you had made him when one jaw wouldn't even meet the other. It was a fifty-dollar trick, and the woman, though no one ever saw her, always left a little bottle of expensive perfume or real linen handkerchiefs and things as gifts. She always wanted young, nice-looking girls, so that was why I got to go," Rusty reminisced. "Don't you ever wonder what you'd feel like if you'd only had one peter stuck in you? The same one, a good one, all your life? Don't you wonder how you'd feel about it?"

"Yeow," both girls admitted.

It was as if the loss of innocence were a greater mystery than all possible, barely conceivable experiences to come.

Wilma had been there three weeks when Mr. Harris came in alone after the midnight tower had come and gone. They were ready to close. Vera had let the girls have their stiff nightcap. He stood there when they came downstairs with his hat in his hands and ignoring the others, asked Wilma, "Are you all right?"

"Yes."

The other girls went back upstairs.

"I heard some of the guys talkin, you know. I just had to come see."

"Well, it's good to see you again. I've often thought about you. Wondered how you were doin."

"Oh, just fine." His eyes kept roving around as if he were uncomfortable talking there. "Well, I just wanted to see how you were doin. . . ."

"I'm fine. Listen. They're just closing up here. If you don't mind, you can give me a lift home."

"Oh, sure!" He was surprised she went home at night.

In the cab of his pickup truck, she explained, "I'm just sort of a fill-in until Bill gets out and comes to take care of us. He's got about another six months to go. He might get paroled. There's a lawyer up there workin on it."

He asked about her boy. "Oh, he's fine. Shooting up like a weed. Twelve years old and he's as tall as me, weighs more, too. I think he's going to be like his dad and grandpa. He's missed so much school. I hope we can get settled someplace before school starts again. How is your, uh, family?"

"My wife's gotta spend most of the time in bed. Her sister's separated from her husband and stays with her. One boy's in Africa. The other can't wait to get out of high school this year and join up. He could come work in the oil fields and get a deferment, but he wants to go. Ain't it funny? I mean, them kids really want to go. Now, I ain't unpatriotic, but they'd have to call me up to go to Africa or them places to fight. I'd fight here in a minute. But they'd have to call me to go over there."

"My father always said the same thing."

"It's a different generation. I just wonder what's goin to come out of all this. Sure, after the war's over we're goin to build cars, houses, airplanes, and stuff for everyone. Peace once and for all. But we said that before. And there's something hollow in the rest of it. I can't put my finger on it, but I remember it was just a little ago we were all out of work. I feel like that depression got interrupted, not reconciled, you know what I mean?"

"Yeow, I think so. But I try to look on the bright side. I never wanted a lot. I'd just like to realize the little I truly do want."

"I sure hope you do." He squeezed her knee. "Because I really like you. You've stuck in my mind."

"I really like you, too."

"What I'd like to do is tell you not to go back there no more. Let me take care of you and your boy. But I got to send nearly everything home. When her sister ain't there, she has to have somebody in and pay them. Then there's the damn house four times bigger than we need. . . ."

"Don't." She stilled his lips with her fingers. "I don't even want to dream. We are both bound. But we can be the best of friends. We'll just keep it that way. No dreams."

"All right, but if I do, I won't tell you about them."

"Can we go to your place?" she asked.

"No."

"There's a motel out on the highway."

"OK." He wondered why she seemed so eager after so busy a night.

Sensing his feeling, she said, touching his muscular forearm, "You're the only man I've really wanted since that time in Houston. But I just realized it now. I love Bill, but we've been down on our luck. And you know how that makes things. I suddenly feel so much better now that you're here. I feel happy! That's funny, too. You know how a person goes along *thinking* they must be happy because they aren't miserable, then something comes along to make them truly happy and they realize they were fooling themselves all along."

"That's just how I feel. I couldn't put it better," he said.

The boy awakened and realized his mother had not come back to their room. He ate, waited around until noon, then hooked on his sunglasses, clamped on his Stetson, and went out. The door to the room across the hall was open behind its screen. Beneath the flowered modesty panel he saw a pair of muddy driller's boots, tin safety hat, and greasy khakis dropped on the linoleum floor. Two men who worked nights on the midnight tower shared the room.

His mother said she was working nights at the local diner. There was only Clayton's restaurant, a family place that closed at ten, and the all-night diner which was set to trap truckers and now found business booming with three shifts of roughnecks. His mother told him he must never come there when she was working or else she could lose her job. When he asked why, she told him, "They just don't want kids hanging around. We are very busy. Now, you promise. We need the money."

So he promised and stuck to it, waiting at night for her to come home before sleeping deeply, then sleeping late the next morning so she could get her rest. He figured she probably stayed on to work in the place of someone who hadn't shown up. Yet, knowing so much about what *can* happen to a person, he worried that something bad had happened to her.

There were people in all four booths, having the big lunch. Every stool at the counter was covered by a roughneck, trucker, local clerk, Railway Expressman. "Here's a seat, sonny." A big man got up, picking his teeth.

"What's yours?" a plump peroxide blonde, letting her hair grow out, showing four inches of dark roots, leaned through the noontime noise to inquire. She snuck a smoke from the cigarette she had in a saucer under the counter.

"I'm looking for my mom. She works here nights. She didn't come home last night. I wondered if she worked over."

"Hunh?" she asked as if she hadn't heard a word. He repeated the whole thing for her. "You musta made a mistake, honey. Nobody on here nights but Archie the night man. You got the wrong place."

"No," he insisted, "this is where she said." His face reddened as he drew the attention of others in the crowded place. The day's special was chicken-fried steak or fried chicken, with chicken wings as a rock-bottom alternative. The deep-fried smell of cooking oil, the humidity of a busy steam table, made him feel queasy. She had given them a phony name, was his first thought, and he worried he would cause her to lose the job; they did not want to know where she was because of some deal of their own; or she was flat lying in her teeth. Then where was she? "She said she worked here."

"What's her name?"

"Wilma Wayne Wild."

"Never heard of her. You know any Wilma Wild?" she called back to the cook.

"Hell, no! Pick up your order."

The other waitress hadn't heard of her, either: a tall girl with dun-colored hair and skin pocked from years of fighting pimples and an expression that demanded someone propose instantly, now that she had conquered her problem, as if such a thing were part of the guarantee that came with her complexion cream.

"Well, we're awfully busy now," the plump one said. "You must have made a mistake. Try Clayton's." They were clearly looking at him as if he were simple-minded.

When he had gone, she asked, "Any of you ever seen that boy around?"

No one had. "Might have seen him on the street," the feed store man said. "Kids all look alike to me now. See my own on the other side of the street and I can't tell one from the other."

"I think he's—" She twirled her finger around beside her head to signal he was nuts.

He walked slowly past Clayton's restaurant twice. There was only a high school girl and a heavyset older woman waiting on the customers. With that kind of help, it was a cinch if she worked there, she wouldn't be in the kitchen. The girl, a blonde with her hair piled on the top of her head, her little breasts cantilevered within an inch of her chin, popping the buttons on her too-small uniform, saw him peering in the window while taking an order, squared her shoulders, and smiled. She wasn't there. He slumped on home, his hands hooked into his pockets, leaning as if into a gale. "She ought to have the damn decency to let me know where she's at!" he told himself. It was a maddening mystery. "Damn her!" he breathed. He settled down on the upstairs porch of their room, which she called a *mirador*, to read her *Horoscope* magazine. She claimed her life ran just like the books said. He was standing up in his underwear eating a peanut butter and jelly sandwich when she came in about 2 P.M., whewing as if she had run all the way.

"Hi! It sure is hot! I see you're keeping cool. Boy! Am I bushed. I'm not working tonight. I doubled for a girl. They said I can take off tonight."

"Who?" he asked, his mouth full of peanut butter.

"The cook."

"Where?"

"You know."

"They never heard of you."

"What do you mean?"

"I went there. I was worried."

"I told you not to. I'm not using my own name."

"Bull! Whose are you usin?"

"Listen, young man, I don't have to answer to you for anything. And I won't have you going around spying on me—"

"I wasn't *spying!* I was worried."

"Don't!"

"You're a liar, though."

"What do you mean by that?"

"You don't work there."

"So *what!* Quit playing detective. I work. You eat. I don't see you gettin out and finding a little something to put anything on the table."

"I went around. There ain't nothing for a kid to do."

"If you wanted to, you could find something." She had turned the attack back upon the boy, so he felt twice as desperate.

He went out and flopped down on the pad they had on the porch to take sunbaths when the sun was just right. "Maybe I'll just run off," he groused loudly. She did not respond. He heard her humming no recognizable tune while she changed clothes. He was thinking about something else when she came out in a pair of pink shorts and a colorful, flowered silk print blouse with clear glass buttons. She had piled her hair on top of her head. She wore her new sunglasses. Not a breeze stirred the big tree that hid the porch from the house across the wide street. No bird twittered in its branches. Heat had driven everything to shade and water. She placed a pitcher of lemonade and two tumblers on a little side table and sat down, crossing her legs to read a magazine, sipping lemonade. "Have some. It's good," she offered. He refused, staring at her over the crook of his arm. He resented her cheerfulness. She tried to keep from laughing. "You look like a little boy peeking out of a hole."

"No!" His eyes welled up with tears.

"Hey," she chided. "That isn't my big man. You aren't going to cry on me, are you?" She reached out to touch him. He jerked away. "Sorry."

*"I wish you were dead! I hate your stinkin guts!"*

"OK," she said evenly, pretending to read her magazine.

"DAMN YOU!" He leaped up, enraged, flicking out his left arm tensely, his teeth set, drawing back his right as if to smash her. She cowered in the chair, drawing up her leg to protect herself, cringing, lifting her hands in a gesture of purely feminine, ineffectual self-defense. His rage collapsed in him. She caught his wrists, her magazine sliding off her knees, pulling him down and burying his sobs in her belly, hugging his head. "I was so worried."

"I'm sorry," she soothed, stroking his head.

"When you're out all night, I just don't know if you're ever coming back," he said.

"I'll never leave you," she promised.

She slid down on the pallet, cradling his head in her lap, turning his head so it would not be so close to her sex. Beneath the perfume, he could smell the unique scent that was her, as pleasant to him as the smell of his own sweat. She moved his head further along her thigh, stroking his eyebrows with her fingertips. "When you were a baby, I could put you asleep like this." Where his cheek touched her bare thigh, their skin felt welded. "Guess who I saw? Mr. Harris. Remember the nice man who gave us a ride to Houston last year? He's a driller here on the midnight tower. He sends his regards. Maybe he'll come over Sunday and take us to Victoria for dinner and a show. Would you like that? You liked Mr. Harris, didn't you?" He nodded yes to both questions, rolling his cheek heavily against her belly, aware of the crush of hair in there. She looked down at his shorts, then scooped his head up with both hands and fell backward on the mat, wrestling playfully. He looked down at her face and saw the fine light fuzz along her jawline, a shallow minute crater left from chicken pox. "You're growing up so fast," she observed, brushing his hair back from his face. "We've got to get you in a school where you can meet some kids your own age. It isn't good for you to spend so much time with me."

"I don't hardly see you! You leave before dark and don't come back until nearly one or two and sleep all morning."

"I mean, you should have some friends your own age." She brushed his lips with her fingertips. "God! Sometimes you're a very beautiful boy. Almost pretty enough to be a girl. All right! I take it back." She forced his head onto her shoulder.

"You don't really like me no more," he said.

"I do so! What makes you say that?"

"You never talk to me anymore."

"Oh, I do. What do you want to talk about?"

"Like we used to. Everything. Now you're always too busy or too tired, or you aren't home."

"Well, I'm sorry if that's so, but we have been kind of on the go for quite awhile now. I get worried. I'm tired of hustling from pillar to post. I want to settle down and live nice for a change. I *really* do."

"But if I try to touch you or anything, you get angry. Like you don't love me."

"I do love you." She hugged him tightly. "I love you more than anyone. If I didn't, do you think I would keep on trying and hoping to make our life as nice as I can? You don't know what I have gone through for you."

"But you don't ever kiss me or anything, anymore."

"I thought you were getting too big to want your old mom to kiss you."

"No, I'm not."

"Then give us a kiss."

He raised up and leaned over her. She licked her lips and looked soft and kind. He lowered his lips upon hers and pressed with increased ardor as he had studied lovers in the movies until with eyes wide she protested, "Mmmm! Mmmmmm!" He reached up and gently covered her left breast with his hand. She quickly covered his hand with her own, twisting her face away. "*Jacky!* Please. Let's not get that started again. We promised."

"I just want to," he protested.

"Now, now. Be a man." She pried loose his hand and removed it from her breast. "Let's be nice, now."

"I don't want to be nice! I want to touch you and love you."

"That's not loving me. If you aren't going to behave, I'm going to get up. Can't you just lie still and we'll—I thought you wanted to talk."

"I want to *do* something!" he insisted, his face wrinkled in agony.

She extricated herself from him and sat up, tucking in a wisp of hair. "You'll have to find yourself a girlfriend," she advised.

"I can't! I don't know no girls. Girls my age don't even have tits."

She smothered a laugh. "Well, you're big enough to pass for fourteen or fifteen. I'll give you a couple of bucks, go out, ask somebody to go to

451

the movies." She stood up. She went to her purse and returned with two singles. Looking up, he could see up the legs of her shorts. "Go on, take it. Go out and scout around. I'll bet you can find a cute little girl who's just dyin to meet you."

He dressed in a hurry and pocketed the money. "Have a good time, dear." She smiled after him.

Two blocks away the little fundamentalist church was holding Wednesday night prayer meeting. The street was broken, patched black-top with old elms and oaks shading the yards of the two-story frame houses. Beside the white frame church, cars and pickup trucks were parked off the shoulder in the grassy ditch, and a saddle horse cropped grass around the base of a chinaberry bush in the front yard to which it had been tied. The sound of the congregation singing "What a Friend We Have in Jesus" *a cappella* came wavering up the street: ". . . All our sins and troubles bear. . . ."

He walked from one end of the town to the other. Two boys and two girls came rattling into town in a '28 Model A roadster, laughing, flying wet bathing suits from the door handles. They were all sitting on the backs of the seats. The driver was steering with his bare feet. "Hey, Claude Dean!" one of the girls yelled and waved at Jack. He waved back. The boy said, "That ain't Claude Dean."

The police chief of the three-man police force, coming from Clayton's, picking his teeth, hollered at the car, *"T. J. Berry, you sit down in that dang car, heah!"* The girl on the back of the rumble turned and thumbed her nose at the officer. But T. J. sat down. "Dang kids," Jack heard him mumble when they passed.

Jack went into Clayton's, the screen door snapping behind him like a trap. The room was high, with a pressed metal ceiling from which hung two electric fans in nacelles like airplane motors. Varnished shelves going all the way up to the ceiling behind the counter made Jack think the place had once been a dry goods store. The girl set a tumbler of murky Texas water on the counter in front of him and whipped her order pad from her pocket.

"Guess I'll have a cheeseburger and a chocolate shake."

She called his order and began making his shake. She looked a little like his second cousin, Babe, a natural blonde with short strong arms, curvy and soft, already at fourteen or fifteen nearly the woman she was going to be for the next fifty years, a rubber woman like his mother who could bounce from man and the wall and back again. She reminded him more of Lana Turner than she did of Babe, he decided.

452

She poured the thick cold shake into the large Coke glass in front of him and set the sweating metal container beside the glass. "I ain't seen you around here much, before. I saw you walk by earlier. Your folks with the oil people?"

"My mom and me moved down ahead. My stepdad's finishing up a job and will join us later."

"I guess you'll be goin to Goliad High, then, won't you?"

"Yeow, I guess."

"You go out for any sports?"

"Football, baseball, basketball, track, wrestling—"

"We don't have no wrestling. You got the pink eye or something?"

"Hunh? Oh!" He removed his big Air Corps sunglasses. They grinned at each other.

"What's your name?" she asked. "Mine's Linda." She jerked her thumb at the pin made from tiny alphabet noodles glued to a background and varnished to spell her name, which she wore at the end of the inrun on her little ski-jump breast. "It means 'beautiful' in Spanish," she informed him, modestly lowering her lashes.

"Well, there you are!" he exclaimed, fulfilling her expectations.

"Oh, no, not *really*. My nose is too pug, my seat's too big. . . ."

"Yeow. You are," he insisted.

"Well, I *was* Pep Queen last year. And I'm just a sophomore. But I don't think I'm beautiful." She posed in a way that elevated her little boobs and made her round rear stick out as if her back were dislocated. She smoothed her blond upsweep. "Most people think I look older when I have my hair up. How old do you think I look?"

"Fifteen . . . sixteen."

"Aw, you been peekin!" she squealed. "Most folks think I look seventeen at least. One fella travelin through here sellin auto supplies was so surprised when I told how old I was he nearly fell off that stool there. He wanted to take me over to Victoria dancin. He thought I was twenty."

"You go out with boys?"

She looked at him as if he were odd. "Sure. I been datin since I was twelve. How old are you, anyhow?"

"Fifteen," he lied.

"I went steady last year with Billy Bob Ocker, the captain of the football team. He's goin to Texas Tech next year and had to go practice with the team. But he still sees me when he's in town."

"Oh."

"But I go with other boys now, too."

"Would you like to go to the show with me?"

"I already seen it."

"Maybe when it changes?"

"OK. But I work until ten every night except Sunday."

"You walk home after work?"

"Yeow. Unless some boy picks me up. Your folks have a car?" she asked pointedly.

"Well, my stepdad does, but it ain't here."

"What kind?"

As long as he was lying, "A forty-one Lincoln convertible. He always likes a heavy car."

"Wow! Does he let you use it?"

"Sure. When he's here."

"What color?"

"Uh, maroon."

"Oh, great! Hey? If you come back around ten, you can walk me home."

When she gave him his change, she let her fingertips touch his palm, and he was sure he was in love. He tipped her a dime. "See you later," she promised low, making it all the more intimate. She all but blew him a kiss.

The movie was a Don "Red" Berry Western with a Bugs Bunny cartoon, chapter twelve of a Red Circle serial, a newsreel, and a Wild Bill Elliott oater. It was a small theater with a single aisle down the center and the folding seats only half cushioned. He sat next to the wall about halfway down eating a huge nickel bag of popcorn, seeing in the blond heroine a hint of Linda strong enough to wish the theater were a big-city barn of a place so he could jerk off under cover of his Stetson hat. "She's had it." He toughly assured himself of the girl's virtue. "She's had plenty stuck in her." He could tell.

"Why do you bite your nails?" She lifted his hand in hers, their fingers laced.

"I don't know. I just do."

"I used to. As bad as you. Then I stopped biting them one at a time. Mom gave me a dollar for every one I let grow out. I sometimes still bite my thumb." She showed him her thumbnail, peeled to the quick as were all his own nails. Every once in awhile as they strolled along the broken walks beneath the big trees, the back of his hand brushed her thigh. It seemed to him such short span to his goal. They left the walk for the shoulder of dirt road where there were only two or three houses to the block, with chicken coops, cows and horses fenced in beside and behind, where gardens grew with tomato vines climbing up laths and broomsticks topped with rags to scare away the birds. "Maybe sometime you can pick me up in your stepdad's car and drive me to school."

"Sure. He won't drive it out to the oil rig."

She squeezed his arm against her. There was nothing in town to compare with his stepdad's maroon Lincoln convertible. And when on the dark porch of her parents' four-room, asphalt-sided house, he kissed her so easily, he resented the rich kid he had made himself out to be. If he had told her the truth, would she have been so easy to kiss? She opened her mouth and searched for his tongue with her own. She broke away. "Don't you French kiss?" He wasn't sure. "Don't tell me you never have?" She obviously thought rich boys where he came from lived sheltered lives. She was charmed. "Let me teach you. I'll do it to you the way you're supposed to to the girl, OK?" She came close, opening her mouth as if to take a bite of him, then closing on his lips and working his lips apart with her own, inserting her tongue between his teeth, finding and caressing his. "See?"

"Yeow."

"Like it?"

"Yeow."

"Hey? You ever laid a girl?"

"Well, not exactly."

"A virgin! Wow. You sure you're fifteen?"

"Yeow."

"Kiss me, you fool." He kissed her as she had shown him, clutching her rigidly to himself. "Don't hold me so tight," she protested. "Let me breathe." When he relaxed, she moved her body against him. When she had the rigid lump in his Levis against her soft mound, she crooned in his mouth and moved against him as if screwing. He moved, too, about fell off his high-heeled boots, his head swimming, so when the spotlight from the road hit him, he wasn't certain if he had come or been shot. Police! was his first thought. Her lips looked so swollen and beautiful in the stark light. Their shadows were nine feet tall on the wall. A piece of her upsweep had come down. He was aware of his front feeling cool after having been pressed against the girl. There was someone running across the dusty front yard; there was someone else just behind.

"Billy Bob!" she cried when his big feet in dusty cowboy boots leaped onto the front porch.

Jack could see a corona of light shining through curly hair. A hard hand coming out of a denim jacket took his arm and flung him away from the girl. "Whatcha doin fooling around with my girl, you sonofabitch?" he demanded. Jack could still only see the dark bulk of him. He didn't know what to say.

"He was just seeing me home," the girl explained in a whining, frightened voice.

"And practically diddlin you standing up on the front porch. I coasted up five minutes ago with my lights off, you bitch. Now who the hell are you, and where the hell did you crawl from?"

"I'm Jack Andersen," he said, his voice sounding in his own ears like a girl's. "We just moved here."

"Break his fuckin face, Billy Bob," the guy behind him encouraged.

"Shit, he's about to piss his pants," Billy Bob snorted. "What the hell you doin with my girl, anyhow?"

"I didn't know she was your girl. She said I could walk her home."

"Is that right?" he demanded of the girl.

"Well, yes. But you didn't say you was comin by. You ain't come over in a week."

"I been busy."

"Well, how was I to know?"

"You just know this. I don't want you messin around little twirps like this when I ain't here." He shook her roughly by the arm. "You hear me?"

"*Yes!*" she said angrily. "But I don't get to have no fun!" she protested. "I don't consider we're goin steady no more."

"I don't give a crap what you consider. I catch you fuckin around with some shitbird like this an I'll break your neck *and* his." He mashed his fist slowly into Jack's face. "And don't let me ever catch you around her again. You understand?"

"Go on, kick his ass so he'll believe yuh," his buddy in the yard advised.

"I ast you, did you understand?" he mashed harder.

"*Yes!*" the boy mumphed around the bigger boy's fist.

"Then you scat. And don't let me see you around here again!" He flung Jack off the porch.

His buddy tried to take a kick at Jack, swore, and swung at him, swearing, "Sonofabitch!" as he spun and dodged away. "Yella!"

"What the deuce's goin on out there?" A man in long johns came to the door to find out. "Eh! Oh, it's you, Billy Bob. Whyn't you put out that damn light and let us honest folks sleep?"

"Leroy! Put out that light," he instructed the other in the yard. He

456

stood there with his arm around the girl's waist. She glanced back, trying to see Jack going away down the dark road.

"Well, daughter, are you comin in or stayin out?" the man asked.

"We was just goin for a little ride, Mister Calkins," Jack heard Billy Bob say nicely. The girl looked trapped.

"Well, try and not wake creation when you come in next time," the old man said. The light went out.

When Billy Bob's Ford passed Jack, it swerved sharply, forcing the boy to leap into the ditch. The laughter of Leroy was what the boy heard. Then he saw it was Billy Bob and the girl in the back seat, and the other guy driving. He remembered how she had taught him to kiss, though the memory faded quickly into the numbness he still felt from the bigger boy's fist mashing his lips. There was a cold slick on his left thigh where he had come a little in his Levis. He imagined them parked somewhere, Billy Bob doing it to her and the other guy watching, standing guard. He felt completely lost between the riches he did not have and the size and strength he had yet to possess.

The door across the hall was closed and locked with a padlock. His mother was sleeping but awakened when he came in. "How'd it go?" she asked sleepily.

"OK," he muttered.

"Oh. . . . Want to tell me about it?"

"No."

"OK." She yawned. "Maybe you'll have better luck next time."

He blamed her for getting him into the scrape he had been in, lying there so comfortable and not caring! He stripped to his shorts and piled roughly in beside her, laying his arms under his cheek, with his back to her.

"I'm sorry, baby," she crooned, stroking his shoulder with her fingers.

"I ain't no damn baby!"

"I know you aren't. But you'll always be *my* baby."

"I don't want to be!"

"I know it's rough being the age you are. It's the hardest time of your life. But you'll come through with flying colors. I can count on you. Come on, roll over here. You aren't mad at me, are you?" He let her turn him. He snuggled into the warm softness of her. "Night, night," she said, intending to give him her standard good-night peck. He forced her lips open with his and drove his tongue into her mouth, finding for an instant her own. Sputtering, she twisted away. "I don't like that!"

"Isn't that how Bill kisses you?" he sneered.

"It is not! I never liked to French kiss. I just don't like it. That's the quickest way to turn me off I know."

"How do *you* kiss, then?"

"Like this." She made her lips very big, very wet, and very soft, but only slightly parted. "There." She leaned back. He preferred the other way but did not say so. "You've been getting around more than you let on, buster. Who taught you to kiss like that?"

He told her about walking the girl home, leaving out the part about her boyfriend, changing it so it was he who walked away from her. "She was just a stupid peapicker," he said.

"But maybe she'd show you something else," she said slyly.

"I wouldn't want to with her."

"Wasn't she a clean girl?"

"Aw, you know. She didn't appeal to me."

"Wasn't she pretty?"

"Yeow. She was pretty. Looked sort of like Lana Turner, only younger, you know."

"Well, that sounds pretty good."

"Yeow, she was. But I just want somebody like you." He cowered in the silence, following his daring.

"Oh? I'm sure she was prettier and nicer than me." And he knew from the tone of her voice *she* was fishing. His heart leapt cunningly in his breast. He snaked his hand up and inside her bodice.

"No she wasn't. No one is."

"No, now. Let's be good." She patted his hand.

"Just let me hold it," he bargained.

"If that's all."

"I promise."

"All right. Night, night, then."

"Night, night." He kissed her shoulder, and she laid her cheek on the top of his head.

He was dreaming of being straddled in his sleep by Rosalind Russell, of all people. He did not even *like* Rosalind Russell. At least he hadn't until that moment when just as she was about to put him in her, he awoke to the clatter of leaves outside in the top of the big tree, stirred finally by a vagrant breeze. He thought he smelled rain.

He reached down to where her gown was rucked up to her thighs and began gently tugging the twists out from under her to slide it up over her butt. She awoke angrily, snatching it back down. "If that's all you think about me, you can just go live with your grandma!"

"It *isn't* all I think of you," he protested to her back. "I just *got to,*

Mom. I *got to!*" He made directly to pull up her gown while she was awake.

"Listen, all I want to do is get a little sleep. *Please!* I told you, I understand. But I can't help you."

"Yes you can if you want to."

"*No-I-can't!* Don't you understand? Can't you go play with yourself or something?"

"It don't do no good. I got to know how it feels. If I don't, I think I'll go nuts. I really do!"

"Oh, it can't be that bad."

"It *is!*" All the while he was tugging to get her gown up, she struggled to keep it down. He got one hand on bare skin.

"Stop it, now!"

"No!"

"Yes!"

"I got to! I'm going to!"

"Now listen here— *Don't!*" He got his hand on her sex. *"Stop-it."* She struggled, only exposing herself more, then clamping his hand tightly between her thighs where he had plunged it, so tight he could only wiggle his fingers, she laughed through her nose. "Ha!" Now he was stopped. But twisting with all his might, he turned his fingers toward her womb. She held his wrist with both hands. As a last effort, she dug her nails cruelly into his wrist. He gritted his teeth and pressed harder. His fingers sought to open her.

*"All right! Here it is!"* She yanked up her gown, spreading her legs wide. "There! Help yourself. Have fun!" She turned her face away from him. "It's always open house with old Wilma."

He just touched the dark hair. He had never seen it all that way before. He explored the total perimeter and depth of it and realized she was crying. "Don't cry," he said. "Why are you crying?"

"Because you don't love me. Because I always have to live like some, some *thing!* Because every man who looks at me tries to get into me. God knows why! I look like an old bag. I never wanted it to be like this. . . ." He covered her with her gown. She turned and threw herself in his arms, her tears wetting his shoulder and throat. Her hair smelled clean. "I just wanted us to live and be like everyone else. I never wanted much, just a nice place and a good husband, and when I found out for sure I couldn't have any more kids, I wanted you with me all the more. You're all I've got. I love you so much and feel so bad about what you've had to go through. I understand how you feel, and if there was anything I could do to help you out, I would, honey, don't you know that? But what you want me to do is wrong, and if I let you, you would never forgive me."

"Yes, I would," he protested.

She laughed a bit through her tears. "Yes, probably you would. Monkey."

"It's just I feel like I'm going to go nuts if I don't get to do something soon," he said. "Like I'll explode. Sometimes I feel like killing you, I want to do it so bad."

"Oh, baby, listen, don't think things like that. Maybe I can help you out."

"How?" He was cunningly wary.

"Well, I know a girl. Maybe she'll give you a chance."

All he wanted was a chance. "When? Is she pretty as you? What's her name? How old is she? Why would she?" She was swept under with his questions. He only half believed her, so his interrogation took the tone of cross-examination until she clapped her hand over his mouth.

"I promise you I will do my best."

"An if she don't, will you?"

"Jaaaaaaack—you! You are *impossible!*"

"I don't care. If she don't, you got to."

"I'll do my best, OK?"

"Yeow. But just in case, you *got* to." He frankly couldn't imagine how she could convince a grown woman as pretty as she said the one she had in mind was to let him do it to her. OK if she did. But she would have to make good if she didn't. He had decided it absolutely in his mind. He could pin her easy. He could hold her down by her wrists so she had to give up. "Now you've promised," he repeated.

"Then let me get some sleep, hunh?"

"OK. But you promised."

"Good *night,* Jack."

"Night." He curled against her back and she cupped his hand on her belly.

"Now lay still and let me sleep or I won't ask her."

He wondered in the dark why he had fallen in love with Rosalind Russell. Of all the stars he could have dreamed about. . . .

# 39

EVERY night when she came home, the boy would ask her if she had fixed it for him with the girl as she had promised. "I'm working on it," she faithfully reported.

Saturday morning they caught a bus to go visit Bill. She wore her seersucker suit, fresh from the cleaners, her sunglasses, and a wide-brimmed straw hat. She caught their reflection in a store window and was stopped for a second with her mouth open. It seemed impossible that the tall weed in Levis and cowboy hat was her son. She had always seen in him the baby he had been. No one looking at them would believe they were mother and son.

"What's the matter?" He turned back.

"Nothing. There was just a dress I wanted to see in that window. I wish you'd take off those big sunglasses. They make you look so much older and tough."

He tried looking even tougher, happier than ever about copping the specs from a Polaroid display in a Rexall store back in Corpus. There were no stores in Goliad big enough to steal from.

Before going out to the prison farm, they had to stop in town to see a man called "Judge," who had an office in the county court house. Inside, though the building was not air-conditioned, the dim marble corridors were cool as a cave. There was no elevator, only a wide, sweeping stair-case up around the rotunda. They found an office on the third floor.

There was a rolltop desk and a wall of books in the small anteroom, an old leather settee, a couple of straight chairs, and a floor fan in a cylinder, like a footstool. The "Judge" wore a sport jacket and slacks, shoe-string tie on a sport shirt, and tan cowboy boots that had low, elastic, gored tops like Romeo slippers. His rimless glasses were tinted a pale green. He told the boy, who was parked on the fan, "Don't sit on that, son. That ain't a chair." He seemed annoyed the boy was there. He sized the woman up obliquely, out of narrowed eyes.

"I'm very pleased to meet you, sir." She smiled and put out her hand. He shook it, staring at her breasts, grunting. "Bill said to come see you about submitting an appeal for a parole. He said you were the man to see."

"Well, can we talk privately?" He obviously meant the boy.

"OK." His mother's voice sounded suddenly shaky. "Jacky, why don't you wait for me downstairs? I won't be long."

"OK." He got up and slouched out. He knew what they were up to. That bastard was going to screw her. Why else couldn't they talk in front of him? She didn't have enough money for a damn lawyer. She'd said she hoped she could pay his fee off in installments. Well, he was about to get his first. Oh, he knew. *The stinkin bitch! To hell with it!* he decided.

A Mexican secretary scooting between offices with a sheaf of papers in her hand smiled at him, her enormous brown boobs in her white peasant blouse jumping along a half a step in front of her. *"But they are old bags by the time they are thirty,"* he heard his mother advise him.

The building sat upon its own square. He went out and lay down on the grass beneath a strange, bitter-looking tree that had slick, greenly primeval leaves. He leaned on one arm, sucking the sweetness from a blade of grass, watching the occasional leggy Texas girl or bouncing Latino pounding the hot walks in high heels. He knew in his heart, as surely as he knew the great ball under the pale sky on which he lay was turning, that she was letting that snotty old bastard put it to her while he waited outside like a jerk. Oh, man, he didn't care. But he narrowly and ruthlessly saw no reason under the circumstances why he shouldn't be getting some, too. "She better, by God, come through, like she promised," he reminded himself.

She came out an hour later wearing her sunglasses, looking into the depths of her purse. They hailed a cab.

"What took you so long?" he asked, the sneer creeping into his upper lip.

"I wasn't *so* long."

"Yes, you were."

"No, I wasn't. There were a lot of things to discuss."

"Oh, you were discussing?"

"Now, what is that supposed to mean?"

"You know."

"No. I don't know what you're acting so smart about."

"Yeow, you do."

She shook her head desperately.

They turned into a gravel road between large level fields of low green vegetation. It was the best gravel road Jack had ever seen, smooth as a table. The little stones pelleted the underbody of the car like a steady hail. In the field on one side of the road black prisoners in zebra-striped suits just like in the funny papers, or at least suits half zebra, half dungaree, weeded the rows in a stoop under the Reising submachine gun of the uniformed guard. They did not straighten up until they reached the end of a row. On the other side of the road, a gang of white prisoners, all in blue dungarees with a big white "P" stenciled fore and aft on trousers and jackets, did identical work. In the distance on both sides of the road other prisoners were at work. There was no sign of machinery anywhere. A State of Texas dump truck whizzed past with half a dozen black prisoners in back chained together and chained individually by the wrists to another chain around their waists that then went down to their ankles. Two guards with sawed-off pump guns rode in the back with the men. Jack was frightened. Two of the prisoners grinned broadly at the woman and the boy in the taxi. The others stared blankly.

The tan brick building sat a long way back from the road at the end of a long concrete walk bordered with limp, nodding bluebonnets. A flower garden in the shape of the State of Texas decorated the lawn. Jack had expected a dungeonlike place. It resembled a consolidated high school or county airport more, until up close he saw the web of bars in front of glass reinforced with chicken wire in the deep-set windows. They went in under a vaulted portico, where a decorative wrought-iron lamp hung overhead. A voice came from the walls: "Halt. Please state your business."

"Wife of Prisoner Bill Wild, four two seven eight six zero."

"Who is the other individual with you?"

"My son."

A buzzer in the barred, reinforced glass door grated until they were inside. A guard popped out of a little office just to the left and asked them to step in and sign the visitors' register. "Are you carrying concealed upon your person any firearms, knives, tools, weapons, or explosives, narcotics, medicines, tobacco?"

"No."

"Sign here." He gave her a pass. "One visitor at a time," he said.

When she had gone away with another guard, the first indicated the boy could sit on one of the straight chairs there. A big piece of varnished plywood was displayed on the wall: *Weapons and Contraband Taken from Prisoners on This Farm. Don't Contribute to Prolonging Your Prisoner's Stay!* There were guns and knives, zip guns, a rifle sawed down to about eight inches overall, all kinds of files and hacksaws, homemade bombs in gas pipes taped to batteries, a Bible hollowed out to hold a snub-nosed .38, dry old marijuana reefers, the whole weed, capsules of dope, hypodermic syringes—the accumulation of years of desperate schemes that never came off, each weapon, weed, or shot the marker of dead dreams of escape. The boy thought of all the men who had never received the things on the board. The effort involved in it all seemed fantastic.

"Anyone ever break out?" he asked.

The guard looked at him suspiciously. "Nope." Then he mellowed a bit. "Once in awhile someone runs off, but we always get them back. How old are you, boy?"

"Fifteen," he lied.

"You can't go back, then. Supposed to be eighteen."

His mother returned, laying the pass on the desk. "He's too young," the guard explained. "Got to be eighteen."

"Doesn't he look eighteen?" his mother asked.

"Go on, kid, but if anyone asks, you swore to me you was eighteen."

Bill was at the barred door of a narrow hall separated from the boy by a barrier four feet away. A guard lounged back against the wall. Bill had on the dungarees with white "P's." He looked a lot older than the boy remembered. His hair was grayer. It had been cut in a prison bowl haircut—no sideburns. The boy grinned at the man's naked temples. He looked a lot less fierce that way than he did outside.

"Ain't that some haircut?" he asked. "You could cut hair better'n these peapickers in here. Well, you're growed almost to a man, now. Your mama says you're a big help. Guess when I get out of here we'll have to see who's best, hunh? That a deal?"

"Sure."

"I'm makin you a hand-tooled belt with a monel and brass buckle I designed myself. We got a good shop here. I'm makin a purse for your mother. If my parole goes through, I can be out of here by Christmas."

"We sure hope so," the boy mumbled. Yet there was something about Bill behind bars that made Jack feel he was somehow happier, or at least less haunted, in there. He did all his talking as if listening to an inner voice or expecting to be called any moment. He wanted out. But in there he had put on weight.

"I sure hate for you to have to see me like this," he said. "I guess you're man enough now, though, to keep it to yourself. I mean, your grandma and grandpa don't have to know, right?"

"Sure, Bill."

"Well, it's been good to see you. Hang in there and tough it out, Jack. It's a hard life if you don't weaken."

In the cab back, the boy said, "Don't you think he seems sort of happier locked up?"

"I do not! Whatever could make you think such a thing?"

"I don't know. He just seemed more peaceful."

"That's because they put stuff in their food to keep them from getting excited."

"What kind of stuff?"

"You ask Bill when he gets home."

"No. Tell me."

"Saltpeter," she whispered.

"Soft peter?"

She giggled behind her hand and shook her head. "Tell you later."

She was a little late getting to work. Her employment was still a big mystery to the boy. She didn't work at either of the cafés, she didn't work at the drugstore. It was three in the morning when she rolled in, playfully drunk. She snapped on the light, calling, "Everybody up! Up! Up! Everybody up. Come on. Surprise!" She had two quart containers of something. "Chicken chow mein!" He had hoped at least for ice cream.

"Guess where I got it," she demanded. "Won't guess? I'll tell you. Mr. Harris brought it to me all the way from Victoria. Wasn't that nice?"

He grunted.

"Oh, well, what do you know? You just like junk. You don't know what's good. I was so pleased. It was more touching than roses." She made a nest of noodles from one container in a cereal bowl and filled it with glop from the other. The remainder she put in the refrigerator. "For our Sunday dinner." She got up when she had eaten, unsteady as she was, and brushed her teeth so not one germ might survive. "Whooo, help me, Jacky." She sailed toward the bed, arms outstretched.

"Where'd you get drunk?"

"You sound like your grandma," she chided him. *"Where'd you get drunk?"* she mocked, speaking through her nose. "I'll do that!" She unhooked her own brassiere. "By the way, it's all set."

"What?"

"Now, *what?*"

"The girl?"

"Right! I'll take you over tomorrow. She's doin this as a special favor to me, so you get a bath and clean up."

He would start now! She pushed him back with her hands, held him at arm's length studying him there in his briefs. "My little boy's going to be a man." And hugged him tight.

He lay awake the rest of the night, frightened of what awaited him that day, yet determined to see it through. He only wished "the girl" weren't some mysterious stranger. He envisioned a kind, blond young woman, barely older than the girl he had walked home from Clayton's late that night, an understanding, intelligent woman. His mom had said her husband was in the Army, which was why she needed a guy. It did not entirely make sense, nor did he fully believe her, but he had to see it through. And this time it better not be one of her lousy promises that never come true. He bid his warning invade her sleep.

Every motor in town was shut off. From distant small churches the songs of Sunday morning services marched the dusty streets. Jack thought of Sunday on Guadalcanal from the movie. The day was warm, but with a breeze. Fluffy white clouds chased each other across the silent high sky. Sticking to a side street, they ambled across town. They passed a few people hurrying to services.

"Nervous?" she asked, smiling.

"Yeow. Sorta."

"She won't bite you. Just relax." She winked at him. Then she laughed. "If these good citizens knew where we were going, they'd flip."

Suddenly there was not a soul in sight. Off somewhere a dog barked briefly. A hawk circled a pasture over the spot where something small had died. They walked down a dirt road where there were no sidewalks for about half a mile. His mother hummed and remarked what a mild day it was. He bore straight ahead. Until it was done, there was nothing else on his mind. "Here we are," she said, turning up the drive to a dilapidated old house. The boy's heart sank. She had done it again. The house was so far from his vision of what the place was going to be he felt insulted and hurt that she thought so little of him as to bring him to a place like that. "Wait here," she said.

Rage, hatred, disgust washed through him like different fevers. He hadn't expected a palace, a princess . . . just a decent place, a regular woman. No girl of his dreams could come out of there. A very fat cat came mewing from under the sagging porch and rubbed against his leg. He bent down to stroke its head and tickle its neck until he felt its motor running. "Like my pussy?" a woman's voice that made him think of a St. Louis aunt cracked behind him. He turned. A tall woman with a high-cheekboned face beneath a sleepy mop of reddish hair stood in the doorway, wrapped in a silk kimono open in a slit from the hem to the waist, where she hugged herself, a cigarette in one hand, so her leg looked a mile long. His mom was nowhere in sight.

"I'm Rusty," she said as if it were a joke. "What's your name?"

"Jack."

"You a little shy?"

He shrugged. She came near and squatted down on her high heels to take her cat. She hung her cigarette in the corner of her mouth, squinting against the smoke that trailed upward across her right eye. He could see in the gaping top of her kimono her long, big breasts. They were the shape of large mangoes. In spite of her flaming hair, her skin seemed tawny as a Mexican's. "You like to come to my room and play with my pussy?" she asked slyly, squinting over the cat.

"I don't know," he stammered. He *thought* he was certain what she meant. But she did not at all fit the description of the girl his mother said he was to meet.

"How old are you, honey?"

"Twelve and a half," he said.

"WHAT!" The cat yowled and hit the porch running. It dove off the end and darted back under the house. She was up, yanking her kimono tightly about her, bellowing, "WILMA!" His mother came out at a trot.

"*What?* What's wrong?" She plainly expected to find them twisted into some tragic scene.

"How the fuck old you tell me he was?"

"Uh, fourteen."

"You damn right. An how old does he tell me he is? Twelve and a half! What kind of shit are you tryin to pull on me? Get me up there tryin to fuck some twelve-year-old boy! What are you, crazy? I thought you were straight, had good sense. Wantin me to screw some goddamn baby."

"Listen, he's as grown-up as most fourteen-year-olds," she protested to the tall young woman who had gotten out of a Sunday morning bed and put on her makeup as a special favor to her friend.

"Yeow, then you better see a quack. That boy's got somethin wrong with him or he's some kind of yellow-haired nigger."

"I'm sorry," Wilma whimpered. "It's just he's gettin *too* much to handle. I had to do something. I thought—"

"Forget it. Fourteen, OK. Twelve and a half, no go. Get him an operation or something." She let the screen door slam behind her. He heard her carrying on inside. "Man, now I've seen everything!"

In the road he tried to take his mother's hand. "Don't!" She was mad as hell.

"I'm sorry. I didn't know you meant, uh, whore."

"What? Did you think I could just go out and knock on the door of some cute little housewife?"

"Well, she wasn't like you described. You said short and blond—"

"Rita wasn't feeling good today. Rusty agreed to do me a favor and take her place. You're just too dumb to know what you missed."

"Now that I do understand, I'd go back."

"It's too late now. You had to shoot your mouth off and tell her you were only twelve. Any other time you would have lied. So why didn't you?"

"I don't know. I didn't think it mattered."

"Well, I've done all for you I can. I stuck my neck out for you, embarrassed myself in front of my—embarrassed me."

He would always remember the look on the woman's face when he told her how old he was. She looked shocked, horrified—"Stinkin whore!" he mumbled.

"What's that? There's no need to call me names, young man. I did what I said I would do."

"I wasn't calling you names." And suddenly he knew that was where she worked. He saw her dressed like the girl on the porch, greeting a boy like himself about fourteen, a dark-haired boy who followed her into the house. The cat sat there looking at him.

Back in the room she changed clothes, putting on her shorts. She lay down on the pallet on her stomach to read the Sunday paper. It was all over as far as she was concerned, he could see that. He put on his bathing trunks and followed her out. "Want some oil?" he asked.

"I'll put it on," she said, reaching for the bottle.

"Will you put some on my back?" he asked, when he had done his front.

"Oh, roll over." She slapped oil on his back. "There. Now let me read the paper."

"Are you mad at me?" he asked.

"No. I just want to read this paper."

"You're mad. I can tell."

"I'm not mad."

"You know what you promised?"

"What now?"

"You know. You promised if she wouldn't do it, you would."

She flung down the paper. "Now-I-didn't-promise-that-and-you-know-it. Now I *am* getting mad!"

"You did! And I'm holding you to it, too. You got to!"

"Well, you're just mistaken there, young man," she huffed, sitting up. He caught her wrist. "Don't! You're *hurting* me," she complained.

"I don't care. You promised."

"I did no such thing—*Jack!* Now let me go."

"I'm going to, damn it! I'm going to." He pitched himself upon her, forcing her down so she grunted like an old cow.

"Stop it!" He stabbed at her breast, hoisted up her halter, baring her breast. He had a knee between her legs. They scuffled about on the papers, wadding and tearing them. "Going to rape me? Is that it?" she huffed, twisting and hissing. "Better men than you have tried." He snapped the button off her shorts. "*Now* see what you've done. Stop it right now! *Don't!* This is terrible, Son. This isn't you. You should see your face. Please don't, baby. You're only going to be sorry and disappointed."

"*You let all those others. Why not me?*" he cried out.

She ceased struggling. He plunged his hand down her belly under her shorts. She caught his wrist but could only restrain him. "Don't, baby. Don't do that, now." He cupped her sex in his hand, buried his face in her bare breast, finding the nipple with his mouth. "Don't do this," she pleaded, stroking the back of his head. She tried to pull his hand away once, then when he resisted gave up. He entered her with his fingers. Once he had forced his way in, she was very wet. "Listen," she said. "I'll make a deal with you. Come to church with me, and when we get home if you still feel this way, OK."

"It's too late to go to church," he argued, wary of her tricks.

"It isn't very long until evening services. Let's take a nice nap, get up and have a shower and go to prayer meeting. It's just too hot now, anyway. Come on. OK?"

"When we come back, though, you'll let me?" He wanted a definite commitment.

"I want you to ask God to show you what's right. And I'll ask Him, too."

"But even if God tells you *not* to let me, will you?" he insisted.

"Yes," she sighed wearily. "Just, please, don't act like this."

"OK. But no matter what." He let her extract his hand, rolled away, and covered his eyes with his forearm.

"This paper is just ruined." She got up, gathering up the torn paper. *The Katzenjammer Kids* was faintly transferred to her damp thigh. She went and lay down on the bed. He remained on the pallet on the porch and dozed, dreaming of a house where Rosalind Russell reigned in a red kimono, and where just as he was about to get between her enormously long, outspread legs, he was devoured by a dragon in one fire-breathing snap. He sat bolt upright. She was gone.

THE BITCH! he screamed in his dry throat, though only a squeak passed his lips. He ran and threw open the closet. Her things were still there. He was trying to determine when she had dressed and gone when she came humming in the door from the shower, her hair wrapped in a towel turban. "What are you looking for?" she wondered.

"Nothin."

"Go take a shower. It's wonderful. You'll feel much better."

When he returned, she was sitting on the edge of the bed, smoothing on her best pair of hose. She hooked them up and lowered her slip over the tops. "Hurry up. I laid out your clothes."

He dressed in clean slacks, a white shirt, and a pair of crepey-soled blue canvas sport shoes he hated and hadn't worn in months. Birds had come to their tree beyond the porch and were piping evening songs. "It's so still," she observed. "It seems like there isn't a breath."

"It's probably going to rain," he said, tying his shoes.

She was ready except for a last touch at her hair and her lipstick. "Come here. Bend down." He bent his knees so she could wet her comb at the sink and plaster down his cowlick. He stared at the thin blouse in the vee of her jacket, all ruffles and froth and alive because of the skin under it. Her spectator pumps were a little smeary where he had run the white over onto the brown, but she looked good. She always looked good.

On the way up the street beneath the darkening trees they heard a deep distant roll of thunder like a heavenly bowling alley. She said, "Woooo," and hurried a bit as if it were going to pour any minute. Then there was another. Off beyond the town the sky was darkly boiling. High-flying birds were hurrying home. The leaves of trees were turned bottom side up, a sure sign it was going to storm.

"Well, we certainly need it," she said as if she had planted crops. "It's been so dry."

It was a plain, small church with two banks of pews separated by three aisles to facilitate taking up the collection and passing communion. But the preacher in the businessman's suit was sporting Argyle socks in the service of the Lord. Wilma choked, coughing in her song book. "What's the matter?" Jack asked.

"Nothing. Just nothing," she said. There were tears in her eyes, and she gripped his hand tightly along her thigh while the congregation sang "Shall We Gather at the River" as if it were not a question.

The preacher was strictly a four-square fire and brimstone hell-shouter. "And God *said!*" He banged the Bible in his hand as if he had a direct wire. "And God *meant!* . . ."

She sat there with her eyes glazed, holding the boy's hand. He figured she was praying. Every now and then her lips moved. Once she bowed her head and covered her eyes for a minute.

"Are you praying?" she asked him.

"No."

"Pray!"

He shook his head he did not want to.

She prayed for them both.

Then they were standing for the Invitation. "Come now brothers and sisters, and any of ye who have backslided, sinned, strayed from the comforting arms of Jesus Christ our Saviour. Come now while we stand and sing."

Cutting in over the preacher the song leader sang, ". . . Weary prodigal come. Come. . . ."

Wilma looked at Jack as if she expected him to hear the call. She sort of nudged his shoulder. He shook his head. A workingman with a face like a Norman Rockwell cover, wearing a gabardine windbreaker, his face burned a deep red, inflamed further by his embarrassment, staggered toward the mourners' bench, his cap in his hand, where the preacher threw an arm over his shoulder and they both went down on their knees, their faces in the pew. When they came up—the song leader running in an extra chorus to give the preacher time to save the man's soul—the preacher's right hand was still on the penitent's shoulder, the left pointing toward the steeple. "Praise God! Praise *Jesus!* This brother who has strayed from the paths of righteousness, who has drank too much from the cup that kills, been less than the faithful husband and father he ought to be, has repented of his transgressions and beseeched our most merciful God and His Son Our Saviour, Jesus Christ, for forgiveness. And herewith rededicates his life to Christ. Stand up, brother! Walk once more in the light of Our Lord. Praise God!"

"Amen," rose from all over the hall.

"Blessed be His name!"

"Blessed be."

"How beautiful His mercy."

"Amen."

"In the name of Jesus Christ, amen."

Everyone rushed up to congratulate the brother on his return to the flock.

The preacher stood there in the shallow vestibule shaking every hand that passed. There was no way to avoid him. He caught her hand, then dropped it as if it had been electrified. Recovering, he retrieved it. "Sister . . . ?"

"Wild," she said.

"Yes. Yes, of course. And this is your, ah—"

"This is my son, Jack."

"Yes, of course. Well, it's a pleasure to see you at church. Fine-looking boy, there."

She took a step, then said, "You're a pretty good little preacher," and they passed down the steps.

"You know him?" the boy asked as they went along the walk.

"Yeow. I know him." He was happy to feel her opinion of him did not differ greatly from his own. She looped her arm through his and pressed it tight against her. "We have to stick together. The whole damn world's screwier than we are. Every time I start getting way down on myself, I meet some lousy hypocrite that makes me feel in my heart I'm as good a Christian as anyone. If it was between that guy back there and me before God, I'd take my chances. Oh, Jacky! What's going to become of us?" She hugged him quickly, tightly. The first big, half-dollar-sized drops of rain dotted the dry walk.

He had taken off everything and sat waiting on the edge of the bed, feeling small and younger than ever. He could hear the rain fall in big, single, wide-spaced drops through the leaves of the tree. It was kind of like living in a tree house. Only the lamp beside the big chair was lit. She put on the radio and found some dance music. She wore only her slip. She flipped it up so he saw her bare white bottom when she sat beside him. "I wish you would just forget this," she said, threading her fingers in his hair. He shook his head no. "I just got to," he piped.

"My baby." She took him in her arms. "I do love you," she told him. "I hope you won't hate me later."

"I won't," he promised. He felt the room was spinning. She took his penis between her thumb and forefinger and stroked it until she could hide it in her hand. She lay back beside him, slipping the top of her slip to give him her breast. She scooted up with her head on the pillow, raised her hips, and lifted her gown. "Come on," she whispered.

"Take it off." He wanted her to remove her slip.

"No. This is all right." She led him over her, opening her legs just enough for him to lie between them. "I hope I'm doing right," she prayed, her eyes looking beyond his head at nothing, reaching down between the quaking, silent boy and herself to draw his penis into her. "Just push a little," she said.

He felt the hot liquid of her and froze, then collapsed, weak as an exhausted runner. She stroked the back of his head crooning, "It's all right, honey. It's all right. I'm here. Go ahead and cry." She made a subtle move and he was out of her. It had just been too much. He had wanted it so badly the achievement was too much to fulfill. "Just lay here beside me and let me soothe your brow. You're wringing wet!" She was shiny with his sweat. She stroked his eyebrows with her fingertips until he dozed.

He did not doze long. He awoke feeling he had missed something. It had not rained, after all. Just those few drops. The thunder still rumbled away toward the Valley. But it was very still and close in the room. The radio continued to play music from some hotel ballroom. When he lifted her hem, she said, "Jacky, why don't you just be still, honey?"

"No. I got to, Mom."

"You did. Wasn't that enough to satisfy your curiosity?"

He did not answer. He played and probed her sex until he felt ready to try again. With her arm over her eyes, she let him roll on top of her once again, but this time she let him find the way himself. In her, he tried to kiss her lips. She would not remove her arm. Her lips were cold. "Just get it over with," she said.

She lay unmoving, moved only as his weight and strength moved her. She wondered at the quickness with which he learned how it all went. It must be instinctive, she decided, her breath beginning to become labored in spite of her indifference. She bit her lower lip. He was no longer such a little boy.

"I love you!" he cried desperately. "Mom!" She rolled her hips upward then so he felt himself completely contained in her warmth. She held him tightly with both arms around his back, moving just a little. Just a little. He kissed her cheek, tasting the salt of her tears.

When he rolled off her, he still held her fast. She covered her sex with the tail of her slip. "Was I OK?" he asked. "Did I do it right?"

She patted him. "Let me get up and go to the bathroom."

"Was I?" he insisted.

"You did OK. Come on, let me up."

He let her go. She sat on the edge of the bed for a minute. "Didn't rain after all, did it?"

"No."

"Sure could have used it. It's sticky." She peeled her slip away from her skin.

"Mom." He stopped her just at the door.

"What?"

"Thanks."

"Don't mention it," she said, going quickly into the hall.

# 40

THE boy stretched on the pallet in the sun, so content between earth and sky he feared neither death nor blindness. His mother came onto the *mirador* wearing shorts and a flowered crepe blouse, carrying a lemonade. She sat cross-legged on the floor and began flipping through a magazine in her lap. She tore out a recipe for some kind of colorful casserole. She looked so young with her hair pulled back and tied with a pink ribbon to match her shorts. He stretched flat on his back with his hands behind his head. Her tan knees looked polished. The world hadn't ended. They hadn't been struck by a bolt from the blue. There wasn't a cloud in the high pale sky for as far as he could see. Grass grew. Birds tweeted.

"You goin to work today?" he asked.

"Um. Got to," she said without looking up.

"I sure wished you didn't."

"Got to eat."

The idea of men being able to come into that place where she worked and do it to her for money raged in his brain. It was a trap in which they were both caught. Yet, he had known all along she was doing something like that. She always had. "What do they pay you?" he wondered cruelly.

"Jack. . . ."

"Well? What do they?"

"Five."

"How many you let do it?"

"Jaa*ack!* I'd rather not *think* about it."

"But you got to do it every night, don't you? Two? Three? How many?"

"If you're going to act like this, I'm going inside. It doesn't mean any-

474

thing, what I do. The men don't mean anything to me. I don't mean anything to them. They just use me and pay me."

"Why?"

"Well, because that's all I can do here."

"I mean them."

"Oh. They are lonely and need a woman for a few minutes. Or their wives don't treat them right. I don't know. Some men just need to go to a place like that."

"Big *boys,* too?"

"Now, that's enough. I don't want to talk about it. On my own time, I like to forget about it. Now, come on. You're just going to make yourself upset."

"I just don't like to think of all those guys and you. What does Bill say about it?"

"I'd never tell him. He knows I love only him. People do what they have to do to live. Except with Bill, it means nothing."

"Never?" He felt in pain.

She tousled his hair. "You think too much, that's your trouble. You've got to get out and enjoy life more."

"I enjoy life when I'm with you."

"Well, you'd enjoy it even more with kids your own age."

Mr. Harris' pickup truck stopped in front. The large man, like a khaki bear, unfolded from behind the wheel and moved smoothly toward the house. "Here comes your boyfriend," he said gloomily. She gave him a disgusted look.

The man tried to ignore the fact the boy was lounging around the house in nothing but a pair of faded light blue swimming trunks in the middle of the day, but he kept glancing at him in spite of himself. Finally he asked, "You *been* swimmin or goin?"

"I was taking a sunbath," he informed the man, who inwardly cringed at the thought.

"I wish there was something for him to do," his mother said. "Some little job or something to take up his time."

"Why, I think they're lookin for a boy over to the hotel. They had one who quit. They never keep one very long."

"Why don't you run over there right now?" his mother suggested. "Maybe if you hurry, you can get it."

He reluctantly dressed and slouched out the door. He didn't want to be a goddamn bellhop. He wasn't going to wear no damn little monkey suit.

He had little to worry about. The hotel did not sport uniformed bellhops. The best it could spring for was a used band jacket and hire a boy to fit it. The clerk, a small, balding man, pink where he wasn't tanned, dabbed at his neck with a wadded handkerchief.

"Let's sit down over here and you tell me about yourself," he offered. Jack told him where he had come from and where he had been. He said he and his mother were waiting for his stepdad to join them. He was going to work in the oilfield.

Jack noticed the man bit his nails even worse than himself. The nails were like a child's at the tips of small pudgy fingers that were nevertheless covered with moist dark hair up to the first knuckle. But he wasn't burly—a pear-shaped man in a narrow-shouldered, rumpled summer suit. His jowls where he shaved were dark with shadow and chapped. He clapped the boy on the knee. "Well, you can start this evening. You come on at four and work until midnight. OK? Oh, I almost forgot. It's two dollars a night and tips."

His mother was so happy to learn he had found employment.

When he came in that evening, Mr. Weefer was having his lunch at the desk, looking over a girlie magazine. When he saw who it was, he did not bother to hide the book. Jack kept glancing at it. It was full of pin-up girls in underwear and high black hose. "You got a girlfriend?" the man asked while he got into the red and black band jacket that still had gold bullion music stands sewn above the braid on each cuff.

"Naw," Jack confessed.

"You like girls, don't you?"

"Sure."

"You ever go to bed with one?"

"Yeow."

"You know what I mean, screw her?"

"Yeow," he admitted.

"Not much, I'll bet."

"Once."

"That's what I thought."

"How'd you like to do it with somebody like that?" He indicated a stripper called Busty LeGrand in such a way Jack wondered if the guy could arrange an introduction. "You like big boobs?"

"Yeow," the boy admitted.

"You ought to meet my wife, then. She's got the biggest ones you've ever seen. Bigger than that."

The boy stared at the picture. It was hard to imagine any bigger than Busty's.

"We were show business people originally. We were with a show that

476

went broke near here and just stayed. Maybe we'll hook onto another show one of these days. Would you like to meet my wife?"

"Yeow, sure. . . ." He couldn't figure the man. He tried imagining him with a wife like the one in the magazine. Well, it was a screwy world.

"I'll take you up later. She's a big woman. But she likes to meet young boys like you. Does looking at pictures like that excite you?" he inquired, shoving the book beneath the boy's nose. Jack shrugged. "I've got some real pictures upstairs. Shows everything. Would you like to see them?"

"I guess," the boy said.

"Watch the desk for me. If the phone rings, answer it. If they want a room, you take this plug and stick it in the hole under the room number and ring by pushing this lever. Listen until the room answers, then hang up. When they're through, the little light will go out and you can disconnect them. Got it?"

"Yes, sir." While he was gone, Jack looked at the rest of the book. He sometimes bought such magazines and hid them to look at and masturbate. He was very suspicious of grown men who carried magazines like that around with them, folded in their pockets, haunting public toilets and parks, a look so much different from a thief's or conneroo's in their eyes—men with private, selfish eyes. Weefer wasn't quite like that. There *was* a lot of the con job in the way he came on. Jack knew something was cooking, and wary, he was willing to go along at least until he had seen his wife's big tits. He looked at Busty LeGrand. Man, that Mrs. Weefer had to have some pair of jugs, for either one of Busty's was bigger than her head.

"Look at these." Weefer laid a deck of playing cards illustrating fifty-two ways to screw before the boy. The Joker was a photo of two dogs doing it—wirehaired terriers—which made Jack think whoever had made the cards was expressing an opinion of the entire pack. Then Weefer sprung a packet of fuck books from another pocket; cartoon books of *Maggie & Jiggs*, with old Jiggs looking like a round pole vaulter running after his daughter, the end of his dong like a 200-watt light bulb. . . . *Tillie the Toiler, Popeye, Etta Kett, Jane Arden, Blondie,* all of his favorite funnies, characters he knew better than his own relatives, stripped bare, fucking until the fur flied. "Give you a hard-on?" the man crooned close by, reaching down backhanded to feel beneath the skirt of the boy's jacket.

"Hey!" he protested. "Watch it."

The man chuckled. Then he said, "Dodge it!" and scooped up the books, stashing them quickly out of sight. A middle-aged couple—a gray-haired, tall, but paunchy man and tall, black-haired woman, so evenly black of hair it had to be dyed—got out of a green Chrysler sedan. The man horsed two suitcases through the door. The boy leaped to be of help. The bags nearly pulled his shoulder sockets loose. The man sized up the lobby. "I told you you should of stayed in San Antone," he reminded the woman.

"Well, it's only for a few days."

"You got a suite or bed-sitting room?" he barked at Mr. Weefer, grabbing the register and pen.

"No, sir, but I can offer you a nice large front double room with bath."

He grunted and attacked the register, threw down the pen.

"That's two oh one, boy." He handed Jack the key. "If you need anything, please just call the desk." He smiled at the large man, almost bowing.

Jack struggled up the stairs with the heavy cases. He let them into the room, lifted the bags on the bag racks right side up, and offered the man the key. The woman was removing her jacket and opening the windows at the same time. Jack turned on the wall fan.

"Will that be all, sir?" He extended his hand about waist high. The jacket was a bit too large, so the damn cuffs almost came to his knuckles.

"Yeow. Bring me the biggest damn pitcher of ice water you can find. And some drinking glasses."

"Yes, sir." He bowed out.

"He's with the oil company. Some kind of supervisor or something," Weefer informed him excitedly.

Jack got the ice water and glasses on a tray and took them upstairs.

The man came to the door in his trousers and sleeveless undershirt. He had gray hairs on his pale shoulders, but his arms and face were sunburned. A golfer, Jack decided. His wife looked up at him blankly from where she sat on the edge of the bed in a black slip peeling a stocking from her pretty left leg. The man tipped Jack a dime. "I was a bellhop in the Muhlebach Hotel in Kansas City when I was a boy your age. If I showed up for work needin a haircut like you do, I'd of been fired on the spot."

"Yes, sir," the boy said.

"Here. Get a haircut." He flipped the boy another quarter. The woman was removing her other stocking when the door closed.

All the exclamations from the fuck books bounced through his head to the tune of "A Tisket, a Tasket." The possibilities of what could be happening behind all the hotel doors at any given time made his mind reel, and every sound was full of erotic portent, every suggestion by Weefer a mere cover for the flaming truth underneath. What were they going to do, Weefer just take him up to his wife and say, "Hey, show him your tits"?

"She likes young fellas, particularly innocent young fellas." Jack did not feel particularly innocent. He tried to look innocent. "It doesn't bother me," Weefer explained. "We have an understanding. We love each other dearly. You understand?"

He did not at all. "Yeow," he said.

A little before midnight, just before Jack was to go off, Weefer said, "Come on, I'll take you up now." Jack's knees felt weak on the stair. Outside the louvered outer door, Weefer gently tapped. "Honey?" he called softly. Jack straightened his band coat, slicked back his hair with his hand, licked his lips. Beyond the door waited the better of Busty Le-Grand.

"It's open, come in," a lilting voice sang. Weefer opened the door for the boy and let him pass, following behind, closing the door after them. Jack was stunned.

"Baby, this is Jack."

He started to smile, thinking it was a joke.

On the bed was a woman in a pale see-through baby-doll negligee who had been the fat lady in a carnival. She looked inflated. She was monstrous. She wore teeny blue satin slippers with four-inch heels. Her little cupid's-bow mouth looked to have been carelessly made in her billowing cheeks by a sculptor's thumb. Her hair looked like a Little Orphan Annie wig. "He doesn't like me," she sniffed at her husband.

"Sure he does. Don't you? Come on over and get acquainted. Don't be shy. She'll treat you fine." He patted the bed beside her.

"Come give me a kiss. I like little boys." She puckered her mouth deep in her face and held out her arms. Her upper arms were like hams. "Because we never had one of our own," Weefer explained. One monstrous elephantine cheek of her pale butt could have crushed him. Her belly rose so before her there was no way she could feel her own cunt. Weefer stripped the nightie from her right shoulder, unveiling her breast as if hauling a basketball out of a tow sack. It was like a living pillow, billowing and rather square. "Here." Weefer took his wrist and drew him toward the woman. He guided Jack's limp hand against her amazingly cool breast. It was almost cold, though damp with tiny drops of perspiration.

"I don't think I want to," he mumbled.

"Take him away, he don't like me!" she shrieked, looking at him as if *he* were the freak; as if he were just some *thing,* a dish she could order removed. *"Take him away."* Whether she repeated it or it merely reverberated in his ear, he heard her say it over and over. *"Take him away. He don't like me!"*

"Sure he does. He's just a little shy," Weefer insisted. He had more hands than his wife had dimples. He was behind the boy, fumbling open his belt, getting his pants down and his cock out with one hand, mooshing Jack's left hand all over his wife's cold acres of flesh with his other hand, keeping Jack's free hand busy with *another* hand, and getting his own prick out and shoving it at the boy's bottom with yet another hand. He had Jack tipped forward, off balance on his toes, trying to keep from being pressed down into the swamp of a woman. The little man was everywhere. Jack got fleeting glances of his intently busy face behind him over both shoulders. Maybe he was *twins,* was a sudden terrible thought. While the woman shrieked all the while, *"Take him away! I don't want him. He don't like me!"*

"Tell her you like her," the man insisted, huffing busily behind the boy. His jeans were around his knees. Weefer was trying to work his own cock in over the top of Jack's jockeys with a forefinger that had to have come from a trapdoor below his navel.

*"If you want him, take him to another room!"* his wife squealed. *"I can't bear this!"*

Jack had borne about all of it he cared for, too. He gave Weefer a shot in the solar plexus with his elbow that made the little man go "Oaf!" falling backward long enough for Jack to slip to one side, hook up his pants about halfway with his left, fending the guy off with his right as he came on again, his dark, thick dong in his hand and a purposeful look in his eye. Jack pushed his sweating face, feeling like a piece of meat in a kennel, got his trousers up far enough to kick the little man in the groin and see him back away holding himself, a pleading look in his eyes. The woman on the bed gulped for air like a beached giant white grouper. He backed out the door and kept right on going. That little guy was a lot stronger than he looked; he was amazed. Then remembering the woman, he wanted to laugh, but it did not really seem funny. "God! Anything goes. Anything goes," he chanted to himself, hurrying along through the deserted streets of the dusty little town. Homeless dogs slunk along in the shadows with the attitude of coyotes.

He had a headache. He had no plan but found himself on Mile Road humping along in the dust in his cowboy boots, bearing on the house that just leaked a little light around every drawn shade. The old cottonwoods chattered like old men with loose dentures when he passed. A '36 Ford two-door skidded into the driveway and ran up in the yard where two other cars and a pickup truck from Akins Hatchery already sat. Four boys led by a bruiser in a letterman's jacket leaped onto the front porch. They opened the front door and went in. When the big one stood in the light, Jack saw it was Billy Bob Ocker, All-State fullback, the boyfriend of Linda Calkins, who worked at Clayton's café. The idea that he might be with his mother drove Jack mad. He ran to the shiny old Ford. There was a pair of girl's lace panties hanging from the rearview mirror. He tried stabbing the tires with his pocketknife but succeeded only in breaking the blade and cutting his hand. He tied the hand with a dirty handkerchief, using his teeth to help make the knot. He crept around the house, trying to listen through the walls under the high, shaded windows. Something brushed against his leg and he screamed, flattening himself against the weathered boards, tasting the old dusty wood, flat against the house, wide-eyed with terror. The cat mewed and the boy recovered, one remove from dying. His heart pounded furiously. "Goddamn cat," he chided himself.

He went all the way around the house. Which was *her* window? He looked upstairs where the eaves of the house were black angles against the dark blue velvet sky. An owl or hawk passed the peak. There were clouds up there somewhere. Everyone hoped they would get rain. He had felt the house all the way around with his hands. He knew the splintery feel of the old boards, their dusty smell. There was music in there and laughter. *Was that her?* It sounded like her laugh. Laughing with Billy Bob. He came back around the front. He tiptoed across the porch. Taking a deep breath, committing his life to eternity, he opened the front door. He followed it one step inside. An old guy in khakis sitting on the couch looking at that day's paper glanced up. The cute blond girl in shorts and halter talking to two of the guys who had come with Billy Bob looked past them to where the boy stood in the open door. Down the hall an old colored woman paused before scooting into the kitchen. A tall woman in a robe came quickly out.

"Well, come in or go out," the young girl in the parlor said. "Don't stand there with milk on your chin."

*"Get out of here!"* Wilma screamed from the stairs. She turned around, her terribly myopic eyes squinting through her own eternal fog. Her face was made up so garishly she looked like a cartoon of herself. Her hair frizzed out below her pompadour like a witch's. Her lipstick looked purple, her mouth drawn on like a clown's. She had drawn lashes

under her eyes, darkened and arched her brows; there was a mole on her cheek she had never had before. Her breasts leaped in their loose halter as she bent screaming. Behind her stood Billy Bob in his letter jacket with the big "G," laughing, his hand on her hip. The woman in the hall was coming toward him. He backed out, closed the door.

"What the hell was all that about?" some guy wanted to know.

"Some punk kid," Vera said.

"That was Wilma's son," Rusty confided to Rita and led the chicken man, who had been waiting for her, upstairs.

He awoke when she came in, his eyes hard and red under the overhead light. "Don't you ever pull a trick like that again!" she warned, shaking her finger at him. "What the hell got into you, anyway?" The garish makeup was gone. Her face looked naked, glistening with the residue of cold cream she had rubbed in and left on her face, her lips soft and pale. Her hair was tucked back under a kerchief. "I could have killed you when I saw you standing there in the door."

"You let that guy in the jacket, didn't you?"

"What? Oh, for godsake!" She turned her back and got ready for bed, undressing in the closet. She brushed her teeth frantically at the sink as she always did, gargled, put out the light, and crawled into bed.

"Night," he said in the dark after awhile.

She pounded her pillow. "Good night," grudgingly. He rolled over and put his arm over her, snuggling up to her back.

"I'm sorry. I just did it. I just wanted to see you."

*"There?"* She moved a bit away from him. "It's too hot," she muttered.

"Yeow. Yeow, there." He told her about the desk clerk at the hotel and his fat lady wife. "Thirty-five cents." He told her what he had made.

"How big was she?" She thought he must be exaggerating, or more than likely making up the whole thing.

"Like a fat lady in the circus. Four hundred pounds."

"And that really happened?"

"You never believe nothing I tell you."

"Well, you do exaggerate."

"She was *big!* And he's tryin to cornhole me and she's like something ugly hidin inside herself. . . ." He scooted back over against her bottom, tightening his arm around her waist.

"Listen! I'm still mad. You just get to your own side of the bed."

"Why do you wear all that crap on your face?"

"I don't know. They like it. Or maybe it's my mask."

"Show me sometime."

"No!"

He cupped her left breast in his hand. "No, you don't!" she hissed. "You roll over there now and leave me alone."

"I just want to. I need to."

"No, you don't! I let you work me into doing something I knew I'd be sorry for, now that's the end of it. Do you understand?" She pried loose his hand.

"But I've got to! If I don't, I'll go nuts."

"I don't *care!* It's over. If you want that, you'll have to get it from someone else. I mean it, Jack. I don't want to hear any more about it! Be a man," she sneered.

"Man, you!" he hissed. "Damn you! *Now be a nice boy. Be a man.*" He mocked her. *"Be a mama's brave boy!* You goddamn whore! I need it. You let me before. You let everybody in this goddamn town. Even that big dumbass bully bastard Billy Bob and his goddamn gang. You let 'em all! Turn over!" He yanked her around. She fought back, pushing him away, her teeth set and bared.

"I said *no,* and I mean *no!*" she insisted.

The top of her gown tore. *"Now* see what you've done!" He slapped her hand away from trying to tuck up the strap. She slapped his face hard. Tears coursed down his cheeks. He threw himself on her, weeping.

"You let me before. *Please,* just once more. What will it hurt?"

"No! I'm not going to. You aren't talking me into it again. Go ahead and throw a fit. It won't do any good. I said no, and I mean no."

*"Please!"* he begged. *"Please,* Mom. I'm dyin. I just got to. You let everybody else. What difference does it make? *Please!"*

"Oh, for godsakes. What a mess. I come home tired and all I want to do is get a little sleep. And I have to go through all this noise."

*"Go on, give him a little and we can all get some sleep,"* one of the roughnecks across the hall called out.

They froze in bed. It was so still they could hear the breeze stirring the leaves of the tree outside the open doors to the *mirador.*

"Now see what you've done?" she whispered angrily.

He hadn't any notion what had seemed so private and in his head might carry beyond their own walls. He was conscious then of every creak of the bed. But he did not worry, really. After all, he hadn't been telling a lie.

# 41

WHEN the boy came into the diner, a derrickman on the midnight tower with the name "Buck" painted on the front of his tin hat nudged the roughneck next to him, and their conversation stopped. The boy did not notice or realize that he was the cause of a lessening in the noontime buzz. He took a stool at Shorty's girlfriend's station, figuring to give business to people he knew. Shorty worked on the same tower as the men at the other end of the counter and shared a room with Buck across the hall from the one the boy and his mother had.

"Do I *have* to wait on him?" the tall, plain, pockmarked girl asked the cook.

The boy was aware of Buck staring at him. He smiled. The man plainly said, "Shit!" and threw his fork in his plate and looked away. His thin lips looked white.

The cook came from the kitchen, wiping his hands on his grease-stained apron. His paper cap was greasy yellow around the part that touched his head. He hadn't shaved that day. A sallow, thin man with bloodshot eyes and a tremendous Adam's apple. He told the boy, "Sorry, kid, we can't serve you."

"Why?" He felt slapped in the face.

"Look, you just better haul on out of here. We don't want any trouble."

"What trouble?" The boy nevertheless got up. Everyone had stopped eating and turned to stare at the thin, tall kid in a faded Levi suit, dusty runover boots, sweated Stetson, and Air Corps sunglasses.

"I'll break his goddamn dirty neck!" Buck vowed, whirling off his stool. The stocky, sandy-haired roughneck beside him pushed him back against the wall.

*"For chrissake, kid, get out of here!"* the chubby, bleached-blond waitress yelled.

"Get out of town!" the other waitress sneered. "The further the better. Get off the world!"

He did not understand. He hadn't done anything. He thought they must be making some kind of mistake. He went into the drugstore to think about it. He had a ham salad sandwich and a lime Coke. He left the drugstore and walked down to the station to watch the train come through and snatch the mail bag and milk cans from their hooks, determined not to let what happened at the diner upset him. He honestly could not think of anything he had done that would warrant such treatment.

The train barreled through. The engineer waved to him from the cab. It snatched mail and milk without a hitch, people in the wide windows blurring past. His eyes went crazy trying to hold an image. The train highballed away, sucking a tunnel of turbulent, dusty air behind it. The boy got up and walked back to the room.

Buck, Shorty, and the man the boy had seen with Buck in the diner were in the hall with his mother when he went up.

"*Go!*" she yelled at the boy as soon as he appeared at the top of the stairs. "Run away!" Her face was twisted agonizingly. She reached out toward him with both hands as if to push him away.

"Come here, boy, we want ask you somethin," Buck said narrowly.

"He's goin to run!" Shorty warned. "Get 'im!" Buck leaped to stop the boy. Shorty pushed the woman back against the wall when she moved as if to help her son.

Buck grabbed the front of the boy's jacket. "No, you don't! Come on, you little sonofabitch!" He got behind the boy and pinned his arms, hustling him to where Shorty held Wilma pinned against the wall.

"We want to hear you say it," Buck demanded. "You fuck her or not?"

"YEOW!" the boy cried out when the man yanked his arms.

"That's all we wanted to know," Buck said meaningfully.

"Oh, listen! *Please!*" the woman pleaded. "He doesn't know what you mean. He doesn't know what he's saying. He doesn't know what he's doing." The words tumbled from her. "Let him be. He's sick. He isn't responsible. He fell on his head when he was a baby and he gets funny ideas. I know I ought to have him put away. But he's all I've got. I can't see him in one of those places. He's harmless. He just gets ideas."

*What was she saying?* Buck had him bent almost double, standing on his toes to take pressure off his arms.

"Looks all right to me," Buck grumbled.

"We just know what we heard," Shorty put in. "And we heard him say you'd let him before. We heard him. Buck and me."

"But he didn't know what he was *saying!*" she insisted.

"*I did so!*" he insisted. "Why you making me out a liar?" He truly wondered, agony twisting his face, straining from the double nelson in which he was being held.

"Is that right, boy, she let you put it to her, hunh?" Buck insisted, putting the pressure on his arms. "Tell the truth or I'll break 'em off."

*"I was telling the truth!"*

"Town whore or not, by God, we got a right to expect some decency," Buck proclaimed righteously, almost femininely.

Wilma felt like a public utility. "Please, *believe* me. You all know I've always treated you fair. You *know* that. But he just goes snap sometimes." She snapped her fingers for emphasis. "Let him go. We'll get out of town if you want. But, please, he isn't responsible for what he says."

"Maybe it's you who's responsible," he said menacingly. "Know what we do to someone who does such a thing where I come from?"

"Come on, Buck," the third man, who had until then stood aside quietly, said. "Let's go. This ain't accomplishing anything."

"I just want her to know what we do to lousy motherfuckers and such where *I* come from. We'd breed you to a boar or pack of dogs; shove a live rattlesnake up you; cut off his plumbing and make you eat it—*then* we'd beat you to death like a goddamn fox and feed you to the gators 'cause you're unfit for a Christian burial. Or maybe they'd chain you to a tree and burn you alive. There's an old nigger oak at home still black in the shape of an old swamp widda who they said wouldn't leave her family alone. Burned the whole fucking family, all 'cept one, a girl who run away. Say she lived in the swamp like an animal, tongue-tied and crazy as a loon from what all she'd seen."

"TURN ME LOOSE!" the boy yelled, kicking and spitting.

"You little cocksucker! Kick at me!" Buck spun the boy around and busted him in the face with his fist. The boy saw stars and went flying backward onto the floor.

*"Don't!"* he heard his mother scream. He tried to clear his head and get to her. She was down, cowering against the wall, her arms wrapped around her head to protect it.

"Let me at her, R. T.!" Buck insisted to the stocky roughneck who was fending him away from the woman.

"What the devil's goin on up there?" the landlady hollered from the foot of the stairs. "If there's any more ruckus, I'm callin the law!"

"Come on, let's go." R. T. shoved Buck toward the stairs.

"It's just there's some things people fit to live don't do," Buck protested.

"Yeow. But you don't know."

"I *heard* what he said! Shorty heard!"

"But like she said. You can see he ain't all there, man."

"Looks right enough to me to know *that* much."

"Naw. Come on, forget it."

"Little bastard kickin at me. Cussin ME!" He tried to kick the boy, but R. T. wrestled him away and bulled him to the stairs.

"You ain't heard the last of this!" Buck warned.

All three tumbled down the stairs and argued out to R. T.'s car. The landlady huffed up. "Now, what was all that about?"

Wilma got to her feet. The boy got up. The man's blow had knocked the point of his broken front tooth through his lower lip. A rivulet of blood ran down his chin and dripped on his tee shirt. "I was afraid there would be trouble when I rented to you. Always is when there's a woman without a husband around."

"We're all right now," Wilma said. "Please let us alone."

"I'll let you alone! You can just start looking for other digs. I'm givin you a week's notice."

"OK." She led the boy into the room. "You all right?" she asked. He nodded that he was. "Come to the sink." She washed his face, examined his lip, put merthiolate and a Band-Aid on it.

"I don't know what we're going to do now," she sighed, casting about the room. "Where'll we go? I don't have enough money to get us out of town. I sent Bill ten. The bus has gone. You sure got us in a fine mess."

"I'm sorry. But why did you say all those things about me?"

She acted like she didn't have time to explain. "I had to say *something*. Listen, those two would have really done something if that other one hadn't been with them. You don't *know* how lucky we are. Look, we've got to do something. Goddamn it, why couldn't you just do like any other kid? It must be retribution." She looked on high.

"I never lived like no other kid."

"OK. OK. I'm a rotten mother and a town pump— Shut up. I've got to figure something. . . . Look, I'm going down and ask Mrs. Blier to let us use her phone. I'll be right back. Wait! Take this." She gave him a butcher knife. "If they come back, you're going to have to fight for your life. If you let them take you, you'll be done for. I probably won't be able to help you."

He looked at the knife she had left in his hand, at the mottled brown varnished door out which she had gone. She could just leave him standing there, he realized, and darted to the porch, where he could watch the front of the house.

"Jack?" she called when she did not immediately see him when she came back into the room.

"What?"

"What are you doing out there?"

"I was afraid you'd run off and leave me."

"Don't think it isn't a temptation," she growled.

"Then do it! I don't give a shit! Go ahead. I don't care."

"Oh, dummy up and give me a hand. Just pack what we can, forget the kitchen stuff. Mr. Harris is coming to take us. So hurry." She blocked the door with a chair hooked under the knob, just in case.

"Get that box from the bottom of the closet. I want to take that." It was the beat-up box which contained all her special personal junk that had trailed them around ever since he could remember.

Mr. Harris honked when he pulled up out front and came right up. She unhooked the door and pressed herself against his big chest. "I'm *so* glad to see you. It was *horrible!*" Jack saw tears in her lashes.

"Yeow. I'd guess. They're talkin around about it. We better get movin. I just told Art to take my tower for me tonight if I ain't back in time. So we better get gone before word gets around."

"You don't know how much I appreciate this. I just don't want you to think that there's any truth in what they are saying—"

"Don't make no difference," he stopped her. "You don't owe me no explanations."

"I just don't want you to think—"

"Forget it. I'm doin what I'm doin because I want to. That's all. We better get goin."

It took the man and the boy one trip to get their stuff secured in the back of the pickup truck. They got in and started up. "They're down at the pool hall drinkin, so we'll get a good start," the man said. He kept to back streets and took Mile Road out to catch the highway below town. When they passed the old silvered farm house where the shades were always drawn and ruts from many cars scarred the front yard, they all pretended not to see it.

It was dark when they rolled into McAllen. "Too late to look for a room tonight," Harris said. "I remember a motel out here somewhere." Presently, he turned into a gravel drive where there was a lighted sign: VACANCY. "Want me to go in?" he asked.

"No. I don't know how I can ever thank you. . . ."

"Don't mention it. Just didn't want nothin to happen to you."

The boy unloaded their stuff in the drive. It was only a couple of suitcases and two cardboard boxes. When he came back around, Harris was pressing some money in his mother's hand. "I don't want to take it," she insisted.

"Don't be a fool. You need it. Call it a loan. When we run into each other again, you can pay me back."

"I *will!*" she promised.

"Well, so long and the best of luck to you."

"Thanks. Really. You've saved our lives. You know how I feel. . . ."

"Yeow. . . . Well. I better be pushin on. If you need anything, you can reach me, I guess. So long."

"So long," the boy said. The man did not answer.

She had specified a room with twin beds. He was already in bed when she finished her shower and came to get in her bed without putting on the light in the room. She had sent a collect wire asking the boy's grandmother to send some money. She wasn't sure she would get it. She had to find a job right away.

"Mom?" he said in the dark.

"What?" she answered finally. Her back was turned toward him, a gentle hill under the distant blanket.

"You forgot to kiss me good night."

"Not tonight. Just go to sleep. One more thing today and I'd just blow my cork!"

He lay there for a few minutes. "Mom?"

"What now?!"

"Do you really think I'm crazy?"

*"Go-to-sleep!"*

"But *do you?*"

For an answer she angrily threw back her covers and flounced into the bathroom, closing the door.

He really wished someone would tell him.

# 42

TRAPPED between poverty that was a personal moral failure and the lure of material reward for citizenship they could never achieve, they were outsiders wherever they moved. Their history was a crazy spider's web of fact, fantasy conceived cinematically, instinctive self-protective lies, and truth shaded toward a modest, acceptable American dream.

After all, what woman would admit to a prospective landlady her husband was in jail while trying to rent a room with only four dollars to put down as a deposit?

The landlady at first thought they were married. The first thing she wanted to know was if they had children. "No! Ah, uh—" Wilma sputtered. The woman cut her off.

"Well, I like kids as well as the next one, but we are just so crowded here and they're always getting into things, you know. Don't get me wrong. I love them, but we have people tryin to sleep at all hours, you know, and babies *do* cry."

"We aren't married."

The woman looked puzzled. "I don't know, then. I'm a—"

"This is my *son!*"

"My land! Oh, I feel so foolish." She blushed and hid her face in her hands, peeking through her fingers. "I just thought— Why, you don't look half old enough to have a boy that big. Forgive me."

"A lot of people take us for brother and sister," she admitted. "He's big for his age. And those sunglasses he insists on wearing make him look older."

"I thought he was in the Army," the woman said, squinting at his khakis.

She showed them the room. A bedroom off the front downstairs hall, a screened-in back porch which provided them with access to the kitchen, which they would share with two Army wives who had rooms on the same floor. "There's only the one bed, but if you want, you can put a cot up out there, I don't mind. It's eight dollars a week," she said as if expecting them to protest the price.

Wilma had found a job at the local Rexall drugstore as a clerk and "cosmetician," as she liked to call herself. It made her much happier than the fountain job she had expected to get. Jack toured supermarkets, bowling alleys, poolhalls, stores, looking for a job, but in the Rio Grande Valley, where 75 percent of the population was Latino and Mexico itself was just across the bridge, jobs normally held by boys were fought for by grown men with families to support. He was suddenly, by virtue of his skin, in a class above that which was hired for stoop labor, and the harvest of citrus. He was a Texas citizen by default. He spent his days haunting park and levee, a movie theater at the height of tropical day, smoking cigarettes, daydreaming, praying for the time he was old enough to enlist.

There was a training base for navigators and bombardiers nearby. A lot of the men were washouts from pilot's training up at Randolph Field, so there was a kind of wounded, emasculated, second-rate feel to the military atmosphere which washed against the Mexican soul, whose war had already been fought and pissed away. Mexico was not at war with anyone.

"We're going over to Reynosa and buy an electric iron," the boy's mother announced happily after work one afternoon, bouncing into the room towing a tall, paunchy, goosy-gander-looking Texan about sixty behind her. He wore a tan gabardine Western suit, Martinez boots, a neutral 6X beaver Stetson, and half-rim glasses. He was a real estate man who had an office above the drugstore where Wilma worked. He had a big cream-colored Buick that purred like a watch and rode like a ship.

The border guards waved them right across. They were immediately surrounded by a moving bazaar of hucksters both shrill and blandly confidential. "You want tires? Nylons? Toaster? Marijuana? You want girl? Boy? Love? You wanta see a show, *amigo?*" They parked nose to the curb. The streets were so potholed and narrow it was better to walk.

"We'd like to get an electric iron," the Texan said, looking down imperiously through his sincere glasses.

"Sure! You come with me. General Electric, Westinghouse, Sunbeam. Follow me, please."

She got a Sunbeam that might have been brand new, though there was no box for it. It cost less than she would have paid back across the river even if it had been available.

"Tires, gasoline?" the steerer offered. "Coffee, rubber, leather?" He shifted to general categories of rationed items.

Carrying her iron, Wilma let the Texan lead her and the boy into Joe's Place for dinner. They had a feast with three kinds of meat, vegetables, and salad, served family style in huge bowls from which they could take all they wanted. But his mother felt it was probably unsanitary. "They aren't going to throw away what you don't eat," she reasoned. "They'll just serve it to someone else." Because the water was parasitic the man let the boy drink Mexican beer, which was stronger and tasted better than American beer in the boy's opinion. The man and Wilma had tequila with lemon and salt just for the fun of it, then switched to Margaritas. By the time they were through eating, they were feeling very pleasant. A band had come while they dined and alternately played U.S. dance music and South American stuff. Wilma wanted to dance. The man begged off. He never danced and had a bum knee from having a horse fall on him.

"You dance with me, Jacky." She stood up, offering him her arms. He did not like to dance much. He did not do it well. And she danced with him just as if he were Bill or anybody, as if she were not aware how it made him feel holding her tight as she always insisted, moving that way together to a rhythm. "I think you're going to be as tall as your father," she said and led him to execute a dip she had taught him. "But neither of you could hold a candle to your stepdad when it comes to dancing."

"I don't care," he said.

"Now, don't go pouty on me. I'm enjoying myself."

The floor show began with a beat-up Anglo couple on roller skates who had faces that no longer reflected anything of life outside of their act, completely inward faces with totally outgoing, grim smiles, their eyes those of old fighters who still fight though they can no longer string together a coherent sentence or recall the town in which they last lost. His limbs were like bundles of jerky in ill-fitting, shiny tux pants and a stained satin blouse and scarlet cummerbund. Her legs in net hose that had a dollar-sized hole beneath her left buttock could have carried a marathon runner. Her little blue costume reminded Jack of Christmas decorations left in some side-street shop window all summer. Her hair was like bleached sisal. And through it all were those sad, fixed funhouse grins and insane, persistent eyes.

When they completed their act with a wild airplane spin, the woman solicited the audience for a volunteer to take a ride. Finally, a sailor was launched onto the floor by his buddies, stumbling forth self-consciously, tugging down his jumper. The gaunt skater hoisted the gob high overhead, using centrifugal force to lift his weight, gaining speed rapidly until the sailor was a white blur in the spotlight, a head at both ends. Then he slowed, stopped, set the sailor on his pins, and stood back, sweat popping through his makeup, to watch the sailor fall rubber-legged to the floor, which was still careening for him, trying desperately to get a handhold in the tiny cracks between the boards lest he be swept overboard. Three times he tried to arise, to be swept away by an uncontrollable pull to port. Finally he crawled on hands and knees back to his table to the roars of the crowd.

Then came a pretty, short Mexican woman crying *rancheros* that had the sound of murder, rape, arson, and the wail of a coyote in them.

"Miss Superfortress with her twin Bee Forty-sevens!" the Latino MC in a white tux jacket that was not his own announced loudly. A big stripper who was fifty if she was a day leaped into the spotlight as if she wanted you to believe she had flown there on her own power, propelled by her big tits in a red, white, and blue bra with three-bladed propellers on the tips. Her legs were too short, muscular, bowed, which caused her to stumble around in a crotchy kind of crouch that made the boy feel embarrassed for her because she wasn't better-looking. She kept lifting her huge breasts in her hands and letting them drop to the limits of her bra's ability to withstand stress, to the accompaniment of a bass drum. Baroom. . . . Then she spun the props and looked cute, making little moues that showed the vertical wrinkles across her lips.

She dropped directly before the boy at ringside, rolling her bottom around on her heels. Between her pasty white thighs the big mound of her sex was caught in a G-string darkened along the edges with sweat. *"Ooooou!"* she squealed, popping it at him, spinning her props and jumping up and moving on. She finished face up in the spotlight, her meaty legs spread and bent back beneath her, arching her snow-white old belly higher than her head, both props whirling on her big flattened boobs.

The second girl was a lithe young Mexican beauty with really great legs. Jack's mother nudged him and winked. "Now, there's one for you. That other one was just grotesque."

Toward the end of the girl's performance she invited someone from the audience to join her. From airmen and sailors jostling for position, she selected a gangling cadet with a shock of red hair growing like the fronds of a palm from his otherwise clipped, country noggin. She led him into the spotlight by his tie, leaned back with her fullsome G-string a scant inch from his fly, and slowly undulated her pelvis, and Jack felt a sympathetic twinge in his lap. She led the cadet that way all around the floor. He followed like a child being led in a walker. She lay back on a little stage, locking one long, beautiful leg around his waist. She aped the sounds of sexual intercourse, grinding away so it looked as if the dolt were actually in her. Then when there was nothing more that could be done in public and the cadet began to look as if he were losing sense of time and place, she hopped up, kissed him passionately on the mouth, stepped back to a fanfare, and simultaneously whipped off her wig and bra. There was nothing there but a *pachuco* haircut and two boyish paps. The cadet vigorously wiped his mouth on his uniform sleeve, looking as if he were going to be sick, while the *maricone* skipped away behind the band before he got killed. The middle-aged Anglos loved that act best of all.

The man patted Wilma's bare knee when they said good night in front of the house, promising meaningfully to see her soon. She thanked him for the iron and patted his hand.

Jack hadn't dared to touch her since they were run out of Goliad. Beyond the fact that they had to share the same bed once more, she was careful to dress and undress modestly with her back to him, slipping her nightie on over her slip, which she slipped off underneath as the gown came down. If he even nudged her accidentally in his sleep, she woke him and made him move over. As soon as she could afford it, she was buying him his own bed.

Only a faint breeze stirred the curtains. The Valley was a magic place to Jack, where winter was only a violent kind of summer and forty degrees was a cold wave. Grapefruit grew on a tree in the backyard, and no one rushed to pick them, so common was the miracle. In the backyard of the house the owner had built a wooden platform on which he pitched a large tent divided into two apartments, both of which were rented. Every habitable space in town was rented, some spaces twice when the shifts could be worked out. The beds never cooled.

His mother lay sleeping on her back, her short gown across her thighs. She did not stir when he lifted her nightie and carried it back above her belly. He fluffed up her hairs with his hand, and she only shivered once and said, "Um?" as if it were a question, dropping her chin on her near shoulder. Her face seemed happy. He thought there was a faint smile in the corners of her slightly parted lips. Her feathery breath smelled of Ipana and alcohol. He rose to look upon her. He traced the line of fine hairs from her puckered navel down over the incredibly soft, loose flesh of her belly, which looked slightly gathered like Victorian drapery, the tissue broken and minutely scarred, yet softer somehow than healthy skin, to where her bush bloomed and drew him in a wave of love and inexplicable desire to lower his face into its tender, electric mass, seeking to kiss the lips there. She groaned and lifted the leg near him slightly, putting her hands beside his head, murmuring low as though half asleep, "Don't do that, honey. That isn't good." And drew his head onto her breast. He was not certain if she was asleep or awake when he lifted her breasts from their bodice. Yet her legs were parted enough for him to play all along the long, slick lips of her sex. His fingers went in so easily he could feel the curious velvet cone way in the back. After awhile she muttered something and stopped his hand with her own. Yet she lay there on her back, uncovered, one leg cocked slightly to one side, making sounds as if dreaming . . . asking something, a tiny frown flickering between her eyes. "Umm?" on a rising inflection. "Honey?" a whisper. Her left hand lifted and fell limply toward him where he crouched on his knees beside her on the bed. "Humm?"

He stripped off his shorts, lifted his left leg astraddle her, suspending himself on arms and toes above her, expecting at any moment to be stopped, looking down between them, quaking as if his elbows were eccentric joints, watched his penis disappear into the dark hair between her legs. It was as if she moved without visibly moving, and his thing went into her as if it had eyes. *She had done it!* Pretending to be asleep, she had just slid up somehow without seeming to move a muscle and taken it. "Ummmm," she murmured and moved as if trying to get comfortable. "Ummm, Bill . . ." she crooned and snaked both smooth arms around his neck, drawing his face into the junction of her perfumed neck and shoulder.

"It's not Bill, it's Jack," he insisted.

"Umm. Bill, honey," she emphasized, moving more purposefully, stilling his lips with her own. She slipped her left leg out from under him, then her right, rolling upward in a long, slow slide that made him feel the way he had once felt on a roller coaster. His stomach felt as if it had turned over inside of him.

"Open your eyes," he said. "See, it's me." She kissed him again, wet and long, but she did not open her eyes.

She began rolling her bottom around in a way he could never have dreamed possible. He would never have supposed a person was built that way—on her back, one leg over his back, moving as if she were on top of something. His notion of sexual intercourse had until that moment been a quickly furtive back and forth sort of vision. During his other, solitary actual experience he thought all lateral movement on her part had been simply evasive. He no longer had a sense of "up." He perceived her face as a glow in a luminous nimbus. He hung on for his life, trying to move, moving instinctively, but mainly hanging on tight, riding a cork raft on a warm, heavy night sea. There was a momentary perception of all his parts as if they were strung together on cord like a Popeye pop-up character on a board. In the roaring shell of his skull, his brain felt diminished, yet swollen and on fire. His insides felt loose within his taut carcass. His penis felt both enormous and infinitesimal in the hot puddle of her body, which seemed to emanate in rings from an indistinct point beneath him to some point in the dark beyond the creaking bed. He became aware that the bed sounded the way it did when she and his stepfather did it. *He* was really doing it! The reality shot through him, drawing everything together, giving him back himself. He began to ape the motions she was making beneath him. She went, "Uhah!" quite loud and began moving wildly at a tempo that blinded him, had him breathing through his mouth. Then, just as suddenly, she closed on him like a kind of long, lingering kiss, at the end of which she slid slowly and tightly back on him. She repeated the movement several times, only twisting and snapping in such a way that he could feel real muscle under the soft covering of her belly. The game grew into a rhythmic grinding at an ever faster tempo, while she strained against him, clutching him to her with her hands. She began forcing him to move faster and around and around more with her hands. She licked the inside of his ear with her tongue, raised herself on one leg clear off the bed and took his testicles in her hand, threw her head back as if in pain, the cords in her neck standing out, her right leg wrapped high over his back. She began moving in short choppy strokes, blowing through her nose, then saying, "Oh!" and trying to move faster. He hung on to her wild buttocks and wished he knew what to do. He felt himself start to come. "Kiss *me!*" she commanded, bending her head back down, searching for his mouth, kissing the blood out of his lips, raising them both off the bed, holding them there, writhing on her left knee, which was twisted under her, kneading his back with her fingers until he felt her nails hurt. "Oh! *God!* God. God. God. . . ." She collapsed, twisting her face away, recoiling from the boy's sex lost in the flow of her, contracting to sense it in spite of herself, again and again, yet repulsed, her body and mind at odds. She could not open her eyes. Her face was contorted. Tears ran with sweat down her face. Her hair was a damp tangle. The sheet was wet beneath them. She was exhausted and yet tortured. Her climax seemed such a small and distant thing— like a catastrophe on the moon—a soundless, distant awareness separated from her by the horror and self-hatred which twisted her so cruelly, gnarled her fingers, spread her toes like those of a stricken cat. Her gown was a soggy wad around her waist. In the light from a street lamp falling on them through the window, sweat glistened on their skins. She heard the boy calling, "Mom? Mom? Are you all right? What is it? Mom?" He had slipped from inside her. She became aware he had gone. He tried to kiss her cheeks. "No! Don't." She wrenched away.

"Are you mad at me?" he asked.

She shook her head no. "Let me get up," she said, trying to rise. She opened her eyes and for the first time looked at the face near hers. She had borne him, this strange, hard, skinny boy with a look in his eyes she had known since he was only a few months old. She brushed back the damp hair stuck to his brow. "This is *crazy.* You know that?"

He shook his head that he did not. "I love you," he argued.

"No," she protested, cringing again, tears flooding her eyes, trying not to cry. "Don't love me. I'm no good. There's nothing I haven't done now," she mourned.

"You don't French kiss," he offered as if that were a saving grace.

"Jack! Oh, listen, baby—" She caught his face between her hands. "This is *so* wrong. You're a little boy. I'm your *mother!* . . . Oh, God, how'd I ever let this get started? I knew it would come to this. I *knew*." She got up, hooked her gown back over her shoulders. The wrinkled body of it fell crumpled and cheap-looking to her knees. She stood there beside the bed, her stomach pushing out the front of the gown, her breasts sagging, looking suddenly so old and ugly to the boy he felt like laughing out loud from his own sense of superiority in having got her to do what he wanted to do. She pushed at her damp, stringy hair in a familiar gesture that now seemed pathetically futile. He had to bite his tongue to keep from calling her "ugly old whore." His inclination so shocked him he wasn't sure he had not said it aloud while the dumpy little woman fussed with her crummy gown. Her face, which had been washed with her sweat and tears, now looked haggard, her eyes blinking, dark coals that could not focus on the other side of the room. *Fucked her,* he told himself. *Just fucked her, man.*

She stood in the middle of the floor looking at him sprawled on the bed, holding her left elbow in her right hand, and said, like someone growing feeble before his eyes, "I just don't know what we're going to do. . . ."

After that he could pretty much use her whenever he wanted. She would protest, beg him to be nice, but in the end she almost always gave in, processing him mechanically and only occasionally losing control and becoming aroused herself. She began to put on weight. When she had gained ten pounds, she went to a doctor, but he could find nothing wrong with her. Every time it happened she swore it was the last time and vowed the first thing she was going to do the next day was get him his own bed. But she never got around to it.

He thought for awhile he no longer loved her, perhaps even hated her for being such a whore. Then he realized what he loved about her were the regular goofy things he had thought before were the things he disliked most. He loved her for her broken nose that would prevent her from ever being pretty again. He loved her superstitions and how she looked sitting cross-legged in bed, eating an apple and reading their goddamn horoscopes. He loved her phony airs and feeble attempts to pass the two of them off as citizens to all the gray people of the world who were crowded around them, except for the time they were alone in their room and when between her legs and within her body all time stopped in the madness of the criminal moment.

Then Bill got out of prison and showed up at the door with his hair almost entirely gray and a new, more desperate look in his eyes, which now gazed beyond both the boy and his mother toward something in the distance. "This is it," he told her solemnly. "This is our last chance. If we don't make it this time, honey, we ain't never going to make it at all." He had an offer of a job on a wildcat that was being drilled outside Rio Grande City. He left the next morning. They followed in a few days.

The place he had found for them was two rooms in a dusty alley tacked on the back of a store. And when Jack saw the empties already piling up by the door, he knew with Bill it was going to be the same old oil. So he slept more often than not in the cemetery between Richard Villareal and Augie Navarro, his head on some old Anglo grave and his toes turned up at the still Mexican stars.

# 43

JACK began to be considered the boyfriend of Augie Navarro's sister, Berta, who was called Tiny. Though Jack was only thirteen and Berta was nineteen, no one thought it strange that he was her *novio,* for in a town where the local *curandera* had only the year before turned a mean man into a coyote who yet howled on the distant bank of the Rio Grande when the moon was right, the only person in town with blond hair was protected and catered to as if they really would like him to stay. Old witches in perpetual mourning for all they had survived, with faces and hands like the gnarled dead drift of the desert, would snatch at him behind his back to touch his hair for good luck.

Berta had graduated from high school, and she could type. She wanted to get married and move someplace North where she thought she would feel less Mexican. Her brother was a year older than she was, but he treated Jack as an equal, sharing fiery muscatel and marijuana with him. Their mother ran a line of six shoddy cabins under the rise of the levee on the slow, shallow, red river. Their father had gone to live with a younger woman back in Mexico. Berta did not want to marry a man like her father, or her brother, or anyone she had known up to then. She dreamed of having golden-haired babies by Jack and living in a nice house in Minneapolis, though she knew no more about Minneapolis than she did about Bombay. "I just like its name," she confided. He took the opportunity to kiss her for the first time. He felt strange being the boyfriend of the sister of a guy with whom he lay out in the cemetery at night planning an expedition together across the river to see the little painted girls of San Pedro de Roma.

Bill had begun there with a dedication that exhausted Wilma and drove the boy to stay away from the house. He began as a derrickman on the eight-to-four, then when a man fell on the four-to-12, Bill began pulling two towers for twice the pay. He also cut down drastically on his drinking. . . . But he was so mean, absolutely brutal to both Wilma and the boy, that they secretly wished he would go back to his usual fifth a day.

They hadn't any dishes, so they ate on paper plates. One morning when Bill's eggs were not to his specification, he squashed Wilma in the face with them, eggs, plate, and all. When she tried to slap back, he threw her on the floor. Jack made a move to help her, and the man drew back in a crouch as if he faced a mortal enemy. The look in his eyes so frightened the boy he made a note never to tackle Bill unarmed. The panic in his eyes that they had seen when he returned from prison had deepened, and his pupils were dilated as if it were night.

Then one day he did not make his first tower. He also missed the second, having dressed, taken the sack lunch Wilma had made for him, and stopped at Timo's Café for a couple of beers and a shot. He ended up across town in the shack of the *curandera*, bartering unsteadily for a bottle of her homemade, unlabeled mescal and a cartouche of marijuana. The whole works cost him four dollars, and she had overcharged him. It was like finding a secret well. He giggled all the way home. He got Wilma to taste the mescal, after which she was willing to try the weed. He had long experience with rolling his own and fashioned her a neat reefer clean as one made by a machine. She complained it made her throat dry, so he passed her the mescal. Around eight o'clock they ate his lunch sitting on the bed in front of the picture window like two kids at a picnic. He took her there then the way he hadn't taken her in years, both of them muttering dreamily about making the little blond girl she so desperately wanted and could never have, with the light on, the blinds open, and half a dozen little kids outside in the alley ranging in ages from four to twelve watching and giggling. A couple idly jerked off while they watched. And Bill never went back to work again.

Jack came in a couple of days later and found them both sitting inside with all the shades pulled down to keep out the over-100-degree heat, higher than the highest tree. "Whooo, baby, where you been?" Wilma swooped upon him dreamily, smelling of rotten cactus, Bill, and pot. He had never seen her like that before. "Give your old lady a kiss, if you ain't too good for us anymore." She pursed her lips out exaggeratedly. He turned away. "Look at that," she demanded. "Too good to give his mother a kiss. Where the hell you been for the last week?" she wanted to know.

"I was here day before yesterday."

"He's got 'im some little spic couse down by the river."

He resented Bill talking about the girl that way.

"How is she?" Wilma leered, leaning toward him, sitting on the edge of the unmade bed sucking on a reefer she held in the corner of her mouth. She so rarely smoked tobacco it was a very unpracticed skill. He wanted to slap the thing out of her mouth. "She got a nice little tight one?"

"I don't know," he said.

"You mean you haven't? You?" She swelled up her chest in a mocking swagger that was supposed to be him. "You just don't want to tell us about it," she pouted. "You probably think she's too good for us. Why don't you ever bring her around to meet me? You ashamed of me or something? I'd like to be friends with my son's girl. What mother you know has more of a right?" she demanded, sitting up and thrusting her chin at him. "Hunh? *Look at me!*" She wrenched his face around to force him to look at her. Her face was naked and sagging. She hadn't bathed or put on makeup in two days. Her hair was a stringy mop caught behind her head with a plastic barrette. Her mouth looked like a wet little trap in her doughy face. She had continued to put on weight. Her belly and buttocks bulged in her slacks, which were straining at the seams. The zipper on the side was only partially closed, the opening bulging with a bubble of hip encased in pink panties like a bladder about to pop through the broken seam of a basketball. "Look at him!" she commanded Bill. "He can't stand to even look at his own mother." She threw his face away and went to flop on the couch beside Bill, who sat in his undershirt and work pants, barefoot, a bottle of mescal in one hand balanced on his left knee and the roach of a weed in the nicotine-stained fingers of the other. She put her arm around Bill's shoulder as if posing for a snapshot. "What do you think about a kid who's ashamed of his own mother?" She solicited an impartial opinion.

"Fuck 'im," was his counsel.

The boy's eyes and hers met for a moment. There was a flicker in her eyes. He almost smiled. Then she shook her head to clear it, tightly squinting both eyes.

"He never was no fun," Bill complained. "Goddamn dopy, peapickin Swede. If he's so much like his daddy, I don't understand what you saw in him. We don't need him," he decided blearily. "He's his grandpa and grandma's boy. Let him go the hell back to 'um. We don't need him, them or nobody, right, babe?" He set down the bottle and reached over to catch her between the legs, bending her head back cruelly on the couch in a rough, long kiss. Her arms wrapped around his shaggy gray head, and she opened her legs as if they were alone. Jack let the door slam behind him. And from the end of the alley heard them laughing like crazy.

He walked Berta toward her home from the ice cream parlor, telling her what had happened. "I ain't going back there, Tiny."

"What are you going to do?"

"I don't know. I can work. I can work in the oilfield."

"You want to do that?"

"No."

"What do you want to do?"

"I want to join the Naval Air Corps when I'm seventeen, sign up for pilot training."

"Carmen's boyfriend, Jimmy Hinojosa, is in the Marines, and he is only fifteen. He lied about his age, changed his birth certificate, and he is a PFC. He is no bigger than you."

Jack wondered if he could. The boy who had lived above them when he lived with his grandparents on Cleveland back in Wichita had gone from the CCC's right into the Marines when he was fifteen. His grandmother had sent a picture of the kid cut from a local paper. He had been the first man to land in the Marshall Islands. "You think I could pass?"

"Yes. I know it." They stopped in the middle of the road. She gripped his shirt with both hands like a child, moving close and looking up at him. "And if we were married, there would be no doubt about your age. I could get a place. You could send me money. I would wait for you."

"Yeow," he said, thinking of something else.

"I love you!" she said in a way that tripped some gate in her. She threw her arms around his neck and kissed him. It was so different from the chaste single kiss they had shared before, it made the boy wonder, even as he pressed against her little belly, his right hand straying over her surprisingly full hips, surprising for she was the only flat-chested Mexican girl he had ever met. She was small and boyish, so the femininity of her hips and the warm skill of her lips and tongue were a surprise. Someone in the cemetery loosed a wolf whistle and called out in a singsong, "Tiny . . ." followed by a string of Spanish he did not understand.

"*Burrito!*" she hissed. "Come." She led him along the road fast until they came to a stile. "Help me," she requested, tucking her skirt up to keep from snagging it on the barbed wire. In the field beside a cotton shed he kissed her again, mashing her with his body against the rough boards of the wall, squeezing her small breast, trying to catch the tiny nipple between his thumb and forefinger. He tried to force her onto the ground. "No. Inside. I am afraid of snakes." She led him into the shed, open on one side, and kicked a little cotton that was in a corner around with her feet to make a bed and sat down carefully, fully expecting to be bitten by a snake or stung by a scorpion but willing then to make that sacrifice. She took his hands and pulled him down beside her.

He was surprised at how easily he went in. She wasn't a virgin. He hadn't asked her. He had just assumed she was. He was even more surprised that she knew how to do it pretty well. The valentine sentiments with which he had always regarded her were worn away by the clever way she moved her bottom, and he did her every way he knew how. Eerily, her eyes rolled up under her half-open lids until the pupils almost disappeared. She kissed as if their mouths and sex were two ends of the same experience. He grabbed her by the hump with both hands and fucked her. He came in her as if she were his own. He felt she was snuffling him in by mouth and her sex. Tiny, she had made him feel so big.

She vowed her undying love in both Spanish and English while he stood up to button his pants, now more than a little concerned about getting bitten by something himself.

When they came up the road toward the house, their arms around each other's waists, their heads tipped so he could smell her hair, her brother came running out to meet them. "Jack, you gotta go home right quick. Your father is beating the hell out of your mother. You better hurry or somebody is goin to get hurt."

He ran all the way home. A gang of Mexicans was gathered stoically in the alley, the children rooted in front of their parents. The women generally stood flatfooted, feet turned out, their arms folded over their large bosoms. A kitchen chair exploded through the big plate glass window that was the pride of the alley, dragging the curtain with it.

"*Open this door!*" he demanded, kicking hell out of it. And heard nothing but maniacal laughter behind it.

"OOOOOOW!" his mother screamed. There was the thud of her body on the other side of the door, the sound of her begging Bill not to hit her any more. Then she was yanked up and towed away. Jack kicked the remaining glass out of the broken window and went through, flinging aside the drapery, coming out standing on the bed like a kid playing king-of-the-mountain. His mother was peeking from the closet. Bill, naked, a small mantislike figure with huge head, sunken chest, spindly legs making the equipment swinging between them appear all the more amazing, caught his lower lip between his teeth and smashed the door with a forearm, catching Wilma's fingers in the crack, and she screamed.

"I said stay in there!"

"*Stop it!*" the boy shouted. Bill turned as if he barely heard him, a puckish, conniving look on his face that was almost disarming. Then he was coming on all fours, growling like some ape. The boy kicked him right in the face. He leaped on the man. They tumbled over once on the floor; Bill was on top of him, his face the insanely happy visage of a totally destructive infant. He made a snap at the boy's face. Jack threw his forearm up between them in time to save his nose, but lost a small chunk out of his arm. It was his mother, as wild-eyed as Bill, her face puffed and puffing, one lip twice as large as the other, wearing only a striped polo shirt, and it ripped and soaked with liquor, spittle, and blood, who grabbed two handfuls of Bill's hair and yanked him backward long enough for the boy to wriggle free. Bill immediately turned on her. "I told you to stay in that closet," he reminded her as if she were letting him down. "Now here you are again out of there. I want you to stay in there until I say you can come out."

"I don't want to stay in that old closet, Bill," she whined. "Why do I have to stay in there? I don't *want* to go in there!" She stamped her bare foot. He backhanded her perfectly across the mouth, knocking her face up and away, warning her with a single finger when it came back to focus. "I'm goin! I'm goin!" She scampered in terror toward the tiny closet, her big white bottom gleaming. She dutifully shut the door after her.

Bill seemed to forget the boy was there for a minute, fumbling as if he were trying to find a shirt pocket, then accidentally spotting the boy standing there casting wildly about for something to brain the man with.

"Now it's you," he said, stalking the boy, his head lowered between his shoulders. "Don't think I don't know what you and her been up to when I was away. You don't slip nothin past ole Bill, kid. Come on, get yours." He carried his right fist low in front of him, tensed, waiting to pull the string. It was as if he expected to mesmerize the boy with eyes and crooning voice and destroy him with a coiled right. "Here it is, come an' get it," he sang lullingly. The boy backed through the door into the kitchen. Then Bill was coming in a rush. The boy came straight forward to meet him, aiming the top of his head at the man's chin. The murderous right wrapped across his back so it was like being whipped with a hawser. But Bill was staggering backward, tumbling off to one side, a glazed look wiping the impishness out of his eyes. The boy swung a kitchen chair over his head and brought it down on the man's skull. He cowered on the linoleum, wrapping his head in his hands, scooting toward the toilet door, which was standing open just across the room. The boy cracked him again with the chair, yet he continued to crawl. Blood was running into one of his eyes from his scalp. A leg was broken from the chair. Bill's single big testicle was caught between his bare legs as he wriggled on his side toward the door. Jack kicked him with all his might, and he only groaned like a dying bear and made the door. It was a tiny toilet room and shower. The door opened out into the kitchen. When Bill closed it behind him, the boy wedged it shut with the back of a chair.

"Someone go get the constable!" he shouted out the back to the Mexicans standing in the alley.

"Someone has already gone, *señor*. He will be here pretty quick now."

His mother would not leave the closet until Bill was taken away.

The constable was a Mexican-American who had his pearl-handled .45 in his hand when he came through the door. The boy told him what he knew. He opened the toilet door carefully, and Bill darted out, trying to make a break for it. The constable knocked him off balance with the first rap of his gun butt and decked him with the second. "Let's get something on him," he said with distaste. He was locking no one up naked. He put thumbcuffs on him and led him away, Bill on tippytoe, his total attention on getting to jail as soon as possible and out of those cruel come-alongs.

Wilma peeked out of the closet. When she saw Bill was gone, she threw her arms around Jack's neck and cried on his shirt, blubbering about all the cruel things Bill had done to her. "Look at me! Look what he did to your mother," she wailed. She swore she was through with him forever. "Nobody's going to beat me around like some old punching bag! I don't need him. What has he ever done for me, anyhow? Nothin! Just used me, let me do his dirty work, get him out of jail, *everything!*"

"Yeow. It's OK now," he soothed and parked her on the couch long enough to secure the blinds and so hide them from the eyes in the alley. She hung herself again around his neck. "We don't need him. We can make it. You and me. We can take care of each other. We can move to Brownsville on the Gulf, get jobs and save our money and live decently, have something. Not see everything we get be drunk up or left somewhere. We could do it, baby. You can be my big man, can't you? Hunh?" She nuzzled him with her puffed lip. It looked like a kidney. "Hunh? We could make it, couldn't we?" Her breath was like the lingering high part of the smell where a skunk has been killed in the road a few days before. "We could make it. We don't need him. I'd treat you right. Don't I treat you right?" She rubbed against him.

"You need a shower. Your breath stinks."

She twisted like a little girl being reprimanded. "Don't be mean to me. Talk nice to me. There's no need to talk like that to me. I'm your mother." She squared herself dramatically, took a sight on the donicker, and marched like a little bare-assed soldier into the shower. He made a pot of coffee and straightened up the room, shook glass from the bed and put on fresh sheets. Then he began packing a suitcase for her and one for him.

In the bottom of the closet was that damn box they had shipped around behind or before them. He dragged it into the middle of the floor and cut the clothesline that secured it. There were just a lot of clippings from magazines, special horoscope books, photos, a lot of crap. Before he dug below the bottom layer of what seemed to be all the same sort of shit, he decided he had better see how she was doing in the shower.

She sat in one corner with her head on her knees, the cold water pelting her. He roused her and fished her out, getting soaked in the process. He threw one towel over her head and, propping her against the wall, dried her with another. Curiously, he thought, her legs and pussy were the only things that still looked young. Her waist had visibly thickened, making her bottom look a bit too flat. He wrapped her in a towel and led her to the bed. He fed her the hot coffee with a spoon, then had her sip from the cup. "What's that doing out there opened like that?" she asked.

"I'm packing. I've lugged that damn thing around all over hell and gone. I just wanted to see what was in it. What are you saving all those recipes and crap for?"

"Someday maybe we'll have a place where I can cook. I never have fixed you one of my good meals. It's just things I want to keep."

He dug through the stuff. There were poems clipped from the newspapers. There were newspaper clippings from the thirties about his father's accident and death. "He does look a little like me, doesn't he?"

"Put it back, hon. You're just going to mess everything up. Those are my private things."

Rummaging through the box, he said, "I'm wiring Grandma first thing in the morning to send us enough to get home on. We ought to be out of here by dark at the latest."

"We don't want to go back *there!* You don't want to go back there to bedbugs and living on relief."

"I don't see as how this is much better."

"You don't?" She raised herself and crossed over to him, resting her arms on his shoulders, a smile trying to twist through her battered face. "Put out the light and come to bed. We can finish packing in the morning." He did as she told him. She had thrown off the towel under the sheet. She drew his arm over her, placing his hand on her large, flaccid breast. She reached down and snapped the elastic of his shorts. "Don't you want to take them off?" she whispered.

He shook his head no.

"What's the matter? Don't you like me no more?" She rolled toward him, wrapping him desperately in her arms. "I love you. Haven't I proved how much I love you? Who would have done for you what I did? Don't leave me, honey. Please. I *need* you. Take care of me. We got to stick together." She pulled down his shorts in back and played with his buttocks, slid her hand around and lowered his shorts until she could take his penis in her hand. "I'll treat you right," she promised, rocking her belly against him. "I'll treat you good." She laid her right leg over him and rolled him on top of her.

And he did it to her, this time for her, because the more loving and intimate she became, the greater his revulsion, until he was whoever he was, and she was just a poor old whore.

"We'll stick together, won't we?" she asked afterward.

"We're going back to Wichita," he said.

"I don't *want* to go there!" She pounded the bed with her fists.

"We're goin," he said.

The next morning he sent the wire, convinced her Wichita would be best, and spent the rest of the morning hunting for her glasses.

"Bill's hid them somewhere. That cunning devil. I remember! When he started acting like an animal, I told him I was going to leave. Then he snatched my glasses and hid them because he knew I'm too blind to go anywhere without them."

"I can guide you. When we get home, you can get another pair."

"No. We'll have to go to the jail and get them to make him tell us where he hid them."

Jack was afraid to go to the jail, afraid Bill would talk her into staying.

"No, sir!" she assured him. "I told him I was finished. And I am finished. I never said it before, and I only had to say it once."

In that case he would take her there. She had on her good summer suit to travel in, her spectator shoes. She hid her face under a floppy straw hat that tied under her chin and a pair of drugstore dark glasses. He led her through the sun as if she were blind, her hand resting lightly on his arm. "Curb," he warned.

"I can see a *street*," she insisted.

They had Bill upstairs where there were windows on three sides of the building guaranteeing a nice breeze, except there was no breeze at all. The Mexican turnkey led them up, chuckling at what a time they had been having with him. "He say there are little men with electric switches sticking them at him all the time. He see many things, boy! We give him a little of this, it quiet him down." He showed them a quart of paraldehyde half full and a nearby tin cup.

In the cell nearest the door a Mexican was curled like a sick dog on the floor with his hands thrust down between his legs, shivering as if he were on an ice floe. It was over 100 degrees up there. All the cells were in the center of the big room, with a four-wall walk-around outside. Bill was up on the bars of the back cell, craning to see out the adjacent window. "Now see him," the guard chuckled. "Know what he's seein down there? A grand bullfight." He nodded indulgently.

Bill cried, *"Ole!"* and waved a bit of cloth torn from his trousers like a handkerchief, his arm sticking out of the bars.

"Hi Bill," Wilma said, just as if he were a rational man and she expected an apology.

"Look at *that!*" he enthused. *"Ole! Ole!"*

"You can stop the nutty act with me," she said bitterly. "You might fool them, but you aren't fooling me. I want to know where you hid my glasses. I need them. I can't see without them."

"Shhh!" He beckoned her to come near. Jack stood back a bit near the wall to take a peek out the window. With Bill you could never tell. There was just a bald field out there where not a blade of grass grew, in the center of which was a dry well that had once served the church whose grounds were next to the jail. "If I don't keep awake, they come when I'm asleep and stick me in the ass and balls with electric rods." He glanced around furtively to make sure he hadn't been heard. His trousers hung on his skinny hips. He looked as if he had lost ten pounds since the day before. A crusty scab was formed in his hair on the top of his head. "Who's that?" he demanded, as if just spotting Jack.

"You know who that is," she said wearily.

"Never saw that funny-looking peapicker before in my life. Nobody ask *my* permission to let him up here. Guard! *Guard!*"

"Just tell me where you hid my glasses and quit clowning around."

"Tell you nothin, that geek standing there staring at me." He stuck out his tongue at the boy and waggled his fingers in his ears. He ran to the corner of the cell and rattled the bars, screaming, "You stop that starin at me!"

"Wait downstairs, honey," she said, gently touching his arm.

"Wait downstairs, honey!" Bill mimicked. "Let old Bill rot in a goddamn border jail. *Wait downstairs, honey!* You'll never get your goddamn glasses now!"

She was up there a long time. When she came down, she looked drained. Jack took her arm. They walked across the churchyard.

"He tell you where your glasses are?"

"Hunh? Unh, no."

"Why not, for chrissake?"

"He's afraid I'll go."

"You are going!"

"I can't leave without my glasses."

"We have looked everyplace in the house"—he thought a minute—"but one."

There they were, dropped in the tank of the toilet. He fished them out, dried them, and watched his mother gloomily hook them over her ears. There was a notice of a telegram on their door when they came in. The money had come.

Then she confessed she loved Bill. "I can't leave him like this. I guess we've just been over too many jumps together. I can't go back and live with Mom and Dad and leave him here. They want too much of me. . . . I just can't leave him." She looked up and smiled feebly. "Joke's on me, hunh? Hate me?"

"No," he said, staring at her shoes.

She pulled him to her. "I don't blame you if you do. But I did my best. It maybe wasn't the kind of best to be proud of. But it wasn't *all* bad times and heartaches, was it?"

"Pretty much, Mom." He could not lie.

"Yeow, I guess so." She sort of drifted off, perhaps looking back. "Anyway, you're almost grown up now. If you work hard, you can make up the schooling you missed." Tears flowed from behind her glasses. "Finish high school and maybe you can get to college." She always was an optimist.

"I'm going to join the Marines."

"You're too young."

"I can pass for seventeen. I'll change my birth certificate. I'll send you the papers and you can sign them. I know lots of guys who did it. I'll be fourteen in May."

"My baby. Forgive me?"

"Shit. There's nothing to forgive."

"Well, anyway. Give me a kiss good-bye."

He kissed her the way he did his grandmother, backing away when she tried to hold him longer. "See ya."

"Be careful, Son." He grinned about that all the way up the alley.

The bus was due in about half an hour. He hung around the depot, not wanting to be spotted by anyone he knew. He did not want to tell Berta good-bye. Richard Villareal, going past in his dad's ramshackle pickup, braked to a screeching halt and yelled, "Hey, *compadre! Que pasa?*"

"I'm joining the Marines."

"No shit! Hey, give them hell. I will look after the home front for you."

"You do that."


In Oklahoma City a sailor who looked no older than himself got on the bus with a buddy. He studied every G.I., measuring himself against them. He could see his own reflection and the sailor's across the aisle in the dark window. He could do it, he was certain.

In Tulsa a tall woman in a good suit, wearing gloves, got on and looked for a seat. He swung his feet out of the one next to him, the last vacant one left. She took it, smiling gratefully, plainly a woman unaccustomed to riding a bus. She was over forty, Jack guessed. She had sort of buck teeth over which she had to consciously lower her upper lip after speaking.

"Where are you going?" she asked kindly.

"Wichita," he said. "I'm going home. I'm going in the Marines next week."

"Oh? But you look so young."

"I'm seventeen."

"They all look so young to me. My son was on the *Wasp*."

"Sorry," he sympathized.

When the lights were out, he nodded off, his head falling accidentally on her shoulder. He awoke when she covered them with her coat. It had grown chilly. When his left hand strayed accidentally to her left breast, she pretended she was asleep so as not to disturb him.